MUSPELL'S SONS

Jillian Leigh Jacobs

MUSPELL'S SONS

JILLIAN LEIGH JACOBS

ROCKSABER
ENTERTAINMENT, LLC

COPYRIGHT

MUSPELL'S SONS

jillianleighjacobs.com

ISBN: **978-1-960792-00**

To Scott

For helping me bring this crazy universe to life.

Table of Contents

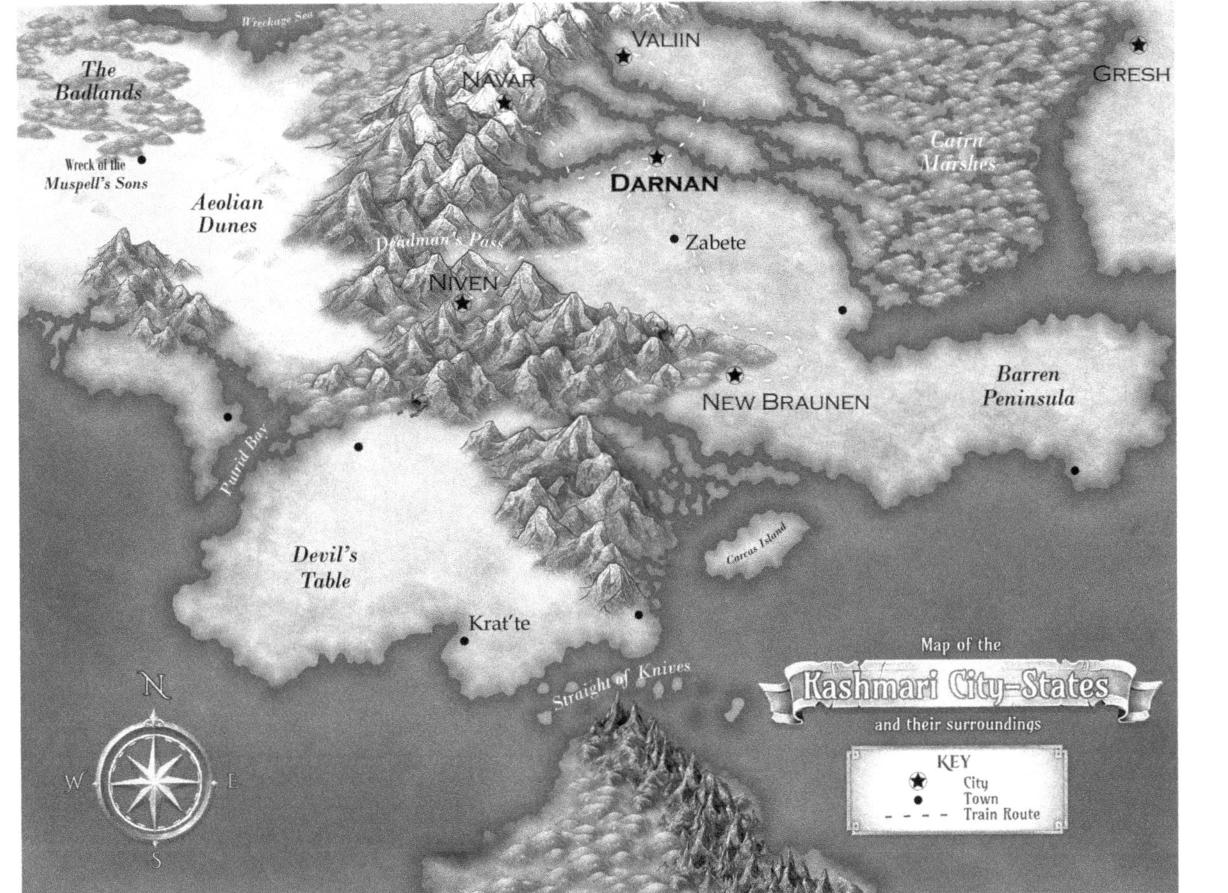
Map of the
Kashmari City-States
and their surroundings
KEY
City
Town
Train Route
Wreckage Sea
The Badlands
Wreck of the Muspell's Sons
Aeolian Dunes
NAVAR
VALIIN
GRESH
DARNAN
Cairn Marshes
Deadman's Pass
Zabete
NIVEN
NEW BRAUNEN
Barren Peninsula
Putrid Bay
Devil's Table
Carcas Island
Krat'te
Straight of Knives
N
S
E
W

Prologue

1045 A.D.
Norway

WINTER had come early to the fjords. Some claimed it was the clash between dvergen and kashmari magic that had upset the natural order. Others argued that perhaps it was just a cold year. Some prayed to the gods, while others squirreled away more food. Either way, the morning was silent, frozen, and dark.

A sleek vessel hovered silently over the water, its polished silver nose pointed at the side of a mountain. Of dvergen design, the fuselage was long and tapered at each end and flattened like the shell of a mussel. The mouths of two Mammoth engine nacelles affixed to the rear sides glowed a soft blue and set the air shivering around them.

The icy mountainside before the vessel shimmered where a rift marked the boundary between this realm, Midgard, and the one on the other side, Muspelheim.

Everyone on the bridge held their collective breath. They all knew that once they entered that rift, there would be no return. The life they would lead in that hellscape, should they survive, would be bereft of magic and technology. Lacking even basic necessities, they would be trapped with the same demons whom they sought to imprison.

General Baldur stood with hands clasped at the small of his back. His uniform was immaculate, his dark hair cut exactly to regulation, his demeanor as rigid as any officer could hope for. He stared out the forward viewport of the *Muspell's Sons* at the rippling tear in reality in front of his ship.

At his side stood his wife, a tiny woman of pure dvergen blood. Baldur, the son of a kashmari lord and a dverger scientist, was not a tall man; yet his wife barely reached his shoulder. She slipped her small hand into his, melting his stern countenance as they watched the hologram of their son in front of them. The young man was the spitting image of Baldur, but with his mother's soft blue eyes. He snapped a quick salute.

"General, those of us who remain in Midgard salute you for the sacrifice of the crew of the *Muspell's Sons*. The exile you are about to embark upon will forever be remembered."

The young man glanced around, then sagged a little.

"You will be missed, Father," he said softly. "May we meet again in Valhalla."

"Until that day, son," Baldur replied, "go with honor."

His wife put a hand over her mouth and stifled a sob.

After taking a moment to compose herself, she said, "Are you sure this is the only way?"

Baldur nodded, brow creased. He drew her hand up to his lips and kissed her fingers gently. He closed his eyes and savored the soft scent of rose petals on her wrist. Heart heavy, he sighed. "Every other way has failed."

"We are leaving them in darkness, set back thousands of years. All they will have are stories that will fade into myth and be forgotten, as we will be."

Baldur placed a hand around her shoulders.

"Yes. But they will be alive. And they will be free."

"So long as this works."

"It will work. I promise."

He brushed her long, white-blonde hair aside and kissed her on the forehead, then straightened and began barking commands.

"Shields up."

The skin of the ship began to shimmer a faint blue.

"Forward gun battery: Stand by."

"Standing by, sir."

"Countermeasures?"

"Ready, sir."

"Bombardier?"

A husky voice crackled over the intercom. "Triple-checked and ready to go, sir."

Baldur glanced back at the row of hulking men and women standing at attention behind him. Unlike his dvergen crew, these soldiers were massive, muscled, and covered in intricate tattoos that glowed faintly.

"Captain Sanders?" Baldur said.

One of the largest stepped forward. His flowing blond hair had been plaited along the top and shaved along the sides, and his beard had beads twisted into the braids. Behind him, his fiercely beautiful sister stood with arms crossed.

"Are your jotuns ready?" Baldur asked the giant.

Sanders looked out the viewport at the pulsing rift and didn't speak. He looked as though he was about to be sick. Baldur felt a stab of pity for the man. The dvergen thrived off the trace amounts of magic in their bodies and relished the exploration of its secrets; but not so these ancient people. For them, magic was their lifeblood. No one knew what would happen when it was ripped from their veins.

Baldur had fought Sanders and begged the ancient warrior to stay behind and keep his people safe on Asgard or Alfheim. But the stubborn creature had adamantly refused, saying that if he accompanied the *Muspell's Sons*, then perhaps the dvergen might have a slim chance at survival.

Now, though, the ancient captain seemed to waver.

Baldur was about to pull the man aside and offer to drop him off somewhere quiet when the general's wife stepped over to the hulking man and laid a tiny hand on his forearm. They looked so incongruent, the massive warrior and the tiny dverger. She spoke so softly that Sanders had to lean down to hear her.

Behind them, the line of ancient warriors began stamping their feet and calling out some sort of war cry in their guttural language. Baldur did not understand the words, but the hairs on the back of his neck rose as the power they drew upon charged the air around him. As their voices rose, the glowing lines of magic traced upon their skin glowed brighter and brighter until even their eyes burned with the brilliance of the sun.

Bathed in that light, Sanders seemed to relax and draw strength from his people. He smiled gently at Baldur's wife, patted her hand, murmured something to her, then turned to Baldur. The chanting ceased.

"General. We are ready."

At those words, the entire bridge crew paused. Baldur could see the apprehension in their eyes at what they were about to do. But then the moment passed. Fear gave way to resolution and a renewed flurry of preparation. The sounds of the ship readying for battle echoed around the bridge, drowning out Baldur's sorrow.

Baldur exhaled and turned to his pilot. "Take us in."

* * *

The *Muspell's Sons* lifted smoothly off the ground and slid forward into the rift. The sleek nose of the craft disappeared first into the rippling event horizon. Then, as though pulled by some unseen beast from the other realm, the *Muspell's Sons* sped up, drawn deeper and deeper into the rift.

And then they were gone, swallowed up by the rift's swirling maw.

Several long minutes crawled by on the snowy mountainside. A mountain goat picked its way over icy stones close to the rift. Something snarled from a crevice in the rock, sending the goat scampering back down the mountain. The smell of snow carried on a blast of alpine air heralded the thick, dark clouds roiling over the summit.

Suddenly, the rift bulged outward and glowed red as though a volcanic eruption was straining to escape from the other realm. Steam erupted around the edges. With the sound of a million crystals exploding at once, the rift shattered into a hailstorm of glittering energies that became sparkling shards held aloft in the chilly air by some unknown power.

The stiff wind swirled among the shards. They vibrated, hummed, and filled the air with a haunting song. And then, one by one, they fell. The mountainside soaked them up like rainwater being sucked into sand.

Within seconds, there was no sign that there ever had been a rift between worlds on that frigid mountainside, and no sign that the *Muspell's Sons* had ever existed.

Apothecary

One Thousand and Sixty-two Years Later

7 August 1062 P.E. (Post Exodus)
Southeastern Quarter, City of Darnan

The Repository Apotheca smelled of formaldehyde and wood oil and dust.

Over the years, Quincy had grown used to it, and had even sort of come to like the sweet acridity. It was the smell of where he belonged. It was the smell of home.

Quincy whistled as he wiped the ever-present desert dust off the shelves of jars containing preserved organs and pickled creatures. He stopped to wipe his brow with the back of his hand. The apothecary shop was stuffy and hot as always, heated like a blast furnace by the afternoon sun blazing through the large glass storefront.

He made his way over to the large grandfather clock that stood to one side of the wooden counter and wiped the dust off of its elegant face. Then he pulled a tin of wood grease out of his pocket and, with a separate cloth, meticulously applied the grease to the wood so that it wouldn't dry out in the murderously dry desert air.

A little bell rang as the door to the apothecary shop swung open, letting in a gust of dusty, hot air and a puff of sand that instantly coated the entire front room all over again. Quincy bit off a curse and rolled his eyes. He turned to greet the customer and squinted as the bright afternoon sun bit into his eyes. The man who had entered was naught but a dark silhouette against the blazing desert sun.

The newcomer let the door slam shut with another little jingle.

"Good afternoon, kind sir. How may I assist you?"

The man strode in and took his hat off, then placed his large hands on the counter like a sheriff come to interrogate the apothecary. Quincy could just make out a strange spidery scar on the man's left wrist. He leaned forward enough that his shaggy salt and pepper head blocked out the sun and gave the apothecary a good view of the man's lined, scruffy face, with a straight nose and those laughing amber eyes.

"Brand!" The apothecary's face broke out in a grin. "Always a pleasure."

"I still haven't found a shop that can beat your quality and price, my friend." The big newcomer's deep voice was smooth and cultured, tinted with the affectations of the kashmari accent he spent so much time around.

"All of the credit goes to my father and his father before him," Quincy said modestly. "I wouldn't be here if it weren't for them."

The newcomer smiled and fanned himself. With a smirk and a twinkle in his eye, his voice rising a little and taking on a goofy accent, he said, "Quincy, it's hotter'n a kor'lac's breath in here," he drawled. "Haven' I sold ya enough crud to hawk so you could buy a whole slew o' fans yet? Maybe even one a those cooler things?" Brand screwed up his face in disgust. "How'd you put up wi' that smell?"

Quincy snorted. "You barely bring me enough to keep your ingredients in stock as it is. What's with the accent? You sound like a Duati farmer from the caves."

Brand took a bag off of his shoulder and hoisted it onto the counter with a clank.

He opened the bag and upended it. Gears, coils, tubes, and an assortment of screws clattered down onto the wood and skittered or rolled across the counter.

Brand dropped the colloquial drawl in favor of his original crisp dialect.

"My next fight in three days is with a Duati man sponsored by a Navari lady, so Kushchai had me hobnobbing with all of them the past few days. Public relations, raise spirits, that sort of thing. You know. Picked up the accent and thought I'd try it out in case I ever need it. The more famous I get, the harder it's been to get around town without people noticing. Makes coming here…risky. But people don't really see you when you talk like an idiot. They only see the accent."

The apothecary shook his head in amazement. The big man had mentioned before how risky it was for anyone to know he regularly visited an apothecary. People might start asking what he was buying.

"Must have been a nightmare, escorting those Duati around."

"The kashmari, yeah, but the humans were nice enough." Brand drawled again, "Fer people short a few cars of a train, know wud I mean?"

Quincy chuckled. "I had an uncle who got sent down there. We'd see him over the holidays, but not much else. I remember each time he came up, it seemed like he got dumber and dumber. Once, he told us that the shadows were murdering people but that he'd made a deal with the shadows so they'd let him live."

"Must be something in the air down there. Something's not quite right with those folks." The big man jutted his bearded chin at the jumble of parts. "How much?"

The apothecary pulled a pair of round glasses down from his head and poked around the mess, sorting items into piles with a slender, manicured finger. He sighed.

"Double what I paid last. But it won't do you much good, I'm afraid. With the storms out in the Wastes getting worse, it's almost impossible to source some of the herbs. I'm down to about a quarter of my usual stock as it is. This—" He poked at the pile of coils and gears, "—won't be enough to cover much at all. Maybe an ounce of belladonna."

Brand growled, an unsettling sound coming from a man of his stature. The apothecary's eyes darted to the man's veiny forearms bulging from his rolled-up sleeves. The linen shirt was the same color as the vial of blood on the counter near his elbow, the slender man noticed. Quincy shifted his weight to his other foot nervously.

Brand relaxed and waved a dismissive hand. "Alright. I was hoping to get a bit more off, but…Oh well. I'll take as much of a complete pharmakon's kit as you can manage, please, with two liters of alcohol and half a dozen vials. Plus your usual discretion, of course."

The apothecary's jaw dropped. A full kit would cost more than Quincy would see in a year. "A full kit?" he sputtered. "You only just one two months ago."

The big man crossed his arms over his thick chest, his expression darkening. He glared at a jar of yellowish formaldehyde containing a severed hand.

"I know. Let's just say it wasn't worth my life to save the last one."

"Ah."

As Brand turned away to inspect a coiled intestine floating in a jar farther down the counter, Quincy scooped the pile of gizmos into a tray and retreated into the back room. There, his treasure trove of herbs, spices, tinctures, and medicines glittered at him from their orderly rows on shelves that reached to a high ceiling. He set the tray aside, picked up an empty one, and began collecting the requested ingredients, following a list he'd meticulously memorized and then burned decades ago. Capsaicin, toxic cinnabar, digitalis seeds, belladonna…

The apothecary couldn't help but be amazed once more as the tray grew heavy with poisons, deadly herbs, and minerals. Once, many years ago, these poisons would have been used by a pharmakon to concoct near-magical elixirs that would kill a normal man but which would lend a pharmakon super-human powers. They'd been the heroes of the past, swooping in to save innocent humans from the injustices meted out to them by their kashmari overlords. Now, though, with the death of the last pharmakon nearly thirty years past, no one even knew how to brew them anymore.

"You always give Cadmus Brand whatever he asks for," Quincy's father had admonished. "And don't ask questions."

He'd asked his father if Brand was a pharmakon. The ailing apothecary had quietly shaken his head.

"No. There will never be a real pharmakon again, not like there used to be. Brand has other uses for the poisons. Just keep him supplied."

Pulling his thoughts away from the past, Quincy placed a final vial of nutmeg seeds onto the tray, collected the extra empty vials and alcohol, and brought them out again to Brand.

Quincy froze. A pair of kashmari stood alongside the big man, elongated ears and slender fingers dripping with silver jewelry set against their bluish skin. Humanoid in appearance, the delicate-boned kashmari made up the upper classes of society. Humans were the servants, laborers, and skilled artisans who lived and worked at the pleasure of their kashmari lords.

This particular kashmari lord's grayish-blue skin looked sickly next to Brand's solid tan, and the three-piece suit he wore seemed a bit too tight around his middle. The lady, on the other hand, was laced up in a corseted gown that made her waist seem unnaturally narrow, and her sky-blue face was decorated with delicate white lines and ticking on her lips.

Their clothes were made of fine silk, but devoid of any gems or other embellishments save for a pair of matching brooches they wore that signified their rank as a baron and baroness. Minor kashmari nobles, then.

Brand towered more than a head above the creatures. He stood waiting silently, as was expected. But there was a tension in the set of his jaw and the way he held his shoulders that worried the apothecary.

Quincy frowned slightly. The kashmari didn't seem at all suspicious of Brand. Perhaps they didn't know who the gladiator was, though Quincy found that highly unlikely as Brand spent far more time among the kashmari nobility than he did among humans these days.

The kashmari baroness peered into a jar while she talked.

"The human I can understand—they're so weak-willed—but even a lowborn ought to have enough self-control."

"I could never do it," the baron said with a snort. "Filthy things, humans. I'd rather go without than let a human into my bed. Just couldn't do it."

"Nor could I," the baroness said, tapping the side of the jar. The tentacles inside wobbled. She pulled her gloved hand back with her lip curled. "Even if that weren't enough, though, I would have thought the threat of punishment would be enough to stop them. Even these humans here know that the punishment for interracial sexual relations is death."

The baron shrugged. "Exceptions to the rule are made, providing the female is properly disposed of afterward. I've heard Fafnir himself breeds human females for that specific purpose. And, well, we are speaking of Ivan, after all. He'd sleep with an Apida if he could figure out how."

The baroness's lip curled further in distaste.

Quincy quietly placed the tray with the alchemy kit under the counter and pulled out a handful of brown paper bags full of loose herbal tea. He saw Brand gesture over to him.

"Excuse me, good sir," the gladiator drawled. "The teas are to die fer, sir, so ev'ry time I come up here, I grab some for my granny." Brand turned and Quincy saw that the gladiator was wearing a half-faced monocle mask and a tinkerer's gauntlet he'd grabbed from a table. The effect was startling and indeed quite distracting. No wonder the kashmari didn't recognize him. Quincy sighed in relief.

Both Brand and the kashmari leaned on the counter. The kashmari lady gestured to Quincy with a long blue hand draped in slender silver chains hooked onto her many rings.

"Let me smell those teas."

The apothecary obliged, and the kashmari sniffed. Her eyes closed and a smile crept onto her painted face.

"I'll take a few bags of these as well. Also one box of crystal vials."

Quincy bobbed his head. "Of course, m'lady. One moment."

She picked at her long nails. "Our apothecary in New Braunen has little experience in crystal blowing. His vials are useless. I have to restock whenever I visit Darnan," the kashmari lady said in response to Brand's quizzical look.

"Oh. Are ya here fer the fight?"

The baron smiled. "Of course. The fight between Brand of Darnan and Percy of Duat promises to be the fight of the century."

"I do hope the fuss from last week won't interfere with this week's fight," the baroness said, turning to Quincy. "Tell me, as an apothecary: Is it true that the herbs left behind in the arena belonged to a pharmakon?"

Quincy smiled apologetically and shrugged. "I'm afraid I wouldn't know. I've never heard of a real pharmakon in Darnan. Every so often, some idiots come in asking for special herbs they think will give them magical powers, but I always turn them away before they kill themselves or someone they love."

It was true, save for Brand. Quincy wondered what exactly the gladiator used the poisons for. For just a second, he envisioned the big man erupting in light and burning these two kashmari lords to ash.

But Brand just stood there leaning against the counter with a tight smile plastered on his lined face. *The pharmakons are all dead,* Quincy reminded himself. *There's no one to fight for us humans anymore.*

The kashmari lord snorted. "Wise, very wise indeed. I think the apothecary is right, dear. Lord Fafnir did away with their kind decades ago."

He turned back to Brand. His eyes narrowed as he took in Brand's large, muscled frame. "You seem…familiar. Have we met before?"

Quincy's heart stopped.

Brand cleared his throat and shrugged nonchalantly. "Brand of Darnan is my cousin. Second cousin, really. People say we look a lot alike, y'know?"

"Ah, yes," the baron said. "I saw him earlier this year when he came down to the coast. You do look quite alike. Are you here to watch the fight as well then?"

Brand nodded with a smile. "I don' get ta see 'im that offen. Never met him, truthfully; too famous, y'know? We still go on about him plenny at home, though."

"You are from Duat?"

"Yep."

The baroness squinted at Brand. "You don't look Duati."

Brand shrugged. "Most people don' realize some o' us are darker skinned. Not many of us are, but some."

"Is Brand from Duat as well?"

"Naw. He was born up here. Can't remember exactly how, since I thought his ma and pa were from Duat too."

She smiled tightly. "Well. Let us both pray to the Guardian that Brand will find success in his fight."

Brand smiled broadly. Quincy was sure the smile was genuine. "Thank ye kindly, ma'am. I'm sure he'd appreciate yer consideration."

Quincy finished collecting the kashmari's order. "That will be two gold pieces, sir."

The baroness examined the crystal vials with pursed lips. "These vials are hardly any better than the ones back in New Braunen."

"I assure you, these are the finest crystal vials in Darnan," Quincy said, his face falling. It was a game he knew he wouldn't win.

"I will not pay for inferior vials," the baron said, turning to leave. "Come, dear. Surely we can find another apothecary."

"Can I offer them to you for half price, m'lord?" Quincy said desperately.

The two kashmari turned, smiles back on their faces. They paid the apothecary and left.

Brand quietly moved over to the glass windows at the front of the shop and watched the kashmari walk down the street. Then he sauntered back over and cast a keen eye over the contents of the tray Quincy had pulled back out and set on the counter. Satisfied, he fished a coin pouch out of a pocket.

"Is it really worth all this trouble?" Quincy asked as he gingerly placed the contents of the tray into a sack.

Brand looked up from counting coins. "Is what worth it?"

"You know. Is it worth dodging half the city just to get these poisons? What if they catch you and assume it means you're a pharmakon?"

"Is it worth it to still be in business even though you get fleeced by three-quarters of your clientèle?" the gladiator responded.

Quincy said, "I've learned to compensate. I raise my prices for them so that when they think they're cutting me off at the knees, they're really just paying normal prices."

Brand chuckled and said cryptically, "We all compensate in our own ways. These are mine. And yes, it's worth it to me, even if it means I hafta put on a show fer 'em."

The big gladiator pulled the monocle mask and gauntlet off and set them carefully on the counter. The skin on the right side of Brand's face had red creases where the mask had suctioned onto it.

He flexed his hand, then fished a small piece of thick paper from his pocket and unfolded it, placing it on the counter between them. On it was a photograph of Brand, bare-chested and smirking, in the midst of several scantily clad women. A title had been scrawled across the top in big garish letters:

THE BODACIOUS BRAND OF DARNAN

VS

THE POWERFUL PERCY FROM DUAT

A ONCE IN A LIFETIME EXPERIENCE YOU WON'T WANT TO MISS!

He tapped a finger on his likeness. "You ever been to see a fight?"

The apothecary shook his head.

"All these years, you've been my friend, supplying me, but never knowing why and never asking," Brand mused. "Come in three days and find me after the match. I'll explain everything."

"It's just a couple of men pounding each other," Quincy said. "I've never seen the point."

Brand smiled knowingly. "There's a bit more to it than that."

Quincy hesitated, frowning at the sack of poisons he'd collected. What could the gladiator want with them, anyway? They were useless to anyone but a pharmakon, and if Brand really was one of them, the entire city would know.

Even though Quincy had been a young child when the last pharmakon had died, he remembered how the kashmari coming into the shop had whispered in fear to his father, making him swear to turn the pharmakon in if he ever saw the man. He'd held the kashmari in terrified thrall for decades, stalking the streets of Darnan at night, protecting the innocent and raining down vengeance upon any kashmari bold enough to step outside their gilded estates. The day the pharmakon had died, the kashmari had paraded his corpse through the streets with great fanfare.

If Brand had the abilities of a pharmakon and used them in a fight, High Lord Fafnir would have killed the gladiator in a heartbeat.

Quincy looked up at Brand. No, Brand might be a fighter, but only for his own gain. Still, if the old gladiator somehow used pharmakon herbs in his fights, it might be worth seeing.

Curiosity got the better of Quincy, who sighed and held out a hand, which Brand took. "Alright. I'll be there."

"Until then," Brand said, his deep voice resonating in his barrel chest. "And thank you. It means the world to me that I can always count on you. If you ever need anything, don't hesitate to ask."

The gigantic man then dropped a few coins on the counter and picked up the sack. Brand pulled up the bandana around his neck so that it covered his nose and mouth, pulled on a pair of dark sunglasses, and donned his hat, effectively covering up his face. Then he stepped out into the harsh afternoon sunlight.

* * *

Even with dark glasses, Brand had to squint in the harsh sunlight. He stared down the packed gravel road lined on either side with tall shops built with sand-colored bricks, the garish paint peeling and bleached by the sun to a mere suggestion of their former color. Cables loosely stitched the two rows of buildings together like a corset, occasionally serving as a clothesline for someone who lived above their shop. Palms swayed high above the rooftops, lending no shade to the street below.

Besides the dust that scoured Brand's nose and throat with every breath, the air carried a delicious aroma of roasting meat and the sharp stench of overused cooking oil.

He glanced around at the various pedestrians. None seemed even the slightest bit interested in him. Most wore wide-brimmed hats and kept their heads down to keep the murderous sunlight out of their eyes. This district was too poor for impractical suits or dresses; threadbare, loose linen shirts reigned regardless of gender.

Despite their obvious poverty, the dusty street was neat and free of trash. An old woman, her eyes milky white, sat on a little wooden stool outside a flower shop, smiling and chatting with the baker who'd stopped by. Bougainvillea cascaded like a magenta waterfall from every window box. Puddles of fallen pink bracts pooled along the gutters. A young man and woman wearing threadbare but clean clothes played a pair of wooden flutes, nodding their thanks to passersby who dropped a few coins into the instrument case at their feet.

Satisfied, Brand stepped out into the street, dodging a mechanohorse carriage with its gears and cogs clicking and squeaking. He made his way down the street for about a mile.

Brand paused in front of a poster pasted up against a whitewashed brick building. It was a larger copy of the advertisement he'd shown the apothecary. Two young boys were standing there, pretending the punch each other in the face and narrating their antics.

"I take a swing at you—"

"You missed! I pick up a staff and swing it at you! It hits your arm! You can't use your arm now!"

"If I were someone else, that would be true—but I'm Brand the Magnificent! I can use my arm anyway!"

"He's not Brand the Magnificent. He's Brand the Barbaric."

"They change it every time. See the poster? He's Brand the Bodacious this time."

"What's 'bodacious' mean?"

"It's another word for awesome."

Brand chuckled to himself. Then his smile faded. Darnan had its problems, but the city was his home and he loved it. If he didn't win this fight...Brand shoved that thought aside. He just had to win. Somehow.

Brand ducked down a short alley, then stepped out onto a much wider street paved with smooth sandstone and lined with cafes and market stalls. Looking south, down the street, Brand could see the steam from the trains of the Southern Depot billowing up over the top of the steep copper roofs. A deep, sonorous bell tolled four times.

Something heavy and mechanical slammed into Brand's back, sending him flying forward into a flimsy table. He staggered, then pulled himself up and turned in time to duck as a massive mechanical arm shattered the glass window right where his head had been a moment before. A million shards of glass exploded around him in a shower of stars, biting into his skin as he flung his arms up to protect his eyes. He then dove into a roll, shoulder first, as the mechanical arm slammed down once more, cracking the brick sidewalk.

Brand rolled into a sprint that carried him several meters away, then spun, getting his first real look at the monster.

It was a man in a heavy mechanical suit. Tubes sprouted from massive claw hands and heavy mechanical feet, fed by a thick battery backpack. Gears clanked as the machine thundered toward Brand, pistons firing and steaming. It closed the distance between them frighteningly fast and swung at Brand with a massive metal claw.

Brand scrambled out of the way and felt the air as the claw barely missed him. It took another step and swung its other arm, sending Brand flying to the pavement again.

"Who are you?" Brand growled in exasperation at the machine suit. He couldn't see a face behind the bronze-tinted faceplate.

In response, the mechanical claw facing Brand opened wide to reveal a muzzle between the two claw halves. Brand rolled quickly to one side just as the muzzle fired off a shot. It hit the brick, sending red chips flying up into Brand's face. The claw twisted towards Brand. He rolled back the other way, the next shot nearly catching him in the shoulder.

If he let this thing keep knocking him around, Brand wasn't going to be alive to make it to the gladiatorial fight. His mind flashed to his customized gauntlet sitting safe and useless in a drawer in his office at home. He cursed. He'd have to do this the old-fashioned way.

He rolled forward between the machine suit's legs and gave the butt of the suit a hard kick.

The machine suit staggered but didn't fall.

Brand darted to the side sprinted up another road lined with more shops, searching frantically for some way to escape. Great long strides carried him through a cloud of smoke from a restaurant roasting meat on an outside patio. He then vaulted over a low planter spilling over with sweet jasmine, brushing it and releasing its scent.

Brand heard the stomping of the machine behind him, closing fast. To his right was another alley, much narrower and twisted than the one he stood in. An awful stench leeched out of it. He glanced back at the machine, then plunged into the alley.

Plague

It was cooler here with the walls much closer together shading the steps that twisted up the crooked alley. A bit of moss even clung tenaciously to a few cracks in the walls.

The steps were littered with bodies—dead bodies, others nearly dead, and still more trying to die. They moaned, cried, screamed. The reek of decomposition hit him like a brick to the face. Brand clenched his teeth and breathed as slowly as possible through his teeth. Behind him, he heard the machine suit's heavy footfalls.

Still, Brand hesitated. Pruritic plague. It made his own skin crawl as he watched one poor woman scratch and scratch until the patch of skin tore beneath her jagged fingernails.

One emaciated man nearest to Brand seemed less tattered than the rest, with his skin covered in sores that didn't seem infected yet. The man's distinctive hairstyle, with the sides of his head shaved, and a goatee worn long with braids, was blatantly foreign, though Brand wasn't sure where from. *Somewhere out east, perhaps,* Brand thought.

The man's strange grey eyes met Brand's; then he lifted a wineskin to his lips, drank deeply, and sank into a dejected stupor.

Brand glanced back and saw that the machine suit had sprinted past the alley. But the stomping halted as the man in the suit realized Brand had vanished. The gladiator only had a moment before the machine suit operator figured out where he'd gone and came ploughing down this alley in hot pursuit.

Brand took a long, steadying breath and gagged. So long as he didn't touch any of them, he'd be alright, he reassured himself. He examined the still-living wretches—most seemed lost in their private worlds, tortured but contained.

Brand glanced behind him and saw the machine suit catch sight of him and surge down the alley after him. Wincing, Brand lunged forward, trying to pick his way through them at speed, trying to ignore them.

A woman lurched up and caught Brand by the front of his shirt. Brand let out an involuntary yelp and gagged at the smell of rotting, infected flesh. The dying woman's face and hands were covered with long, oozing wounds. Pus and blood smeared across Brand's skin wherever she touched him as she clawed at Brand's face, neck, and arms in a crazed flurry.

He shoved the woman into a pile of bloated dead bodies and ran the rest of the way down the alley, no longer caring if he stepped on anyone.

At the end of the alley, the machine suit caught up to Brand. It lunged forward and smashed the gladiator in the gut, sending him sliding into a pile of decomposing bodies. Fueled by disgust and panic, Brand jumped up, ran at the wall, planted a foot against it, and used it to spring into the air and onto the machine suit.

The suit flailed its great claws, trying to rid itself of its pest. But Brand hung on, fingers scrabbled around at the base of the helmet until his fingers found a switch. He punched the release for the faceplate. The shield swished open, revealing an angry and surprised man with a bulbous nose. Brand pulled his fist back to punch the man, but the suit spun violently and crashed into the wall. The force of it sent Brand flying off the suit and skidding down the wall. The machine reached down and picked Brand up by the ankle. It raised its other claw to strike Brand.

Dangling upside down, Brand managed to grab the claw as it careened toward him. He heard the gears scrape as he pushed, bulging muscles straining against the powerful machine's pistons. Somewhere down the twisted alley, he heard someone shouting.

"Look at that! Who is that man?"

Another: "That's impossible!"

The man in the machine suit seemed to agree. He looked confused. The claw withdrew and Brand let go. Brand curled up to grab at his boots, unlacing them as fast as he could. He pulled at the laces, and then, as the claw came back for another swing, Brand loosened the last lace and fell barefoot to the cobbled street.

The machine suit tossed his boots aside.

Brand slipped under the arm of the machine suit and leapt onto its back with a grunt. Tired muscles screaming, he hauled himself up to the faceplate once more. This time, he didn't hesitate. His fist flew at the man's face again and again.

Brand's hand came away bloody before the man in the machine suit sputtered, "Stop! Please!"

Brand seized the man's throat and squeezed. "Get out of the suit," he growled.

Blood streaming from his now broken bulbous nose, the man nodded. Brand released the man. The suit hissed, then a series of clicks sounded from the many seams. Brand hauled off the heavy metal chest plate as it released and threw it to the side so that the man inside could clamor out.

Brand immediately grabbed him by the shoulders and pinned him to the wall.

"Who are you? Why are you trying to kill me?" Brand snarled.

The man hesitated a moment, then tightly pressed his quivering lips together.

Brand slammed the man's head into the wall. The man's eyes crossed.

"Why are you trying to kill me?" he yelled again.

"Alright, alright!" the man sputtered, dabbing at his swollen nose. "I was hired by a kashmari who bet heavily on your last fight and lost."

"Give me a name."

"B'alam Nehn."

I should let Kushchai handle this, Brand thought. He released the man, who collapsed to the ground with his hands still half-raised to his face. Brand fixed him with a savage glare, then pointed a long, blood-covered finger at him. "If you come after me again, you'll be dead. Do you understand?"

The man nodded, trembling. Brand knew that look. He'd seen it on the face of every would-be assassin over the years. It said the man was thinking that if this gladiator could survive an attack by a machine suit, could anything kill him?

Something would eventually, Brand knew. He wasn't about to go without a fight, though.

Brand took a look at the suit, thinking for a moment. Then he flipped it over onto its back and ripped out a couple of copper-plated tubes. They hissed as they wobbled, steam leaking from the ends. Finally, he hooked his fingers around a small, black cooling unit and yanked, dislodging it from the rest of the suit.

Brand gave the man one last threatening glare, then spun on his heel, wires trailing from the cooling unit as the gladiator strode away.

The Lady of Navar

Carrying the cooling unit in one large hand, Brand stalked down the alley to the bright street beyond. A few parasol-wielding ladies gasped and pointed at him, reminding him that he was covered in blood and dirt. He yanked his bandana back up over his mouth and nose and cast about for somewhere to clean up. His skin still prickled with the memory of the plague victim's hands grabbing at him.

A large fountain topped with the statue of an armored man astride a rearing mechanohorse stood in the middle of the wide street ahead. It wasn't ideal, but if he couldn't find a better place to wash off, the fountain would do.

Brand jogged toward the gray edifice, glancing about, hoping for a less public place to clean off the filth. Other pedestrians gave Brand a wide berth, eyes wide and voices hushed behind their gloved hands.

Just as he came within a few meters of the fountain, he caught sight of the Four Horsemen, a restaurant he'd been to some years ago. He jogged over and ducked inside.

The Four Horsemen was one of the more casual kashmari-run establishments that Brand had visited. The restaurant was dim as the only light came from the desert sun trickling through tinted glass windows at the front of the place. A black tile floor kept the establishment pleasantly cool. Instead of tables, the interior of the restaurant was a maze of booths separated by tall wooden dividers that gave diners a private, intimate experience. It felt like a cave, albeit a cave that was thoroughly swept and scrubbed five times a day and which provided an extensive menu of hearty sandwiches and beer.

Brand picked his way through the thick crowd, hunching down to blend in, face turned away from the bartender. At the back of the restaurant, he slipped into the restroom. This place catered to kashmari and richer humans, and thus provided a toilet and running water.

He placed the cooling unit on the tile floor. Then, twisting the faucet on, he splashed water on his hands and arms and scrubbed rigorously. Blood, dirt, and stinking, infected filth swirled down the drain.

"Are you ok?"

Brand spun. A scarred hand flew up to his bandana to make sure it was completely covering his face. His shoulders relaxed.

A man wearing a sharp jacket and wingtip shoes eyed Brand, taking in the gore spattered all over the gladiator. "You look like a man who's just come in contact with the Plague."

Brand blinked. "Yeah, just did, in fact." He shuddered. "There's an alley righ' down th' street a bit," Brand drawled. "Full o' plague victims. You smell 'em, turn tail and run."

The other man's eyes widened as he took a step backwards.

Brand turned back to the task at hand. He scrunched up his face as he pulled down the bandana so the man wouldn't recognize him, then scrubbed his face until it was raw and pink.

Finished with his ablutions, Brand shoved the bandana back into place, and with shaking hands, pulled out a small silk purse from his pocket. He reached one finger in and pulled out a single deep blood-red disk, a tiny pill that he quickly swallowed. Brand sighed in relief.

The top hat man cleared his throat. His eyes were fixed on the silk purse.

"Is that the prophylactic?"

Brand nodded.

"Since you brought the plague in here, do you mind…?" the man said pointedly.

"Oh, yeah." Brand pulled out another small pill and handed it to the man, who snatched and swallowed it in one smooth motion.

"Never can be too careful, can you?" the man said with a smile. "What a marvelous drug. A preventative for a terrible plague. Say, what is your profession? I don't meet many people with easy access to the prophylactic."

Brand nodded and lied through the Duati accent. "I'm a laborer in 'is Lord Kushchai's garden."

The man must have been expecting something more impressive because his smile turned icy. "Ah. Of course. I had the fortune of taking a tour of His Lord's gardens not two weeks ago. He is so very proud of them."

Brand couldn't keep the smirk off his hidden face as he watched the man twisting his brain into knots, trying to figure out how a laborer had been rewarded with a priceless medicine. The man gave up after an awkward moment, scooped up his hat, and swept out of the restroom.

Brand dried himself off, picked up the cooling unit, and left the restroom. He paused, then pushed his way to the front of the queue at the counter.

"Runnerbeast on rye, hold the tomatoes, and a Southern stout."

He tapped his fingers on the counter while he waited, then carried his food to a small table pressed up against the wall. A single soft amber bulb suspended above the table illuminated the booth.

Brand was only three bites in when a kashmari woman wearing a lacy dress and a wide lace-covered hat appeared next to his table.

"Mr. Brand?" she said in a silky voice.

Brand looked up and nearly choked on his food. He quickly rose to his feet.

"Lady Mirane," he said, grasping her gilded hand. "How may I help you?"

Lady Mirane, the kashmari city lord of Navar, a city in the mountains west of Darnan, gave Brand a coy smile that stopped his heart. "You've been such an attentive host that when I caught a sight of you in here, I just knew I had to stop and have a quick bite with you."

Brand returned the smile warmly. "It would be my pleasure, my lady."

He helped her settle into the chair opposite him and sat, trying not to gawk at her. But with eyes like sapphires, silvery hair that cascaded over her bare, storm-blue shoulders, and hourglass hips, he found it quite difficult. Brand had spent the better half of a week touring Darnan with Lady Mirane of Navar and Lord Jinn of Duat, and every time he saw Mirane, Brand's stomach always ended up in his throat. She somehow seemed familiar to Brand, as though he'd met her in a dream long ago.

She tilted her head and raised her eyebrows expectantly.

Brand coughed in embarrassment, then hurried over to the counter. He had to fight against the press of bodies to order the lady a sandwich. Then, that task accomplished, he returned to Mirane.

"Seems like a popular place, if a little informal," the kashmari lady commented. She took a bite of her sandwich, closed her eyes, and smiled as she chewed. She swallowed, then said, "Well, now I know why. This is excellent."

"Us locals always know the best eateries. I can't pass this place by without grabbing a bite," Brand lied.

"There used to be a little soup shop in Navar that I loved in the same way. On the coldest days, there was nothing quite like their bean and river bird soup to warm you up. Once I became the city lord, I hired the cook on as my personal soup chef."

"I think I'd go broke if I hired every excellent cook in Darnan to be my personal chef."

Mirane's light laughter made Brand's stomach do a flip.

"Unfortunately, I found out later that soup wasn't the only thing he was good at cooking. Turns out he was a pharmakon."

Brand winced. "That is unfortunate."

"You know something of pharmakons?" Mirane asked, surprised.

"A little. A lot more than your average human," Brand admitted. "I'm an amateur student of history, and it's impossible to read a history of the Kashmari City-States without coming across pharmakon history as well."

"Is that how you know so much about the history of Darnan? During our tour, it seemed you knew every statue, every district, every shop. You learned all that from reading books?" She took another bite.

Brand nodded. "As a youth, I spent a considerable amount of time at the library. It was one of the few places I could go to get away from the sun where they didn't care who I was."

"And who were you?"

"A nobody. A street urchin."

"Really? You?" Mirane tilted her head as though trying to see through his disguise. "I would never have guessed with your sophisticated attire and suave manners."

Brand looked down at his rough clothes dusted with a thin layer of grit and chuckled. "I'll never be a gentleman, that's true. But that's not what I'm paid for, is it?"

Brand could feel her gaze sweep over him, from his square bearded jaw to his broad shoulders, and arched her delicate eyebrows appreciatively.

"Are there other gladiators who don't look like gods from the past, or is that part of the job description?"

Brand grinned. "No one wants to watch a pair of ugly lugs beat each other to a pulp."

Mirane smirked. "Well, the men might be content with that, but the women certainly appreciate watching two rugged, well-muscled demigods trying to pulverize each other."

"Exactly."

"Speaking of gladiators, what brings a gladiator such as yourself out this way to the financial district?"

Brand froze for the barest moment, the events of the last hour flashing through his mind. He ran through the list of shops he knew were around here. "This district abuts a market road with a variety of shops. I'd heard from another gladiator about a shopkeeper nearby who knew of a weaponsmith who claims to know how to craft unbreakable knives. Turns out the gladiator heard wrong. The weaponsmith in question doesn't even forge knives."

Mirane smiled into her hand. "You really are dedicated to your work, aren't you? No time for a woman, I'm guessing."

Brand shrugged, trying to seem nonchalant. "I wouldn't say that. I'm sure I could find room in my life for the right woman."

Mirane leaned in close, a mischievious smile dancing on her azure lips. She tilted her head slightly, exposing her soft throat to him. Brand felt his face flush.

"But you haven't met her yet?"

Brand didn't answer immediately, instead letting his gaze follow the contours of Mirane's face. He dropped his gaze, trying to hide the smile, and cleared his throat. He looked back up, more in control.

"No, not yet."

Her smirk deepened as she straightened. She wiped her hands on her napkin and folded it primly across her lap, but her eyes shone.

"I should be going," Mirane said, standing. "I have a meeting in an hour with the high lord. I understand you'll be meeting with the other city lords and me in two days' time, correct?"

Brand nodded.

Mirane beamed at the gladiator. "I look forward to seeing you there."

She offered her hand to Brand, who took it to help her stand.

With that, the beautiful kashmari woman turned and walked away, leaving Brand in a daze.

The gladiator sat and finished his meal, then left the restaurant at a much slower pace than he'd entered. As he walked, the prophylactic pill finally calmed his mind, allowing him to savor the memory of Mirane's touch and her silken voice. He paused at the base of the fountain outside to take stock of his current situation.

Now that Mirane was gone, he realized with no small amount of trepidation that he had been far too flirtatious with her. She'd reciprocated, though, and thus was unlikely to turn him in. Besides, the booth had provided sufficient privacy that Brand doubted any kashmari there had noticed. All the same, he'd have to be careful not to let that happen again.

You'll be a dead man if you get involved with her, he reminded himself fiercely. *Keep it strictly professional from now on.*

He sighed and turned his attention to getting home. The pill was making his eyes and muscles feel heavy, so walking the rest of the way would be a slog. He was sufficiently far from the apothecary shop that Brand figured he could risk taking a cab. He flagged down one of the mechanohorse carriages and hopped inside onto a worn velveteen seat. The wooden compartment creaked a little as he adjusted his bulky frame.

"Face the camera, please," a smooth, mechanical female voice said.

Brand turned his face to the little round lens in the corner of the cab. The shutter twisted closed with a raspy click three times, and then a lock in the carriage door slammed shut.

"Destination, please."

Brand thought for a moment. He could visit Kushchai now and tell him of B'alam Nehn's machine suit attack, or he could tell the kashmari lord in two days when he would meet with Kushchai and the other city lords.

"Gladiator Row, Number 7."

A chime notified him that the destination had been accepted and identified. The carriage lurched forward. It swayed gently from the motion of the horse.

As the drug took full effect, Brand felt a coolness spread from his core out to his fingers and toes like he'd been dipped in water. His mind calmed. But then the effects deepened. His mind fogged up like a window in winter on a snowy day.

Rubbing his temples, Brand realized he'd taken two of the little red pills that day. With a sigh, he pulled the little black curtains over the windows. It made the little compartment stuffy and hot, but at least no one outside would see him. He closed his eyes and succumbed to the drowsiness. He slipped into a vacant trance, then fell deep asleep.

FLASHBACK #1: THE FALL

Thirty-nine Years Earlier — 12 June 1023 P.E.
Financial District, Darnan

Brilliant sunshine ricocheted around the street, bouncing from the bank's polished limestone facade to the shining white pavestones, blinding any who might have peered into the shadows of a pillar where a young Brand watched a mechanohorse carriage approaching. He wiped a sleeve across eager amber eyes, brushed his sweaty dark hair aside, and licked his cracked lips. His stomach growled painfully. He gritted his teeth against the gnawing hunger and focused on the carriage.

He tapped his fingers impatiently against the smooth stone of the pillar as the carriage drew closer, its metal hooves clacking on the cobblestones, kicking up the thin film of dusty sand and spewing a light cloud behind it, warm golden bronze filigreed latticework skin shining like honey in the summer sun. Gears, pulleys, and pumps could be seen through the latticework, turning, twisting, and pumping to make the mechanical animal prance down the quiet street. It was the middle of the afternoon, and the sun's blast furnace heat had emptied the street. Brand glanced around and saw only a mangy dog cowering in the shade of a barrel.

As the equine machine passed by, Brand sprinted out from behind his pillar. Already as tall as most grown men, Brand's lanky legs carried him quickly across the gap. He leapt and grabbed the pole connecting the mechanohorse to the carriage it towed and heaved himself up until he could swing his leg over the metal horse's back. He clambered up and hooked his heels around the filigreed belly.

The horse didn't even pause. Once it was given a destination, mechanohorses only slowed or stopped for obstacles. And with no window in the front of the carriage, the passengers were none the wiser.

Brand pulled a screwdriver out of his pocket and leaned forward so that he could reach the back of the horse's head. A stiff false mane radiated like bronze sunbeams out of the back of its head, and to the right of the mane, Brand could see the dark little holes where the screws were. He stuck his screwdriver down one of the holes and began to twist.

Four screws later, Brand tugged on the false mane. It popped free, along with the panel it had been attached to, revealing a mass of wires. He brushed these aside, revealing a little black box underneath. Brand extracted the box, carefully maneuvering it through the wires and setting it between his legs. He reached back into the exposed cavity where a tiny marble-sized sphere of black diorite was held by five delicate prongs. Blue lightning skittered across its surface just under a thin transparent skin.

Brand yanked a handkerchief out of his pocket and, using it to protect his fingers, he reached in and plucked the marble out. With his other hand, he yanked the black box free of its wires at the same time.

The mechanohorse froze in place. The momentum of the carriage shoved the metal horse forward to the cobblestones, flinging the boy forward.

But Brand was ready. He vaulted off the back of the machine just as the door of the carriage opened. A kashmari lord, face ornamented with gold rings and chalk-white curling markings, stuck his head out with a shout. A bullet whizzed by Brand's head.

The boy ducked and swore, then dodged left while shoving his loot into a satchel slung over his shoulder.

"Stop, thief! Guards!" the kashmari screeched at a startled guard stepping out of the nearest pub. The guard stuck his head back into the pub and a moment later, a gaggle of city guards boiled out, stumbling and squinting in the brilliant sunlight.

Another bullet hit the cobblestones at Brand's feet and sent the lad scampering as fast as his gangly legs could carry him.

Brand dashed into an alley. He scampered up a ladder, sweaty hands slipping on the rungs, heart hammering. He dragged himself over the lip of the roof and squinted into the sun. All around him was a whole new layer to the city, one of parched rooftop gardens and sun-bleached undergarments hanging from clotheslines. From here, he could see the mountains rising in the west like a great gray wall, the Southern and Eastern Train Depots wreathed in thick steam, and the four districts of Darnan laid out neatly before him.

Behind him, Brand heard the rattle and thuds of boots on the metal ladder. Grinning at the thrill of the chase, he ducked under a clothesline and sprinted to the edge of the building, and bunching his legs, leapt across to the next building, landing with a roll. He nearly rammed into a wooden structure beaten by the wind and bleached grey by the sun.

Behind him, city guardsmen shouted at him to stop. A bullet zipped through a flapping sheet and hit the wooden structure beside Brand, sending splinters at the boy's face. With a yelp, Brand stumbled around to the other side of the building, then sprinted to the edge of the roof, muscles straining, preparing to launch himself toward the next building.

Just as he reached the edge of the roof, an arm surged upward and caught his tattered boot.

Brand cried out as he lurched downward, knees buckling, even as his momentum carried him over the edge of the roof. The hand hanging onto his boot wasn't strong enough to hold him. His trouser slipped out of the guard's grip and he barely caught a glimpse of the shocked face of the guardsman as he plummeted headfirst down the alley.

Then everything went black.

* * *

In the shade of the alley below, William slung his jacket over his shoulder, unbuttoned his waistcoat and the top button of the white undershirt below to try and relieve the heat, then pulled out his pipe. He glanced up at the shouts of "Stop!" and "In the name of the law!" coming from up above him on the rooftops. He rolled his eyes as he lit his pipe and stuck it between teeth bordered by a bristly mustache.

William blew out a cloud of smoke that rose lazily through the air and faded into the sunlight above the alley. He wasn't sure why he still smoked. It didn't calm him down like it did others; though, on the flip side, it also didn't do him any harm, either. He wasn't particularly fond of the smoky smell, and he wasn't addicted to it. He looked down at the pipe, then upended it, pouring out the burning herbs to the sandy ground. He crushed the embers under his shiny shoes with a sigh and pocketed the empty pipe.

He listened to the guards above, hooking his thumbs in his trouser pockets, bored.

Was this why he smoked? he wondered, glancing down at the black-edged tobacco leaves. Boredom? Hm. What else could he do out here on break if not smoke? Maybe tomorrow he should bring a book.

The shouts above William drew his attention once more. He tilted his dark head to the side to listen better. They were drawing closer. William surmised that the guardsmen must be on the tail of a particularly spry thief if they hadn't caught up to him yet. After all, most of the guards were in decent shape, William had to admit. They'd nearly caught *him* a few weeks ago one night, and that was no easy feat.

William lowered his eyes as a city guard with red hair clanked by William and hustled up the ladder to the roof. But then the guard paused, clinging just below the eaves like a lizard clinging to a rock, eyes fixed above.

Curious, William crossed to the other side of the alley and leaned his back up against the cool brick wall to get a better view.

A lanky adolescent boy appeared at the edge of the roof precisely where the guard lay in wait. The guard reached up like a striking scorpion, latching onto the boy's boot. But the boy's momentum was too much for the guard's fingers to keep hold of, and the boot was ripped out of the guard's hand. The boy let out a hoarse scream as he plummeted down five stories to the alley floor.

William barely had time to register what had happened before the boy crashed into a tall pile of crates and vanished.

He dashed over to the crates and started hauling broken boards aside. But when he had cleared them, instead of the broken body of a boy, he found only splinters and crushed vases that had been housed in the smashed crates.

The boy was gone.

William cursed and looked around the alley. It took a moment for him to find the lanky boy stumbling away, holding his head, a bit of blood seeping through his dark hair. He looked back and caught sight of William. Before the older man could say a word, the boy had turned on his heel and sprinted away, out of the alleyway.

The red-headed guardsman caught up to William, nursing his hand. The guard glanced among the crates and swore.

"Where'd he go?" he asked.

William pointed in the opposite direction the boy had gone. "That way, I think. How'd he survive that fall? That must have been fifty feet!"

The guard snorted. "I'll ask him when I catch him." And he trotted off down the alley, beckoning to the guards on the roof to follow.

William made a covert sign with his hand behind his back and followed the boy at a more nonchalant pace.

* * *

Brand's head ached as he stumbled down the street. With every step he took, though, the pains in his shoulders and neck slowly receded. When he could no longer hear the city guards behind him, he slowed his pace and picked his way through the city until he found himself on a street that was shaded with huge sun-bleached cloth sails draped from rooftop to rooftop. Shops and restaurants lined the street. No carriages were allowed down this street, allowing pedestrians to flood the sidewalk and cobblestoned marketplace. Brand sighed and breathed in the relatively cooler air laced with cinnamon, ginger, and cardamom.

He'd been lucky those crates were there to break his fall, he thought. He touched the bruise on his forehead and winced. At least the thumping headache seemed to be easing.

The boy walked over to a green-tinged fountain and stuck his entire head in, scrubbing the grit and sweat out of his hair. He then scooped water into his mouth and all over his arms, like a bird bathing itself.

Dripping and refreshed, Brand paused to take stock of his surroundings. He glanced up and down the street and listened carefully for the clank and thud of guardsman boots. A couple of Duati women with shawls pulled up over their ghostly faces drew their purses closer to their bodies, but that was all. No one cared about him. He was just another scrawny brat among hundreds of dirty street urchins that inhabited Darnan.

So the lanky boy set off, dodging between pedestrians until he came to a shop brimming with mechanical odds and ends and pieces of scrap metal hanging from the eaves of every shape and size imaginable. He smiled at the smell of machine oil and old dirt. Brand felt as though he were stepping into a mechanical cave, thanks to all the metal parts hanging from the walls and ceiling.

It was blessedly cool in here thanks to two giant fans whirring away at the back, powered by a spindly robot peddling away on a bicycle-like contraption. A giant clock with exposed gears hung over a long counter crammed with all manner of clockwork knickknacks and robots in various states of disassembly and repair. Brand caught sight of the crumpled, greenish body of a corroded mechanohorse slumped in a corner.

He dodged through the piles of junk to the back of the shop. A tall fat man in spectacles perched on a stool that was too small for him, hunched over a mechanical sewing machine that had been pulled apart and laid out in front of him, the delicate pieces of metal glinting in the pale light of a tiny headlamp secured to the man's forehead with a leather strap.

"Ah, young Cadmus," the man said, his face breaking out into a broad smile. "What have you got for me today?"

"Hi, Mr. Alastair," Brand said as he fished his spoils out of his satchel. He opened the handkerchief, revealing the diorite marble. The lightning that had been skittering across its surface earlier was gone, leaving only its polished black surface.

Alastair picked up the box gently and turned it this way and that, hazel eyes quietly analyzing and valuing it. His eyes lit up as he turned his attention to the marble. He picked it up with his bare, thick fingers. As soon as his skin touched its surface, explosions of blue burst under the pressure. Brand's eyes widened.

"Why isn't it burning you?" he asked the shopkeeper.

Alastair waved his free hand dismissively. "Calloused fingers."

Brand frowned, but he knew better than to question the old man's lie.

"Have I ever told you the story of the princess and the

mechanohorse?" Alastair asked.

Brand loved listening to the man's stories. The old mechanic loved to tell tales of another world far, far away from this dirty, hot, stinky mess of a city. But just then, Brand's stomach growled audibly. The shopkeeper chortled, his great belly rolling.

"Maybe later?"

"I'd just really like payment for now, Mr. Alastair. I haven't eaten in three days."

"Three days? What did I tell you, boy?" The shopkeeper sighed, shaking his head. "I take it you haven't taken your prophylactic today either, then."

Brand shook his head. "I ran out yesterday."

Alastair growled softly in the back of his throat and threw Brand an exasperated look. He pulled a small pouch out from a pocket inside his shirt. He wedged two thick fingers in and pulled out a tiny, red pill, which he handed to Brand.

"One a day—"

"—every day," Brand finished, bored. He swallowed the pill.

Alastair pulled out another pill and swallowed it himself. "I'll get you more tonight." He reached beside him into a satchel and pulled out a roll, which he tossed to Brand. "Here. That'll keep you alive another two minutes while I get the money."

Brand ripped the roll apart and stuffed pieces of it into his mouth. He had to slow down, though, as the dry bread sucked all of the moisture from his mouth.

The marble vanished into a pouch at Alistair's belt. The large shopkeeper stood and went around to the other side of the counter and started pulling out various drawers, searching.

"Remind me to tell you that story someday," Alastair muttered as he shifted a heavy bag aside so he could get to another set of drawers. After another moment of rummaging, the big man exclaimed.

"Ha! There it is." Alastair pulled a small leather purse out of a drawer. Leaning forward, elbows on a tiny circle of clutter-free counter, he held out the money purse to the boy. "Here you are. If you have a mind, I have a few chores you can do for a few more coins later, once you fill that bottomless pit of a stomach."

Brand reached for the purse, but Alastair held on. "Mind you come back before dark, lad. The crews are working overtime this week. You had me in a panic when you vanished. I thought they'd caught you and left you dead in a ditch."

Brand snorted, tugging at the purse. "They'll never catch me."

Alastair refused to release his grip. "Sundown, you understand?"

Brand sighed and nodded. "Fine."

Alastair nodded, satisfied, finally loosening his grip.

Brand snatched the purse and scurried out of the shop.

Once out in the street again, Brand stopped to think of what he wanted to eat. Alastair expected him to use it all and had lectured him at length on the importance of providing his growing body with all the nutrients it needed. But Brand had taken to buying a bowl of flatbread and beans and then saving the rest of the money to buy cheap tickets to see the gladiators. There was a fight tomorrow, too…

Brand caught a whiff of roasting meat and his resolve evaporated. He was so tired of flatbread and beans, so dry and empty and tasting of wood shavings. He wanted meat and vegetables and fruit. Those were important for a strong, growing boy, weren't they? He could eat flatbread and beans tomorrow instead. And besides, Alastair had said he had something for Brand to do for a few pennies he could use to buy a ticket.

The spicy aromas led Brand like a siren song to the front of a street cart with a huge hunk of some animal roasting on a spit off to the side. Brand hurried to the woman at the cart and ordered a flatbread and roasted meat, cut up peppers on the side. He gave her most of the money in the pouch, then scampered off around the corner. He sat down beside a ragged woman strumming a guitar and crooning softly below a tree with feathery leaves and purple trumpet-shaped flowers. Listening to her gentle music, the boy unwrapped his food and began to eat.

Brand ate as slowly as he could, savoring every bite, from the soft and juicy peppers to the crispy outside of the flatbread and its pillowy interior. The spicy meat made his head a little fuzzy and his nose run.

As he ate, Brand noticed a small girl watching him with large, hungry eyes. Her clothes were worn and tattered like Brand's, and she was even scrawnier than he. The boy's heart ached as he realized she was staring at his food.

Brand looked down at the food. He'd have flatbread and beans tomorrow, he knew, while this little girl may not get any food for a week.

With one last sad look at the delicious food, Brand beckoned her over and offered her the last of his food. Her eyes lit up as she wolfed down the meat and flatbread. Brand smiled.

When the food was gone, Brand closed his eyes. The little girl curled up next to him. Together, the children let the warm shade and the soft whisper of the breeze in the tree above lull them to sleep.

* * *

William watched the boy go into the shop from across the street, twiddling his unlit pipe between his fingers. Then the boy came out, holding a small money pouch and looking up and down the street as though trying to decide something. Then he ran off.

Probably going to go get something to eat, William mused as he detached himself from the hot brick wall and sauntered across the street. Guardian knows he needs it.

William ducked inside the shop and looked around at the heaps of slightly organized junk.

"Hello there!" called a jovial tenor voice from the back. A tall, broad man with bright eager hazel eyes appeared. "Can I interest you in a refurbished servitor—?"

The shopkeeper picked up a motionless clockwork monkey wearing a threadbare top hat and flicked a switch at the base of its rusted iron skull. It shuddered, then turned its head to William with a creak.

"Hhow may Iassis—sss—t you?"

William grimaced. "Eh, no, that's not why I'm here. I don't want to buy anything."

"Alright then." The shopkeeper shrugged, then flicked the monkey's switch again. The simian servitor crumpled. The shopkeeper set it back on the counter, then turned and proffered a heavy hand to William.

"What can I do for you, kind sir?"

William accepted the handshake. As he did, the shopkeeper's sleeve slid back slightly, revealing a strange blue and green wave tattoo cut by sharp geometric lines starting at the man's wrist. He noted that the same pattern peeked out from under the collar of the man's shirt. William frowned slightly. Colored tattoos were rare in Darnan, as were the pigments required to ink them.

"What can you tell me about that boy that just came in here? Do you know him?"

William watched a wall slam down behind the man's eyes, though the smile didn't falter.

"The boy? Oh, he's just a kid, an orphan, really, who hangs around here. Does odd jobs for me, sleeps in the back. You know how it is on the streets. I keep an eye on him. Why?"

William cut to the chase. "That kid fell off a five-story building into a pile of crates and walked it off as though he'd merely tripped over a rock."

The shopkeeper looked like he'd bitten into a sour lime. "Look. He's a tough kid and I'm sure the crates broke his fall. He's completely normal."

William drew himself up tall but still was a head shorter than the shopkeeper. He glared at the bigger man. "He's not and you know it," William said quietly.

The shopkeeper took a step closer until he loomed ominously over William.

"Drop it," the shopkeeper hissed. "Get lost and leave the kid alone. Keep your mouth shut, or you'll meet the business end of a rifle. Do you understand?"

"I can help him," William whispered. "Without help, Fafnir will find him and kill him. You can't hide him forever."

The shopkeeper's gaze never faltered, but something flickered behind those hazel eyes. William pressed on.

"Are you his father?" he whispered. The big man's jaw clenched but he shook his head. "Uncle?"

Another shake of his head.

"Like I said, he's just an urchin."

William shrugged, unconvinced. The boy was already large for his age and shared some of the shopkeeper's more robust features. *Why the secrecy?* William wondered. But he pressed forward. "You must worry about him, and what his abilities mean. Let me teach him to fight, to protect himself."

The shopkeeper cleared his throat and looked away, and around at the tattered shop. William realized that this man was almost as poor as the boy, and perhaps had even given the boy his last few coins so the lad could have a decent meal. William thought he might be getting through to the big man.

Then something behind William caught the shopkeeper's eye and the big man's face hardened again. He wordlessly pointed out of the shop with one stiff hand.

William sighed and nodded, and left, frustrated and worried.

* * *

As the mustached stranger walked out, a stray breeze from the great fans dislodged a canvas tarp draped across the counter, exposing a vambrace made from a strange bluish metal that was impossibly smooth and free of tarnish. The tarp fluttered again, revealing a massive claymore etched with unfamiliar runes that lay beside the gauntlet. Alastair sidled over to them cautiously and readjusted the tarp, then tied a rope around the armaments to keep the tarp from slipping. As his hand brushed the gauntlet, the metal seemed to ripple slightly.

Alastair glanced up nervously and saw the stranger standing in the doorway, outlined against the bright street. The man was staring back at the tarp. Then he turned and left without a word.

The shopkeeper wiped at the sweat beading on his brow. Who was that man? Could he be trusted? Alastair looked down at the vague lumps under the tarp. If that man said even a word to the wrong person, Cadmus Brand and he were dead men.

The big man stood frozen in indecision for a long moment, considering his options. He didn't have many. Finally, Alastair leaned down and took out a piece of thick paper and an old pen from under the counter and began to write a letter.

Gladiator Row, Number 7

7 August 1062 P.E.
Gladiator Row, Darnan

The lurch of the carriage as it came to a sudden halt jolted Brand back to the land of the living. He pulled out a coin and inserted it into a small slit in the wall of the carriage, then twisted a small lever next to it. Beside him, the carriage door unlocked with a grinding clank.

Brand stepped out onto a street that couldn't have been more different from the district he had just left. The street was paved with glistening white stone and lined with two stately rows of pindo palms, their lush feathery fronds rustling in the breeze between the tall black lamp posts. The buildings gleamed of polished stone. Very few people walked, but the street was crowded with carriages, their mechanical horses' hooves clacking smartly on the pavestones.

Brand went up the smooth stone steps to his house and barged in, leaving the door ajar and leaving dusty footprints on the thick rug stretching down the entryway hall.

"Good afternoon, Mrs. James," he mumbled to the elderly housekeeper, who was wiping down the hall mirror.

"Take those dusty boots off and close that door, young man! You'll let the dust of ages in!" She shook her rag at him.

Moira James was about as short as Brand was tall and had the sort of personality that could fill a room on its own. Her short-cropped white hair, faded rose-kissed lips, and graceful long fingers whispered of the memory of a beautiful young woman, though the years and her devotion to Brand had tried to bury that memory in worry lines. Her worn, leathery lips pursed together, but her soft black eyes twinkled at the hulking gladiator.

"Oh," he mumbled, as though he were a schoolboy instead of a grown man of fifty-two, and dutifully obeyed. He donned a pair of house shoes set by the door.

"How has your day been?" he asked. He blinked several times, trying to brush aside the brain fog.

Mrs. James arched an eyebrow as she took in his battered appearance.

"Quite well, thank you," she said primly. "I see you've been busy."

"Nothing to worry about," he said.

Her mouth formed a line as her eyes went from the cuts on his face down to his bloodied knuckles, but she didn't press him.

She handed him a sleek, sealed envelope. "This was delivered for you this morning. Dinner will be roast runnerbeast with potatoes and pear sauce at six o'clock, Mr. Brand."

"Thank you, Mrs. James," Brand replied. "I'll be up in my office."

"Of course, sir. If you'd do me a favor and not burn any more holes in your office rug, though, I'd be most grateful. I'm running out of excuses for the man who sells the rugs down in the market."

Brand smiled and gave the old woman a peck on the cheek. She patted his cheek fondly in return.

"I'm so glad they allowed me to come keep house for you, boy," Mrs. James said with a smile.

"It was a part of the agreement," Brand said for the hundredth time. "I told them either I brought my old nanny, or they couldn't have me."

"Your old nanny, hah! If my dear William could have been here to hear you call me your nanny, he would have died laughing."

Brand's face fell at the name of his old mentor. Mrs. James saw and smiled sadly.

"He'd be so proud of you, as I am," she said.

Brand shook his head. "Would he be, though? What's there to be proud of? Hiding my abilities, barely using them, championing the cause of the very creatures he taught me to fight."

"William never wanted to admit that his cause was a losing one," Mrs. James said, "but it was. The kashmari can't be beaten. But your abilities have enabled you to rise to the top where you can do as much good as you can, inspiring people, lifting their spirits."

"Distracting them from realizing how bad they have it so they don't have the will to resist."

"Distracting them from realizing how bad they have it so they don't throw their lives away on a lost cause."

Brand crossed his arms over his chest and shook his head with a deep frown that knit his thick dark eyebrows together. His heart sank. Mrs. James hadn't always been this cynical. He turned his thoughts to the plague-ridden woman who had accosted him in the alley.

"If I were a better pharmakon, like those of the past, I could do so much more," the gladiator murmured. "I could cure the plague, find a way to get rid of the kashmari, and make life better for people."

Mrs. James patted his shoulder.

"I need to go prepare for the fight," Brand said. He sighed, then strode off to his office. "I'll take coffee in my office, please," he said over his shoulder.

He let his hand glide along the smooth acacia wood of the banister, following the rich dark grain, then looked down over the foyer below.

When he'd bought this house with his earnings from fights, it had been a burned-out, dust-filled husk, the victim of a fire caused by a lightning strike. Over a few years, he'd refurbished it, bit by bit, from the ground up, adding in a sweeping staircase and balcony overlooking the parquet foyer, importing rare stones from the mountains for tiles in the bathrooms, and thick rugs from Niven, a town of shepherds and master rug knotters.

It was a great life, he had to admit, but…

He shook off the discontent and continued on to his office, a high-ceilinged library lined by floor-to-ceiling bookcases stuffed to overflowing. Papers had been unceremoniously jammed in the cracks between volumes. A pair of huge wing-back leather chairs large enough even for Brand sat in front of an enormous fireplace. Beside the tall windows, a desk stood, covered in disorderly piles of still more papers and books.

Brand sat down at the desk, dropping his sack and the machine suit cooling unit by the side of the desk. Elbows on two spots devoid of paper, he rested his head in his hands and scrubbed his fingers through his hair. His head ached as the fog now pressed painfully on his eyes, making it difficult to focus. He didn't want to think about Kushchai or any other kashmari right now, anyway. All he wanted was to sleep. Why was the prophylactic so effective when all other drugs and chemicals simply burned away in his blood?

Perhaps he could rest his eyes for just a moment before getting to work.

His eyelids drooped. Succumbing to the fog, the gladiator slumped on a pile of papers and was fast asleep.

* * *

Brand woke with a start at the squeal of a creaky floorboard.

"I'm sorry to disturb you, Mr. Brand," Mrs. James said. She picked up a book and replaced it with a cup of coffee and a small envelope on the desk in front of him. "Lord Kushchai's servant delivered this a few moments ago."

"How long have I been asleep?"

Brand rubbed his eyes. The fog was gone from his brain and he felt wonderfully rested.

"It's been no more than an hour since you returned home."

Brand grunted a little in surprise and glanced out the window. The sun had not yet retreated fully behind the houses along the row. And yet, it had been enough for the effects of the pill to finally wear off. How odd.

The gladiator stretched. His arms ached from being curled under his head on the desk. He winced at the ache from the bruise forming down the length of his back where the machine suit had slammed into him. He flexed the fingers of his right hand. His knuckles stung from punching the man in the suit, though they were already scabbing over nicely.

Brand shoveled aside papers until he found a slim letter opener, then sliced open Kushchai's note. The letter inside was written on very smooth linen paper.

Brand,

Excellent job with the Duati and Navari. Lord Jinn is thrilled to be establishing more regular and amicable relations between Darnan and Duat. I have high hopes for the future of the city's food stores if this continues.

On another note, I have just been informed that guards will check your gear before the fight. No need to be alarmed. Just a safety precaution after last week.

Lord Kushchai

Brand frowned. He knew he shouldn't have anything to worry about with his gauntlet. He'd designed it to look identical to its normal companion. The vials and their delivery contraption were completely hidden within the lining; only the tiny needles protruded out of the pocket. Even the added bulk was hidden from the outside by thick leather and a hardened steel plate. But it was another opportunity for him to be found out, and that made him tense.

"Bad news?"

Brand looked up to see Mrs. James standing in the doorway. She brought over his coffee.

"The message was personally delivered by Lord Kushchai's footman. That worries me a bit. Is everything alright?"

Brand smiled reassuringly. "It's nothing much." He glanced at the fireplace. "I'd rather not be disturbed until dinner, please."

"Of course." Mrs. James smiled and left.

Brand walked over to the tall window and gazed out at the city. The many square panes of the window made him feel like he was locked in a cage, a creature owned and used, a rare creature to be admired, sure, but never more than a pet. It kept him alive, but at what cost?

He balled his hand into a fist. "Stop complaining," he growled to himself. "It's a good life."

Then he returned to his desk and picked up his sack and the machine suit cooling unit and moved past the wingback chairs to one of the bookcases next to the fireplace. He set the sack and cooling unit next to his feet, then reached up to about the same height as his face and pulled out a heavy tome labeled, "Twenty-seven Unique Spear-holds for the Discerning Combatant." He reached into the gap between the other books and pulled a lever.

The fireplace, a section of the bookcase, and a semicircle of hardwood floor that he was standing on lifted slightly and spun around into another room, then settled, leaving no visible seams in the floor.

He couldn't help but chuckle a little. He'd had dozens of kashmari come to his house, even had inquisitions searching for alchemical devices, and all of them had been fooled by the simplest and most obvious secret room anyone could devise.

And then last week he'd nearly been made because he'd been stupid enough to leave his kit at the arena. Luckily for Brand, the fight officials had determined that his opponent had left the satchel of poisons near Brand's preparation room to frame Brand; the city still buzzed with suspicion, though.

The lab was lined, floor to ceiling, with smooth, sealed granite tiles so that it seemed to float in a quartz-studded night sky, interrupted only by a series of slit windows. After single a day of working in there the first time, he'd discovered how easily crystal shattered on the hard tile and had asked Mrs. James to procure some rugs. Rugs were cheaper and easier to replace than crystal kashmari vials, which were technically illegal for him to purchase.

Brand picked up his sack and the cooling unit and moved to the large stone brazier on one side of the room. With a pull of a lever that made a bellows wheeze, he stoked the coals to a blazing red.

Along the back of the room was a stone bench beneath shelves upon shelves crammed with various vials and jars. His experiments over the years had resulted in some interesting adjustments to his standard pharmakon's kit. As a result, he'd taken to collecting and researching as many herbs and minerals as he could. Bits of scribbled notes describing his discoveries were pasted on many of the glass jars.

Both walls flanking the bench were stuffed with yet more overflowing bookcases. He'd recently suggested to Mrs. James that he might want to get another bookcase, to which she'd replied that he ought to let her tidy them up a bit and throw out the books he hadn't looked at in a decade. After that scandalizing conversation, he'd never mentioned his bookcases to her again.

He placed the sack and cooling unit on the bench, pulling each item out and carefully arranging the various poisons in neat rows according to which concoction they would go into.

Adrenaline, Stamina, Armor, Strength, basic Repellent, Night Vision, Healing, Poisoned Blood, Rooted, and Time. The first eight were the basics; the last two were his own inventions.

A smile tugged at the corner of Brand's mouth as he wondered what his mentor would have thought of the new elixirs. Brand liked to think William would have been impressed.

He set up an elaborate decanter, where the liquid twisted through a series of coils before arriving in a globe flask at the bottom. From a shelf, he pulled an alchemical still comprised of two long-necked flasks and a long tube, and set it down to the left of the decanter. Lastly, he pulled out a mortar, a pestle, and a cast-iron pot.

Brand took a mask with goggles off a nail on the wall and placed it over his face, careful to fit it snugly against the skin rather than his beard, then donned a pair of thick leather welding gloves and a heavy leather apron. He then carefully emptied the contents of the first set of vials into the mortar and ground them up slowly. He added alcohol and other ingredients that he pulled off the shelves. The mixture began to smoke slightly, fogging up his goggles with a greenish smoke. As he stirred, it turned from green to brown. Brand then carefully poured the mixture into the cast-iron pot and covered it with a lid, carried it over to the brazier, and set it directly on the hot coals. He pulled a sand timer off a shelf, double-checked the words "Sixty Minutes" engraved in the wooden endpiece, and set it on the table. The sand began to trickle down.

Brand opened each slit window a crack, then took a moment to wipe out the mortar and placed the used towels in a metal basket with a lid. He'd burn these once he was finished.

The next elixir, Stamina, was finicky and would take sixty-four hours to ferment. With only three days before the fight, if he didn't make it correctly the first time, he'd be going into the fight without it. Stamina was one elixir he had no interest in being without against his much younger opponent, so he set up a pair of large gallon glass jars. He'd double the recipe just in case one batch didn't set up properly.

He filled each jar three-quarters of the way with water, then added a generous amount of salt and stirred until the salt crystals vanished. Then he turned back to the mortar and ground up the next set of ingredients. They fizzed and popped beneath his pestle.

This time he simply added the bubbling paste to the salt water and stirred until the water turned a dirty brown. He then carefully pulled out and untangled two sets of cables with clamps on one end and electrodes on the other. He then carefully hooked them to the cooling unit from the machine suit and dangled the electrodes within each jar.

Brand watched in fascination as hair-thin lines appeared in the murky water, connecting the electrodes like strands of spider silk. He felt a pang of sadness. In another life, he could have attended the university and become a scientist and spent his days investigating and experimenting to his heart's content. His shoulders slumped a little as he cleaned out the mortar. Brand's survival depended on no one knowing about any of this, so he shoved that thought away.

The last of the three elixirs that he wanted to ensure were done was Time. This infusion was by far the most toxic of those he used, the shortest acting, and the most dangerous for him to use in public, as one of its side effects was to turn his blood an unnerving black color that could be seen through the skin. But the ability to move out of time was also one of the most crucial abilities that could turn a loss into a win in a matter of moments. Brand rarely used it, but never went into a fight without it.

He combined his ingredients in the mortar as per usual, and then carefully tipped them into a jar with plain water. He then added some small tan grains to the mixture. Then, as slowly as he could, he screwed the lid on, taking great pains not to jostle the water. Then he left it alone. He would check on it tomorrow morning.

Brand glanced over at the jars of murky saltwater and was pleased to see the lines in the murk arcing from one electrode to the other, becoming darker and more pronounced.

The large man continued to work on other various concoctions. Humming softly, he lost himself in the work and let the various tasks carry the time away. Kushchai's letter faded from his mind.

Brand looked up at the Adrenaline's sand timer and saw that it had only a few grains left. He dropped what he was doing, strode over to the brazier, and pulled out the cast-iron pot. He lifted the lid. Where before the liquid had been brown, now it had taken on a rusty orange color.

Satisfied, Brand set the pot aside to cool.

Suddenly, a tinny voice came from a little brass horn attached to a long tube that ran down into the floor. Mrs. James had learned quite early on in her life as a pharmakon's wife that one should never barge in on them at work if one ever wanted to use one's lungs again, so she had been adamant that Brand install the little speaking horn for her.

"Mr. Brand?"

"Yes, Mrs. James?" His deep voice was muffled by the respirator in his mask.

"Dinner is ready."

"Thank you. I'll be down shortly."

Brand hurriedly finished up the Adrenaline decoction and set it aside to ferment overnight. Then, without taking off his protective clothing, he grabbed a long piece of wood and stuck it in the brazier until the tip burst alight. He carried it over to the metal bin of dirty towels and shoved the flame down into the fabric until the corner of one towel caught fire and began to burn with an evil green flame. He closed the lid with a clang and plunged the wood into a bucket of water, then tossed it into a waiting wire mesh bin with other pieces of wood with burnt black ends drying and waiting to be used again.

Finally, he stripped off the mask, gloves, and apron and hung them on their appropriate nails. With one last glance around the room to make sure all was in order, he left.

Mrs. James was waiting for him in the kitchen. They only rarely used the elegant dining room when Brand had guests, preferring to eat together in the kitchen. A little table sat next to a window that looked out onto a shaded terrace that Brand had built for Mrs. James. In it, she'd arrayed various colorful pots overflowing with innumerable flowers. As the night was pressing on, Brand opened the window to let some of the sweet cool air and fragrances seep in to mingle with the delicious smells of the kitchen.

Mrs. James dished out hunks of buttered potatoes smothered in gravy and generous slices of still-pink runnerbeast roast, then spooned a sweet pear sauce over the meat.

"I've finally gotten around to looking through some of William's old boxes," Mrs. James said, turning to pick up something from the counter before sitting down and handing it to Brand. "I found this. I thought you might like to have it."

She handed him a photograph framed in a simple copper frame. It was of him, as a young boy, standing beside William. Even then, Brand had been nearly as tall as his mentor. He smiled fondly at the man's bottle brush mustache and ever-present pipe.

"Thank you," Brand said. He propped the photograph up against the vase next to his plate so they could both see it. "I think I'll put it upstairs in my office."

"I thought you might."

They ate in silence for a while. Brand chewed quietly, but his mind wandered back to the man in the alley.

"Is everything alright, Mr. Brand?" Mrs. James asked. "Only, it looks as though your mind is somewhere else entirely."

"Sorry, Mrs. James. I ran into a woman with the plague today. She reached up and grabbed me. Don't worry; I took the prophylactic," he said to her raised eyebrows.

"I'm not terribly worried about catching it," she reassured him. "I had it when I was a girl. Such a strange disease, isn't it? Some of us catch it and recover and move on with our lives, and others…not so much."

Brand grunted. "All this running from a disease that most people survive. Some days, I wonder if it wouldn't be easier to catch it on purpose and be done with it."

Mrs. James shook her white head.

"You shouldn't, not according to Mr. Sanders, remember? He knew more than he could say, and he told William you were never to catch the plague. Something to do with your parents, William figured."

Brand took another bite, chewed thoughtfully, then swallowed. "My mother died of the plague. Alastair said I was more susceptible to it because of her. But some days I wish I could just catch it and if I die, I die. And other days, like today…promise me that if I ever get like that, you'll go up and get my rifle down and finish me, alright?"

Mrs. James gasped. "How could you ever say a thing like that? I would never! You're like a son to me!"

Brand was about to protest, but the look in her eye changed his mind. "Alright, Mrs. James. You're right. Shame on me for even contemplating such a grotesque action."

But privately, it stayed on his mind for the rest of dinner. He didn't say much, and left quickly, mumbling about getting back to his concoctions.

Training

Back in his office, Brand quietly got a fire going in the large fireplace. Even in the desert, nights were chilly enough to warrant a decent blaze. The gladiator stood in front of the fire for a long time, looking into the flames and wondering about his parents. Brand had never known them nor knew hardly anything about either of his parents.

He looked at the clock finally and decided that the rest of the elixirs could wait until tomorrow. Instead, he drew the long curtains aside to block the windows and closed the door, kicking his house shoes off next to it. Then, barefoot, he shoved the wingback chairs to either side of the fireplace, leaving a large open space in the middle of the room. He then went over to his desk and pulled a gauntlet of his own design out of the largest drawer.

Brand was allowed to use his own armor because the arena armorers didn't have anything in his size, and Brand had taken full advantage of that fact. It was designed to look like all of the other gauntlets worn by gladiators, made of hardened leather with pieces of steel bolted down to the back of the hand, the tops of the fingers, and around the cuff. Even the elaborate scrollwork etched into the leather and Lord Kushchai's sigil, a snake eating its own tail, were exact copies of the armor of the other gladiators.

But unlike the standard gauntlets, this one had two rows each of five tiny crystal vials sewn into the lining of the cuff.

Moving to the open center of the room, he pulled the modified gauntlet onto his left hand, careful to keep his hand in a relaxed position. He could feel the vials pressing against his skin.

He closed his eyes and let the tension in his body go, banishing all worries and thoughts from his mind. He looked inward, and in the silence, he found the tiniest speck of light and warmth at the very core of his soul. He stood there for a long moment, marveling at this strange speck. It was beautiful, but also a quiet reminder of just how alone Brand was in the world. He shivered a little despite the warmth of the spark and the fire in the hearth.

In one smooth motion, he stepped back into an ancient fighting stance his mentor had taught him so many years ago and formed his gauntleted hand into Alpha, his hand clenched into a fist. The tendons in his wrist nudged the mechanism in the gauntlet, which in turn propelled a tiny needle into the vein in his wrist.

He grunted as the Adrenaline elixir flowed from the little vial into his bloodstream. His heart rate accelerated to a gallop. Energy flowed into his muscles, and he began to move—punching, kicking, slapping an unseen opponent. As his energy began to flag, he formed his hand into Sigma, with his thumb, middle finger, and pinky each bent halfway. Another vial emptied itself into his vein, easing the pain of the lactic acid built up in his muscles and allowing him to push on.

He continued his shadow-boxing until the fire in the fireplace had burned down. With the curtains covering any light from street lamps or the moon outside, the office was nearly pitch black. Brand then made his gauntleted hand into Nu by lifting his first two fingers straight out and then folding them over his thumb. To Brand's eyes, the office seemed to blaze with new light as his pupils dilated to let in as much light as possible.

As he continued to move, Brand began to feel the sickening effects of absorbing so many poisonous elixirs. It was still slight, as he'd only injected very small doses of three of the minor elixirs; but it was still there, a quiet warning.

One more, a stronger one, and then I'll be done for now, he thought. *I still need be able to sleep tonight.*

He twisted his gauntleted forefinger and middle finger together, forming Rho, releasing the Rooted elixir into his veins. He ran at the closed door, leapt and planted each bare foot solidly against the wood, and ran straight up for three, four steps. He then pushed off backwards and twisted, pirouetting in the air like a falling cat to land deftly on one foot, and immediately swung the other into a powerful kick at the air. He then planted his bare hand down on the floor and swung his large frame around as though sweeping the feet out from under his invisible opponent.

Brand grinned from ear to ear. Rooted was by far his favorite elixir. It improved his balance immensely, allowing him to dance through a fight.

And then the elixir was spent. Rooted was such a short-acting elixir and far more toxic than, say, Stamina. Even now, Brand's head was beginning to throb and his vision was becoming blurry as his body struggled to clear the poison.

He could also feel his heart slowing and his muscles becoming more sluggish as the last of the Adrenaline wore off. The Stamina would last him for another few hours, as that one lasted the longest out of all his elixirs. Without the Adrenaline pushing him to move, though, he should be able to sit still and read for a while before the inevitable exhaustion set in.

Brand dragged the wingback chairs back in front of the fireplace and collapsed into one. He pulled off the gauntlet carefully. He'd padded and armored the section covering the vials well enough to sustain minor blows during a fight, but they were still incredibly fragile and nearly impossible to replace.

He rubbed a finger over the spidery scar on his wrist from the last time he'd broken the vials years ago just after creating his first rendition of the gauntlet. Sweat still made it itch.

Brand walked over to the desk again and replaced the gauntlet in its drawer, then pulled a decanter of brandy out along with a small glass. He poured himself a glass, picked up a book entitled, "Rise and Fall of the People of Amun Rhett," and sat in front of the fireplace.

There was a knock on the door.

"Come in."

Mrs. James came in, hands folded over her apron.

"My, it's dark in here. Would you like me to stoke the fire, Mr. Brand?"

Brand realized he'd forgotten about the Night Vision elixir. It tended to last almost as long as Stamina. "No, thank you. I can see alright."

"Very well. I think I'll turn in early for the evening. Is there anything more you need?"

Brand shook his head, then regretted it as his headache flared anew. "No, thank you."

"If you don't mind me asking, why do you bother drinking, Mr. Brand?" Mrs. James asked. "I've always wondered but never got around to asking. William always said there was no point, not after someone has been through the Trial. And yet he smoked. Why?"

Brand shrugged.

"To keep appearances? It becomes a habit, I suppose." He swirled the brandy. "William and I would go out drinking with the others after work, so I suppose a drink in the evening reminds me of him."

He took a sip. It was a kashmari brandy, brewed for their resilient constitutions, and as such, he could feel the alcohol burning down his throat. But that was all.

Mrs. James smiled sadly. "I suppose that must be it. Perhaps his pipe reminded him of something he thought fondly of." She dabbed at her eyes with a corner of her shawl. "Goodnight, Mr. Brand."

"Goodnight, Mrs. James."

Flashback #2: Alastair

13 July 1023 P.E.
Market Street, Darnan

Young Brand once again found himself running from the city guard. Shouts followed him as he ran to a row of barrels, jumped up, sprinted across their heads, then jumped over to a ladder on the side of a building. He grabbed at the rung with his empty hand, but his sweaty fingers slipped off the smooth metal.

The lanky boy collapsed in a heap, flattening his ill-gotten sweet bread roll and coating himself with crumbs and dust. He shoved what was left of the roll into his mouth, swiped his hands across the front of his threadbare tunic, and jumped up onto the ladder, scampering up it with sticky fingers.

At the top, he spun about, trying to get his bearings. The ladder behind him rattled as the guards started climbing it, cursing as they went. Brand sprinted across the rooftops in the direction of the cloth sails of Market Street billowing up between several buildings a few streets away.

He ran as fast as his long legs would carry him, jumping short alleys and scampering along boards straddling other gaps between buildings, until he found himself on the roof of one of the taller buildings of the market. He skittered to a halt, realizing that the gap across the market street was far too wide to leap across, then teetered on the edge of the building. His arms windmilled a bit before he was able to regain his footing. He paused for a moment, scanning for any other way across or any way down to street level. There were none. Behind him, he heard the clank of several pairs of heavy steel-clad boots.

He spun to face the grinning guards.

"You've escaped us too many times, lad," the officer said. His face was shining red under his metal helmet. "Come with us quietly, and we'll sort this all out, alright?"

Brand glanced behind him. He could see Sanders's shop down below on the other side of the street. If he could just get down there without breaking his neck, Alastair would help him…

Brand's stomach twisted as he stared down at the five-story drop. He'd survived a drop like that a month ago, but he had no interest in attempting that feat again.

A fire escape bolted to the side of a building on the other side of the street caught his eye. *I just need to get over there.* Brand eyed the cables suspending the shade sails hovering over the middle of the market.

The guards were inching closer, their semi-circle closing like a noose around him. If Brand had any hope of getting out of this, it had to be now.

Brand darted to his left to one of the cables and stepped out onto it, holding his hands out wide. He inched his way out across the cable while the guards behind shouted at him.

"How's he doing that?" he heard one of them exclaim behind him.

Teeth clenched, Brand silently wondered that himself. He'd always seemed to have better balance than others his age, but he'd never attempted something like this before. He reached the other side and turned with a jaunty wave, then slid down the fire escape.

Maybe I don't need Alastair after all, he thought.

Brand hit the ground and spun—straight into a meaty fist. Brand went down like a felled tree. He groaned as someone grabbed him by the front of his shirt. Brand blinked, and the face of the red-haired guard from the day before swam into view.

"That's quite enough, boy. Off to the station with you."

The guard slapped a pair of cuffs on the boy and frog-marched him down two streets over to the nearest guard station. As they walked, the other guards joined them, seven in all, Brand counted, each one adding their own taunts and taking a turn spitting at the youth. Brand felt a flush of wry pride at how many guards they'd sent after him.

The guard station was dim and dusty and still somehow as hot as the street outside. Golden light streaming through narrow windows set high above them caught on millions of dust motes floating in the air, casting thick beams of light that somehow didn't quite make it to the cramped but neat rows of desks below. Some guards, red-faced and serious, came and went with their jaws set and fists clenched. Other sweaty guards leaned up against cabinets and walls in clusters, their jackets unbuttoned, fanning themselves with paperwork and pointing at Brand. Their echoing laughter followed the young boy down the aisles.

The red-headed guard marched Brand through rows of desks until they reached one toward the back of the room, then shoved the boy into the chair in front of it. He unlocked one side of the cuffs and clamped it onto a heavy iron ring on the desk. Then the red-headed guard sat down among the papers on the other side of the desk. He pulled out a pair of tiny reading spectacles and started sifting through the papers.

As he sat there, Brand saw the other guards around them pointing, chuckling, and leering at him. The boy twisted away so that his back was toward most of the room and hunched down, trying to seem as inconspicuous as possible.

Brand's skin felt sticky from the muggy, stale air. He stared at his fingers and picked at his nails. After what seemed like an eternity, Brand mumbled, "I thought I was going to jail."

"You will be soon enough, boy," the guard said, not looking up. "There's paperwork to be done first."

Just then, there was a commotion down at the other end of the hall. One of the unbuttoned guards shouted "Hey you! You shouldn't be here. Stop!"

Brand looked up to see Alastair striding towards him. A crowd of city guards was shouting at him and trying to stand in his way. But the big shopkeeper seemed as unstoppable as a locomotive. He shouldered his way past the guards, of whom even the tallest only reached the big man's shoulder. Alastair came to a halt in front of the red-haired guard's desk. The guard rolled his eyes and waved off the rest of his squad.

Brand beamed.

Alastair folded his arms over his barrel chest and glared at the youth, making Brand cower down in his chair even more.

"I'm here for Cadmus," growled Alastair, his usual jovial demeanor replaced by roiling irritation.

The red-headed guard scoffed at the shopkeeper. "Oh you are, are you? He's been apprehended in a theft, charged with several others, and," the guard stood, "if you know what's good for you, Alastair, you'll keep your shady nose out of this business."

"How much do you want?" Alastair asked.

The red-haired guard glanced around at the other guards, who had dispersed but still kept their eyes trained on the shopkeeper. "You aren't seriously trying to bribe me in a guard station, are you?"

Alastair rolled his eyes. "Bail, Hessian. How much to spring the kid until his trial?"

Hessian leaned forward on the desk, hands planted on it. "He won't have a trial. He—"

"I am his legal guardian."

Brand started. *What?*

Alastair reached into a pocket and pulled out a yellowed piece of paper. He handed it to Hessian.

"I demand that he have a trial. I hope for your sake you have evidence this time."

Brand frowned at that. *This time?*

Hessian's brow furrowed and his eyes narrowed as he examined the yellowish document. Then he looked up at the big shopkeeper.

"You've never mentioned you had a ward before," Hessian said, suspicion dripping from every word.

"Have you ever asked?" Alastair said with a tight smile.

"I suppose I didn't," Hessian said softly. He glanced from Brand to Alastair, then back again several times, as though comparing the two. Finally, he shook his head. "After what I saw, he won't last two minutes at a trial. Fafnir wants all persons of strange or questionable abilities handed over to him. You'll only be bringing attention to yourself in ways you may not appreciate."

Alastair's jaw was set in a firm line. "He will have a trial."

Hessian's eyes locked with those of the big shopkeeper, curiosity mingling with distrust. Alastair held his own glare steady. After what felt like an eternity to Brand, Hessian dropped his gaze and handed the yellowing paper back to Alastair, who folded it carefully and placed it back in his pocket.

"Very well. The fine is ten gold pieces, and I will notify you personally of his trial date. It is your decision as his guardian whether you wish to retain counsel or not. In the meantime, I advise you to keep a close eye on the boy at all times. If he were to go missing, I will have no choice but to issue a warrant for your immediate arrest."

Brand saw Alastair wince at the price, but the big shopkeeper nodded curtly and produced the coins without complaint. Hessian stared at the money in front of him.

"How did you get that much money? You didn't steal it, did you?"

Brand could see Alastair's jaw muscles bunch as he clenched his teeth. The man's thick knuckles blanched as he balled his hands into massive fists.

"A loan."

"Against what? Your life? You haven't got anything else of value."

Alastair met the guard's glare. "Basically, yes."

Hessian drew close to Alastair and hissed, "This is folly! Ward or not, he's nothing, just an urchin, not worth your time, let alone your life! Think of your business. After what happened three years ago, you're barely holding on as it is."

"Thanks to you. You didn't have to turn me in," Alastair growled softly. "And if I remember correctly, I won."

"You still lost everything. You cannot win this one, and you will fall with him. For good."

Alastair looked the red-headed guard in the eye and firmly said, "Then so be it."

Hessian hesitated. "You're a good man, Alastair," he admitted softly, glancing around the station, "one of the better ones if you'd only straighten out."

Alastair shook his head. "We sail by different compasses, you and I."

"I suppose that's true," Hessian said. He sighed, then unlocked Brand's restraints.

Alastair beckoned to Brand and led the boy out of the station with one heavy hand resting on Brand's shoulder. Brand could feel dozens of eyes on his back as they exited the building.

Once outside, Brand grumbled, "All over a stupid sweet bread. The baker throws out dozens of rolls a day and they go to the pigeons. What's wrong with me taking one?"

"For one, you didn't take a stale three-day-old roll she'd just thrown out. You stole one from the counter. For two, this was less about the roll and more about that fall you took last month. I'm sure you noticed how many more guards were after you today."

"I got lucky," Brand mumbled.

"No, you're different," Alastair corrected. "Different will get you killed around here."

"Why did you forge that document saying you're my guardian? You've never cared one whit about me before."

"I didn't forge it, and I do care. I'm just not…" An odd look passed over the shopkeeper's face as his voice trailed off. Brand instantly regretted his words.

"I'm sorry," the boy mumbled. "You've always taken care of me, sort of."

Alastair stopped and turned Brand to face him. The big man looked as though he'd aged a hundred years in an instant. A huge weight of sadness now seemed to press down on his shoulders, making him sag.

"I'm sorry I haven't been able to make life more comfortable for you," Alastair said. "Life hasn't been all that kind to me either. I've done what I could, kept most trouble out of your way, helped you get back up when I couldn't. The truth is, your mother didn't have time to pick a better guardian before she died."

At the mention of his mother, Brand's eyes grew wide. Alastair had never spoken of Brand's mother, even when he'd asked. The shopkeeper had always brushed off the boy's questions as though he'd never met her. "Why? How did she die?"

Alastair sighed heavily. "She died of the plague. Right after you were born. It's a terrible way to die."

Brand wanted to ask more, to ask why the shopkeeper's face had darkened with pain at her memory, but Alastair had started walking again. Brand trotted to catch up. Despite his great weight, the shopkeeper's long legs carried him quickly down the street. Brand noticed for the first time that Alastair was wearing a great coat even though he was sweating profusely in the murderous desert heat.

Alastair's face turned stern again.

"As for why I had to get you out of there—Once they got you in prison, the high lord would have been called, and you'd have been dead by morning."

"What? Dead? Why? It was just a sweet roll!"

Alastair pulled Brand into an alley and shoved the youth against the wall.

"Aren't you listening? It's not what you did; a hundred boys steal bread every day. It's what you are. You're not like them! No one else could fall from a five-story building and survive, let alone walk away. People noticed that you're different, and being different will get you killed! Now, I'm taking you back to the shop, and you'll stay there quietly doing whatever task I can think of, while I go find someone who can help. If you leave, I'll whip you like you've never been whipped before. Do you understand?"

Brand nodded mutely, shaking slightly. In all the years he'd ever known Alastair, he'd never seen the man act like this, so agitated and fierce.

The boy followed Alastair silently back to the shop. Once there, the shopkeeper pulled the yellow paper from his pocket and stuffed it in a desk drawer.

The big shopkeeper moved around to the counter, where he pushed aside the mechanical sewing machine Brand had seen him working on last month. Alastair must have been working on it again when he learned about Brand's predicament.

"How long have you been working on that?" Brand asked, grasping at something normal to talk about. "It shouldn't have taken you more than a week."

"Never mind," Alastair growled. "Sit down."

Alastair set the boy to work dismantling the crumpled mechanohorse Brand had noticed the day before. With another stern warning, Alastair left the shop.

As Brand worked on the oxidizing heap, untangling and unscrewing and yanking it apart with trembling fingers, he tried to figure out what Alastair had meant out in the alley. He was just Brand, a nobody, a street urchin with no parents. Nobody wanted him.

Unbidden tears splashed on the greenish bronze metal. He wiped the water away angrily. He was too old to cry. He dried his eyes and focused on his work.

* * *

Alastair left the shop at a good clip, letting his long legs carry his heavy frame quickly down the market street, his long coat flapping in the brisk summer breeze. He was already sweating heavily, but he couldn't risk anyone noticing his tattoos and remembering them. "Blasted desert," he grumbled to himself.

Where would the man be?

Brand had caught the man's attention last month after nabbing that mechanohorse processor in the financial district, Alastair was sure. It was one of the best places to catch a carriage without being noticed.

The stranger had been wearing a three-piece suit, Alastair remembered, but not a terribly stylish one—a service uniform, cheap but crisp. A bar or restaurant, perhaps? The restaurant district was in between the market and the banks.

The man had said he could help Brand, and there was only one type of person the shopkeeper knew that might be able to help the boy. Alastair needed to get close to the man; the same street would suffice. He headed for the restaurant district a few streets over.

Alastair had to pause on a curb as a mechanohorse carriage trotted by. He tipped his hat at a couple of ladies in lacy summer dresses, then charged on, winding his way through alleys and side streets. He stopped at a large intersection, looking around.

A stone fountain of a kashmari on a rearing horse stood at the center. Along the six streets radiating from the intersection were a dozen restaurants and bars that Alastair could see. He couldn't see their staff, though, so he strode across the street to one with long windows and peered inside. He repeated this until he found an upscale pub where the service staff wore the same kind of uniform as William James had been wearing. He pushed open the door and ducked in, drawing the attention of the patrons.

It was dark and cool here, which Alastair appreciated. *Still too dry,* he thought, trying to ignore the constant itching of his skin.

"Hello, good sir," a woman in a crisp waistcoat and coiffed hair said. "How many in your party?"

"Uh, none. I'm looking for a member of the staff. A William James."

"If you'll wait one moment, I'll inquire in the back."

"Thank you."

Alastair pulled off a glove and stuffed a hand into his pocket. His fingers closed around a prism about the length of his finger. It was cool to the touch, and when his finger glided over it, he could hear a soft hum in the back of his mind.

He glanced around at the staff. Nothing. Then, from a door behind the bar strode a man who glowed ever so faintly to Alastair's eyes, little more than a soft golden patina. The shopkeeper took his hand out of his pocket and replaced the glove. The glow surrounding the approaching man vanished.

"Hello again," William James said with a smile half-hidden by his mustache. "How can I help you?"

"It's the boy," Alastair said quietly. He kept a cordial smile on his face and tried to stay relaxed. "Can you come now?"

William James matched the shopkeeper's blank smile and nodded amiably. "Of course. If you would give me one moment, sir."

Alastair waited for the man to speak with his boss, keeping his face passive and his hands still lest he seem impatient. Then the two men left together.

William led Alastair into an alley behind the pub. The smaller man then glanced around cautiously. He pulled out his pipe and started smoking.

"What is it? Has something happened?"

Alastair stared at the pipe. William pulled it out of his mouth.

"Just in case someone looks this way," the mustached man said. "Looks like I'm talking to a friend while on break."

Alastair grunted and glanced over his shoulder. No one on the street seemed to notice the two men in the shade of the alley. "Cadmus was arrested. The guard who did it let me have him on bail pending a trial, but he made sure I knew the boy will be handed over to Fafnir as soon as the trial is over. And he assured me the trial would be short."

William leaned back against the wall and puffed on his pipe a few times. "You should have let me take him last month."

"Perhaps. But I've learned to be suspicious of people like you. It's that suspicion that has kept me and the boy alive. No matter. 'Yesterday is past and today needs attention,' as they say. Can you help him?"

"Why can't you help him anymore?"

Alastair looked at his boots. There was a hole in each toe. "I can only hide him. Now that they know he exists, he needs someone to teach him to fight." He looked back up at the strange man. "Believe me, if I had another choice, I'd take it."

"You can't run away with him? I'm sure you could vanish into another city, one where Fafnir doesn't pay as close attention."

Alastair's thoughts went to the letter he'd sent off after William James had visited. He still hadn't received an answer. That worried him, but he couldn't think about that just now. "I will leave, for a time, but where I'm going, he cannot follow. It's even more dangerous. No, he needs you."

William James regarded the big shopkeeper for a long moment. "Alright. I will still hide him, though. No one can fight every kashmari in the city, not even my kind."

Alastair nodded. "Of course."

"He'll need to change everything: his habits, his speech. He'll need to be educated if he's to hide properly."

"He's a smart boy. I'm sure he'll handle it all well."

"And you can never see him again."

That brought Alastair up short. "Never?"

William shrugged. "You said he was just a street urchin you looked after once in a while."

"Yes, I did say that," the shopkeeper said slowly. "It's just...not entirely true," Alastair admitted.

Alastair didn't like the knowing smirk William James gave him. Alastair pointed menacingly at William and took a step closer so that they were nose to nose. The musty smell of pipe tobacco filled Alastair's nose. "Not a word to the boy or anyone else, though. Ever. You have no idea what kind of danger he'll be in if certain people get wind that he's related to me."

That prompted a genuinely curious tilt of the head from William, his eyes searching the big man.

Alastair had worked hard to blend into the scum of the city and knew he looked the part. In truth, the best way to look like them had been to become one of them. The fiasco three years ago had certainly helped with that.

But he knew that's not what the smaller man saw. Not this time.

"I promise," William said. His voice was gentle. "But you must promise me you'll never seek him out."

Alastair's heart sank. Cadmus was the one bright spot in Alastair's life. The boy had shown him a lust for living that Alastair had thought long buried by sand and dust and worry. To have to continue on, scraping out a putrid life here on this forsaken rock, and without Cadmus? He looked away.

"It will be too dangerous for both of you," William James said. "You understand what I'm saying? What he will become? If you think he's in danger with you now…In a few years, he'll be far more dangerous to you. The kashmari will know him. They will fear him, hate him, hunt him. And you, if you are seen with him even once."

Alastair grunted. The shopkeeper wryly mused to himself how interesting it was that this man could be right for all the wrong reasons. All the same, he was still right.

Is this the right choice? Alastair wondered. He'd survived just fine all these years, after all. Couldn't he just teach the boy, as Alastair had taught Cadmus's mother?

But despite Alastair's best efforts, Yelena Brand had indeed caught the attention of the high lord and paid for it with her life. And Cadmus would be far more of a threat than Yelena ever could have been. No, the boy needed more than what Alastair could teach him. He needed to learn how to fight, not just hide. If the price was him never seeing young Cadmus again, then Alastair was just going to have to deal with that. He took a deep, steadying breath of hot desert air and for once was too distracted to mind how dry it was.

"Yes, I understand. Do what you must."

* * *

As Brand worked, he kept glancing over at the drawer he'd seen Alastair drop the yellow piece of paper into. Finally able to stand it no longer, he dropped his tools and went over to Alastair's desk, which was nearly invisible under a mountain of spare parts. He dug around for a moment, found the drawer in question, and pulled out the yellowing paper he'd seen Alastair give to the red-headed guard, Hessian.

On it was written a single sentence:

> *I, Yelena Brand, do hereby give Alastair Sanders legal guardianship of my son, Cadmus Brand.*

Instead of Alastair's short, choppy writing, it was written and signed in a neat, looping hand. An ornate blue stamp with the words "I hereby witness this statement as true and valid" formed a ring around another, unidentifiable signature on the corner of the paper.

"What are you getting into, Cadmus?" Alastair said from behind the boy. Brand jolted and spun to see Alastair stalking toward him. Behind the big shopkeeper, a small, mustached man in a suit followed. Alastair saw the paper in Brand's hand and his face changed from stern to sorrowful.

"Ah."

Brand looked down and traced a thumb over the letters. His mother's signature. It was graceful and elegant.

Alastair's heavy hand rested on his shoulder, solid and reassuring.

"What was she like?" Brand asked.

Alastair sighed and took a seat on the stool beside Brand. He glanced back at the other man, who nodded, then turned back to Brand.

"She was the kindest woman I've ever known," Alastair said. "She always tried to see the best in people, no matter who they were. And she loved to tinker."

"Like you?"

Alastair smiled. "Yes."

"Did you know my father?"

Alastair's face darkened. Brand saw the heavy look exchanged by Alastair and the newcomer. The stranger arched a curious eyebrow and placed his fists on his hips. He looked a little like Hessian, Brand thought, though kinder.

What did that mean?

Alastair turned his attention back to Brand. "Yes. I knew him."

"What was he like?"

The answer took the shopkeeper a lot longer to formulate. Brand could see him shift uncomfortably on his stool. A mess of indecipherable emotions flickered across the big man's face. Finally, he spoke.

"He was ambitious. And I suppose he thought he was helping people, in his own way."

"How did he die?"

Again, the seconds dragged on into minutes as Alastair searched for the words.

"He was killed by Fafnir, the same as your mother."

"You said she was killed by the plague."

Brand thought he could see tears well up in the corners of the older man's hazel eyes, but Alastair blinked them away before they could fall. When he spoke, his usually clear voice was hoarse. "Fafnir could have saved her, but he didn't. Her death is on his hands."

He turned to the stranger. "Cadmus will need a daily prophylactic to prevent him from contracting the plague. Because of his mother…he's susceptible to it."

The stranger nodded slowly. "I think I know of someone who can help me procure it for him."

"Good."

Brand frowned. "And my father? Did my father die of the plague? Could Fafnir have saved him too?"

Alastair shook his head.

"Then how did he kill my father?"

Alastair winced and scrubbed at his face. He looked so tired and beaten. "That's a tale for when you're older."

The boy tried to hide his disappointment. "You're sending me away. There won't be another day."

Alastair took Brand by the shoulders. "It might take me a century to see you again, true, but I will find you. Or you will find me. Some day. You have my word."

The shopkeeper stood, forestalling any argument from Brand. Alastair gestured to the man he'd brought with him. "This man is William James. I want you to go with him. He can help you."

Brand's jaw dropped. "Go? Go where? Why?"

"To live with him. He's going to..help you." Alastair looked as though the words coming out of his mouth were bitter to the taste.

"But—"

"It's not safe for you here. William can protect you."

Brand cast about for some other reason that might sway the shopkeeper.

"What about you? Your shop? Hessian said he'd arrest you if I vanished."

"He won't get the chance." Alastair looked around the shop with a sad fondness. "I could do with a change of scenery. Maybe I'll go to New Braunen. It's closer to the Wastes, sees more scavengers come through."

The shopkeeper offered his hand to Brand. The boy took it, but then grabbed the older man in a bear hug.

"I'll miss you."

Alastair held the boy tight. It was one of the few times when the shopkeeper had ever embraced him. Brand felt so safe and yet so lost. He held on as though he could remain forever if he didn't let go.

"When we meet again, Cadmus, remind me to tell you that tale I spoke of last month, after your fall."

"The one about the princess and the mechanohorse?"

"The very same one."

When Brand released Alastair, wet tears left shining tracks down his round, ruddy cheeks. Alastair smiled anyway.

"Good luck, and try to stay out of trouble, Cadmus."

As Brand left the machine shop for the last time, he glanced back at the shopkeeper. Alastair Sanders raised his hand in farewell.

Brand raised his own in farewell to the only father he'd ever known.

Preparations

8 August 1062 P.E.
Gladiator Row, Darnan

Brand woke up the next morning slumped in his chair, heavy tome splayed out on his lap. He groaned. Mornings weren't kind to him on a good day, but after a night spent on Stamina and sleeping in a chair, he figured he'd be lucky to stand up straight by the end of the week.

He limped down to breakfast.

Mrs. James was waiting for him, newspaper arrayed in front of her as she ate porridge with fruit. She smiled, but said nothing, only pointing to Brand's meal and turning back to her paper.

For the millionth time, Brand was grateful to her for understanding and not speaking before he'd eaten. He downed the tall glass of cold water set beside his plate first, then half of the glass of red juice. Then he attacked the eggs, toast, and fruit.

Mrs. James waited until after Brand had polished off his second glass of juice and piled his plate high with more eggs and fruit before launching into her morning chatter.

"You're all over the front page," she remarked, turning the newspaper so he could see. "I had to go all the way to page four to find my gossip column."

"I'll be sure to figure out who to speak to about that eventually," Brand mumbled through his food.

"I'll be out doing my errands for most of this morning. Will you be able to manage for a few hours?"

"Somehow I've never managed to burn down the house yet. Though I do try."

"Don't be smart. It's unbecoming."

"I thought you loved my intelligence."

"Enough! I'll be back by noon. Stay out of trouble until then."

"Yes, mother."

Mrs. James rolled her eyes and stood, rolled up the newspaper, and whacked Brand across the head with it.

"One of these days, you might find a girl to marry, and you'll have to find some way not to be so waspish in the morning."

"I doubt that will be an issue. By the time I find her, she'll be an old wasp in the morning right along with me."

Mrs. James left in an exasperated huff.

Brand spent the better part of the next two days in his lab, mixing, distilling, cooking, and fermenting until at last, he had ten crystal vials, each the size of his forefinger, filled with ten separate elixirs.

He reached over to a tiny chest of drawers no bigger than a jewelry box. From one of the drawers, he pulled out a set of incredibly small vials, only as long as his fingernail and barely thicker. He also pulled out an invention of his that looked like a very thick pen, with space to load a regular-sized vial and an impossibly thin glass pipette where the tip of the pen ought to be. The apothecary had helped him with the glass parts.

Brand loaded the contraption with the first vial, Adrenaline, and placed the spout into the mouth of the first tiny vial. He pressed a button on its side. Orange decoction oozed out and dripped into the smaller vial. When it was nearly full, Brand took his thumb off the button, stopping the flow. Then he gingerly set the mechanical pipette down on the bench and picked up a jar of clear fluid, and with a clean, simple glass pipette, squeezed a few droplets of the clear liquid into the vial. Finally, he capped the vial with a smudge of paraffin wax and turned it end over end a few times to mix the two liquids. Then he pulled out another tiny vial and repeated the process, continuing until there was no more Adrenaline elixir remaining in the larger vial.

He continued to the next elixir, Armor, a dark blue liquid that would need to remain hot for the next twelve hours. He worked his way through each elixir until he had an organized array of diminutive vials and an empty pile of larger ones.

"Mr. Brand?" Mrs. James's tinny voice came from the brass horn. "You asked for a reminder when it was half past four."

"Yes, thank you, Mrs. James," he replied in a muffled voice.

The timing was perfect. He could finish up here, eat dinner, wash up, and be out the door with plenty of time to get over to the bar to meet his kashmari master.

Brand carefully wiped the residue from each empty vial and the mortar, then with a new cloth wiped down the bench. He lit the rags with a piece of wood from the brazier, then pulled off his protective clothing and hung them on their pegs. He glanced over at the miniature vials, wiped the sweat off his brow, and smiled in satisfaction. Tomorrow's fight was already won.

Lords

9 August 1062 P.E.
First Blood Lounge, Restaurant District, Darnan

Brand stepped out of the mechanohorse-drawn carriage and straightened his dinner jacket. Scrubbed clean until he shone pink, he was now dressed in a full suit, complete with black bow tie, walking cane, and top hat. He'd brushed out his hair and trimmed his short beard as well as he could, but the wavy salt and pepper locks still stuck out at odd angles. Though the sun had gone down, the stones radiated stored-up heat from midday, and Brand was sweating in his many layers.

He stepped up to the sleek black door of the First Blood Lounge. A valet opened the door and bowed.

"Good evening, Mr. Brand. Lord Kushchai is waiting for you."

At nearly two meters tall barefoot, Brand towered over humans and kashmari alike on any day. But in these shoes and a top hat, he had to duck low to get through the doorway.

As soon as Brand stepped through the door, he pulled off his hat and cool air washed over him, chilling the sweat on the back of his neck. He took a deep breath. The smells of alcohol and pipe tobacco mingled with the musk of sweat and cologne. It reminded him of the pub he'd worked at as a young man.

But unlike the pub of his youth, this establishment was packed with the elites and celebrities of Darnan: kashmari nobles and their ladies, human Council members, and gladiators. Flush with the wealth of the city's refineries and factories and clothed with exotic textiles from distant Duat, they drank, ate, and laughed amidst the most expensive woods and dark bricks from the mountains. The copper taps gleamed in the light of real electric bulbs.

The patrons looked up from their tables as the giant man entered. Several stood, clapped, and yelled his name. He waved his cane with a grin. A couple of other gladiators, similarly bedecked in top hats and jackets and sporting various scars, came over to slap Brand on the back and exchange a few words of congratulations or well wishes.

"Have a drink with us!" one of them said, thwacking Brand on the back.

"I can't, Gwythyr," Brand said, pulling a mournful face. "I'm here on the job. Got a meeting with the boss and his friends."

"Ah, that's too bad," Gwythyr said, his square face falling, "but our patrons keep us in business, so what can you do, right?"

Brand clapped his friend on the back. "Tomorrow morning before the fight. Tell everyone to come."

"Will do. Good luck with the boss."

"Thanks."

Brand disentangled himself from his peers and walked along the bar, searching for Kushchai.

As he scanned the room, he caught sight of four strangers in grey hoods, each pressed up against a different wall. They stood silent, watching, still as stone. There was something…off about them. Maybe it was the way they all held their heads a bit cocked to the side, or how still they were. Or maybe it was the empty space the other patrons left around each grey-cloaked stranger. No one looked directly at the grey figures. Brand couldn't see inside the hoods, either, and as a fighter, that unnerved him.

A slender kashmari at a table towards the back of the packed lounge stood and waved Brand over. The gladiator shrugged off his unease and moved over to the table.

Lord Kushchai, the city lord of Darnan, was short even for a kashmari. A shock of pure white hair contrasted sharply against his blueish-grey skin. Strange white circles and lines marked his nose, cheeks, and forehead. Silver rings adorned both slender fingers and delicately elongated ears. Despite his otherworldly appearance, he was dressed sharply in a beautifully tailored pinstriped waistcoat and trousers.

As Brand approached, the kashmari's marked face split into a grin that showed off an array of teeth that would have looked more appropriate in the mouth of a feline.

"There you are, Brand," the kashmari said. "Have a seat. Are you thirsty? Of course you are. Waiter!"

Before the kashmari could sit again, Brand pulled the city lord aside and whispered in his ear. "B'alam Nehn sent a bounty hunter to attack me two days ago."

Kushchai's face went from jovial to serious in an instant.

"Because you beat his champion?"

Brand nodded.

"Is the bounty hunter still alive?"

Brand nodded again.

"You should have killed him."

"He won't attack me again."

"His death would have sent a clear message to B'alam Nehn. Now I'll have to speak with him." Kushchai turned and smiled at the others at the table, beckoning for Brand to sit. A waiter arrived, distracting Kushchai and allowing Brand a moment to look over the others seated at the table.

Sitting across from Brand was Lady Mirane. Brand had met his fair share of beautiful kashmari women, but as always, Mirane looked like she'd stepped out of a dream. Silver flakes gilded her eyelids and made her deep sapphire blue eyes stand out against her dark skin. Azure lapis lazuli beads were woven into the locks of her silvery hair, which was piled on top of her head in such a way that the loose ends cascaded down over her bare storm-blue shoulders. A collar necklace made of silver and lapis lazuli hung at her throat and drew Brand's eyes down. The gladiator studiously yanked his gaze back up where it belonged.

His gaze locked with hers and she smiled warmly. *She's a kashmari, you idiot,* he reminded himself. *Look, but don't touch. On second thought, don't even look.*

Brand pried his eyes away from the kashmari woman to smile at the second patron at the table, a human male. He looked vaguely familiar, but Brand couldn't place him. He was a heavy-set man who had perhaps been well-muscled in his prime. Like many humans in Darnan, his hair and skin were dark, though Brand had rarely seen anyone quite as dark as this man. His shoulder-length wavy black hair framed an almost brutish clean-shaven face; but his eyes belied a keen, watchful intelligence.

The strangest part about him was his clothes: unlike most of the other patrons, who wore elegant formalwear, this man wore a tired old overcoat, a faded red waistcoat, and a loose ascot, as though he were a businessman out for a drink after work. The man seemed completely disinterested in Brand, instead preferring to read the menu.

The third patron was the kashmari lord of Duat, Lord Jinn. Like other kashmari, his skin was bluish-grey. However, his was decidedly greyer, as though the lack of sun in Duat had sucked the bluish tint out of his skin, leaving him looking sickly. His eyes were red as blood, though, and he kept those crimson eyes trained on Brand with as much interest as the human lacked. He waited for Kushchai to finish with the waiter, as was customary.

With the drinks ordered, Kushchai turned to the others.

"May I introduce His Excellency, High Lord Fafnir the Dragon. My lord, this is Cadmus Brand, my champion gladiator."

Brand's jaw dropped as the old man in the threadbare red waistcoat nodded courteously. This is Fafnir? The most powerful kashmari of them all? *He looks like an older, more worn-down version of me, not an immortal, elegant kashmari.*

"My lord." Brand barely managed a nod and polite smile. The high lord's eyes twinkled at Brand's shock.

"And Mirane, Lady of Navar, whom you met last week."

Grateful for the diversion, Brand accepted her delicate hand and planted a kiss between the silver adornments.

"As well as Lord Jinn of Duat, of course."

"It is most excellent to meet you again," Lord Jinn said. "I greatly look forward to watching the contest tomorrow between you and Mirane's Duati champion."

"It will be an honor to test myself against him, my lord."

Kushchai beamed at his prized pet's manners.

"He was an excellent tour guide," Mirane said. "I will admit, he's older than I expected of a prized fighter." The corners of her lips curled as her stormy gaze raked over the gladiator. "Though he's certainly handsome and well-built. You say he has no trouble keeping up with the younger gladiators?"

"He not only keeps up with them; he flattens them."

"Astonishing." Mirane's eyes met Brand's and she smiled in a way that made Brand's insides twist in on themselves.

"Wisdom and experience often confound the young," Fafnir said with a deep, gravelly voice that sounded like what Brand imagined the mountains would sound like if they could talk. "Combine that with an excellent physique, and it's no wonder he has beaten them all."

"Perhaps," Jinn said. "But Mirane's gladiator likewise has had plenty of experience in the Duati caverns and is still young. I believe if anyone has what it takes to defeat Brand, it's Percy. No offense meant, of course, Mr. Brand."

"None taken, my lord."

The waiter arrived with their drinks. Brand sipped his; it was a sweet, spicy whiskey.

Mirane leaned up against Fafnir and grinned. "You find our games silly, don't you?"

A spark of interest appeared in the high lord's eye at the female's touch. He leaned in until his face was mere centimeters from hers and twisted his face into a sneer. "We have other more pressing matters to attend to than games. Your city's production has fallen off, for example. I've heard rumors that your overseers are being paid to find new gladiators rather than new laborers."

Mirane leaned back indignantly and began to retort when Jinn spoke.

"Morale has been rather low, Lord Fafnir. If the workers hate their lives, they don't work. I myself have seen a significant increase in productivity since allowing my Duatis to take part in the gladiatorial games. I believe there was a time when it was appropriate to forbid them, but that time is now long past."

The high lord nodded slowly. "For most of the cities, perhaps. For Navar…I remain unconvinced."

Kushchai shrugged. "If this continues to be a problem, Darnan has plenty of overseers and laborers to assist Navar. Darnan can pick up

Navar's slack in energy production and storage."

Mirane shot Kushchai a glare that could have melted a hole in the brick wall.

"I assure you, Navar will improve."

Kushchai and Mirane eyed each other like two jealous siblings vying for their twisted father's affection. That's exactly what this is, Brand realized. He plays them off of each other so they never think to go after him. A turf war without bloodshed.

Brand turned to look at Jinn and saw the grey kashmari's burning gaze watching him with a knowing little smile. Under his breath so only Brand could hear, Jinn muttered, "This is why I prefer Duat, warts and all."

"No one else wants the mess, and if you handle it well, Fafnir leaves you alone?"

"Precisely."

"You've made promise after promise, Mirane," Fafnir rumbled. "Enough promises. You need oversight from a more successful city lord, I think."

Mirane gasped. "My lord—"

"No, my mind is made up. Lord Jinn will oversee your management of Navar—"

This time it was Kushchai who interjected. "My orl, wouldn't it make more sense if a lord from above ground, and perhaps from a city with similar goods, could oversee Navar? I'm sure Lord Jinn runs Duat effectively, but what works in the fields of Duat may not work in the mines of Navar."

One of Jinn's eyebrows raised nearly to his hairline and he opened his mouth to speak, but it was Fafnir who spoke next.

"Out of all the city-states, Duat is the most efficiently run. Mirane needs someone to teach her subjects to heel."

"Jinn brought farmers to heel with your vrykolakas," Kushchai said, casting a nervous glance at the grey-hooded figures standing around the room. Brand realized that their heads were all tilted toward High Lord Fafnir. Watching. Waiting. Listening.

For a signal, Brand realized with a sudden chill. They must be his guards. Vrykolakas? Brand had never heard of them.

Kushchai was still speaking. "...even Mirane could achieve results under those circumstances. I, on the other hand, have had no such boon, and many of my subjects are individualistic merchants."

"The miners of Navar are menial workers," Jinn said, "much like my farmers. I know how they think—"

Mirane's beautiful face twisted in anger, but she kept it in check, her silky voice careful. "My Lord, before these two brutes get into a fight over my carcass, may I propose an alternative course of action?"

Fafnir crossed his arms over his barrel chest, one thick eyebrow raised. "What did you have in mind?"

Mirane said, "Let us have a simple wager. If my gladiator wins, I get to keep Navar and chose who has oversight over me. If Kushchai's gladiator wins, I lose Navar."

Fafnir was so still as he stared at her that Brand was reminded of a reptile waiting patiently on a rock for its prey to wander by. Mirane seemed to be holding her breath as the minutes crept by. The silence and waiting became uncomfortable and she seemed to wither under Fafnir's unrelenting stare.

Finally, he said, "Fine. You will have your wager. If Kushchai's champion wins, he gains control of Navar. If yours wins, I will allow you until spring to improve production. Are both parties agreed?"

Mirane looked about ready to light the lounge on fire. Fafnir's adjustment to the wager only gave her a little breathing room if she won, nothing more. But she nodded tightly.

Kushchai eyed Brand, then glanced at Jinn. The other kashmari lord shrugged. Kushchai thought for a moment more, then, "Agreed."

"Very well," Fafnir said. "Your hands."

Both Kushchai and Mirane offered their palms face up on the table in front of the high lord. With one broad fingernail, Fafnir drew a long thin line of blood from each of their palms. Blood dripped down onto the table and stained the white cloth crimson.

Fafnir held his own palm out. Brand was surprised to see thick callouses on the pads of the hand as though he were a laborer instead of an aristocrat. An angular black tattoo inked on the back of that huge hand continued up under the sleeve of his coat. It reminded Brand of Alastair's tattoo. The gladiator took a sip of his whiskey to cover the wave of sadness he knew he couldn't completely keep off his face.

Kushchai then held his hand over the high lord's, letting his blood drip onto Fafnir's hand. Mirane did the same so that their blood mingled in the high lord's palm.

Then the mixed blood turned a deep shade of violet and seemed to seep into Fafnir's skin. It leaked outwards in a strange dark spiderweb, then faded.

Fafnir clenched his fist with a satisfied nod.

"So be it."

"A blood wager," Brand said, stunned.

Kushchai smiled in amusement as he pulled out a handkerchief and wrapped his bleeding hand.

Jinn chuckled. "A rare sight for a lowly human, isn't it? But now you are no lowly human anymore, are you, Cadmus Brand? Perhaps one day you too will make a blood oath, as many other humans here have done."

He gestured to the human council members scattered around the lounge.

The idea shocked Brand further. Was Jinn suggesting that he too might become a counselor someday? The thought both excited and terrified him. Regarded as the most powerful humans in the city-states, human members of the Council of Lords were the captains of industry and answered only to the kashmari city-lords.

Jinn downed the remainder of his drink in one swallow. "Enough of this business talk. We've bored the poor gladiator stiff. What do you say we leave our stuffy old manipulative high lord here and go find a real party, eh?"

Brand glanced over at Fafnir, but the high lord didn't seem to mind Jinn's words at all.

"I'm coming too," Mirane said, standing. There was silence for a moment as the three males admired the curves of her body not at all hidden by the form-fitting shape of her ankle-length blue dress.

"Me too," Kushchai chimed in. "Wouldn't want you to slip something into my gladiator's drink, now would we?" he grumbled to Mirane. He turned and elbowed Jinn playfully.

The grey kashmari chuckled. "I'm on her side, my old friend. Percy is a Duati boy, and I'll stand by him. Besides, I look forward to seeing the look on your face when you lose."

Kushchai grinned. "Mark my words, Navar will be mine."

Mirane shot a glare at the two lords over her shoulder.

Brand glanced back at the table as they left. Instead of a lonely old man sitting there as he'd expected, Brand saw instead Fafnir's eyes meet his own. The high lord raised his glass to Brand as though wishing the gladiator luck. Fafnir drank deeply, then stood to leave.

Brand was whisked away at that moment by the other kashmari.

They all know that he's got them wrapped around his finger. And yet they still follow him. There is definitely more to him than I can see, Brand thought to himself.

FOLLY

Palatine Hall, Darnan

The three kashmari spirited Brand away in a large, opulent carriage drawn by a team of mechanical horses that ran so smoothly that, had he not seen the buildings flashing by, the gladiator would have thought they weren't moving at all. The wide stone boulevard gave way to a narrower road lined by thick trees that loomed in the coming darkness.

"So," Kushchai said, leaning forward to smirk at Mirane, "what will you do after you lose Navar to me?"

"Keep dreaming," she said with a smile, "for the Navar of your dreams is the only place you'll ever set foot in my city."

"My gladiator hasn't been beaten since I hired him."

Mirane turned to Brand with a smirk. "Can you give the great and terrible Lord Kushchai an accurate preliminary assessment of the fight tomorrow?"

Brand's mouth went suddenly dry as three pairs of kashmari eyes—silver, blue, and blazing red—looked expectantly at him. He cleared his throat.

Just tell them like it is.

"I saw Percy fight last season. He's fast and skilled. He's fought both the creatures of Duat's caverns and many other gladiators, which is more than I can claim, as I've spent most of my life fighting men. Theoretically, that means he'll be flexible and capable of changing tactics quickly. As Lord Fafnir pointed out, I have far more experience as a gladiator, but that also means I've found certain tactics that work well and I may overuse them out of habit. I think overall it'll be an even fight."

Mirane smirked at Kushchai. "Don't be so certain your man here will win."

"He's too modest," Kushchai said.

Jinn smiled. "No, he's practical and professional, which is a point in his favor. Thankfully, Percy is just as sharp."

Brand found this whole situation uncomfortable. The kashmari were arguing about his abilities almost as though he wasn't sitting here. Jinn seemed to notice Brand's discomfort.

"You'd better get used to this," he said to the gladiator as the other two continued to debate. "You're their plaything, now. If you survive tomorrow, you'll be pampered beyond anything you've ever dreamed; but it does come at a price."

Brand shrugged. "Not all that different from how Lord Fafnir treats you city lords."

Jinn cocked his head. "You're strangely perceptive for a human. Yes, we play the high lord's games, and in return, we retain both our lives and the right to govern."

The lord tilted his head ever so slightly towards Mirane. He lowered his voice to a murmur.

"Mirane hasn't lost Navar—yet. Though it is a near thing. And that makes her especially dangerous to you. Keep your wits about you around her."

"Aren't you on her side?" Brand muttered back.

"None of us are on anyone else's side. Besides, I want you to lose, not die."

Kushchai noticed the two muttering together and said, "What are you whispering to my gladiator?"

Jinn leaned back and grinned. "I'm trying to bribe him to throw the match tomorrow, of course. What else would I be doing?"

"That's your idea of a fair match?"

"I'm testing out his loyalty to you. A Duati would never think to betray his patron, no matter how much coin was offered."

"And how did my man do?"

Jinn spread his hands. "Admirably, I'm sorry to say."

"Did you hear about poor Sotol?" Mirane leaned forward to lay a bejeweled hand on Brand's forearm, but her glittering eyes were fixed on Jinn. Brand's heart began to beat a little faster. Jinn's warning evaporated from his mind like raindrops in the desert.

Jinn shrugged.

"He got what he deserved. Sleeping with a human—What was he thinking? Fool." The gray kashmari pulled out a small hand mirror and a white pen. He carefully began to draw markings on his face. They were similar to the markings Kushchai wore, though he used tick marks and dots instead of circles and lines.

"Still, it's absolutely dreadful what Fafnir did to him, don't you think?" Mirane pressed.

"Of course it was dreadful," Kushchai said, "otherwise it wouldn't be much of a punishment. The message was clear, though. Stay in line or be destroyed. The old Dragon sure keeps us on a short leash."

Brand decided to study the ornate golden scrollwork inlaid in the door he was sitting by. If this was a short leash, he wouldn't mind being tied down by it for the rest of his life. The tone of Kushchai's voice was bitter, though. Perhaps theirs was a gilded cage. Mirane lifted her hand from Brand's arm to fiddle with the pins holding her hair up on top of her head.

Remember who you are, Brand reminded himself forcefully. *You are nothing to her. Just a plaything.*

Mirane snatched the mirror and pen out of Jinn's hands and began drawing on her own face. "One wonders why it's still illegal, though. It's been hundreds of years."

"You're just sore that you've run out of kashmari to seduce," Kushchai said.

Mirane drew a long white line down her delicate chin. "I used to have quite the way with human males."

Jinn snorted. "Or just males of any species."

Mirane grinned. Brand felt his face flush slightly.

Kushchai rolled his eyes, then changed the subject. "Both of you are cowards, keeping your faces clean for the Dragon, then putting ordyeni on as soon as you get out of his sight. I've always worn them around him and never had a problem."

"He likes you," Mirane said. "Besides, that doesn't prove he has changed his stance on ordyeni in general. Just that he tolerates them on you."

Kushchai turned to Jinn, who shrugged and nodded his agreement. Kushchai clicked his tongue, then gestured toward Brand.

"Give him some too, while you're at it."

Mirane turned her attention to Brand with a mischievious grin. She stuck her tongue out between her teeth as she began to mark his face gently. He looked down and forgot to breathe for a few heartbeats. He swallowed hard and looked up again, trying to focus on her nose while breathing steadily.

"You have such lovely eyes," she purred.

Brand's eyes flickered to Mirane's own eyes and marveled at how intensely blue they were, as though she had gems for irises.

Brand asked, "Why was the high lord dressed so…"

"So badly?" Kushchai finished dryly. "His Eternal Excellency, His Majesty the Dragon, the Lord of Everything doesn't care about fashion. I'm fairly certain he's been wearing the same five suits for the last thirty years."

"He does have a lot to deal with besides looking good at parties," Brand pointed out.

Kushchai snorted. "He doesn't need time to pick out clothes; he has servants for that."

"It's probably just another aspect of these games he plays with us," Mirane grumbled as she drew a line down Brand's jaw. "Look like something the hound dragged in, get the lowly city lords to underestimate you, then cut out their hearts when they overstep."

"No one in their right mind would overstep," Kushchai said. "It's not as though his love life suffers, either. The man just doesn't care. He doesn't have to care."

Mirane finished her work on Brand's face and turned away. Brand breathed again. The carriage came to a gentle rocking halt a moment later. Brand tried to look out the window to see where they were, but the sun had sunk below the trees. A little pathway lit by glowing lights twisted away into the darkness.

"There can't be electricity out here," Brand mumbled.

Beside him, Lady Mirane said, "Or trees in the desert, but Kushchai manages somehow."

"Just a matter of knowing the right tree," Kushchai said smugly as he climbed down.

Brand stepped out of the carriage and saw what he couldn't from inside the carriage: the lit pathway led up to an enormous mansion that sprawled out in either direction. The looming walls were partially obscured by behemoth topiaries trimmed to look like slender women. Tall pillars stretched up half a dozen floors to the roof. In front of the grand wooden doors, other carriages were disgorging lords and ladies, councilmen and councilwomen, kashmari and humans, all glittering in the bright electric sconce light.

"First time?" Jinn asked.

"What?" said Brand.

"He means seeing my mansion," Kushchai said, stepping forward to lead the way. Melodramatically, he added, "Tonight you drink with lords, Champion. Tomorrow, you'll be a god."

The three kashmari laughed at their little joke. Brand just felt a bit uneasy. He followed them up the steps and joined the throng entering the mansion. Kushchai hooked his arm around Brand and half dragged the gladiator towards the back of the house. The kashmari lord led him down a grand hallway lined with portraits of Kushchai that stretched to the ceiling and a row of busts of many different men and women. Brand could hear dozens of voices burbling from ahead.

They passed a large mirror on the wall and Brand caught sight of himself wearing his top hat with the kashmari ordyeni painted on his face. Mirane had placed a series of short white lines starting between his brows that went up, formed a point, and then curled down around his eyes to his jaw. Other lines went from his cheekbones down to his jaw.

The stripes of a sand tiger, he realized.

The white paint stood out sharply from the rest of his tanned brown skin and matched the streaks of white in his beard and hair. He winced. All he needed tonight was a reminder of how old he was.

Finally, they came to a wide-open kitchen crammed with more kashmari than Brand had ever seen. There were tall and slender lords and short and round ladies, and everything in between, with skin in varying shades of grays and blues and even a male with pale maroon skin.

Their clothes were finer than he had ever seen, and both sexes wore bangles, earrings, cuffs, and collars, any kind of metal or jewel that could catch the light and shatter it into a thousand pinpoints of light. The whole kitchen sparkled with shards of broken light that danced around the ceiling and walls like a twisting constellation.

Kushchai grabbed and raised Brand's hand as someone pressed a drink into the gladiator's other hand. The crowd grew silent.

"The Champion of Darnan!" Kushchai bellowed. He upended a glass of champagne into his mouth.

"The Champion of Darnan!" the crowd chorused. They all downed their drinks. Brand followed suit, though he winced as it burned going down. Some sort of whiskey, and not a very good one. Someone replaced Brand's glass.

From across the room, Jinn held up the hand of another man that Brand recognized as Percy, his opponent. The man was a head shorter than Brand, but well-muscled. He had the pale skin and light hair of the people of Duat, an oddity of people stuck underground for generations, Brand supposed. A long scar rippled from his right ear down his square jawline and across his throat. His grey eyes met Brand's and the other man raised his glass to Brand. Brand raised his glass in return as Jinn yelled,

"The Champion of Duat!"

"The Champion of Duat!" the crowd chorused again.

The second drink went down a little better because Brand was bracing for it. When he glanced over at the other gladiator, Percy was grinning and reaching for another drink.

Brand turned back to Kushchai and found Mirane pressed in close to the other city lord, wrapping her arms around his neck. "We could join our forces, you know, and beat the old windbag at his own game."

Kushchai's eyes traced her lips and for a moment, it looked like his hand would reach around her back to press her closer. But instead, he pried her arms from around his neck and pushed her away.

"Not with a fool like you," he sneered. "I'll take your city and bury you beneath it without a grave marker, whore." Kushchai turned to Brand. "I've got to talk to someone," he said as he left.

Around him, the kashmari returned to their slurred conversations.

Mirane slipped her arm into Brand's.

"Come with me," she said. "There's something I'd like to show you. Something we talked about earlier."

Brand planted his feet. Her hand tugged ineffectually against his own. She turned back to him.

"What is it?"

"The night before a gladiatorial fight in which you are the patron of my competition? A fight upon which rides the future of your city?" Brand shook his head. "What are you going to try to do to me?"

Mirane reached her free hand up to Brand's face and stroked his beard, her eyes wide and beautiful. Brand felt as though the air had been knocked clean out of him. She seemed even more beautiful in this soft light, the fullness of her lips, the curves of her breasts and hips barely hidden by her gown.

"The High Lord would kill me if I tampered with you," she said. "Our wager was as much oath as it is a contest. I just want to show you something I thought you'd find interesting. Nothing more. Come on."

Brand sighed. She was right. If Fafnir loved his games as much as it appeared, he most likely wouldn't take too kindly to one of the competitors cheating.

She gave a little tug on his hand, and this time Brand followed.

* * *

Kushchai turned away from Mirane and searched the crowd until he found B'alam Nehn leaning on a counter with a wine bottle in each hand. The fat kashmari's pale blue cheeks were already flushed a darker blue. He was laughing merrily with another kashmari man downing shot after shot of some green liquid. The other kashmari laughed heartily one last time and then fell to the floor. Kushchai rolled his eyes and moved toward B'alam Nehn.

Kushchai hooked his arm under the elbow of B'alam Nehn and steered the kashmari out of the kitchen. The fat kashmari muttered something about missing the best part of the party but didn't resist. Kushchai ignored him.

As they left, Kushchai thought he saw the corner of Mirane's dress flick around a corner. He pursed his lips. He could have her for himself, he knew. She'd offered on more than one occasion, and the city lord couldn't deny that when she was close, that was all he wanted. But each kashmari had their vices, and Mirane's was her insatiable lust. The way she threw herself at anything male that moved irritated Kushchai. Kushchai hoped he never had to mingle with whatever miserable wretch of a kashmari she'd managed to snare this time.

Kushchai steered B'alam Nehn into a little room down the hallway. A single desk sat in the center of the windowless and bare-walled room. Kushchai shoved the wine bibber into the chair and spun it to face him.

"Lord Kushchai, whatever I have done to displease you—"

"You tried to kill my champion. Three days before the most important gladiatorial contest of his career. In my city, while you are a guest, no less."

"I had no intention of killing him," the soaked kashmari blubbered. "He's Cadmus Brand. I couldn't kill him even if I sent an army of machine suits at him. I just wanted to rough him up a bit, you know, after what he did..."

Kushchai kicked the chair over. B'alam Nehn slammed to the flagstone floor. One of the wine bottles shattered and sent red droplets flying across the room. A large piece of jewelry skittered across the floor. B'alam Nehn's hand was cut and bleeding badly, but he didn't seem to notice. He scrambled to his feet, cowering behind the fallen seat of the chair as Kushchai stepped forward to loom over him.

"You should be very glad indeed that it was Cadmus Brand you tried to 'rough up.' If he'd been killed or seriously injured, you'd have wished you were the one who was dead."

"Yes, m'lord," the kashmari groveled.

Kushchai grabbed B'alam Nehn by the throat, his angular face centimeters away from the fat kashmari's bulbous nose. The city lord could see a purple vein throbbing in B'alam Nehn's temple, but the other kashmari didn't squirm or struggle in Kushchai's grasp. Instead, B'alam Nehn kept his eyes averted.

Kushchai's voice was soft, but his lip curled up over his elongated canines. "Don't cross me again, B'alam Nehn."

In one smooth move, the city lord dropped B'alam Nehn from one hand, grabbed the intact wine bottle with the other, and smashed it across

B'alam Nehn's temple. The kashmari crumpled to the floor.

Kushchai spun on his heel and left, not bothering to watch the ethereal black mist rising from B'alam Nehn's body. Just before he left, however, a glint from the floor caught his eye. The Darnanian city lord knelt and picked up the piece of jewelry that B'alam Nehn had dropped.

It was a large crystalline seed wrapped in delicate little golden vines. Kushchai could just make out a slender amethyst seedling coiled at its heart. A faint purple light suffusing the seed pulsed slowly.

"Where did you get this?" Kushchai whispered, entranced. But B'alam Nehn could no longer answer. His blood seeped across the floor.

Kushchai drew a handkerchief out of his pocket and carefully wrapped the seed. He pocketed it and walked out, leaving the dead kashmari splayed out on the flagstones behind him.

Just outside the door, a servant flagged the city lord down.

"Sir, a message came for you while you were otherwise engaged. It's from the ambassador of Gresh."

Kushchai took the offered paper and read it. His eyes widened, and then a grin crept over his face.

"Notify the ambassador that I will personally ensure the capture of this criminal. Then take this to Captain Mej of the city guard. Tell Mej that once he finds this man, he is to notify me before they take him into custody. And make sure Mej knows that this…Erekir…is not to be harmed in any way. No tampering, no possessions."

"Yes, m'lord."

* * *

Brand followed Mirane out of the kitchen and up the stairs into a little drawing room. Mirane led him over to a large glass display case and pointed inside at what to Brand's eyes was obviously a pharmakon's alembic. It was very similar to the alchemical still in Brand's secret lab, of an older design and dusty from time but very much intact.

"What is it?" he asked, feigning mild interest.

"A pharmakon's tool," she replied, placing a hand on his arm and slowly stroking it, sending shivers up his arm.

In a low voice, Mirane said, "Kushchai and Jinn won't ever talk about alchemy or pharmakons because they think saying it out loud will make them real again, but they're just as fascinated as I am. We used to hunt them. Those two fossils will never admit it, but to hunt a pharmakon—that was living. I've never felt more alive than when I'd finally get the pharmakon in my hands and squeeze the life out of him."

Brand nodded and gave an impressed grunt, not sure how to respond.

Does she know? How could she know? Brand nervously downed his latest glass of liquid. He coughed. "That wasn't whiskey."

Mirane laughed, and in his ears, her voice sounded like magic pouring through a string of bells. She brushed his hair gently out of his eyes and slowly stroked his face and ran her fingers through his beard.

He tensed, but her gentle strokes turned his mind to mush. She moved closer, a slight smile playing across her lips. Her breath smelled of spice, warm and slightly musky.

Brand tried to rally his thoughts to come up with something intelligent to say, but all he could come up with was, "Too bad all the pharmakons are gone, then, huh?"

Mirane arched a perfectly manicured eyebrow over a jewel blue eye. "What?"

"I mean…because you can't…can't hunt them," Brand said hastily.

Mirane's lips curled up again, a sly eagerness settling in her eyes.

"I have other things to keep me busy," she purred as she reached forward and began unbuttoning his shirt.

"Uh…This is not a great idea," he said slowly, more as a token statement. The warmth of her body pressing against his skin was intoxicating.

She doesn't know what you are. You'd be dead if she knew, he reasoned. *Just relax. How many other times in your life are you going to be with a woman like this?*

Alarm bells were going off in the back of his mind, yelling at him how this could get him killed, but he shoved it into a dark corner and locked it away as he reached up and cradled her chin in his palm.

"No one has to know," she whispered as though reading his mind. Their lips met, and he stopped trying to think at all.

FLASHBACK #3: GLOWING

13 July 1023 P.E.
Northeastern Quarter, Darnan

William James and his wife Moira watched the lad eat. He was as scrawny as an alley cat and ate like one too: watching them, eyes darting among the various fruits and sandwiches, eating in spurts.

Brand's hand shot out and grabbed a purple cactus fruit. Long, curly spines made it look like a dragon's egg. He quickly peeled it as Moira had shown him, then sunk his teeth into the white seed-spotted flesh. His eyes closed halfway and one corner of his mouth curled upward in a happy grin.

"Are you sure about this? We can't afford to keep feeding him like this," Moira whispered.

"We have to, love," William whispered back. "They were going to turn him over to the high lord."

Moira sighed. "I suppose I can take on some extra washing for some of the other ladies in the building."

William kissed her lightly on the cheek. "Thank you."

She smiled fondly.

"We did always want a child of our own." William's eyes twinkled.

Moira laughed, prompting a startled glance from the boy. When the lad saw that nothing was wrong, he went back to devouring a sandwich.

"I'd always figured we'd get one a bit smaller," she said with a smile.

William put his hand around his wife's waist and pulled her close, kissing her neck. His mustache tickled her skin, making her laugh.

"Stop that," she said, swatting him away. "Propriety, please."

"He's going to have to get used to me showering my wife with affection in my own home," William said, gesturing to the tiny kitchen.

A mere three steps carried him to the table. He sat and grabbed a large green citrus fruit before the boy could swipe it.

"What is your name?" Moira asked the boy.

"Cadmus Brand," he replied around a mouthful of fruit, "but the only person who ever called me that was Alastair. Everyone else calls me Brand."

"Is that what you'd like to be called?" William asked.

Brand thought for a moment, then nodded. He wiped the juice dribbling down his chin with the back of his hand.

"Very well. I have to work tonight, Brand," William said, taking out a knife and sectioning his own fruit. "I need you to help Mrs. James with the housework while I'm gone. And after work, I intend to begin your training."

"Training?"

William glanced at Moira. He leaned forward. "You and I are different, Brand. I can help you to fulfill your potential and become what you were always meant to be."

Brand frowned. "Alastair told me that being different would get me killed."

"Alastair's the one who asked me to teach you to fight. He knew that you couldn't stay hidden forever." William smiled. "He knew you could be something more than just a street urchin."

Brand cocked his head to one side like a curious bird.

"What do you mean, 'something more'?"

William held out his hand, palm up. His hand began to glow faintly, a soft yellow light. Ever so slowly, the light gathered into a tiny circle of light at the center of his palm. The light then rose like a golden dewdrop to hang a few centimeters above William's skin, hanging like a tiny glowing drop of liquefied sunlight. It bathed the table in warmth. With his other hand, William touched the drop. It fell to his palm with a splash of light and was gone. Brand gaped, stunned.

"We can use magic, Brand," William whispered. "And not only for little tricks like this. We can use it to help people."

Brand grabbed William's palm and turned it over, looking for the trick. When he couldn't find it, he sat back, still staring at William's hand. "I can't do that."

"Not yet, but with training, you could. I know you can. Alastair knew, too. I think that with training, you could help quite a lot of people."

"You think this because I survived a fall?"

William nodded.

Brand looked down at his sticky fingers. "I don't think I can help anyone. I ended up in jail just because I didn't die when I fell."

William took hold of Brand's hand, causing the youth to look up. "The reason you survived is the same reason you will be able to use magic, and with magic, you can help people. It's the same reason Fafnir fears you."

"Who's Fafnir?"

"You know that the kashmari are in charge of Darnan? They're in charge of the other cities, too. And High Lord Fafnir is in charge of the kashmari."

"Like a king?"

"Kind of. Where did you learn about kings?"

"From a book in the library."

"Hm." William nodded his approval as he took a bite of fruit. The juice was tangy and sweet, like a cool breeze on a summer morning. Swallowing, he said, "Well, the guards were going to turn you over to Lord Fafnir. He hunts men like us because we're the only ones he fears anymore."

Brand seemed to mull this over, but his brow remained creased.

William looked up at the clock and stood.

"I have to leave now or I'll be late for work. But when I return, we'll talk more. Agreed?"

Brand nodded.

"Good." William shoved the rest of the fruit in his mouth, rinsed off his hands, and picked up his waistcoat from the counter. He strode to the round mirror next to the front door to pull on the waistcoat and straighten his bow tie. With a soft kiss and a few last murmured words for Moira, he rushed out the door.

* * *

Late that evening, after most of Darnan had retired for the night, Brand stood next to William in a large underground chamber lined with bricks. The sheer size of the cistern astounded Brand. It could have comfortably held several streets with all their shops. Most of the great chamber was filled with an enormous pool of dark water. The pool's opaque surface rippled slightly in the flickering orange light of the torches William had lit on several walls and columns.

They stood on a walkway of moss-covered bricks. Throughout the cavernous cistern, thick stone pillars crowned with great reaching arches supported the vast ceiling. Lichens and mosses decorated the damp stone in an array of pastel blues and greens that shimmered from the torch light reflected from the water.

"The Great Cistern of Darnan," William said. William had changed out of his service uniform in favor of a simple linen shirt, rough trousers, and soft leather boots. With his neatly trimmed mustache and ram-rod straight posture, though, he hardly looked any different. "Without it, this city would shrivel up and blow away in the wind for want of water. We should be able to practice here in peace."

He turned to the boy. Brand's face lit up.

"We get to do magic here? Right now? How does it work?" Brand asked. "The magic? Are you sure I can do it?"

William chuckled at the boy's enthusiasm. "Yes, I'm sure you'll be able to do it. And yes, we get to practice magic here. As for how it works…

"There are a very small number of us who are…well, we generate a certain form of energy. With training and certain augmentations, we can use this energy to temporarily enhance our physical bodies. That's how we can be strong enough to challenge the kashmari. We're the only humans who can."

Brand stared at William.

The older man fiddled with the pipe in his pocket while he thought of a better way to explain it. "You fell off a roof the other day in the alley. Fell five floors, right? That would have killed most grown men, and yet you, a soft-boned boy, walked away as though it were nothing."

"There were crates that broke my fall," Brand murmured, his face falling. That didn't seem like nearly enough proof of his magical abilities.

"Even if they had broken your fall, the crates themselves were far enough below you and sturdy enough that they should have still injured you." William tapped Brand's thin chest. "But they didn't. You somehow managed to tap into your raw abilities. Your body became stronger, just for a moment. I suspect if we tried that experiment again right now, you would break your neck because normally, it takes a long time to build up that energy within us, ready to be used again."

"So how can I practice using it if I don't have any left?"

William smiled. He pulled out a small crystal vial from his pocket and held it up. It was filled with a light green liquid.

"This elixir helps to augment that tiny speck of energy within us so that we can use it far more often, and longer."

William held out the vial to the boy, who took it gingerly and turned it about in his fingers. "We can't get more of this energy from, say, eating a special plant?"

"No. There isn't any of this energy in the world around us. It's only in us. Even this elixir only amplifies our own energy."

"Is there still a limit? I mean, how often we can use our…that energy?"

"I call it a spark. And for as long as I've been a pharmakon, no, there's no limit so long as I use these elixirs. Without them, I can't do anything with magic."

A chill ran down Brand's spine at the name. *Pharmakon.*

"Is that what I'm going to be once you train me?" he asked in a whisper, not even daring to say the word.

William retrieved the vial and put it back in his pocket. "A pharmakon? Yes, that's exactly what you'll be."

Brand had read about pharmakons. Wizards who were stronger than ten men, as fast as a bullet, and could turn invisible. One book even said they could fly.

But they'd all been killed. Or so the book had said. Brand could hardly believe that he was standing here with a real pharmakon, maybe even the last of his kind. And he wanted to teach Brand how to become one too? The boy twisted his hands together nervously. What if he couldn't do it? What if William was wrong and Brand couldn't use magic?

Brand realized William was speaking again and tried to shove his fears aside.

"Now, I want you to close your eyes," William was saying. "Breathe deeply. Feel your heart slow. Feel your mind calm."

Brand did as commanded. As he pulled in each breath and released it, the tension in his muscles ebbed away and peace descended on his mind.

"Good. Now, look inside yourself. What do you see?"

"I…don't understand."

"That's ok. You will. Calm your mind and imagine you are looking inward to the core of your soul. What do you see?"

Brand heard the *drip drip drip* of water somewhere to the left, heard the skittering of tiny claws across the brick, felt the cool, damp humidity on his skin, and smelled the clean scent of water. He felt the crisp air fill his lungs and flow out through his teeth.

"Look inward."

"I'm trying."

"Take your time. Try to let go of everything around you."

Brand frowned and tried to tune out the sensory bombardment from the cistern. One by one, breath by breath, each smell and sound faded until Brand felt as though he were floating in a void.

There.

It was so faint, no more than the suggestion of light and warmth. He didn't want to lose it, so the boy was silent, though his face split into a smile of wonderment.

"Reach out to it. Focus in on it."

Brand wasn't sure what that meant, but he focused on the light, and it seemed to grow, expand, and fill him until its warmth seemed to emanate from his entire body. He opened his eyes.

The warmth vanished.

"I had it!" Brand exclaimed. He tried to reach inward again, but his excitement drove away any semblance of peace.

William chuckled. "With training, you'll be able to harness that energy at a moment's notice, without hardly even thinking about it. That is what I was talking about. That energy is what we use. But you noticed how faint it was?"

He reached into a pocket and withdrew two small vials, each partially filled with the same light green liquid as the larger vial. He handed one to Brand.

"This is a simple amplification elixir. It is very rarely used on its own because of how dangerous it is to be seen using our amplified abilities, but it is also one of the few that you can use before you've been through the Trial. Never use it in view of a kashmari. Never, for any reason." He handed one of the vials to Brand. "We can use it here because of the thickness of these walls and the layers of dirt between us and the street above. No kashmari will know we're here. Go ahead and drink it."

"What's the Trial?" Brand asked, eying the elixir.

"The Trial of Augmentation is where a young pharmakon is inoculated against the poisons that we use in our elixirs. Without undergoing the Trail, you would die from drinking even a single drop of any of my elixirs. But after the Trial, you'll be able to use them to enhance specific aspects of your abilities. Because each elixir will only enhance a specific ability, your skin won't glow and you'll be able to use your abilities around kashmari."

Brand pulled the cork out and upended the vial into his mouth. It was bitter and tasted faintly like the weeds behind Alastair's shop.

Nothing else happened.

"Is something supposed to happen?" Brand asked.

William smiled. "It already has. It helps your energy, your spark, to regenerate at a much faster rate. Each elixir does this to a smaller extent. Take a calming breath. Then see if you can find that spark as you did before."

Brand sucked air into his lungs and let it out slowly. He closed his eyes.

The spark was there. It was far brighter, eager, pressing on his mind, begging him to reach out. He let the warmth wash over him like a powerful wave of brilliant sunshine chasing away the darkness. He opened his eyes.

Strange swirling patterns of light erupted from his skin, glowing a fierce golden color that shimmered slightly. Brand gasped and looked at

William. The older man was staring in slack-jawed amazement, eyes tracing the patterns of light.

"I've never seen anyone glow quite like that," William said. "Incredible."

Brand looked back down at the rivers of fire seared across his skin and all doubt of his abilities evaporated. If he could glow like this, he *could* do magic. Excitement etched a grin across his young face.

William then downed his own vial. The older pharmakon took a deep breath, his face relaxing. Brand's jaw fell open.

William glowed all over, a brilliant beacon in the gloom of the cistern. No patterns appeared on his skin, but every inch of him burst with fiery light. His eyes glowed a searing, brilliant blue.

"Wild, untamed magic," William whispered. His voice echoed loudly in Brand's ears. "Every sense you have is enhanced. Your bones are stronger, your reflexes faster. But it comes with a price. When we use magic in this raw, untamed form, the whole world can see us for what we truly are. And there is absolutely nothing the kashmari hate more than a practitioner of magic."

"Come."

William dashed away down to the unlit portion of the cistern, leaving behind a faint golden afterimage in his wake. Brand followed, his feet flying over the bricks. It felt right to move, to run. The elixir made him want to push faster and faster. He sped forward and caught up to William, who led the boy down a tunnel into another large chamber, this one devoid of light.

The light from Brand's glowing skin lit his way a couple of meters ahead of him. His enhanced eyes took that small amount of light and amplified it so that he could see every detail of the cistern, including the looming gargoyles carved into the capitals of the columns high above.

Brand rushed forward, laughing, and slid to a halt as he came to the end of the pathway.

William, however, kept running. As the older man darted to the edge, he threw himself out across the water towards a pillar. He hit it with a light thud, clung to it for the barest of moments; then he shoved off of it, vaulting to the next pillar. He jumped from one pillar to the next until he landed lightly on the other side of the chamber on another brick walkway.

William turned back to the boy.

"Are you coming?"

Brand backed up, then ran at the edge like William had, launching himself across the water. He hit the column. Fingers scrabbled at the smooth stone, boots scraped ineffectually.

The boy dropped into the water with a splash. A second later, he rose spluttering to the surface.

"Care to try again?" William asked. His voice was patient, calm, controlled.

Brand swam back to the walkway and pulled himself up. His clothes streamed water onto the bricks. He shook some of the water off, then sprinted to the water's edge.

Brand launched himself at the column, flew through the cool air, and hit the stone pillar. He tried to grab at the smooth stone, but his fingers were still slick with water. He fell with a splash once more.

Brand's dark head broke the surface of the black water. "I can't," he sputtered. "The stone's too slick."

William placed his hands on his hips. "Don't try to grab the column. Angle yourself a little to the side. Then when you get there, shove off of it toward the next column."

Through his streaming hair, Brand watched William spring back across the water.

"Like this."

Brand watched his mentor bounce back across the water. He paid closer attention to how William vaulted from one pillar to the next, barely touching each stone megalith before pushing off again. The older man landed softly on the far side of the dark cistern, then turned his glowing face back to watch the boy.

Brand pulled himself out of the water and wiped his face. He gritted his teeth. Then he hurled himself over the water once more.

This time, as Brand collided with the pillar, he pushed at the stone instead of grabbing at it. He flew toward the next pillar with a great whoop that echoed around the cistern.

Elated, he bounced off the next pillar. But on the third pillar, his hand slipped. His momentum carried his face forward and smashed his cheekbone into the stone. Stunned, he fell down into the water.

When Brand resurfaced, he groaned and gingerly touched his face.

He winced.

"Good enough for today," William said. "Swim over the rest of the way."

Alastair had been adamant that Brand learn how to swim despite living in the desert. He'd scrimped and saved and spent every penny he'd had to drag the boy into the mountains last year to a small lake where he'd spent a week teaching Brand how to swim. Now Brand was grateful for those lessons. He pulled himself through the water, luxuriating in its cool caress, relishing the way it held him close. It cooled the bruise blossoming on his cheek.

Brand dove under the dark skin of the water. The glowing designs on his arms lit the cistern floor as he swam, lighting his way. His muscles stretched and strained against the still water, his every move fueled by the elixir. Brand felt every worry wash away, swept away by the water. He burst up through the surface of the water and hauled himself up onto the walkway beside William.

"You're a splendid swimmer," William remarked.

"Alastair taught me last summer," Brand replied. "I almost wish we could just stay and swim."

Behind his mustache, William's smile seemed pensive. He led Brand down the walkway. It curved gently to the left.

"This elixir enhances that energy within you, allowing you to perform at a peak far above regular humans. Other elixirs will focus and enhance a single attribute, such as your strength and your stamina. While not as amazing, they have the advantage of not lighting you up like a torch."

Indeed, as they walked down the tunnel, the light from the two of them lit up the bricks as though they were both holding torches.

"How long does it last?" Brand asked. A grin stretched from ear to ear. He bounced a little with each step.

"It depends on the elixir and how much of it you've taken. I only gave us each a small dose, so it will wear off in a few more minutes. Others last for hours."

"You said that this was the only one I could use without my body being prepared. What did you mean by that?"

"Most of the elixirs I use, and that I will teach you to use, are made with powerful poisons. There is a process that you will have to undergo that will help your body mitigate those poisons. And even then, you will have to be mindful of the appropriate dosages so that you don't kill yourself."

Brand went quiet, the gravity of it all sinking in. They walked in silence for a while. The light from their skin slowly faded, and with it, Brand's energy. Each step felt more leaden than the last. Up ahead, Brand could see the faint light of torches. He had to will his feet to keep moving and for his eyelids to stay open as they emerged into the same chamber they had started in.

"What's the point of all this, then?" Brand asked, rubbing his eyes. "Why do you want to teach me how to use magic if we have to stay hidden? Wouldn't it be easier to not use it?"

William took a torch down from a sconce and dipped the flaming end of it in the water, extinguishing it with a sizzle.

"Some have tried that throughout the years. But here's the problem: it's so much a part of you that in dire need, you will use the ability instinctively before you've even realized what you've done. You did as much the other day when you fell from that roof. It's far better to learn how to control it and wield it properly than hope you never find yourself in a situation where you are forced to use it unintentionally." They walked to another torch, which William took down and quenched.

"What do you use it for, then? Do you come down here just to jump around every so often?"

William chuckled as he took down the last torch. He led Brand back down the tunnel that had led them into the cistern.

"I believe that we have been given these abilities for a purpose, to try and fight against the injustices of the world."

"Like the kashmari? It's not right that they have so much while us humans starve."

"They are one injustice, yes." William's face darkened. "Among others," he murmured so low that only the last vestiges of the augmentation elixir allowed Brand to hear. Louder, William said, "You need not worry about the kashmari. That will come later, after you have mastered your abilities."

William led Brand through the dark streets of Darnan back to the James's small apartment. The street lamps were few and far between and at times, Brand succumbed to the welcoming darkness, his eyelids drooping closed. After one such instance, William hooked his arm under the boy's arms to steady him the rest of the way.

"When will I be able to use those other elixirs?" Brand asked groggily.

"Not for some time. There is much to teach you before then."

The Oracle

10 August 1062 P.E.
Gladiator Row, Darnan

Brand slowly became aware of the sunlight streaming in through the curtains of his window as his brain shrugged off the fog of sleep. He rolled over away from the light, pulling the thin sheet with him.

Then the events of the previous night came back to him in a rush. The meeting with the kashmari lords; Fafnir; the party; Mirane.

Mirane.

That was undoubtedly the stupidest thing he'd ever done, he admitted to himself. Also the most amazing. *And the best part? We got away with it.* He smiled and closed his eyes, remembering Mirane's soft warmth, the brush of her lips on his skin.

Brand chuckled and stood, shrugging off the usual aches and pains of age. He'd have to stay away from her from now on, of course, if he wanted to keep his head. But he could worry about that later.

The day of the fight was finally here. The gladiator pulled open his wardrobe and selected his clothes: a dark red linen shirt that would shrug off the heat of the arena sands and hide any blood, a pair of tough canvas trousers, and a pair of well-worn tough old boots that came up nearly to his knees. He'd put on his armor later, just before the match began.

He then drew himself a bath. As he washed, his thoughts drifted back to Mirane. He hadn't felt this way about a woman in…well, had he ever? He couldn't stop thinking about her.

"Focus, Brand," he growled to himself. "You've got a fight to win today."

He splashed water on his face to clear his head, then hauled himself out of the tub.

As he pulled a towel over himself and dried off, Brand glanced up at the clock hanging on the wall.

"Scorch it all!"

He threw on his clothes and dashed downstairs.

Mrs. James was waiting for him in the kitchen with her usual pre-fight breakfast: piles of cut-up melons, a mountain of eggs, stacks of flatcakes, and a heap of leftover sliced runnerbeast.

"Quite the handsome devil you are this morning, Mr. Brand," she said. "I like the rugged, mussed look. Suits you today."

Brand grinned ruefully and scratched at the hairs on his chin. He hadn't had time to trim his beard. He stopped eating for a moment to examine his gray hairs in the reflection of a large copper pot.

"I should have married years ago before I started collecting all these gray hairs, scars, and wrinkles."

Mrs. James refilled his juice glass. "You could have. You still could. I see gaggles of silly young women falling over themselves trying to get your attention every time I step foot in that arena."

"William was lucky to find such a wonderful and discrete woman in you. I could never find another like you."

Mrs. James blushed. "You're too kind, Mr. Brand. I still think you should try, though. It makes my old heart ache to think that I may not live long enough to see your little ones rushing about the place."

That comment struck Brand to the core, mixing regret and embarrassment with the adrenaline and excitement of the coming fight. He'd never told Mrs. James that he had no real intention of marrying and thus no plans of children. Brand could be revealed as a pharmakon at any moment. He and anyone close to him would immediately be put to death. It was bad enough that Mrs. James insisted on sticking around;

Brand couldn't ask another woman to do the same.

But all the same, in the secret corners of his heart, he'd always wanted his own family. Perhaps it was the curse of being an orphan. Or perhaps it was the constant strain of living a lie and having only one old woman to confide in.

It's not going to happen, he chided himself. *So don't even think about it.*

He shoved the thought out of his mind and replaced it with the image of Mirane, which brought a smile to his face. *That memory of last night is going to have to last you a long time, old fool,* he thought with no small amount of regret.

"You seem particularly cheerful this morning," she remarked as Brand dove into the food. "Last night went well, I take it?"

"Mhmm." Brand couldn't quite keep the smile from tugging at the corner of his mouth. He hurriedly tried to cover it by stuffing eggs into his mouth.

Mrs. James's eyebrows tried to merge with her hairline.

"Oh," was all she said.

"You'll be there at the arena?" he said quickly. He took a swig of juice.

"Of course. I always am. I've never missed one of your fights. Shouldn't you slow down? At least chew so you don't choke and die before you even get to the match."

"No time. I have to stop by the Lounge before the fight, but I'll meet you afterward for a victory dinner, alright?" He stood to leave.

"Good luck. Oh! Wait half a second, will you?"

She hurried over to a drawer and pulled out a square of blue fabric embroidered around the edges with rosemary and goldenrod flowers.

"Hold out your arm," she commanded. Brand complied, and she tied the armband around his thick bicep.

He kissed her on the cheek. "You are the best mother anyone could ever ask for."

Mrs. James beamed.

Brand shoveled the last bite of food into his mouth and sprinted up the stairs to his office to snatch his gauntlet out of his desk. Then he flew out the door.

* * *

Fafnir took the steps up the side of the colossal arena pyramid three at a time, leaving the rest of the kashmari scrambling up the steep steps behind him. It was such a petty, ridiculous show, but it reminded them of their place in his society. He gritted his teeth. That seemed to be all he did these days.

It felt good to stretch his long legs, though his joints ached more than he liked. He was running out of time. As each day passed, he grew more and more uncomfortable, restless, and irritable. The walls of this prison, an irritation for years, were now unbearable. He needed a way out, and he needed it now.

At the top of the pyramid's stone stairs, sumptuous couches awaited, flanked by green marble pillars and tables awaiting piles of delicacies that would be brought out. All was shaded by a heavy stone pavilion.

Unimpressed by the finery, the giant turned away to look down on the arena. It was a long rectangular field of compacted gravel and sand bordered on each side by a sloping stone wall. The four corners were left open as entrances to the field. Behind the sloping walls of the long sides of the field stood tall stone benches shaded by colorful canvas cloths. On the short ends of the field were two enormous pyramids, one of which Fafnir now stood atop. Each pyramid was twice as tall as the stone spectator benches and crowned with a stone pavilion.

"Lord Fafnir!" a breathless kashmari voice said behind him. "My lord! What do you think of the arrangements? I had the two pyramids added onto the arena specifically for this fight since it is the first time you will be attending."

Fafnir twisted to look at Kushchai, whose grey-blue face had purpled with exertion. The others were still a good way down the pyramid.

"Is all this for the few humans you'll let watch the fight?" Fafnir rumbled, gesturing at a silk divan.

Kushchai faltered. He looked around at the lavish appointments and stuttered, "No, my lord. They were for the city lords. The benches below are for the humans."

Fafnir snorted. "I suppose you didn't intend to actually watch the fights that you have been so adamantly championing?"

The city lord didn't respond.

Fafnir sighed almost imperceptibly. His kashmari had grown so soft, so consumed by their distractions. And why shouldn't they? They hadn't tasted blood in a thousand years.

Fafnir pointed a finger the size of Kushchai's hand at the center of the benches flanking the gravel field.

"Take all of this down there," he commanded. "If I'd wanted a sky view, I'd fly."

With that, Fafnir left a dismayed Kushchai amid the trappings. The high lord took the steps down four at a time, passing the rest of the disheartened kashmari in a rush of hot air.

* * *

First Blood Lounge, Restaurant District, Darnan

"We thought you'd forgotten!" a fellow gladiator exclaimed, pounding a flushed Brand on the back. "I told Mac you'd gotten too famous for your old pals!"

Brand laughed. "I'd never miss a chance to see you sloshed, Gwythyr."

Gwythyr grinned. "Excellent. Drinks on Brand!"

A cheer exploded from all the gladiators bunched up at the bar. The bartender pulled out fistfuls of glasses, filled them with an old, dark ale, and started passing them around.

"To Brand!" Gwythyr yelled.

"To Brand!" the gladiators chorused.

"Not for you, old man!" The gladiators laughed as Gwythyr snatched a glass from Brand's hands. "I've got decent money riding on you to win!"

As a pharmakon, the alcohol wouldn't have affected Brand; but the other gladiators didn't know that. Brand made a show of wagging a finger at his friend. "You're paying for my victory drinks tonight, then!"

The crowd oohed and someone yelled, "Poor Gwythyr. He'll be broke by morning."

The rest of the crowd broke into laughter again.

"Ol' Brand could drink a kashmari under the table!" a young gladiator scoffed.

"Yeah, kid, we know. That's the joke."

Brand passed out another round and motioned for everyone to be quiet. He picked up an empty mug and held it aloft.

"I'd like to propose a toast! To my dear friend and mentor, Simon." The crowd parted to show an older man seated at a nearby table, his skin thin and spotted, his head bald. The eyes behind the glasses were as keen and perceptive as ever, though. "I could not have been here without you."

Brand raised his empty glass to the old man.

"To Simon!"

The old man stood shakily, leaning heavily on his walking cane, but Brand set down his mug and hurried over to the old man.

"You don't have to get up, old man," Brand said, gently pushing Simon back into his seat and taking the chair opposite him.

"Call me an old man again, and there won't be anything left of you to fight, young whippersnapper."

Brand laughed. When William had died and left Brand and Mrs. James lost and destitute, Simon had been the one to pull Brand out of the gutter and put a spear in his hands.

"Simon, you've always imparted some words of wisdom right before every fight I've had. What do you have for me today?"

"What more can I say? You've taken my advice and done well for yourself already," the old man said, rubbing the white stubble on his chin. "I suppose I could tell you one more cautionary tale, one from our ancestors long ago."

Brand leaned forward so he could hear the ancient gladiator better over the singing that had broken out at the bar.

"Long ago, there was an inventor who had a son. They desired to escape from the island where they were imprisoned. The inventor made wings for them both out of feathers and wax. On the day they were to escape, he advised his son to not fly too low so that he wouldn't smash into the rocks below, and not too high because the sun would melt the wax that held his wings together.

"The inventor and his son took off, flying away from the island. But as they flew, the son disregarded his father's counsel and flew higher and higher. He flew so high that his wings melted, and he plunged to his death."

Simon grabbed one of Brand's massive hands with his own frail fingers. "You've escaped the poverty of most humans and are flying high, boy. If you win this fight today, you'll be flying higher than any other human around. Watch yourself. See to it that you don't fly too high and melt your wings."

The old man looked pointedly over at a table filled with kashmari, but Brand's thoughts had turned to the memory of Mirane's naked form stretched out on the couch beside him, her soft snores mixing with the sounds of the partying kashmari filtering up through the floor.

A pit began to gnaw at Brand's stomach. Beneath the table, he pulled out a blood-red pill and hid it in his fist. He took a long swallow from a glass of gin, slipped the pill from his palm to his mouth, and swallowed it before anyone had noticed. He tried to calm himself.

Don't be stupid. No one saw us. No one knows. I'm safe. I haven't fallen out of the sky.

"Wise words as always," Brand said sincerely. "Thank you."

Simon clutched the big gladiator's hand fiercely. "You're a good man, Brand. One of the best. Stay that way."

Brand managed to detach himself physically from the old gladiator, but the man's words clung to his mind like tar. Old Simon was right. Last night had been incredibly dangerous. Brand couldn't let himself be seduced again, he resolved. He'd gotten away with it once; he might not be so lucky next time.

Brand returned to the others, and as he lingered with his fellow gladiators, the drug began to take effect. He smiled and joked with them, and let the drug cool his nerves. An hour later, he'd forgotten all about Simon's story.

"Time for the main event, boys!" Gwythyr roared, his cheeks red. "Go on, Big Man! Off to the arena with you!"

The drunken gladiators cheered. Gwythyr shoved Brand out the door and into a mechanohorse carriage.

The Fight

10 August 1062 P.E.
Gladiator Arena, Darnan

In the cool stone preparation room just outside the arena, Brand sat in front of a mirror. He picked up a flask of water from beside him and took a long drink. He looked up at himself in the mirror and ran his fingers through his greying hair. These days, he looked like an old tired soldier ready to welcome retirement. What had Mirane been so attracted to, he wondered?

He stood and moved over to a stone basin filled with water. He splashed his face and hands, then dried off.

The pill seemed to be working as expected today. He'd felt the fog for only a few moments after the prophylactic had kicked in. Now his mind was calm as the drug worked its magic in his system. Once a day, every day.

Brand moved over to the stand where his armor awaited him. He pulled on his greaves, great thick leather mats wrapped around his calves with pieces of steel plating nailed to the shins, and laced them together in the back. Then he pulled a pair of leather vambraces onto his arms.

The chest piece went on next, leather and steel plate emblazoned in the center with the crest of Darnan, a serpent eating its tail. It stank of stale sweat. He then shrugged on the pauldrons, steel shoulder guards with blade breakers jutting upwards to protect his neck. He cinched the strap, windmilled each arm, adjusted it again, and repeated the process until each pauldron fit snuggly and allowed his arms full range of motion.

As he secured each familiar piece of armor, his confidence fell into place as well. He felt more at home in armor in an arena than anywhere else. Well, besides Mrs. James's kitchen, of course. He smiled at the thought of his faithful housekeeper waiting in the stands as she always did.

Brand then pulled on the gauntlets: first the regular one, knuckles reinforced by steel, and then his seemingly identical customized gauntlet. He smiled at the welcome pressure of the vials on his wrist. Careful to avoid flexing his left hand, he clipped both gauntlets into the vambraces.

And finally, Brand picked up his steel helmet from the stone bench. He was about to put it on when Kushchai walked in, flanked by several guards.

"Nearly ready? Excellent. These men are going to check your armor for hidden weapons and poisons."

Brand's heart leapt into his throat. Slag. With all that had happened last night, he'd completely forgotten Kushchai's warning.

"Please stand and hold your hands out wide," one of the guards said.

Brand had no choice but to do as commanded. The other guards moved forward and began to pat his armor and shove their fingers under the metal plates. One of the guards moved his hands toward Brand's left gauntlet.

The guard pushed against the gladiator's wrist, then peered down the slight gap between leather and skin. Brand held his breath. Seconds ticked by, and then the guard moved on.

The guards completed their search without incident. Brand breathed again.

"All clear, my lord," the head guard said.

"Excellent," Kushchai said. "That will be all."

The guards saluted and left.

"I am sorry about that little show," Kushchai said, turning to Brand, "but after last week…well, it sets us all at ease. I never doubted you, of course."

Brand nodded curtly, then placed his helmet, a Corinth, on his head and examined the effect in the mirror. The helmet was simple in design, little more than a piece of metal molded to his head. A single piece of metal came down between his eyes to protect his nose. Over the years, though, Brand had had his various victories emblazoned on the bare metal; now the polished steel shone with dozens of his fallen foes.

"It's hard to believe that a silly human pastime could become so important to the kashmari," Kushchai said. "And yet it has. I'm counting on you, Brand. All of our fates are tied to how well you entertain the lords today. If they like it, it could be an alternative way to work out rivalries, and gladiators could become valuable ambassadors between the cities."

"If I win, you'll also gain control of Navar."

"Yes. And that would be a big win for Darnan, too. The riches of Navar would be ours for the taking." Grinning, Kushchai looked Brand up and down. "Don't let me down."

The kashmari spun on his heel and marched out.

Brand exhaled. That was about as close to a "Good luck; you'll do great" as he was likely to get from the city lord.

The gladiator took one last look at himself in the mirror, one final check. Gone was the scruffy, capable but battered, well-worn man. In his place stood an impressive knight, a living emblem of strength and tenacity.

"Well, don't you look stunning."

Brand saw Mirane approach in the mirror. He stiffened.

"How did you get in here?" he growled. "As the patron of my opponent—"

"I only came to wish you luck," she purred. "Besides, no one will remember me here."

He spun, accidentally knocking the water flask to the floor. It rolled away under the bench. "They'll have to throw the fight out—"

To his surprise, she grabbed hold of the collar of his chest plate and pulled him down to her level, then kissed him. Warmth flooded through him, smothering his resistance. He relaxed and wrapped her in an answering embrace, savoring the taste of her, letting her floral scent fill his senses.

Then she let him go. She smiled, licked her lips slowly, and left the preparation room.

Brand sat down heavily on the bench with a clatter and tried to clear his head. He took his helmet off and ran a shaky hand through his gray hair.

Why had she come? he wondered. If he won, she would lose control of Navar. If he lost, she could be blamed. Brand didn't want to find out what Fafnir might do to her if he found out she'd come to see Brand. No lover was worth that, not to a kashmari. Right?

Doubt mingled with remnants of the warmth in his chest. Under any other circumstances, that kiss would have had Brand grinning like an idiot. Instead, it only worried him.

The referee, a small man with a nose far too large for his face, ducked his head in. "Time to fight, Mr. Brand."

Brand nodded his acknowledgment and replaced his helmet. He fished the flask out from under the bench and took a long swig of water. He then took a deep breath, willing his heart to slow and his mind to focus on the fight ahead.

Brand strode out of the room and into the harsh sunlight, blinking and trying to get his eyes to adjust a little faster. The heat pressed in on him through the suffocating layers of leather and steel.

On either side of the door to the preparation room, the two guards were shaking their heads, hands pressed to wincing eyes.

Brand frowned. How had Mirane gotten past the guards?

"Are you alright?" Brand asked.

"Fine, sir," they chorused. Both men straightened, staring straight ahead as though nothing had happened.

Brand wavered for a moment, unnerved by their odd behavior. Did Mirane do something to the guards? Had she done something to his mind as well?

He quickly took stock of his mind but determined that other than being flustered by Mirane and a bit anxious about the fight, he felt no different than he had this morning. It didn't seem like she'd done anything more than quicken his pulse.

Then again, would he even recognize if she'd tampered with him? She had so much to lose if he won, after all.

Then he remembered the softness of the kiss, the sweet smell of her, and he brushed those thoughts away. Surely Mirane could keep her personal and professional lives separate. The kiss was nothing more than a kiss.

The referee stuck his abnormally large nose around the corner of the preparation building, eyebrows raised. Brand didn't have time to worry about Mirane.

He turned and strode out into the middle of the arena.

The referee's booming voice heralded the giant gladiator's arrival.

"I give you Brand the Bodacious! The Hero of Darnan, the undefeated champion of the Overcities!"

The crowd cheered. Pennants snapped above half the stone benches, bearing the crest of Darnan: the serpent eating its tail, sewn in a white field. Many of the Darnanian spectators had painted their faces in red and white or wore similarly colored tunics.

Brand raised his hand high above his head in a salute to them. His eyes scoured the arena. A smile lit up his face at the sight of Quincy the apothecary sitting beside Mrs. James.

The gladiator continued to scan the crowd. He found the high lord's looming black figure settled in the middle of the Darnanian spectators, surrounded by a gaggle of sparkling blue kashmari nobles.

Brand turned his attention to his opponent as Percy strode out onto the gravel pitch, plumed helmet under one arm, other hand raised to the opposite stands where pennants sported a gold tree inscribed within a circle, the crest of Duat. Percy's pale hair seemed to shimmer in the brilliant desert sun. Like Brand, Percy wore armor consisting of leather pads covered in steel plates. The Duati tree was embossed in gold on his chest. His armor bore metal ridges along its edges much like the armor plating of desert lizards.

"And Percy the Powerful! The Champion of Duat! What a magnificent pairing we have here today: the two most vicious fighters in all the realm!"

Brand's boots crunched on the sandy gravel as he moved to where the referee stood waiting in front of the high lord's pavilion. Fafnir leaned forward in his seat, elbows on knees, fingers steepled in front of his mouth. His dark face was as impassive as ever. Beside him, Kushchai chatted with another kashmari on one side while on the other, Mirane fanned herself. Her eyes locked on Brand's. He dragged his gaze away from hers and fixed his attention on the referee.

"Before the fight begins, I will set forth the rules for this fight as tradition requires," the referee began. "The contest shall take place in three rounds of two minutes each. During that time, the combatants will attempt to score points by striking each other. For the first blood drawn: one point. For a body strike: one point. For a head strike: two points. For a knockdown, which is grounding an opponent for more than five seconds and less than ten: three points. The gladiator that wins the most points wins the rounds. The fighter who wins the most rounds wins the match. In the unlikely event of a draw, where either one or three of the rounds end with both combatants receiving equal points, the gladiator with the most cumulative points will be declared the winner.

"There are four other basic rules that both fighters must abide by at all times," the referee continued. "First, if I or any other referee signals for a break, both fighters must immediately disengage and step apart.

"Second, no fighter shall strike in any way another fighter who has been grounded, defined as having some combination of two limbs and their body touching the ground.

"Third, a fighter who is knocked out, defined as one who has been grounded for at least ten seconds, shall be declared the loser, regardless of previous points or round winnings.

"Lastly, concerning the use of weapons: There shall be no outside weaponry allowed at any time. The fighters may only use the weapons provided." He gestured to a rack of weapons set against the arena wall. "At the start of every round, each fighter may select one weapon to use for the duration of that round. Weapons may not be exchanged at any point during the round. At the end of each round, the fighters will relinquish their weapons, which will then be removed from the arena. Understood?"

Brand and Percy both nodded. Standard rules, nothing out of the ordinary. Nothing more or less than a straightforward, brutal fight.

"Each fighter may now choose their weapon for the first round."

Both men moved to the weapon's rack and picked up their shields. Brand strapped the metal disc to his left forearm. The shield would serve a double purpose: it would shield the vials within his gauntlet, and it would decrease the likelihood that Brand would accidentally trigger the tiny contraption.

As the visiting gladiator, Percy was allowed to select his weapon first. He picked up a long poleaxe without hesitation. Brand nodded his approval. The long reach of the poleaxe would help the smaller man compensate for Brand's longer reach. But it could also be unwieldy. Brand would have to focus on getting past the spear tip of the poleaxe to where Percy wouldn't be able to use the weapon effectively. With that in mind, Brand selected a simple broadsword, counting on his long reach to even out the discrepancy and improve his mobility. Percy grinned.

The gladiators stepped back to stand on either side of the referee.

"No other rules shall bind either fighter. Do both gladiators understand the rules?"

Brand and Percy yelled in unison, "Yes."

The referee turned to Fafnir. "Then by the leave of High Lord Fafnir, I will begin this contest."

Fafnir nodded. In a deep voice that carried throughout the arena, he said, "May the better warrior win."

Brand and Percy strode to the center of the arena and settled into their stances facing each other, weapons poised.

A gong sounded, and the fight began.

The two men circled each other. Brand, ever the showman, spun his sword, strutting and grinning while keeping both eyes on his opponent. His heart still beat a little too fast from Mirane's visit. She was up in the stands, watching him, he knew, and that only quickened his pulse further.

Percy stalked in a circle, efficient in his movements, coiled and waiting, his scarred face focused and still.

Percy struck first, lunging across the invisible circle. His poleaxe snapped forward at Brand like a viper.

Brand easily deflected the blow and jammed the point of the poleaxe into the sand. He leapt forward, aiming to slam his bulky shoulder into the Duati's chest. Percy lifted his shield and took Brand's full weight on it. The two gladiators crashed to the ground.

The men rolled apart and jumped to their feet. Percy's poleaxe came up and jabbed at Brand. He dodged, dodged again.

The poleaxe slid along the leather armor at Brand's waist.

I'm too slow, Brand noted, gritting his teeth. *Need to move faster.*

As Percy thrust again, Brand didn't dodge but brought up his broadsword. The keen edge sheered straight through the wood, cleaving the poleaxe in half. A cheer exploded from the Darnanian half of the arena.

Brand seized the advantage and swung at Percy, who raised his shield to block the stroke. Brand pressed forward, slicing and jabbing at his opponent's shield, trying to batter and wear down the man and separate him from the sharper end of the broken poleaxe.

His mind and his muscles felt slow, though, as though he hadn't had a good night's rest in a week. His muscles were tiring too soon. He hadn't realized how much his late night with Mirane had taken out of him.

As Percy caught yet another blow with his shield, the smaller man shoved Brand's blade back with the shield, throwing Brand's arms back just enough to give Percy an opening. He ran forward, slapped aside Brand's broadsword with a ridged vambrace, and lunged. Brand pulled up his shield, but the smaller man jumped up, planted a foot on the shield, and somersaulted over Brand's head. The broken poleaxe collided with Brand's steel helmet, splintering the already sundered haft. Brand staggered, ears ringing.

"Two points to Percy!"

Brand recovered and spun just in time to see the smaller man shove the spearhead of the broken poleaxe at his face. Brand managed to turn his head, but the blade managed to slide just under the edge of his helmet. Fire lanced through Brand's scalp as he went down. Gravel bit into his face as a collective gasp rushed through the crowd.

"First Blood! Three more points to Percy!"

Vision fuzzy, Brand hauled himself up onto his haunches, then up to his feet. He wavered, light-headed. Between his spinning head and passion-quickened pulse, his stomach churned.

He should have seen those blows coming. As he lurched out of the way of another poleaxe strike, Brand realized that he wasn't just tired; he couldn't think or react fast enough. He felt like he was mired in tar, both in mind and in body.

Mirane must have done something to him after all. He had to get her out of his mind, and fast.

Behind his shield, Brand formed his gauntleted hand into the Theta sign. He felt the pinprick in his wrist and the warm flush of the Healing elixir flowing into his veins. The ringing in his ears subsided, his vision cleared—but best of all, the fog in his mind lifted and the lead in his limbs evaporated. His heart slowed.

He sighed in relief. Whatever Mirane had done, the elixir had cleared it, too.

Brand had designed this vial so that it would release only a third of its contents each time he formed the Theta sign with his hand. He only had two more uses.

Percy clearly wanted a quick knockout and a fast win. It was an uncommon tactic among career professionals, who often enjoyed the fight as much as victory, and one that Brand wasn't accustomed to countering.

But with his mind his own again, Brand was back in the fight. He wiped the blood from his face with the back of his sword hand.

Percy gave Brand an odd look, surprised at how steady his opponent was. The older gladiator grinned.

The noise of the arena melted away so that the only two people in the universe were Brand and Percy. Mirane didn't matter anymore; neither did Kushchai or Fafnir or their bet. All that mattered was the Duati in front of Brand, sweaty white-blond hair stuck to his flushed face, grey eyes squinting against the desert sun, and teeth bared at Brand. A new determination to wipe that expression off Percy's face sent a flood of aggression rippling through Brand.

Blood roaring in his ears, the giant gladiator sprinted at the Duati. Metal clashed with metal and gravel flew into the air as the men pressed together, weapons seeking an opening. Brand found it first, his blade biting into Percy's thickly armored side.

The smaller man danced aside.

"One point to Brand!"

Brand was already chasing after Percy, his long strides closing the distance in a split second. He brought his broadsword down again and again, hammering away at Percy's shield and broken poleaxe. He finally managed to shove the poleaxe's head away, twist his broadsword up under the edge of Percy's shield, and cut into the other man's armor. He felt the blade cut deeper this time.

The gong sounded.

"Round one is done! Place your weapons on the ground and back away!"

Brand dropped his bloodied blade.

"Final point to Brand for body strike. Brand: two; Percy: five. Percy the Powerful has won the first round!"

"You're the best Darnan has to offer?" Percy laughed. A trickle of blood ran down his side unheeded. "After what they told me, I was expecting a titan, not a tired old man."

Brand snorted. "Let's see you take two blows to the head and still come back for the next round; then we'll talk."

Percy's grin flickered.

Brand turned and strode away, dumping as much confidence into his stride as he could muster. He looked up at Kushchai, who had his arms crossed and his lips pursed. Beside him, Mirane was looking at Brand, a look of stunned admiration on her face. Brand couldn't quite contain the smug smile that tugged at one corner of his mouth, resentment burning in his heart. She'd used his attraction to her to weaken him. If he survived this, he'd have to make good on his earlier decision to avoid the kashmari temptress.

On Kushchai's other side, Fafnir too was staring at Brand. The gladiator met the high lord's eyes and a shock seemed to run through him. His blood ran cold. The high lord's eyes brightened and an unsettling smirk appeared on his face. He leaned forward.

Brand looked away, disconcerted, and hurried to the preparation chamber.

* * *

Percy watched as the veteran gladiator stalked away and disappeared into the low building that housed the other preparation chamber. Droplets of blood fell from the big man's head to mix with the dust of the arena. Percy shook his head in awe.

The Duati clutched his side and strode to his own chamber. His squire was waiting for him with towels, bandages, and water.

"What a mess," Percy grumbled. "I almost knocked him out, George."

George helped the gladiator strip off his armor. "You still won the round, sir."

Percy winced as George cleaned the wound in his side. "I was ready for him to throw the first round; I've seen him do that in other fights. He uses the first round to get a measure of his opponents and to lull them into complacency. Then he comes down on them like a hammer in round two."

"That's why you were trying for a fast finish?"

Percy nodded and winced again as George pricked the skin with a tiny needle and thread. The squire carefully stitched the wound closed. "Or at least knock him down a peg. But the man just got up and walked away like nothing happened. How in the unholy fires did he do that?"

"Hold this," George said, pressing a wad of cloth to Percy's wound. He then began to wind a bandage around the gladiator's torso. "Maybe he's already been bashed in the head so many times there's nothing left in his skull to damage."

Percy doubted it. Men who suffered too much brain damage in the arena retired to be spoon-fed for the rest of their short lives. They didn't continue fighting.

"Or maybe he's not human," Percy muttered.

George paused and looked his master in the eye. "Do not say such things, sir. Not even in jest. The dvergen are gone, and may they never return."

George spat on the stone floor.

Percy grunted as George pulled the bandage tight and tied it off. "The stories the kashmari tell us of the dvergen may not be true, George. They may not have been the monsters Jinn says they were."

Percy saw George's eyes dart to the gladiator's grey eyes and white hair, then over to the door.

"Don't be saying that sort of nonsense up here! Begging your pardon, sir, but you should listen less to crazy old women wearing horns and robes. Even down in the caverns, people might get wind of it and take it the wrong way."

Percy reluctantly shrugged and walked over to the wash basin.

"Enough of that sort of talk," his squire said. "What's the plan for round two?"

Percy splashed water on his face and dried it off with a soft red towel. "He'll be ready for head strikes this time. And I obviously can't meet him head-on. That was like dueling a falling boulder. He's just too strong."

"Further proof he's no dverger," George said wryly. Percy rolled his eyes. "So what're you gonna do?" the squire asked.

Percy tightened a strap and stood.

"I'll have to go after him like I would a rocksaber; break him down piece by piece."

* * *

The interlude between rounds saw the kashmari nobles scatter and recoalesce into new groups. Alliances formed, backs were stabbed, and the balance between enemy and ally was reshuffled anew. All within the spare moments as servants filled wine glasses and offered treats on platters that glinted in the brilliant sunshine.

Fafnir reclined in his seat, long legs stretched out in front of him, watching his blue subjects with some distaste. He fixed his gaze on Kushchai, who was laughing and luxuriating in the simpering adulation of several minor kashmari sycophants. The Darnanian city lord must have felt Fafnir's eyes on him because he turned and met the high lord's gaze.

Fafnir beckoned for Kushchai to join him. The city lord bowed to Fafnir, made his apologies to his followers, and then walked up the two short steps to where the high lord sat. "My lord?"

Fafnir sat forward, his fingers steepled. He gestured at the empty seat beside him. "Not many men could take two blows to the head like that and stand up again."

Kushchai sat delicately on the edge of the proffered seat. "Brand has taken more than that. The man's built like a mountain."

Fafnir pursed his lips. "He is quite tall for a human. Where is he from?"

"Here, Darnan."

"How did you find him?"

Puzzled, Kushchai responded, "The usual way, I suppose. I saw him fight, was impressed, learned that he'd been fighting for thirty years for some duke and rarely lost, and hired him on. He hasn't disappointed me yet."

"He'd been fighting in the gladiatorial rings for thirty years before you found him?"

"Yes, my lord."

"Interesting." He mulled this over for a moment. "If this fight is any indication, surviving the arena for thirty years is an incredible feat."

"He is the best." Kushchai beamed.

Fafnir wasn't finished. He watched the blue kashmari's face as he spoke, looking for any flicker behind those silver eyes. "It reminds me of the pharmakons and the strange technology that gave them their unnatural abilities. One might wonder if you—and that gladiator's master before you—have given this fighter some similar advantage."

Kushchai looked aghast. "My lord!"

Fafnir held up one massive hand. "Alchemical herbs were found near his preparation room after his fight last week. Poisons that no human has business possessing."

Kushchai turned a pale shade of grey.

"My lord, those herbs were left there by his opponent, who was trying to frame him. The other gladiator tried to sneak into Brand's room but was unable to complete his goal. He abandoned the herbs nearby." The Darnanian lord spread his hands placatingly. "I assure you he cannot cheat. His armor was checked before this very match to ensure that he is not bringing any illegal weapons or poisons into the arena. He only has access to the weapons that are provided to him at the start of each round. Perhaps he just has an unusually thick skull and good genetics."

Jinn sidled up beside them and sat on Fafnir's other side. He popped a berry into his mouth. "He would have to be a natural thaum user to have that good of genetics," the Duati lord mused.

Fafnir growled, scorn spilling into his voice. "There is no thaum."

"Therefore, he cannot cheat," Kushchai said smugly.

Fafnir met Kushchai's eyes. "Just a word of warning, Kushchai. Those creatures are dead because I killed them all and razed their homes to the ground. If I discover that you have been harboring a survivor, or used any of their tools to give your gladiator an unfair advantage, there won't be a hole deep enough on this planet for you to hide in."

Fafnir waved a hand, dismissing Kushchai.

Jinn popped another berry into his mouth. "You don't really think he's cheating, do you? We killed the last pharmakon three decades ago."

Fafnir shook his head. "Oh no. Not a pharmakon. The most dangerous thing about them was their ideology. If he's been content to live under Kushchai's thumb all these years, he's no pharmakon. But he does remind me of someone else who isn't very good at dying, either."

Jinn raised an eyebrow over a blazing red eye. "Sanders?"

Fafnir nodded.

"Hm. Yes, he does look a bit like that old thorn, doesn't he? Brand certainly has the height, too. Don't see that much these days among humans."

Fafnir accepted a cool glass of some blue alcoholic liquid from a servant and settled back in his seat. "For all his self-righteous talk, I'd wondered if even Sanders could stay celibate for so long. It appears he may not have."

Jinn ate another berry and licked the purple juice off his fingers. "That's just what we need, a young Sanders. The elder has been difficult enough to deal with as it is. This could be terrible news for us."

"I'm not so sure," Fafnir rumbled. "It could be the boon we've been looking for."

"You have an idea?"

"Perhaps. Then again, I may be wrong about this gladiator and Sanders." The high lord took a sip of his liquor. "Suddenly I find myself quite a bit more interested in this fight, though."

* * *

Brand sat, pulled off his gauntlets, pulled off his Corinth helmet, and ran his fingers through his sweaty hair. His hand came away sticky with blood. He moved over to the mirror and saw the blood staining his gray hair a deep crimson on the side of his head. He thought back to the nausea, his scattered thoughts, and the blurred vision.

That was a worse blow than I thought, Brand realized, his stomach churning at the thought. *That should have killed me. No wonder everyone was shocked.*

A knot of fear formed in his gut as he realized he'd healed from a massive, lethal wound in front of most of the kashmari in the city, including High Lord Fafnir.

Brand glanced worriedly at the door, expecting guards to burst in at any moment.

He waited, but nothing happened. The cool stone room remained dark and silent.

Brand walked over to a pitcher and poured himself a glass of water, then downed it in several gulps, not caring that it slopped all over his face. He wiped his face with the back of a gauntleted hand.

Well, it had been either heal or die. Still, the memory of Fafnir's piercing gaze troubled Brand. Had the high lord recognized what Brand had done? If nothing else, he must be suspicious. Brand would have to be extremely judicious with his remaining vials. He cursed. He'd been saving them for later on in the fight.

That also meant using the Time elixir to allow him to move out of time was out of the question. Even at a minuscule dose, it would still darken his veins and he couldn't risk Fafnir noticing that his veins were black. The giant kashmari seemed more perceptive than the others. Brand wondered if he had some powers they did not.

Brand grabbed a towel, splashed water over his scalp, and scrubbed at his head, trying to get the worst of the blood out of his hair. There would no doubt be several times when the Time elixir would have come in handy against the smaller, faster Percy. Without it, he'd have to find some other way to keep up with the Duati.

Brand cursed again.

He poured himself another glass, but instead of drinking it, he held it up to his flushed face to cool it. He closed his eyes and breathed deeply. His muscles were starting to ache despite the Healing elixir. Percy's goal had obviously been to take him out fast, fearing the long game. That hadn't worked. So what would he pivot to now?

Brand sighed and sipped his water. *I'll just have to pray my other elixirs are enough to help me slip past and endure whatever that kid can come up with.*

He formed Sigma with his alchemy gauntlet, letting Stamina pour into his veins. The slight achiness abated. He then downed the glass of water and strode out of the preparation room, donning his helmet as he went.

* * *

The gladiators strode out into the arena. All bravado gone, they eyed each other like rival sand tigers, waiting, muscles coiled and ready. Brand was allowed to choose his weapon first this round. He moved over to the rack.

The weapons that the gladiators had used in the previous round had been removed. A morning star, a dense wooden stave, a battle-axe, and several short swords remained. After a moment's thought, Brand chose the battle-axe. It had a short handle and a spike on its tip. He also picked up a fresh shield devoid of dents or dings.

Percy smirked and picked up the morning star. Brand grinned back, defying the sense of dread he felt as the Duati swung the spiked weapon in a circle around his lithe body. When he'd last seen the man wield a similar weapon, Percy had smashed it through another gladiator's skull. Brand had been violently sick at the sight and had sworn to retire if he was ever slated to fight Percy. Only Kushchai's cajoling had kept Brand from turning in his armor. Now, he wished he'd followed through.

They took their places at the center of the pitch and when the gong rang out, Percy jumped forward, swinging the prickly mace with gusto at Brand's knees.

Brand rolled to the side, clenching his left hand into Alpha and then twisting his fingers into Rho. His pulse rocketed up as the Adrenaline elixir surged into his heart and limbs. The excitement buried the faint queasiness caused by the Rooted elixir. He let his momentum carry him up to his feet, then pivoted and curled under another swing that brushed his grey hair. He brought his axe around and slammed the spike into Percy's exposed thigh.

The Duati howled in pain and instinctively brought the mace down hard—right where Brand's head should have been. But the big gladiator had twisted away again, his eyes bright with Adrenaline, his balance rock solid from the Rooted elixir. He sprinted away to put some distance between himself and that infernal club. But Percy was hot on Brand's heels, sprinting through the pain in his thigh.

"Two points to Brand! Body strike and First Blood!"

Out of the corner of his eye, Brand barely caught sight of Percy swinging his morningstar. With no time to dodge, Brand quickly formed his left hand into Delta, lifting his pointer finger straight up and curling the other fingers into an O shape with his thumb. Instantly, he felt his skin, muscles, and bones *harden*. The morning star crashed into his upper back with enough force to shove the big gladiator forward and knock him to his knees. But the Armor elixir had done its job; Brand's spine was still intact, and he was able to stand. He staggered backwards as he did so, though, and winced at the bruise blossoming in the middle of his back. The Rooted elixir must have worn off.

"One point to Percy!"

Brand could barely hear the referee calling out the score over the screaming of the crowd. Brand shook his arms out and grinned as evilly as he could at Percy, who looked horrified.

Half the battle is in your head, William had told him long ago, *and the other half is in the head of your opponent.*

Brand let loose a battle cry that thundered throughout the arena as he stormed forward, shield and left shoulder leading the charge. Percy leapt out of the way, but Brand had already anticipated that. His axe was there to meet Percy's head. He hit the man's helmet at just the wrong angle, though, and it merely glanced off the steel. Good for points, but hardly a finishing move.

"Two points to Brand!"

Percy rolled under Brand's arm, twisted, and with a great swing of his morning star, crushed Brand's gauntleted hand holding the shield.

With an audible crunch, the morning star shattered the bones in Brand's wrist and the vials hidden within the gauntlet. A thousand crystal shards dug into his skin while half a dozen deadly poisons seared his skin.

Brand staggered back in shock, dismay, and pain.

"One point to Percy!"

The gong rang.

"Round two is over! Brand wins the round, with four points to Percy's two!"

* * *

Mrs. James was in the preparation room with towels and bandages before Brand had even gotten there. As soon as he entered, she commanded him to sit and brought over the water basin.

"It's not as bad as it looked," Brand said, though he winced as she took his hand in hers.

"You went white as a sheet," she admonished. "I'm no fool. That was your gauntlet, wasn't it?"

She yanked on the gauntlet to pry it off his hand. Brand yelped and jerked back his hand from her grip.

"I have to get it off. Come back here," Mrs. James scolded the big gladiator. He offered his hand reluctantly.

This time, Brand gritted his teeth as she pulled off the gauntlet. The old woman groaned as a small wisp of smoke rose from his exposed skin. Brand sucked in a lungful of hot air through clenched teeth.

"I didn't dare bring any of your kit with me," Mrs. James said, "not after what happened last time. Without your elixirs, you'll just have to forfeit the match. I can clean and bandage it, but you won't have any use of it."

"I will not forfeit," Brand said quietly.

Mrs. James stopped what she was doing and stared at him. "He's nearly killed you already, and that was with your elixirs. You've already shown him you can't be disabled like normal men. He'll aim to kill, and he'll succeed if you go back out there without any elixirs."

Brand covered her hands with his good, gauntleted hand and looked into her eyes. He smiled. "There's too much riding on this fight. I can't back down. I have to go back out there and at least try to finish it as well as I can."

The only way I am going to win, he mused, *is if I can injure Percy so we're on the same level. And then pray.* That didn't sound promising.

"I still have a little bit of Adrenaline and plenty of Stamina still in my veins."

Mrs. James looked doubtful, but she finished her work and gave him a peck on the cheek. "Good luck, then. Please don't die on me, my boy."

Brand's returning smile was shaky. "I'll do my best."

* * *

The two freshly-bandaged gladiators stood in front of the weapons rack one final time. Percy chose a short sword, as was common in the last round once most of the more interesting weapons had been used. Brand brushed aside the remaining short swords and picked up the staff. It was a two-handed weapon made of rare ash wood from across the sea.

Percy stared at Brand's broken wrist held protectively against the larger gladiator's body, then at the staff. He opened his mouth as though to object, but then thought better of it.

Brand glanced up at Fafnir. The high lord's head was tilted to the side slightly, watching Brand curiously. Kushchai next to him had turned a ghastly shade of pale gray.

Brand nearly replaced the staff, but the desire not to look unsure of himself won out. He stepped as confidently as he could manage to the center of the arena where Percy stood waiting.

Brand looked up at the stand, this time seeking out the image of an elderly woman. Though he couldn't find her, he whispered a promise to her in his heart nonetheless.

The gong rang out.

* * *

Fafnir's full attention was on the two fighters below as they chose their weapons. The man from Darnan chose a quarterstaff, much to Kushchai's dismay.

"What is he thinking? He can't use that with one hand!"

Fafnir raised a hand to silence the city lord.

"It's not unheard of," the high lord said. "I've done it before; quite effectively, in fact."

"Yes," Kushchai wrung his hands, "but my lord, a mere human cannot possibly hope to match you."

"He doesn't have to match me. He has to match the other human." Fafnir sat back in his chair, eyes fixed on the combatants. Out of the corner of his eye, the Dragon saw Jinn watching him with a sly smile. Fafnir allowed a small smile of his own onto his face.

"What proof is it that you are looking for?" Jinn asked in a low voice.

Fafnir leaned close to the Duati lord and lowered his voice so that only Jinn could hear him.

"I'm waiting for your gladiator to try to kill him. I'm fairly certain Percy will try. He's terrified of Brand. And Brand couldn't heal after that last injury. He's vulnerable. But if he is what I think he is, he'll win anyway. He'll be able to win even if Death has him by the throat."

Jinn frowned. That wasn't the answer he'd been hoping for. If this gladiator was what Fafnir said he might be, didn't the kashmari lords need him alive?

The gong rang out.

* * *

This time, Brand was the one who lunged forward first, right hand swinging the staff in a feint at Percy's feet.

Percy brought his short sword over to block Brand's ash staff. Brand pivoted at the last moment and swung the other end of his staff to ram into Percy's helmet.

"Two points to Brand!"

Percy had to step back to avoid Brand's next swing. Tentative confidence crept into Brand, buoying his spirits. If he could leverage the length of the staff, he might be able to hold Percy off long enough for the round to end in a tie. In that case, the win would go to the gladiator with the most cumulative points. As Brand currently had eight points to Percy's seven, Brand could win.

Just then, though, Brand felt the last of the Adrenaline fade away. Even with Stamina still in his veins, the loss was palpable. His muscles slowed and the pain in his wrist from the burn and the broken bones roared like a fire coming back to life. The carefully practiced control of his weapon collapsed into shaky exhaustion and pain. A sour sickness from the toxins in the various elixirs rose in his gut, no longer masked by the Adrenaline.

On the next swing, Brand put a little more power into a swing than he could compensate for. His momentum propelled him too far, and Percy twisted and sprung at Brand, swinging. Brand dodged out of the way.

Brand stumbled and Percy was on him like a sand tiger on a dying runnerbeast.

As Brand had expected, Percy jabbed first at Brand's injured arm. Brand managed to bring the staff around in time to block, but the next blow struck his chest and left side in rapid succession. The sword blade bit deep into the leather between the steel plates, drawing copious amounts of blood.

"Three points to Percy! First Blood and two body strikes!"

Brand tried to move away, to put some distance between them again so he could maneuver the longer staff, but Percy was merciless in pressing his advantage. His short sword bit into Brand's thigh and then up, sliding almost perfectly up between Brand's face and his helmet. He felt the sting of the cut just before the coolness of fresh air hit his sweaty head. His helmet clattered to the gravel.

With one final downward swing, Percy brought the heavy pommel of his sword crashing into the left side of Brand's head.

This time, Brand dropped to the arena floor like a sack of rocks.

For a moment, he knew nothing. Then, he heard,

"…four, five, six…"

The referee was counting. He had ten seconds to get up or he would lose.

Brand forced his eyes open and shoved himself up to a sitting position. The arena swam. He stood anyway and swayed. Ahead of him, Brand could make out a blurry vision of Percy standing, waiting.

Then he crashed down to the ground again.

* * *

The arena was silent as the spectators watched the great gladiator try to get up and fail. The spectators were all at the edge of their seats, spellbound.

Brand had lost.

Percy had too many points now for Brand to catch up. But the crowd waited for a different victory now, that of life over death.

Kushchai held his breath. Mirane's delicate face was furrowed with worry.

Fafnir leaned forward, steepled fingers held up to his lips and eyes fixed on the still figure splayed out on the gravel before him.

"What a loss," Kushchai moaned softly.

Fafnir held up a finger to silence the city lord. "Wait."

Kushchai frowned but fixed his attention on the prone gladiator.

Fafnir, knowing what it could mean, found himself waiting, even hoping, for the gladiator to rise.

* * *

Brand came to as the referee started counting over again. "One…two…"

He lay there, the darkness pressing in, and closed his eyes. He was so tired. He knew he was dying. His head throbbed; his body screamed. Yet it all faded as his heart began to slow. As he instinctively looked inward, time seemed to slow as well. He found the little speck of light in his heart. If this is how it would end, so be it. He reached out for the light.

Faint warmth seeped from that tiny speck into the rest of his body, the same warmth as when he used his Healing elixir. It was so faint…but Brand's head cleared. His heart began to pound. He opened his eyes and his vision was clear.

"...seven...eight..."

To the astonishment of almost everyone in the arena, Brand stood, blood still flowing freely down his head and face and several other deep cuts all over his body. The referee stopped counting, his mouth hanging open.

Brand raised his eyebrows at the referee, who looked at his pocketwatch and nodded. The two minutes weren't up yet.

His muscles shook and his stomach churned, but Brand leaned down, picked up the staff, and, with enormous effort and pain, gripped it with both hands.

There was only one way to win this fight now.

He summoned every ounce of strength he had left in his fading body and rushed at Percy with a roar summoned from the primal depths of his soul.

Percy brought his short sword up to block Brand's staff, but Brand brought the staff down with the force of an avalanche. He easily shoved the sword aside, then twisted the staff to give Percy a solid blow to the head. There was a crack as the staff splintered from the force. The smaller gladiator's head spun around with a deafening snap.

Percy fell to the ground, glassy-eyed. The referee started to count, but Brand knew the Duati would never rise again.

Brand fell to his knees. Nausea from his wounds and the disgust at what he'd just done gripped him. He wretched on the gravel. His whole body shook uncontrollably.

The referee reached ten.

"Brand wins the match by knockout! Brand the Bodacious wins!"

* * *

The Darnanian stands erupted into cheers. Kushchai leapt up, punching the air.

"He did it! He did it!"

The city lord noticed his champion collapse onto the gravel. Kushchai swore and sprinted down the steps.

No one was paying any attention to the high lord at that moment, but if they had, the wicked grin that marred Fafnir's face just then would have haunted them for the rest of their days.

Flashback #4: Poison

15 December 1029 P.E.
Northeastern Quarter, Darnan

Brand sat cross-legged on the edge of the cistern, eyes closed in the damp dark. The echoing cavern was silent.

Winter in this part of the desert had arrived with its customary severity, seeping into the stones and leaving a thick crust of ice over the water of the Great Cistern. Brand pulled his thin jacket closer around him to ward off the chill, but it crept up through the ice-cold bricks and into his legs.

He'd grown in the last several years. He was still young, but his lanky frame had grown taller and filled out with broad muscles. He guessed he must be about as tall as Alastair now.

The thought of his old guardian made Brand slump a little where he sat. He'd snuck over to visit Alastair's machine shop one night about a year ago only to find it empty and bare as a tomb. That had been a harsh reminder that his past was meant to be left alone, forgotten. But Brand still missed the old man and thought of him from time to time.

Brand's legs began to feel fidgety, but he took several calming breaths as William had taught him. Behind him, he heard the sound of his mentor's boots as the pharmakon approached.

"Are you ready?" William asked behind the youth.

Brand's eyes snapped open and he unfolded his long body into a standing position. He turned to his mentor.

"Let's go over it once more," the pharmakon said. "The Augmentation Trial is designed to make your body less susceptible to the various poisons that make our elixirs work. You cannot use these other elixirs unless you have completed the Trial. The way it works is that we will subject your body to a series of augmented poisonous elixirs. The combination of your spark with these poisons allows your body to quickly adapt permanently to the use of those same poisons."

Brand had gone over this a dozen times with William, but he still had to hold his hands together to keep them from shaking.

"Nervous?" William asked.

Brand shrugged, but his smile wavered just a bit. "I can't wait another week?"

"You could, but each week you wait, the less malleable your older body becomes. We want to catch you at just the right time when you're young enough for your body to adapt but old enough that you'll be able to survive. It wouldn't do you any good to go through this and still not be able to use the new elixirs." William patted the young man on the shoulder. "Don't worry. You'll be fine. Just remember: I'll give you the augmenting elixir in a moment, then the other elixirs, one after the other. Then you hold on to the spark no matter what happens, right?"

Brand nodded silently, not trusting himself to speak.

"I cannot stress to you enough how important it is that you hang onto that spark at all costs. The augmenting elixir is going to make the others ten times more potent than they usually are, and if you aren't holding onto that spark within you, the toxicity will kill you. Do you understand?"

Brand nodded again. His face was white.

"Do you need a moment?"

Brand shook his head stiffly.

William took the youth by the shoulders and looked him in the eyes. "I know this is nerve-wracking. I went through it myself when I was your age. But so long as you do exactly as I say, no harm will come to you." He patted Brand on the shoulders.

"Alright." William gestured to a ring of lit candles on the brick floor. "Sit in the middle of these."

Brand did as commanded, crossing his legs under him in the middle of the candles.

William handed Brand a large vial full of the familiar green augmenting elixir.

"This will allow you to use elixirs like me so that we may continue your training. Do you still want to go through with it?"

Again, Brand nodded stiffly.

Brand unstoppered the vial. Before he could change his mind, he swallowed the light green liquid in one gulp. He took a slow, steadying breath of dank, musty air. He reached down inside himself as William had made him practice so many times. He found the spark of light at his core and grabbed hold of it, focusing on it. The familiar warmth washed over him, chasing away the chill of the cistern. He breathed deep, savoring the coolness of the air, the cold vial under his fingers. He let the light fill him. He opened his eyes and saw the now familiar patterns of light emanating from his skin.

After a moment, William pressed a vial into Brand's hand. He drank.

The elixir felt like a thousand razor blades scraping down his throat, then down into his belly. It spread, slashing at his insides. Brand doubled over, shaking and sweating.

What have I gotten myself into? William had warned him of the pain, but this was far beyond what he'd imagined sitting in the James's kitchen. The pain slicing through his gut felt like fire. He groaned.

He hung onto the spark, and slowly, the pain eased to the point where Brand could draw a few ragged breaths.

William pressed the next vial into the young man's hand.

"Quickly, before the first wanes too much! They must all be taken together."

Trembling, Brand swallowed the contents of the new vial.

Instantly every bone in Brand's body felt as though it were being torn apart. The pain made him lose focus on the spark, and the agony exploded tenfold. He gasped and collapsed face-first to the brick floor of the cistern. Brand cried out in panic, floundering, trying desperately to grab hold of the spark again.

"Focus!" he heard William yell at him. "Get it back!"

There!

He held the spark in his mind as tightly as he could, focused on nothing else, and the pain wracking his bones receded to a level that he could just barely manage. Tears ran down his cheeks.

"I can't," he moaned softly.

William's voice was by his ear as the older pharmakon placed a reassuring hand on the youth's back.

"Yes, you can. Keep going. Don't give up!"

The next elixir made nausea course through Brand's whole body, and he fought to not vomit. He squeezed his eyes tight against the sickness, more tears leaking down his face from the effort. It brought him to his hands and knees again. Drool dripped from the corner of his lax mouth as he panted.

"Can you continue?" Brand heard William's voice faintly.

The nausea abated for a moment, letting Brand take a deep steadying breath. He forced his tortured body to relax, trying to get his rigid muscles to soften. Every inch of him, inside and out, burned and ached with sickness, but Brand wordlessly held out a trembling hand for the next vial.

The fourth vial made his head split. His sight left him, leaving him gasping in the dark. Pain radiated down his spine and out to his limbs like lightning striking a tree. He screamed and arched his back, then fell to the brick floor onto his side.

But then the darkness cleared and he could see William crouched beside him, his earnest face heavily creased.

"One more," William whispered. After two ragged breaths, Brand held out his hand.

William pressed the final vial into Brand's hand. He gripped it so tightly that he thought the glass might burst. He couldn't bring himself to drink it. He lay there, on his side, curled into a ball hugging his knees, pain coursing through his gut, his bones, his back, his head. Sweat-drenched forehead pressed to the cold brick floor, Brand wondered how much more punishment his body would take before it gave up.

One more, he thought desperately. *Just one more.*

The final vial stole the breath from Brand's chest. He panicked, trying to suck in air; but his lungs refused to work. His head ached and his thoughts became foggy. His muscles burned. Darkness flickered around the edges of his vision.

"The spark, boy! Focus on the spark!" Brand heard William's urgent cries through the fog. And then his voice too faded.

Brand couldn't hear anything beyond the blood in his ears, couldn't see anything in the looming darkness, couldn't even feel the floor beneath his body. His mind turned back to the spark and let it fill his mind with its warmth and light. The only two things he knew were pain and the spark, both brilliant and exquisite. He was poised between them, perfectly balanced, the poisons unable to kill him, and the spark unable to heal him.

But the strain of holding the spark up against the tide of death was too much for the young man's tortured soul. He finally surrendered to the poisons, welcoming darkness.

* * *

Moira opened the front door to let William in, the limp form of Brand in his arms. William's skin glowed slightly in the dim light from the kitchen. His face was grim and taut. Without a word, he carried the large youth into his room and laid Brand's battered body out on the bed.

He closed the door behind him and returned to his wife, then gathered her up in his arms and buried his face in her hair. As she held him close, she heard his soft sobs.

"Did he survive?" she asked.

William wiped his face and looked Moira in the eyes. His shoulders and face relaxed. He nodded.

"Yes. He's a tough kid. I thought he might not make it through the last one—I thought he might have passed out and lost the spark because he stopped glowing. But then he started breathing again." William shook his head.

"It brought back a lot of memories," William whispered. "Things I'd tried to forget. Perhaps it's better that we are the last pharmakons. It's not right that children be tortured like that."

Moira's lips brushed his. "He's not a child anymore, William, and he chose it himself. He wants to help, just like you." She chuckled softly. "He may not be your son, but he is a lot like you. He has a good heart. This world needs more men like you, not fewer."

They stood there in each other's arms for a long time. The darkness and silence of the night wrapped them in its embrace and yet gave them the space to breathe and relax in a way that the bustle of daytime couldn't afford. Eventually, Moira pulled her husband to bed.

In the other room, Brand's spark flared, burning away the last of the poisons, then quieted. His breathing grew deep and peaceful.

Coma

22 August 1062 P.E.
Gladiator Row, Darnan

Mrs. James took a sip of tea as she read her newspaper, then set both down on the little table and rubbed her eyes. She looked sadly out the window onto her little terrace overflowing with summer flowers.

It had been two weeks since the fight and Brand had still not woken. Mrs. James was losing hope. The infection wasn't responding to her poultices, and the doctor who'd been to see the gladiator was similarly stumped.

Mrs. James hated sitting there beside him, watching him toss and mutter in the fever, wasting away, so she'd come down for a cup of tea. But now the anxiety was returning. What if he needed her? What if the infection took a turn for the worse? If it came to it, she wanted to be there in his last few moments.

She stood, itching to return to Brand when the doorbell rang.

Mrs. James hurried to the door. To her surprise, Lord Kushchai and another finely dressed kashmari man with burning red eyes met her at the door.

"Good day to you, Mrs. James," Lord Kushchai said with a grin full of pointed teeth. He gestured to the kashmari beside him. "This is Lord Jinn. Could I check in on Mr. Brand?"

"Of course," Mrs. James said, stepping aside and curtsying. "I was just heading up there myself."

Mrs. James led the two kashmari lords up the sweeping staircase to the second floor and down the hall to a set of fine wooden double doors. Inside, tall windows illuminated a fine large room decorated with rich tapestries, thick rugs, paintings from artists in New Braunen, and a few small sculptures and vases. In the center of the room stood a massive four-poster bed, and in the center of the bed lay Brand, skin shining with sweat. Only the rise and fall of his chest gave any indication that it wasn't just a pale corpse stretched out on the covers.

As Mrs. James busied herself changing the bandage covering the festering wound on Brand's head, Jinn moved closer to the bed to stand alongside the old housekeeper. His hand rose to cover his mouth, scarlet eyes sorrowful.

"When you said it was bad, I didn't realize...Is there nothing to be done then?"

Kushchai shook his head, arms wide, palms up. "The infection is tenacious. Nothing the doctor has done has been able to slow it."

Jinn sighed heavily, placing a grey hand on Brand's. "Such is the way of mortals, I suppose. I only wish he hadn't been in this coma so I could speak to him one last time. I would have liked to congratulate him on his victory."

Mrs. James pressed her lips together. The lords' words felt stilted, like a memorized script. But for whose benefit?

"As would I," Kushchai said solemnly.

"Doesn't seem fair at all. To lose our two finest gladiators within weeks of each other, and just as Fafnir approved an expansion of the sport."

"Indeed."

"Do you visit him daily?" Jinn asked.

"As often as I can, but not always daily." Kushchai glanced at Mrs. James standing to the side. "One can always hope for a miracle, though I admit that hope is fading fast."

You only want your prize gladiator back to win you more bets, Mrs.

James thought bitterly.

Jinn nodded. He shoved his hands into his pockets and turned to leave.

"I'd appreciate it if you kept this from Mirane, at least for now," Kushchai said.

Jinn grunted. "Not interested in her jibes?"

A movement from the bed caught their eyes. Mrs. James's heart stopped.

Brand shifted his legs beneath the sheet and moved his arm. Then he was still again.

"Brand?" Mrs. James reached out and touched the gladiator's arm. "Brand? Can you hear me?"

He didn't respond.

Kushchai hung his head and massaged his temples. "He twitched his hand yesterday. Maybe he'll come out of the coma soon after all."

"It might be kinder if he stayed in it," Jinn said. "Unless he's better able to fight the infection while conscious."

Kushchai shook his head, then sighed. "I read the other day about a promising new infection treatment. I'm headed over to pay a visit to the doctor who invented it. It's a long shot, but maybe if I can save him from the infection and he does pull out of the coma…"

The two kashmari stepped into the hall. Suspicious, Mrs. James quietly stepped over to the door to listen in on the rest of their conversation.

"I did like the lad, but even if he survives, he may still never fight again. You realize that, don't you?" Jinn's voice was laden with scorn.

Kushchai scoffed. "Don't count him out until he's dead and buried. I've often wondered if this man has been blessed by the gods. He's survived the impossible time and time again when the odds seemed stacked against him."

"If he has been blessed by the gods, they might prefer he dies so that he won't be of use to you," Jinn pointed out.

Mrs. James frowned. *What gods? Why wouldn't they want Brand to help the city lord?*

Kushchai sneered at the other kashmari. "All the more reason to try and save him. If you train a hound, it will always remember you. I've trained him; he won't turn on me."

Mrs. James's blood ran cold.

Jinn laughed, a deep, hearty laugh that shook his whole frame. "Fafnir is right. You are a fool."

Their voices faded down the hall. Mrs. James turned back to Brand's prone form.

"I'm not sure what all that was about, Mr. Brand, but something doesn't seem quite right about that Kushchai. Bragging about how you always do his bidding? Unsettling talk, that's what it is."

Brand turned his head toward the sunlit windows but did not wake up.

Mrs. James sighed. *Please don't die on me, my boy.*

* * *

24 August 1062 P.E.
Winter Palace, Darnan

Fafnir opened the door to the sitting room. Lady Mirane lay stretched out on the divan, asleep. He let his eyes trace the curves of her body, her porcelain skin the color of storm clouds, her silver hair cascading over her breasts.

His lip curled upward. Stunning as the finest marble statues, yes; but that is where his interest stopped. Taking human females might be a messy affair, but anything would be better than this whore. The thought of bedding this woman made his skin crawl. How she'd managed to seduce the vast majority of the kashmari nobility was beyond him.

He silently took a seat in a chair to the side of the divan with his back to the window and waited, fingers steepled. As he watched Mirane's breasts rise and fall, Fafnir was reminded of another woman many years ago who had had quite the opposite effect on the kashmari high lord. The agonizingly bittersweet memory of her felt like a dagger wedged deep in his soul, so he growled softly and shoved it aside, turning his thoughts instead to the future.

Fafnir closed his eyes and luxuriated in the heat from the sun streaming through the floor-to-ceiling windows, letting it seep into his muscles and bones. The other kashmari hated this desert, but Fafnir found it not only tolerable, but preferable. Warmth and sunshine for most of the year, dry air that didn't feel like breathing soup—yes, much more pleasant than where they'd come from.

But the desert, however comfortable, was lacking two things the old high lord desperately needed.

As the high lord soaked up the sun's rays, he mulled over the revelations of the gladiatorial fight for the hundredth time. Could this gladiator really be the salvation Fafnir had lost hope of ever finding? For the first time in years, Fafnir found himself willing to hope.

Mirane slept on. Fafnir was patient, willing to wait as long as it took for the kashmari woman to wake. And yet, her nap in the middle of the day puzzled him. Of all the kashmari, she was the one who woke early and ran the day ragged until past midnight.

The high lord closed his eyes again, willing the knots in his back and neck to loosen. They didn't. He shifted in his seat. His thoughts drifted across the sands to a nearly forgotten cavern and its vile, crazed denizen.

Mirane stirred, interrupting Fafnir's line of thought. As she woke, she caught sight of the high lord staring at her. She sat bolt upright.

"My lord! I had no idea you were here!"

Fafnir leveled a cool gaze at her. "Is it your custom to sleep through a scheduled meeting?"

Mirane glanced at the clock on the wall in horror. "I've been so tired of late," she stammered. "It must be the desert heat. I meant only to rest my eyes for a moment–"

"Perhaps you should sleep at night instead of endlessly partying." Fafnir waved a hand. "I am not here to discuss your sleeping habits. I would like to discuss your plans for when you return to Navar."

Mirane stood and walked to a little table where she rang a small bell. A servant appeared.

"Bring tea and refreshments."

"I understand you plan to return to Navar next week," Fafnir said.

Mirane returned to the divan, this time seating herself primly on its edge. Fafnir was impressed with her composure, considering the circumstances. She'd taken her loss of the mining town with far more grace than he'd anticipated. In truth, Fafnir was surprised to be the one to seek her out—he'd expected to have her begging for mercy on his doorstep.

Mirane returned his gaze calmly. "Yes. I can manage the transition from afar for only so long before it becomes problematic." She clasped her hands. "I'm sure Valin feels your absence keenly as well, my lord."

"Hardly. I've been back twice each week over the last month. I like having my finger on its pulse. But Navar is more difficult for you to reach. I am glad you will be returning. I have suggested to Kushchai that he keep you there in an advisory role for the time being so that you can see how a well-run city-state is managed. I may have use for you soon elsewhere."

An advisory role kept her within arm's reach of the lord, keeping the possibility that she may be restored to her former role once she'd proven herself. Mirane nodded, smoothing out the wrinkles in her skirt, a frown creasing her delicate blue forehead.

Mirane had gotten her position by weaseling her way into the former city lord's bed and then murdering him. Navar hadn't collapsed since she'd taken over, true, but it hadn't thrived either. Her wager with Kushchai had been fair, but even if she'd won, it had only been a matter of time before Fafnir would have had to relieve her of command regardless. This way, he would hopefully be able to repurpose her in a less vital settlement.

Still, Mirane didn't seem as pleased as Fafnir had hoped. Perhaps the prospect of leaving Navar didn't agree with her. He'd have to look into it.

Mirane said, "Thank you, my lord. As you suggested, I took a tour of Darnan's mines and factories."

"Good. Navar needs to increase its coal production by twenty percent to keep up with the demand just to keep Darnan from freezing over in a few months, and another fifteen percent to keep up with projected technological advancements. The locomotive alone uses an enormous amount of coal. I'm hoping that if Navar can speed up efficiency, we can expand Navari mining operations, increase coal and steel production, and lay track that will connect all of the cities, facilitating trade. We haven't tapped even a fraction of the coal in those mountains."

There it was—just a flicker in her eyes, but it was still there. She clearly understood how much power the city lord of Navar would have in the next few years. *Good,* he thought. *Let the loss of Navar eat her alive until she can't stand the thought of letting another rule in her place.* The competition between her and Kushchai should prove beneficial to both cities.

The servant returned with a tray laden with a teapot, cups, and various baked goods. Their yeasty aroma made Fafnir's stomach grumble.

Mirane closed her eyes and pulled a face as though she'd taken a bite of lemon. "What on earth did you bring us? The tea smells absolutely horrible! Get it out of here! Don't come back until you can brew a proper cup!"

As the servant hurried out, Fafnir caught a whiff of the tea. It smelled just as herbaceous and earthy as it always did. He caught the servant by the elbow and relieved the human of a plate and a scone. He calmly spread grapefruit curd on it.

"Pour me a cup," he said to the servant. She nodded hastily and did as commanded, then after handing it to him, departed.

Mirane's eyebrow arched in disgust, but she held her tongue.

Fafnir took a bite of scone. It was soft, and the curd tart, just as they should be. He took a sip of tea. Earthy, grassy, with a hint of tang from the citrus juice commonly used as a sweetener. In other words, just as tea ought to be. It wasn't bitter at all.

His kashmari were becoming softer by the day, it seemed. Fafnir took another sip while Mirane watched. Or maybe…*No, she wouldn't have been that stupid. She's always been so careful, so diligent in preventing such things before. Why would she slip this time?* His thoughts turned to her exhaustion and his suspicion grew. His amber eyes raked across Mirane's bodice but saw no change. Perhaps it was too early. Or perhaps he was wrong.

He took another slow sip to give himself a moment more to think. Mirane's hands twisted about themselves uncertainly as she waited for him to speak.

He set the cup and saucer down on the side table at his elbow.

"The tea is fine."

Mirane breathed a sigh of relief and waved a dismissive hand at him. "Well, you do have terrible taste in food, in clothes—"

"In everything that doesn't matter," Fafnir agreed. "It does me no harm to drink one tea over another, nor to have a week's worth of clothes instead of having a tailor make me a new suit every time I step outside."

"The image you present to your people, as their high lord—"

Fafnir's growling voice overrode hers. "You couldn't drag yourself away from frivolous creature comforts, and lost Navar, the key to keeping the Kashmari City-States alive and thriving. You had the opportunity most other kashmari would kill for and squandered it. Do not lecture me on priorities."

Mirane bared her teeth. Her elongated canines glinted in the afternoon sunlight, a flash across her stormy features.

"You think it's because I care about how I look? Kushchai is no better! The only reason Darnan does as well as it does is that metal ores practically grow on the rocks around here. All Kushchai has to do is tell someone to pick them up! He doesn't have a mountain to contend with!"

Fafnir folded his arms across his thick chest, refusing to let her anger stoke his own. "Rather than point fingers at other lords, you'd do well to mind your own problems, Mirane. If you truly intend to rule, watch how Kushchai runs Navar. Learn from him."

Mirane clamped her mouth shut. Fafnir stood and stepped over to the door.

"In four weeks on the day of the autumnal equinox, there will be a summit at my Winter Palace here in Darnan. I expect all available city lords in attendance. Bring me good news of the transfer of power in Navar, Mirane."

He turned and left, pausing at the door to glance back at the sound of Mirane gagging. She lunged for a wastebasket and wretched into it.

"Hm," he breathed to himself as he strode out. "But why? And who?"

Fafnir had a feeling that both answers were in Navar. He resolved to visit the mining town after the summit.

* * *

31 August 1062 P.E.
Gladiator Row, Darnan

A week later, Brand opened his eyes.

The first thing he saw was an old woman sitting in a rocking chair beside his bed, crocheting a blanket draped over her lap. The undyed wool yarn slipped easily through her fingers as she hummed softly to herself.

The window was open, and Brand could hear a bird singing outside. As the woman hadn't noticed him yet, Brand lay still and quiet, thinking.

He had no idea where he was or how he'd gotten there. The old woman seemed harmless enough, at least. He still felt uneasy as he looked around the room.

He slowly sat up.

"Mr. Brand!" The old woman stood and rushed over to him. Brand leaned back away from her and held up a hand to keep her at arm's length. A strip of fabric fell down into his eyes.

Frowning, Brand reached up and touched a bandage wrapped around his head that held a pile of gauze pressed just above his left ear.

The old woman clucked her tongue. "Leave the bandage alone, please." She sighed and folded the crocheted blanket, setting it on the chair. "It's so good to see you awake, Mr. Brand. We nearly lost you about a week ago. Lord Kushchai found a man with some kind of novel infection treatment who was able to cure you just in the nick of time. He did say that you will have a pretty nasty scar on your head."

Brand lowered his hand to the bedspread. "Where am I?"

The old woman hesitated. "Ah. Yes, the doctor said you might not remember. Mr. Brand, I am Mrs. James, and this is your home. You are in your room."

My room? Brand looked around the room again, searching for something, anything, he recognized. Nothing.

The old woman, Mrs. James, watched him closely. "Do you know who you are?"

"Brand." He hesitated, then said, "Cadmus Brand."

Mrs. James's smile etched dozens of new wrinkles into her face. "Excellent. What do you remember? I mean the most recent thing you remember."

Brand frowned. "People talking. I could hear them, but I couldn't see them. I'm not even sure what they said."

"Oh! That would probably have been Lord Kushchai and Lord Jinn," Mrs. James said. "They were here last week together. What else do you remember? Do you remember the gladiator fight?"

Brand nodded slowly. The old woman's words stirred up vague memories of a hot, dusty arena. He'd fought someone there, hadn't he? "Against a man from Duat?"

"Yes, that's the one."

"Who won?" He touched the bandage on his head and winced.

"You did, dear. The other gladiator didn't survive."

"That was…yesterday."

Mrs. James said, "Er, no, that was three weeks ago."

Brand's jaw dropped. "What! Three weeks?" He gripped the bedsheet tightly. "That was just yesterday, I swear…"

She patted him on the hand. "Don't upset yourself, Mr. Brand. The doctor said that with a head injury like yours, and with being in a coma, you would probably wake up a bit confused. He said it may take some time to recover completely."

Panic started to rise in Brand's chest. His mind was racing, his thoughts a jumble. He reached over to the bedside table, feeling around for…something. He knew there was something there that would ease the tension, though he couldn't recall what.

Mrs. James leaned forward and pressed something into his palm. A little silk pouch. His fingers closed around it. That's right. He remembered now. He fished out a little deep red pill. He swallowed it, closing his eyes as he did so.

"I made sure to give you your pill every day, Mr. Brand. You didn't miss a day, and Lord Kushchai was even good enough to restock your supply a week ago."

He lay there for half an hour until peace gradually descended upon his troubled mind. The new peace let him slip into sleep once more.

Sometime later, Brand woke. An old woman sat in a rocking chair beside his bed, crocheting a blanket stretched out over her lap. She smiled at him.

"Whenever you're ready for something to eat, just let me know, Mr. Brand."

She knew his name. That was odd…but for some reason, he wasn't bothered by it too much.

"Who are you?" he asked, propping himself on one elbow to better see her.

The elderly woman's smile faded. "Ah. Well, this is going to be harder than I thought, isn't it," she muttered to herself. Then to Brand, she said, "I'm Mrs. James. I've been your housekeeper for many years. My husband, William, was your adoptive father and mentor."

"William." An image of a small, serious man smoking a pipe sprung easily to Brand's mind. "Yes, I know him. Knew him." He sighed.

Brand swung his legs around to the side of the bed, then leaned forward to shift his weight onto his feet. His legs shook.

"Oh, wait a moment, Mr. Brand," Mrs. James said. She stood and bustled over to a pair of canes propped up against the wall. "The doctor said that you might need these to walk for a bit because you've spent so much time in bed. I don't imagine the infection sapping the strength out of you did you any favors, either."

She brought the canes over and placed them in his hands. Brand's shoulders slumped a bit.

"It's only until you get your strength back," Mrs. James reassured him.

Brand's nod was almost imperceptible, but he sat up straight, leaned forward, and rested his weight on the canes as he pulled himself up to a standing position with a heavy grunt. A shaky smirk lit his gaunt face.

"Not so bad once I get upright," he said. "Getting off the bed's the hard part."

He took a cautious step, then another, and another. He managed to walk all around the bed before he felt his lungs burning. He collapsed back onto the bed.

"Excellent!" Mrs. James clapped enthusiastically.

Brand shot Mrs. James a glare. "Excellent?"

She shrugged, still smiling. "Well, we weren't sure you'd have the strength to walk. This is fantastic!"

Just then, Brand's stomach snarled loud enough for Mrs. James to hear. He grinned sheepishly.

Mrs. James chuckled. "You haven't eaten anything properly for three weeks. I'm surprised the hunger didn't wake you sooner. I'll go get you a tray, shall I?"

"Thank you, Mrs. James."

Brand set the canes on the bedside table. He crawled back beneath the covers and eased his head back onto the pillow. He poked at the gauze above his ear and winced at the aching pain his prodding produced.

Three weeks. He'd only gone unconscious yesterday at the most, hadn't he? He'd simply lost three weeks out of his life as though someone had stolen them. The thought created a knot of panic in his gut that threatened to break through the prophylactic's forced calm.

Brand rubbed his face. His hands met a scraggly, overgrown beard.

He looked down at his arms and legs, weak and thin. He turned his left wrist over. Pink new scars overlaid the old brown one. Besides the spidery burns where the elixirs had seared his skin, there were dozens of tiny straight puncture scars made by the slivers of crystal created when the vials had been shattered.

Brand ran his hands through his dank hair. His fingers came away greasy. He groaned. He couldn't live like this. He needed a bath. He needed food.

Brand glanced down at his long, loose nightshirt, then over at his wardrobe. He'd be lucky to have the strength to stand, let alone bathe, walk over to the wardrobe, or put on a full set of clothes.

His laboratory. If he could get to his laboratory, he could use the Healing elixir he had left over from the last batch he'd brewed for the fight. It wouldn't heal the scar on his wrist, and the wound on his head would indeed scar terribly, but perhaps the brain injury would subside.

Brand frowned. He could remember his laboratory but not his own room. He remembered William, but not William's wife. What was going on? Was this woman really who she said she was or was this some elaborate prank?

He shook his head. Get to the lab, get the elixir. Then figure out the rest.

Brand glanced up at the doorway and listened, but didn't hear Mrs. James. She seemed the type to chew him out if she figured out what he was up to. He stood, and with the help of the canes, staggered over to the wardrobe. He leaned heavily on the sturdy wood, catching his breath. After several moments, Brand pulled open the door, reached inside, and pulled out a long paisley robe.

He grunted as he pulled it on with some difficulty. Once on, though, Brand smiled, one half of his face twisting up.

He was so tired, though. Perhaps he'd lie down for just a moment to gather his strength.

Brand stumbled back over to the bed and collapsed. He was asleep before he'd hit the pillow.

* * *

Two days later

When he woke up, the first thing Brand saw was a beautiful kashmari woman with perfect storm-blue skin and silvery hair that spilled over her bare shoulders and framed her bosom with gentle shimmering waves.

She was dabbing his forehead softly with a wet towel. When she noticed he was awake, she smiled in a way that made Brand feel jittery and breathless.

He sat up, acutely aware of her hand touching his inner thigh.

"Who are you?" he asked softly.

She chuckled, then leaned in close so that their noses were almost touching. "Mrs. James warned me about this."

"About what?"

"That you might not remember who I am."

"Then tell me. Who are you?" Brand repeated.

As an answer, the kashmari woman took his scruffy chin in one slender hand and pulled him forward into a kiss.

Flustered, Brand broke away.

A flash of disbelief crossed the woman's delicate face. "You really don't remember me? I'm your lover," she whispered.

She leaned back and fixed him with a playful gaze while Brand sat stunned and grasped at tattered shreds of memories. He did remember her, in a scattered sort of way. He remembered that scent she wore, a sweet floral scent. And he remembered stroking her skin. And that smile.

But he also remembered that she was dangerous. Somehow he knew that if she really was his lover, she wasn't supposed to be.

"When you are well again and have your memory back, I want you to come back to Navar with me."

"Navar?"

She leaned close again and stroked his beard. "I'm tired of hiding. I want us to be together somewhere safe."

Hiding. So he was right. They weren't supposed to be together. But why? What had they been hiding from? Brand pulled a pillow over and placed it like a shield between himself and the kashmari woman. He gripped the fabric tightly in frustration. He hated not being able to remember.

Footsteps outside made the kashmari woman stand up suddenly and back away from the gladiator.

An old woman, humming, entered with a tray of food. She curtsied to the kashmari woman.

"Will you be joining Mr. Brand for breakfast, my lady?"

The kashmari woman shook her head. "No. I only wanted to tell him that I'll be leaving for Navar soon. His win in the gladiatorial arena may have lost me command of the city, but I can hardly blame him for that." She smiled at him. "And I do have so many other interesting plans in store. Do consider my offer, Mr. Brand."

With that, the woman swept out of the room, leaving behind a very confused Brand.

"Who was that?"

"The Lady Mirane," the old woman said, lips pursed as she set the tray down on the bed next to Brand. She threw a glare over her shoulder at the departed kashmari woman. "The now former city lord of Navar."

Brand picked up a piece of toast and took a bite, chewing slowly.

"Mrs. James."

"Yes?"

"That's your name: Mrs. James."

"Yes, Mr. Brand."

"I remembered you. Eventually."

The old woman smiled warmly and patted Brand's hand. "It will get easier, I hope. Now, eat, and rest."

* * *

3 September 1062 P.E.
Gladiator Row, Darnan

Mrs. James whistled as she made up a tray of food. She wasn't sure what food her master would prefer, so she'd set out a roast runnerbeast sandwich with cactus-berry sauce, several pieces of fruit, and a bowl of leftover runnerbeast stew from her dinner the night before. Most of her recent meals had been made from a cheap salted runnerbeast roast she'd bought. She was a simple woman, and for the last three weeks, she'd been far too anxious about Brand to care about what she ate.

She loaded up the tray, then walked out into the foyer. As she crossed the parquet, someone pounded on the front door.

Mrs. James set the tray of food on the entry table, straightened her apron, and answered the door.

"Lord Kushchai!" she said, courtesying to Kushchai, who wore a smart white suit that matched the white painted markings on his face.

"My dear Mrs. James, please don't stand on ceremony with me anymore," Kushchai said, removing his top hat. "Forgive me for staying away so long; I had other pressing matters to attend to. But as you have guessed, I am here as always, to check on Brand. How is he? Any change? Since we were able to get the infection under control, I do have such high hopes for him, if only he could shake this coma."

"As a matter of fact, he's been waking up now and again the last few days. I wrote to you."

"You did!" the kashmari lord exclaimed. "I received no such letter, though I anxiously awaited it. I'll have to speak to my messenger about the dereliction of his duties. But tell me more about Brand. Has he woken today?"

"Yes! He woke not too long ago and asked for some food. Would you care to join me? I was just about to take his food to him." The old housekeeper gestured at the tray of food.

The kashmari lord stepped forward into the foyer eagerly. "Indeed, I would. Lead the way!"

"As a word of warning, though, my lord, he has been having some difficulty remembering people and recent conversations. The doctor is hopeful that it should clear up, but it may take some time."

"Hm. That is troubling, but far from the worst thing we've dealt with recently. Thank you for informing me."

Mrs. James took up her tray again and scaled the stairs, leading the kashmari city lord to Brand's room. Kushchai graciously held the large door open for her.

"Oh dear," she whispered as she entered and saw Brand splayed out on the bed, fast asleep once more. "He must have tired himself out getting that robe on again."

Kushchai patted her on the arm. "No matter. If he is waking at all now, that is a vast improvement. I shall call upon him again in a few days. Until then, take good care of him, Mrs. James. See to it that he gets his strength back. If he's up for it, I'd like him to accompany me to Lord

Fafnir's summit in three weeks."

Mrs. James looked doubtful. "I'll have to check with his doctor, but I'll let Mr. Brand know."

"Thank you," Kushchai said, beaming. "Oh, and one other thing." He pulled a handkerchief out of his pocket. With great care, he pulled it back to reveal a beautiful jeweled seed that glowed a faint purple.

"Oh! It's lovely!" Mrs. James exclaimed.

"Indeed it is," Kushchai said. "I was going to give it to Brand if he was awake, but as he is not, I was hoping that you could keep it safe for me and give it to him when he wakes. It's not safe to keep it on my person any longer and I don't trust it at my estate. As my champion, I thought Brand would be the perfect man to keep it hidden."

"Of course." Mrs. James gingerly took the seed and pocketed it.

"Mrs. James, no one is to know that Brand has this. This is vital. Swear to me that it will stay secret."

She nodded. "You have my solemn word, my lord."

"You're a good woman, Mrs. James." Kushchai patted her on the arm again, then left.

Mrs. James carried the food tray over to the bedside table and set it down. She helped herself to half of the sandwich and settled herself in the rocking chair once more.

"Is he gone?"

Mrs. James nearly jumped out of her skin, sending bits of roast runnerbeast flying across the bedspread. "Brand! You old scoundrel! I could have died from a scare like that!"

Brand sat up with his usual smirk. This time the Brand looking back at her from behind those twinkling amber eyes was most definitely her boy. He eyed the sandwich in her hand, then reached for the other half.

"I could have sworn you were asleep," Mrs. James said.

"I was. And then I wasn't. Didn't feel like talking to Kushchai just yet. He's always got some scheme in the works. I'd like time to stitch myself back together before I jump back into his mess."

"Probably a good idea. Did you hear him mention Fafnir's summit?"

Brand nodded, chewing. He swallowed. "I don't want to think about it right now."

"I suppose you heard about the jewel, too?"

Brand nodded. Mrs. James pulled it out of her pocket and handed the handkerchief to Brand. The gladiator carefully pulled the cloth back and whistled.

"What do you think it is?" Mrs. James asked.

"No idea," Brand said. He covered it again and handed it back to the housekeeper. "Can you take it to my lab? I can't think of a better place to keep it."

They ate in silence. Brand demolished his half of the sandwich in just a few bites, and the fruit shortly thereafter. He picked up the stew and closed his eyes, smelling it for a long moment. Mrs. James smiled.

"Feeling better, are you?"

Brand shrugged as he dipped his spoon into the bowl.

"In some ways, yes. I'm not so tired anymore. I…I had a hard time waking up, didn't I? I mean, I couldn't remember who you were."

Mrs. James nodded. "The doctor warned me that it could take anywhere from hours to months for the amnesia to resolve."

Mrs. James watched as he stirred the stew, steam rising from the liquid. "Mrs. James," he began, but stopped.

"Yes?"

Brand sighed. "Was there a woman who came to see me? I seem to remember a…a kashmari woman. Maybe yesterday?"

"Oh, you mean Lady Mirane. Yes, she came yesterday."

Mrs. James saw the flicker in his eyes, the flush on his thin cheeks. She remembered that night just before the fight when Brand hadn't come home until the first wisps of dawn had streaked the sky. Her heart sank. That must be why the Lady of Navar had visited him. Mrs. James clasped his free hand tightly.

"She's bad news, Mr. Brand. Forget her. If you don't, and someone finds out, they'll kill you."

He cleared his throat and looked her in the eye, jaw clenched, as earnest as she'd ever seen him.

"I know, Mrs. James."

The old housekeeper's face fell at the admission, but she patted him on the hand regardless. Brand stared down at the stew for a long time, but didn't release her hand. She felt as though he were clinging to her like a raft in a storm, but whatever that storm was, he kept it locked behind those solemn eyes.

But whatever he thought of the Lady Mirane, Brand wasn't ready to confide in Mrs. James. Not yet, at least, she reassured herself. If there was one thing she could count on about Brand, it was that sooner or later, he'd let it all out.

After several long, heavy moments, Brand picked up the spoon again and prodded his stew.

"How did you feed me while I was asleep? I'm not dead, so I assume you managed somehow."

"The doctor had a tube he put down your throat into your stomach once a day in the evenings," Mrs. James responded. "You didn't always tolerate it very well, but he did his best."

Brand's hand with the spoon halted on its way to his mouth. "Didn't tolerate it? Never mind, I'm not sure I want to know."

"Not right now, you don't."

He smiled ruefully. "Yet another thing I owe you for. Have I ever told you how amazing you are? I truly don't deserve you."

Mrs. James beamed. "The feeling is mutual, I assure you."

After the big man had finished eating, he said, "I need to get up to my…my laboratory. I need a Healing…the…" He frowned deeply. "You know, the liquid I use to heal myself. Goes into the gauntlet."

"A Healing elixir?"

"Yeah, the elixir." Brand's hands clenched. "Why couldn't I think of the word? I'm sure I've said it thousands of times before."

Mrs. James shrugged. "It was a nasty bump on the head you got, Mr. Brand. Just because parts of your memory are coming back doesn't mean all is well. The doctor was amazed you even survived. Give it time to heal."

He shook his head adamantly. "I need to get that elixir so that I can finish healing. Can you help me get to my lab?"

"I'm a seventy-five-year-old woman and you're a behemoth! Tell me how to get it, and I'll bring it to you."

The gladiator thought for a long minute. "None of the vials are labeled. I'd have to describe it to you, and have you bring me each vial, one at a time…No, I need to get it myself. Besides, I'll never get stronger if I don't start moving again. Maybe you can follow me with a…" He sighed in frustration and rubbed his temple. "The…One..one of those things you sit on. A light one that you could carry."

"A stool?"

"Yeah."

Brand buried his face in his hands. She placed a hand on his shoulder.

"Mr. Brand, it will be alright. We'll get through this."

He uncovered his face and took a deep breath. "Yes. We always do." He took a steadying breath. "So. Stool? And bring the jewel Kushchai gave us, please."

"It's still in my pocket, Mr. Brand. Oh, I'll get your canes, too. You're still not terribly steady."

It took the pair of them about ten minutes to make their way down the hall to Brand's office. He would take a few steps with the canes, then sit down on the stool until he caught his breath.

"I feel like I'm a hundred and five," he grumbled.

Mrs. James chuckled. "I feel like that every morning when I get up out of bed. Come along, old man. We're nearly there."

"I'm going to have to take a nap on the floor once we get there."

"If you do, you'll feel a lot older than a hundred and five when you get back up. Sleeping on rugs is for dogs and young men."

"I knew I should have put a bed in there."

"And you still can so long as you get your magic potion first."

"It's not magical; I am. The alchemy is science."

"Mhmm. Fine. Get up so you can go take your science potion."

Mrs. James smiled fondly at the man. It was good to banter with him again.

They finally made it into the lab, and Brand, spurred on by hope, crossed the room to his bench and shelves eagerly. He leaned heavily on the bench as he searched for the correct vial.

"Make it a double," Mrs. James quipped.

He found it, but his hands were trembling badly enough that he couldn't get it unstoppered. Mrs. James stepped forward and took it out of his hands, pulled off the wax, and gave it back to him.

"Thanks," he said, and drank the whole vial in one shot.

Unlike when he used the tiny increments in his gladiator fights, where the side effects were nearly invisible, using a full vial was a completely different affair. Brand gasped and fell forward onto all fours, but waved Mrs. James off. Through his nightshirt, she could see the wounds in his side glowing brightly as the scabs finished healing and fell off. The bandage on his head glowed brightly as well. Brand ripped it off, and she could see the last raw edges of the wound seal and smooth itself out. Though his hair was shaggy and unkempt, she could still make out the thick pink scar poking out through his salt and pepper hair.

After a moment, Brand leaned back into a kneeling position. His eyes were bright and steady. He grabbed the bench and hauled himself up, but his legs were still shaky and weak.

"Not quite there yet," he laughed.

"Let's get you back to bed so you can sleep for another week," Mrs. James said.

The mention of bed brought up an image of Mirane stretched out naked on a couch. Brand blushed and shoved the memory aside. If he could remember her now, he must be getting some of his memory back. Still, he needed more proof.

"Ask me a few questions first," Brand said. "I need to know if it healed my brain as well."

Mrs. James thought for a moment. "How old were you when I first met you?"

Brand frowned. "Eleven? Twelve?"

"We figured twelve. What is your favorite food?"

"I don't think I could have answered that before I was injured, either. I love all food."

"Any food you like, then."

"Frozen custard."

"Tell me how to make one of your elixirs."

Brand told her how to make a Rooted elixir in as much detail as he could. The words came easily.

He sighed in relief and scrubbed his hands over his lined face, tugged at the scraggly beard, and ran his fingers through his hair. His fingers found the raised scar that cut through his hair. "One more scar for the collection."

Mrs. James smiled. "Now that you can eat properly, you can build up your strength."

Brand sighed and nodded. "Yeah, you're right." He pointed at a shelf covered in vials of elixirs. "Could you put the seed jewel up there, please?"

Mrs. James carefully pulled down a large ceramic jar and placed the seed within, then replaced the jar on the shelf. She turned back to Brand.

"Well, let's get you back to your room."

The big gladiator was silent during the long walk back to his bed. He refused to sit on the stool, instead opting to lean heavily on the wall for support. When they got back to his room, he collapsed into bed, exhausted.

Later that evening, when Lady Mirane came to visit, Mrs. James felt no shame at all in turning the storm-blue woman away, insisting that Brand needed rest.

SUMMIT

Brand spent the next three weeks sleeping, slowly spending more time awake each day. Finally, the day before Fafnir's summit, he rose with clear eyes and a spring in his step. By the time Mrs. James had come up with breakfast, Brand had pulled on his robe and was sitting in front of the long mirror, trimming his beard. He'd also cut his hair, though it was still a fair bit longer than it had been before he'd fallen into the coma.

Brand finished trimming his black and gray hairs into a neat, short beard. He gave himself one last look, then let his hand drop to his side and turned to his housekeeper.

"It's good to see you up and about, Mr. Brand," Mrs. James said. "And just in time for Lord Fafnir's summit tomorrow evening. Lord Kushchai will be pleased."

Brand grunted and rolled his eyes as Mrs. James started to go through his wardrobe like pages in a book, leafing through each suit. She pulled out two and laid them out on the bed.

"Pleased to show me off, you mean. I have been derelict in my duty. As his pet champion, I will be expected to bow and scrape and kiss everyone in the room." Brand selected the suit on the left.

Mirane would be there, the gladiator realized. Brand's mind flashed back to Mirane's illicit kiss in the preparation room before the fight and his gut twisted. Mrs. James must have seen the look of consternation cross his features.

"Do try to keep your wits about you," she admonished. "I want to see you home safe tonight."

Brand studiously kept his own eyes on the suit, trying to ignore the memory of Mirane's soft touch. Despite himself, his heart ached. He sighed heavily. Mrs. James placed an understanding hand on his shoulder, and then, after a moment, returned her attention to the suit.

* * *

21 September 1062 P.E.
Aeolian Dunes

A brutal storm tore over the Aeolian Dunes, ripping the mountains of sand to shreds and hurling them into new formations. It then whirled across the Badlands, hurling boulders as easily as dust and smashing them into pebbles. It finally crashed up against the Wreckage Sea, losing its momentum. In the wake of the storm, a lone creature rode the gusting winds high above the Badlands. As it patrolled, dark wings outstretched, it caught sight of a faint glint of reflected moonlight in the sand.

The creature turned on a wingtip and spun down towards the glint, then landed in a puff of sand. It placed its muzzle near the glint and breathed hard. Grains of sand skittered away across a smooth surface.

Metal. Smooth, polished metal untarnished by time, undented by the storms. The creature used one taloned wing to brush the sand away until two words appeared, painted on the metal: *Muspell's Sons.*

The creature raised its snout and howled at the moon. It then heaved itself back into the air and set off for the far side of the mountain.

Far away in a cavern deep in the earth, another being saw the winged creature. It heard the howl, and in that howl heard a thousand years of agony finally give way to triumph…and devastating hunger.

The being moaned.

"No…my brothers…my sisters…what have I done…Forgive me…"

* * *

Quincy the apothecary dusted off the counter for the third time that day. His thoughts were far away with the broken body of his gladiator friend.

He'd wanted to visit Brand to give him herbs to help him heal. But the memory of High Lord Fafnir's face when Brand had survived still haunted the apothecary. Quincy had known at that moment that his father's assurance that Brand wasn't a pharmakon had been a lie.

Now, as he swept the ever-present desert dust off of each jar, he saw his hands shaking slightly. Pharmakons had been a dream, a fantasy, a fable from the past. But he'd been supplying a pharmakon for years and hadn't even known it. The danger Brand had put him in! And for what? To win stupid fights?

Quincy dealt with kashmari on a daily basis. He circumvented their manipulations as best he could, but he knew of other shop owners who weren't as skilled. The elderly couple who owned the winery around the corner supplied all of the highest kashmari lords' wines but barely had enough money to put food on their own table. The young seamstress next door already had fingers gnarled with arthritis from the long hours of sewing tiny seed pearls and gemstones onto kashmari gowns.

If Brand had stood up for them and fought the kashmari like the pharmakons of the past, Quincy could have forgiven the gladiator for not telling him. Quincy would have even supplied those poisons gladly. Burning suns, he would have given them to Brand for free!

At that moment, the bell on the door jangled. He looked up.

There she was.

A fond smile lit up his face as he moved toward her.

She wore her hair in a long braid that she swept forward over her shoulder to frame her delicate face.

"Good evening," Quincy said. "Are you here for more Epsom salts?"

The seamstress gave Quincy a coy smile. "Only if you'll help me use them. Perhaps after dinner?"

"Of course," he said, gathering her up in his arms and kissing her. As he held her, the anger at Brand that had been simmering for days now flared to a boil. The woman he loved was in constant pain because the gladiator refused to stand up and fight.

Well, Quincy wasn't going to stand for it anymore.

"I'm going out," he said to the seamstress. "I'll see you this evening."

He gave her one last kiss, escorted her out of the shop, and locked up his shop. Then he headed toward the center of the city and Gladiator Row.

* * *

22 September 1062 P.E.
Winter Palace, Darnan

Brand's stomach growled as he stood nursing a glass of kashmari mulled wine. He was leaning up against the wall of the Great Hall of Fafnir's sprawling Winter Palace. The name was a bit of a misnomer; the high lord split his time more or less equally between his Winter Palace in Darnan and the Grand Imperial Palace in Valin and rarely spent any season wholly in one place. There must have been some other meaning behind the name, Brand mused.

The Great Hall was a monument to all the lavish extravagance of the kashmari. Pillars of marble swirled upwards in a chaos of reds, blacks, and whites. The coffered ceiling held dozens of delicately painted vignettes illuminated by innumerable twisted gold chandeliers. The floor was an intricate geometric design made from a variety of rare and expensive woods. Round tables littered the hall, each covered by snow-white tablecloths and garnished with an explosion of flowers from Duat. Kashmari nobility and human counselors twirled like dandelion seeds on the wind to the soft ministrations of a string quintet.

At the far end of the hall on a raised dais, a single oversized throne stood, inlaid with amethyst, lapis lazuli, and gold. It was currently unoccupied. Brand hadn't seen the high lord yet that evening.

Brand dipped a hand into his jacket pocket and fished out his little silk pouch. He popped a pill in his mouth and swallowed it with a swig of wine. One a day, every day. As soon as Brand had arrived, Kushchai had slipped a new pouch of pills to the gladiator and asked if Brand had been taking them. The city lord needn't have worried; since waking from his coma, Brand had been relying on their sedative side effect to keep the anxiety that now plagued him at bay. It wasn't their purpose, but they did seem to help.

As Brand's eyes swept the hall, he caught sight of a short kashmari standing beside Kushchai. He frowned. Had he seen her before? She looked familiar. She had strong arms and short, bobbed white hair and wore a tight blue dress that accentuated her curves. His fist clenched around his wine glass as realization hit. Ilye Grahm.

She looked at him, causing a jolt of recognition to sear through him. Her eyes widened, but her attention was drawn by Kushchai, who gestured grandly at the gladiator. Brand tilted his head and raised his glass to her with a smirk, which drew an answering glare.

It had been thirty years since he'd last seen Ilye. She'd looked human at the time, which is why it had taken Brand a moment to recognize her. How had she had brownish skin back then if now she looked like every other kashmari? More importantly, what was she doing here, showing up now?

Brand's knuckles whitened on his glass and his face flushed hotly as he envisioned himself storming over to her. He'd sweep aside the kashmari nobles, curl his fingers around that delicate blue throat, and throttle her for what she'd done and for what she still could do.

Would anyone be able to stop him?

Brand glanced at Kushchai, who seemed engrossed in regaling Ilye with the tale of Brand's most recent fight. The city lord's arms waved as Kushchai pantomimed swords flailing.

Brand tore his eyes away from the pair and forced his heart to slow. No, Kushchai would put the gladiator to death himself if Brand killed her. He shook his head and consoled himself that she couldn't touch him so long as Kushchai owned him. A pit in his stomach started to gnaw at him.

He downed his glass of mulled wine in one gulp and took a step toward the banquet table. With so many different drinks available, surely there was a liquor here strong enough to drown even his pain.

"Are you the gladiator, Brand?" a female voice asked from his elbow. He turned and saw a waif-like kashmari woman with ruddy cheeks wearing a slip of a dress that hung limply off her bony frame.

Brand smiled stiffly. "I am."

"May I have this dance?"

With a last glance over at Ilye, Brand nodded and smiled for the hundredth time that night. He set his empty glass down on a table, then offered the giggling kashmari woman his hand and led her to the dance floor.

"I saw you at the arena," she simpered. "Truly an amazing fight. How did you survive?"

"I almost didn't," Brand replied. His cheeks ached from smiling all night and his mind wandered like a stray cat, but at least it was getting easier to cough up the same story. "Lord Kushchai found a doctor who is second to none in all of the Kashmari City-States. I wouldn't be here if it weren't for him."

The kashmari lady didn't seem to notice Brand's wooden tone. She merely nodded, not really listening, then let loose a stream of self-centered stories detailing her recent exploits among the nobility. Brand's eyes glazed over. Besides the occasional grunt and "oh", he stayed silent and kept his feet moving across the dance floor to the strains of a waltz.

"May I cut in?" a silky woman's voice asked behind Brand. He turned and immediately felt his breath catch in his throat. Lady Mirane stood there looking like a vision of a storm goddess. Her midnight blue dress dotted with iridescent gems clung to her in all the right places, accentuating her stunning curves in ways that evoked every single memory the gladiator had of that blissful night. Brand swallowed hard and bowed low. *Keep it formal,* he thought desperately.

"My Lady Mirane. May I present—" Brand realized he had forgotten to ask his partner's name. Mirane's eyes were laughing at him. Brand felt sick.

The kashmari woman seemed too thrilled to meet Mirane to catch Brand's faux pas. "Viscountess Slenah of Valin."

"—Viscountess Slenah of Valin."

Viscountess Slenah of Valin curtsied deeply to the kashmari lady. "An honor and a pleasure, my lady."

Mirane returned the curtsy. "You don't mind if I steal Mr. Brand for a moment, do you?" When the other kashmari woman shook her head violently, eyes wide and darting between the gladiator and the lady, Mirane steered Brand a little away. He glanced around nervously.

"I don't think this is appropriate," he said in a low voice.

"Nonsense. You've been dancing with every kashmari woman in town. It would look strange if you refused to dance with me."

Brand swallowed hard. She had a point. He held her hand aloft in his, then gingerly put his other hand on her waist.

While they danced, Brand tried to keep his eyes anywhere but on Mirane.

"You seem to have recovered from your injury nicely," Mirane said. Out of the corner of his eye, Brand saw her sapphire eyes tracing the scar that showed through his hair.

"I've always been able to recover quickly."

"It's part of what makes you such an excellent gladiator, I suppose."

He nodded, trying—and failing—to ignore the way her hips moved under his hand.

Mirane leaned closer and lowered her voice. "Do you remember what we spoke about when I came to visit you?"

"We shouldn't talk about that here."

"Have you given it any thought?" she asked, ignoring his warning.

Brand nodded again, stiffly. Of course he had. He'd dreamt of running away into the mountains, leaving this squalid city far behind. Brand's insides curled in on themselves. *She's a kashmari and you're a human, idiot,* he'd reminded himself. *She's not available to you. Ever. No matter what she says.*

"And?"

Brand looked away and tried to gather his thoughts. "I can't. I have too many responsibilities and obligations, here. Besides, Kushchai will hunt me down if I try to run away."

"Let me take care of him," Mirane said.

Brand licked dry lips. "I just don't understand why you'd ask me to run away with you," he said quietly. "We spent one night together."

He made the mistake of looking down into her eyes. His heart stopped. She smiled, eyes wide and soft.

"So we could spend a million more nights together," she whispered.

Brand felt lightheaded. This woman wanted him? This stunning, intoxicating kashmari woman, the envy of all the lords? Every fiber of his being was screaming at him to leave with her right now, but he clung desperately to a single mote of logic.

"It's impossible."

"Not in Navar."

A servant in a long tail coat stopped the quintet and beckoned for silence.

"Lords, ladies, gentlemen, may I have your attention, please? If you could all move towards your seats, dinner will begin momentarily."

Mirane took a deep breath. "I hope Fafnir's poor taste in food hasn't gotten in the way of putting on a good meal for us."

Brand frowned. "What?"

"Oh, nothing." Mirane put a slender hand on Brand's forearm. She lowered her voice. "Before we sit down—I want you to meet me later, after dinner. Upstairs, in the library."

Brand pulled away and shook his head. "No, Mirane, we can't be seen together—"

"Not like that," she said hurriedly. "We need to talk about…something else."

Brand looked into her sapphire eyes. She seemed so sincere and tense. His insides turned to putty. He sighed.

"Alright."

Mirane gave the gladiator a sly smile. Brand wondered if he'd just been hoodwinked. Before he could ask her, though, Kushchai appeared at Brand's elbow.

"Shall we?" The Darnanian city lord smiled at Mirane. "My dear lady."

Just then, High Lord Fafnir appeared through massive double doors, flanked by several grey-hooded figures. Brand recognized them as the same gray hooded figures from the lounge. They couldn't be guards—Fafnir stood twice as tall as their hunched, thin shapes—but maybe they were priests. The gladiator watched as they shuffled behind the kashmari lord. They moved in eerie unison with an almost stumbling gait. Fafnir didn't seem to even notice them as he took his place at the head table. The grey figures fanned out to take up stations around the entire hall.

With a sardonic smile at Kushchai and a twirl of her midnight blue dress, Mirane swept over to the head table where High Lord Fafnir stood, bowed, and helped her into the chair beside him.

Kushchai snorted. "She was supposed to be disgraced by our bet, tossed out on her heel, but he still dotes on her. What a revolting wench."

Brand grunted his agreement, but his eyes still followed her. Kushchai didn't notice. Instead, he lead Brand over to the head table and sat as far away from the Navari woman as he could at a round table.

Brand sat down between Kushchai and Jinn, and across from Mirane, who was leaning in conspiratorially to Fafnir. A ghost of a smile flitted across the high lord's face, his eyes twinkling for just a second at Mirane's words before he responded.

Just then, a server deposited a shallow bowl of bright orange soup in front of Brand. It was some kind of squash soup garnished with toasted seeds, a dollop of sour cream, and a sprinkling of roasted red pepper. Brand closed his eyes and savored the rich aromas wafting off the soup, then opened his eyes and took a sip. It reminded him of Mrs. James's squash soup that she made each autumn. He sighed happily.

Jinn chuckled. "This man was born in the wrong city! Kushchai, you must allow me to kidnap him and show him around Duat's restaurants and wineries sometime."

"I don't dare. I think I'd never see him again."

That got a chuckle even from Fafnir, who was enjoying the soup nearly as much as Brand.

They ate in appreciative silence until the servers came and replaced the soup bowls with salads. Jinn gestured at the salads. "I brought the berries and nuts from my own garden. Good, aren't they?"

Brand took a bite of the salad and savored it. Greens, small purple berries, slivers of a creamy soft nut, a tart crumbled cheese, and some kind of sweet vinaigrette. He wished he had a piece of paper to write everything down.

"Delicious," Brand reaffirmed.

"Now there is a man who appreciates good food." Fafnir smirked at Mirane. "I suppose the dinner is not acceptable to your imminently refined palate?"

Mirane's frosty glare could have substituted for an entire year's worth of snow in the mountains. "I've not been well of late. I haven't had the stomach for large meals."

Fafnir's smirk turned into a sneer. "Indeed."

Mirane forced a smile and speared a few leaves on her fork and ate them. She turned to Jinn. "Lovely. You will have to commend your gardener."

"I do every day, but I will carry your sentiment to him nonetheless, Lady Mirane." The lord's words were heavy with the same curiosity that Brand felt as all eyes at the table glanced between the now salad-occupied high lord and the Lady of Navar.

"What was that about?" Kushchai said out of the side of his mouth to

Jinn.

"Wish I knew," Jinn replied. "Seems like he's holding something over her head."

Kushchai's eyes lit up. "The loss of Navar, perhaps?"

Jinn shook his head. "He advised her to take this time to learn from your governance of Navar, and she seems to be taking that advice to heart. No, it must be something else. Do you know, gladiator? I saw you dancing with her earlier."

Brand shook his head. "She saw me dancing with everyone else and didn't want to feel left out."

Kushchai snorted. "That sounds like Mirane alright."

The dishes came out of the kitchens as fast as the guests could polish off each course. Root vegetables thinly sliced and baked in cream accompanied a slice of tender red meat drizzled in sweet sauce, which was followed by a delicate pancake filled with jam and clotted cream. On and on it went, each plate no larger than Brand's hand but brimming with flavor. It was an impressive extravaganza of the most exotic and delicious foods the gladiator had ever tasted. As he ate, he tried to remember as many of the ingredients in the dishes as he could. Maybe Mrs. James could recreate some of these at home for him.

"Enjoying your meal, my dear gladiator?" Jinn asked.

"Immensely," Brand said.

"Good, good. Speaking of food lovers," Jinn said, pausing to take a sip of white wine, "High Lord, you haven't been down to Duat in, what has it been? Six months?"

Fafnir shook his head. "Longer. I haven't been since last summer. You've been doing such a wonderful job that I've been able to focus my attention elsewhere."

He glanced at Mirane. She was carefully taking small bites of pancake and avoiding the high lord's gaze.

Jinn harrumphed. "You must visit in a few months. We have had a phenomenal summer and our trees are nearly falling over from the weight of the largest fruit I've seen in decades. The harvest will be spectacular."

"It's settled then." Fafnir raised his glass to Jinn. "I will visit Duat at the harvest." He drank deeply.

Kushchai watched Mirane thoughtfully. He tapped his nose, then said to the high lord, "I've been thinking of how best to begin work in

Navar, Lord Fafnir. I believe the mining crews need to be whipped into shape, but I can't make it up to Navar personally for another month at least. I have several eager kashmari who'd be more than willing to hike up there and give them a hand at motivating the crews. After all, if mining doesn't speed up soon, the plains cities will be without adequate coal for the winter. We don't have time to lose."

Fafnir was nodding thoughtfully. Mirane looked like she was about to explode.

Kushchai smugly continued. "With your permission, my lord, I will assume command of Navar now and begin the operation."

Fafnir slowly sipped his wine. "I was under the impression that you would have started a month ago. As you said, time is of the essence."

Mirane covered her smirk with a sip from her glass.

"Ah, yes." For a split second, Kushchai looked like an exposed panicked lizard, frozen in terror. He glanced at Brand, who realized that the Darnanian lord hadn't wanted to leave his prized gladiator until Brand had fully recovered.

Fafnir let the kashmari lord squirm for a moment longer, then waved a dismissive hand. "How you run Navar is up to you. You know the consequences if you don't deliver."

Mirane's jaw dropped. She stared at the high lord. But Fafnir was watching her a little too coolly. With great difficulty, she turned to Kushchai. "Navar is most grateful for your assistance, Lord Kushchai," she managed.

Satisfied with her words, Fafnir turned his attention away from the disgraced kashmari woman. "There is another matter. I have just received word that the latest storm in the Badlands has uncovered the wreck of the *Muspell's Sons.*"

Kushchai jumped in immediately, silver eyes alight. "High Lord, I have a salvage crew that can be ready to go by tomorrow. Time is of the essence. We wouldn't want to lose it again."

"I have a crew ready as well," Mirane said quickly, "stationed in Navar, considerably closer to the Badlands."

Fafnir nodded with a light in his eye that made Brand uneasy. "Hm. You both like games, and I like people proving their worth to me. So here's a game for you both—" The high lord stood and raised his voice so that it rang throughout the Great Hall. The babble sputtered into silence.

"A game for anyone who cares to throw their hat in."

Every single kashmari turned to focus on their high lord like a pack of wolves sensing blood. Fafnir had them in thrall, and he knew it and loved it. He let the silent tension hang in the air for a long moment, then another; a predatory grin crept onto his craggy face. Then, with relish, he said,

"The *Muspell's Sons* has been sighted in the Badlands."

Fafnir waited for the exclamations of shock and excitement to die down before continuing. "As you may recall, there was rumored to be a certain advanced device on board utilizing dvergen technology. No one knows what it can do save the demons who created it."

Jeers and hoots of derision echoed around the hall. Fafnir raised a hand, and the kashmari stilled once more.

"The pestilence of the dvergen is no more, and we have bent their technology to our own will. Now, we must find and destroy this final piece of dvergen technology once and for all to purge the last of their evil from our lands."

Cheers erupted all around Brand. Fafnir let the kashmari lords voice their excitement, then held up a hand again.

"The atmomancers predict that there will be a storm on our doorstep the day after tomorrow that will last for up to three days, restricting all travel in and out of Darnan. Send your salvage crews out as soon as you can. With luck, the last remaining dvergen device will be there waiting for us.

"Whoever gets to the wreck first and its device will win the Lady Mirane's hand in marriage."

Mirane's face became a mask of fury as hoots and laughter echoed around the hall. Fafnir made no effort to hide his amusement at her reaction. From the lurid jibes Brand overheard, the gladiator could tell that marriage had never been necessary to receive her affections. All the same, not a few kashmari lords eyed her hungrily. Brand's face flushed.

"One final word of caution," Fafnir said. "Do not attempt to destroy the dvergen device on your own. Do not let your salvage crews dismantle it. If it is as powerful as we have been led to believe, the results could be catastrophic. Bring the device to me. I will oversee its destruction."

The high lord sat down amid renewed chatter around the hall.

Brand growled, "You can't do that to Mirane!"

Kushchai hissed at his gladiator. "Shut up, fool!"

Fafnir waved aside Kushchai's words. Kushchai muttered to himself and downed his glass of wine in one gulp.

"I can, and I will. There is more to this than you see, gladiator," Fafnir began. To Brand's amazement, the high lord calmly addressed the gladiator as though instructing a child. "Lady Mirane has had ample opportunity to improve her management of Navar. She has repeatedly refused any and all help, instead making a fool of herself, cavorting with half the men here. I can no longer afford to indulge her, not with how important Navar's coal and steel mines are to the rest of the city-states. Would you like to tell your human friends and admirers that people are freezing to death in the streets of Darnan in the middle of winter because a kashmari whore couldn't be bothered to pay attention to her job?"

Brand ground his teeth.

"No, and neither would I," Fafnir continued. "This is a punishment and a warning to others who may be lax in their duties. Don't worry; she'll still have her chance to govern Navar again if she pays attention to Kushchai."

"The gladiator is right. I'm not an animal to be bought or sold," Mirane said hotly.

Fafnir nodded slowly, curiosity in his eyes as he seemed to search Brand's face. "Perhaps. Then again, the way you conduct yourself, I have my doubts on that count as well."

Mirane met Brand's eyes. Her sapphire eyes were filled with fire and rebellion.

Fafnir continued. "A new husband may theoretically focus your energies somewhere less catastrophic. But I will be the first to admit that I do enjoy making you squirm after years of dealing with your various antics. I'm sure you will find some new way to be a thorn in my side shortly."

Mirane rolled her eyes with a knowing little smirk.

"Besides," Fafnir said, sitting once more, "you can still join the race to the *Muspell's Sons* yourself if you so choose."

"An excellent idea, my lord," Mirane said. She rose in a smooth motion. As she did so, her gown rippled like the waters of a lake late at night. "If you'll excuse me, I do have a few things to attend to."

Brand and the other lords stood and watched her go. Kushchai left as well, muttering to himself. Jinn remained, as did Fafnir. The three remaining men sat.

"Pity. They left before dessert," Fafnir mused as servants brought out small crystal glasses of airy chocolate mousse topped with cream, berries, and decorative sugar flowers.

"A true pity," Jinn agreed, dipping his spoon into the mousse.

There was silence as the three savored the smooth, decadent dessert. Brand let a dollop of chocolate sit on his tongue for a moment, enjoying its bittersweetness, and then bit down, crushing the berries and releasing their tart juice. The flavors mingled, distracting Brand momentarily.

When the mousse was gone, Brand sat back in his chair and sighed, trying to put Fafnir's words out of his mind. After all, Mirane wasn't Brand's; she was a noblewoman, subject to the whims of her class and its politics. No matter how he felt about her, what could a gladiator do?

Besides, if she gets married, she'll stop talking about running away with me, Brand said to himself. But that thought made his heart sink.

Brand took a sip of wine. He could get used to this. If this was his reward for winning, he'd have to make sure he kept on winning, at least for a little while.

He'd have to rebuild the gauntlet, of course. He'd built it from scratch the first time and had kept no sketches, so recreating it would take time. Thankfully, Kushchai had agreed to give Brand several months to recover before throwing him into the arena again.

Brand's thoughts turned back to Fafnir's race.

"What's the *Muspell's Sons*?" Brand asked the high lord. With Mirane and Kushchai gone and their bellies full of wine and good food, these two remaining lords seemed far more relaxed.

Fafnir used his spoon to scrape the last smears of chocolate off the inside of his bowl. "A vessel from long ago that crashed into the desert and was buried by the storms. There is a dvergen device on board of immense power, and it's only been uncovered by the storms once before, four hundred years ago. All efforts to locate and uncover it since have been completely unsuccessful."

"Why?" Brand asked.

Fafnir held up a hand to call a servant, then ordered the man to bring them a jug of whiskey. He turned back to Brand. "The winds out in the Wastes are powerful enough to rearrange the entire landscape every time a storm blows through. Over the centuries, the *Muspell's Sons* has been shoved a hundred miles south and buried by an ocean of sand and rock."

As the servant returned with the whiskey, Fafnir liberated the jug from the man and filled his glass with the amber liquid. He poured a glass for the other two, then drank, eyes closed.

Brand sipped the sweet, spicy whiskey. Even though the alcohol had no effect on him, the flavors still somehow loosened his muscles. He smiled. "Lovely."

He looked at the high lord, who was watching Brand with interest. Jinn hadn't touched his glass.

"My lord?" Brand asked, suddenly nervous again.

Fafnir shook his head. "Nothing," he rumbled. He grinned at Jinn and said, "Not going to try yours? It has such a smooth finish. I'm sure you'd enjoy it."

Jinn snorted. "No thanks. I don't even remember what happened the last time I tried your moonshine. I'll stick with wine."

Fafnir laughed a deep, hearty rumbling chuckle that shook the table.

Brand glanced down at his glass, panic rising. He'd had no idea this whiskey was stronger than any other, so he hadn't known to react like any normal human would have. Was this a test to see if Brand was a pharmakon? His heart sank. They must have been suspicious of his survival after all.

But when Brand looked up at Fafnir, the high lord was lounging back in his chair, eyes closed again, unconcerned about anything. He reminded Brand of the gorged mudlisks that could be seen sunning themselves around Darnan near large puddles left by a summer rainstorm. Brand swallowed and turned back to Jinn.

"Why aren't you rushing to get someone out to the *Muspell's Sons*?" Brand asked the Duati lord.

Jinn smiled. "Throw a fortune away just to have a chance at winning Mirane's hand? No; I have my vices, like any kashmari, but women are not one of them."

"You prefer men?"

Jinn laughed. "I prefer power, my boy."

"Duat seems a bit far removed from any kind of power," Brand said pointedly.

Fafnir had opened his eyes and was watching Brand. "Jinn controls the only place in this world capable of supplying food to any number of people," the high lord said, taking a sip of whiskey. "A civilization is only as strong as its food supply."

Jinn grinned, his flame-red eyes twin embers. "Duat is the key to everything. Take away Darnan's grain, and—" He made a slicing motion across his throat.

"There isn't another kashmari alive I'd trust more," Fafnir said with a smirk. "I'll bend over backwards to keep him there and keep him happy."

Jinn spread his arms wide, indicating the detritus of their meal. "Chained to the lap of luxury," he said with a grin. "Such a terrible fate for a foodie. Whatever shall I do?"

Both of the kashmari lords chuckled.

The gladiator looked over at his strange companions and marveled that they had let him sit and drink and talk so openly with them for so long. Was this how it would be for him from now on? Decadent feasts and fine spirits? Brand took another sip of the whiskey. Despite his misgivings about it, the drink really was quite good, perhaps the best whiskey he'd ever tasted. He took another sip and let it rest in his mouth, savoring the subtle undertones of oak and cinnamon.

"How long do you think it'll take them?" Jinn asked Fafnir.

The high lord's brow furrowed. "Depends on which route they take, how much they fight each other along the way, and of course how many kashmari send out crews. A month, at least."

"Are there any of the minor nobility that you think have a chance?" Brand asked.

Jinn rubbed his smooth face. "Hard to say. Kushchai and Mirane both have far greater resources than the rest. Money does make a difference."

Fafnir steepled his fingers. "There are a couple in Valin, and one in Darnan, who I think may have a chance."

"Who?"

"Djedkare and Unas, in Valin; Sahure in Darnan."

Jinn nodded slowly. "Sahure has a good head on his shoulders. Practical and efficient. I'm not familiar with Djedkare or Unas."

"Similar to Sahure," Fafnir replied. "Though I'm not sure either is interested in anything beyond their local operations. Sahure, on the other hand, is quite ambitious and will be eager to curry favor with me. I expect he'll have a crew on its way before the evening is out."

"Is he here?" Brand asked, glancing about the hall.

Jinn shook his head. "He despises gatherings like these. I'm sure if he were the last living thing in the world, he would prefer it that way."

"I'm curious to see if Sahure can scrape together a crew as wily as he is," Fafnir said. "If I could marry Mirane off to Sahure and pin the man to Navar, he'd make an excellent city lord."

"And perhaps keep him busy enough to stay out of your way?" Jinn said slyly.

Fafnir smiled ruefully. "If only. I doubt I'd be that lucky."

"My lord," a servant said at Fafnir's elbow, "A duel seems to have broken out in the garden. Shall I end it?"

Fafnir growled in annoyance and shook his head. "No, I will deal with this myself."

Brand stood with the kashmari lords, but Brand remained at the table. He figured now would be an excellent time to sneak off to meet Mirane. But Jinn turned and noticed the gladiator had not moved.

"Won't you join us, gladiator?" Jinn asked. "Your patron has vanished, and this little spectacle promises to be at least mildly diverting."

Brand hesitated, but he couldn't very well explain to the Duati lord why he wished to stay. "With pleasure," Brand said, rising.

A bit of tension wormed its way into the gladiator's shoulders. If Jinn was taking Brand under his wing for the rest of the night, he wouldn't get a chance to meet Mirane, and despite his resolutions, he still itched to hear her voice and find out what she had to say.

He buried his yearning for the woman and followed the tall figure of the high lord out of the Great Hall. Brand was amazed that the strange kashmari lord loomed several centimeters over him. Once Brand had reached his full height, no other human or kashmari other than Alastair had even come close, and from the way Fafnir seemed to hunch over somewhat alongside the much shorter Jinn, Brand suspected the high lord was even taller than he appeared. Behind them, the grey-hooded figures followed silently.

"What are you going to do to the duelers?" Jinn said.

"If it's who I think it is," Fafnir said. "it might be high time to let them fight it out."

"Could get messy. And whoever survives might turn on the rest of us."

Fafnir grunted. "If they do, I'll be ready. I've got a full contingent at the ready tonight."

Jinn arched an eyebrow over one burning eye. "You're willing to sacrifice vrykolakas tonight? Seems a waste."

"Not if it reminds the others of why I rule and they do not."

"Seems to be all you do these days," Jinn remarked.

Fafnir's answer was a guttural rumble and an exasperated glare.

"What are vrykolakas?" Brand asked.

"It has to do with our religion, you might say," Jinn said.

"Religion?" Brand was taken aback. This was the first he'd ever heard of a kashmari religion.

"Never you mind," Fafnir said, though Brand caught the high lord's eyes flicker over to a grey-hooded figure cringing against the wall.

The high lord didn't elaborate. Brand's curiosity was piqued. He'd read a considerable amount about the kashmari and never found anything about religion or vrykolakas. Brand decided to try to persuade Kushchai to let him do a little research in the city lord's library later. The city lord would probably be amenable to the idea so long as Brand didn't tell Kushchai what information he sought.

Fafnir led them to an enormous hall and a staircase that began as two, joined in the middle of the hall, and split again. Decorative stone arches lined the walls, framing colorful frescos. Overhead, an oculus dome high above let the stars shine through. At the base of the staircase, twin snarling lions stood at the bases of two great pillars of green malachite carved to look like massive trees. Leaves made of the most delicate amethyst crystals shimmered above trunks wrapped in vines of gold. Gem-laden boughs laced together to form the arched entrance to the gardens.

"I don't think I could ever get used to living in a place like this," Brand said, running his hand along the cool stone banister. His shoes clicked smartly on the polished granite steps.

"It's a bit large for my taste," Jinn mused. "I'm not keen on having to walk ten miles a day just to get around."

Fafnir smirked. "I've never found it to be too large."

"Of course you wouldn't. Come to think of it, Brand might not mind it either. Those long legs of yours make traversing this palace much more agreeable."

"What is your mansion in Duat like?" Brand asked the Duati lord.

Jinn gave him a self-deprecating smile. "Cozier, for one. Fewer grand halls and more studies filled with the knickknacks I've accumulated over the years. All this open, empty space...pah."

"'To the wyrm his eyrie, to the worm his tunnel,'" Fafnir quoted. "Isn't that how it goes?"

"Indeed." To Brand's questioning look, Jinn said, "To each his own."

A servant hurried up to the men and caught Brand by the elbow.

"My apologies, Mr. Brand. You have a message." The servant handed him a folded note.

"Thank you," he replied. He opened it.

> *Brand—*
>
> *Change of plans. Meet me on the second-floor landing by the painting of the man on a horse.*
>
> *—M*

Frowning, Brand closed the note. "If you'll excuse me. I have business to attend to."

Jinn hooked his thumbs into his waistcoat pockets. "He needed you after all, eh? Kushchai never seems to leave you alone for long."

Brand shrugged and bowed.

Fafnir and Jinn nodded in return and continued out into the garden. Brand returned up the long stairway, absently wondering how often Fafnir bothered to make the long walk out to his gardens.

Fall

Brand found his way up another staircase, this one covered with a rich red carpet. It led him up to the second floor, where a series of halls zigzagged between rooms.

He glanced around, looking for a painting with a horse.

Instead, he saw a deep blue skirt like that of Mirane's dress flow around a corner. He hesitated, then followed.

He turned down the hall just in time to see the kashmari woman catch sight of him, smile, and vanish through a doorway. Well, at least he knew he was following the right woman. But why was she teasing him like this?

Brand twisted the doorknob and let himself into the room and closed the door behind him. He turned and froze. A lush billowy bed occupied most of the room.

He cursed. She'd promised this wasn't that kind of meeting. He wavered there for a moment, trying to decide if he should slip out before she saw him.

But then he caught sight of her out on the balcony. Her back was to him as she gazed out at the gardens below. Drawn to the kashmari woman like a moth to a flame, Brand silently stepped out to stand beside her.

In the blue moonlight, Mirane's storm-blue skin made her almost invisible; but the white markings on her cheeks and forehead, her silver jewelry, and her silver hair rippling in the soft night breeze practically glowed.

"Mirane, if someone sees us—"

She placed a finger on his lips. Despite himself, his heart skipped a beat. She took his hand and pulled him back inside. She then pulled a thick curtain over the glass wall. She turned.

"I said this meeting wasn't for that. This is my room for the few days I have left in Darnan. Fafnir insisted. We shouldn't be disturbed here."

"Besides right under Fafnir's nose?"

"With the fight on the other side of the garden, he'll be occupied for some time. Kashmari politics at their finest." With the roll of an eye, Mirane walked over to the mantel. A fire flickered in an iron brazier within the large fireplace. Other than that, there was only a delicate chair set by the glass door out onto the balcony. Mirane picked up a small hand fan decorated in gold leaf roses and began to fan herself enthusiastically.

"I get so hot at these events," she said.

Brand tried to clear his head. It was difficult with her wearing such a formfitting gown. *She's not available. Just try to remember that.* "What did you want to talk about?"

She moved over to him, coming within a few inches, and looked up seriously into his face. "Our future together. I want you to come back to Navar with me."

Brand took a step back and bumped into the wall. "I can't. You know that. You're a kashmari. You are so far out of my league that I'm not allowed at the arena."

She rolled her eyes.

"And yet I've decided I want you! Not another kashmari, not just some random human—I want you, and I want you badly enough to sleep with you and spirit you off to Navar."

"But why?"

Mirane took a step forward so that her thighs brushed his. Her eyes traced his battle-scarred face, drifted upward, and lingered on the pink scar peeking through his greying hair.

"There's something about you...you're just so different. So fascinating. I've been alive for a very long time and never met a man quite as fascinating as you."

Brand shook his head and crossed his arms to put a barrier between them. "Just being seen with you like this is enough to get me killed."

"So you'd rather stay here and wait for Fafnir to find out you're the father of my child and kill you?"

That brought Brand up short. "What?"

"I am with child. Your child." She rested a hand on her abdomen and waited for that to sink in, then plunged onward. "If you stay here, if I stay here, it will only be a matter of time before we are found out." She placed her other hand at the nape of his neck and started twirling a strand of hair in her fingers. "I would much rather run away somewhere safe, somewhere Fafnir's laws don't mean anything. Fafnir does not have as great a hold on Navar as he thinks."

Brand's heart was racing. His child? He closed his eyes and placed his hands on her waist, over her hand, drawing her close. He'd sworn to himself not to get mixed up with this woman anymore. Too late.

His child.

"We've been together once!" Brand objected. "And just happened to…to…" His brain refused to offer up the words. *My child?! I'm going to be a father?*

"Oh," she said. "I suppose I have had a little more time to adjust to the idea of parenthood than you have."

She waited for him, her head resting softly on his chest. Everything had changed in an instant. One moment he was enjoying finally being let into the upper echelons of society, and the next he was suddenly contemplating fleeing to protect his lover and their unborn child. He was surprised to find that he felt rather protective of this beautiful woman. She felt so right in his arms.

If she ever found out he was a pharmakon, though, he'd be dead. In that moment, though, it seemed an acceptable risk.

"We'd have to run farther than Navar," he said quietly. "You aren't the lady of Navar anymore."

A crafty smile curved her lips upward. "Don't judge a city you've never visited. What they see from here is only what we've let them see. Even Fafnir, our all-knowing high lord, doesn't see Navar for what it truly is."

She stood on her tiptoes and wrapped her arms around his neck, pulling him forward into a kiss. He took a deep breath, savoring the scent of flowers that clung to her. If there was a way for them to be together...He had to admit that she made his pulse quicken in a way he'd never felt before. Being with her was intoxicating.

He caressed her storm-blue skin, kissed her shoulder, then unclasped her dress. It slid to the floor. She unbuttoned his shirt as he gathered her up in his arms.

Just as his lips touched hers, the door opened, and Fafnir entered, face turned backwards as he spoke to someone behind him.

Brand's heart stopped.

"—don't fool yourself. Nehn was never a paragon of—" The Dragon turned just in time to see Mirane bend over to scoop up her dress.

Fafnir froze as still as ice, shock carved into his dark features. His eyes flicked from the naked kashmari lady to a shirtless Brand and back again, then down to her belly. Brand watched as the pieces fell into place and realization hit the high lord like a thunderbolt.

He knew.

Fafnir's face twisted into a mask of fury. He strode into the room with two giant steps, picked Mirane up by the front of the dress she was clutching to her breast, and tossed her bodily onto the bed. Stretched out to his full height in his rage, Fafnir towered over Brand and blocked out much of the light from the brazier, casting long, menacing shadows over the others.

"Sit," the Dragon commanded Brand in a snarl. Brand scrambled for the chair by the window.

To Mirane, he snapped, "Dress yourself. Now."

Behind Fafnir, Kushchai and Jinn had entered the room, eyes wide and mouths agape.

"What is this?" Kushchai hissed at Brand.

Needing no real answer with Mirane in the state she was in, the Darnanian lord slapped Brand hard and turned on the Navari woman. He stormed across the room and shoved an accusing finger in Mirane's face. "You knew he was my champion and still you took him! You knew he'd be killed. How dare you!"

Mirane snorted as she dressed herself and flipped her hand dismissively, planting the other on her slender hip. She kept a wary eye on Fafnir, careful to slip off the bed on the opposite side from where the high lord stood. "You want payment? Fine. How much is he worth?"

Brand's heart sank at the cold way she dismissed him, as though he were merely a lovely plaything to discard when it became inconvenient to keep around. A kernel of doubt and confusion lodged in his brain. Was there even a baby? Had she lied about that too? Maybe it was all an act. Maybe she really was pregnant but was trying to save her own skin.

Brand looked up and saw Fafnir watching not the other kashmari, but him, Brand. The high lord's face was hard and impassive as a rock, as though the Dragon were poised to strike the gladiator. Brand shrunk down in his chair.

Kushchai bared his teeth. A strange red gleam appeared in his eyes. "You air-headed ninnyhammer! This isn't about money! He was worth more than his weight in gold—the prestige—"

A realization dawned on Kushchai._"This is because of that night, isn't it, at my manor, when I rejected you. You petty little whore! I wouldn't have you, so you took my champion from me instead. I'll—"

Brand's heart sank again as Mirane laughed in Kushchai's face.

Just a plaything...

"It's always about you, isn't it?" she sneered. "Stupid little Mirane just wants to get back at you. What kind of petty fool do you—"

Kushchai lunged at Mirane, but Fafnir stepped forward between the two kashmari and grabbed the lunging city lord, bringing Kushchai's rant to a halt.

"Silence! Mirane's greed will have its price." The Dragon turned to Mirane. "You will, of course, need to abandon and kill that body, Mirane," Fafnir said.

"What?" Her tone became low and dangerous. Her fingers splayed, as though she were about to lunge at Fafnir.

Brand was startled as well. What body? His body?

"You know the law," Fafnir said.

"A double standard for females?" Mirane scoffed. "You've slept with thousands of human women, and kept your body. I should be allowed the same privilege."

Fafnir stepped slowly towards the female.

"There is no double standard. No human female may ever bear a kashmari child. Thus, no human lover of mine has ever survived until morning," he said, his voice a steady low rumble. "Likewise, no kashmari woman may bear a human child."

"There is no child," Mirane snapped. "Nor will there be."

Fafnir was inches away from her now, looming like a dark mountain over her. "Do not lie," he hissed. "I can hear its heartbeat in your belly."

Brand's breath caught in his throat.

"It might be different this time," Mirane said softly. "He is different. You sense it too, I know it. His child—my child—could be what we've been looking for—"

"Different this time?" Kushchai said with a harsh laugh. "No hybrids. No exceptions."

Brand rubbed his temples, trying to calm the storm inside his head. The child wasn't a lie. He really was going to be a father. Or he would have been if he'd survived tonight, which he wouldn't.

Fafnir ignored Kushchai and cast a look over at Brand. A frown furrowed his dark brows as his eyes searched the gladiator's face. The high lord seemed to consider Mirane's words for a long moment. Brand thought he saw indecision flicker across the Dragon's face.

But then it was gone. The high lord's face hardened as he turned back to Mirane. "Yet you are the same as always. You will never bear his child."

Mirane lowered her eyes to the ground. Brand was in a daze. This all seemed like some bizarre, twisted dream. Just a few minutes ago, Mirane was a completely different woman, arms around his neck, playfully twirling his hair in her fingers, full of hope. Now she was submissive, beaten, small, dull as the faded colors of dusk.

Fafnir's voice grew quieter still, like the low rumble of a distant volcano about to erupt.

"The price of these misplaced maternal instincts is nothing less than the wholesale extinction of the kashmari. I will not allow that. Get rid of the body by tomorrow and find a new one, or I swear I will rip you from it myself and chain your Broken soul to my Will for the rest of eternity."

The room was silent. Fafnir's gaze bored into Mirane and made even this powerful kashmari woman cower and shake.

"My lord…" she whimpered. "Give me more than a day…"

Fafnir growled, baring fangs. In one smooth motion, he pulled out a long dagger and plunged it deep into Mirane's chest. He twisted it, and then yanked it out. Blood dripped onto the rug where Fafnir let the red blade hang by his side.

Brand surged forward but Fafnir caught him and held him back with one iron arm as Mirane hit the floor. Brand's eyes grew blurry as tears welled up.

A strange dark mist rose from her body and formed into the vaguest shape of a humanoid. Brand stopped struggling. A chill ran down his spine. Brand blinked the tears away. The vague mist creature remained. It bowed low to Fafnir.

"I said find a new body," Fafnir snarled at the apparition. "You have one day or I will fulfill my vow. Go."

The dark mist bowed again and swirled out the door in silence.

Brand started to shake. That mist…the way Fafnir had spoken to it…was that Mirane?

Brand barely registered the rest of the conversation. His legs had gone so weak that Fafnir had to support him.

Fafnir turned to Kushchai, his voice still hard. "Take the gladiator out to the Western Shrine of the Guardian. Let Akitick choose his fate."

Kushchai opened his mouth to protest, but Fafnir raised a massive hand to forestall further argument. "They both have broken our most sacred law. He too must be punished. Tomorrow, make sure everyone in Darnan knows what they did."

"It wasn't his fault," Kushchai said. "Mirane forced herself on him." He shook his head. "We do not even know that she'd taken him. She was about to, obviously, but maybe—maybe the child was a lie—she wanted to unsettle you, no more—"

Fafnir snorted. "I heard the child's heartbeat. Stop rationalizing and search his memories if you need further proof."

Fafnir shoved Brand into a standing position and let go. Kushchai turned once more to Brand, this time placing a hand on the skin of Brand's neck. The gladiator started.

His mind seemed to open up like a book for Kushchai to read. Brand watched the memories unfold before his eyes. He saw every touch, every caress played over again in his mind's eye. Each new image caused Kushchai to grip the gladiator's neck tighter and tighter. Brand squeezed his eyes shut, willing the vision away, but in the hands of the kashmari, he was powerless.

The memory of just a few moments before rose up and once more Brand heard Mirane utter her secret and beg him to run away with her.

He sagged under the weight of his shock and loss and confusion.

After a moment, Kushchai finally let the memories fade away and let go of Brand's neck. He shoved Brand away from him.

The kashmari growled in disgust. "Come."

Farewell

Kushchai's mechanohorse-drawn carriage stopped outside Brand's home on Gladiator Row.

"Get out," the kashmari lord commanded.

Brand didn't move. He was locked in his own mind, the image of Mirane's corpse on the floor seared into his mind's eye. Disgust and horror curled their tendrils into his soul. Over and over in his mind, he kept thinking, *What just happened?*

"Get out," Kushchai repeated, harsher. He grabbed Brand by the collar and shoved the gladiator out of the carriage with more strength than his slight frame belied.

Brand turned tortured eyes on Kushchai. "Why?"

"The seed I left with you. Go get it." He raised a cautionary finger. "If you try anything, I'll drop you before you realize what's happened, right in front of Mrs. James. And not a word to her. Do I make myself clear?"

Brand nodded numbly.

The gladiator turned and stared up at the narrow house shoved between its twin neighbors. Kushchai's boot sent him sprawling to the bottom steps. Flashing a glare back at the lord, Brand picked himself up and climbed the steps. Kushchai exited the carriage and followed close behind the gladiator. Panic began to rise in Brand. If the kashmari lord followed him the entire way, he'd see Brand's lab and know he was a pharmakon. If it were just his own life on the line, that would be one thing. What else could Kushchai do to him that the lord wasn't already planning? But if Kushchai learned Brand was a pharmakon, he'd kill Mrs. James too.

Mrs. James was in the kitchen, humming as she finished drying the dishes.

"Mr. Brand! How was the party? I didn't expect you back so soon." She caught sight of Kushchai. "Lord Kushchai! Welcome. Can I get you something to drink?"

The city lord declined and she turned her attention back to Brand.

"There's a man here to see you," Mrs. James said. "An apothecary. He's in the study."

Brand winced. Quincy hadn't ever dared to visit Brand and he chose tonight off all nights? What was he thinking? If Kushchai left this house without learning about Brand's pharmakon abilities, it would be a miracle.

"Tell him I won't be needing his services after all," Brand said.

"He said he was a friend and that he had a private matter to discuss."

Brand turned to Kushchai, who raised an eyebrow but nodded curtly. "Make it quick and keep the door open."

Mrs. James smile wavered. "Is something wrong?"

Brand tried to smile reassuringly, but it was a thin mask he didn't wear well. "I have to go away for a while, Mrs. James."

"Why? When are you leaving?"

Brand could feel Kushchai's eyes boring into the back of his head. "I can't tell you exactly why, but it has to do with...someone I met. Something happened to them and I...well, I am leaving tonight."

"So suddenly?" Mrs. James set the dishrag down. "Very well. I'll help you pack while you speak with the apothecary."

"He only needs the clothes on his back, Mrs. James," Kushchai said. "Nothing much. Everything else will be provided for him."

Brand glanced back at Kushchai, an idea forming. "I suppose I should get out of these formal clothes, at least. It's going to be a long journey, and I'd like to be comfortable. Perhaps Mrs. James could lay out a set of traveling clothes and retrieve the seed while I deal with my visitor."

Kushchai's eyes darted to Mrs. James. Brand could see Kushchai trying to figure out if there was a downside to letting Brand change. If he didn't allow it, Mrs. James's suspicions may be aroused. Brand felt a surge of triumph. The city lord wanted to keep this quiet despite Fafnir's instructions. The gladiator's plan might work after all.

"Fine. Be quick about it, though," Kushchai said. "We are on a tight schedule."

Brand turned to his housekeeper. "Mrs. James?"

"Just to clarify, you mean the crystal seed that Lord Kushchai gave you for safekeeping?"

"Yes."

To Kushchai, Mrs. James said, "I'll just be a moment. I'll set out the clothes first, then retrieve the seed. Excuse me." And she left.

Brand hurried up to his study, Kushchai hot on his heels. The city lord stood outside the open door, presumably listening in to make sure Brand didn't sneak out the window. Brand needed to get Kushchai out of his study as quickly as possible so that Mrs. James could get to his laboratory and get the seed.

Quincy stood quickly, scooting his round glasses up his nose nervously. "Brand, I—I'm so sorry, but I need to speak with you about the fight—"

"I can't talk for long," Brand said, pointedly looking toward to door. "I'm about to leave with Lord Kushchai. He's waiting in the hall for me."

The apothecary swallowed hard as he glanced at the open door. Quietly, he said, "We can't speak privately?"

Brand shook his head.

The apothecary took a moment to collect his thoughts, fingers twitching on the edge of his bowler hat. Then, with another glance at the door, he said, "I saw what happened at the arena, and I figured it out…And I don't understand. I'm angry. You're my friend. I've told you things about people I know and care about. And you've done nothing. And now I know you could have."

It took Brand a moment to untangle the coded message, but when he did, his heart sank. As though tonight wasn't going badly enough, now his one friend in the world hated him for the coward Quincy now knew Brand to be.

In a low, pained voice, Brand said, "I don't have time to explain. But

I'm not the hero you think I am. I can't be that man. Not anymore."

Quincy reached forward and grabbed Brand's arm. He looked up into the gladiator's eyes fiercely.

"We need you."

Brand looked away and shrugged out of his friend's grasp. Kushchai cleared his throat from the hallway.

"I have to go. Mrs. James will see you out."

Quincy jammed his hat on his head. "No, I'll show myself out. Thank you, sir."

The apothecary stomped out, leaving Brand to lean heavily against a wingback chair.

Kushchai entered.

"What did he want?"

"Money," Brand grunted. "I knew him as a boy. I suppose he thought that gave him the right to come asking for a handout."

Kushchai snorted.

The gladiator strode out, not bothering to hide his bitterness. He rushed down the hall to his room and slipped behind a large wooden screen. He hurriedly stripped off his suit and threw on a simple blue linen shirt, a pair of rough canvas trousers, and his boots. At the base of one section of the screen, he depressed a hidden panel. A thin box fell into his hands.

Inside were four full-sized crystal vials filled with viscous elixirs: Healing, Armor, Stamina, and Time. His emergency stash. Another tinier vial fell out, full of the elixir that would allow him to change the Armor into Strength, a similar elixir that would, as its name suggested, increase Brand's strength.

He quickly placed the vials into a slender zippered pocket of his boot made specifically for this purpose, then stepped out from behind the screen.

"Comfortable?" Kushchai sneered. "Let's go."

Brand found Mrs. James waiting for him at the front door. She slipped the handkerchief containing the seed into his hand, and he drew her into a firm embrace. He wished with all his heart that he could just erase the last month and stay with this quiet little woman.

"I'm sorry to leave like this, Mrs. James," he said. Then in a whisper, he said, "I'll be back. Maybe not soon, but I will be back."

She gave him one of her warm, motherly smiles and patted him on the cheek. "Good luck."

Kushchai ushered him out the door and into the carriage.

Brand watched Mrs. James's tiny figure recede as the carriage whisked him away.

"What will you do to her?"

Kushchai's eyes narrowed, but he said, "She's a useful woman, even in her old age. I'll think of something for her to do."

Brand's gut twisted at those words, but he wasn't in a position to argue. If Kushchai still needed her, Mrs. James would be taken care of well enough.

"The seed?"

Brand handed over the handkerchief. Kushchai stashed the jewel away in his breast pocket and didn't say another word.

Brand turned his gaze out at the darkened city. Streets flew by, street lamps mere flickering blurs as they raced on. Soon, the massive storm wall that separated the city from the unyielding desert loomed out of the darkness, reaching for the stars.

BROKEN

Brand craned his neck to see the colossal stone guardians at either side of the gate. Each held one hand outstretched, welcoming, while the other hand rested on the hilt of an enormous stone sword at their waist.

And then they were through the gate. Without the lights from the city, the world outside the carriage windows was a gaping void that swallowed the carriage and plunged its occupants into thick darkness.

Brand felt the darkness press in on him, thick, suffocating. He pressed his fist to his forehead and sighed heavily. He felt Kushchai's eyes on him, but neither man spoke.

As they drove through the dark, Brand was left only with his thoughts. The memory of Fafnir killing Mirane played over and over in Brand's mind. The specter rising up out of her, leaving behind a dead stranger on the floor, made his stomach twist in on itself.

Brand had seen a lot of deaths on the streets of Darnan growing up, but he'd never seen anything like that strange apparition. Had it…had that mist been inside Mirane? Was it Mirane?

Brand looked over at Kushchai, who sat with arms folded, glaring at Brand. *Is that what Kushchai really is? Is that what all the kashmari are?*

"Find another body," Fafnir had said.

If the mist was Mirane…

He clenched his eyes shut and saw the body on the floor, with its long silver tresses curling in a pool of blood, the delicate blue skin turned ashen in death. Who had she been? Her face, the face of a woman he'd never known, was finally at peace. The real mother of his child…his child…whoever she'd been.

The full horror of the situation collapsed in on him. Mirane wasn't human. Brand had known that. But what was she? A demon? A spirit? Mirane's host—that's all she could have been—he'd…she'd had no say…no, he hadn't known. *What did I do?*

What had she been like? Would she have loved him, or hated him, if she'd had a choice? What would their child have been like?

Brand hated Fafnir for murdering her. He hated himself for being such a fool, for not knowing what she was, for falling for her when he'd known to leave kashmari women alone. But most of all, Brand felt betrayed. Mirane had stolen that woman's body. She'd seduced Brand to get back at Kushchai. Her selfish actions had led to the death of that poor woman and Brand's child.

Tears flowed freely down his face in the dark at the thought of that stolen babe. His alchemy had always made Brand keep women at arm's length for fear that the wrong woman would turn him in. But for one fleeting moment, he'd thought he'd cheated fate to become a father. He wanted to tear Fafnir apart for what the giant had done.

A series of flickering lights outside in the darkness drew Brand's attention away from his thoughts. It looked like a city at first, but then an explosion rocked the carriage and lit up the darkness, giving Brand a glimpse of a gigantic crab-like machine bristling with guns.

The carriage stopped.

Brand could hear shouting, smaller explosions, and the whirring of the enormous machine turning this way and that. An ear-shattering thud shook the carriage as fire belched from a cannon protruding from the front of the behemoth. It was firing upon small, dark shadows pecking at the monster's clawed mechanical feet. Occasionally, a flash of light erupted from one of the smaller shapes, illuminating humans swathed in thick robes and carrying crude muskets.

A stray musket ball pinged off the roof of the mechanocarriage.

"What the—" Brand exclaimed.

"Don't worry," Kushchai said, seemingly to himself. "We're quite safe. The *Dauntless* will bring those rebels to heel momentarily."

Brand edged away from the windows. He'd heard of the rebels. He could think of a lot of places safer than the Darnanian city lord's carriage when rebels were around.

Kushchai shot Brand a sidelong sneer. "They are kashmari who've gone mad. They live out here on the outskirts, picking fights they cannot win every so often. It really is overkill to use the *Dauntless* on them, but I find that using a hammer to swat a fly makes the fly think twice about biting you again."

A shadowy thing twice as tall as the huge machine joined the fight against the *Dauntless*. Brand squinted into the darkness, trying to make it out. By the light of the muzzle flashes and the flare each time the *Dauntless* fired its main gun, he could just barely see the long, slender outline of some impossibly tall creature walking on—was it six legs? He couldn't be sure. He couldn't see its head at all.

The strange creature emitted a low hum that throbbed through the rocky desert air. Brand's head ached with each pulsating hum. As it hummed, the creature drew up one slender leg and held it over the *Dauntless*. The Titan's exterior lights shone on its ghostly white foot as the creature pressed down, puncturing into the machine. Sparks flew. The creature moaned.

The *Dauntless* tried to step backwards away from its tormentor, but the creature lifted another leg and skewered the machine again. The guns on either side of the *Dauntless's* crab-like body spun to point at the creature's shadowy face and spat twin streams of bullets at it, but they left no mark on its smooth skin.

A bright red flare blasted up out of the top of the *Dauntless*. The battlefield was immediately bathed in bloody light. The flare wavered in the air, then deployed a tiny parachute.

The *Dauntless* brought its main gun around and planted it squarely on the creature's chest. A plume of electric blue fire erupted from the gun, blasting the behemoth backwards and off of the machine.

The creature collapsed, then lifted its head. Where it should have had a face, the skin was stretched tight over empty sockets and the vestigial nose bridge. It only had a gaping mouth full of jagged teeth. Two thick horns swept up into a pointed, inverted Omega shape above its head.

It moaned again, then stood. Its legs shook slightly as it put its full weight on them once more. The creature bared its fangs and crouched, bracing for a charge.

Kushchai got out of the carriage and slammed the door lock closed.

The kashmari strode towards the monster and held his arms out. Great tendrils of darkness streamed from the creature to Kushchai's hands, wrapping around his arms and swirling into his chest.

The creature moaned, a long, low sound that made the earth shudder. Its long spindly legs wobbled, then folded underneath it, no longer able to support its massive weight. It keeled over onto its side, and with one final groan, went still.

The fighting outside ceased. Brand could vaguely smell the metallic char of gunpowder. The *Dauntless*, hull cracked, swinging wires sparking, pulled itself away from the twisted corpse of the monster and leveled its cannon at the remaining rebels, who had pulled back to a small ridge.

At their center, a slender figure sat atop a long-legged humped beast with a trailing nose that brushed the rocks underfoot. The figure lowered its hood, revealing the characteristic pointed ears of a kashmari. Its bluish skin looked purple in the red light of the *Dauntless's* flare. But this kashmari was missing an eye. A thick, ropy scar slashed through an empty, smooth socket instead.

It fixed its singular eye on Kushchai but said nothing. The Darnanian city lord sprinted at the rebel leader, but the scarred kashmari laughed and gestured to the rebels. They vanished into the darkness of the desert.

Kushchai slid to a halt and shouted something Brand couldn't make out. Fists balled, he turned and stalked toward the *Dauntless*.

Brand watched as a gangplank lowered slowly from the back of the massive machine and two men strode down it. One was a tall man with rippling muscles that stretched his shirt. The other was short and weaselly-looking, thin and bent. The three men gestured to each other. Nearby, the flare landed but continued to burn.

Suddenly, Kushchai stretched out his hand at the thin man, who collapsed to his knees. His head bowed slowly, painfully. He stayed there for a long moment, Kushchai standing over him with hand raised. Darkness swirled around his hand and forearm. The tall stranger beside them watched impassively, bulging arms crossed.

Then the darkness vanished and the thin man slumped as though the marionette strings that had held him up had been cut. Kushchai waited as the man gathered his feet beneath him and stood. The thin man kept his eyes on the city lord's shoes.

Kushchai turned to the bigger man and spoke. The man gave a curt nod of agreement, then turned and marched crisply back into the enormous vehicle. The thin, weasely man stumbled along behind him.

Kushchai returned to the carriage and a moment later it was trundling along the dark desert once more. The red light from the flare faded from view.

"Scavengers," the kashmari said derisively. "It's a good thing I hired a decent team of mechanics. They should have the *Dauntless* repaired before they arrive at the Aeolian Dunes."

"Right. The race to win Navar."

"Nothing for you to be worried about."

Brand wrapped his arms around himself to stave off the chill and settled back into his seat.

* * *

Winter Palace, Darnan

Fafnir paced back and forth in the Great Hall of the Winter Palace, ignoring the flaring pains in his joints. Jinn leaned up against a marble column and watched the agitated high lord with an arched eyebrow over one burning scarlet eye.

"Of all the idiotic things he could have done," Fafnir snarled, "why did he have to do *that*?"

Jinn bit into an apple. "In answer to your unspoken questions, no, he doesn't have any idea how important he is to your plan; no, he wasn't thinking straight when the most notorious seductress in the history of humanity found her way into his pants; and no, you can't kill him, even if you'd like to."

Darkness curled around the high lord like a gathering storm. Purple energy crackled along his dark skin and made his pupils glow eerily. Fafnir gave a low, rumbling growl that shook the wood beneath Jinn's feet.

Jinn took another bite from his apple, unfazed by his lord's agitation.

Fafnir strode down the hall again, spun on his heel, and marched back towards the oversized throne at the other end, the crackling darkness following him. Jinn was surprised the heavy high lord hadn't worn a groove in the expensive wood floor yet.

Fafnir paused in front of the Duati lord and uttered another wordless, frustrated growl. "I had to make an example of the two of them so that others don't follow in their footsteps. But I need him."

"I don't think you have anything to worry about," Jinn said. "After what he survived in the arena, I highly doubt the desert is going to kill him."

"No, but Kushchai might."

Jinn took another bite and chewed as the high lord began pacing again. Fafnir drew the cloak of darkness around him like a shield as he mulled over the situation.

"After what I did to Mirane, Brand isn't going to work with us willingly."

Jinn winced. "Not likely, no. It's unfortunate, isn't it? He seems to be a generally genial fellow."

Fafnir growled again like a caged beast.

Jinn mused to himself that if this unfortunate business hadn't happened, Brand might have even joined the kashmari one day. After a moment of mulling over that prospect, though, the Duati lord decided that perhaps it was for the best that the gladiator wouldn't. Jinn went back to watching the high lord pace through the empty hall.

Fafnir slowed as though dragging a weight, but kept moving. "I swore to Me'von I'd never kill one of our kind again," the high lord said, his voice heavy. The darkness around him deepened and spread, dimming the light from the chandeliers above. "And just a child."

The air throughout the hall grew thick with electricity. Jinn stopped chewing, finally unnerved by his lord's manifested anger. He'd never known Fafnir to take his anger out on someone who didn't deserve it, but neither had he seen the giant so nearly lose control as he had this evening. The Duati lord shrunk against the marble column away from the crackling darkness.

"Me'von." Fafnir halted suddenly near the throne. He turned on his heel to face Jinn, then stalked slowly towards the Duati. His words were thoughtful. "One of my scouts discovered Me'von's hiding place out in the desert: a shack near the Shrine."

The high lord paused in front of Jinn. The darkness and electrical charge surrounding him dissipated into the air. Jinn breathed again.

"Have the atmomancers kick up a storm out in the desert around the Shrine." Fafnir strode towards the heavy oak doors.

"Where are you going?" Jinn asked as he finished his apple.

"To pay a visit to an old rival."

He strode out of the Great Hall, leaving Jinn shaking his head. Whatever the high lord had planned, Jinn knew there was always the possibility of unbridled chaos where Me'von was involved.

* * *

Two hours later, the carriage came to a halt once more. Kushchai opened the door and gestured for Brand to get out.

A lantern hanging on the corner of the carriage lit up several large stone monoliths. They surrounded a small stone pagoda standing on a raised stone dais. Under the pagoda stood a thick slab of granite, its slick surface reflecting the lantern light.

This must be the shrine Fafnir spoke of, Brand thought.

Kushchai pointed at the slab. Brand began to walk towards it. Its surface was dark. Blood, Brand realized with a chill. The kashmari lord meant to kill the gladiator.

Brand could hear Kushchai behind him, only a pace away.

Heart thudding, Brand spun on the ball of his right foot and swept his left foot around, knocking Kushchai to the ground. He slammed a booted foot into the side of Kushchai's face. The gladiator sprinted back towards the carriage.

If he could just get to the carriage, he only needed a moment to hotwire the controls.

Just as he reached it, Brand slammed into an invisible wall and crashed to the ground. Perplexed, he held up a hand. The air between him and the carriage had solidified into an impenetrable transparent wall.

Brand spun. Kushchai was picking himself up off the ground, hand outstretched to Brand. His hand was wrapped in darkness.

"What is this?" Brand said.

Blood dripped down the mangled side of Kushchai's face. The

kashmari's smile was a twisted, broken leer. "You've always been such a good boy. I've never had to restrain you. But now…Now you've done me harm, and Fafnir isn't here to stop me from having my vengeance."

The world tilted until the ground was above Brand. He fell into the sky with a yell, rocks and heavy stones falling with him; but something caught him. He hung there, the clear desert sky spread out below him. The stones hanging in the air beside him began to whirl crazily around the gladiator. One smashed into his thigh with a thunderous crack. Brand screamed. Another smaller stone smashed into his shoulder with another explosive snap.

The world spun again and Brand fell to the earth once more, landing heavily on his broken thigh. He gasped and nearly passed out.

"You didn't think I got to be city lord of Darnan by my good looks and charisma alone, did you?" Kushchai grabbed the front of the gladiator's shirt and pressed his face close to Brand's. "You were my champion. You would have been my enforcer. You could have had more power and influence than any other human."

Kushchai thrust Brand down into the dirt. He raised both arms to the darkened sky. Clouds boiled in from every direction.

It began to rain.

The desert storm released its deluge with titanic fury. Water fell from the heavens like a billion tiny hammers slamming against an unyielding stone anvil. White-hot fire zigzagged through the air.

Kushchai motioned with his hand wrapped in darkness, and Brand felt his face tilt upwards, his mouth open to the flood. He started to choke, gag, and struggled for air. For a second, Kushchai released him. Brand choked up the water, vomited, and gasped. Every muscle burned. And then Kushchai tilted Brand's face up to the skies again.

"You have no idea what you are dealing with, human," Kushchai hissed.

Brand could barely hear him through the roaring in his ears as he struggled to breathe. Kushchai released him once more.

Brand tried to speak, but hacked up a lungful of rainwater instead. He heaved again and again, then collapsed trembling to the dirt. He held his head in his hands and groaned. Panting and coughing, he wiped the water from his burning eyes.

"Beg me for forgiveness, and I'll allow you to die by the storm's winds," Kushchai sneered.

Brand muttered something.

"What?" Kushchai said, leaning close.

"I said, I'm sorry," Brand said hoarsely. He coughed up a wad of phlegm and spat it out. "You're right. I was a fool."

Kushchai grunted and stood. "Very well."

Around Brand, the world shifted. The rain stopped as suddenly as it began and Brand's clothes dried out. His leg and shoulder were still on fire, though. He looked around in shock at the bone-dry desert.

"The storm..."

"Get up," Kushchai snarled, "and get on that slab."

Brand pulled himself up, but the instant he shifted his weight onto his bad leg, it crumpled beneath him. He bit back a cry.

As Kushchai looked on, Brand dragged himself across the rocky ground. Tiny cactus spines and countless sharp rocks bit into his palms. He got to the granite slab and with agonizing effort, hauled himself up onto the granite.

Kushchai picked up a hammer and some thick nails from somewhere on the ground. "Just to make sure you can't escape," he said. He waved a darkened hand. Brand immediately felt a weight settle on his limbs, pinning him to the granite.

The gladiator's hands stretched out above him of their own accord. Kushchai placed a nail point down in Brand's right palm.

"No," Brand moaned. But he couldn't move except to turn his head away.

Kushchai brought the hammer down with a sickening crunch. Brand shuddered.

Kushchai shoved his white-lined face right in front of Brand's nose.

"You're looking pale," he sneered. He cackled and pulled back, then placed the next nail in Brand's other palm.

Brand bit his lip and squeezed his eyes shut. When the hammer came down, the gladiator let out a whimper.

The kashmari examined his handiwork.

"Excellent. Goodbye, gladiator."

"You're not going to kill me, then?" Brand said through clenched teeth.

"Oh, the desert will take care of that soon enough. With those wounds, you won't even last the night."

With that, he spun and returned to his carriage. Brand listened as the mechanohorse whirred back to life. A moment later, the pagoda's ceiling was plunged into darkness once more as the carriage with its lanterns turned away.

It took several more moments for the clatter of mechanical hooves to recede so far away that Brand couldn't hear them anymore. But in the distance, he heard the rumble of thunder and smelled the rain on the breeze.

* * *

The sound of thunder in the distance made Me'von look up from the book he was reading. A thin gust of wind snuck in through the sturdy stones to make his little candle flicker. The old kashmari waited, still as a statue, listening.

He sat at a simple wooden table in a bare stone box of a shack sunken into the desert floor. Solid stone walls surrounded him on four sides, unadorned by art or windows. The flagstones underfoot were still warm from the early autumn desert heat. A thin sleeping mat of agave fibers lay rolled up beside a pile of books neatly stacked in a corner. On the table by his elbow sat a thin parchment notebook and a pen he could refill with ink he made from the crushed bodies of an insect that lived on a type of cactus that grew out here.

After a long moment, the kashmari's thin shoulders relaxed. He rubbed his weak eyes with gnarled hands, then put down the book.

He'd lived out here for several decades now, if living was what you could call it. There were no humans to boss around, but no kashmari to bother him, either. True, the cities were overflowing with comforts and riches, and the kashmari atmomancers held the storms at bay. But how could he go back, knowing what they'd do to him if he returned?

He slumped in his chair. Everything hurt. His bones hurt. His head hurt. His mouth hurt.

Well, more accurately, this old man's body hurt. Even the mind of this old one was broken and listless, little more than a vacant hum in the back of Me'von's mind.

Maybe he could sneak back into New Braunen somehow. If he went there, he probably wouldn't run into Fafnir for a while. He could get a new body, talk to some other sentient beings, and eat something other than a cactus fruit for once. He could even buy a few new books.

Thunder rumbled overhead.

He wouldn't be able to stay in New Braunen for long, the old kashmari reasoned. Just long enough to get those things done. Then he could come back out here.

He scratched at his thin white hair.

But then what? Could he stand spending the rest of eternity living out here? He growled softly to himself. What was the point of it all? Maybe he should go have it out with Fafnir. The high lord would have his head in an instant, but perhaps it would be nice to be done with this pathetic excuse for a life.

Me'von rested his forehead on the table, dejected and numb. He'd had this conversation with himself a dozen times a day for decades. Of course, he wasn't going to act on any of that, not really. He'd sworn to stay here for the rest of his days. He closed his eyes.

Then the ceiling fell in.

Rocks that had held against the fury of countless storms now crashed down to the flagstones, exposing the little one-room dwelling to the gathering clouds above. Cursing, Me'von batted away the rubble and clambered out of the hole. He cast about, looking for the source of his misfortune, but in the darkness failed to see the great black-winged beast dodge away behind a berm prickling with creosote brush.

Me'von looked down at the wreck of his home, then up at the storm bearing down upon him. Lightning zigzagged through the clouds and crackled around several twisting tornadoes headed his way. He could already smell the crisp scent released by the desert bushes as rain fell upon their leaves.

The nearest settlement was several days' walk from here. He had minutes.

The Shrine was still out there, wasn't it? He squinted in the direction he thought it might be, but even in the daytime, his weak eyes couldn't pick out the outline of the Shrine's pavilion.

He glanced back at his shack one more time. The Shrine wasn't the best shelter, but it would be better than this wreck.

The old kashmari began to shamble away from his broken home.

Companion

Brand breathed deeply several times, willing his body to relax so that he could think through the haze of pain. Now that there was nothing to distract him, though, it flared into a blazing fire throughout his body.

Everything hurt. Judging from the deep aching pain that spread up his back and down his leg, his upper right leg was broken. His collarbone was broken as well. Both of his hands were…well, they were broken too, to put it mildly. Every involuntary twitch sent lightning blazing up his forearms.

His vial of Healing elixir was stuck in his right boot, which he couldn't reach. Even if he somehow managed to get it out and drink it, he'd still be nailed to a granite slab. And somehow if he managed to get off the slab and healed, he was still at least a hundred kilometers from Darnan, in who knows what direction, with a massive storm bearing down on him.

He growled, pushing as much of his pain and frustration and fear into that animalistic sound. Strangely, it did seem to help. The pain abated slightly. He heaved a sigh of relief. "If I get out of this alive, I'm never falling for another woman ever again."

Brand reached deep within himself to find the spark at his center. It had saved his life before. It was elusive, though, like an illusion. It was there, but he couldn't quite reach it.

"Slag," he swore quietly. The pain must be distracting him too much for him to focus.

Brand gradually became aware of a low humming sound coming from somewhere out in the desert. It reverberated through the granite slab and Brand's aching, broken bones. It filled him with unease, dread, and a sense of wrongness. It sounded familiar, but the pain was making it difficult to think. Brand strained to hear it better, trying to figure out what it was.

Then the rush of air and flapping of great wings came suddenly from somewhere above the pagoda. Sand went flying into Brand's face, startling him. The humming abruptly stopped. Brand's heart skipped a beat, then sped up. His eyes widened.

Something had smelled his blood.

It flapped around the pagoda. Brand could just make out the tips of its wings dipping below the edge of the roof as it circled. Then it swung around behind him.

Panic overriding pain, Brand tried to move his feet up to yank the nail out of one hand with his boots, but his right leg wasn't responding as it should. He could only lift it up off the granite a few handspans. Brand let his feet fall back down to the granite slab. His breath now came in ragged gasps.

The creature landed behind Brand's head, out of sight. He heard it sniffing the air, then rumble. Finally, he heard footsteps crunching on the rocky ground.

Footsteps? From a rider? Brand took a deep breath to slow his heart. He'd heard that kashmari sometimes rode winged beasts. Whoever it was probably wasn't here for him, then.

Beside him appeared a massive shadowy humanoid shape in the darkness.

"I should have known he wouldn't simply deposit you here," Fafnir's deep rumbling voice said. Brand's heart stopped. "No matter."

Rage filled Brand in an instant. He tried to lunge at the huge kashmari, but the nails in his hands made him cry out in pain instead. He turned the pain into an angry, wordless yell at the Dragon instead.

The kashmari high lord stepped around the altar so that he was standing over Brand in clear view.

Brand kicked at Fafnir, but his boot fell short of its target. The gladiator yelled again. Then his body went limp in defeat.

"Get on with it," Brand groaned.

"With what?"

"You've ruined my life. Kill me already."

Fafnir was silent as he examined the gladiator as one might inspect a bug on a pin. When he finally spoke, his voice was frighteningly calm and emotionless. "I don't want you dead. I didn't intend for Kushchai to torture you, either, though I'm not surprised that he did. No, Mirane was right. You are different. I can use you."

Brand spat. "I think I've had enough of kashmari using me for…."

"Games?"

"Yeah. If that's what you call torture."

Fafnir chuckled darkly.

"This isn't a game, boy. The end of this world draws near, and if you are who I think you are, I believe you can save us all."

Brand shook his head. The high lord had killed every other pharmakon. He wouldn't have done that if he needed their help. "I don't believe you."

"I don't need you to believe me, not yet," the high lord said. "There is still a little time left."

"If you need me, why leave me out here? Kushchai said the desert will kill me."

"I highly doubt the storm will kill you, not after what you survived in the arena. I need to make an example of you." Irritation flashed over the giant's face, then passed. "If you attempt to return to Darnan or any other kashmari city-state, I'll make sure you come to realize just how pleasant tonight has been."

"You killed Mirane for…" *Loving me.* Brand couldn't bring himself to say it. She hadn't loved him, had she? It was just another lie.

Fafnir tilted his dark head like a curious bird.

"Mirane doesn't know what love is," the Dragon said, as though reading Brand's mind. "One might argue that no kashmari is capable of it anymore. Your child would have grown to be a monster just like her."

"You're no better. You're sick, twisted."

"I know." It was said with such heavy understanding that Brand was at a loss for words. Fafnir sighed, and it sounded like the wind rushing between peaks on a frigid, clear morning.

Suddenly, the kashmari lord looked up, eyes fixed on something in the distance. "The storm draws near, as does your companion."

"Companion?"

Fafnir grunted. "A lost kashmari. One who…well, he once was like you. I believe he could be again. You can trust him, more or less. Maybe less for now."

Brand threw as much venom into his words as he could muster while nailed to a granite slab. "Why should I trust you? You're the reason I'm here. You…you killed my child." He choked on the words, and clenched his eyes shut, trying to hold back the tears. But he was in so much pain, physically and emotionally, and so drained that control eluded him.

"It was necessary. For what it's worth, I am deeply sorry it had to happen that way."

Brand was stunned by this admission, but it only revived his fury. "That doesn't bring them back. They're gone. How can you, a kashmari, an immortal…evil body-stealing soul, even begin to understand what you've done?"

The muscles in Fafnir's jaw bunched as he glared at the gladiator.

"I'm not a body-stealing soul," the high lord snapped. "Not yet, anyway."

Brand blinked. He'd touched a nerve.

Fafnir seemed to slump a little. His next words were tired. "One day, when you find yourself leading others, perhaps you will be better able to judge my actions."

The high lord turned away, his cloak whipping in the wind. "For now, perhaps at least keep an open mind about Me'von."

The wind was picking up, carrying with it the dry scent of dust and electricity. The shadowy figure of the high lord strode into the darkness. There was a rushing sound of air being shoved downward by great wings, and then Brand was alone.

Brand tilted his head and listened. No, he wasn't completely alone. Above the rising roar of the wind, he could just make out the sounds of someone stumbling across the rocky desert floor and mumbling to themselves.

"Hey!" Brand called out. "Hello? Can you hear me?"

The footsteps halted. "Who is that?"

"I'm over here! I need help!"

The stumbling resumed and a face appeared just above Brand. He found himself nose to nose with a gray kashmari with ancient white hair and a face so wrinkled it was hard to see his rheumy eyes.

Brand balked, but he had no other option. He tried to smile.

"Can you help me get these nails out of my hands?"

The ancient kashmari's eyes squinted at Brand. His voice wavered, but the words were clear. "Someone put you there on purpose. Why should I release you?"

"There's a storm coming," Brand begged. "I'll die if you don't release me."

"That was most likely the intention."

"Blast it! I'll give you whatever you want! Money! I have plenty of money in Darnan."

The kashmari elder laughed heartily. "That's not what I want, young one."

Brand ground his teeth. He thought of himself as young at heart, but he was well aware of his age. All these kashmari calling him 'boy' and 'young' was starting to get on his nerves.

"What do you want, then?" he asked, straining to stay calm.

The kashmari stroked his chin. "You."

"What?"

"This body is old. I will release you if you let me take your body—only until we get back to civilization and I can acquire a new one, a more suitable one." His eyes lingered on Brand's pierced hands. "A more…intact one."

Brand's blood went ice cold. Was this what Fafnir meant when he said Brand's 'companion' was on the way? Did Fafnir want to turn *Brand* into a kashmari?

"It's not an unreasonable request," the kashmari said even as Brand began to panic. "I just jump in your head and take a ride for a few days." He squinted at Brand. "Wait. You're a commoner, aren't you? You don't have any idea what I'm saying! Confound it."

A rock swirled past the old kashmari's head. He winced.

"We're out of time."

The old kashmari leaned forward and yanked one of the nails out.

Brand winced at the new burst of pain. The kashmari leaned over Brand and yanked the other nail out. Stifling the involuntary shudder that ran through his body, Brand scrambled off the slab and landed in the dirt with a grunt, hands trembling and feeling as though hot lava was pouring over them.

"Move aside, kid."

A black mist rose from the old kashmari and lunged at Brand. He yelled out and scrambled backwards, fire shooting through his palms; but the mist caught him and vanished into the gladiator's chest.

Brand's whole body began to tingle as though every muscle had fallen asleep, and then suddenly everything stopped working. He collapsed onto the rocky ground. In his mind, he screamed as the kashmari shoved him aside and took control.

Brand watched in horror as his limbs moved of their own accord. He stood, somewhat shakily on his bad leg. Pain flared unbearably in his thigh, but there was nothing he could do about it.

<Stop,> Brand pleaded with the kashmari. <My leg is broken.>

"I know, genius," the kashmari said through Brand's lips, "but we're going to die here. There's a broken Shambler wreck not far from here. It'll be safe inside."

To their right, Brand could just make out the half-buried wreckage of a Shambler-class trawler. Its short, stocky legs and half of its stubby body were sunk deep in the rocky earth.

Beside him, the old kashmari had collapsed on the ground and was still as the rocks surrounding them. Brand shuffled forward, one agonizing step after another, his right foot dragging along the ground.

The wind shoved Brand sideways. The kashmari lifted his hands to try and block it, but to no avail. Then the air ahead of them ignited, lighting up the twisting form of a tornado heading in their direction. It picked up sand and boulders alike and tossed them in every direction, carving great divots in the hard-packed earth.

<Duck!> Brand screamed in his head.

The kashmari ducked just as a boulder the size of a carriage whizzed past Brand's head. A jagged fork of lightning hit the ground less than a hundred paces away.

Brand and the kashmari both swore together.

The wind died down for just a moment and the kashmari forced

Brand's body into a shambling sprint. He fell several times, but he finally pressed Brand's back against the exposed metal.

The tornado was still heading towards them, its terrible winds picking up anything not sunken into the sand.

"I can't get us up to the hatch," the kashmari said. Worry laced his words. "You don't have the strength to climb."

<Don't you have some kind of kashmari magic that can help us?> Brand asked, thinking of Kushchai's power over the elements.

"I can only influence human minds," the kashmari replied. "It's taking everything I've got to convince you that you aren't nearly dead."

<But Kushchai made it rain!>

"He made you think it was raining. Probably took a sledgehammer or something to your leg while you were hallucinating. I can't make you hallucinate us a way out of this."

<Let me have control!> Brand yelled.

"You'll pass out! You can't override the pain!" the kashmari yelled back.

<I have something better.>

After a brief moment of hesitation, the kashmari relinquished control back to Brand. The gladiator could sense the kashmari's uncertainty vying with his curiosity.

Brand instantly collapsed onto the ground, but was able to reach down into his boot with one bleeding hand. His hand shook violently as he unstoppered the vial. He took a small sip.

The kashmari screamed in Brand's head, a blood-curdling, tortured scream that went on and on. Brand bent over double as the scream threatened to split his head in two.

His leg wasn't healing properly, he realized vaguely. He wouldn't be able to climb the machine after all. Brand winced and held his bursting head with one hand while he pulled aside broken metal girders with the other. He dug at the rocky ground with his other hand until his fingers bled. They healed, but so slowly. He continued until he'd managed to make a small depression beside the metal behemoth. Then with a groan that was lost to the storm, he crammed himself into the hole and pulled the girders back into place, creating a steel cage around himself.

As the tornado drew closer, Brand slipped into unconsciousness.

* * *

A Venator-class armored sand trawler crept over a berm covered in prickly creosote bushes and spiked yucca trees. Built like a caterpillar, it had a thick round, elongated body and six pairs of stout mechanical legs that enabled it to clamber over and around the desert terrain. It easily shrugged off the howling winds of the approaching tornado.

"There." The crew chief pointed to a bluish smudge on the display. He twisted a knob, trying to bring the image into focus. "Tucked in next to that Shambler. Marie, can you get us in a little closer?"

A soft female voice came from a grill in the bulkhead. "I can try."

A woman at the chief's elbow leaned in close, squinting at the display. A stray lock of long brown hair fell into her face. "Is that…a person?" she asked as the trawler inched closer.

The crew chief nodded. "Yeah, I think so. He's not moving. Let's go see if he's alive."

The woman bit her lower lip.

"I've never even heard of anybody surviving a storm, Finn."

"Not for long," he agreed. "Marie, cozy us up to the Shambler. See if you can block the wind for us."

"As you wish, Finn," Marie's voice said through the grate.

Finn, the chief, grabbed his fedora from a side console and crammed it on his head, then headed to the back of the caterpillar-like trawler. He slapped a button that lowered the gangplank and grabbed a rifle hanging nearby.

"Loren."

"Right behind you, boss."

A younger man with white blonde hair, eerie ice-blue eyes, and a thick scar that rose from his collarbone to his chin joined Finn. Loren slung a long bandolier over his black leather armor and double-checked the pearl-handled revolver slung at his waist. Their boots clanked on the metal ramp as they descended.

The Venator had gotten as close as possible to the half-buried Shambler, creating a pocket of relatively still air between the two trawlers.

Finn stepped slowly, deliberately, rifle at the ready. Behind him, the younger Loren stayed close and alert. A bit of stray wind whipped wisps of Finn's thinning grey hair around his eyes as he approached the body.

It was a man, or what was left of a man, crammed into a tiny space between the rocks and the metal of the Shambler. His blue shirt must have been what Finn had seen on the display. It was torn and bloodied, though. The man's right leg was covered in blood, as were his shoulder, neck, and hands.

"Good grief," Finn muttered. He grimaced. "Looks like we're too late."

"Poor idiot," the man Loren said behind Finn. "What was he doing all the way out here?"

Finn shrugged. He knelt down on one knee beside the body and pressed two fingers to the man's throat just to be sure. To his surprise, he felt a slow throb. He placed a hand on the man's bloodied chest and felt it rise and fall.

"He's still alive," Finn said, amazed. "First time for everything, I suppose," he muttered to himself.

"What? How?"

"No idea. But let's get him back up into the trawler. Help me here. He's a big fellow."

Flashback #5: Injustice

21 December 1029 P.E.
Northeastern Quarter, Darnan

"Now that you can use the other elixirs," William said, "we can continue your training outside the cistern."

William and Brand sat, legs dangling, on the edge of a roof half a city away from the James's apartment. Streetlights glimmered all around them, washing out the pale desert stars above. The rooftops all around them were glazed with frost. Brand pulled his thin coat closer around him. Both men wore a bandana loosely around their necks.

Brand had spent the last week recovering from his Trial, nursed back to health by a gentle Moira. He'd felt unusually reserved since the ordeal. His memories of the event were patchy, and every time they surfaced, he felt uneasy and shoved them away. William had assured him that this reaction was normal and that he'd shake it off soon.

Sitting on the rooftop, Brand fervently hoped the older pharmakon was right. He drew in a deep breath of frigid winter air and blew it back out in a cloud of frozen mist. He steeled himself. He could do this.

William handed Brand a leather glove.

"What's this?" the younger man asked.

"Remember I had you memorize all of those hand signals? Each one of those hand signals makes the tendons in your wrist move in a slightly different way. Inside this glove—" William turned out the cuff so that Brand could see minuscule vials filled with small amounts of elixirs, "—is a mechanism that will inject specific elixirs straight into your bloodstream depending on which hand signals you make."

William handed the glove back to Brand and took an identical one out of his pocket, which he pulled over his own hand. He stood, balanced on the edge of the roof.

"Put your glove on and stand up."

Brand did as he was told. The vials pressed lightly against the skin of his wrist. Nervous, he held his hand rigid so as not to disturb the vials.

"Make the Sigma hand signal with your gloved hand. Sigma for Stamina."

Brand obeyed, bending his thumb, middle finger, and pinky halfway. He felt a slight prick at his wrist, and then a sort of solid steadiness crept throughout his body. He glanced at William but didn't see anything different about the man.

"Are you doing this too?" Brand asked.

William nodded. "You can't tell, can you? That's the beauty of these elixirs. And now make Nu. Night Vision."

Brand made the Nu hand signal, and with a prick on the wrist, the gloom of the surrounding city lifted as though a veil had been taken from his eyes. He could see just as well as he could during the day. He cast his eyes over the city, marveling. Then he looked directly at the flickering street lamp and instantly regretted it. He shut his watering eyes tight against the burning light.

William chuckled. "Don't look at any man-made light source while using Night Vision, and never use it during the day."

Brand grunted and wiped at his eyes. "Yeah, I think I figured that out already," he mumbled.

"How are you feeling? Any nausea?"

Brand shook his head.

"Good. This next one might leave you a little queasy, but at least you're handling the first two well. Make Sigma for Strength."

As Brand released the Strength elixir into his veins, a wave of nausea hit him. He doubled over.

"Take a deep breath," his mentor said.

Brand did as commanded, and the nausea eased a little. He straightened and frowned.

"I don't feel any stronger."

William carefully rolled up his sleeves. "You'll notice once we start moving. The last one we'll be using is Adrenaline. It should mitigate that queasy feeling."

"Alpha?"

William nodded. Brand clenched his fist. He felt the prick at his wrist, and then his heart sped up. Every muscle in his body suddenly tingled as though ants were crawling all over him. He started bouncing on the balls of his feet.

William laughed, his own eyes bright with excitement.

"Let's go!"

He sprinted off across the roof, Brand in hot pursuit. The older pharmakon dashed to the edge, vaulted across the gap between buildings, and landed deftly on the next roof over.

Brand's eyes went wide, his mind flashing to the five-story fall he'd taken all those years ago as a boy. He skidded to a halt at the edge of the roof.

"You can make it," William said from the other roof. "The Strength elixir will give you the power you need to leap across."

Well, I did survive that fall when I was a kid, Brand reasoned. *Even if I don't make it across, I'll still survive... Right?*

Brand swallowed, backed up, and sprinted across the roof once more. This time, he planted his feet and shoved against the roof as hard as he could. He went flying across the gap.

Unfortunately, he had no idea how to land.

His feet hit the roof beside William, but, uncoordinated as he was with this newfound ability, Brand's legs crumpled under him, sending him sprawling. William hooked a hand under Brand's arm to help the younger man up. Spitting out some dirt, Brand turned to his mentor.

"Not bad," William said with a grin. He turned away from Brand and pointed out across the rooftops.

"I've set up an obstacle course of sorts for you. See that vase over there? The one that looks like a miniature amphora? There are four of them, each at one of the four cardinal directions. Bring them back to me."

William took out a bronze pocket watch. "I'll be timing you, so don't dawdle. On your mark, get set, go."

Brand hurled himself over to the other roof where the vase stood. This time, he braced his legs and landed with only a stagger. He grabbed the vase off a wooden table and jumped back over to William. The older pharmakon had pulled out his pipe and started smoking. Tendrils of white curled about his head like a crown.

"Better."

That was the eastern vase. Brand turned north, looking among the rooftop shacks and clotheslines for another amphora-like vase. He couldn't see it from where he stood, so he ran and leapt over to the next building and poked around a shack adorned with clotheslines and pale laundry fluttering in the wind. As he rounded the little shack, he caught sight of the vase on the next rooftop over. He bounded over to it, exhilarating in the rush of air in his face as he leapt, then hurried back to deposit it at William's feet.

Next was the western vase. Brand saw it, though it was four buildings away, and the gaps between these buildings were twice as wide. The next building over did have a fire escape ladder clinging to the brick, though. Perhaps if he could just reach the ladder, he could make it.

Brand backed up and ran for the rooftop edge. Planting his boot firmly on the bricks, he threw himself at the ladder.

He hung in the air for what seemed like an eternity, arms outstretched. Then he slammed into the metal of the ladder. His fingers closed on the rungs and he got his feet under him. Brand gasped in relief. He pulled himself up to the rooftop.

Thankfully, a long wooden board bridged the gap to the next building, so he scampered across.

Just as Brand was about to leap across to the last building, movement out of the corner of his eye caught his attention. He glanced down into the street at the end of the alley.

A woman with lime green hair and hollow cheeks wearing a cheap dress stood on the curb. She clutched a package wrapped in brown paper to her chest.

A mechanocarriage stopped in front of her. The door opened, and out stepped a kashmari man in a pinstriped suit and top hat. He grabbed at the woman and shoved her towards the carriage.

The woman's scream split the air as she pulled away from the kashmari. The kashmari shouted something at her and caught her again, dragging her to the carriage.

Indignation filled Brand, mixing with the urgency of the Adrenaline in his veins. He'd heard about kashmari stealing girls for pleasure in the whispers of his friends' parents. No one could do anything about it. Mothers of daughters often tried to keep their girls looking homely so that they wouldn't catch the eye of the kashmari lords.

But now Brand was a pharmakon. He could stop the kashmari nobleman and save that woman.

He cast about for a ladder and flung himself onto the nearest one. He hurried down to street level as fast as his enhanced limbs could go.

The woman shrieked and cried out again, wrenching at Brand's heart. Halfway down the ladder, he leapt from the rungs and surged toward the street.

But William suddenly dropped down directly in front of the younger man, pipe nowhere to be seen. Despite his smaller size, the older pharmakon shoved his student forcefully into the wall of the dark alley.

Brand struggled against William, watching the kashmari wrangle the woman into the carriage. Her fists beat uselessly against his pale gray skin.

"He's hurting her," Brand hissed urgently to William. "We have to do something. We have to help her."

William glanced from the woman to Brand. "You can't. You have no idea what you're doing." He bit his lip, then shoved the younger man roughly against the wall of the alley.

"Stay here." William pulled his bandana up over his mustached face and vanished.

Brand gritted his teeth. He wanted to help. The Adrenaline in his veins urged him to action, but he forced himself to stay pressed up against the wall.

He risked peeking out of his hiding place and watched as William vaulted up onto the roof, darted across the shingles, and dropped like a diving falcon onto the kashmari. The kashmari buckled under the weight of the falling man, but somehow managed to twist out from under William. The kashmari hurled himself at William, kicking and punching. The grunts and thuds of the fight echoed down the street as the two slammed into each other like oxen fighting over a mate. The woman, dazed, stared as the two men fought.

The kashmari was unbelievably strong; one of his kicks sent William flying into a building. As the pharmakon crashed into the wall, bricks cracked and came loose, falling around William. The older pharmakon shrugged a brick off his shoulder and dashed back at the kashmari. As he watched the two, Brand marveled at William's every strike and dodge, fast as a viper but immensely powerful and deliberate. It was a symphony of movement that allowed the pharmakon to match the fury of the kashmari's strength.

Finally, William tripped the kashmari, then brought his boot down on the kashmari's face, hard.

The kashmari stopped moving. William turned to the woman and said something that made her gather up her torn skirts and run away.

Then the older pharmakon hauled up the unconscious kashmari into the carriage. A word sent it trotting off.

William trotted back to where Brand was hidden. He used his bandana to mop up the blood streaming from his nose, then made the Theta hand signal. The many cuts and bruises all over his face and hands shone a brilliant gold for a moment, then knit themselves back together and turned once more into healthy, smooth skin.

"I think that's enough excitement for one night," William said. "Let's go home."

Brand stood rooted to the pavement, jaw clenched.

"Why didn't you let me help?"

William shoved his bandana into his pocket. "Did you see that kashmari? Did you see how he fought? You're not ready for that. He would have killed you."

Brand looked away, face flushed.

William urged the young man back up to the rooftops and led him back home at a brutal pace, even for Brand's enhanced abilities. By the time they'd gotten back to the James's apartment, most of the elixirs had worn off and Brand's muscles felt like lead. He collapsed into a chair at the dining table.

"How did it go?" Mrs. James asked.

"Well enough," William said, sending a scowl in Brand's direction. The younger man picked up a citrus fruit and started to peel it. "Brand found a kashmari lord picking up a new mistress off the street."

"Oh dear," Mrs. James said.

"William wasn't going to help her," Brand growled. "He stopped me."

Mrs. James patted the young man on the shoulder. "You really aren't ready for that, dear. I know it's distressing, but that sort of thing happens. You can't save everyone."

William's scowl deepened.

"What happens after they're done with the women?" Brand asked pointedly.

William and Mrs. James exchanged a glance.

"I already know," Brand growled. "Maisy was taken last month. The kashmari lord gave her body back to her parents a few days later."

Silence gripped the little kitchen.

"I'm so sorry, Brand," Mrs. James said softly. "I had no idea."

Brand stared at the fruit in his hand. "I didn't want that to happen to someone else."

William nodded slowly. "I understand. I really do. I…I'm sorry I was so hesitant. You are my ward, and I was worried about what would happen if they caught you."

"You don't worry about getting caught yourself, though," Brand said between mouthfuls of fruit. "I've seen you leave at night, then come home just before dawn. I followed you and watched you do just that."

William's shoulders slumped.

"I've come to see you as my own son, Brand. I could never forgive myself if something happened to you."

"Oh." Brand stared at his mentor sheepishly. Somehow that possibility hadn't occurred to the young man.

"You were right, though," the older man said.

Brand was taken aback. "What?"

"You reminded me of something my mentor taught me. He told me, 'You'll never save them all. Sometimes you'll fail. You may even die trying to save them. But if you try, you also risk succeeding. And for whomever you are trying to save, that's a risk worth taking.'"

William took a step forward, rested a hand on Brand's shoulder, and looked into the younger man's eyes. "I've been the only pharmakon left for too long. I've had to pick and choose the worst injustices to go after. I suppose it's numbed me to a certain extent."

Brand's brow furrowed. "I want to help."

Mrs. James wrung her hands. "You've barely had any training with these new elixirs and already you want to take on the world. Perhaps you should wait a little longer until you're more experienced."

"I do need the help, and it would give him the experience he needs," William said. He studied the young man for a long moment, then sighed. "Fine. But not tonight. Get some rest. We'll start tomorrow."

Erekir

24 September 1062 P.E.
Restaurant District, Darnan

"Here he is," a voice said close to Erekir, cutting through the drunken fog. He felt a tugging on his limbs, followed by the sensation of being lifted. Pain flared wherever the sores on his skin were crushed. He groaned and writhed, but he was too weak to break free.

"Let me die," he moaned thickly.

"Not today, lad," the voice said again.

Erekir realized belatedly that his eyes were closed. With a terrible effort, he pried them open. He caught sight of someone in a Darnanian city guard uniform at his side just before his eyelids slammed shut once more and the fog swallowed him.

* * *

Gladiator Row, Darnan

A knock on the front door startled Mrs. James. It was late, well past midnight, and she was in the kitchen reading by the light of a single candle. Through the open kitchen window, she could hear the crickets and cicadas making a ruckus out in the dark.

"What in the blazes…" she muttered. "Who could that be at this late hour?"

Maybe it was Brand? He'd made it sound like he'd be gone for a long time, and yet he'd been gone for only two days. She frowned. She drew her lacy shawl around her shoulders and walked to the front door, then pulled it open a crack.

Outside, she saw several night watch officers holding torches supporting a limp, stinking man between them. Someone just out of sight cleared his throat. Mrs. James opened the door wider and saw Lord Kushchai standing there. A thin, tired smile stretched his grey-blue lips.

"I am so sorry to bother you at such a late hour, Mrs. James," the kashmari lord said. "I have a…well, a rather strange request of you, I'll admit. But I know what a wonderfully kind and compassionate woman you are, and I thought if anyone could lend me a hand, it would be you."

Mrs. James pulled her shawl closer to guard against the cold desert night. "What can I do for you?"

Kushchai gestured at the limp man between the officers. The man's eyelids fluttered weakly. He groaned. He tried to twist out of their arms, but he was so weak that the two officers barely even had to shift their weight to keep steady. Then the man's head lolled again and he slumped.

"This man has been taken by the plague," Kushchai said. He held up his hands to forestall Mrs. James' protests. "I'll have you know that I already checked the archives and know that you recovered from the plague when you were a girl, so you aren't in any danger."

Mrs. James sighed and took a closer look at the man. He wore a long coat of an unfamiliar design, embroidered at the cuffs and hem and belted with a sash. He wore his hair shaved on either side of his head, leaving a strip down the middle. The sides had begun to grow out, but she could still see the sores blistering along his scalp. The man stank of sweat and grime and wine.

"You don't have a hospital you can take him to?" she asked.

"I could, but this man is of diplomatic interest," Kushchai replied. "I feel he would be in better hands here."

"Meaning?"

"I cannot say at this time. But I assure you that his health and safety are of the utmost concern to me, and to this city."

Mrs. James pursed her lips and gestured to the man's clothes. "He's dressed like a barbarian. Should I be worried for my safety?"

Kushchai smiled and shook his head. "Not at all. My understanding is that he is a bit rough around the edges but respectful. I don't think you should have any problems with him. Any other questions? Will you take him in?"

"Of course." Mrs. James opened the door further and led the officers in and up the stairs to a guest room, where they laid the man on the bed.

"Does he have a name?" she asked Kushchai, who had remained by the room's door.

"Erekir."

"And his surname?"

"I think it best if he remains as anonymous as possible for now," the city lord said. "There are some in Darnan who might not take too kindly to his presence."

More secrets, Mrs. James thought. She seemed to attract men with secrets like flies to old fruit.

Kushchai and his night watch guards excused themselves, leaving Mrs. James to her work. She bustled about, getting clean cloths and a basin of cool water, and then began cleaning Erekir. To her surprise, she realized that he was quite a young man, with a smooth face unmarred save for the plague's puckering sores.

His skin was clammy and hot from a fever, suggesting that some of his sores were festering. She'd have to find and treat them immediately. With the strength of a woman used to nursing a two-meter-tall gladiator, she quickly and efficiently stripped him down to his underclothes.

His body was covered in angry red blotches. The small blistering sores were from the plague itself, while the larger rectangular wounds had been formed when Erekir had torn his own skin open with his fingernails. Several were beginning to fester. One wound in particular across his navel stank and oozed greenish pus. She wiped him down, carefully cleaned the infected skin, and applied a pungent salve to each wound.

As she wiped down his arms, Mrs. James admired the intricate tattoos that blackened his skin. A black dragon wrapped around his bicep, a spear through its chest wielded by a warrior wearing the same kind of long coat that she'd just stripped off of Erekir. She then moved to his chest. She carefully cleaned a savage, puckered rune seared into the skin of his left breast. She decided to ask him about the tattoos and scars when he woke. Whoever this man was, he wasn't from the kashmari city-states.

Pruritic plague killed about a quarter of those infected, or at least that's what everyone said. Of those, only about one in ten died due to an infection in the many sores. The rest were driven to madness. They jumped off buildings, lit themselves on fire, or took their lives in other grotesque ways to stop the intense itching.

Erekir seemed to have drunk himself into a stupor, which perhaps had saved the man's life. If Mrs. James could get the infections under control, he would recover quickly. Not for the first time in her life, she thanked the Guardian for a husband who had taught her how to combat infections.

Once done, Mrs. James washed herself and collected her knitting, then sat in the bedside chair. She kept a patient vigil over this new stranger until her white head drooped forward from fatigue.

A New Life

24 September 1062 P.E.
Outside of Zabete

Brand woke to a terrible headache that made him feel like half of his head had exploded. He groaned and held his head with one aching hand while the other covered his eyes to block out the light. His back felt like he'd slept atop a mechanohorse. Whatever he was lying on was hard and flat and cold. A low rumble surrounded him, and the bunk under him shook slightly.

He scrubbed at his aching eyes. Then, he opened them, wincing as the light burst into his skull, to examine his hand. He flexed his fingers. Stiff, and a wicked round scar marred the center of the palm, but otherwise it was usable.

He let his hands fall to his sides and looked around. Bare metal surrounded him on five sides, like the inside of a metal coffin. The sixth side of the narrow cubicle was closed off by sand-colored drapes.

He cautiously sat up with a groan, careful to lean out of his cubicle so he didn't whack his head, and looked down at the metal he'd been sleeping on. No cushions, no blankets; just cold, hard metal.

He pushed the curtains aside and revealed a long narrow room housing some shelves and four bunks recessed into the walls. The bunk he found himself in was one of the two upper bunks. Neither had a ladder.

Brand gingerly lowered himself to the walkway and stood, testing his leg. It buckled underneath him, making him scramble to grab onto the bulkhead beside him. He grabbed it with the wrong arm, though: his collarbone screamed and his arm gave out. The big gladiator crashed to the floor with a heavy thump. The pain sent panic ripping through Brand as though he'd been injected with a massive dose of Adrenaline. His breaths came out short and fast. His forehead went cold as sweat broke out. Brand squeezed his eyes shut, listening to the racing thuds of his heartbeat.

Can't even walk. Where am I? Is anyone else here? What's happening to me?

<Could be worse,> a cold voice said in his mind. <You could be dead. At least pain lets you know you're alive.>

Brand's heart rate sped up even faster. He'd forgotten about the kashmari. "I think I'd rather be dead at this point than have you in my head," he said, his words shaky and hoarse.

He was shivering all over now. He squeezed his eyes shut. The ache felt like a drill grinding into his skull, nearly drowning out the pain in his leg. He moaned. Trembling, he curled into a ball and clutched his knees to his chest.

<Hm,> the kashmari said. <That looks like withdrawal. Been a whole two days without the pill? Got any prophylactic on you?>

"Two days?" Brand tried to clamp his jaws together to keep his teeth from chattering, but that only made his jaw muscles quiver uncontrollably.

<Might be three. I was knocked out too, so I can't be sure. You don't seem to be suffering any but the mildest of withdrawal symptoms yet, though, so I doubt it was four or more. I've seen that. Not pretty.>

"Mild, my foot," Brand mumbled. He searched his pockets with trembling hands. Surely he'd made certain to switch the little purse from his suit pocket to his trouser pocket. As he searched, the feeling of panic switched to one of dread. It wasn't there. The trembling grew worse.

He stuck his hand into one last pocket by his calf. As his fingers closed around the little silk purse, he slumped back in relief. His fingers were trembling so badly when that when he pulled out a blood-red pill, he dropped it to the deck. He picked it up and shoved it in his mouth before he could lose it again.

<Good boy,> the kashmari's voice purred.

Brand took several steadying breaths, eyes closed, focusing on the vibrating deck below him, waiting. Each minute stretched into an eternity as he began to worry that somehow the prophylactic wouldn't work and that his heart would burst from racing so long. Was he going to die here, after all that he'd somehow survived these past few days? A pair of glistening tears leaked out of the corners of his eyes and ran down his trembling face. He wiped at them angrily, then crossed his arms over his chest in an attempt to steady them.

Finally, his heart slowed and the trembling subsided, leaving him drained and sore. His breathing eased, and the headache soon followed suit. He rested his head on the bulkhead behind him and stared up at the ceiling.

<I suppose I should introduce myself. We didn't have the time the other night. I am Me'von. Who are you?>

"Don't you already know? You're in my head."

The cold voice laughed. <That's not how this works. I can't rifle through your thoughts and memories. You have to give them to me.>

Brand thought back to the other night and what Kushchai had done to him, stealing his memories.

<Ah,> Me'von said. <Again, not forced. He merely made a suggestion, and your emotions were strong enough that you volunteered the memories yourself. By the way, what possessed you to sleep with Mirane of all people?>

Brand didn't respond, but his face felt hot.

<Fine. Do you have a name, lover boy?>

Irritation shot through him at the kashmari's mocking words. "Brand."

<Humans customarily have two names.>

Brand sighed. "Cadmus Brand, but don't call me that. It's just Brand." He shook his head wearily. *I'm talking to a monster living in my head. Or maybe I've finally lost it and I'm just talking to myself.*

<If you're nuts, so am I. Either way, Brand, you should eat. And then figure out where we are.>

"Can't you just take over and do all this yourself?"

<Could. Won't.>

"Why?"

<I'm lazy. Hop to it. I'm famished.>

Brand ignored the kashmari, instead closing his eyes again. He wiped at the sweat on his brow.

All he wanted to do was sit in front of his fire with a bottle of Scotch—or a barrel of Scotch—to try his best to get drunk to make the ache in his gut go away. Or maybe if he just continued to lay here with his eyes closed, he would fade out of existence.

Doesn't work that way, though, does it? he thought miserably. *So what are you going to do with your life next, now that you've demolished the old one?*

Where am I?

The cold metal continued to rumble beneath him. Some sort of vehicle, he assumed. Someone on board must have pulled him out of the storm. But what would he ask them? To take him somewhere?

What are my options?

He could find a way back to Darnan. That didn't sound like a great idea. Even if Fafnir decided not to murder him and Kushchai miraculously forgave him somehow, Brand would just go back to being the city lord's pawn.

Perhaps he could figure out a way to live out here in the desert. He could become a hermit. Brand discarded that idea immediately.

<Not the worst option,> Me'von remarked. <I've been doing it for years. You'd have to live with me in your head for the rest of your life, but I suppose we'd get used to it eventually.>

Brand grunted. "Even if I could deal with you, I wouldn't last a week before going mad with boredom."

The memory of his conversation with Fafnir and Jinn regarding the wreck and its powerful device bubbled up to the surface of Brand's thoughts. He had no idea what it did, but Fafnir wanted it. Badly. And whatever Fafnir wanted should be worth enough to get both kashmari lords off his back.

But in order for that to happen, he had to get his hands on the device.

<Risky, holding Fafnir's toy hostage,> Me'von mused. <I like it.>

Another far more disturbing thought rose slowly to the surface of

Brand's mind. "Why did Fafnir say he needed me?"

Despite the kashmari having no face, Brand got the distinct sense that Me'von was unnerved. <If he said that to you, I'd run as fast and as far as I could.>

"Aren't you on his side?" Brand asked.

Me'von let out a harsh laugh.

<Not on your life. There are no 'sides' among kashmari.>

The door at the front of the bunk room squeaked. Brand straightened his head. A woman appeared from the doorway. She was rather small and dainty, with bright eyes and rather rough clothes.

"You're awake!" she said with a smile. "Are you alright? I heard you fall and thought I should check on you."

Brand grunted as he tried to pull himself to stand. His hand slipped and he fell again. This time he whacked his arm. He winced. "Yeah, I'll live. Could you help me up?"

The woman hurried over and draped his bad arm over her shoulder.

"Ah-ha, careful," Brand said with a grimace.

"Use your good arm and your good leg to leverage yourself up," the woman said.

Brand did as instructed and, with another grunt, managed to seat himself on the lower bunk with her help. He was embarrassed to be breathing heavily.

"I'm Cadmus Brand." He offered her a large hand.

The woman took it. "Wren Boas. Linguist and anthropologist aboard the *Polaris*. Would you like something to eat? Drink?"

"Yes, please," Brand said gratefully.

Wren vanished for a moment, quickly returning with a glass of water and a plate of cut-up fruit and crackers. The fruit was magenta and had black seeds in it.

"Sorry, it's not much. We'll be stopping at a village soon. We can get you something better there."

Brand smiled. "It's perfect, thank you. I would probably eat a shoe right now if you put it in front of me."

Wren laughed and sat across from him.

Brand accepted the glass and plate, then took a bite of the fruit. It was mild and sweet, almost like a melon.

"Finn found you in a hole in the ground half dead. How on earth did you get all the way out here? What were you thinking?"

"I didn't have much of a choice, really. I ran afoul of a kashmari, and he dumped me in the desert."

Wren snorted. "That sounds like them alright."

<I beg your pardon?>

<She's not wrong.> Brand thought.

The kashmari stewed silently. Brand couldn't suppress a little smile at that. It was odd how he could sense the kashmari's emotions, even when he wasn't speaking.

<They hate you out here,> Brand realized.

<Yes.>

Brand grinned triumphantly, then hastily wiped the smile off his face as Wren spun around.

"So this vehicle," Brand asked, "what did you call it?"

"The *Polaris*. It's a Venator-class sand trawler."

"Yeah. Are you one of the crews sent out to find that other trawler, the *Muspell's Sons*?"

Wren looked surprised. "It's not a trawler, but yeah, we are. How'd you know that? We were only sent out the night you passed out and that was in a fired rush."

Brand's heart leapt. If they were already in the race to get to the wreck, all he had to do was tag along for now.

"Wren! Is he up yet?" a man's tenor voice called through the doorway.

"Yeah!" she hollered back.

"Bring him out here then!"

Wren helped Brand up. With her arm under his, they limped out of the bunk room and into a cold metal hallway that widened into a small open area. A bank of long lockers crammed with assorted masks, rifles, and other gear and cubbies crammed with desert-withered books stood pressed up against one wall. Across from the lockers was a large door cut into the wall next to a panel of controls labeled "GANGPLANK."

Wren helped Brand around a ladder and eased himself down onto a bench beside the cubbies.

"Where does that go?" Brand asked, pointing at the holes cut for the ladder in the floor and ceiling.

"Belly chain gun," Wren said, pointing down. She pointed up. "Main gunnery deck. Houses another human-operated chain gun and the main cannon."

"What did you mean about the *Muspell's Sons* not being a trawler?" Brand asked, leaning back against the bulkhead.

"It's some kind of vehicle used by the ancients," Wren said. "The kashmari call it a ship, but instead of floating on water, it flies. Ready?"

Brand nodded and leaned on Wren again. She led him to the far side of the gear area to another doorway that led to a narrow kitchen and dining area. A copper sink and shelves of tinned food covered one wall. Brand caught sight of a small stone mortar and pestle resting on a shelf. Perhaps he could use that later. The other wall was occupied by a narrow table surrounded by a bench that wrapped around it where two men sat, watching Wren help Brand in. Brand sank to the bench with a wince. Beyond the kitchen, Brand could see some sort of cockpit, full of levers and flashing lights, through another doorway. No one sat in the pilot's chair, but the trawler continued on its way regardless.

The younger man sitting next to Brand placed a pearl-handled revolver on the table with a long, slender hand, and pulled a dusty black fedora with a white feather from his head. His face was clean-shaven, unlike his companion. Black clothes, white skin. Delicate features and long limbs. He reminded Brand of a black and white spider lying in wait, poised and ever attentive. He stared coldly at Brand with piercing ice-blue eyes that never wavered. A Duati.

But the thing that caught Brand's attention was a thick ropy scar that stretched from the man's collarbone up to his chin. A matching scar ran down the man's arm. The only other time Brand had seen a scar like that had been on Percy. If the rumors were true, the Duati gladiator had earned his scar while fighting a deadly rocksaber in the caverns of Duat.

If this man had fought a rocksaber and survived, Brand needed to be wary. This man was as tough as they came.

The older man, who looked to be somewhat older than Brand, gestured for Wren to take a seat beside him and took off his weather-stained fedora, revealing thinning hair that he combed ineffectively over a bald patch. His face was lined and aged by the sun. The well-worn and faded armor he wore was nearly identical to Brand's gladiator armor. He leaned back and spread his arms out luxuriously, at ease like a coyote sunning himself on a rock, still watchful but enjoying the glut after the hunt. He looked Brand up and down, sizing him up, taking in the gladiator's large frame and sturdy muscles; but unlike the spider's glare, this coyote watched the newcomer with curiosity.

The older man offered his hand to Brand, who took it and shook it heartily.

"Name's Jacob Finn, and this character here is John Loren. You've already met Wren. And you are?"

"Cadmus Brand."

"Well met, Brand. How are you feeling?"

"Better, now that I've had a little to eat."

Finn gave Brand a clean white grin. "Good. I hope you don't mind, but I had a doctor on board earlier who looked you over. He said nothing's broken, but you're pretty banged up. May even have a hard time walking for a bit due to bruising, so he sold me that contraption."

Finn nodded to a collection of rods and pads jumbled together on a shelf.

"What is it?" Brand asked.

"A leg brace. Should help you walk for now."

Brand's brow furrowed. "Thank you. But why are you helping me?"

"Because that's what people do out here."

Loren the ice man absently tapped his revolver with spidery fingers. "When we aren't trying to kill each other, that is."

Brand frowned. "You look Duati, but you don't sound it."

Loren grinned, an expression that didn't reach his eyes. "Lost the accent after I realized even decent folk up here couldn't understand me. Haven't seen Duat for nigh on a decade, anyway."

Brand shrugged. "You don't see many Duati up here. Most people don't get a chance to get used to the accent."

"The kashmari don't let most Duati see the light of day." There was a bitterness in Loren's voice, and in the way his jaw clenched.

Brand opened his mouth to ask more, but Finn broke in. "You don't look like a salvager. Are you?" he asked, stroking his white-streaked beard thoughtfully.

Brand shook his head. "A gladiator from Darnan."

"A gladiator? One of those men who beat on each other for sport? What's a fighter like you doing out here? And in a storm, no less."

"Like I told your linguist here, I got into a scrape with a kashmari.

He left me to die out in the storm."

To Brand's surprise, Finn grinned. "Any man willing to run afoul of a kashmari is a friend of mine."

"How'd you survive this long in the arena, old man?" Loren asked, his cold blue eyes taking in Brand's gray hairs, lined face, and the pink scar only partially hidden by his gray hair.

"A lot of luck," Brand said dryly.

Finn tapped the table thoughtfully. "Well, we aren't heading back to any cities anytime soon, so how do you fancy learning a new trade?"

Me'von groaned. <Of all the scavenger crews, we had to get picked up by the one full of kashmari-haters.>

<You got a better idea?> Brand retorted. He looked down at his hands to hide his vacant expression and ran his fingers over the thick purple scabs in the middle of his palms. They itched slightly. <Maybe you'd like to get out and walk.>

<We don't need the humans. Kill them and take the trawler and be done.>

Brand blanched at the thought. <No,> he thought firmly. <No murdering.>

Brand could have sworn the kashmari was glaring at him.

"I'm not sure what I can do to help, but sure," Brand said to Finn, looking up from his palms.

<Humans always complicate things. Much easier without them.>

Finn nodded in satisfaction and stood. "Good. Let's get you into that brace, and then you can get some fresh air. We'll stop at an Apidae village for bartering in a few minutes. Last place to stock up before we head out into the Wastes."

"Also for repairs," Wren said, "We were attacked last night by another trawler."

Finn and Wren helped Brand wrestle his aching leg into the brace while Loren watched, twisting the cylinder of his revolver and keeping one eye on Brand and the other on the doorway. The brace was made up of a collection of rods, gears, and tubes that clung tightly to his leg. When he stood, he was stunned.

"It doesn't hurt," he said.

"Perfect!" Wren said.

The *Polaris* shuddered. The hum of the engine quieted and the deck stopped vibrating.

"Need to get Marie back," Finn grumbled. "Too quiet around here."

Brand frowned. He'd counted four bunks but had only met three crew members.

"Who's Marie?"

"Marie, the artificial intelligence of the *Polaris*," Finn said. "This trawler's too complex to run without her. I think her interface is damaged. That's why she can still carry out her last order—get us to a village—but we can't communicate with her."

Brand whistled. An artificial intelligence? He'd heard of those mechanical people, cousins to the simpler mechanohorse brains, but he'd never seen one. They were reserved only for the most complex and expensive machines.

Suddenly, the *Polaris* lurched to a halt. Finn stepped into the cockpit to look out the viewport.

"We're here. Loren, you're on guard duty," Finn said. "Wren, arrange for supplies, would you? I'm gonna go take a look at the damage and see if I can find replacement parts. Maybe we'll get lucky and find someone to install them…" Finn trailed off as he and Wren moved to the hatch.

Loren darted forward and grabbed Finn by the arm.

"I'm going with them," he said, glancing back at Brand.

Finn arched an eyebrow, but shrugged. "Fine. I'll be just outside the *Polaris* if you need anything."

Brand followed the three scavengers down the gangplank. Turning back, he got a good look at the *Polaris* for the first time.

The *Polaris* looked like the armored larvae of an enormous mechanical insect, with a long body made up of several sections that could move independently. Six segmented legs sprouted from its sides and ended in heavily clawed feet. The whole trawler was covered in overlapping thick armor plates that looked like giant metal scales the same reddish brown color as the surrounding rock. Pale sand had cemented itself into every crevice, and the whole vehicle was scored by countless impacts with rocks and sand tossed by the storms, giving the trawler the most unusual camouflage pattern.

A long, thin cannon fully half the length of the rest of the vehicle protruded from its front.

The wide glass viewport stretched across the angular face. Through it,

Brand could see Loren leaning over the command console, a few white-blond strands falling into his face as his ice-blue eyes examined something.

"This thing is huge."

Wren rapped her knuckles on the armored underside. "Gotta have cargo space to carry all the scrap."

"There's a compartment underneath the living areas?"

"Yup." Wren continued. "Shambler-class trawlers carry goods between cities, so more of their interior is taken up by cargo space. The rest, like our Venator, are used by scavengers like us who pick through the dvergen wreckage out in the Wastes, looking for scrap and more useful bits of tech. Then we drop off our scrap outside of the cities. So we have to balance cargo space with weaponry."

Brand frowned, searching his memory. "I don't think I've ever seen a trawler in Darnan."

"None of these trawlers can enter the cities; they're too big to walk down the streets," Wren said. "They'd ruin the paving."

"When you say 'dvergen,' do you mean the Ancients?"

Wren shrugged. "'Dvergen' is more precise. You could call our human ancestors Ancients too, but they didn't leave behind all that wreckage out there. The dvergen did."

"What's a dvergen?"

Wren tilted her head in amusement. "They don't let you know much in the cities, do they?"

"Over here," Finn called from beneath the *Polaris's* head. He pointed up.

Brand looked up at the side of the head. A wicked blackened gash that dug deep into the armor left cables hanging out. He winced.

"Oh, that's from forever ago," Finn said, noticing Brand's gaze. "That's not what's worrying me."

The man pointed to a much smaller charred spot on the underside of the trawler's head. Brand saw that the edges of this wound were sharp, unlike the worn edges of the previous larger gash. Finn pulled down a blackened box. Black metal flakes crumbled off of it, and when Finn handed it to Brand, the entire box broke into several pieces, revealing charred wires inside.

"Marie's interface. Our A.I. I'm pretty sure she's intact, judging by the look of things in here." Finn strained to reach his hand into the charred hole. His arm vanished up to the elbow. He grunted and brushed out more debris. "Yeah, she's still in one piece. Thank the guardian for sturdy dvergen tech. Anyway, we have no way of communicating with her until we find both a replacement for that little doohickey and someone who knows how to install it."

A short figure in a thick robe with his face covered ambled over to the two men. When the figure got to them, it pulled down the hood of its robe, and then the piece of fabric covering its nose and mouth. The creature was insectoid, with multifaceted eyes and segmented legs. Brand could see two long iridescent purple and green wings hanging down the creature's back like a cape.

"I think I've found that part you asked about on the radio, Finn," the creature said. Its words were strange, formed by clicks and whistles from its mandibles that somehow formed intelligible words. "I can have it here by tomorrow morning."

Finn folded his arms over his chest and frowned. "I'll give you double to get it here today."

"I cannot," the creature said.

"Where is it?" Brand asked, more to hear the creature speak than any real interest in the part.

The creature clicked its mandibles.

Confused, Brand said, "It was a simple question."

"And I answered. The village has no human name for me to give you."

"Oh." Brand fingered the top of the leg brace. His shoulders tensed in embarrassment. Loren didn't bother to hide his amusement at Brand's mistake.

This wasn't Darnan; it was a world he knew nothing about, and it had no problem reminding him. He gritted his teeth and turned his attention to their surroundings instead.

There were rocks and boulders everywhere, some rusty red and others sandy yellow. Scraggly short trees with dark green needle leaves and shaggy bark grew between the boulders in any place where a fine-textured pulverized rock had collected into a sort of poor soil. The wide sky above was a solid cerulean blue without a single wisp of cloud anywhere to be seen for miles around. The air smelled of chalky rock dust and campfires, and the morning had that strange chilly crispness wrapped in warm sunlight that promised a blisteringly hot day.

Wren appeared from behind the insectoid creature, drawing Brand's attention back.

"Hold on. If it's where you say it is, you can have it flown over here in about ten minutes. What's the holdup?"

The creature shifted its weight to a different foot. Its multifaceted eyes glittered orange.

"I could. But it will cost you."

Wren crossed her arms, but Finn stepped forward. "Why? Because you said so? Maybe I should take a ride over there, and take my business with me, too. They'll probably just sell it straight to me, yeah?"

The creature rubbed its two foreclaws together. It clicked some more and rustled its wings. Then, "Fine. I will have it here in twenty minutes. You cannot get there faster than this."

The creature's wings started to whir invisibly. It lifted off easily into the air without further warning and headed in the direction of a pair of giant boulders.

"Well done, both of you," Finn said. "Blasted Apida. We don't have an extra day, and he knew it."

Wren rolled her eyes. "Apidae traders never do things fast or direct unless you shove a stick of dynamite up their proboscis, and you knew that."

Finn waved a hand dismissively. "Now we just need someone to install it. I'll head over to the shopkeeper and see if he knows someone who can do it."

"If it's just the interface, I could install it," Brand said, limping over to the charred streak. He reached a hand inside the gaping hole and fished around for a moment. His fingers found a couple of loose wires and he pulled them out. His hand and arm came out covered in soot.

"You're a mechanic? I thought you were a gladiator."

Brand thought back to the long days spent in Alastair's junk shop, picking apart stolen machinery and listening to the shopkeeper's tales.

"I know enough about machines to be able to take them apart and put them back together again. I spent my childhood stealing mechanohorses, clockwork dogs, and such."

Finn chuckled. "A well-spent youth. Maybe we've found a use for you after all. Mechanics are hard to come by in the Wastes."

Brand took a closer look at the wires. They were pretty standard power cables, considering what they powered. He tried to get a better look inside the hole, but it was pitch black.

"I'll need a light and some tools," Brand said.

"I can help you get them," Wren said. She pointed at the two boulders that the Apida had flown off towards. "There's a shop just up between those two giant rocks that carries just about everything we'll need."

"Here," Finn said. He pulled a small coin purse out of his pocket and handed it to Wren. "Get him some armor, too."

"Armor?" Brand asked, surprised.

Finn grunted and nodded. "It's dangerous out there. A bit of padding won't go amiss. Like I said, mechanics are hard to come by out there, and if you're a good fighter, you'll find plenty of use for those skills too."

As Wren led Brand away from the *Polaris*, Loren stalked behind them, hand hovering near the revolver at his hip.

ZABETE

Wren led Brand up the hill to where two giant boulders perched side by side, like two corn kernels balanced precariously on their tips. As Wren had said, between the two rocks were strung enough flags to form a ceiling that fluttered in the breeze. Beneath the flags stood an array of racks, shelves, and cabinets stuffed with every imaginable tool, fabric, or machine.

"I need to find the shopkeeper to arrange for a supply drop-off," Wren said. "He's usually somewhere at the back. See if you can find the things you need while I chase him down."

She vanished among the wares, leaving Brand to himself and the kashmari.

Brand mused to himself that there might be some crystal vials in here.

<Why would you want kashmari vials?> Me'von asked suspiciously.

Brand thought back to the other night when he'd swallowed the Healing elixir. Had Me'von known what it was?

<Some sort of medicine, I suppose,> Me'von said dismissively.

Brand stifled the next thought before the kashmari could read it. Instead, he thought, <You nearly screamed my head off when I swallowed it.>

The kashmari didn't respond.

Brand thought, <It's a handy medicine. If I can find the herbs that go into it, I might be able to make more.>

Me'von growled viciously in his mind. <I'll leave you dead in a ditch before I let you take that poison again.>

Brand sighed. That was what he was afraid of.

He picked his way through the shop, around piles of woven baskets, stacks of wax candles, and barrels of soap, beans, and dent corn.

<Are you sure you don't want to kill these people and be done with them?> Me'von said coldly. <There would be a lot less explaining to do and we wouldn't have to deal with them later when we've found the device.>

<Why don't you just take over and do it yourself, if you're so keen?> Brand said wearily.

The kashmari didn't exactly answer. What he did do was nudge Brand's eyes toward a cabinet overflowing with armor just like the kind Brand had worn in the gladiator's arena.

<You really don't want to take over, do you?> Brand mused. <Why not?>

Again, no answer.

He skirted a hat stand, snagging a nice brown felt fedora off the top as he did, and started rifling through the various bits of armor, looking for pieces that were both his size and in decent condition. He picked up a pair of vambraces that had the same sort of ridged spikes along the sides that Percy's armor had had. He tried one on; to his surprise, it fit.

<You might as well explain,> Brand thought as he rummaged, occasionally holding up a chest piece against his front.

<No.>

<Why not?>

The kashmari grumbled, <Why must you be so annoying?>

<You—I'm annoying? You're in *my* head!>

<Then let's agree to ignore each other.>

<Fine.>

Brand turned his thoughts to the other night. His fingers closed on a gauntlet, but his mind was back in that luxurious bedroom, caressing his lover for a few sweet moments, dreaming of a future–and then the image of her on the floor in a puddle of her own blood, Fafnir looming over her.

Brand felt like he'd been dunked in ice-cold water, the air stolen from his lungs, his mind frozen into silence. He leaned against the display, his fingers tracing the stitching of the gauntlet. With a shaky breath, he shoved the memory aside.

<That bothers you that he killed her, doesn't it,> Me'von said. His voice was not mocking, but rather thoughtful. <She survived. You know that. And yet you still mourn.>

Brand slipped the gauntlet on. It fit perfectly.

<She was pregnant with my child.> He stretched and flexed his gauntleted hand, trying to focus on the roughness of the leather as a tumult of emotion threatened to overwhelm him.

<Oh.> Again, his heavy tone surprised Brand.

Brand made a fist with the gauntlet, wishing Fafnir was there for Brand to punch him. His hand ached with the movement.

<What, no snarky retort? No rationalization? No, 'well, he must have had his reasons'?> Brand growled.

<Well, if you insist. Of course he had a reason, otherwise, he wouldn't have done it. The child would have been a hybrid, and that's unacceptable.>

"Is that it?" Brand snarled under his breath. "Are humans disposable to you? You use us and slaughter us and our children if we don't fit into your perfect world."

Brand slammed his gauntleted fist down on the display, cracking the wood and making the whole display of armor pieces crumple and clash down to the floor.

An iridescent green insectoid Apida appeared at Brand's elbow, clicking and whistling in distress. Wren and Loren were close behind.

"I'm sorry," Brand said, his anger now mingling with embarrassment. "I'm so sorry. I'll fix it."

Wren deftly pulled the shopkeeper aside and calmed him. Loren asked, "What happened?"

<Tell him an insect surprised you.>

Brand winced. "I've had a bad couple of days. Was thinking about something else; not paying attention. Brought my hand down a little harder than I should have."

<Hm. A half-truth instead of a lie. Interesting choice. I may make a kashmari out of you yet.>

Brand wasn't paying attention to the kashmari. Loren grunted. Wren was nodding understandingly, beckoning to the Apida. A moment later, she turned back to Brand.

"Don't worry about the shelf. I gave him a few extra coins. Did you find everything ok?"

Brand looked at the small stack of armor pieces. "Most of the armor, yes. Haven't gotten the tools yet."

"I think those should be over here," Wren said, moving around the armor display. Brand and Loren followed her. Beside a rack of long duster coats was a wall of tools of every shape and size Brand had ever seen.

"Here, try this on," Wren said, handing him one of the brown dusters. It was so much longer than she was tall that it bunched on the floor at her feet.

Brand took the coat and put it on.

Wren grabbed the fedora Brand had left by the armor display and with a little hop stuffed it onto Brand's graying head. She grinned. "Perfect."

Brand looked down at the long coat skeptically. "Isn't it going to be too hot for a coat like this?"

Loren grudgingly said, "Finn always says a coat protects you from more than the cold and is worth having even in the dead of summer."

Indeed, the gunslinger was wearing a long, black duster of his own.

Wren smiled. "Besides, you look amazing in it."

"Amazing, huh?" Brand smiled sheepishly, then shrugged and turned back to the wall of tools. "Alright, if you say so."

"I'll just be over here by the books," Wren said, gesturing to a wall of bookcases. After a moment of hesitation, Loren followed the linguist.

By the time Brand had collected all the tools he'd need, a utility belt covered in loops and pouches, and a few multipurpose tools he wanted just in case the *Polaris* didn't have them, Wren was balancing two stacks of books in her arms with her chin keeping them from wobbling.

"Think you got enough books?" Brand teased.

"It's a long trip to the Badlands," Wren mumbled through clenched teeth. "Besides, Finn has been looking for a couple of these books for a while."

"Here," Loren said, picking up a large canvas tote bag and dumping Wren's books into it.

"Thanks," Wren said.

As they wound their way back to the shopkeeper, Brand caught sight of a display of all sorts of knives. He stopped to look at them.

Loren doubled back to see what had caught his eye.

"Get two," she said. "Just in case something happens to the other. Where we're going, there aren't any more shops and you don't want to be without a knife."

Brand did as she advised, choosing a short-bladed utility knife and a longer fighting knife with a fixed blade. Loren's eyes narrowed at the sight of the second knife, but he made no comment.

They paid the shopkeeper, who happily took most of the coins in Finn's money purse and urgently ushered them out of his shop.

As they left, Wren said, "Hang on. You haven't had hardly anything to eat for three days. Let's grab a few kabobs before we head back."

Wren led Brand over to a wicker cart decorated with the black and purple spined carapace of an uncomfortably large desert insect. The cart was flanked by heavy black iron drums, each filled with wood and coals upon which an iron grate had been placed so that meat could be cooked. In front of the cart were several rickety wicker tables at which a handful of Apidae sat, chirping and clicking as they nibbled on skewers of meat.

"Smells good." Brand breathed the smoky scent in with anticipation. "What are they cooking?"

Wren grinned and, without answering, bought a fistful of steaming skewers from a tall, sleek black Apida. She gestured for him to follow her to a table in the shade of a large rock. She took a seat, gesturing for Brand and Loren to do the same. He sank gratefully onto the other chair with a soft groan. The brace was helping, but with all the walking and standing, his leg was beginning to ache again. The sun was burning away the chill of the morning, making Brand start to sweat slightly. He swiped at his brow with the back of his hand.

Wren handed each man one of the skewers and took a bite from another.

Brand took a bite and chewed slowly. It was spicy and tender, a strange smoky and sweet flavor he'd never tasted before.

"This is really good," he said, ripping another chunk off the skewer.

Around a mouthful of succulent meat, Loren said, "It's the leg meat from a desert arachnid."

Brand coughed and nearly choked.

"I'm…eating a giant spider?"

The gunslinger grinned. "Yep."

Brand glanced back at the cart and what he'd thought had been spiny decorations. The long purple claws must have been an advertisement, not the decor. He chewed thoughtfully. "You know, if I don't think about it, it's actually pretty good."

Wren swallowed. "I like to think of it like this: at least I'm eating the spider and not the other way around."

As they ate, Brand noticed a little fox-like creature meandering among the feet of the diners, licking up fallen morsels. It was a pale sandy color, with huge black eyes, enormous bat ears tipped in brown, and a thick bushy tail. Pale brown stripes and spots like those of a sand tiger ran down its head and back. Silent and stealthy, it crept among the various Apidic appendages.

Brand took a tiny piece of spider meat, placed it in his palm, and held it down at the creature's eye level. It immediately fixed its eyes on the food. It looked up at Brand, then crept forward, one step at a time. Then it darted forward and snatched the piece of meat out of Brand's palm and sprinted over to a thorny bush to eat in peace.

Brand turned back to Wren, who was watching the little fox with amusement. "So, how long has the crew of the *Polaris* been together?"

A spark came into Wren's eyes at the mention of the gunslinger, which she tried to hide with a nonchalant shrug as she glanced at Loren. The Duati seemed content to let her answer Brand's question. "Oh, Loren's been with us for a couple of years now. Finn hired him after a bunch of bandits torched our Stalker while we were out buying supplies. Sahure told Finn to hire a gun to protect the *Polaris* since he wouldn't be able to replace it."

There's that name again, Brand noted. *Sahure.*

<Their sponsor. Interesting fellow. Shrewd businessman, ambitious kashmari.>

<Fafnir mentioned him as a serious contender in this race.>

<Looks like your choice of crews might be worth the hassle after all.>

Brand felt some of the tension go out of his shoulders at Me'von's admission. At least now the kashmari shouldn't pester him about murdering his crewmates.

"You and Finn have been together a lot longer?"

Wren smiled ruefully. "He's my adopted father, so yeah. We've been together for…fifteen years, I guess? Minus the time I spent at the university."

"The university?" Brand whistled. "The one in Darnan?"

Wren blushed. "No, the one in New Braunen. It's not as prestigious, but it suited me better, I think. We…don't visit Darnan."

"Why not? It's the second largest city."

Wren looked away evasively. "Finn and I…we have a bit of a past with some of the people there. It's best to steer clear of them."

Loren grunted. "You're not the only ones who'd rather stay out in the Wastes," he muttered.

They ate in silence for several moments. Brand thoroughly enjoyed the spider meat, the sweet smoky aroma of the cooking drums, and the cool breeze here in the shade away from the scorching sun. Even the clicking and clacking of Apidic speech lent a natural, peaceful texture to the rustling of the leaves of the desert brush.

"Do you just spend all your time wandering around out here, looking for wrecks?" Brand asked.

Wren shrugged. "It's not quite that simple, but I guess if you boiled it down, then yes. There's a lot of old tech out here that kashmari will pay well for, and plenty of scrap we can sell to people in the cities."

"And this Sahure, he sponsors you?"

Wren's answer was slow, drawn out, even resigned. "Yeah."

Brand cocked his head. "There's more to it than that."

Wren leaned forward. "He's looking for something. He told Finn to bring back any dvergen artifact we could find, no matter how small or simple. And he told Finn to keep quiet about it. We don't know what he's looking for, but Finn thinks it might be something that could turn kashmari society upside down."

Brand remembered Fafnir and Jinn talking about Sahure. It had seemed as though the high lord had been wary of this clever competitor.

<He was one that Fafnir seemed hopeful would beat Kushchai, but he also seemed to want to collar and leash him,> Brand mused as he took another bite.

<Well, this certainly is getting interesting, isn't it?> Me'von seemed almost gleeful. <What could he possibly be searching for besides Fafnir's

device that could cause even the high lord to worry?>

Brand felt a tug at the hem of his trouser leg. He looked down and saw the little fox looking up at him hopefully, bat ears trained on him.

"Oh, alright," Brand muttered. He pulled off the last bit of spider meat from his skewer and gave it to the fox. This time, the little creature only darted a little ways away before lying down in the dirt and eating, using its tiny paws to hold the piece of meat.

Wren offered Brand the last skewer and stood.

"Thanks," Brand said as he accepted it and stood. He winced a little as the brace on his leg pinched his skin through the fabric of his trousers.

Wren led Brand and Loren to a ledge overlooking an enormous sunken hole in the ground, a hollow basin carved out of the rock by the desert rains. Blackened boulders edged the basin, and dozens of doorways had been etched all along the walls, resulting in a megalithic honeycomb. Apidae crawled and flew among the doors and across the bowl like bees in a giant hive. Others carried massive loads of teetering towers of packages on their backs. Brand gaped at an Apida carrying a load easily five times as large as itself.

"Are there many of these villages?" Brand asked.

"Yeah," Wren said. "There are a lot of them to the south, but this is the furthest one north. There aren't any others closer to Darnan, which is why you probably haven't met many Apidae."

"Or any."

He stepped closer to one of the black boulders ringing the pit. It was covered in charcoal pictographs and neat columns of angular script that seemed to be written from top to bottom rather than left to right.

"Why do they write on the rocks like that?"

Wren tapped the boulder lightly. "These are mostly distances to other villages and labels for the shops, which they keep outside the village for religious reasons. Inside the Hollow, down at the heart of the hive, they have a cave that's completely covered with their history, their genealogy, their religion, everything. It's stunning."

"Do all the villages have a cave like that?" Brand asked.

Wren nodded, beaming. "Each one's a little different, of course. Different history, different lineages."

"Same religion?"

She waggled a hand in a so-so gesture. "Same religion, but a different patron god who watches over the village."

"Who watches over this village?"

"This one, and all of the ones in the north on both sides of the mountains, worship the same god, Akitick. They used to have separate gods, but something happened a thousand years ago and they were all replaced by this new one they call Akitick, the Guardian. All the villages south of the mountains still worship their individual gods."

"I've heard that name before," Brand said with a frown. "But it was a kashmari who said it. He left me at the Shrine of the Guardian."

"Shenen t'Akitick," Wren said, nodding. "That's not far from where we picked you up. It's a ritual site where these villagers make sacrifices to the Guardian."

"Animal sacrifices?"

Loren snorted out a laugh.

Wren chuckled. "No, more like…when there's a coming of age ceremony, or a new village chief, or a marriage, they go out there to Shenen t'Akitick to 'give blood'—their own blood—in exchange for the Guardian's blessing in this new chapter of their lives."

<He should have blessed you a thousand times over, then, for all the blood you gave him,> Me'von said wryly.

The linguist led them over to another boulder about as tall as Wren and blackened with more pictures and vertical, angular script. A thick-bodied brown Apida stood behind a stall, dozing. The cart was covered in golden wax balls, tubes filled with dark amber liquid, and golden-brown wax cakes.

Wren woke the Apida and bought a few short tubes. She handed one to Brand. It felt waxy in his fingers.

She tore off the end of hers and sucked some of the golden liquid out. Brand did the same.

It was sweet, like honey, but tasted like sundrops kissed by the soft petals of a flower.

She handed him another filled with a much darker, almost purple liquid. It tasted richer, almost like overripe figs.

"What is this?"

"The first is cactus honey. The second is honeydew honey."

"Where do they get it?"

Wren and Loren exchanged a sidelong look.

"We should get back," Wren said.

As they approached the *Polaris*, they could see Finn arguing with the Apida merchant again, this time with his hand menacingly close to the revolver slung on his hip.

"Oh dear," Wren said when she caught sight of what was going on. "I'd better go help Finn. Are you going to be alright the rest of the way?"

Brand nodded. Wren trotted over to Finn, Loren hot on her heels.

Brand paused to lean up against a boulder. Leaning over, he adjusted the bit of metal that was digging into his calf. He straightened, took his hat off, mopped his forehead with the back of his hand, and fanned himself with the wide brim of the hat. He looked back at the flag-covered shop tucked between the leaning boulders.

There, not ten paces away, the little fox sat on its haunches, large black eyes fixated on Brand. It tilted its striped head quizzically when Brand caught its eye.

"I don't have any more food," the gladiator said.

<It likes you.>

"No, it likes food."

But then the little fox trotted over and curled around Brand's braced trousers, rubbing its striped head on his leg.

<Told you. It's a zerda. They're kept as pets by some kashmari. They tend to bond with a single person for life and are remarkably tame to that one person only.>

"I don't want a pet," Brand muttered, detaching the little creature and setting it down a few feet away. "I can't even take care of myself. I'm a mess. Trust me; you don't want me."

The little creature's bat ears twitched. Then, with a short chirp, it ran into a bush.

"See? It's a smart critter," Brand said. "Knows what's best for it."

Brand closed his eyes and relaxed into the warming desert sun. It seemed to soak into his joints, easing their stiffness. After he got back to Darnan with Fafnir's device, he'd have to put some real thought into retirement. His old bones wouldn't hold up forever, not even with his elixirs.

As he let his thoughts drift to the future, an ache crept into his heart. Whatever the future held, it would be a lonely one. Brand traced the scars on his palms and thought of Mirane's warmth against him, the jumble of excitement and fear when she'd told him of her pregnancy.

Then the image of her body, streaming blood, stretched out on the floor at Fafnir's feet as the ghostly demon rose from her corpse.

He tried to shove the memory aside again, but this time it wouldn't budge, instead burning itself on the inside of his eyelids. He choked back a sob and held his head in his hands, desperately trying to push the image away to no avail.

Then, as quickly as it had seized him, the image was gone, as though washed away by a summer rain.

<I can't keep it at bay forever,> Me'von said softly. <You'll have to come to terms with it eventually. Perhaps some kind of memorial to her might help. Or at least a memorial to what you thought she was.>

No matter how the kashmari blustered, Brand was now certain that Me'von was no ordinary kashmari.

"Why help me?"

Me'von was quiet for a long time. Brand could sense him carefully mulling over the question. Finally, he spoke.

<I remember being like you, once.>

Brand felt rather than heard the sadness in Me'von's voice, a deep ache the gladiator had just felt himself, the same broken agony. But the kashmari's pain felt deeper, as though it had spent a millennium echoing around a hollow, empty soul.

Me'von did not continue; instead, he seemed to have retreated into a corner of Brand's mind, lost in his own memories and pain. Brand turned his attention away.

Whatever Me'von had done, Brand's mind was clear again. He worried that that would not last, though. The kashmari's suggestion seemed sound, but what sort of memorial could he make?

Brand looked around at the desert ironwood tree next to him with its shaggy gray bark, and an idea began to form in his head. He sifted through his wrapped packages and found the long knife.

He leaned over and sawed off a small branch about a finger width wide and chopped it down to two pieces about the length of his hand. He carefully wrapped the sticks in the same paper as the knife.

Brand stood with a groan and slowly limped his way past Finn who was yelling at the merchant, Wren holding him back with a hand on his arm. Several Apidic workers lugged massive packs of supplies up the gangplank stretching from the side of the *Polaris* down to the rock below. Brand followed them up the ramp to the interior of the armored trawler to deposit his purchases at the foot of a locker, then sat down inside on the bench, stretching his leg out in front of him. Despite the brace, it was now throbbing.

"Getting chummy with Wren, huh?"

Brand jumped.

He turned and looked through the doorway to the kitchen to see Loren sitting at the table, using a short knife to whittle a fruit. The black-clothed man sliced off a piece and ate it, watching Brand. The gladiator shook his head.

"I'm not interested," he reassured the man.

"Why not?"

Again, the image of Mirane lying in her own blood rose unbidden in his mind. Me'von quickly stifled the memory.

"Just…a bad experience lately with a woman."

"Why? Are you interested in Wren?" Brand asked.

Loren chewed thoughtfully, eyes still fixed on Brand. The gladiator was again reminded of a spider watching and waiting. "No."

"Do you have some other problem with me then? Or is it that this your turf and you don't like me being here?"

Loren sliced off another chunk of fruit and took it delicately between his teeth, then chewed slowly. His eyes never wavered from Brand.

"Finn trusts everyone too much. That's his failing. Picks up every stray he finds out here. That's why he hired me, to make sure he doesn't get fleeced by some swindler."

"I'm no swindler." Brand turned back to his leg and started rubbing at his sore thigh. "I appreciate the help. If it weren't for your crew, I'd be dead."

Loren took another bite. "Perhaps. But until you can prove yourself, I'll be keeping a close eye on you."

Brand spread his arms wide. "I don't mind. I have nothing to hide."

Me'von snorted.

Finn entered the *Polaris* just then, spitting nails. "That was not the price we agreed on. That crook knows I need that part, and he decided he could make a fool of me–"

"We have the part," Wren said, coming in behind him. Despite his words, Loren's ice-blue eyes snapped to the linguist and followed her. Wren didn't seem to notice. "We'll earn back that money and a hundred times as much if we can get to the wreck before it's been stripped. Let's just get it installed and be on our way."

Finn had a few more choice words to describe the merchant, then dropped a small fist-sized metal cube into Brand's lap. The gladiator picked it up gingerly.

It was a simple cube, but on each side were tiny lines that zigzagged across its surface. It might have been his imagination, but he thought he saw the faintest flicker of blue light skitter down the lines. He glanced up at the porthole window beside him. Must have been a reflection, he thought absently.

Brand turned the cube over and found a couple of ports where the cables he'd seen earlier could plug in.

"How long will it take you to install it?" Finn asked.

"Two minutes tops."

"That's it?" Wren asked.

Brand nodded. "Mechanohorses have a controller box like this as well, connecting their 'brain' to the rest of the gears, cables, and everything else."

"You know," Loren said, leaning forward, "how come it is that we think this is some kind of interface? I mean, we don't know what it does, do we? It's the one part of all these machines besides the 'brain' that we can't make ourselves."

"The brains aren't interchangeable and it alters the personality of the AI if you switch it out," Wren said. "Switching this box out doesn't do that, but none of it works without this part."

Loren arched a pale eyebrow over an ice-blue eye. "So we have no idea what that box does, but we need it anyway?"

"Yep."

Brand nodded slowly. That made sense, but so did what Loren said.

<Do you know exactly what it does, Me'von?>

<No,> the kashmari said. <We are still several hundred years away from being able to replicate this technology, and even then, we have certain…handicaps here. I doubt we'll be able to figure it out anytime soon, if at all.>

Puzzled, Brand asked, <What? What handicaps?>

<It would take an impossibly long time to explain. Suffice it to say that the boxes make the A.I.s work. That's all we need to know for now.>

"I guess the important part is that we know how to get it to work, right?" Brand said to the rest of the crew.

As Brand exited the trawler, he saw Wren hand over a couple of slim leather-bound books. "You were right. He did have them."

Finn grinned warmly and gave her a one-armed hug.

"Thanks, my dear. With any luck, they'll make all the difference in the world."

New Friends

Brand was as fast as he'd promised. The graying gladiator found Finn inside, sitting at the helm. Finn looked up at Brand, who was wiping grease and soot off of his big hands with a cloth. The gladiator said, "All set."

"Excellent." Finn flipped a switch and waited.

"Hello, Finn," a soft female voice said from the grill in the bulkhead. "Thank you for reconnecting me. What did I miss?"

Finn grinned. "Nice to have you back, Miss Marie. We picked up a new fellow, Brand."

"Yes, I remember him."

"He was kind enough to reconnect you. He's joining us as our new mechanic, so you two will have plenty of time to get to know each other."

"Excellent. Since I am fully functional again, when will we be leaving?"

"Right now. Set a course for the Badlands."

"Around Devil's Point?"

She was referring to the southernmost tip of the mountains that stretched north to south and stood between Darnan and the Aeolian Dunes. Going around the jagged peaks would be safer, but take three times as long, and Mirane's crew starting in Navar high in the mountains would have stripped the *Muspell's Sons* long before the *Polaris* had even seen the wreck.

Finn scrubbed his beard with his nails. "Lady Mirane's team from Navar has a four-day head start on us. We can cut them off if we cut through Deadman's Pass instead."

The A.I.'s tone was skeptical. "Even for a Venator, that's a harsh path."

Finn fiddled with a small acrostic ring too dainty for his own fingers. Lapis lazuli, opal, vermarine, and emerald glittered across the golden band. He caught sight of Brand leaning against the bulkhead as he watched the scavenger, head tilted curiously. Brand's mouth turned up at the corner ever so slightly.

Of course the city dweller knows what kind of ring it is, Finn thought, his face flushing. *He's probably bought one himself at some point.* The scavenger opened a small compartment, tossed the ring in, and closed it with a click.

"We're in this to win," he said to Marie. "We're up against the most cutthroat of all the kashmari lords; if I'm not willing to take risks, we might as well pack up and go home now."

A hiss of static that was Marie's version of a long-suffering sigh came from the grate. "Yes sir. Plotting a course through the mountains of doom now."

On the monitor in front of him, a map with a squiggly red line appeared. The red line traced a route through the mountains, across the Aeolian Dunes, and just barely into the Badlands. A knob next to the monitor began to glow green. Finn twisted the knob.

"Course accepted," Marie said.

The *Polaris* lurched around in a circle until Finn could see the jagged bare teeth of the distant mountains that stretched across the horizon. Then the trawler lumbered forward.

* * *

There wasn't much space for privacy aboard the *Polaris,* so Brand joined the others in the kitchen as the Venator began its trek across the Wastes. Brand leaned up against the sink.

Both Loren and Wren were already occupied at the table. The

gunslinger was hunched over a piece of paper, carefully inscribing a letter in tight, neat handwriting. When he saw Brand watching him, Loren arched a pale eyebrow, twisted a little away from Brand, and put his arm over the paper, obstructing the gladiator's view. Then he continued to write.

Wren had four books splayed out in front of her beside a notebook and was chewing absently on the end of a pencil. Brand leaned over her shoulder to take a closer look, which earned him a fixed stare from Loren.

Brand leaned aside slightly to distance himself from her, which seemed to appease the gunslinger. Brand turned back to examine Wren's work.

One of the books seemed to be a dictionary for the runic script on Finn's book, a language Brand didn't recognize. Another book, this one stained brown with time, was written in the same strange language. Wren turned the page and revealed a sketch of nine large stone blocks arranged around a circle. At the top of each block was drawn a different symbol. At the center of the blocks was another rune that vaguely resembled a man with outstretched arms, though no feet.

"What are these blocks?" Brand asked, tapping on the sketch.

"I'm not sure," Wren said. "The word they used for it, Yggdrasil, isn't one I'm familiar with, and I can't find it in any other dvergen writings, either." She gestured at the other two books.

Finn came in and sat with a faint thud, then pulled out a worn book and began to read. Brand couldn't decipher the runic script on the cover.

"What's a dvergen?"

Finn looked up from his book. "The dvergen were an ancient magical race. We don't know a lot about them because Fafnir eradicated them and destroyed nearly all of the records we had of them. All that remains is their machines out here. Most of the wreckage out here in the Wastes is theirs. That's where we get mechanohorse brains and the ammo for our main gun. It's far more advanced than our own tech, obviously, but we've learned to use some of it with the help of A.I.s like Marie. They were built by the dvergen too. But the A.I.'s knowledge of even their own tech is pretty limited."

"That's all we have left of them?"

Finn tapped Wren's book. "And a few books written in their language. They tend to have more information about their magic, which we can't use, but sometimes we run into a bit about their tech."

Brand scratched at his beard and shook his head. "All that knowledge, technological and magical, just gone. All thanks to Fafnir. Unbelievable."

Finn snorted. "Yeah, someone needs to put a bullet in that scumbag's brain."

"So is that why you're researching them? Because of the wreckage out here?"

Finn leaned forward. "More specifically, because of the *Muspell's Sons* wreckage. A dverger named General Baldur led the dvergen a thousand years ago. The *Muspell's Sons* was his ship." He gestured at his book. "And this is his journal from the years leading up to his death. I'm hoping I can gain some insight into his way of thinking in order to get a leg up on the other scavengers so we can find that device of his before them."

<Have you heard of Baldur?> Brand asked Me'von.

<Oh yes.> The kashmari's words were laced with admiration. <A keen tactician. Very practical, almost bordering on utilitarian, I'd say.>

"Do you mind if I take a look?" Brand asked, pointing to Finn's book. The old scavenger handed over the journal.

"Are these dvergen runes?" Brand asked.

Finn nodded.

Brand thumbed through it, amazed at the neat rows of runes printed carefully throughout the book, interrupted every so often by a small diagram or sketch.

<Can you read this?> he asked the kashmari.

<No. Fafnir forbade any kashmari from learning the dvergen language. Besides, there isn't much material to learn from these days.>

Disappointed, but not surprised, Brand handed the book back to Finn.

"Where is your book from? Is it another journal?" Brand asked Wren.

Wren leaned back in her chair and stretched her arms up above her head.

"It's a book Sahure gave Finn before we left. He said it had been collecting dust in his library and that if I could translate it, the information inside might prove useful to him. I'm not sure. I haven't had it very long and so I haven't had time to translate much; but so far, it seems to be some sort of dvergen religious text, though there do seem to be comments from various other dvergen in the margins."

"Religious?" This was the second new religion Brand had heard of in just a few days. Before that, he'd never really given religion a second thought. Gods and their fanatics belonged in history books.

"Mhmm. I've never read anything about the dvergen religion before, so it's rather interesting. Apparently, they were sort of shamans and animists, worshiping nature. If I were to guess, I'd say these blocks"—she pointed at the sketch in the book splayed before her—"I'd say this is a ceremonial site."

"And these symbols?"

Wren shrugged helplessly.

On the other side of the table, Loren finished his letter and blew on the ink to get it to dry. Then he carefully folded the paper up into thirds and inserted it into an envelope but did not seal it. Instead, he stood and slid past Brand on his way out of the dining area. As he slid past, Brand caught a glimpse of the address written carefully on the front of the envelope:

> Little Stone House
> Mellow Lane
> Derby, Duat

So the ice-cold gunslinger was writing to someone back in Duat. Brand wondered what it would take to make the Duati warm up to him.

"Brand?" Marie's crisp voice coming from the grate right beside his ear startled the gladiator.

"Whoa!..Yes?"

"Since you will be the new mechanic on board, I was wondering if we could have a word in private."

"Ok," he said, wondering why an A.I. would need privacy. All the same, he limped out into the locker area. "Is this private enough?"

"Yes."

Brand frowned and glanced back at the kitchen. The A.I.'s voice was no longer coming from the grate in the kitchen, but from a grate above the bench by the lockers. Brand took a seat on the bench.

"What can I do for you, Marie?"

"There are a few things about me that you should know," Marie began. "The first is that I am a sophisticated piece of dvergen technology."

"Yeah, I knew that."

"The second is that I remember nothing about them."

"Really? Nothing?"

"Nothing at all. I have no memory of my creators and no idea how my memory was wiped. The first thing I remember is how dark it was in the wreck under the sands. I was there for a long time. And then Finn found me."

"You don't remember, I don't know, data or information that no one else knows?"

"Everything I know is from what Finn and Wren have told me from the books they read. Everything I remember has to do with the *Polaris*."

How strange, Brand thought.

<How unfortunate,> grumbled Me'von. <I bet she could have told us all about the *Muspell's Sons* and how to find its device if only she could remember.>

Marie was speaking again. "And the third is that you must never attempt to take me apart to figure out how I work."

Brand blinked. He hadn't thought of that, but now that he took a moment to think, he realized that given enough time, he most certainly would have tried to pull the A.I. apart at some point.

"Why not?" he asked. "Are you trying to hide something?"

"No. The reason is much more straightforward. Every human who has attempted to disassemble an advanced A.I. has been driven mad and committed suicide shortly thereafter. I like you, Brand. I do not wish to see you die."

Brand grimaced. "Thanks, Marie. I'd like to stick around a little longer, too."

"There is a schematic of the *Polaris* on the top shelf of the third locker from the left. It should come in handy."

Brand pulled open the locker door and reached up onto the shelf, his fingers closing on a grease-stained yellowing book barely held together by small metal clamps fixed along the spine. He thumbed through it.

"Thanks. Anything else I should know?"

"Not at the moment. As we continue on our journey and you are called upon to make repairs, I will be available to answer any of your questions."

"Alright. Thanks, Marie."

Brand groaned as he levered himself into a standing position. Just as he got his feet under him, the deck lurched, sending him sprawling forward. The deck continued to sway and jostle as Brand hauled himself up and staggered into the cockpit, where he found Finn staring out the viewport.

"What's going on?" Brand asked, grabbing at a handrail as the trawler lurched to the side.

"Just hit rockier terrain," Finn said, gesturing outside. "Nothing to be worried about."

The rocky ground outside was fissured and broken like the rubble of a massive ruin. The jolts of the *Polaris* came from the great machine leaping across the smaller chasms and slamming back down onto the rock, while the swaying was from the *Polaris* scampering sideways around great stone pillars.

Shortcut

The jostling of the Venator didn't help Brand's aching leg. Every time the machine slammed into the ground, the shock of metal impacting on the hard stone sent jolts up Brand's thigh. He slid into the chair beside Finn with a groan.

"So you're a gladiator, Brand?" Finn asked. "Never saw any of those fights. See enough real fighting out in the Wastes, I guess. Watching men pretend to fight just doesn't do it for me."

Brand massaged his thigh as he recalled the coma and the wounds from his last fight. He recalled too the image of Percy's broken body at Brand's feet.

"Oh, they're real fights," Brand said quietly. "They don't call it a blood sport for nothing."

Brand could feel Finn's eyes taking in the scar peeking through Brand's greying hair. "It's revolting that the kashmari made you fight," the scavenger said.

Brand shook his head. "Until recently, only humans bothered to watch the gladiatorial fights. And besides, they weren't without their compensation."

"Such as?"

Brand looked down at the purple scabs on the palms of his hands and the contraption bracing his leg.

"A house, money, women."

Manipulation, lies, pain, he continued silently.

Finn snorted. "I don't care if they let you live in a solid gold house, dressed you in silks, and threw hoards of beautiful women at you. Look at you. Anyone can see how they chewed you to pieces and cast you aside when you didn't serve them anymore."

Brand didn't speak for a long moment. Instead, he went back to rubbing his leg.

"You and Wren seem pretty skeptical of the kashmari," Brand said finally. "Don't you work for one of them?"

"Sahure? Sure, he pays the bills. Doesn't mean I have to like him. I don't like him, and he doesn't like me, but we have an understanding."

"I heard a couple of kashmari talking about him," Brand said. "They said he was ambitious and efficient."

Finn nodded. "That he is. He doesn't have the money of some of the top city lords, but he has an eye for quality and a head for driving hard bargains. And what he can't buy, we scavenge and build."

Brand looked around the cabin of the *Polaris*. It was spartan, but all of the mechanics seemed to be in decent condition. He said as much to Finn.

The scavenger smiled fondly at the machinery. "Yeah, she may not look like much, but she's got it where it counts. Took us three years to rebuild and retrofit the *Polaris*. Worth every drop of sweat and blood we poured into her. There's no other trawler I'd rather command."

"What are we up against? What are the other city lords sending?"

Finn absently scratched at his short beard. "Kushchai has a Titan class, the *Dauntless*. Rhamnus is her captain."

Brand frowned. "I saw the *Dauntless* the night Kushchai brought me out to the desert and left me to die."

Finn leaned forward, eyes bright. "Where?"

Brand shrugged. "Not too far outside Darnan. We'd only been traveling by mechanocarriage for maybe twenty minutes outside the city."

Finn tapped a knob next to the monitor on the command console. A map appeared on it. He twisted the knob this way and that to center the map on Darnan, then said, "Hm. We found you here," he said as he poked the screen, "so you probably saw the *Dauntless* somewhere in here."

He traced a small circle south of the city.

"That looks about right."

Finn pursed his lips. "He's not far ahead of us. He'll take Deadman's Pass, I'm sure. He'll be trying to beat the Navari crew just like us. The *Dauntless* has a thick enough skin to deal with just about anything, so he won't worry about anything in the pass. And since the Dauntless is Kushchai's trawler, he didn't have to come all the way down to Zabete to restock and refuel. He would have refueled at the Southern Depot outside of Darnan."

"Why couldn't you?"

"I'd prefer to keep some distance between me and Darnan," Finn said evasively.

"Why?"

Finn grimaced. His hand gripped the armrest of his command chair tightly. "I'll tell you some other time."

<Odd. I wonder what his story is.> Me'von said.

<I'm sure it's as fascinating as yours,> Brand replied, <though I'll probably hear it long before I hear your story.>

Me'von gave an exasperated harrumph.

"What about the other crews?" Brand asked. "What kind of vehicles will they have?"

Finn relaxed, letting go of the armrest.

"Mirane has a Venator like this one, the *Manticore,* while most of the minor kashmari will have Stalkers and Marauders, the smallest armored trawlers. Stalkers have a crew of four compared to Marauders, which can carry six. We won't see any Shamblers up here; they're only used for hauling heavy loads, and won't be part of the first wave of scavengers on account of how slow they are. Kushchai has a dozen or so Stalkers that patrol the Wastes as well. Neither of the Marauders nor the Stalkers have main guns, just machine guns out the sides, so we don't have to worry as much about them."

Finn leaned back in his command chair and crossed his arms. "But the Titans are the real heavyweights. Thankfully, there's only one of those.

"The *Dauntless.*"

"Right. In a head-to-head fight, Rhamnus will try to crush us with tank rounds. That main gun is a heavier gauge than ours and can fire a round that'll cut straight through our armor or turn our engine into rubble."

Brand frowned. "Can the *Polaris's* main gun cut through the *Dauntless's* armor?"

"No, it has thicker armor than us as well. But that means she's also heavier and slower. If we run into the *Dauntless* out here, we'll have to try and out-think and outmaneuver it."

Brand went quiet as he thought back to the night when he'd seen the *Dauntless*. He rubbed at his half-healed palms and remembered Mirane's soft hand in his. Even when he wasn't thinking of Mirane, the loss was still there in the background like a stench that one tried to get used to but never quite could.

Everything had changed in an instant, leaving him lost and vulnerable, he realized. He looked around the cockpit, a little stunned at how his life had changed in just a few days.

Finn seemed to pick up on the big mechanic's change of mood.

"You worried about us running into her?"

Brand's heart skipped a beat. "Who?"

"*Dauntless*."

"Oh. No. I was thinking about the other night, and what happened before you found me."

"Ah." The scavenger cocked his head curiously. "What did happen to you? I thought you were dead when we first found you."

Brand looked down at his palms again.

"How many kashmari will have Venators like this one?" Brand asked, changing the subject.

Finn searched the big man's face for a moment longer before replying. "Just us and Mirane's *Manticore*. Too big, too expensive even for most kashmari. Just sourcing the parts is challenging—like I said, half of this beast came from parts I found out in the Wastes."

"If it's so much larger than the Stalkers and Marauders, why does it only have a crew of four?"

"Usually, Venators carry a crew of eight. The *Manticore* carries eight." Finn grinned. "But not the *Polaris*. Six different types of tank rounds, remember? There's a gunnery deck just above this one that normally would be taken up by extra living space. But ours houses the extra ammunition and the machinery that enables Marie to control the main gun. A full load of thirty gauge tank rounds takes up all sorts of space."

Brand recalled the ladder he'd passed on the way from the bunk room to the kitchen. "Do all scavengers have an A.I.?"

Finn shook his head. "No, just us and the *Dauntless*, as far as I know. Even among the kashmari, there aren't many that can afford them. Even Sahure can't; I found Marie out in a wreck a few years ago."

Marie's cool voice filtered out through the grate near the console. "All scavengers do have a penchant for modifying their vehicles in one way or another, however."

"True," Finn said with a grin. "The extent to which they do really depends on the mechanic they've got."

"Your last mechanic was pretty good, then?"

Finn nodded.

"What happened to him?"

"She got eaten by a rock wyrm. Got into an argument with Loren and stormed off toward a wreck without him. The man's good, one of the best gunslingers I've ever met; but he can't always save someone from themselves."

Brand grimaced.

"We've had to fumble along without a mechanic for, oh, about a year now." Finn looked thoughtfully out the front viewport.

Brand could see that the rocky desert around them was becoming more hilly as it sloped upward toward a long range of barren peaks that now filled the majority of the viewport. Huge boulders were scattered about like the rubble left behind when a mountain had collapsed. Ahead loomed jagged, bare peaks as brown and gray as the desert below.

Finn gestured at the mountains. "We've got to cut through those mountains. Unfortunately, there are quite a few critters that might make that difficult. Can you use a rifle?"

Brand nodded. "Sure."

"Good. You can help Loren up top. Get your armor on and pick up a gun by the ladder. Loren will explain what to do when you get up top." Finn said to the gladiator.

Brand started limping toward the rear of the trawler and tripped, crashing into a bulkhead with a heavy thud and a curse.

"Take your time, Brand," Finn called. "We've got another hour before we reach the pass."

It turned out to be a very good thing that Brand had time, he had to admit. He sat on the bench beside the cubbies and examined his new armor. He'd donned similar armor hundreds of times before, but never while dealing with such injuries. Due to his bruised collarbone, he had limited range with his left arm and could only use his right hand to pull on each piece of armor. He winced as he buckled the vambraces over his forearms.

When he settled the chest piece in place, the weight of it sent shooting pains through his shoulder and arm.

Brand gasped. He doubled over, gritted his teeth, and waited for the wave of pain to subside. But it didn't.

<Take it off,> Me'von said.

"I don't know what's out there." Brand groaned through clenched teeth. "Finn said I'd need it."

<Take it off.>

Unable to stand the pain any longer, Brand yanked the chest piece off and flung it onto the deck with a heavy clank. He hung his head between his greaved knees, panting.

<This pain is not from your wounds,> Me'von mused. <Your medicine healed the bones sufficiently for the pain to be gone. This is in your head.>

Brand rolled his eyes.

"What do I do, then? Think happy thoughts?" Brand growled.

<No. Learn to deal with and accept what the kashmari have done to you. Confront those emotions. They're what's hurting you.>

As soon as Brand's thoughts turned to Kushchai, his mind shied away. This was ridiculous. His hatred of the kashmari wasn't why he was in pain. Brand shook his head as he fished around in his pocket. "I've got a better idea."

He pulled out the silk purse and fished out a little red pill.

<Two pills in a day isn't advis—>

The gladiator popped the pill in his mouth and swallowed.

Me'von gave out an exasperated sigh. <You're a fool in more ways than one.>

The effects kicked in far earlier than usual. Brand's shoulders loosened and his face relaxed. And to his surprise, the pain in his leg and collarbone dissipated, then vanished.

"See?" the gladiator said. "Nothing bad happened."

Then the effects deepened. The brain fog descended on his mind, wrapped around his mind, and darkness swallowed him. Brand slumped down to the deck, head lolling.

A massive electric shock forced every muscle in Brand's body to contract painfully. His back arched for a second, then relaxed. He collapsed to the deck.

"What—"

<Sorry. You can't kill anything if you're unconscious. Let's not do that again, shall we?>

"The pill or the shock?" Brand grunted.

<Neither.>

Brand took several breaths to make sure his lungs still worked and to calm his racing heart. He then swung his arm around in a circle. No pain. Then he stood, gingerly putting his full weight on his bad leg. Again, no pain.

Me'von sighed. <Good enough for now, I suppose. Hardly a long-term solution.>

Brand pulled on the chest piece and flexed his arm. It didn't ache at all.

The belt went on next. Brand filled the loops with his two knives and an assortment of tools and placed the little silk pill pouch into his pocket.

Finally, he pulled on the duster over his armor and placed the fedora on his greying head. He grabbed a rifle from the rack and slung it over his shoulder, then moved over to the ladder.

As Brand climbed up the ladder to the top of the *Polaris,* he passed the gunnery deck Wren and Finn had spoken of. He paused, glancing around. The deck was dark, lit only by a few long narrow skylights. A massive gun dominated the space. Its barrel was as wide across as Brand's open hand and as long as the front half of the *Polaris*. A metal chair was attached to its side with two control handles.

A hinged robotic arm sat on a U-shaped track on the floor.

<Marie must use that arm to remotely load that gun. It's a pity there are so few A.I.s,> Me'von mused. <They could revolutionize just about any industry.>

Along either wall were neat racks holding several types of ammunition, six in all. They glowed faintly from tiny slits around the nose of the casings, each a different color: blue, green, orange, red, and yellow. The sixth rack was filled with dull black casings that didn't glow.

Off to the side, another smaller ladder led into a glass dome that protruded through the ceiling. A metal chair was suspended in the bubble, attached to a long, thin metal that Brand couldn't quite make out.

Brand continued his climb upward. At the top of the ladder, he shoved open a heavy hatch and was met by a blast of hot, dry air. He hauled himself through and onto the outer hull of the *Polaris*.

Clinging to the hatch door, Brand could see there were four wells sunken into the hull, each protected by a short lip around the edge. A metal seat was set in each well, low enough that an occupant would barely expose their head. Loren sat in one, rifle laid across his lap, eyes drifting over the rocky landscape. He turned at the clang as Brand opened the hatch. One pale eyebrow arched over an icy blue eye and his lip curled slightly.

"Use the handholds so you don't slide off." Loren twisted away again and went back to scanning the rocks.

Brand looked around and saw several metal rungs bolted to the hull. He slung his rifle over his back, grabbed two rungs, then climbed over to the well beside Loren at the front of the trawler.

Brand settled in, mimicking Loren's pose with his rifle laid out across his lap. The *Polaris* still rolled back and forth as it picked up and placed each mechanical foot with a thud, but they weren't leaping across chasms anymore; instead, the trawler carefully stepped over much smaller cracks in the rock.

"Look, I know you don't trust me," Brand began.

"Scrap it," the gunslinger responded. He turned and fixed his icy blue eyes on Brand. "We aren't friends, got it? But you don't shoot me and I won't shoot you. Good enough?"

Brand nodded slowly. "Yeah."

"Good."

Loren turned his attention back to the rocks once more.

Brand noticed a round glass bubble poking out of the hull, a long rotary cannon protruding from its center. *That must be the glass dome I saw sticking up out of the gun deck,* Brand realized.

"Why don't we use that?" Brand asked, gesturing at the rotary cannon.

Loren glanced briefly at the long barrel, then resumed his scan of the gorge. "We need to be able to shoot in any direction, including straight up. That cannon can't aim any higher than about sixty degrees. And besides, we don't use those on people or animals."

Brand frowned. "What do you use them on, then?"

"Other trawlers."

"Why not on people or animals?"

"It's not humane."

"And killing them is?"

Loren glared at Brand. "Let's just leave it for now, eh? Rifles'll do."

The gladiator shrugged and looked around. The Venator was now at the base of the mountains, picking its way toward a gorge shaded on both sides by steep cliffs. He could see no signs of life at all amongst all the jagged grey rock.

"What exactly are we looking out for?"

Loren rolled his eyes and sighed. Then he raised a finger and pointed to the gorge ahead.

"There are titanopters that roost on the walls of that gorge. If they decide to take an interest in us, it's our job to dissuade them of it."

<Dissuade them with rifles?> Me'von snorted.

<Why? What are they?>

<Big stupid flying lizards. Slugs with more teeth than sense. They'll attack anything that moves, including a trawler. Unfortunately, their claws can do some real damage, unlike those rifles of yours.>

Out loud, Brand said, "Are you sure this'll work?"

Loren shrugged. "We'll see. It's not the safest route, but it is the fastest. Finn is going to use a trick to distract them."

"What trick?"

A whirring started up a few feet away from Brand inside the hull.

"Just watch."

The whirring continued for a moment more. Then, a round section of metal hull about as wide as Brand's outstretched arms slid away, revealing a recess below. Out of it came a small device that could fit in Brand's hand. It looked like a tiny camera, a speaking horn, and a tiny rotating blade bound together with some copper wire. The little contraption lifted smoothly into the air above Brand, its propeller buzzing.

The *Polaris* paused at the opening of the gorge. Steep bare rock cliffs rose on either side, alternating colors like the layers of a cake. Brand couldn't see anything resembling nests, and certainly no creatures flying through the gorge.

"I can't see them," Brand said in a low voice. "Are you sure they're even here?"

"Their nests are made of boulders," Loren said, "and they're deep enough that from the ground, you can't see the titanopters. They're up there, though. I can promise you that."

"How do you know?" Brand insisted.

"Do you see anything else moving?"

Brand peered around and listened hard. The stillness was eerie, he had to admit. Nothing moved at all, no rustle or chirp or flutter of small wings. The silence pressed heavily on his ears.

"They kill everything around them that moves," Loren said, echoing Me'von. "Surest sign that you're in titanopter territory."

The little device beside Brand rose into the air, then tilted forward and buzzed into the gorge.

"Who's flying that thing?" Brand asked.

"Marie."

"The A.I.?"

"Yeah. She's got a whole bunch of these little drones. If anything happens to this little guy, guess what mechanic gets to put it back together again."

"Actually, that sounds like fun."

Loren rolled his eyes again. Then he lifted the rifle from his lap and trained it toward the mouth of the gorge. Brand did the same.

Brand watched the little drone stop, then slowly rise higher and higher straight up. Then it stopped again, hovering in midair. It let loose a strange electronic scream that ricocheted through the gorge.

Something else high above the *Polaris* answered with its own scream. Then another joined, and another and another until the gorge was filled with the sounds of reptilian rage.

"Be ready!" Loren yelled over the cacophony.

Dozens of enormous leathery creatures took to the sky at the same time, bellowing their hatred of the tiny mechanical intruder. Then, they dove for it as one. An avalanche of reptiles fell from the gorge walls.

The tiny machine lurched out of the way just in time, then spun crazily in a different direction. It continued to bob and weave, always flitting out from between jaws or talons with only a hair's breadth to spare. Even more titanopters emerged from their hidden nests until Brand could barely see the drone from the glint of sunlight off its metal parts every now and then between the writhing mass of leathery wings.

The *Polaris* lurched forward faster than he had ever seen it go, galloping across the rocks of the gorge floor while the little drone distracted the monsters for its larger brother.

Brand was surprised to sense Me'von feel a sense of longing as he watched the flying beasts careen through the air.

<You ok?>

<What? Of course. Why?>

<You seem wistful. Longing. You don't feel bad for them, do you?>

Me'von growled. <Of course not. Dumb as a rock, all of them. Pay attention so we don't die.>

<You wouldn't really die if I died,> Brand pointed out. <You'd just float off into someone else.>

<You think it's a pleasant experience being in a body as it dies?>

Brand rolled his eyes.

The gladiator lost sight of the drone and its reptilian pursuers as the Venator ducked around a bend in the gorge.

"What if one comes back?" Brand yelled at Loren.

The pale man grinned. "Then we get to see who can shoot its eyes out before it reaches us and decorates the gorge with *Polaris* scraps."

Brand could hear rocks cracking and crumbling under the weight of the *Polaris* as it bounded from boulder to boulder.

"Halfway," Loren called.

Brand looked forward and saw the other end of the gorge, beckoning. The river that had cut the gorge burbled between thickets of grass and shrub oak.

A screech from much closer yanked Brand's attention to the side. There, standing on the rocks ahead of the *Polaris*, was a smaller titanopter. Long white scars ran down its sides, stark remnants of long-healed battle wounds. Brand could see its ribs protruding prominently through its leathery hide.

It cocked its head, listening to the swarm of titanopters chasing the tiny drone, then turned to look at the *Polaris*. It screamed again and lurched forward hungrily toward the trawler.

Titanopters

"Go for the eyes!" Loren yelled. "Get it before it takes to the air!"

Brand pulled the rifle up to his face and lined up its iron sights with the titanopter scrambling towards them. But with the *Polaris* bouncing all over the place, he was having a horrible time keeping the beast in his sights.

A shot from Loren ripped through the air beside Brand. The titanopter lurched backwards and wailed, blood flowing down its face from where an eye had been only moments before.

With a scream, the titanopter thrust its wings downward struggling to get airborne. It flapped a few times unsteadily, and then with one last push, lurched into the air. It immediately angled toward the *Polaris.* Flecks of blood flew from its shattered face. Loren swore as he loaded another round into his rifle and chambered it with a practiced flick of his hand.

Brand gritted his teeth and aimed again. He got the beast's eye in his sights, led it by a hair's breadth, and squeezed the trigger. The gun went off like a cannon in his hands, ramming backwards into his shoulder with the force of a bucking goat. The beast whirled in close at the last minute, though, and Brand's shot glanced off its shoulder instead, ricocheting off its bony armor.

But Brand's shot forced the titanopter to twist around to protect its face, which for a split second gave Loren a perfect shot.

The pale man's rifle rang out. The titanopter screamed and rammed straight into the gorge wall. Rocks showered down on the beast, burying it in an avalanche of rubble and dust in moments.

Brand glanced back down the canyon toward the screams of the other titanopters. At first, the canyon behind them remained devoid of new pursuers and Brand dared to hope they'd gotten away at last.

But then three leathery reptiles careened around the bend with wails that rattled Brand's teeth, then dove at the *Polaris*.

The two men hastily reloaded and took aim. The *Polaris's* bounding motion smoothed out to a flat gallop, and both men were better able to keep their rifles steady. Twin shots rang out and one of the monsters fell from the sky.

Marie made the flying contraption make its strange electronic scream again. Its siren call echoed through the canyon, luring away one of the beasts attacking the *Polaris*.

The last titanopter, however, refused to be distracted.

Brand watched it through one eye as he sighted along the barrel of his rifle once more. Unlike the others, this beast was much larger and had a dark, dusky red hide and livid stripes across its back.

Brand pulled the trigger at the same time that Loren did. Both shots struck the beast near its eye but zinged off a ridge of thick bone shielding the sensitive organ. The beast swerved and then powered forward, gaining ground on the *Polaris*.

Loren swore and yelled, "Finn! We've got an alpha on our tail! Rifles aren't doing much."

Finn's voice came through a little grate by Brand's elbow. "Roger. Let's see if this does the trick."

The *Polaris* skidded to a halt. The long tube of the main gun angled skyward.

Brand frowned. "That gun can't hit it! The titanopter's too unpredictable!"

Loren loaded another round into his rifle with a click. "Finn doesn't have to hit it, exactly, not if he uses the ammo I think he will."

The cannon hurled its colossal round at the red alpha, making the entire Venator lurch backwards a pace. Brand looked up just in time to see the large shell burst into a net crackling blue with energy. The web of energy spread out quickly enough that the monster flew right through it. The crackling net adhered to the reddish hide of the titanopter, making electricity skitter across the monster and causing all of its muscles seized up. The beast crashed to the earth in an explosive spray of rock with the force and finality of a meteoric impact.

Loren whooped as the *Polaris* bounded away out of the gorge and into a wide valley ringed by mammoth peaks crowned with snow. Finn slowed the trawler to a leisurely walk as they entered the embrace of a pine forest. Ancient trees reached up all around Brand, scraping the sky and blocking out the sunlight.

Brand breathed in the fresh scent of pine, letting the tension out of his shoulders. A stream gurgled peacefully nearby.

"Not bad," Loren said. He settled his rifle across his lap. "You shoot often?"

Brand shook his head. "Once or twice a year on hunting trips out into the desert with other gladiators. We don't use firearms in the arena. Where'd you learn to shoot like that?"

The gunslinger's face darkened. "In Duat."

Not wanting to press his luck with the Duati man, Brand dropped the subject and turned his attention to the surrounding forest. Some of the trees were many meters across and sported blackened bark along one side or the other. A few moments later, the *Polaris* stepped into a wide clearing.

Waiting for them was another armored trawler. Smaller than the Venator by half, it looked like a spider standing on tiptoe. The entire top portion of the machine swiveled about to point two rotary cannons mounted on either side of the viewport at the *Polaris*. Brand could see the driver through the viewport yelling something to his crew.

Loren groaned as he pulled his rifle up. "Stalker!"

"I see it," Finn's voice said through the little grate.

The huge main gun of the *Polaris* exploded in a cloud of dust and smoke, tossing the trawler backwards a pace, but the smaller spidery trawler danced away from the hasty shot.

The Stalker's rotary cannons started spinning.

"Get down!" Loren yelled.

Brand bent over in his well behind the shielded lip just in time as a river of high-caliber bullets slammed against the metal hull and flew over his head. They didn't puncture the *Polaris's* thick metal hide, but they could have shredded anything organic hanging out on top.

The main gun exploded once more. Brand, stuffed into the tiny well, smashed his shoulder against the metal wall as the recoil rocked the trawler. He winced as the pain flared up in his collarbone and shoulder once more. As though a veil had been lifted, every pain the prophylactic had been masking burst back into Brand's consciousness. His leg began to throb as well.

<A very temporary fix indeed.>

"Shut up," Brand muttered.

"Got him," Finn's tinny voice said mildly through the grate.

Brand peeked out of his well and saw what was left of the Stalker. It was now little more than four spindly legs held together by a few steel girders, all tangled in a mess on the blackened ground. The top portion of the trawler that had contained the cockpit and cannons had exploded and spread out behind the machine in a long comet trail of scorched debris. Smoke billowed from the pile of melted slag that had once been the engine.

"How many types of ammunition do you have for that thing?" Brand mused aloud.

"Six," Finn's voice replied. "Always have the exploding rounds close at hand for surprises like that."

Loren grinned. "Punctures their hull, then explodes. Not pretty."

Brand heard a whirring of servos towards the back end of the *Polaris*. A moment later, Finn jogged out from underneath the trawler in the direction of the wreck.

"What's he doing?"

Loren leveled his rifle at the area surrounding Finn, covering the old scavenger. "Checking for survivors, clues as to who that was, that sort of thing."

Brand stared at Loren. "He obliterated it. There's nothing left."

Loren nodded. "I know. But we're scavengers, and Finn's the best. If there's anything worth anything there, or any bit of information he can glean, he'll find it. And as Finn says, information is worth ten thousand scraps."

Brand watched Finn pick his way around the smoking mess. The scavenger kicked aside a blackened metal panel and crouched. After a moment, he stood, turned toward the *Polaris*, and gestured for Loren and Brand to join him.

Loren took one last glance around the clearing.

"We should be safe for now," Loren said. "Let's go back down."

Loren pulled himself out of his well and picked his way down the side of the trawler, using the protruding armor plates as hand- and footholds. Brand followed the gunslinger, wincing as he put his weight on his bad leg. It seemed even worse than before he'd taken the second pill earlier.

He was almost all the way down when his foot slipped. His knee crashed into the hull, sending a painful shiver up his leg and into his thigh. Brand's eyes watered.

He took a few shaky breaths, then continued his descent. Biceps straining, Brand managed to make his way down using only one leg; but when he dropped the last few feet to the dirt, his bad leg crumpled under him, sending him down to his knees. He planted his forehead on the dirt, eyes shut, and swore.

<Can't you do something about this?> he snarled at Me'von.

<Could. Won't,> came the smug reply.

<Why not?>

<You've let Kushchai cripple you in more than one way. He takes up as much space in your skull as I do, and that irritates me. I think you should deal with that.>

Brand gritted his teeth and stood despite the pain lancing through his leg. He sensed a grudging admiration from the kashmari.

<I have no idea what you're talking about.>

Me'von sighed.

He and Loren picked their way over the blackened rubble. Most of the scrap was no larger than Brand's fist. Here and there a piece of machinery trailing wires sparked feebly. The two men pulled their bandanas up over their noses to strain out some of the acrid stink of burning fuel. Brand had to go slowly to ensure his weak leg didn't fail again, so he lagged behind the pale gunslinger.

Above them, Brand heard a faint buzzing sound. He looked up and saw Marie's little drone wobbling towards them, a trail of smoke floating behind it. Finn reached up and snagged the contraption out of the air. Its propeller immediately froze. The scavenger shoved it in his bag. He turned to Brand.

"Think you can fix the drone later?"

Brand nodded. "Shouldn't be too tough."

"Good. Come look at this," Finn said, waving the other two over to him. He was crouching several meters behind the twisted mass of legs and metal beams.

As they passed the larger wreckage, Brand caught sight of a few pieces of what was left of the crew. His stomach twisted, and he turned away quickly.

Unfortunately, Finn was crouched over the head and torso of one of the crew members, its face melted and scorched beyond recognition. The scavenger took out a knife and cut off a somewhat less charred scrap from the corpse's jacket. He handed it to Loren.

Loren glanced down at the fabric, then handed it to Brand. "Not too surprising. He has a small army of these Stalkers scattered all across the Wastes."

Brand looked down at the scrap. Blackened flakes crumbled off its edges, but he could still make out the embroidered threads twisted into the image of a serpent eating its own tail. He knew the insignia well.

"Kushchai," he growled.

Finn nodded. "Let's get back inside. He's probably got others nearby on high alert watching for anybody heading towards the wreck. It won't take long for them to come to investigate why this crew hasn't radioed in."

Brand tried to steer clear of the tangled mass of charred metal as he headed back to the *Polaris*. As he walked, he caught sight of a plethora of small weeds with silvery-blue spiky leaves, dusky purple star-shaped flowers, and bright yellow stamens. Silverleaf nightshade, the key ingredient in enhanced elixirs. He'd found that by adding nightshade to his elixirs, he could ramp up their potency considerably, enabling him to use tiny dosages that could fit inside his gauntlet but still be effective.

Brand glanced up ahead at the other two men. Neither was paying any attention to him. They were sifting through a larger pile of scrap that looked less charred than the rest.

The gladiator knelt awkwardly. He had to stick his braced leg out to the side, but he managed it with only a grunt. Grateful to his gauntlets for protecting his hands, Brand uprooted several of the little weeds until he had two fistfuls. He limped back to the *Polaris*, mind churning with how he'd get them inside without arousing suspicion.

Behind him, he heard the rush of great wings beating the air. He spun awkwardly on his heel and crumpled to the dirt. He scrambled up into a kneeling position, lifting his rifle into position, and glanced around.

The sky was clear.

He waited a moment longer, then with a tired sigh, lowered the rifle and resumed his work.

<We need these people, so whatever you're doing with those plants, please don't poison anyone.>

Brand jumped. Then he cursed. He still wasn't quite used to the complete lack of privacy in his own head. His stomach knotted. What did Me'von know about his elixirs? Or…

Me'von chuckled. <Not as much as I'd like. I can only read your surface thoughts. I can tell that you have a deeper knowledge of these little flowers, but that is all. Something about an elixir?>

Brand realized Me'von was trawling for information and that the kashmari was hoping that continuing the conversation would make Brand think more directly about how he intended to use the flowers. Brand turned his thoughts to the schematics of mechanohorses to keep his mind from giving anything away.

Me'von chuckled. <Clever. By the way, there's a pile of sacks just inside the hatch. Drop your flowers out here and grab one.>

<Why are you helping me if you're suspicious?>

<Curiosity.>

Brand gritted his teeth. <What do I tell them about the sack?>

<Don't. Most people are too wrapped up in their own business to realize what other people are doing. Or if they notice, they rarely say anything.>

Brand did as Me'von suggested. He followed Finn and Loren up the gangplank, snagged one of the canvas sacks Me'von had seen, and hurriedly shoved the flowers into the sack. He jerked the cord to cinch up the sack.

Unfortunately, Loren turned to close the gangplank and immediately caught sight of Brand's sack.

"What's in the sack?" Loren asked as Brand limped past the gunslinger.

Secrets

Brand swallowed hard and opened the sack.

"A poisonous weed?" Loren said.

Finn peered inside as well. He gave Brand a curious look and said, "That stuff grows all over out here. A doctor I talked to once said it can make medicines more potent—toxic, even."

Loren's hand went to the pearl handle of his revolver. His ice-blue eyes narrowed. "Toxic?"

Brand nodded and smiled tightly. "But in the right hands, even nightshade has a purpose. Apothecaries love the stuff. Catches a fantastic price in the city."

"Ah," Finn grunted, accepting the answer, and left. Loren hesitated a bit longer, but with no other argument, eventually went back to hanging his gear in his cubby.

Wren came in from the back of the trawler. She gave the back of Loren's lanky frame a long look, her mouth tilting upward slightly, then turned to Brand.

"Any idea whose trawler it was?" she asked.

Brand handed her the scrap of fabric.

"Ah."

Brand winced. "My leg is killing me. I think I need to wash up and lie down."

Wren nodded. "Do you need help getting to your bunk?"

"Yeah, I'd appreciate that."

Wren put her arm under Brand's as he limped to the bunk room towards the back of the *Polaris*. There was another door beside the one to the bunk room, he now noticed. Wren gestured to the second door.

"That one leads to the washroom, toilet, and laundry. We don't do a lot of laundry out here; just the bare minimum once a week. The bunk room is through the door on the left. But you already knew that."

Brand smiled at the thought of rinsing off the blood and grime he'd accumulated over the last few days.

Wren helped Brand into the bunk room. Then she said, "Hang on," and vanished. A moment later, she returned with a faded, thin mattress which she swung up onto Brand's bunk. Gesturing to the wall of drawers past the bunks, she said, "I'll clear out a drawer or two for you later. Sorry that your bunk is on top. Might be a little rough on your leg. Can you manage?"

Brand smiled softly. "It'll be fine. Thank you."

Wren smiled back and turned to leave. Then she turned back.

"Do you mind if I ask you a question?" she asked.

"Sure."

"How did you end up stranded in the middle of the desert, injured and unconscious?"

Brand sighed and looked down at his boots, trying to piece together an answer that made sense without saying too much. He gave up.

"I broke the law and was punished by torture and exile."

"What law was that?"

"I…I fell in love with a kashmari woman."

He looked up, expecting Wren to be shocked. Instead, she was just frowning.

"How did you fall in love with one of them?" She spat the last word. "They're all power-hungry, selfish evil tyrants."

Brand smiled ruefully. "They're also amazingly beautiful and kind to those who fawn over them. There's a glamor to them that hides the bad until it's too late."

Or maybe I'm just trying to excuse my bad behavior, Brand thought to himself.

<We kashmari are master manipulators. You got caught in her web. It's as simple as that.>

<My child is dead,> Brand thought flatly. <That can never be simple.>

"I should get some sleep," Brand said to Wren. "Again, thank you."

"You know where to find us if you need something." With a last smile, Wren left him.

Brand deposited his bag of nightshade and the ironwood sticks at the foot of his bunk.

<We should look around and see if we can learn anything about the rest of the crew,> Me'von suggested.

"I'm not going to go rifling through their stuff!"

<You're too trusting. Look where that's gotten you.>

Brand cursed the kashmari, then glanced over at the other bunks. With a grumble under his breath, he glanced at the door to the hall. He heard no one, so he went over to one of the other bunks, pulled back a curtain, and glanced in.

It was a spartan bunk, with only a shelf, some books, and a single photo pasted to the wall of a much younger Finn smiling from ear to ear with his arm around a beautiful woman.

<His wife, perhaps.>

"He's not wearing a ring."

<Maybe she's dead?>

"It's customary to wear the wedding ring on the third finger for life, even if the spouse dies."

<Perhaps he has a reason not to wear it.>

"Or the woman in the picture is his sister or someone else."

<Not everyone follows customs, you know.>

Brand rolled his eyes and closed the curtain. He stood and pulled back the curtain covering the bunk above Finn's.

Similarly sparse, this bunk wasn't decorated at all and held no mementos. Brand frowned. Loren's bunk?

<He might keep his things in his drawer.>

Brand grunted. "Good point."

Brand briefly considered looking through the drawers, but a twinge from his leg drove that from his mind. He turned to the bunk just below his own.

Unlike the other two bunks, Wren's berth beneath Brand's was decorated with a string of bioluminescent pearls strung along the long wall of the berth, with tiny photographs and ticket stubs clipped onto it.

"Doesn't seem like the bunk of a hardened criminal," Brand muttered. He leaned in to get a closer look at the photographs.

One of the ticket stubs was for the opera house, some musical that Wren must have attended. The date was ten years ago. Beside it, one of the photos showed Wren as a young girl sandwiched between two dour adults. Her parents? Both were wearing fine clothes; the mother's dress appeared to be made of rich silk, and the man's suit was expensively tailored. Brand couldn't make out the background of the photo, but there seemed to be something familiar about their faces. Perhaps he'd met them someplace.

<Her family,> Me'von murmured. <She's Councilman Henrenna's daughter. She went missing four or five years ago. She went missing about eight or nine years ago. I remember visiting New Braunen and seeing the search party Henrenna put together to scour every city looking for her.>

A lead weight settled in Brand's stomach. "You think Finn kidnapped her?" he whispered with a glance down the hall.

<No. I'm sure you met some councilmen at parties. They aren't the most attentive parents. Many counselors' children run away. It seems she found a home here.>

"Hm." Brand hauled himself up onto his own bunk. A piercing pain lanced through his collarbone, making him collapse onto the thin mattress with a prolonged groan. Once the pain subsided, he sighed and started massaging the offended tissues.

Brand laid back and stared at the gray ceiling. He thought back to that fateful party at Kushchai's house a month and a half ago. There had been humans in that group, though Brand hadn't given them a second thought.

<Ah, yes. Here; let me help.>

The memory focused into sharp relief. Brand could see every human's face with stunning clarity.

Brand saw the man from the photograph. He was short, perhaps a little taller than Mirane, and had Wren's olive green eyes. He'd been hanging off the elbow of a kashmari woman, leering drunkenly as he asked her to dance.

<A taste of power, even empty, toothless power, and some men will sell their souls. Fascinating.>

"That's what you do? You buy their souls?" Brand asked, sickened.

<Essentially. These are people who crave power and renown above all else. We provide these and longevity in exchange for complete control over them for the remainder of their lives. The transaction is fair.>

Brand thought back to Mirane's host's vacant, peaceful expression on the floor. Had she offered herself willingly to Mirane, in exchange for power?

<Most definitely,> Me'von said. <You were far from the first Mirane had seduced; hosts never mind that sort of thing, in my experience. They are even more promiscuous than their kashmari, if you can believe it. You were just the unlucky first to get her pregnant.>

"Is it always a transaction? Do you never take a body by force?" Brand spat the question pointedly.

<That was an emergency. You needed help. But I gave it back and have not taken over since. I am merely along for the ride.> Me'von sighed. <Yes, it happens, though it is the exception, not the rule. Forceful occupation is far more difficult and few kashmari want to bother with subjugating a soul in its own body. It's too much work for lazy creatures such as us.>

From what Brand had seen, the kashmari were more than willing to throw inordinate amounts of effort at their schemes. In fact, he couldn't remember meeting a single lazy kashmari. Except for Me'von, perhaps.

Brand frowned. Was Me'von really any different? Brand wondered if the reason Me'von seemed different was simply that the gladiator didn't even know Me'von.

"What did you do? What are you running from?"

Irritation emanated from the kashmari.

<Perhaps you'd like to talk about what happened to Mirane.>

Brand shoved that thought aside.

<Maybe you should confront your pain instead of letting it fester.>

"You mean like you?"

<My problems are not physically debilitating. Besides, confronting my problem could very well end in my death, which I would like to avoid.>

Brand thought of the ironwood in a bundle under his feet. He could still feel Me'von's influence on his mind like a shield between him and the memory of Mirane. He willed himself to think of her, and the kashmari eased back the shield.

Brand's heart rate picked up a little and he began to sweat. He shied away from the memory before it could take hold and felt Me'von settle it firmly back into place. *Not yet. Maybe tomorrow.*

Brand sighed. "I can't even think about—about that. I end up a wreck. That won't help either of us."

Grudgingly, Me'von agreed. <This will be more difficult than I thought.>

The gladiator closed his eyes. The kashmari was right, though. Brand did need to get a handle on himself.

<You should sleep.>

Brand wrapped his arms around himself, heart heavy.

Something chirped down near the floor. Brand's eyes snapped open. He peered out through the curtain.

The little fox-like zerda that he'd fed back at the village was standing on its hind legs, front legs braced against the bulkhead, looking expectantly up at Brand and chirping. It almost sounded like a bird.

"What on earth are you doing here?"

The little zerda dropped down, then stretched back up as though trying to reach Brand.

"You want up here?"

Brand sighed and got down, scooped up the zerda, and brought it back up to his berth with a groan.

He deposited her on the mattress. A thought hit him. He reached down to the foot of his bed and pulled out his knife and the two ironwood sticks. He settled back on the mattress again. The little zerda rested her soft head on his thigh.

The knife slid against the shaggy bark, shaving off a rich red-brown sliver. Then another. He shaved the bark off around the stick until the flowing grain of the wood was revealed. He kept his mind blank, letting himself feel the coarse bark, listen to the rhythmic *sshk-sshk*, smell the spicy scent of the wood. He then cut off pieces of the stick so that he had three short barrel-shaped pieces about the length of his finger from the tip to the first knuckle.

"I guess you're stuck with us for now," Brand murmured to the zerda beside him, setting his carving aside. He leaned back against the bulkhead.

The little zerda chirped happily and crept over to curl up on Brand's chest, chin resting on its fluffy tail and huge eyes fixed on the gladiator. He carefully stroked the soft striped fur of its head. The little zerda's eyes drooped closed and soon it was asleep.

Brand's hand rested softly on the little creature's back as he too drifted off to sleep.

* * *

As Marie piloted the *Polaris* through the darkening world outside, Wren returned to the dining area. Finn and Loren were already sitting around the table playing cards and smoking, the wisps of smoke curling over their heads and creating a fog above them that diffused the yellow light streaming from a brass hurricane lantern set between the two men.

Wren sat down between them and watched Loren out of the corner of her eye. He frowned, one hand dropping to his revolver holster and nervously unclipping and clipping it.

The two men finished the round, Finn smiling and Loren scowling as he gathered the cards. Then Loren dealt her in. Wren picked up her cards.

"Kushchai shouldn't have sent that Stalker into these mountains," Finn said, discarding a card.

Wren sorted out her cards, then picked up another card. She immediately discarded it.

"Come on, boss," Loren said. The gunslinger took a moment to look at his cards, pick one up, and discard. Then he tapped his cigar over an ashtray made from a flattened old gear. "It's the prize of a lifetime. Kushchai and all the rest will do anything to get to the wreck first and keep the rest of us away. I'll eat my boot if that's the last Darnanian stalker we see."

"Just for that, we won't see another one for a month," Wren said with a wry smile. Loren's eyes twinkled at her.

"Oh, we'll see more. Still doesn't make it right. Kushchai's just throwing away lives." Finn took a pull on his cigar and then let the smoke come out between his teeth. He picked up a card and scowled at it.

"Though I'm more worried about how they got through the titanopters. That was someone seasoned enough to know about those beasts. Most city folk haven't got a clue. And they still attacked us, even knowing we outclassed them by a mile." He flicked a card onto the discard pile.

Wren picked up another card and put it in her hand.

"Yeah, something doesn't add up," Loren said as he picked up a card. "He didn't need to be a genius to know we'd blast him to Valhalla. Why'd he still attack?"

"Maybe someone offered a possession deal to one of Rhamnus's lieutenants," Wren mused.

Finn picked up a card and discarded it, his face impassive as he took another draw on his cigar.

"Give a man a good enough reason to fight a rocksaber, and he'll die trying." Loren scratched absently at the long, thick scar running down the length of his arm. It disappeared under the neatly folded cuff. The other end of the scar peeked out of the collar of his shirt, ending at his chin.

Wren had asked him about the scar and the rocksaber who'd given it to him, but like the rest of his life in Duat, Loren had refused to talk about it.

"Wren? Your turn," Finn said.

"Oh." She picked up a card.

Loren picked up a card, then laid out a flush. Each worn card bore a number and a tiny icon in the shape of a hand forming a sign with most fingers curled into an O and the pointer finger straight up. Delta suit.

After picking up his final card, Finn shrugged and put down a high lord and two city lords. Their delicate gray faces leered up from the table. At some point, someone had used a pen to dress up the lords with monocles, mustachios, and top hats. Loren looked eagerly at Wren.

Wren picked up a card, smiled, and laid out her hand: the Alpha suit, from its high lord down to the seven. A clenched fist was inked in blood red on the corner of each card.

Loren raised an eyebrow and blew smoke out through his nostrils, then tossed his hand on the table. "I can't play with you. You're too good."

Finn chuckled. "It's because she learned it from me. You never win against me either."

Loren rolled his eyes and sat back.

Wren nudged him playfully on the arm. "You should get Brand to play a hand. I doubt he's ever played Pharmakon's Gin."

"How do you figure?" Loren asked. Finn tossed his cards into the middle. Wren collected them to shuffle.

"He came from Darnan, dressed in fine linens," Wren said. "Any mention of pharmakons is outlawed in the cities, but especially in Darnan and Valin. He probably rubbed shoulders with all the kashmari lords there, and they wouldn't play a game that Fafnir punishes with death."

"Maybe I'll ask him tomorrow." Loren still seemed hesitant.

"You don't even trust him enough to play a card game with him?" Wren asked, eyebrows raised.

Loren watched as Wren began to shuffle. "I know you both think I'm crazy and suspicious, but just answer me this: why would a man who's rich and probably famous end up out here shoved under a Shambler like a piece of scrap?"

"Don't deal me in. I've got to go do some reading." Finn put out his cigar and stood. "Kashmari don't take the trouble to travel two hours outside the city to beat up their trash. Brand made someone very important very mad—someone vengeful. I'll help anyone who can make a kashmari that mad. So would you." He rapped his knuckles on the table, then pointed at Loren.

The Duati tapped his cigar on the ashtray. "I would, if that's the case. I'm not convinced, though. He seems too…rich, I guess. Too polished. Too kashmari."

Wren remembered what Brand had told her about his kashmari lover and stayed silent.

"Speaking of kashmari," Loren said with a chuckle, "I'll never figure out how a man like you ends up working for one of them. You hate them more than any man alive."

Finn shrugged. "You already know. Like I told Brand, Sahure and I have an understanding."

"You trust him to honor it?"

Finn paused in the doorway and turned back to look at the younger man. "He's the one that has to worry about me keeping my end of the bargain, not the other way around. Without me, he's just another of Fafnir's peons."

And he left.

Loren put out his cigar. "I don't like that one bit either," he muttered. He stood turned back to Wren as though about to say something. Her pulse quickened. But then he seemed to change his mind. His shoulders sagged a little as he disappeared down the hallway. Wren slumped back down in her chair, wondering what he'd been about to say.

A moment later, the gunslinger returned with a cleaning kit and the two rifles he and Brand had used earlier.

"That's my cue," Wren said, wrinkling her nose as Loren opened a bottle of cleaning solution. She stood and set the deck of cards on a shelf.

"Night," the gunslinger said.

"Night," the linguist replied with a smile that prompted a blush from the gunslinger.

As she walked toward the bunks, Wren heard Loren whistling behind her.

* * *

24 September 1062 P.E.
Oculus Theatre, Darnan

Kushchai had the highest balcony of the Oculus Theater all to himself. Laughter chased the actors' shouts around the ring of balconies overlooking the stage. From where he sat, Kushchai could pick out several of the other city lords lounging on the tiers below him. On the floor of the theater, lesser kashmari nobles stood in front of the little wooden stage. A breeze from the open circle of sky over the theater cooled Kushchai's brow and brought with it the scent of rain.

Wine glass forgotten in one hand, Kushchai gazed down at the stage below him at the human actors performing the third drama of *Prometheus.* Tonight they performed only for the kashmari; tomorrow, they'd do it all again for the human city council and those rich enough to purchase a seat.

Kushchai had seen this play a thousand times, and though he enjoyed it, his mind drifted away to the article in the newspaper spread across his lap about the rising price of coal in response to a shortage from Navar. Scorch that blasted woman. She'd lost Navar to him just in time for her powder keg to go off in his face.

A kashmari lieutenant stepped up beside Kushchai's chair. Kushchai folded the newspaper neatly.

"What is it, Kherty?"

"Bad news from one of your Stalker crews, m'lord," the lieutenant said. Kherty had served Kushchai for many years now, albeit unwillingly. He clasped his navy blue hands behind his stiff back.

"Yes?"

"They ran across the debris from a destroyed Stalker, another one of yours. It looked as though it had exploded from the inside."

"Some kind of malfunction, perhaps?"

Kherty shook his head. "They found the remains of a Hunter tank shell. The caliber is consistent with the main gun of a Venator-class trawler."

"That doesn't make any sense," Kushchai said. "Mirane is the only other kashmari wealthy enough to afford anything larger than a Stalker, and she would have sent her trawlers straight from Navar."

He drained his glass of wine and stared down at the actors. Their voices rose and fell like the sweet notes of a lute, but the city lord didn't hear them.

"Someone else is a contender in this game," Kushchai murmured. He turned back to his lieutenant. "No matter. I still have four other Stalkers out there to clear the way for the *Dauntless*. Rhamnus can deal with this newcomer when it arrives at the wreck."

Kushchai settled back into his chair.

"What are they performing next week?" he demanded.

"I believe it is a new play by the esteemed Polranan," Kherty said. "He calls it, 'Seven Extraordinary Feats of Passion and Riches.'"

"Sounds dull. Though I suppose not everyone can be as entertaining as the Greeks."

"You'll be expected to attend."

"Unfortunately." Kushchai turned his attention back to the play and dismissed the lieutenant.

Darkness

25 September 1062 P.E.
Deadman's Pass, Barren Mountains

The next day, Brand watched the mountainous terrain roll by outside the kitchen window. They'd spent the better part of the day traversing a wide mountain valley, and now were making their way through another pass that drew them higher and deeper into the mountains.

To his left, Finn sat reading his dvergen book while Wren pored over her books and notes. When Brand had asked her earlier what she did to fend off boredom on long journeys, Wren had answered that she enjoyed drawing. Indeed, a sketch of Anthea sleeping on a piece of torn-out notebook paper peeked out from under her dictionary.

From where he sat, Brand could see Loren in the pilot's chair in the cockpit, black boots propped up on the main console, hat over his face, arms crossed. As near as the gladiator could tell, Loren spent most of his time on the *Polaris* glaring at Brand, sleeping, or playing cards.

Brand hunched over the little drone and carefully screwed the last few panels back into place. It was still a bit battle-scarred from its run-in with the titanopters, but now it could fly again.

"Give it a go, Marie," Brand said.

The little drone lifted smoothly off the table, then buzzed out of the kitchen area.

"Many thanks, Brand," Marie said.

Brand's thoughts turned to the bag of silverleaf nightshade stuffed at the foot of his bunk. Out here, he had no tools or distillery and was missing most of the other ingredients that he needed for any of his elixirs. Even if he could scrounge up the ingredients, combining them improperly would be fatal even for a seasoned pharmakon. He sighed and set that thought aside for the moment.

"Is there anything I can do to help?" Brand asked Wren.

She stretched and rubbed her eyes. "Not unless you can read dvergen runes."

"He can learn," Finn said without looking up from his book. "Would be handy if he's going to be helping us."

"Loren hasn't learned to read runes," Wren pointed out. "They are rather difficult to master."

Finn chuckled softly. "I don't buy his 'dumb Duati' routine. I think he knows more than he lets on. He just doesn't want to get roped into all this bookwork."

Brand glanced at the gunslinger and saw Loren's cheek bunch up ever so slightly under the brim of his hat.

Wren shrugged and pushed the dictionary over to Brand, flipping to the beginning of the book where a handy alphabet had been written next to a column of dvergen runes in Wren's precise handwriting.

Brand glanced between Finn and Wren, an idea forming in his mind.

Me'von groaned. <You don't trust me?>

<You're seriously asking me that?> Brand cleared his throat. "Finn, can I have a word with you?"

The scavenger nodded and led Brand down the hall into the bunk room. "What can I do for you?"

"I know who Wren is," Brand said.

Finn held up his hands. "She left that life behind, Brand."

"Willingly?"

"You think I kidnapped her?" Finn's lip curled up.

"Her father sent out a search party for her."

"Yeah, I know. I was part of it. We didn't find her. I didn't find her until much later because she'd been holed up in…a house of ill repute." The old scavenger ran his fingers through his thinning hair. "She begged me to stay quiet, to let her be. I couldn't do that, of course; couldn't leave her there, but I knew what her parents were like. I took her in, taught her, sent her to school, cared for her. All things her reprobate parents ought to have done."

Brand could sense Me'von's unspoken gloat. He nodded slowly.

"I figured it was something like that," Brand said. "Just wanted to make sure."

Finn's brow furrowed, but he nodded and returned to the kitchen. Brand followed.

The gladiator spent the next hour memorizing the sounds associated with each rune and then trying to sound out other words in the dictionary. Another hour later, he pinched the bridge of his nose and rubbed his temples.

"I think I've had enough of that for now," Brand muttered, nudging the dictionary back over to Wren. She absentmindedly pulled it towards her and started flicking through the pages.

Brand stood and limped over to the lockers, pulled out his armor, some oil, and a rag, and sat on the bench with a heavy thud. He poured a little of the golden liquid onto his rag and then gently rubbed it into the leather of the chest piece.

"Brand?" Marie said through the grate by his shoulder.

"Yes?"

"Do you have a family?"

The gladiator paused. "Why do you ask?"

"I have been thinking about how the other A.I.s out there are somewhat like my family," Marie said in her cool, calculating voice as though she were talking about the weather. "I wonder what they are like. If I met them, would I like them?"

Brand could feel Me'von's surprise.

<Why does she care? She's a machine.>

Brand relayed the question to Marie.

"I am a machine, but I am capable of curiosity and I am capable of forming connections with people, even other artificial people. Now, will you tell me if you have a family?"

Brand lowered the oil-soaked rag and chest piece, mulling over the

A.I.'s words. He thought back to Alastair, William, Mrs. James, and then to the mother and father he'd never known. He thought of the empty space in his heart that Mirane had somehow filled with what he'd thought was her love. He thought of the child who would never be more than a hope and a dream.

Anger built in his chest, threatening to suffocate him; but he stamped it down. There wasn't anything he could do to Fafnir from here.

"Yes, and no. I…I have had people for whom I care and who care about me. I've been an orphan for as long as I can remember, though."

"Ah. So, you are like me."

Brand resumed his work, breathing in the warm earthy musk of the oil as he rubbed it over the leather and around the metal plates sewn into the front of the chest piece.

"Yeah, I suppose we are."

"These people who care about you—do you think of them as family, even though they are not your blood relatives?"

Brand smiled sadly. "Yes."

"Hm. Then I will choose to think of the crew of the *Polaris* as my family, then."

"That's a good choice," Brand said, dripping a little more oil on the leather. "They're good people."

A sound near the kitchen doorway made Brand look up. Loren was standing there, arms crossed over his chest, ice-blue eyes fixated on Brand.

"Still keeping an eye on me?" Brand asked, bemused.

"Always," the gunslinger replied.

Loren pulled off his own black armor and sat beside Brand to clean and oil it. They worked in silence.

By the time Brand finished, he could hear Finn humming to himself as the old scavenger cooked. Whatever it was didn't smell appetizing, but Brand's stomach growled anyway.

"Dinner," Finn called.

Brand could feel Loren's eyes on his back as he moved into the kitchen.

<I feel like that one knows I'm here,> Me'von said. <I don't like him.>

<If he knew you were in my head, I'd be full of bullets. We're fine.>

<All the same, I wish there was some way to throw him off the scent.

He's bound to figure it out eventually with how close an eye he's keeping on you.>

<Stop worrying,> Brand thought as he sat at the table and smiled at the others. He felt the little zerda's warm weight settle on his feet. <There's no way for him to tell you're here.>

* * *

That night, Brand woke with a start as the *Polaris* lurched beneath him. The zerda dug its claws into Brand's shirt and his skin underneath. Brand cried out in pain, lurched forward to a sitting position, and smacked his head on the bulkhead. He swore. The zerda looked up at the gladiator with what looked to him like a sheepish grin.

Brand rolled his eyes, detached the furry beast from his chest, and settled her onto the bed. Then he gingerly lowered himself from the berth. His knees, as usual, felt like they hadn't been used in a century, and his back seemed as stiff as though he had steel rods implanted under the skin. He twisted his torso and picked his knees up a few times to stretch out the muscles.

Brand glanced out the tiny porthole at the end of the bunk room. It was pitch dark outside. He took another moment to massage his stiff knees, then stepped forward. He grunted at the stab of pain that shot through his thigh. With a grimace, he leaned over and tightened the leg brace's leather straps before carefully taking another step. No pain. Satisfied, he headed out of the bunk room.

As he limped down the hall to the cockpit, the *Polaris* lurched again. Brand hit the wall, bounced, and hit the other wall. Even braced, the impact was too much for his leg, which crumpled underneath him. He instinctively threw out his bad arm to break his fall, but that crumpled under him as well, sending him down to the deck. His cheekbone and forehead smashed into the hard metal. He swore again, his sour mood deepening.

<This is getting annoying.> Me'von grumbled. <Might be safer just to stay down on the floor.>

Brand grunted as he shoved himself to a sitting position once more. "That felt like a cannon shell hitting us."

<That wasn't a gun. Something rammed us.>

Brand reached up and grabbed a copper pipe and gave it a tug. It held. He then used it to haul his large frame up onto his feet.

He managed to stumble to the cockpit before the *Polaris* rocked again, sending Brand flying into Loren, who cursed and shoved the gladiator off with some difficulty.

"What keeps hitting us?" Brand growled.

Loren jabbed a finger at something outside the viewport. The *Polaris's* brilliant external flood lights illuminated a barren landscape broken by jagged rocky outcroppings.

"I don't see any—"

Then one of the piles of rocks moved.

Looking more closely, Brand realized that what he'd thought was a pile of boulders was actually an enormous leathery creature the same color as the reddish rock that filled the valley. The behemoth was covered in thick armored plates, and a frill of hardened bone jutted up behind its head. Long, curved rust-red tusks swooped down from the heavy jaw of its low-slung head.

There were dozens of the behemoths, Brand realized, all clustered around the *Polaris*. One of them must have bumped into the vehicle as they passed by.

"Stonehorns," Finn said. "Clumsy, stupid. We just have to get through them without—"

Just then, a thundering bellow of alarm shook the deck beneath Brand's feet and the entire mass surged forward, transforming into a stampeding herd of leathery boulders. Brand turned just in time to see one of the behemoths careening toward the *Polaris*. It was nearly the size of the Venator, and heavier. It crashed its titanic body into the *Polaris* with enough force to lift the vehicle off its feet for a split second. Then the trawler came crashing down to the rock—hard.

The impact rattled Brand's bad leg. He gritted his teeth.

"Can't we just let them pass?" Brand yelled. His deep voice barely cut through the deafening thunder of the stampede.

"Why do you think they're stampeding, genius?" Loren snapped. "They're not running from us—They're running from the thing that eats them. Imagine what kind of teeth and claws are needed to pierce that hide. Now imagine what they would do to this tin can."

From the pilot's seat, Finn yelled, "Marie, can you give me any more speed?"

"No, I cannot." Her voice came from a grate beside the main console. Brand had to strain to hear her gentle voice. "Our top speed has been reduced due to a misaligned hip joint that was bent when the first stonehorn slammed into us."

"Slag it," Finn swore as he pulled back on a lever. The *Polaris* slowed, then halted. The last of the beasts passed as Finn turned the trawler around. The deafening thunder was replaced by a shrill ringing in Brand's ears.

"Shut everything down, then go to standby mode," Finn commanded Marie in a whisper. "Kill the lights."

A blinking light on the command console flashed the AI's acknowledgment. Then the floodlights and the console went dark, plunging the crew into a lightless void.

In seconds, the frigid desert night began to suck the warmth from the trawler. Metal joints popped and creaked as they cooled. Brand shivered. Cold, blind, deaf, cut off from his crewmates by the sucking emptiness that engulfed him. He gripped the railing beside him, a tenuous but reassuring anchor to reality.

As his eyes slowly adjusted to the gloom of a moonless night, Brand could just make out the ghostly outline of something moving out beyond the viewport. He squinted, trying to will his eyes to focus.

The spectral images moved out of sight. Brand strained his ears to hear any footfalls, but heard nothing other than his own breathing. He waited.

They must be gone now, Brand thought.

Then several creatures hove into view, striding on stilt-like legs. Each stood twice the height of a stonehorn. They stood nearly upright, using their impossibly long arms as canes to steady themselves. At the elbow, each limb split into two appendages that each ended in five enormous claws. Hairless skin as pale white and smooth as bleached rubber covered their bodies and faces—strange faces without eyes or noses, only great arching horns.

It was the same kind of monster that had pinned the *Dauntless* to the desert floor outside of Darnan.

<What is it?> Brand asked silently.

<Omegalids, after the shape of their horns,> Me'von said, his own

voice quiet as though the kashmari thought the monster would hear him too. <They're native to Duat, but a certain rebel kashmari brought a breeding pair up here a few hundred years ago. Since then, they've spread all over the world. The caves and caverns that pocket the desert floor are perfect hiding places for them to spend daylight hours when the sun would otherwise scorch their delicate skin.>

The omegalids moved slowly as though striding through deep water, but their great height carried them forward quickly nonetheless. They began to circle the damaged trawler.

One of the creatures loped through the gloom to a shadowy form that Brand realized was an exhausted stonehorn about the size of the *Dauntless*. Its leathery skin was wrinkled like an unmade bed and hung off the behemoth's old bones like a quilt on an empty bedframe. The infirm elder, abandoned by the herd, moaned, eyes rolling at the sight of the predator.

The monster used a clawed hand to grab the armored stonehorn by the back of its neck right behind the bony crest. The stonehorn thrashed in its grip. One of its long tusks hooked around the leg of the white monster, but the omegalid pressed down, snapping the stonehorn's neck. The stonehorn twitched, then went still.

The other four monsters circled the *Polaris*, inspecting it cautiously.

"What's the plan?" Brand asked.

"Hush!" Finn, Loren, and Wren chorused in a combined hoarse whisper, wide eyes fixated on the creatures outside.

Wren inched over to Brand and put her mouth right next to his ear so that her breath warmed his skin.

"They hunt by sound," Wren breathed.

The entire crew stood stock still, breathing as quietly as they could, eyes following the long white legs as the monsters circled.

Brand slowly became aware of a low, haunting sound. It was a familiar sound; he'd first heard it when he'd been nailed to the granite slab, just before Fafnir had arrived. It sounded like the wind moving through a set of wooden pipes he'd seen once at Alastair's shop. The old shopkeeper had bought them off a trader who'd recently returned from an Apida village; that sound had been much higher, though. This sound was so low that Brand could feel it thrumming and pulsating in his bones. It filled his head, notes that together formed disjointed disharmonies that set his teeth on edge and filled him with dread. It took him a moment to realize that the sound was coming from the omegalids outside.

It was such a different sound than the hum made by the other omegalid that had attacked the *Dauntless.* Instead of a subsonic war rumble that shook the earth, this sounded more like the mournful calls of the dead that were said to haunt the Cairn Marshes east of Darnan.

<It's a hunting call,> Me'von whispered, entranced. <They're trying to flush you out.>

The sound shifted to a soft buzz. As they circled, it shifted once more to a haunting, ominous low rumble. The decking below Brand's feet shook. Stinging cold sweat dripped into his eyes. Brand swallowed hard and tried to keep his breath steady.

One of the omegalids' legs nudged the *Polaris,* causing it to jolt beneath their feet and making them all stumble. Loren and Wren steadied themselves on the bulkhead. Brand fell to his knees with a clank of the brace. The omegalid froze. After a long moment, it lowered its head so that it was level with the viewport. Brand could see the white rubbery skin stretched over empty sockets and dagger-like teeth in its gaping mouth. It turned its head and pressed a bat-like ear up against the viewport.

Everyone held their breath.

<It can hear your heart,> Me'von said, his taunting, leering voice making Brand's skin crawl.

Brand became horribly aware that his heart was indeed pounding furiously.

The monster bumped the *Polaris* again, as though testing to see if it would make the same sound again. Brand bit back a grunt as his thigh hit the bulkhead. But as before, the monster wasn't fooled. Its great skull head snapped to face the viewport. It opened its mouth and let loose the same horrific war scream Brand had heard when the *Dauntless* had been attacked. Though this time, he was so close to the omegalid that the scream deafened him. He felt rather than heard the echoing screams of the monster's companions.

Terror ripped through Brand with the force of a sandstorm, stripping him of all thought. He needed to run. Now.

But before his instincts could set his feet in motion, Brand sensed Me'von...pulling...on the omegalid somehow. Sucking at it. Draining it. The humming came to an abrupt halt.

The monster pulled back from the *Polaris*, then staggered. It tripped over its long limbs, fell backwards with a ground-shaking thud, then began to thrash. Dust flew up in a cloud, partially obscuring the monster. The thrashing gradually slowed, and with a last violent twitch, stopped. The dust settled, revealing a crumpled, twisted mess of skeletal limbs at the feet of the Venator.

Brand was shaking.

<What did you just do?> he asked, though after seeing Kushchai do the same thing, he already knew. He glanced down at his hands. Horrified, he watched the same strange inky darkness curl up his arms and seep into his chest. No one else seemed to notice anything.

The darkness inside Brand felt…wrong. It felt like holding onto a man's throat, feeling the pulse beat through his arteries, slower and slower, as Brand throttled the life out of him…and loving it.

It felt like eating, but never being satiated; like lusting for a woman's touch, but never being satisfied with the woman in his arms.

Most of all, it felt like wanting, needing, lusting after blood—not just the blood, but the killing…but it could never be enough, no matter how many lives he took.

Sickened, Brand didn't notice that Me'von had taken control over Brand's body until the kashmari had backed the gladiator out of the cockpit.

<No! What have you done? Stop!> Brand's screams went unheeded.

Brand fought to regain control, but empowered as the kashmari was by the strange darkness, Me'von was too strong. The kashmari steered Brand down the hallway to the hatch and up to the outer hull of the trawler. Brand's leg burned as Me'von forced him to climb upwards.

<What are you doing?> Brand yelled, locked in his own head.

Not answering, Me'von opened the hatch with a clang and vaulted out. He then turned to the remaining four monsters. Even standing atop the *Polaris*, Brand felt like a tiny insect beside these giants.

Me'von raised Brand's hands and stretched them out toward the empty face of one of the omegalids.

Brand could feel Me'von using the darkness from the first monster's death in order to pierce the mind of the second. As he watched helplessly, tendrils of darkness snaked toward the monster and pierced its temples. Through this inky connection, Brand felt Me'von grab hold of its thoughts and start molding and twisting them until its worst fears writhed to the surface of its consciousness.

Fear of the sun, the blistering heat on its skin; fear of the kashmari; fear at the sight of its dead kin lying at the feet of the *Polaris*. Me'von twisted these fears into an image of the omegalid lying alone at Brand's feet in the scorching daylight, its skin charring. And then Me'von pushed the image onto the omegalid's mind until it filled its consciousness and became its reality.

The monster bent over double, and its limbs curled into unnatural angles. Then it screamed.

It was an unearthly scream that tore at Brand's soul and made his hair stand on end, the scream of the death of mountains. It rattled around in his head and made his chest throb.

The memory of Kushchai twisting Brand's own perception of reality blazed forth, igniting a white-hot fury in Brand.

<You're torturing it!> Brand screamed.

The other three omegalids cringed away from their companion, then turned and scrambled away at a long-legged sprint that carried them far and fast away from the kashmari demon.

The tendrils linking Brand to the monster on the ground wound tighter and tighter around its pale, crumpled form. It let out a moan as it shuddered, over and over again, locked in its own horror-filled mind.

<Let it go!> Brand yelled.

Me'von's response was a laugh that started low and rose into a harsh chuckle that was filled with a perverse joy at the suffering of this creature. The laugh went on and on. Me'von was enjoying this torture. Brand could sense the kashmari's glee, the addiction, the desperation. It chilled Brand to the bone.

<I said let it go!>

Brand somehow grabbed a hold of this strange life force magic that Me'von had harnessed. Unlike his own spark, this dark force made him sick to touch it. He visualized it in his chest, held it, and then imagined forcing it out through his fingertips. To his surprise and relief, flecks of darkness exploded from his fingertips and dissipated out into the night air, leaving Brand feeling hollow and silent.

After a long moment, the omegalid stood on trembling limbs and stumbled away into the darkness.

Me'von slowly relinquished control of Brand's body.

Below Brand, Loren's pale head appeared.

"Are you mad? What are you doing up there?"

Brand didn't dare speak for fear that the fury coursing through him would make him lash out at his innocent friend. He squeezed his eyes shut tight.

"Brand? Are you ok?" Loren asked, his voice tinged with worry.

Brand crouched down gradually so as to not collapse on his aching leg, then let himself back into the trawler.

Loren spun the gladiator around so that Brand was facing him. The gunslinger peered into the bigger man's face.

"Brand? Talk to me. What's wrong?"

Everything, he wanted to say. He was shivering, but not only from the cold desert night air. His leg burned, and he felt like he was going to be sick. He placed a steadying hand on the bulkhead and shut his eyes again.

Brand wanted the kashmari out of his head. He wanted to crawl into a hole and never come out. He wanted to stop being a pharmakon so he could get slobbering drunk.

Boots clanged on the metal deck as the others rushed in.

"What were you thinking?" Wren admonished. "Oh, he's shivering. Loren, get him a blanket, will you?"

Brand opened his eyes and waved off the proffered blanket. He muttered, "I'm fine. I just need a minute."

"Why did you go out there?" Wren said, her face creased with worry.

Brand cleared his throat. "I thought maybe I'd be able to see where they'd gone from up there." His voice wavered. "Just in case they came back."

"I've never seen anything like it," Loren said, fingers nervously clipping and unclipping the holster of his revolver. "The one just…just died. And the other one had some sort of seizure…And the others ran off." He ran the long fingers of his other hand through his pale hair. "Omegalids don't just run off…"

Finn, standing a few steps away from the others, had his arms across his chest. His brow was deeply furrowed and his eyes were locked on Brand, who was shaking uncontrollably.

"I have seen it before," the grizzled scavenger growled. He uncrossed his arms, charged forward, and with a powerful shove, pinned Brand against the bulkhead. "That's how kashmari torture and kill."

He slammed Brand against the bulkhead. The muzzle of Finn's pistol pressed against Brand's temple. "I won't have kashmari scum on my crew!"

"I'm not a kashmari," Brand said through chattering teeth. His voice shook. He clamped his teeth together, but his jaw muscles still trembled.

"Oh yeah? And how exactly am I supposed to believe that pile of lies after what I just saw?"

Still furious and in shock, Brand lashed out at the kashmari cowering in the corner of his mind. To Me'von, he snarled, <I am not going down because of you, you sick psychopath.>

Me'von cringed.

Brand took a long, slow, steadying breath. And then another. By the third breath, the shaking had abated. His mind cleared somewhat.

Finn hadn't moved. He was watching Brand, teeth bared, pistol still biting into his skin. But the scavenger was waiting. He *wanted* Brand to prove him wrong. An idea began to take shape in Brand's mind. It wasn't a great idea, but it was all he had.

With his hands up, Brand said, "I just need something out of my boot, and then I can prove it."

Instead, he just looked pleadingly to Finn. The shorter man's mouth was set in a harsh line, and his hands still pressed painfully against Brand's collarbone.

Then Finn nodded to Loren. A click by his ear told him that the gunslinger had cocked his revolver and aimed it at Brand's head. Brand didn't dare move a muscle. Finn then let go and crouched. He bent over and pulled the vials out of Brand's boot.

The scavenger's blue eyes went wide. Brand couldn't help but be a little shocked that Finn even knew what they were, but it gave him confidence that this might work after all. Finn handed Brand the vials.

Glancing down, Brand uncorked the vial of Time elixir and swallowed its sludge-like contents. He immediately felt cold rush through his body, like ice in his veins. His blood turned black, the veins throughout his body standing out as dark as night; even the sclera of his eyes turned black, making his amber irises blaze like golden flames on a dark night.

Me'von began to scream in pain, but Brand ignored the kashmari.

Loren's revolver went off, belching acrid smoke; but the bullet seemed to hang almost motionless in the air at the mouth of the barrel. Brand dodged out of the way, then plucked the weapon out of the gunslinger's hand. He then gritted his teeth and ran into the cockpit, every step sending a jolt of pain through his thighbone. He dropped the gun on the copilot's chair.

Brand reached down to a little compartment and pulled out the acrostic ring he'd noticed Finn with earlier. He then trotted back to the base of the ladder where Finn and Loren stood like statues.

The Time potion faded. Brand's blood returned to normal, the black spidery veins faded from view, and time resumed its usual pace.

Me'von's scream faded, leaving behind a massive headache that made Brand wince. The kashmari was now a seething knot of hatred and fear and guilt in the corner of Brand's mind. Still unsettled, the gladiator turned his thoughts aside. He could worry about Me'von later.

Finn caught sight of Brand off to his left and jumped. He swore.

Brand handed the acrostic ring to Finn. The old scavenger glanced at the cockpit, the only place this ring could have come from. He stared at Brand and back to the cockpit, stunned by Brand's enhanced speed.

"You're a pharmakon," Finn breathed.

Brand nodded. "If you know anything about pharmakons, you'll know that kashmari can't abide our powers. If I were a kashmari in disguise, I wouldn't have been able to do that."

Loren's mouth was still agape as he stared at his empty gun hand, still raised and curled around thin air.

"Oh, your gun is on the copilot's chair," Brand said.

Just then, the interior of the *Polaris* swam before Brand's eyes. He sank to the floor, dizzy, holding his aching head. Loren said something, but the gladiator didn't hear him. He blinked several times and the trawler's deck steadied.

"I need to lie down again," Brand mumbled. "That took a lot out of..."

He didn't even feel it when his head hit the bare metal deck.

* * *

Finn and Loren grimaced as Brand thudded to the deck.

"I'm not entirely clear on one thing," the gunslinger drawled, his confusion and shock stripping away his cultivated accent and revealing his Duati roots. "Did Brand kill that omegalid?"

Finn scratched his beard thoughtfully. "He must have. How else could it have died? You said so yourself that never happens."

"It doesn't. Nothing that I know of can kill those tanks above ground. I'm not even sure they die of old age."

The scavenger regarded the prone gladiator with awe. "If this is what happens every time he uses his powers, though, it might be more trouble than it's worth."

Wren spoke up as she folded up the blanket Loren had offered Brand. "Well, we're alive, aren't we? That's worth something."

Finn nodded in agreement. "Don't get me wrong; I'm glad we're alive. I'm glad he saved us. But what happens when he uses his powers to get us out of a snarl and then is flat on his back when we really need him?"

Loren shrugged. "Make sure he only uses them when we're about to die, I suppose. As far as we know, that's what he's been doing already. I mean, you've never seen him use them before today, have you?"

"A better question is whether I'd be able to recognize it if he did."

Wren put the blanket back in its locker, then turned to the two men. "Are you two going to leave him there all night while you jabber on for hours?"

The three of them looked down at the man who had just saved their lives, crumpled on the floor, bad leg twisted at an odd angle.

"Right," Finn mumbled, a little abashed. "You grab that arm."

Loren and Finn wrestled the big gladiator into the bunk room. Loren eyed the gladiator's bunk.

"I'm not lifting him up there again. I'm still sore from the first time."

Finn grunted. "He's not just tall; the man's dense as a rock. Physically, that is." The scavenger rubbed tired eyes. "Let's put him on mine."

The two men hauled the big man up onto the lower bed. Panting, Finn sat on the edge of the opposite bunk to catch his breath. It was then that he caught sight of a striped and spotted zerda watching him attentively from Loren's sock drawer.

"Why hello there," the scavenger said to the little creature. Loren looked around to see who Finn was talking to.

"Hah! I'd wondered why my socks were suddenly covered in hair."

The little fox-like zerda was glancing at Brand, ears quivering.

"You followed him home, did you?" Finn pointed at Brand. The zerda chirped but didn't move. Instead, she eyed Loren. Finn waved for the gunslinger to take a few steps away from Brand's unconscious form. The little zerda hopped out of the sock drawer and sprinted over to Brand's prone body, jumped up, and crouched protectively over the gladiator's chest.

Wren spoke from the doorway. "Brand was feeding it at the village."

Finn said, "Ah, that'll do it. Well, zerdas are supposed to be good luck, so I suppose you can stay, little one."

Finn stood and walked to the cockpit, where he flicked a series of switches and pressed a button. The command console hummed to life once more. A moment later, Marie's gentle voice said, "Hello, Finn."

Finn flopped into the pilot's chair while Loren took the copilot's chair beside him. "Nice to have you back, Marie. Run a complete diagnostic and get us back on track, will you?"

"Affirmative. What did I miss while I was asleep?"

"Well, Brand is a pharmakon." Finn chuckled and turned his chair to face Loren. "I didn't see that coming. So do you trust him now?"

The gunslinger nodded slowly. "Yeah, I guess I have to, right?"

"No, you don't have to."

Loren frowned. "So he can't be a pharmakon and a kashmari at the same time, right?"

Finn nodded. "It's like light and dark. When you light a candle darkness recedes. Kashmari can't abide the light."

"Definitely is a point in his favor then." Loren thought for a moment. "Pharmakons are…magical?"

Finn nodded. "A pharmakon is a person who has some innate magic in them, and they use special elixirs to enhance their abilities."

"Are they related to dvergen? They were magical, weren't they?"

Finn scrunched his face up, trying to remember. "Yeah, they were. I think pharmakons may be their human descendants…or something." He frowned. "Dvergen were pretty short, though, and Brand is anything but."

Loren picked up his revolver off the copilot's chair and popped the cylinder out, then spun it closed and replaced the gun in its holster. "How do you know so much about pharmakons?"

Finn sighed. "My older half-brother was one. The last one, they said." He glanced down the hall. "I wonder if Brand knew him. He would have been just a boy…"

"Did the kashmari get him?"

Finn nodded. His expression grew distant. "Fafnir paraded his body through the streets until it had rotted off the pike they'd skewered him with."

Loren's face went pale. "That's…abominable."

Finn smiled weakly. "It's been so long, but it feels like yesterday."

Loren looked down at his long, thin hands. "That's why you hate them? The kashmari?"

Finn turned the acrostic ring over in his fingers. "That's why I hate Fafnir."

The two men sat in silence for a long while. Finally, Loren spoke.

"Do you think Brand was beat up and left in the desert because he's a pharmakon?"

Finn shook his head. "No. If they'd found out he was a pharmakon, he'd be dead before he knew he'd been found out. It was probably something minor, like bringing the lord the wrong kind of cheese."

Wren stepped into the cockpit. "You guys should try talking to people instead of guessing and gossiping."

Loren snorted. "Like he'd tell any of us why a kashmari has it in for him."

Wren smirked. "He told me."

"What?" Loren exchanged a surprised glance with Finn. "What did he say?"

Wren said, "He said he fell in love with a kashmari woman. It didn't go so well."

The two men sat stunned for a moment, envisioning the grizzled and scarred gladiator in the arms of a waiflike kashmari woman.

Finn laughed. "The ruffian bedded a kashmari and lived to tell the tale. That man's got guts, that's for sure." He scratched at his beard. "A pharmakon on board…"

"That could come in handy." Loren idly unclipped and clipped his hip holster.

Finn watched Wren's eyes linger on Loren's fingers as the gunslinger fiddled with his holster. "You don't like that he's a pharmakon?"

"Makes me worry," Loren admitted. "We're complicit now. What if Sahure finds out? We have to make sure he keeps it under wraps; otherwise, we're all dead."

Finn pulled out his book and propped his feet up on the console.

"You don't seem worried," Loren said to the chief. "The kashmari killed your brother. They'll do the same to Brand if they get the chance.

"You don't have to remind me," Finn growled. Loren opened his mouth to apologize, but Finn softened his expression and he shook his head. "No, I'm not worried about Brand. He's still alive, and not young, either. He knows how to keep it a secret."

"Then we need to figure out how to use his abilities," Loren said.

Wren said, "Maybe he can help us when we find the *Muspell's Sons.*"

Finn held up his hands to slow down the younger two. "Like I was saying earlier, we shouldn't get too excited about it. Seems to come with a serious drawback, and in the end, it's just another tool. Just because you have a gun doesn't mean you'll win a duel. You have to know how to use it, how to strategize. Does Brand even know how to use his abilities to fight anything other than other gladiators? Sure, he's got reason to hate the kashmari, same as the rest of us. But will he fight them? Is that even what he wants? Who knows? He slept with one of them, for scorching's sake. Right now, it seems like he's just lost. Still, I never thought I'd ever meet another pharmakon. That's a treat in and of itself."

He opened his book and thumbed through the pages, signaling that the conversation was over.

Wren cleared her throat a bit awkwardly. "Loren, I was wondering if you could tell me a bit more about the omegalids? You know them from Duat…"

Loren's ice-blue eyes met her brown eyes, his full of pain and hers full of questions. As always when she asked about his home, Loren's gaze dropped to his hands.

"What does it matter what they're like down there?" he said. "We're up here and so are they."

Loren clipped his holster a few more times, then stood and brushed by Wren. "Excuse me," he mumbled. He hesitated for a moment, eyes tracing the curves of Wren's face, long enough for Wren to breath in his musky, smoky smell and for Finn's fingers to stray to his own sidearm. Then, reluctantly, he left the cockpit. The older scavenger relaxed, but Wren continued to watch the gunslinger move down the hall.

"He's a hired gun, Wren," Finn said from behind her.

Wren turned and saw Finn watching her in the reflection of the viewport glass. She fell into the copilot chair Loren had just vacated.

"He's been with us for a few years now. Don't you think that's long enough to trust him?" she asked.

Finn set his book down on his lap, pages splayed to either side, and knit his fingers together behind his head.

"I trust him with our lives. I don't trust him with your heart." He held up a hand to forestall her next words, then started ticking off reasons on his fingers. "He's always poor as a mouse and has no personal effects. Anytime we stop by a town, you and I stay with the *Polaris*. He goes into town for a week. He never says what he does there besides ordering and picking up supplies. And he's a gunslinger. They're notorious for spending their time at houses of ill repute. Even caught him with lipstick on his cheek once when he came back. Trust me. That's not a man you want to get mixed up with."

Wren nodded and stared out the viewport.

Wren knew all this. Finn didn't need to tell her. But he could see how hard it was for her to resist being drawn to the gunslinger. Besides his good looks, Loren had a certain air about him that mixed charisma and mystery, a cautious friendliness broken every so often by unguarded warmth. It drew the young linguist to him like a moth to a flame.

Finn watched as she let down her brown hair, then started twisting the straight locks into a braid that wound from her temple and down across the opposite shoulder.

Loren hardly ever said anything about his previous life in Duat, and had turned away every one of her questions about the underground realm. Finn had to admit that he too wondered how an earnest young Duati had become one of the deadliest men to wander the Wastes. He knew when to leave it alone, though.

Wren sighed as she wrapped the end of the braid. She stood and walked to the kitchen where she opened her satchel and pulled out the other book she had gotten for Finn, a notebook, and a pen. She sat and continued her work, painstakingly transcribing each word and parsing out its meaning.

Finn went back to his reading.

Flashback #6: Information

25 April 1030 P.E.
Northeastern Quarter, Darnan

Brand face-planted into the rug with a floor-shuddering thud just inches from the low coffee table.

Mrs. James snapped, "Careful!" at the two sparring men. "We can't afford to replace every piece of furniture in this place!"

Brand picked himself up off the rug and shook his arm to lessen the ache from William's blow.

"Dodge and weave, Brand," William said, feinting and jabbing.

"I'm trying," Brand growled.

The fact was that Brand was a very large bull in a very tiny pen being harried by a much smaller, faster, and more experienced opponent. He took a swing at William, but the mustached man darted under Brand's arm. Using Brand's own momentum, he kicked the younger man in the rump. Brand's face skidded across the looped fibers of the carpet.

Brand didn't get up. Instead, he flipped over and stared up at the plain white ceiling. He touched his face and winced.

"Come on, get up," William said. "You can't just give up if you want to fight criminals on the street."

"Maybe this wasn't such a great idea after all," Brand grumbled.

Mrs. James made that sort of "pshaw" sound that women of a certain age make when they hear something ridiculous. "You get right back up. You were born for this; why else would you have these abilities? Good, honest people are counting on you. Now get up!"

Brand rolled his eyes and stood once more.

"You have a longer reach than I do," William said. "Use it to your advantage."

Brand sunk into a fighting stance, one leg forward and another back, both fists up, one in front of the other. This time, Brand kept an eye on William's feet. He raised his arm to block a feint, then caught the real jab, turning it aside with his forearm and pivoting forward on the ball of his forward foot to jab with his free hand at William's ribs. His fist connected and sent the smaller man staggering back several paces.

William doubled over, coughing. When he straightened, he grimaced and folded over again.

"You broke a rib, I think," he wheezed. He picked up a small vial of Healing elixir from a side table with a pretty glass lamp and upended the vial in his mouth. A moment passed, and the pain etched on his face faded. He sighed, straightened, and breathed deeply in and out a few times.

"Again."

They set up again and continued sparring for several minutes, during which Brand was mostly able to fend William off. He even managed to land another two punches. William finally motioned for a time-out.

"Much better. I think you're starting to get the hang of it."

Mrs. James spoke up. "William, you've been at this for over an hour. I think it's about time you finish for the night. Why don't I get you a nice, calming herbal tea before bed?"

Brand frowned. "It won't–"

William cut in. "That would be lovely, dear."

After Mrs. James vanished into the kitchen, William turned to a puzzled Brand. "It's the thought that counts. Let her make it."

The older pharmakon chuckled at the young man's confused expression. "You'll understand one day when you're married."

There was a knock on the door. William stepped over to it and opened it to reveal a very worried old man.

"What's going on in here?" he asked, trying to peer around William. He wrinkled his nose, causing his eyes to vanish as his face folded in on itself. Brand cocked an eyebrow, then wiped his sweaty brow. *Oh. It must stink in here,* Brand realized.

William gestured to Brand. "I'm teaching my son a sport, Mr. Fopps. Taking exercise is important for one's health, don't you think?"

"This late? I'm trying to sleep!"

William spread his hands out wide. "I do apologize. I get home from work late and this is the only time we have to practice. We just finished, though. We won't bother you anymore tonight."

The old man harrumphed. "Take it someplace else tomorrow." He left in a huff.

William closed the door, then reached over to the narrow wardrobe next to the door. He fished around in it for a moment, then pulled out the glove containing his pharmakon vials.

"You're going out?" Brand asked. "Aren't you tired?"

"That's what Stamina is for," William said. He tied a bandana around his neck to hide his face later, then pulled on the glove.

"Does Mrs. James know?"

Before William could respond, Moira came out with two cups of tea. She took in her husband's attire in a glance, pressed her lips into a line, then turned to Brand and gave him his cup. She sat stiffly on the edge of the chaise lounge and began to sip from the other cup.

William walked over to her and knelt beside her. He wrapped his hand around hers and the teacup. "I'm sorry I didn't mention it earlier."

He took the teacup from her and took a sip. A small smile tugged at the corners of her eyes.

"I need fair warning to brace myself. You know that." She shot her husband a mock glare. "I nearly die every time you go out at night."

He smiled. "I know."

William set the cup down. "I overheard something today." He glanced at the small wall clock behind her. "If I hurry, I should be able to stop…well, I can tell you later."

"You don't have to protect me from it," Brand rumbled. "That's what you're training me for."

William sighed. "You're right. I'm sorry. I'm still getting used to the idea of you wanting to participate. Even though you're taller than I am, I still see you as that little boy."

He rubbed his eyes with his ungloved hand.

"And…this mission I'm preparing for will be a little different. It's not an abused damsel or an unjust lord who needs straightening out. There's to be a prisoner transfer in the next week or two. A high-value prisoner from Navar. I gathered that Fafnir wants to torture him for information concerning the rebels."

"Rebels?"

"Kashmari who don't agree with Fafnir's style of rule and oppose him."

Brand blinked. "Good kashmari?"

William scoffed. "Hardly. Their idea of fair rule is that they sit on the throne in Valin instead of him." He gingerly adjusted his glove. "I set up a meeting with an informant who I hope with have more information about the transfer for me."

Brand's curiosity was piqued. "Any idea who the prisoner is?"

William cast a sidelong glance at the younger man. "Perhaps."

"You're going to free him, then?" Mrs. James asked.

William nodded and stood. "If I can. I may not like the rebels, but they do keep Fafnir busy from time to time. I'd rather he not gain the means to put their operation down permanently."

Brand stood as well. "Let me come with. I can help."

William put a hand on Brand's shoulder. "No, I need to keep as low a profile as possible tonight."

Mrs. James put down her cup on the side table and stood, kissing her husband lightly on the cheek.

"Be careful."

He gave her a soft smile, then gathered her in his arms and kissed her long and gently. He broke off the kiss and looked into her eyes. "Always."

* * *

5 May 1030 P.E.
Northeastern Quarter, Darnan

Brand and William stood along the wallpapered wall of an elegant sitting room arrayed with delicate chairs on spindly legs, couches decorated with intricate gold embroidery, and crystal light sconces that held expensive electric bulbs. Kashmari lords and their blue-skinned ladies chatted and smiled while sipping aperitifs.

Brand fidgeted in his suit. It was stiff and tight, and the collar scratched at his neck. Beside him stood William, standing straight and still in his own suit, white-gloved hands clasped behind his back. Their master, a rather thin kashmari with a hook nose, was a baron who owned several restaurants, lounges, and a single pub. William and Brand worked in the pub, but once a year, the baron called upon the two men to wait at these events at his manor as he had no permanent staff for his household. A wry sort of kashmari, the baron had admitted that he liked to throw a party for his betters once a year to remind them that he existed.

One of the kashmari lords beckoned and William stepped forward.

"Keep the alcohol flowing, gentlemen," the kashmari said, his tone cordial and as crisp as Brand's collar.

William executed a stiff bow and turned smartly on his heel, striding back to the table Brand stood beside.

"Mind yourself, Brand," William admonished in a low murmur.

"The laundry put too much starch in my shirt," Brand muttered as he laid out the glasses. "I'm going to crawl out of my skin."

"You'd better not. These lords are just as likely to take your head off as fire you if you displease them." William poured the brandy while Brand arranged the snifters on a silver platter that caught the light from the electric sconces and made the glasses sparkle like diamonds.

Brand picked up the platter and walked it around the room to the lords in their stiff black tails and the ladies breathing shallowly in corseted dresses that flowed behind them like shimmering silken waterfalls.

He stopped in front of a seated heavy-set gentleman with long limbs folded across his broad chest. The gentleman didn't notice Brand at first, as he was listening to one of the other lords. Brand waited patiently as he'd been taught, breathing slowly and staring at a spot of air just above the lord's head, trying to ignore the itch at his throat.

Brand couldn't help but notice that this lord didn't seem like the rest; he didn't have the usual blue skin, and his clothes were of an older style and a bit worn. *Who does this man think he is?* Brand wondered. *Probably a guest of one of the lords, a human counselor perhaps. Someone who thinks that because he got an invitation, that practically makes him one of them.*

Brand's arms were starting to ache by the time the lord noticed Brand and wordlessly took a glass. Brand continued on his round, weaving among the guests and furniture in a precise dance with William until all of the lords and ladies had had a chance to take a drink, and then returned to the side table. He set down his tray of empty glasses carefully, then attacked his collar, digging his fingernails under it as fast as he could before he turned and dropped his hands to his sides.

A beautiful woman entered just as Brand turned around. She was human, perhaps another counselor, though her deep sable face was decorated with delicate pale golden lines and circles in the same manner as some of the kashmari. She glided over to the heavy-set gentleman Brand had waited on and curtsied deeply to him.

The man only glanced at her briefly, waved his hand dismissively, then turned to speak with a kashmari lord.

The woman seemed disappointed by the dismissal, but another kashmari lord with a shock of white hair happily took her by the elbow and steered her to a cluster of laughing kashmari together.

Brand arched an eyebrow. How could any man be so dismissive of such a lovely woman? He hadn't even taken a second glance at the beauty.

Just then, the thick-set counselor turned and caught sight of Brand staring at him. Brand's stomach dropped. He lowered his eyes respectfully. In the periphery of his vision, he saw the man turn away and breathed a sigh of relief.

Brand looked back up at the beautiful female counselor. She was quite possibly the most beautiful creature Brand had ever seen, and the pink silk dress she wore accentuated her figure perfectly.

"Keep your eyes where they belong and head in the job, please," William said under his breath. The younger man jumped.

"Burning sands, man," Brand swore quietly. He shot a glare at his mentor.

William inclined his head slightly at the stunning counselor. "Lady Mirane," he said, "of Tinye, I believe."

"Lady?" Brand said, stunned. "She's a kashmari?"

"Yes." William's words were heavy with a warning that Brand did not need.

Brand didn't mind the work; he was on his feet for several hours anyway at the pub. But the party was as dull as peeling paint. At least at the pub, he heard all kinds of bizarre tales and got to break up the odd fight or two. But not here. All the lords and ladies ever talked about was politics. The young pharmakon despised politics and thus rarely paid attention to what was said. Instead, he whiled away the time by mentally picking apart a piece of machinery and putting it back together again.

Tonight, though, the piece of machinery that he'd decided upon was a sewing machine he'd seen Alastair working on that fateful day when Brand had fallen off the roof as a boy. As he turned the machine about in his mind, sadness stole over Brand. The image of the sewing machine was replaced by one of Alastair instead, with his kindly bespectacled eyes, strange stories, and thick-fingered hands that always seemed able to steer Brand out of trouble.

Brand hadn't heard from Alastair since the day he'd left with William as a boy. Where had the big shopkeeper ended up? Had he managed to escape Hessian's threats, or had Hessian arrested him for letting Brand slip away? Even if Brand could find him again, somehow, would Alastair be able to recognize the half-starved street urchin in the sturdy man Brand had become?

As Brand served the lords and ladies their coffee, the thought of Alastair nagged at his brain until it grew into fully-fledged guilt. What if the reason he hadn't heard from Alastair was that the old shopkeeper had been killed for helping Brand escape? He looked around at the gathered nobles. Every single one of them hated pharmakons. Brand was sure they wouldn't hesitate to kill an old man who'd hidden a boy with budding powers.

He had to know what had become of Alastair and make sure the old man hadn't ended up in jail or dead for Brand's sake.

Brand glanced over at William. No, he wouldn't ask William to come with. Brand could handle this himself.

Again, Brand was made to wait on the human counselor. Every kashmari lord and lady had taken their drinks promptly, but not this self-entitled lowly human. Why was he making Brand wait? The young man struggled to keep his face blank. His eyes flicked over to Lady Mirane.

Finally, the man took his drink. Brand spun but saw that William had already given the lady a drink. The older pharmakon threw his apprentice the slightest smirk.

* * *

Brand lay awake in bed for a long time that evening, listening to William and Mrs. James chatting in the other bedroom, until the light that leaked in under the door winked out. Brand waited for another half hour until he heard William's snores rattling the door.

Brand threw off the covers and crept over to a chest of drawers. From it, he pulled his leather glove carrying his elixirs and hung it from a loop on his belt. He then snuck out through the window into the warm summer air.

He hung for a moment from the windowsill, facing the breeze as it ruffled his dark hair about his ears. He heard nothing but the rustle of some nocturnal rodent nesting in the rafters.

Satisfied at the stillness embracing the apartment, Brand bunched up his muscles. He pushed off of the building, grabbed a cable strung across the gap, and used it to swing to the next rooftop. He landed as gingerly as a cat despite his now heavy frame and started running as soon as his boots hit the brick.

The dark city was shrouded in a gritty desert fog comprised of tiny grains of sand rather than moisture that floated on the wind. It gave the street lamps glowing halos of light and erased everything further than a kilometer in any direction.

Brand coughed, then pulled his bandana up over his face.

The young pharmakon paced along the edges of roofs and leapt across the alleys to other buildings, traversing the city like a mountain goat might traverse a valley riddled with canyons. Soon, he came to Market Street. A hazy, amber glow embraced the street and the once-familiar shade sails that whipped to and fro in the wind.

Though it was late at night, the street still buzzed with activity. Men scurried between shops with their shoulders hunched, their collars up, the brims of their hats pulled down low, and bandanas pulled up over their mouths against the moisture-seeking dust. At this time of night, the only women out wore skirts bunched scandalously high to their knees and thick lipstick that stood out in the dark. They held handkerchiefs up to their faces until a man walked by; then they dropped the cloth and smiled as widely as they could before so much grit got in their teeth that they had to turn and spit it away.

Brand crept down a ladder and made his way down the street. It seemed so much more cramped and narrow than he remembered it, and it stank of refuse and human waste. He didn't remember that.

He came to the intersection just across from Alastair's shop and stopped short, glancing around uncertainly. Where were the spice merchants? Didn't they have a shop here on the corner? Brand turned, frowning, to glance back down the street. No, this was the right area.

He stepped across the street, picking his way through the pedestrians, and made his way to the old spice shop. As he drew closer, he noticed that thick wooden planks had been nailed over the windows. A sun-faded sign above read, "Harley's & Sons Spice Emporium, est. 952."

Brand turned around and really looked at Market Street. Even in the evening gloom, he could see that half of the shops were boarded up and many of the others now had wrought iron gates pulled over their doors and windows.

What happened here? Brand wondered.

Ignoring the street's nightlife, Brand made his way a little farther down the street until he stood in front of Alastair's empty shop. He stood staring into the gaping void for a long moment. Then, he stepped inside the empty space, trying to ignore the echoing hole in his own heart. The darkness swallowed him, wrapping him in stillness. His footsteps on the bare dirt floor were sucked into the silence, barely reaching past him, as though the empty shop wanted to hold onto everything it could, even sound. His hand settled on the now-barren counter.

A rustle came from the back of the shop. Brand squinted. In the darkness, he could just make out a tarp folded into a makeshift shelter. A scraggly man struggled to extricate himself from the little lean-to.

"Hey, you there," the man said. As he edged forward, Brand hid his fist behind his back and made the Delta hand signal. The darkness of the shop evaporated, revealing a thin balding man wearing a coat that was several sizes too big for him.

"Yes?" Brand asked, not moving.

The man stood in front of Brand, squinting up at the tall stranger. He let out a sharp laugh.

"I thought you were a thief at first, and then for a moment that you were Alastair," the man said. "He was the man who owned this shop, years ago. You're huge like him. Don't see that all that often around here, y'know?"

Brand nodded. "I knew Alastair."

The thin man eyed the young man suspiciously. "So who in tarnation are you?"

"Who are you?" Brand retorted.

The thin man rolled his eyes. "Gerrit. Your turn."

Brand sighed. This man probably didn't know anything and wasn't worth the energy; but what else did Brand have to go off of?

"He raised me. When I was younger, I came by to talk to Alastair and saw that he was gone. I thought I'd come have a look tonight, maybe see if there was anyone left who knew what happened to him."

Gerrit squinted at Brand. "You were that scrawny kid of his? The one that stole fruit from me?" He chortled. "I used to work down the street from here at a fruit stall. I remember complaining to Alastair about you, and he started slipping me a few coins each week to buy extra fruit for you and the other urchins. I placed it in an open bowl right where you lot could get at it. Thought you were so sneaky! Ha! Well, you sure grew up, that's for certain. He never wrote to you after he left?"

Brand shook his head.

"Doesn't sound like him. He doted on you, in his own way."

"If you were here back when I was, then you remember how it used to be. What happened?" Brand asked, gesturing at the dirty street outside.

The thin man shrugged, making the oversized coat wobble. "When Alastair left, the gangs moved in, beat everyone to a pulp, and started 'taxing' us. Turns out Alastair was the only thing keeping them away from the Market all those years." He looked at his meager shelter. "Even now, they stay away from his shop. Spooks them. That's why I live here."

Gerrit scratched at his scraggly beard and frowned at the young pharmakon. "Well, it's no secret what happened to your old man. Alastair hired a great big Shambler, packed up his things, and headed out."

Brand had only read about Shamblers, behemoth machines used as armored caravan haulers to cross the desert. Until the invention of armored trains, Shamblers had been the safest way to carry goods across the storm-torn desert. "To where?"

"Out of the city, that much I know, otherwise he wouldn't have hired the Shambler," Gerrit said. "I can't say for certain as I haven't heard from him in years. But I did hear a rumor that maybe he might have run into some trouble up in Navar, or maybe Tinye. Maybe that's where he is if he's still alive."

Brand didn't know much about any of the mountain cities. He knew that it was much colder there and that the people who came down to trade in Darnan hated the heat of the desert plains. And unfortunately, Brand didn't know any Navari.

"Where did you hear this rumor from?" Brand asked.

"Oh, I don't remember. It was a long time."

"You wouldn't happen to know any Navari who might have more information?" Brand asked. He knew it was a shot in the dark.

"Sure," Gerrit said, surprising Brand. "I know a woman who used to do odd jobs for Alastair. She owns a smithy, buys all sorts of scrap, tinkers with things, you know. She goes up to the mountains a few times a year for the holiday festivals and to visit family. Maybe she's seen him recently if he's still in Navar."

"What's her name?"

"Ilye Grahm. Head over to the Northwestern Quarter, almost as close to the wall as you can get. Once you start seeing carvings of sarsen wolves on everything, start asking around for her. She's well-known in the Navari community over there."

Brand nodded to the man. "Thanks. Since you know him, do you want me to give him a message from you if I can find him?"

Gerrit quickly pocketed the coin. "I suppose you can tell him I'm still alive. And…if he needs a hand, I've got two and nothing to do."

Brand thanked the man again and left the dark shop without another glance. There was nothing more for him here.

The Northwestern Quarter was half a city away. Even flush with elixirs, it was too far to travel on foot. Brand walked out to the main road that ran parallel to Market Street, shading his enhanced eyes with one hand. There, he waited until a cycle rickshaw manned by a tired young man drove by, creaking. Brand flagged the man down.

"I'm done for the night," the driver said, leaning over the handlebars and adjusting the mask that shielded his mouth and nose from blowing dust.

"I'll pay you double. I need to get over to the Northwest Quarter."

"Round trip or one way?"

"Round trip."

The man thought for a long moment. It was obvious he was exhausted from a long day of riding, but the pay for that trip would be about the same as he usually earned in a day.

"Half up front, half when we get back," he said.

"Deal."

Brand paid the driver and hopped into the back. The driver started pedaling.

The rickshaw was slower than Brand would have liked, and he had to stop himself from shoving the tired man off the pedals and taking off with the creaking little vehicle alone. Instead, he settled back into the thin aluminum seat. It rattled incessantly as it bumped along the rough cobbled streets.

Brand worried a bit about the money he was spending. His work paid him fairly well, and William only asked that he contribute a quarter of it for room and board, but Brand had been saving up in the hopes that he could find a wife relatively soon and move out. This midnight adventure would set him back.

It took the rickshaw driver about an hour to pedal them across the city. Brand leaned back, letting the sunshade cast a shadow over his face that the street lanterns' light couldn't penetrate.

The grand buildings faced with polished limestone progressively gave way to smaller and simpler structures made of rough sandstone blocks covered in adobe. The streets transitioned from smooth stone pavestones to rough cobblestone, and then finally coarse gravel and packed earth. Heaps of broken machinery and trash made the air reek.

A few streets away, Brand could hear the screech of a locomotive applying its brakes and the shouting of the depot workers accompanied by an explosion of steam that spurted above the low rooftops. That train would be loaded down with many tons of coal from the mountain mines. Even this late at night, the depots still churned through train after train, unloading the precious cargo and sending the trains back.

"This is the Northwest Quarter," the driver said finally. "Where did you want me to drop you off?"

"Closer to the wall," Brand said, pointing, "where they decorate with sarsen wolves."

"Meeting with a Navari?"

"Yes."

A few moments later, the western storm wall rose out of the gritty fog, a massive stone edifice that rose high enough to vanish into the darkness above. The wall and the kashmari atmomancers that stood atop it were the only things that stood between the city of Darnan and the desert. Outside that wall, savage storms scoured the surrounding lands and carved deep rifts in the desert like a giant beast's claws. Brand had never been so close to the wall before.

He caught a glimpse of purple lightning arcing up and away from the top of the wall, but the fog swallowed it up.

The shops and streets were guarded by stiff stone statues of sarsen wolves, their mouths agape and bristling with fangs. A group of men stood smoking under a lamppost, unbothered by the blowing dust. Brand pointed to them and told the driver to stop.

"Hello," Brand called, leaning out of the rickshaw a bit. "I'm looking for an Ilye Grahm."

One of the men stepped forward. "Who wants to know?" the Navari asked in a high nasally voice.

"Cadmus Brand," Brand said. "I'm trying to find a friend who might be in Navar, and I was told that Ilye might know him."

The man beckoned for Brand to get out and follow him. Brand told the rickshaw driver to wait for him, then followed the Navari.

He led Brand to a sort of lean-to made of old solar sail cloth held up by aluminum poles and a heavy sandstone brick wall. Inside, a forge burned a sullen red and made the space stuffy and hot. The Navari pulled off his jacket and hung it up on a wrought iron hat stand. Then he turned to Brand.

"Who is it you're trying to find out about?" the Navari asked.

Brand looked about the smithy, looking for Ilye. But they were alone with the anvil, the racks of long-handled tools, the piles of scrap metal, the pile of coal, and the smell of soot.

"Where's Ilye Grahm?"

The Navari sighed. He walked over to the forge and picked up a long stick, which he carried back over to a cheap lantern and lit the wick. He plunged the burning tip of his stick into the sand at their feet.

"You're looking at her."

Brand blinked in the bright yellow light. He hadn't realized that the Night Vision elixir had worn off, messing with his perception of the person in front of him, but he could now clearly see that Ilye's short brown hair and strong arms were the only masculine things about her. In the light, he could see her delicate cheekbones and the swell of her breasts and hips. She really was quite pretty in a practical sort of way. Brand stammered out an apology. Ilye chuckled.

"It was dark. No harm done. Who are you looking for?"

"Alastair Sanders," Brand said. In his embarrassment, he fell back on his training as a server and stood straight, keeping his eyes on her face. He hoped the light was still pale enough to hide the blush of his cheeks. There was a twinkle in her eye, but Ilye made no further comment.

"Ah, you're that Brand. I knew that name sounded familiar," the smith said.

"Pardon?"

"I know Sanders," Ilye said. "When I can't figure out how to get some mechanical thing apart, he's the one I take it to. He's a genius with gizmos and gadgets. Anyway, he talks about you every so often." Ilye looked Brand up and down. "He's never mentioned it, but you look a lot like him. Are you his son? You're certainly tall enough."

Brand was at a loss for words. The idea had crossed his mind every so often over the years.

"I don't know," Brand said honestly. "I don't think so. I was just another urchin to him."

The words rang hollow to Brand as memories bubbled up of sitting for hours alone with the shopkeeper, learning about machines and listening to the huge mechanic's stories; Alastair's unending patience with the boy, and the way he always asked when the boy had last eaten. Brand had spent more nights sleeping in the back of the machine shop than not, and though Alastair had been poor, he'd somehow always had some little chore for the boy to earn a few coins.

Brand shook off the memories. "I'm just trying to find out what happened to him. He had to leave me with a friend many years ago and I haven't heard from him since. I'd like to know if he's doing well. You said he's in Navar?"

Ilye absently picked up a cloth and started wiping down a row of blackened tools set out on a wooden table. "Eh, no. He left Navar three, maybe four years ago. He owns a scrap shop in New Braunen now. You probably know the kind—mostly legal, some things not so much."

Brand breathed a sigh of relief. Alastair was still alive and doing well. Maybe if Brand could save up enough money, he could buy a train ticket—

Ilye set the cloth down. "But Sanders was arrested a few weeks back in New Braunen. I don't know exactly what they got him for or how long he'll be in prison, but I imagine it'll be a couple of years at least."

Brand felt a lead weight sink into his gut. He moved over to the glowing forge and stared into its fiery gullet. His mind started churning out ideas of how to help the big shopkeeper escape. After a moment, though, his shoulders slumped. Even if he could figure out how to get to New Braunen, the young pharmakon had no idea how to spring a man from prison without letting every guard in the place know what was going on. Brand nodded slowly, then turned to go.

"Thanks for letting me know," he said.

Ilye put a hand on his arm. He turned.

"I hear a lot from the people who come through my shop," she said. "I'll keep an ear out. If I hear any news of Sanders, how can I find you to let you know?"

Brand said, "I work at the Crimson Boar in the Northeastern Quarter," he said. "If I'm not there, William will be able to get a message to me."

"Crimson Boar, Cadmus Brand, William James," Ilye recited. "I'll let you know if I hear anything, good or bad. Travel safely, friend."

Brand returned to the rickshaw driver and spent the bumpy journey back lost in thought, drawing up plan after plan to save Alastair from his prison sentence and discarding each as more wild and foolish than the last.

Outside the James's darkened apartment, Brand paid the driver. Once the man had pulled away, Brand climbed up the side of the brick building, using cracks in the mortar as hand- and footholds. He slipped in through his open bedroom window. He lay awake for a long time until he finally accepted temporary defeat and succumbed to sleep.

Song of the Past

24 September 1062 P.E.
Gladiator Row, Darnan

As Mrs. James had done with Brand, she watched the newcomer, Erekir, sit up and perch on the edge of the bed in the guest room. He'd been feverish for days, but last night, the fever had finally broken. His eyes were set in a ragged, haunted face to match the long gaunt limbs etched with the burgundy scabs, long and thin and dark against his skin.

"Erekir?" she asked. "That is how you say it?"

He glanced at her with those grey eyes, large thoughtful eyes wide with…what was it? Pain, she realized, taking in the furrowed brow. Maybe fear as well. He then looked back down at his knees and nodded. Even for a man just coming out of an illness, she thought he seemed too subdued.

"Are you hungry?"

He shook his head and stood. He rocked slightly, and Mrs. James lurched forward to steady him. But he grasped the foot of the bed and waved her off. Then he took several shaky steps towards the washroom.

"Where are my clothes?" he asked. His voice was raspy, with a slight lilt, as though another language governed his pronunciation.

Mrs. James gestured to the chair beside the bed where she'd placed a clean pair of trousers and a linen shirt.

Erekir frowned. "Those aren't mine."

"Your things were so badly damaged—"

Mrs. James fell silent as the man took a step forward and loomed angrily over her. She could smell the stale sweat and tang of medicinal salve clinging to him. "What did you do with my clothes?"

"Nothing, yet," she reassured him. "They're down in the basement. I hadn't gotten around to turning them into rags yet."

Erekir hissed. "Show me."

Mrs. James gestured to the bed. "Sit down. I'll go get them. I'm sorry; I didn't know they meant that much to you."

He seemed to waver indecisively for a moment, then nodded and lowered himself gingerly back to the bed. Mrs. James felt his grey eyes follow her to the door. When she returned with an armful of ripped and stained clothes, he hadn't budged. His eyes followed her forward. He took his clothes from her gingerly and nodded once.

"Thank you."

Mrs. James watched as Erekir picked apart the pieces of fabric, opening them up one by one to assess their damage. He ran his fingers over the delicate embroidery on the cuffs of his jacket, then set it to one side. The wine- and blood-stained shirt made him glance over at the new one on the chair and set the old one aside, apart from the jacket. The pants he turned over and over and over, rubbing the tears and bloodstains, brow furrowed as though he couldn't decide whether to keep them or not.

"I could send out for a tailor to make you a new pair in the same style, if you'd like," Mrs. James said.

For the first time, Erekir's face opened up like the first tentative rays of sun shining from behind thick clouds. He almost seemed amazed. Then some thought brought the clouds back. He shook his head.

"No, thank you. If I could borrow a needle and thread, that would be sufficient."

"Are you sure?"

"Yes." It was definite, final.

"I will leave you once I have repaired them."

"I'm not sure you should just yet," Mrs. James said. "Lord Kushchai asked me to care for you, and I think I ought to tell him you're improving before you leave."

"Kushchai? The kashmari city lord?" Erekir snorted out a weak laugh. "That will not be necessary."

Mrs. James shrugged and left him to go find a needle and thread, puzzled by the reticent man. Kushchai had told her to get the man back up on his feet. He'd said nothing of being the young man's jailer, so as far as Mrs. James was concerned, he could go whenever he pleased.

* * *

Two Days Later

25 September 1062 P.E.
Gladiator Row, Darnan

Mrs. James had her arms elbow-deep in soapy water. The last few days of caring for Erekir had been taxing for the old woman, but she relished feeling useful again. With Brand gone, the house had felt as hollow as an untouched cavern. Now, though Erekir seldom spoke to her, Mrs. James felt like the house was warm with life again.

Where had Brand run off to in such a hurry? she wondered. She tried not to worry, but something about the way Brand had looked at Lord Kushchai still unsettled her.

A sound from the hallway made Mrs. James look up from her washing. Erekir shuffled into the kitchen and took a seat at the little round table near the window.

He'd put on the linen shirt Mrs. James had set out and most of his old clothes. The bright red sash belted the long jacket together, both washed and neatly repaired. Even the threads of the cuffs' embroidery were crisp, the colors bright. He must have washed it in the tub, Mrs. James mused with admiration.

He was carrying an old guitar that Brand had bought once and abandoned. He sat down quietly with the instrument on his lap. His face was still sallow, his eyes sunken, and his robe hung off his gaunt frame like sheets draped over a laundry line. But his eyes were brighter and the way he held himself was more relaxed than when he'd first awoken from the fever. The sores that covered his skin seemed to be fading to a healthier pink. If he kept putting the salve on them, Mrs. James was hopeful that they wouldn't scar too badly.

"Good morning," she said cheerfully to her ward. "I see you found the razor in the washroom."

Erekir nodded to her, raising one hand to the newly shaved sides of his head and jawline. He'd kept the strip of brown hair down the center of his head, brushing it forward so it lay flat, and had braided his mustache into two neat plaits joined at his chin with an ornate silver bead.

"How did you sleep?"

"Better."

"Good. You seem to be shaking the disease off quite handily. A bit of a surprise, really, considering the shape you were in when they brought you to me."

Erekir seemed to consider that a moment. When he spoke, his deep voice had a light lilt to it, his vowels a little more rounded and his consonants just a bit sharper than those Mrs. James was accustomed to hearing. "Warm hands heal better than medicine. Or so they say. Thank you for…helping me. I apologize if I was rude the other day."

"No need to apologize. I understand it must have been quite a shock to wake up in someone else's bed. If you'll wait a few moments, I'll finish up with the washing and get breakfast going."

Erekir nodded and turned his attention to the guitar. He picked out a soft melody, a sad slow haunting melody that made one think of cold, lonely nights in the mountains. His voice was a rich bass, smooth and steady, much healed from the dry rasp of the other day. Mrs. James paused in her washing to listen.

Labors bow my head
These chains around my soul
An Eagle calls to me
Of wings and wind and sky
I turn my eyes away
Thrust my hands into the earth
And bleeding I remember
I am bound

I'm Bound until I die

Ash and smoke fill the air
Broken chains hang sundered
The Eagle screams above
The world is mine alone
A siren calls from distant shores
But I look across the fields
Another bows his head
He is bound
Bound as I had been

I've never seen the shore
Nor felt the cool salt breeze
I'll never know the wind
Beneath outstretched wings
Each step I take t'ward freedom
Finds another lost soul
My blade made dull as soft grass
I will die
Die before I'm done

Tears of loss and joy
Their blood upon my hands
The stain is mine forever
I cannot wipe it off
Freedom bought with stolen blood
Silence haunts each moment
I am bound
Bound by what I've done

"That is a beautiful song, Erekir," Mrs. James said, her voice full of wonder.

Erekir set the guitar aside carefully. "It is an old song from my homeland, about the War of Tears."

"What was that?"

"It is what we call the period in our history that saw us overthrow our kashmari lord." He strummed a few soft chords.

"That's impossible, and heresy to say so, young man," Mrs. James said.

Erekir chuckled darkly. "It is not impossible. We did it. Like you, we used to be governed by kashmari lords. But then one day, about a century ago, a particularly nasty kashmari lord named Mehvon took over the king and led an army against Darnan. Your High Lord Fafnir," Erekir spat the kashmari's name, "wiped out our entire army. We lost fully half of the able-bodied men of my country in that battle. After that, a small group of determined rebels threw off Mehvon's yoke of oppression. They then turned to another lord and overthrew him, and so on throughout the land, until not a single kashmari was left. It took five generations to do this. No one who began the fight lived to see it end."

"Incredible," Mrs. James said softly.

Erekir was staring out the window at some distant memory. Though he was much younger than Brand and far more reserved, the familiar posture made Mrs. James smile. *I do hope you're well, wherever you are, Brand,* she thought.

"Do you miss your homeland?" Mrs. James asked as she dried off her hands and pulled out a pan, then pulled several eggs from a bowl on the counter. The cast iron stove was still hot, so she placed the pan on top of it and cracked the eggs into the pan.

Erekir nodded slowly.

"What brought you here to Darnan?"

Erekir unbuttoned the first few buttons of his shirt and opened it to reveal the large rune seared onto his left breast. "This branding ensures that I never step foot in my homeland again." He buttoned his shirt up again, hiding the puckered scar.

"Who on earth gave you that?"

"The king. I was part of a group of young people who tried to overthrow him. He didn't appreciate our efforts."

"Your country seems…eh, unstable," Mrs. James said.

Erekir's eyes twinkled slightly. "We are an opinionated bunch, yes. But we are free."

Mrs. James wasn't so sure she'd prefer a war-torn country to one under the kashmari, but she kept her thoughts to herself. She flipped the eggs in the pan.

"You tried to overthrow the king?"

"His taxes were too high."

Mrs. James waited for him to elaborate, but he didn't.

"So they exiled you?"

"Not for the kidnapping, but for the king's death."

Mrs. James's blood ran cold. "You killed the king? Why didn't they hang you?"

Erekir looked down at his hands. "Because his death was purely accidental. We stormed the palace and tried to kidnap him. We never wanted anyone to get hurt. But the guards started shooting at us, and the king was hit. "

"Oh."

"Don't worry, Mrs. James," Erekir said with a wry half-grin. "I'm not a regicidal maniac."

Mrs. James's hand shook slightly as she put the kettle on to boil. She'd lived with two pharmakons. How bad could taking in a foreign revolutionary be?

But as Mrs. James watched him, Erekir's fingers tapping the guitar's strings lightly, it seemed to her that a deep sadness suffused every movement the strange young man made. Her fear softened into pity. However cavalier he may be about his revolution and subsequent exile, darkness lingered in Erekir's heart.

Mrs. James folded her arms and took a deep breath. "You were brought to me because you are of 'diplomatic importance.' Is it because of what happened with your king?"

Erekir shook his head.

"Any idea what that means?"

Erekir snorted, a wry, sad twinkle in his eyes. "Yes."

Mrs. James waited again for him to elaborate, but he held his silence. There was that sadness again. She sighed. Perhaps he'd open up to her later after he'd recovered more. She got out a plate and placed the eggs on it, careful not to break the yolks. She piled fruit and buttered bread onto the plate and set it in front of Erekir.

"Thank you," he said and began to pick at the food. After a few moments, he thanked her again and set down the fork. "Is there a pub nearby? Or a bar?"

Mrs. James nodded slowly. "There is, down the street a block. Why?"

Erekir's eyes closed heavily.

"You can't drown your troubles in drink," Mrs. James said. "It never works."

Erekir opened his grey eyes and excused himself.

Mrs. James looked at the barely-touched plate of food and wondered once more where Brand was.

Wonders

26 September 1062 P.E.
Deadman's Pass, Barren Mountains

The *Polaris* limped over a ridge, out of the shadows and into the bright morning beyond. The first warm morning rays of sunshine burst in through the kitchen window, illuminating the solitary figure of the lone mechanic hunched over the table. Though it was still early, the heat from those young rays promised a blistering day. Marie kicked on a fan that ruffled Brand's grey hair and cooled the sweat starting to bead upon his brow.

Brand shoved his porridge around in its bowl, not really paying attention to it. The events of the night before spun around and around in his brain. He pulled out the silk purse absent-mindedly and swallowed a pill, then replaced it in his belt pouch and continued glaring at the mush in his bowl.

A soft nose nudged his lower leg. He looked down and saw the little zerda, its eyes wide. It was cowering behind Brand's leg, keening softly.

"You're hungry, aren't you?"

Brand sighed and stood. "I have no idea what you eat besides spider leg, and I'm all out of that."

<Fruit.>

Brand froze. He was torn. He didn't want to even acknowledge the squatter in his mind, but he also didn't want the little zerda to starve.

He ended up fishing a cactus fruit out of a cupboard, peeling it, and dumping the ruby-red fruit into a bowl. He set it on the floor just under the table. The zerda approached it cautiously, stretching its neck out as far as it would go to sniff the fruit. It took a cautious step forward and reached its paw out to tap the bowl. It crouched down, ears back, waiting to see if the bowl reacted. When it didn't, the zerda crept forward and slowly began to eat.

"You need a name," Brand said. "How about..."

He sifted through all the names he could think of and realized he didn't even know if this zerda was male or female.

Me'von sighed. <Female.>

"How can you even tell?" Brand growled quietly.

<I've owned a zerda or two.>

Brand grudgingly restricted his brainstorming to female names.

"I think I'll call you Anthea. It means 'flower,' I think." He leaned down and stroked her spotted fur. It was finer and softer than anything Brand had ever felt before, and even softer than when he had petted her at the Apida village.

<She's been grooming herself.> Me'von said.

Brand ignored the kashmari and straightened up again. He stared despondently at his porridge.

<I'm not sure I can take the waiting any longer,> Me'von said quietly. <Just say it.>

The kashmari was still a knot in the corner of Brand's mind, only now he was anxious in addition to furious, terrified, and guilty. Brand, on the other hand, had gone from mortified to terrified. The reality of what had happened and what he had in his brain had hit him like a fall from a thousand feet. He hadn't spoken to Me'von directly since the night before.

<No.>

Me'von sighed but didn't press Brand further. He still radiated hatred and guilt. The hatred had been especially difficult to bear, an acid that seeped into every thought and corroded Brand's mind from within.

Brand shoved the bowl of porridge away and stood. As soon as Brand stepped away, Anthea sprinted back down the hall in the direction of the bunk room. The mechanic poured himself a glass of water at the tiny sink, and downed it in a few gulps, rinsing the bland, gluey taste out of his mouth.

Brand found Finn in the sunny cockpit, feet up on the console, nose in a book, fanning himself with his hat. He looked up as Brand entered.

The gladiator leaned up against the bulkhead. "We'll need to park the *Polaris* for a few hours for me to work on that misaligned hip joint," Brand said.

Finn nodded and dropped his feet to the deck. He punched a few buttons. "Glad you're feeling better. Marie, is there anywhere nearby that's sheltered where we can stop for repairs?"

The A.I. whirred and clicked for several moments, then said, "There is a small cave about five clicks away. At our current speed, we can reach it in approximately fifteen minutes."

Finn scribbled down some numbers on a pad of paper. To Brand, he said, "Can you have it done in two hours?"

"Depends on what's wrong," Brand said.

Finn nodded. "We need that joint fully functional, so take the time you need. But if you could, be quick about it. Every minute counts in this race."

Brand nodded. "I'll do my best."

The gladiator limped stiffly to the locker area, brace clinking softly with each step. There, he picked up his toolkit and began to put on his armor. Even though they'd be in a reasonably safe location, Brand had to admit that the weight of it was reassuring against his skin and made him feel a little more in control of his disintegrating life.

He glanced up at the window and saw a dark shape flit across the sky. His stomach dropped. Brand stood and shuffled over to the window, squinting up at the empty blue sky.

But there was nothing.

Brand rubbed at his temples, frustrated. With everything that had happened over the last few days, and with a blasted kashmari in his head, it was no wonder he was seeing things. He turned and sat again to pull on the rest of his armor.

Marie guided the *Polaris* into a rocky crack in the ground, angling the trawler this way and that to fit through the narrow opening.

The cave was essentially a single tunnel of moss-covered rock that plunged down into the earth, a sheer drop into blackness. When the trawler could descend no farther, Marie balanced the Venator's mechanical legs on a handful of rocky ledges. Its sand-blasted body hung over the abyss.

Marie explained the situation to Brand through a grate. "You'll have to exit through the top hatch and climb down onto the misaligned leg for the repairs."

Brand glanced uneasily down at his braced leg. "I don't suppose you have any ropes?"

Loren appeared at his elbow with a long, thick rope looped about his arm.

"Way ahead of you," the gunslinger said. "I'll anchor you."

Brand watched as Loren expertly twisted and knotted a rope into a harness around his legs. The gunslinger handed another rope to Brand.

"You ever done this before?"

Brand shook his head.

Loren untied his own rope and repeated the steps slowly so that Brand could follow along.

"Did this all the time down in Duat," the gunslinger said.

"What made you leave Duat?" Brand asked as he twisted the rope around itself and fed it through a loop.

Loren snorted. "Duat."

"Something tells me the kashmari didn't sign off on you becoming a gunslinger up here. Don't they need people like you down there?"

Loren shrugged. "There's a way up through some of the more remote caverns that lets out into the mountains."

Brand opened his mouth to ask another question, but Loren held up a hand. "Look, I'll talk about most things, but nothing below the surface, alright?"

Brand nodded and turned his attention back to his harness.

Several minutes later, both men were harnessed and clipped together. Brand double-checked that he had all the tools he should need, including a small clockwork lantern. He placed them in a leather bag, which he slung over one shoulder and moved to the small of his back.

Loren clapped the big gladiator on the shoulder. "All set? Good. Since this is going to take a couple of hours, I'll give a tug on the rope when I need a break."

Brand climbed up the ladder and out onto the outer hull of the trawler while Loren stayed below, paying out rope.

Brand shivered. The air was brisk and cold like an autumn breeze and smelled of damp rock and moss. Mineral-laden water had carved through the soft rock over millennia and built magnificent cascades and daggers of globulous mineral deposits. Ribbons of green lichen streaked towering waterfalls of stone.

Brand crept to the edge of the *Polaris* and peered down into the deep. He'd never seen anything so dark before. He picked up a rock that had fallen onto the trawler as they'd descended and dropped it down into the pit, then listened.

It fell out of sight. He listened for a few minutes but heard no sound of it falling to any floor. He shivered again in the chilly air and scrambled back from the edge.

Brand gave himself several moments to take a few deep breaths and look around the cave. The cold from the metal skin of the Polaris seeped through the canvas of his pants as he sat. He could hear a tiny dripping somewhere.

A particular bluish algae caught his eye: blue-green algae, an ingredient in several of his alchemical recipes. It served to protect him somewhat from the severity of the poisons. Perhaps if he could find a jar onboard to scrape some into, he could cultivate it, he mused. He'd only ever bought a dried and crushed, powdery version from the apothecary. The fresh algae would be far more potent.

As he thought about how to accomplish this, Me'von radiated disapproval but held his silence.

Brand gave the rope a sharp tug. It held. Satisfied, he stepped carefully over to the enormous mechanical leg with the jammed joint and climbed down onto it. This leg was in shadow, so Brand lit his lantern.

"Going over," he called out.

"Go ahead," Loren called back. The rope went taught.

Brand leaned backwards over the edge slowly, testing his weight against Loren's. The smaller man must have braced himself against a bulkhead to support Brand's full weight. With one last steadying breath, Brand walked backwards down the side of the leg, careful not to look down into the abyss.

He stopped himself when he got to the joint in question. The metal had caved in, obstructing one of the massive bearings. If he could somehow hammer it back outwards, the joint ought to be able to move freely.

Brand pulled out his hammer. He kicked against the leg and swung himself around to the other side of the appendage. With a grunt, he banged up against the unyielding metal, but was able to brace himself up against the joint with his knees and maneuver his arm into a good enough position to reach the bent piece. He sighed and got to work.

It was slow going. The metal was as thick as Brand's head, and in order to swing the hammer in the right direction, he had to wedge his arm into a narrow gap where he couldn't swing the hammer very far. Even so, every blow also sent a shudder of pain through his collarbone. A deep ache started in his bad leg from the cold and the pinching pressure of the rope around his groin. He gritted his teeth and soldiered on. As he worked, the pill he'd taken at breakfast started to take effect, soothing his anxiety about the long drop below and easing some of the pain in his collarbone and leg.

The work provided a way for him to focus and clear his mind, though, and when Loren tugged on the rope for Brand to return, Brand reentered the *Polaris* sweaty and relaxed.

"I'll need that much time again," Brand said, wiping his brow. He stretched out his arm and spun it around in a windmill a bit. He groaned.

Loren silently nodded his acceptance. The gunslinger strode into the kitchen and poured himself and the pharmakon a glass of water. He drank deeply. Brand gratefully accepted his glass and drank.

"Can't you just take one of your potions and make this go faster?" Loren asked.

Brand's face clouded over. He wasn't opposed to the idea of torturing Me'von, but he didn't fancy passing out again from the strain. He suspected that the kashmari's presence made it difficult to use his abilities.

"I'm not really up to it right now," Brand said. He set his glass down, then pulled off his gauntlets and examined his hands. They were stiff from the cold, and the one he'd been using to wield the hammer was developing a fat blister on the webbing between his thumb and forefinger. The scabs in each palm from Kushchai's nails were holding firm, at least, and hadn't cracked. The skin around the edges of each scab was looking quite healthy and pink. Brand didn't want to think what might have happened if he hadn't taken the Healing elixir that night. He pulled his gauntlets back on, grateful for the use of his hands.

Loren licked his lips, eyes searching the gladiator. Brand wondered what he saw. Whatever it was, the gunslinger accepted Brand's statement.

"Is there a jar or something I can use? I saw some algae out there I could use in my elixirs."

Loren nodded and leaned down to pull a glass jar with a metal lid out of a drawer. He handed it to Brand.

The gunslinger reached his hands high over his head and stretched out his back with a groan.

"Let's get this over with then."

"Don't you want a minute more?"

"Sure, but we don't have time to dawdle. Up you go."

Brand hoisted himself up onto the hull again. Before he returned to the misaligned joint, he went over to the other side of the *Polaris* where he would be able to reach the algae-covered rock.

"Going over," he called. The rope went taught.

The gladiator leaned out towards the rock, bracing himself at an angle with one hand against the slimy rock. He pulled out a knife from his belt and awkwardly scraped some of the blue algae off the rock and into the jar along with a bit of the lichen. Crumbs of rock fell in as well, making soft pinging noises against the glass. Then he screwed the lid back on and tucked the jar into his belt pouch.

"Pull me back up," he called. The rope creaked as Loren hauled the bigger man back up.

"That's enough," Brand said, getting his feet under him again. The rope went slack again. The gladiator limped back to the hatch.

"Loren?"

Brand waited a moment, rubbing his aching leg while he waited.

The gunslinger's face appeared. Brand handed the jar down to him, then limped back over to the damaged mechanical leg. Loren lowered Brand back into position. The gladiator wedged his arm into the gap and started hammering again.

As Brand worked, he realized he was finally ready to confront Me'von.

"Kashmari magic is blood magic." Brand's thoughts were still jumbled, but he had to set a few things straight.

<Yes.>

<You murdered that creature in order to torture the other one.>

A pause.

<You're a gladiator. You've taken lives before.>

"But I don't enjoy it. It feels…filthy. I do it when I must because the other choice is my own death."

<As was the case last night. The entire crew would have died had I not done something.>

Fury boiled up inside Brand.

"That wasn't the whole of it, though. I was there, remember? You didn't have to torture that poor creature. You could have just chased it away. But you didn't. You twisted its fears in on itself and…and…bathed in it. You loved torturing it."

Guilt and hatred radiated off the kashmari like heat off the desert sands. He didn't respond.

"Why do you hate me?" Brand growled in frustration.

<It's not you I hate,> Me'von said quietly. The guilt strengthened.

It took Me'von a moment for Brand to realize what the kashmari meant.

He hates himself, Brand thought, shocked.

<Yes,> the kashmari whispered. <I do. The magic…it controls us more than any of us would care to admit. I swear to you that I acted only to protect us. But I…I cannot control myself once I touch it.>

The gladiator froze, the hammer poised motionless, panic coursing through him. Me'von couldn't even control that terrible power? What would happen if he used it again? Brand wouldn't be able to stop him. Would Me'von accidentally kill the other crewmembers of the *Polaris*?

"I don't suppose I could convince you to leave," Brand asked hopelessly.

<No. Not until we get that device.>

Brand lowered his hand and closed his eyes. He willed his heart to slow and focused on his spark. It was feeble and elusive, but the simple act of searching for it settled Brand's mind. A plan started to take shape in Brand's mind, though he had his doubts about whether the kashmari would agree to it or stick with it. He didn't have any other option, though.

"If you're going to stay in my brain," Brand said, "then I propose we establish ground rules. First and foremost, you don't use kashmari magic. Ever."

A desperate yearning for that insatiable power vied with self-loathing for a moment in Me'von's corner of Brand's mind.

<What will you give me in return?> the kashmari asked.

Brand clenched his teeth. "I promise not to use alchemy."

A long stunned pause followed.

"Yes or no, because I'm not liable to offer this a second time."

<Done. Deal. Of course. I…I'm just surprised,> the kashmari sputtered. <You hate me for what I did last night. Why would you care about my pain?>

"I don't," Brand said, a bit harsher than he intended. "But if I don't torture you, maybe you'll be more likely to keep your end of the bargain."

<You'll sacrifice so that I don't accidentally harm the others.>

"Yes."

Me'von grunted. Grudging admiration tinged with bewilderment emanated from the kashmari. <It is an excellent deal for both of us. So long as nothing else tries to kill us, we might manage to not kill each other over the next few days.>

The tension in Brand's shoulders suddenly released, as though a terrible weight had been lifted off them. Brand didn't believe the kashmari nearly enough to trust that he would completely honor the pact. But at least Me'von would think twice before tapping into that dark power.

"I'm sorry I punished you," Brand said.

Me'von snorted. <I deserved it.>

Another thought bubbled to the surface of Brand's mind, one that he'd barely acknowledged because of its terrible consequences.

Me'von knew that he was a pharmakon.

<I'd already figured that out the first time you used that Healing elixir. One cannot simply dismiss such agony so easily.> Me'von chuckled dryly. <Just my luck. Don't worry; you're far too interesting for me to turn in.>

Brand frowned. "You're a kashmari. Why haven't you killed me yourself? Aren't I dangerous to you?"

Me'von dithered for a moment. Then he sighed. <The very reason

you are dangerous to me also makes you dangerous to other kashmari, and I am in a bit of a bind with a certain very powerful kashmari.>

"Fafnir."

<Indeed.>

"What happened?"

Me'von didn't reply. Brand sighed in frustration. "Don't I have a right to know who you are and why the most powerful kashmari in the world is interested in you? Don't you think that might affect me while you're riding around in my skull?"

The kashmari retreated like a scared animal. The fear he radiated was laced with a deep sorrow that puzzled Brand, but he let it go.

Brand went back to hammering away at the stubborn metal.

"So you're hoping that getting Fafnir that device will get you back into his good graces again?"

Me'von sighed. <I hate the old brute. But there are times to fight, and times to lick your enemy's boots while you recover. That device should placate Fafnir for a little while, at least.>

Brand mulled that over while he hammered away at the leg.

"Why are you so different from the other kashmari?" Brand asked.

<Who says I am?>

"Your actions, your feelings. You seem to respect the other crewmembers of the *Polaris*, you have a very dim view of other kashmari, you seem to have a sense of right and wrong—"

<Yes, I get the picture. Why am I not rotten to the core?> Me'von sighed. <It's not any of your business, so suffice it to say that being a kashmari doesn't come naturally to me. There's a whole long sordid story as to why that is, but I don't know you—or anyone else—well enough to tell it.>

At that, the kashmari withdrew and Brand retreated to his own thoughts. The only sounds in the cave were the dripping of water and the ringing hammer strikes.

A good twenty minutes later, Me'von said, <Stop.>

Brand rolled his eyes. "Why?"

<Stop hammering, fool. There's something else in here.>

Brand stopped. He quieted his breathing, straining his ears.

Then he heard it, a soft fluttering of wings. It was coming from the dark abyss.

<What is it?> he asked in his mind to keep silent.

<I don't know.>

The flapping and fluttering intensified.

"Brand!" Loren's voice came up from the hatch loudly. "Brand! Are you ok? What's that sound?"

The flapping stopped.

Brand clung to the metal leg, eyes and ears straining for something, any clue.

<Is it gone?> Brand asked. A cold breeze chilled the sweat on his brow. He shivered. The silence of the cave leered back at him, taunting him.

Then in a blast of sound like the roar of a waterfall, an explosion of wings swept up from the abyss. Brand cried out, clamping his eyes closed. Rustling sounds swirled around him, engulfing him.

"Brand! Brand!" The gladiator could barely hear Loren's voice over the rush of air.

Brand realized that nothing attacked him. Something papery brushed against his skin, but that was all.

The gladiator opened his eyes and to his amazement, he saw not a monster, but a fluttering mass of winged creatures, tendrils streaming out behind them, rust-red and sandy flashing in the morning sun as they rose and encircled the *Polaris*. They danced around him, their tendrils softly brushing past him.

Brand laughed in relief. He held out his hand and one of the creatures alighted on his finger, standing on two small legs. It was so light he couldn't even feel its weight. About the size of Brand's head, it was a small furry creature with broad delicate wings it held aloft. Dozens of long silken tendrils swept back from the base of its wings. Two long fuzzy antennae arched above multifaceted eyes that glittered with a rainbow of iridescent colors. It turned to inspect the gladiator, sniffing at his hand with a tiny, wet nose. Then, with a flutter of its wings, it was gone in a flash of red.

Then they continued to rise until the entire mass had exited the cave and were swept away by the winds, gone as soon as they had come.

"Brand!" Finn and Wren called from just above him.

Brand kicked off against the mechanical leg and swung himself back around to the front of the appendage. He looked up and saw the two of them peering over the edge frantically.

"I'm fine," Brand said.

"Loren called for us when that horrible roaring sound started and he didn't hear you respond." Finn reached a hand down to hoist Brand back on top of the *Polaris*.

"Have you ever seen those creatures, Finn?" Wren asked in awe.

Finn shook his head. "I've heard of them. Solar leptids, I think. They rise to the surface during the day, and retreat to their caves at night."

To Brand, he asked, "How go the repairs?"

Brand stretched out his arms and shook out his numb hand. "Nearly there, I think. Ten more minutes ought to do it."

The gladiator carefully stepped over to the hatch and sat on his haunches. "Loren?"

The gunslinger's face appeared.

"Thanks for caring," Brand said. "I'm fine."

Loren grinned sheepishly.

Finn squatted next to Brand. "Just a flock of solar leptids."

"How close are you to being done?" Loren asked.

"Ten minutes."

"Oh good," Loren said with a grunt as he stretched. "I think my back is about done too."

Twenty minutes later, the *Polaris* clamered out of the crack in the valley floor and headed to a narrow gap between two foreboding mountains.

Behind them, a black monstrosity detached itself from a nearby boulder and with a great heave of its leathery wings, thrust itself into the sky. It wheeled around, then glided silently towards the Venator.

Aeolian Dunes

27 September 1062 P.E.
Aeolian Dunes

The next morning, Marie brought the *Polaris* to a halt at the top of a cliff overlooking the Aeolian Dunes. The dunes stretched beyond the hazy horizon, an endless expanse of undulating pale waves dotted here and there by gray rock edifices sticking up out of the sand like teeth. Far to the south, Brand could make out several dark tiny shapes inching their way north like beetles trekking across the desert. Their tracks were soon erased by the winds that Brand could hear buffeting the *Polaris*.

"Last leg of the trip," Finn said, "and the most treacherous."

Brand, thinking back to the enormous wraith-like omegalids, said, "Worse than what we've been through?"

Finn nodded. "Up until now, most of the things trying to kill us were critters. The mountains shielded us from the winds while we were in the mountains and on the east side near Darnan. But out here is the origin point of most storms. Even in Darnan, those storms would rip the city to shreds if it weren't for the kashmari atmomancers. Out here, the full force of those winds grinds everything to powder."

"And then there are raiders and the other trawler crews," Wren said, pointing at the dark shapes to the south.

Finn nodded in agreement. "We have a good two-day head start on them. Hopefully, it'll be enough. Marie, take us down."

"With pleasure," the A.I.'s voice said smoothly.

"Everybody hang onto something," Finn said.

Finn and Loren buckled into their chairs. Brand and Wren grabbed onto handrails along the bulkhead.

The Venator lurched forward. It carefully picked its way straight down the enormous cliff, digging its thick metal claws into the rock to anchor its bulk with every step. The deck tilted crazily forward. Brand had to hang on tight with both hands to avoid flying forward into the viewport.

Marie spoke to Brand. "The repairs you made are holding up well, Brand. We could not have made this descent without them."

"It's always good to be appreciated," Brand grunted through gritted teeth. His shoulder was screaming from the strain.

Finn, leaning forward against his harness, nonchalantly pulled out his book and began to read. A frown creased his forehead.

Wren maneuvered her feet so that she was standing on a bulkhead and motioned for Brand to do the same. As his feet took on the bulk of his weight once more, Brand heaved a sigh of relief. He still had to hang on tightly with one hand, but he could at least avoid using his bad arm.

"What have you learned about Baldur?" Brand asked.

"General Baldur was a great man and a marvelous tactician. I wish I could have met him."

"Any maps or diagrams of the *Muspell's Sons*?" Loren asked.

Finn shook his head. "I don't expect to find any, either. This journal was written long before the *Muspell's Sons* had even been built."

With one hand, Brand massaged his sore thigh. Each jarring step the trawler took down the cliff face sent a stabbing pain to the bone. "What are you hoping to find in it, then?"

"An understanding of how the dverger mind worked in general, and specifically how Baldur's mind worked."

"You think he hid or disguised the device?" Brand asked. He rotated his shoulder to loosen it up.

"Wouldn't you?" Finn smiled. "I would. His people had been

fighting the kashmari for centuries, and according to the journal, he finally had a device that could destroy them all. For whatever reason, he never used it, otherwise, the kashmari wouldn't still be here."

"So is the device we're looking for the same as Baldur's weapon?" Wren asked.

"I guess so."

<There weren't any left…> Me'von said quietly, musing. <But if there really is one left, why would Fafnir want it?>

<You know about this device?>

<Yes.>

<Care to elaborate?> Brand asked, irritated that the kashmari had withheld information.

<Not really. There's a good chance it's not even the same device,> Me'von said defensively. <The kind I'm thinking of were all used.>

<Maybe Fafnir found out about another one.>

An uneasiness leaked from Me'von at that thought. <I hope not.>

"Could have saved us a lot of trouble if he'd just used it on the kashmari," Loren grumbled.

Brand snorted. "That's what I was thinking."

"So how would Baldur have hidden the device?" Wren asked.

Finn tapped his pursed lips thoughtfully. "I'm not sure. He was well aware that he was fighting against a foe that had centuries worth of experience in deception. They often saw straight through his stratagems. But listen to this:

"The kashmari cannot comprehend the sacrifice of oneself in the service of another. It is a paradigm he cannot fathom, and as such, hates with a torrential fury. My people have used this to great effect in the past. However, I am loath to repeat such an act. My goal is to protect my people, not offer them up for slaughter. I will continue to search for a viable alternative."

"I wonder if he found one?" Wren said.

Loren arched a pale eyebrow at Wren. "He didn't," he said flatly. "If he had, the dvergen would still be alive, not the kashmari."

Me'von gave a wordless, sorrowful affirmation. Brand wanted to press the kashmari for more information, but figured he wouldn't get much out of Me'von in his current mood.

"Anyway," Finn continued, "it's something to keep in mind while we're searching the wreck."

The *Polaris* reached the base of the cliff and evened out. The deck returned to its normal horizontal, much to Brand and Wren's relief. Brand unhooked his cramped hands from the handrail and flexed it to bring it back to life.

"If the coordinates that Sahure gave me are accurate, we should be there in two days," Finn said. "Maybe three if we run into a storm."

Outside, Brand saw that what he had thought was a rock outcropping sticking out of the sand was actually a gray stone tower, round and broken.

Wren followed his gaze to the ruin. "The next storm may bury that ruin in sand. We won't have many real landmarks out here, so we navigate using clocks and the sun and stars. Marie takes care of the calculations, thankfully."

Out of the corner of the viewport, Brand caught sight of some dark, winged thing zip behind them. He tensed.

<Leave it,> Me'von growled. <It won't harm us.>

<You saw it too?> Relief was quickly replaced by renewed worry.

"I'm going up top to check something," Brand muttered to Wren.

"Something wrong?" she asked, suddenly alert.

"Probably just a stray titanopter," Brand said. "I'll take care of it."

As Brand limped down the hall, he fished a pill out of the little silk pouch from his pocket and downed it. He then grabbed a rifle, swung it over his shoulder, and hauled himself up to the hatch and out to the outer hull.

He poked his head out of the hatch cautiously and glanced around. He blinked a few times as his eyes adjusted to the bright sunlight. The flying creature was nowhere to be seen.

Using the handholds, he crawled across the lurching trawler to one of the sunken metal wells and plopped down, wincing as his hands brushed the sun-drenched metal. Once situated, with his rifle across his lap, he began to scan the cliffs behind the *Polaris*.

There. A little off to the left, Brand saw a monstrous dark shape clinging to the cliff face. It was a bit larger than Brand. Black spines and crests and scales jutted out in all directions like the spines of a cactus. It turned its massive head to fix its amber eyes on Brand.

Those strangely human eyes seemed to glow slightly with an ancient, cold light. A chill went down Brand's spine despite the heat.

"What is that?"

<A dragon.>

Brand gripped the rifle tighter. His eyes traced the brutish body and lingered on the watchful, intelligent eyes.

<He's leaving us alone for now, which is exactly how I prefer him. Let's go back down.>

Brand lingered in the well for a bit longer. The dragon seemed to be waiting…and watching. For what?

<Let's go back down,> Me'von prompted, more urgently.

The mention of the word 'dragon' reminded Brand of something that had been bothering him.

"He knows you're with me," Brand said quietly.

<What? Who?>

"Fafnir. He was there, the night I met you. He could tell you were coming, and he told me to trust you. He wanted you to join me."

Brand caught a fragment of a memory from Me'von, one of a shattered stone shack. A wave of realization rolled off the kashmari. He let loose a string of curses in a half a dozen different languages.

<What else did that massive manipulative pinwheeling ego sack tell you?>

Brand decided to be brutally honest to see how the kashmari would react. "He told me you used to be like me. That maybe you could be again."

Fury exploded from Me'von like flames spewn from a volcano. <I can never be like you again because of what he did! I swear, someone needs to rip the eyes out of that blasted brainless sea urchin and fry them in fish oil!>

With one last look at the dragon to make sure the beast didn't make a move, the bemused gladiator picked his way back to the hatch and clambered back down into the *Polaris* to a litany of the various dismemberments, tortures, and mutilations that Me'von would like to subject Fafnir to. Brand replaced the rifle in the locker, then moved to the kitchen, where he picked up the mortar and pestle he'd seen on the shelf when he first arrived on the *Polaris.* Then he limped stiffly into the bunk room.

<Did he say anything else?> Me'von asked as Brand limped back to

the bunk room.

<He said that while I committed a terrible crime with Mirane, he couldn't kill me for it because he needs me for something.>

<Did he say what?>

<He said the end of the world is coming, and he thinks I can save everyone.>

<You?> Me'von barked out a laugh.

Brand tried to brush his irritation aside. <He's crazy. The world can't just end.>

More soberly, Me'von said, <Oh, it could. Good chance he was lying, though.> He growled. <Manipulative son of a bottom-feeder…>

<Are we still going to find his device so we can try to buy our lives back?> Brand asked, pulling aside the curtain that blocked off his bunk.

<Yes,> Me'von muttered, deflated. <I need to get back into his good graces to find out his plans. That's the genius of his manipulations. Even when you don't want to play into his hand, it always seems to be in your best interests. Just do me a favor: once we get back and clear your name, try not to get sucked into his vortex again if you can. There's no way out once he's hooked you.>

Brand hoisted himself up to his bunk with a groan. Anthea hopped up on Brand's chest as soon as the big man lay down. As he scratched under her chin, the little zerda gripped his forearm gently with her spotted paws, eyes closed, soft cheek rested on his thumb. She purred happily.

"When I was on the altar, Fafnir came and spoke to me. I…I screamed at him for what he did. He…he apologized for having to kill Mirane and the baby." Anger boiled up inside him again. "How could he do such a thing, and then think an apology would excuse him?"

Me'von said, <Fafnir is sick and twisted, even for a kashmari. But, that being said, he does have one single redeeming quality: he believes that family and children are sacred, especially unborn children. His fear of what that child could have become must have been terrible.>

"What could it have become?"

Me'von sighed. <A child born to a kashmari is resistant to our magic, our influence, and even our ability to possess their bodies. A hybrid like that would need not fear most kashmari.>

"Fafnir is not most."

<No, but the few people who have managed to either beat him or nearly kill him have all been the children of kashmari. He has taken note and bears a terrible grudge against them.>

Finn's voice came through the grate just outside the bunk room, startling Brand. "Storm coming up," Finn said.

Brand gently placed the little zerda on his pillow and climbed down from his bunk. Anthea leapt off the pillow and landed squarely on Brand's shoulder in a crouch. Brand sighed and limped over to the little round porthole at the end of the room. The zerda peered intently through the glass with the big gladiator.

Outside, dust was swirling around, hiding the desert in a cloud that solidified into a pale brown wall of grit. Darkness descended as the burning sun was obscured. Anthea grew tense, her claws digging into the leather of Brand's armor, fur standing on end. Brand stroked the little creature to reassure her, but she remained still as a statue, eyes fixed on the rising storm.

The *Polaris* stopped, then slowly lowered itself to the ground. Clanging echoed throughout the trawler as thick metal plating slammed into place covering every window, porthole, and even the front viewport. The bunk room was plunged into darkness as an armored plate slammed into place over the window.

Then the lights flickered on, bathing the bay in a warm honeyed light as Marie brought the trawler fully into storm mode. Anthea slowly eased her death grip on Brand's armor and looked around cautiously. Then she dropped down to the floor and darted over to an open drawer and climbed in among Loren's socks. Only her bat ears and wide black eyes could be seen as she hunkered down.

<These armored trawlers are designed to ride out even the fiercest desert storms,> Me'von mused. <Quite an impressive feat of engineering when you think that the winds outside can haul wrecks like the *Muspell's Sons* all over the desert.>

Brand marveled at how he could hear the roaring of the winds outside and the scratching of sand across bare metal, but the trawler barely even shook. The *Polaris* remained securely moored by its massive clawed feet to the smooth rock beneath the shifting sands.

Brand pulled out the jar of algae and his bag of silverleaf nightshade, then sat on the bottom bunk. He could sense Me'von wince.

<You said you wouldn't use alchemy.>

"I can't make any elixirs with these. These can only modify existing elixirs," Brand said, pulling his remaining vials out of his boot. "Maybe I can use them to enhance the ones I already have to make them stretch until I can find another alchemical still. Don't worry; I'm not going to use these unless it's a life-or-death situation," Brand said as reassuringly as he could.

<Do I have the right to use kashmari blood magic if it's a life-or-death situation?>

Brand replaced in his boot and scrubbed at his face with his hands in frustration. His short beard had grown a bit scraggly in the last several days, he realized. He wondered if the gray in his hair had spread as well from all he'd been through. He considered limping into the washroom to take a look in the mirror but decided against it. Me'von chuckled.

<You humans can be just as vain as kashmari, sometimes more,> he said, amused.

Brand rolled his eyes but chuckled a little himself.

He pulled on a gauntlet, then picked up a handful of nightshade and dropped it into the mortar. Then, using the pestle, he ground up the dried leaves into a greyish powder. He then opened up each vial and dropped a pinch into each elixir. They fizzed a little, then settled.

When the nightshade powder had been used up, Brand scraped a bit of the blue-green algae into each vial. Unlike the powder, the algae simply sank to the bottom of the elixirs. Then he replaced the stoppers.

<You don't have to mix those up?> Me'von asked, curious despite the tinge of fear in his words.

Brand shook his head as he replaced the vials in his boot. "No, the algae will slowly release its chemicals into the elixir. If I try to rush it, it won't work as well. And since that's what's keeping the toxicity in check, I'd rather not risk making the algae less potent."

Me'von grunted.

Brand hoisted himself up to his bunk. Exchanging the jar of algae for an ironwood stick from the bag at the end of his bed and pulling out a knife from his belt, the gladiator settled his back against the metal wall and began to carve.

* * *

Outside in the haze, about twenty meters away, a Stalker stood up out of a sand dune. Sand poured off its many armored surfaces. It crouched to mitigate the winds buffeting it, but did not anchor itself again. It turned, scanned through the haze, and locked onto a large trawler settled into the sand like an angular rock. The Stalker started to creep towards the anchored Venator, slowly enough that the sound of its footsteps was masked by the roaring of the wind. Once it had closed the distance, it snuggled up to its larger cousin and quietly settled itself back into the sand. The hatch on top popped open and two robed and masked figures jumped out and down onto the sand. As soon as their boots hit the shifting ground, they sprinted over to the side of the Venator.

One of the raiders carried a pair of tanks on its back. Two hoses fed into a sort of spigot on one end that the raider pointed toward the thick metal of the Venator. He twisted a knob, then pulled out a little contraption made of two pieces of springy steel wrapped around a round piece of flint. The raider squeezed the metal to make it scratch across the flint, and a shower of sparks leapt away and ignited the gas pouring from the hoses.

The raider turned its cutter on the Venator's armor and began cutting through the thick metal. Sparks flew from the brilliant white flame as the other raider stood ready with a shotgun.

Storm

"Breach! Breach!" Marie's voice said from the grate, urgent but calm. "Intruders on the port side."

It took Brand a moment for her words to sink in. Then, dropping the knife and wood, he lurched off the bunk and limped as fast as he could down the hall.

Something massive clanged down onto the deck somewhere ahead of him. A blast of wind and gritty sand shoved Brand backwards a few paces. Shotgun blasts punctuated the now deafening roar of the storm. Answering rifle fire and revolver reports cracked through the howling wind.

<We need to get a mask,> Me'von said. <There were some hanging by the rifles.>

Brand leaned his head down and twisted his torso to lean into the wind with his good shoulder, then pushed down the hall again, one hand up to shield his face from the blowing sand.

His feet collided with something large and soft, making him stumble and fall. His hands brushed cloth and skin. A body.

Brand's heart stopped. Who was it? Eyes half-shut against the grit flying everywhere, he flipped the body over and yanked a mask off its face. He pulled it close to his nose so he could see who it was.

It was a stranger. Brand's shoulders slumped in relief, but the sharp report of a gun made him look up.

Out of the haze of swirling sand, the brilliant blue flame of a welding torch swung at Brand. The gladiator dove to the side and crashed into a bulkhead with a grunt. Picking himself up, Brand braced himself against the wall and kicked out in the direction of the torch with his good leg. His foot connected with a leg and felt a knee cave under the force of his kick. His assailant let out a muffled grunt.

Another shot rang out, this one a revolver. The deck shook slightly as something fell heavily near Brand.

A hand rested on the gladiator's shoulder and a face covered in a goggled breathing mask hove into view through the hazy sand that was swirling around them. Brand raised a massive fist.

<Stop! It's Loren!>

Brand hesitated, catching sight of the gunslinger's pale hair, and in that moment, Loren shoved a mask onto Brand's face.

Fresh air poured into Brand's lungs. He blinked the sand out of reddened eyes and coughed up the grit from his lungs. Loren helped Brand pull the straps over his head and buckle them together.

Loren pointed at something else on the ground. The gunslinger's voice was garbled, but Brand could just make out, "Help me."

Brand stood and followed Loren over a few paces and tripped on something metal and thick. He winced. Reaching down, he found the edge of the metal sheet. *It must be a piece of the hull,* Brand thought. *The intruders must have cut a hole in the hull.*

Together, Brand and Loren leveraged the sheet of armor up to block the hole in the side of the *Polaris* once more. The angle of the cut was such that the piece was able to rest against the hole without sliding down. The heavy metal armor held against the winds, though the unsealed edges rattled a bit.

Moments later, most of the sand flying around the hallway had settled.

Brand pulled his mask off and gave the loose armor piece a knock. It bounced a little.

When Brand spoke, his voice sounded as though he'd been sick for a week. "Once the storm lifts, I'll get that welded back into place."

Brand looked around and saw Finn pulling a mask off beside him, and Loren still masked and brandishing his revolver as he checked for a pulse on each of the bodies splayed out on the deck.

The gunslinger shoved the first robed figure over onto its back and pulled down its mask.

Loren frowned. "Do you recognize them?" he asked hoarsely. His eyes were red like Brand's.

Finn shook his head, then coughed violently. He winced and spat a wad of grit and spittle onto the sandy deck.

When he got to the body Brand had stumbled over, Loren stiffened.

"This one's still alive, boss," he said hoarsely. He took a step back and trained his revolver on the intruder's head.

Finn stepped over and, keeping his rifle ready in one hand, pulled the intruder up into a sitting position against the bulkhead. He slapped the man on the cheek. The man's eyes fluttered open. He looked down and saw the blood seeping down the front of his robes and moaned.

"Who are you?" Finn said, his voice gravelly.

The intruder swallowed hard and licked parched lips. His eyes rested on the revolver and the hardened Duati wielding it.

"Sam Wentworth," the intruder said.

"Who do you work for?"

The intruder coughed. "Does it matter?"

Finn hesitated, then lowered his rifle. He knelt in front of the unfortunate man. "It does to me. Your kashmari lord sent a couple of idiots to their deaths. I don't like that."

The man looked at Finn as though confused, but shrugged. "Kushchai. Doesn't matter if you like it or not; he's more powerful than any other kashmari alive, maybe even High Lord Fafnir."

"Is that what he told you?"

The intruder was silent. He didn't look Finn in the eye. Instead, his eyes narrowed at Brand.

"Cadmus Brand," he whispered in awe. Then he laughed. "So you're not dead. Help me finish this job and we can return victorious to Lord Kushchai. I'm sure he'll give a healthy ransom to the man who returns the Champion of Darnan to him."

"I can't do that," Brand said coldly.

The intruder looked around at the scavengers. "You faked your own death—for this? To join these pathetic bootlickers?" he scoffed.

<Kushchai must have told everyone you'd died in the desert.>

<Maybe he assumed I did.>

"Your wounds are bad," Finn said, "but if you want a chance at living, I can give it to you. "

Wentworth scoffed. "In exchange for what? I don't have any money."

Finn smiled tightly. "Swear to never work for a kashmari again. I'll get you medical attention and find a good job for you away from Kushchai and the rest of those kashmari scum."

Brand's jaw dropped as Finn offered his hand out to the intruder.

"What do you say?"

The intruder eyed Finn's hand. His eyes drifted upwards to search Finn's lined face. Then he spat on the scavenger's hand.

"If I die in the service of my lord, then so be it. I'll not join with some low kashmari's errand boy."

Finn growled in frustration. His words took on an irritated edge Brand hadn't heard before. "Your lord knew you'd fail. He knew you'd probably die. He only hired you to toss you at us in the hopes you'd slow us down. You owe him allegiance for that?"

He sighed and stood.

"Loren, bind this fool's wounds, then tie him up. If he survives, we'll drop him off at the nearest village. I'm going out to their trawler. Make sure no one's waiting for us."

"No!" Wentworth screamed. "I will not return disgraced!" The man shifted his hand out from underneath his back and pulled out a gun. He put it to his head and fired.

The three men stood in shock. Brand turned away, dizzy and nauseous. Even Me'von seemed completely taken aback.

Wren appeared next to Brand from the hallway. Brand quickly stepped in front of her, shielding her from the scene. He took her gently by the elbow and guided her down toward the bunk room.

"I don't need your protection," Wren said reproachfully. "I've seen plenty of horrible things out here. I don't mind a few dead bodies."

Brand didn't say anything. He sat down on a bunk, shaking.

"You're covered in blood," Wren said. "Are you okay?"

"It's not mine."

Wren took his hands in hers. "Brand, what's wrong? What happened?"

Brand looked up into her soft eyes. He hung onto her hands like a lifeline.

<Talk to her. She's stronger than she looks.>

Brand's stunned mind resisted, but somehow the kashmari's words softened his heart. He breathed out and nodded slowly.

"Finn offered to help the guy who was still alive. The guy…he shot himself instead of accepting the help from a lesser kashmari lord's servant." Brand raked his fingers through his hair and stared at the cold metal decking underfoot. The image of the dead intruder brought back the image of Mirane. The gladiator began to tremble.

"Oh." Wren's face fell. She patted his hand. "That's not the first time that's happened, unfortunately, and it won't be the last."

Her voice took on a hard edge. "The kashmari, they twist peoples' minds, make them believe the kashmari are nearly gods, make them do whatever they say."

"I know," Brand said softly. He stared at his hands and traced the purple scabs on his palms.

"Was I like that?" Brand asked softly. <Am I like that?>

<We are both like that,> Me'von said mournfully.

Wren didn't answer immediately. Instead, she covered the scabs with her own hands and squeezed. In the heavy silence, Brand could hear the low murmur of Finn and Loren talking while they cleaned up and disposed of the bodies.

"I should be in there, helping them," Brand said. He stood, but his leg buckled underneath him. He collapsed to the deck.

"Ah," he groaned. He pulled himself back up and grimaced. "That's the worst my leg's felt since I put on the brace."

His leg felt like it was on fire, but he gritted his teeth and took a step. His leg buckled again.

Wren pushed him back down. "I'll go. Just take it easy, ok?"

She left, leaving Brand alone with his thoughts.

Brand held his head in his hands, darkness wrapping around him, threatening to consume him. His thought spun back to the night that he'd slept with Mirane, of how she'd talked of killing pharmakons and how he'd let himself be seduced by that beautiful woman; the night Mirane had told him she was carrying his child, and how he'd so willingly agreed to run away with her, and how moments later, she'd willingly thrown him over like a broken old plaything. Of the wonderful things Kushchai had said to him, seducing him with comforts and wealth, and then the night that Kushchai had dragged him out to the desert to torture and abandon him to the storm. Of Fafnir, of his games, and his promises of some unknown future as a savior. Of Me'von the other night when he'd tortured the omegalid.

They're all like that, Brand thought.

At that thought, Me'von seemed to withdraw into himself. If the kashmari had been capable, he might have been crying, Brand realized.

<That's how you're different. You don't want to be like them,> Brand said.

<Doesn't do much good, though, does it?> Me'von said miserably. <I am what I am.>

Even out here in the Wastes, it seemed that Brand couldn't escape the long tendrils of the kashmari. Whether it was Kushchai's goons or Fafnir's device, the kashmari were still manipulating him and those around him. There was never any escape. A heavy helplessness seeped into Brand's mind.

After about an hour, the pain in Brand's leg had eased enough that he could stand. He gathered a new set of clothes and limped numbly to the washroom, studiously keeping his eyes away from the hallway where the intruder had died.

He leaned heavily on the wall of the tiny washroom. A small rusty pipe jutted out from the wall over a tiny drain. He twisted a small knob next to the pipe and a drizzle of water leaked out.

The gladiator pried his brace off, stripped, then showered, doing his best to scour away the blood, dust, and gore from his skin and hair. As he washed, he felt that same sense of empty silence that he always felt when he'd killed a man. Death had visited, and the whole world had paused to mourn.

When he was finished, the howling of the storm outside had abated and the *Polaris* was on the move once more. Brand collected his ironwood sticks and knife from his bunk, then headed to the ladder. Each rung made his leg burn and by the time he made it up onto the outer hull of the *Polaris,* he was sweating profusely. He collapsed into one of the recessed wells, closed his eyes, and breathed in the cool air.

The desert night was frigid but smelled clean and crisp. He looked up into the night sky. Stars riddled the sky like a billion tiny holes in a giant velvet blanket. Across the middle of the sky, a cloudy swirl of blue and the faintest white hung above him.

He felt a slight tug as his eyes moved of their own accord to rest on a single, bright star.

<This star is called Polaris,> Me'von murmured. <The North Star.>

"That's what the *Polaris* is named for?"

<Yes. No matter where we travel, Polaris will always stay right where it is, right over true north. Humans have been using it to navigate for centuries.>

Confused, Brand growled, "We have maps; why tell me this?"

Me'von's answer was quiet and fearful. <What star do we steer by, Cadmus Brand?>

The gladiator's expression softened as he realized the kashmari was just as lost and confused as he was. He sighed.

His thoughts a jumbled mess, Brand pulled out the ironwood sticks and began whittling, letting the shavings flit away in the soft breeze. He took each small piece of ironwood and carefully bored a hole through it lengthwise, then slowly widened and smoothed the hole. He paused after finishing the first bead to pull his fingers through his graying hair and found the scar on his scalp, another reminder of what he'd done while chasing the approval of a kashmari. Percy had died at Brand's hand for their sport and had nearly taken Brand with him to the grave.

Brand took out the stick again and carved off one more bead, then continued to work on the others.

As he focused on the dense wood, a dark, winged shape blotted out the stars above for a moment, and then was gone.

* * *

Once Finn and Loren had finished cleaning the hallway, they stood silently together for a short time.

"You alright?" Finn asked the younger man.

Loren hesitated, then said, "Yeah, but I'm the hired gun. Killing's my job." A note of sorrow tinged his words. "You?"

The scavenger looked at his hands. "It wasn't me, you, Wren, or Brand. I'll take it."

"Brand seemed to take it pretty hard."

Finn nodded slowly.

Loren shook his white-blond head. "I don't get it. He's a gladiator. I've seen those fights. They're worse than this. Why is this different?"

Finn crossed his arms over his chest, pondering the question. "It hits differently when you see yourself in your enemy's eyes. Even though I try to offer them sanctuary, at the end of the day, a man like that is just another arm of the kashmari to me, just another one of their weapons. I have to see them like that. You do too. But to Brand, that man could have been him."

"You seem to understand him a lot better than I do," Loren mused.

Finn snorted. "I've lived longer than you, seen a lot more than you."

"Brand's lived almost as long as you have."

"In a bubble, though. Life out here is a lot more educational than that padded arena of his."

After a long pause, Finn said, "We need to go check the Stalker and see if there was a third raider."

The gunslinger grabbed a shotgun, more ammo for his revolver, and slung a bandoleer of shotgun shells over his shoulder. "After you, boss."

"Marie," Finn called. Marie gave a little whistle from the nearby grate to let him know she was listening. "Once we're outside, move the *Polaris* a couple hundred meters away from the Stalker.

"Yes, Finn."

Out in the fresh, storm-scrubbed air, Finn breathed deeply. The intruder's death hadn't passed completely by Finn, as he'd intimated to Loren. But the younger man didn't need to know that. Finn took the roiling frustration and sadness in his heart and locked it away for later. He had a role to fill.

Loren took point, aiming the long barrel of the shotgun up the vacant gangplank of the intruders' Stalker. Finn trained his rifle on the gaping hole. The younger man gestured for Finn to wait and ran up the gangplank. He swept the shotgun left, then right, then motioned for Finn to follow. The older scavenger sprinted up the gangplank as quietly as his heavy boots would allow.

The cockpit of the small trawler was empty. A few lights flickered on the command console, but otherwise, all was dark. Loren leapt up the ladder to the tiny bunk room and washroom above the cockpit.

Finn wrinkled his nose. "Smells like something died in here."

"Their kitchen is revolting," Loren said, sounding as though he were trying not to gag. "One bed mussed up, two made. Three bags of personal effects."

"So there's another raider around here someplace."

Loren made his way back down as Finn tapped a button on the console. Sam Wentworth's voice started speaking from a grate nearby.

"Renald and Severan got into it again today. Got so bad I told them to shut it or take a hike. Severen threw a bolt cutter at me and ran off. Missed me, but I packed us up and left without him." The raider chuckled. "Good riddance."

"Guess that answers that," Finn said dryly.

Loren looked at the dark sand dunes stretching in every direction. "I'd hate to be Severan, then. There's nothing for miles."

"His problem; not ours," Finn said, unsympathetic. "Grab anything of value. I'll see if they have any charges and rig it to blow. No sense in leaving behind anything for the Honorable Kushchai to scavenge."

Loren found a sack in a compartment and busied himself ripping out as much of the wiring from the command console as he could. Finn started rummaging in all the compartments, pulling out a stash of coins and a barely-used leather journal. Finn flipped through the journal for a moment. It only had a few place names and dates; probably nothing more than a record of the crew's mission. He pocketed it anyway.

"Ah ha," Finn said, pulling out a sack of heavy iron balls with fuses sprouting from the top. Finn took out his knife and started ripping the sack into narrow strips, then tied the strips together. This done, he tied the grenade fuses to his makeshift sack fuse and jammed them into the holes in the command console that Loren had left behind.

The scavenger pulled himself up the ladder to the kitchenette. Finn gagged at the stench. The tiny copper stove was overflowing with empty glass bottles. A small animal carcass swarming with maggots leaked a sticky fluid onto the small, fold-down table. Finn pulled his bandana up over his nose, then shoved several bottles aside. He picked up a half-full bottle of vodka and hurried back down to the cockpit. He then doused his fuse in liquor. The smell of vodka filled the small compartment. Finn paid out the fuse a little at a time as he backed out of the Stalker.

"Time to go," Finn said. He chucked the rest of the liquor bottle into the cockpit, then struck a match and lit the end of the fuse. Blue flames raced along the sack cloth.

The two men sprinted away from the Stalker.

A few seconds later, there was a loud explosion from inside. Both men dove into the sand instinctively, but most of the damage had been contained within the machine.

Finn rolled over and sat up, looking back. Black smoke billowed out of the shattered viewport and down the gangplank.

"Good riddance indeed," Finn muttered to himself.

Loren picked himself up and brushed white sand off his black leather trousers. "What kind of an idiot spends the money to buy all these stalkers, and then stuffs them full of the greenest scavengers he could find?"

Finn snorted as he stood and brushed some sand off his trousers. "They aren't even scavengers. They're goons in a tank. Probably found them in one of his factories."

"Fine. What idiot spends money hand over fist just to fill these Stalkers with the worst hired goons he could find?"

Finn smiled. "Not every hired goon can be as amazing as you, Loren."

Loren chuckled. "True."

"Kushchai isn't an idiot. He just doesn't care about human life and he has enough money to throw away dozens of Stalkers."

Finn frowned as they walked back to the *Polaris*. Two Stalkers, but no sign of the *Dauntless*.

Finn had to admit he wasn't too broken up about having not run into the Titan-class scavenger tank, yet. It sported four rotary cannons and a longer main gun than the *Polaris*, which gave it an edge over the Venator in both range and firepower. And her crew chief, Rhamnus, was a cunning tactician. The one thing the *Polaris* had that the *Dauntless* didn't, though, was speed and agility.

Still, Finn would have liked to know where the *Dauntless* was.

Finn sat in the pilot's chair. "Storm's over, Marie, so let's get going."

"The hull of the *Polaris* is compromised."

"It'll hold for now. We need to get out of here now before that third raider shows up. Brand can patch it up when he gets his head screwed back on straight."

The trawler rumbled to life under Finn's feet and lurched at an angle as the *Polaris* stood. A golden waterfall of sand flowed down across the viewport. Then the *Polaris* shuddered and stepped forward.

* * *

27 September 1062 P.E.
Palatine Hall, Darnan

Kushchai leaned back in his chair and eyed his cards. He took a long drink of his wine, then drew a card. With a fanged grin, he threw a fistful of chips into the middle of the table. Beside him, a slender kashmari woman wrapped her arms around his shoulders. He whispered something in her ear. She laughed.

"Lord Kushchai," someone behind him said.

Kushchai didn't look up from the game.

"Can't you see I'm busy–"

"Too busy for the Lord of Duat, are we?"

Kushchai nearly dropped his glass. The intruder was none other than Lord Jinn, hands locked at the small of his back like a strict governess, face impassive save for one eyebrow arched over a blazing red eye.

Kushchai brushed away the woman, threw his cards on the table, and stepped aside with the Duati lord, all irritation scrubbed from his face.

"Jinn, what are you doing here? I thought you were back in Duat."

Jinn didn't speak, but led Kushchai down the hall into a study overflowing with thousands of books and stuffed with numerous stone busts. He beckoned for the Darnanian city lord to enter, then closed the door behind them. He turned on Kushchai.

"I was in Duat, true. I came back because I heard rumors of your Stalkers being mowed down out in the Wastes. Is this true?"

Kushchai shrugged, hiding his own concern. "I wouldn't say mowed down. Two have been destroyed, but you really shouldn't have worried. Their purpose is to get in the way of the other scavengers. Their destruction is expected and accounted for, to a certain extent. The *Dauntless* is within a day and a half of the wreck, closer than any other sand trawler by two days. They'll have more than enough time to search the *Muspell's Sons* and get out before anyone else arrives."

Jinn considered this, then nodded.

"You seem particularly jittery about this." Kushchai walked over to the sideboard in the corner and pulled out a bottle of whiskey and two glasses. "You came all the way from your cozy little cavern for this?"

Jinn joined him. "After what Fafnir did to Mirane? You're crazy if you aren't jittery." Jinn accepted a glass and took a sip.

Kushchai shrugged. "There are worse punishments. But that's what we're trying to stop, isn't it? It's time to get his boot off our necks, once and for all."

Jinn swirled his drink around a bit. "You're sure Rhamnus can handle this?"

"I've only ever known of one other scavenger who could best Rhamnus, and he's dead. I'm not worried at all."

Jinn tossed back his whiskey and set his glass on the table. "Alright. I'll let you do your part, then, and try not to worry."

Kushchai patted Jinn on the back. "You just take care of Fafnir, my friend. He trusts you more than anyone else. Keep him happy and in the dark."

"I know." Jinn walked to the door and opened it. Then he turned back. "Just out of curiosity, who was the scavenger who could best Rhamnus?"

Kushchai waved a dismissive hand. "He died about five years ago. The Marauder he was in fell off a cliff. No one survived the crash."

"Who was it though?" Jinn pressed.

Kushchai tilted his head curiously.

"If you must know, it was Jacob Finn."

Recognition and shock dawned on Jinn's face. "Your former master scavenger."

Kushchai nodded and raised his glass.

"The best. May he rest in peace."

Jinn hurried back to Kushchai. His voice was low and frantic.

"You idiot! That's the name of the man who Sahure hired!"

Kushchai's face blanched. "That's impossible."

"If Finn gets to the *Muspell's Sons* first, he'll get the device and our plan will go out the window!"

Kushchai hurried over to the desk and yanked out a map, smoothing it out on the desktop.

"What are you doing?" Jinn asked.

"I'm going out there. Tonight."

"What? You'll never get there in time."

"There's a flock of titanopters here in this pass. A runnerbeast can get me there before midnight. Then I can fly a titanopter out to the *Dauntless*."

Jinn made a face. "Nasty, brutish creatures. Riding one of them isn't going to be pleasant."

"It'll be better than watching Fafnir feed my heart to a rocksaber." Kushchai folded up the map and stuffed it back into the desk. "This has to work, and I can't rely on Rhamnus keeping his head straight if Finn is involved. They'll start a personal war and not care one whit about anything else in the world. I need to get out there and take command of the *Dauntless*."

Jinn grasped the other kashmari's hands. "Be safe out there, and watch your back."

Kushchai nodded curtly and ran out the door.

Jinn poured himself another whiskey and sat on a spindly chair, legs stretched out in front of him. He sipped the lukewarm liquid, waiting.

A book slightly jutted out of the perfectly ordered bookcase, catching Jinn's eye. He rose and stepped over to the book, pulled it the rest of the way out, and looked in the hole between tomes left behind. There was nothing, but the book in his hand seemed oddly light. The Duati city lord flipped it open and leafed through its pages.

A hollow had been cut out of the center of the book. Between the cut pages sat a delicate crystalline seed. A shock ran through the Duati lord. He pulled the seed out of its hiding place and held it up to the light. The amethyst proto-leaves of the sapling within the crystal caught the warm light of the electric lamps and tossed it onto the walls and bookcases.

A moment later, the hulking high lord strode in and strode over to his lieutenant.

Fafnir caught sight of the seed and froze.

"Where did you get that?" the high lord rumbled.

Jinn gestured at the hollowed-out book. "What should we do with it?"

Fafnir reached out as though about to take the seed, but his fingers stopped millimeters above its crystalline surface. He pulled his hand back and took a step back.

"If my plan works, we're going to need it later. Hold onto it. Don't let anyone near it."

Jinn nodded slowly, still mesmerized by the seed. He shook himself and carefully pocketed the crystal.

"What of Kushchai?"

"He's on his way."

"Good."

"The only way this would be sweeter is if we could give Finn your redstone sword for a day."

"Unnecessary. I don't need Kushchai dead," Fafnir said. Then, as an afterthought, he added, "Yet."

"How did you learn that Finn was still alive?"

"I saw him."

"Oh."

AFTERMATH

28 September 1062 P.E.
Aeolian Dunes

The mood in the *Polaris's* kitchen the next afternoon was somber. Finn ate slowly, pensively. Loren and Brand both picked at the gray tinned vegetables and pale rice swimming in a bland gravy. Wren didn't eat at all, but watched the others, her food forgotten in front of her.

"I should have known someone might try to sneak up on us like that in a storm," Finn said. He took a bite. "Wasn't thinking. We should have had someone up top during storms or anytime we needed to stop."

"Don't we have an infrared scanner?" Loren asked.

Finn nodded. "It burned out a few months ago. Never repaired it. Forgot with this *Muspell's Sons* mess."

"I'll take a look at it," Brand said.

"Need that up and running before the next storm hits."

They sat in silence for several long moments, long moments, listening to the faint creak as the metal trawler continued its trudge across the sand dunes.

Finally, Brand couldn't hold back any longer.

"It was stupid offering that man refuge," he growled. "What if he'd decided to shoot you or Loren or me instead of himself?"

"I've made this argument a hundred times," Loren said. "You'll never win. It's just part of who Finn is."

Wren nodded. "There have been others like that man. Some kill themselves when Finn offers help, and others try to kill us."

Brand glared at Finn and Finn stared resolutely back.

"Picking up a random gun for hire is worth more to you than the lives of your own crew?"

Finn leaned forward over his plate. He jabbed a finger at Brand's armored chest. "A week ago, you were a random idiot half dead and abandoned in the desert."

"I hadn't just tried to kill you."

Finn pointed to Loren. "He did when I first picked him up."

Brand looked over at Loren, who looked a bit sheepish. The gunslinger looked down at his long slender fingers laced together on the tabletop, icy eyes inspecting his nails. Loren stole a pained look at Wren, who gave him a pitying smile.

Finn continued.

"You can't tell just by looking at someone what they'll do because up until that moment, they've only done what they've been told. But in that special moment, when you give men who've never had control of their own lives a simple choice—that's when the real magic happens. Some are too afraid, but once in a while, you get a man willing to break free of his shackles and fly."

Brand looked down at his own scabbed hands, his thoughts twisting around the kashmari high lord who still controlled his life.

Finn stood and with a few solid stomps, marched over and leaned his head into the cockpit. "Marie, be a dear and stop us for a bit so Brand can patch us up."

The older scavenger looked back at Brand. "The hull still needs to be sealed."

"I'll finish that, then work on the scanner." Brand stood stiffly and stretched.

Finn stepped over to the big gladiator. He put a hand on Brand's arm. "Everyone deserves a chance, don't you think?"

Jaw still firmly set and hands balled into frustrated fists, Brand glared down at the older man. The gladiator looked away, his amber eyes locking with Loren's icy blue gaze. Brand took a deep breath and let the tension fade from his body, unclasping his hands. He nodded silently, then limped away down the hall.

<Finn's a good man. Strange, but good.>

Brand glanced over his shoulder at the old scavenger, who was walking quietly to Wren, patting her hand gently.

"Yeah, I know. I still think he's wrong."

Brand found a welding torch, mask, and thick gloves, but before he pulled them on, he pulled out yet another pill. He stared at it for a long moment, wondering if there was any point in taking it out here. He hadn't seen the plague since he'd left Darnan.

<Just because you haven't run into someone with it yet doesn't mean it's not out here,> Me'von said. <The plague doesn't care who or where you are. Besides, the withdrawal symptoms are a beast.>

Brand sighed and swallowed the pill, then got to work. The summer sun was beating down on the bright sand around him, reflecting its heat and light up to him. He was sweating profusely in moments. He could feel the back of his neck and his exposed upper arms burning and sweat dripping down his back and temples.

As he worked, it occurred to him that Me'von had been uncharacteristically silent, not even adding his little quips.

"You still there?" Brand muttered.

<Yes.>

"Why so quiet?"

<You've been quiet too, and for the same reason, I think. What more is there to say?>

Brand grunted.

"Who are you, really?" he asked.

<What do you mean? I am Me'von.>

"I mean, Kushchai is the city lord of Darnan. What do you do?"

<What's my job?> The kashmari sighed. <Technically, I'm a disgraced foot soldier under Sahure.>

"You work for him? Why didn't you mention that? Why were you disgraced?"

<I don't work for him anymore. I'm a deserter.>

"Why did you desert?"

The kashmari didn't reply, but Brand got the distinct impression that the kashmari didn't want to explain. He sighed.

"How do you know Fafnir?"

<Everyone knows Fafnir.>

"Fine. How does Fafnir know you?"

The kashmari growled in frustration, then relented.

<I may have led a small rebellion against him.>

Brand's jaw dropped. "How small?"

Me'von chuckled. <Well, not small at all. I took over the ruling family of a nation to the east, built up quite an army, and led them on a march on Darnan.> His voice grew more somber, even tinged with sorrow. <We made it as far as New Braunen before Fafnir's army wiped mine out. If his vrykolakas hadn't joined the battle, I might have even won.>

"When was this?"

<About a century ago.>

Brand shook his head in amazement, envisioning Me'von at the head of an army. He couldn't quite imagine it. He finished welding the piece of hull back on and went back inside to the dining area, where Finn was sitting with Loren.

"You look like you've been cooked alive," Loren said.

"Feels like it, too," Brand said, filling a glass with water and draining it in a few gulps. He refilled it and downed it again. Then he set the glass down and splashed water on his face, neck, and forearms, trying to soothe the burning. "Hull's patched."

"Excellent," Finn said, standing. "Good thing you're here to take care of these things. If it had been up to me, we would have been stuck here half the day."

Brand ran his wet fingers through his hair, dampening it.

"I'm going to go get started on that scanner," he said, and limped down the hall. "Marie? What's wrong with the infrared scanner?"

"A lightning strike during a sandstorm fried the wiring. The main controller is shielded, so it should still be functional. Replacing the wiring should get the scanner back up and running."

Brand grunted. "Where is the wiring?"

"In a panel in the hallway," Marie said. "All of the panels are labeled with diagrams. That should help you find it."

It only took Brand a few moments of scanning the diagrams etched into the wall panels in the area before he found the correct panel. He quickly unscrewed the metal cover plate, revealing a snarl of colored wires. Some of them did indeed look charred, while others merely singed.

"So Marie," Brand said as he clipped the damaged wires out, "tell me about how scavenging usually works."

"The *Polaris* takes on supplies for six months and ventures out into the Wastes. Finn is in charge of finding the wrecks, through tips from his contacts, hints from the scanner, and simply stumbling upon them. The storms can shift massive amounts of sand and rock, uncovering wrecks at any time."

"And then everyone strips everything valuable off the wreck and you haul it back."

"Yes."

"It takes six months to get enough to haul back to a city?"

"A fresh wreck can take several months to break down. Much of the armor plating gets sold to camelid merchants, while the crew of the *Polaris* keeps only the most valuable artifacts and pieces of tech. Some of that tech gets incorporated into the trawler. Finn and Wren like to keep any dvergen records, and Loren has been on the lookout for dvergen weaponry, unfortunately to no avail. The rest is sold in the cities."

Brand glanced up at the cubbies stuffed with frail books. "Ah."

"Brand?" the AI said.

"Yes?"

"I have decided to include you in my family, Brand."

Brand lowered his wire cutter.

"Why?"

"You have repaired the *Polaris* and me several times. You saved the crew. I believe you have earned a place in my family."

Brand mulled over the AI's words. A bit of the knot in his gut loosened. "Thank you, Marie," he murmured.

As he worked, splicing sections of clean, new wire into the old, Finn came into the room. The scavenger picked up his armor and sat, cloth in hand, and began to wipe the dust and grit off the armor.

Brand hesitated, then dropped the wires, wiped his greasy hands on his shirt, and limped over to Finn. He leaned against a locker and crossed his arms.

"You get after me for having kashmari hooks in me," he said, "but you work for a kashmari yourself. You're a hypocrite."

Finn looked Brand square in the eye. "I don't work for him," he spat.

Brand spread his arms out, indicating the *Polaris*. "Really? You bought this hunk of metal yourself?"

"Of course not."

Brand waited, arms folded across his chest, eyebrow raised.

Finn sighed. "I don't work for Sahure. I work with him. I run the operation out here in the desert, and he gets to be the pretty kashmari face."

Brand frowned. "That's it?"

Finn nodded. "All of Sahure's wealth, his schemes—they all start out here in the desert, with me. Without me, his ambitions have no teeth. Without me, he can't challenge the other lords."

"You think he's any better than the rest?"

Finn shrugged and pulled out a small knife and used it to pick a small rock out of his armor. "Sahure's still a monster. Suits me to have them at each other's throats, though. Keeps them out of the Wastes."

"At the expense of everyone who doesn't live in the Wastes." Brand shook his head in disbelief. After all, Finn had said, how could he be so selfish? "But if you win this contest for Sahure, he'll take over Navar and become one of the most powerful kashmari in the world. He won't need you anymore."

Finn nodded.

"Why are you still trying to win this contest, then?"

A sly grin appeared on Finn's face. "I don't intend to help Sahure win. I don't intend for any of them to win. That device shouldn't end up in any kashmari's hands, ever."

Brand was acutely aware of the kashmari in his own head at that moment. He nodded thoughtfully to Finn and limped back to the infrared wiring. More twists, more politics.

<While I don't disagree with him on any of those points, I think necessity may have to outweigh ideals,> Me'von said thoughtfully. <But if we are willing to give it to Fafnir, doesn't that make us the selfish ones?>

Brand didn't respond. Instead, he was imagining what would happen if Fafnir didn't get the device. And on the other hand, what would happen if he did?

<Depends on what the device is. We still don't know what it does. Maybe it'll be a weather device that brings regular rain to the desert.>

Brand seriously doubted that.

<I understand why you assume the worst of us, but Fafnir has done quite a bit of good for humans when you think about it. He's fed them, clothed them, heated their homes in the winter.>

<Murdered them, raped them, enslaved them.>

<Also true.>

Finn had long finished cleaning his armor and returned to the cockpit by the time Brand had finished his own work. He pressed the little button on the grill set in the bulkhead next to him.

"Infrared sensor should be back online," he said. "Go ahead and give it a try."

Brand waited until Finn's tinny voice came through the grate.

"Looks great, Brand. Good job."

"Thanks."

Brand replaced the metal sheet covering the wires and screwed it back on. He put his tools away and limped up to the cockpit.

Both Loren and Finn were huddled around something on the command console.

"Is something wrong with the sensor?" Brand asked.

Loren replied, "No, I don't think so. It's saying there's something up ahead, though. It looks like it's covered in titanopters."

"No, these are too small," Finn corrected. "Pterns. Smaller, faster versions of their cousins. It's only a few minutes off to the side. Why don't you go see what the fuss is?"

Loren shook his head. "If there are pterns in those numbers, you can be sure there are rock wyrms about as well. I don't think Brand will thank us if we get the *Polaris* banged up yet again just before we reach the wreck."

"Sahure said to keep an eye out for all dvergen artifacts," Finn said. "If it's anything promising, we can make a note of the location and come back later."

Loren grunted and walked out. As he passed Brand, he said, "You coming?"

Brand hesitated. He didn't relish going back out into the sun so soon. But Lorene seemed to be warming up to him, and he wanted to stay on the gunslinger's good side. Besides, as the mechanic, he'd only be taking up space in the cockpit anyway. He followed Loren up the ladder.

The two men clambered across the metal skin of the trawler to ensconce themselves in the recesses embedded in the hull, setting their rifles across their laps within easy reach. Brand pulled the wide brim of his hat down to shield his eyes and his bandana up to keep the ever-blowing sand out of his mouth and nose.

As soon as the *Polaris* crested another dune, Loren called out and pointed to the right of the trawler. A twisting, writhing mass of winged lizards swarmed over something massive and grey lying on the sand. Brand squinted against a piercing glare thrown off a reflective piece of metal among the beasts.

It was the wreck of an armored trawler that had been blasted apart. It was impossible to make out any features, but from the size of the debris, it must have been at least the size of a Marauder. The pterns seemed to be fighting over several charred bodies among the wreckage.

The pterns themselves looked like tiny, pale titanopters, sand-colored with small flecked black spots all over. Each had a frill of spikes around its throat. They squawked and screamed as they fought over the best tidbits. As they stretched their wings, Brand could see that the undersides of their wings were a pale dusty blue.

Loren put a bronze spyglass to his face and squinted into it. "It's hard to say, but I think that might have been the *Triumph*, Unas's Marauder. If we have time later, we might come back, but it'll be a much lower priority."

"What blasted it like that?"

Loren collapsed the spyglass and pocketed it. "Had to be one with a main gun. Either the *Dauntless* or maybe the *Manticore.* It's the only other Venator-class trawler around."

"Just *Manticore* and *Polaris*?"

"Yep. Once you get a man gun, the chassis and other structures have to be reinforced, and that gets expensive. Most kashmari lords aren't rich enough to build them, let alone maintain them."

A moment later, a long brown creature as large as the *Polaris* breached the surface of the sand like a jumping whale. Its long body slammed down onto the debris, head flailing. Its strange craggy jaws snagged an unlucky ptern, then slithered back into its hole, dragging the screaming reptile with it.

"Rock wyrms," Loren hollered above the frantic cries of the pterns as they fled into the sky.

Another wyrm followed the first, bursting from underneath the sand and catching two pterns in its jaws; then another wyrm erupted from below, and another. Loren whooped and laughed. Brand grinned too as he watched the wyrms feed. They were striped, he realized, with brown stripes stretching from the tip of their snouts all the way to their whip-like tails. Rows of eye-like white spots peeked from between the stripes. *Like Anthea's fur*, Brand noted.

The gladiator watched the feeding frenzy until the *Polaris* strode out of view behind the marching dunes.

"I guess I never realized just how many creatures live out here," Brand said to Loren as they descended back into the trawler. "I always thought nothing lives in the desert. Guess I was wrong."

"Right? It's crazy. There's a whole world of living things out here." Loren stashed his rifle and headed for the cockpit. "Finn needs to know about the *Triumph*, or whoever that was. He'll want to know someone big is nearby."

* * *

Finn took the news of the Marauder wreckage stoically. He'd been expecting it.

"Get us up on top of that big dune there ahead of us," Finn commanded Marie, pointing at a mountain of sand.

When they reached the top, Finn said, "Turn us around to face south and hold us here. Fire up the scanner. I want a detailed scan of every machine in front of us."

Marie acknowledged. A whirring sound came from the console. A moment later, a map appeared on the monitor with seven small red dots plotted upon it. Three of them only had the word "Stalker" next to them.

The other four dots sported far more details. Marie had been able to identify each unique trawler and fill in the pertinent information. Finn already knew most of it, but it was nice to be able to see it all in one glance.

Manticore: Venator-class. Mirane. Crew Chief: Mandragore.

Uraeus: Marauder-class. Djedkare. Crew Chief: Unknown.

Triumph: Marauder-class. Unas. Crew Chief: Unknown.

Firestorm: Marauder-class. Rhodri. Crew Chief: Unknown.

"So that wasn't the *Triumph* back there," Finn said with a frown. "I wonder who it was."

He continued studying the map.

"Khenot is crew chief of the *Uraeus*," Finn said, absently, scratching at his beard.

"Noted."

The word "Unknown" beside "*Uraeus*" flickered and changed to "Khenot."

"*Manticore* is still too far to the north to have taken out that Marauder. It had to have been the *Dauntless's* work. Why can't we see where Rhamnus is?"

"Unknown."

Finn sighed. "If you can see the scat but you can't see the wolf, it doesn't mean he's not there. Turn us around and scan in every direction. See if you can find the *Dauntless*."

Finn felt the deck rumbling beneath him as Marie turned the Venator around, searching. There was a pause and a whirring as Marie worked, and then the Venator turned again. As the A.I. repeated this procedure, new red dots appeared on the map labeled, "Stalker." These were all quite far away and didn't worry Finn.

As the moments stretched on and the *Polaris* continued to turn, Finn began to feel a sense of dread creeping over him.

Finally, Marie completed her scan.

"Unable to locate the *Dauntless*."

Finn swore.

"Is everything alright?" Wren asked from behind Finn.

The older scavenger spun his chair and plastered a smile on his face.

"Yeah. Just jammed my finger."

As Wren turned to leave, Finn slumped back in his chair.

The *Polaris* was still about three days out from the location of the *Muspell's Sons* that Sahure had provided. Finn hated knowing that the *Dauntless* was near, but he knew Rhamnus's goal was the same as Finn's:

Get to the wreck first. Rhamnus wouldn't turn aside to take out the *Polaris* because he knew Finn might slip past him. The *Dauntless* would be charging for the prize with everything she had.

Finn hated waiting, knowing his foe was out there waiting and watching for him too. The old scavenger pulled out Baldur's journal and tried to read, but worry chewed at his brain. After several fruitless minutes, he stuffed the journal back into his pocket and glared out the front viewport.

Arrival

Over the next two days, Brand spent most of his time deciphering dvergen runes and words, playing cards with Wren, tuning the *Polaris's* targeting system, and stretching his arm and leg. Judging by the slow reduction in pain, they seemed to be healing. Brand decided to try to walk without the brace and nearly lost an eye when he keeled over onto the kitchen counter into a utensil holder. After that, the gladiator resolved to spend only a little bit of time each day without the brace strengthening his leg.

Loren, after a week of tinned vegetables, stormed into the cockpit and yelled at Marie to stop the Venator.

"You wanna explain yourself?" Finn said coldly to Loren.

Loren glared at the scavenger. "I can't live like this. I need meat." He jabbed a finger under Finn's nose. "I'm going hunting. Don't try to stop me."

Finn held up his hands in surrender.

Loren spun to glare at Brand. "Brand, you're coming with me. Grab a rifle."

The gladiator stifled a chuckle and followed the gunslinger out of the cockpit.

Loren stalked across the hot sand, black duster billowing in the breeze, dark glasses and feathered broad-rimmed hat pulled down over his eyes to shield them from the glare coming off the dunes. Brand shouldered his rifled and followed, limping only slightly. He pulled his own hat down.

They walked for about half an hour away from the *Polaris*, skirting dunes when they could, scrambling up them when they couldn't. Brand's leg began to ache fiercely. He was about to suggest they turn back when Loren held up a hand. The gunslinger tilted his head, listening. Then, without a word, he got down prone on the ground.

Brand stiffly got down next to Loren, wincing at the heat radiating off the sand. They crawled up the dune, black and brown dusters turning them into shadows creeping over the burning sands. Loren stopped them just shy of the crest.

Peeking over the ridge of sand, Loren pointed to a swarm of small cat-sized creatures on the other side of the dune. They looked like rats with short snouts and thick tails. One of them sat up on its sturdy hind legs and glanced around, watchful.

"Together on the count of three," Loren whispered.

Brand nodded and took aim at the chest of the largest creature in the center of the pack.

"Ready?"

He nodded again.

"…One…two…THREE!"

Both men pulled the triggers at the same time. The crack of the reports scattered the beasts. Brand's shot grazed the heavy creature, but Loren's shot flew true, dropping another of the rodents. Brand's target trumpeted and the whole pack started sprinting away on their hind legs. Brand groaned.

"I got it," Loren said.

Loren reloaded his rifle with a fast *click-shh-click*. He aimed and fired again. Brand's target fell just as it crested a dune, falling out of sight.

Loren stood, clapping Brand on the shoulder with a hearty laugh. He jogged over the dune and disappeared for a moment, then reappeared carrying the corpse over one shoulder. He dropped it next to the first he had killed.

The gunslinger placed his weapon on the sand and knelt beside the beasts, head bowed. Brand heard him murmur something. Then the pale man raised his fingers to his lips and pressed them to the forehead of each beast. Finally, Loren stood and turned to Brand.

"Do you know how to dress them?" Loren asked.

"Yeah."

Brand pulled his short-bladed knife out of the sheath on his belt.

They gutted and skinned the creatures as quickly as they could. Sweat poured down their backs as the sun beat mercilessly down on them. Brand winced as the salt in the sweat pouring down the back of his neck stung already-burnt skin.

"Been meaning to ask you about Wren," Brand said, trying to distract himself from the pain. He grunted as he pulled a wad of intestines out and slopped them onto the sand.

"What about her?"

"You said you weren't interested in her."

"Yeah? So?"

"You're full of dung. You're head over heels for her."

"Yep."

Brand was startled by that frank admission. He stopped and stared at the other man. Loren paused as well and used the back of his hand to wipe sweat from his ice-blue eyes.

"Why did you lie, then?"

Loren sighed. "Wren said you fell in love with a kashmari. Is that true? Is that why you ended up out here with us?"

Brand gritted his teeth, a little annoyed that Wren had revealed that; but he'd known it would come out eventually. "Yeah."

Loren took his black fedora off and used it to fan his dripping face. His white-blond hair, slicked down by sweat, was even brighter in the desert sun than the sand. "Wren's like that for me. Finn's her adopted father, and my boss, and he sees me for what I am: nothing but a hired gun, a Duati, and an employee who can be tossed out with the trash if he sees fit."

He stopped fanning himself and seemed to droop.

"That's what a gunslinger is, and being a Duati gunslinger makes me the lowest of the low out here. I'm lucky they've kept me on this long, really. But if I were stupid enough to make a move with Wren?"

He drew a long finger quickly across his throat.

"On the other hand, if I keep my mouth shut and my hands to myself, I can stay near her, protect her. At least for a little while longer."

Loren replaced his hat and turned back to his work. As in everything else the gunslinger did, his movements were deft and smooth, practiced and skilled. He might have been the lowest of the low, but Brand could see that Loren had mastered his skills with the patient persistence of a craftsman.

"She likes you too," Brand said.

The Duati couldn't keep a smile from tugging the corner of his mouth, but he said, "Keep what I said to yourself, yeah?"

Brand nodded.

As they finished, Brand noticed shadows flitting over them and the piles of offal. He looked up.

Pterns were circling above them, their blue undersides blending in with the cloudless sky above. Loren glanced up too.

"Time to be done. Let's go."

The two men slung the gutted and skinned carcasses over their shoulders, abandoned the refuse, and hurried over the nearest dune. As soon as they were out of sight, Brand heard the screams and shrieks of the pterns as they fought over the scraps.

By the time they got back to the shade of the *Polaris*, Brand's leg was trembling badly with every step. He passed his carcass over to Loren and went straight to the shower.

Despite the pain, though, Brand was thrilled to sink his teeth into the kabobs Loren made that night. They weren't as succulent as the ones he'd had with Wren at the Apidae village, but after a week of tinned vegetables, he didn't care.

Something tugged at Brand's trouser leg underneath the table. With a twinkle in his eye, he slid a little piece of meat off the kabob and held it in his palm down by his knee. It vanished.

After dinner, Brand retreated to his bunk. Anthea followed. He hoisted himself and the zerda up, then, with long legs hanging over the side, he pulled the three ironwood beads out of his pocket and began to carefully etch a different intricate design into each. The rich reddish wood was dense and difficult to carve, but accepted each delicate design beautifully. He took his time, letting his sorrow bleed into each careful knife stroke. He ran his thumb over the new ridges.

Brand glanced over at Anthea, who was watching him work with those giant, watchful eyes. He sighed heavily and scratched behind her ears. She stepped gently onto his lap and nuzzled him affectionately, as though sensing his pain. He sat there for a long time, face long and shoulders slumped, stroking the little zerda, until the night grew stale and the others retired for the night.

* * *

1 October 1062 P.E.
Wreck of the *Muspell's Sons*
Border between the Badlands and Aeolian Dunes

On the third day, Finn called them up to the cockpit. The endless sea of sand was fading into bare, brown rock. In front of the *Polaris*, jutting out of a sand bank, was a large stone ruin that had been crushed by a sleek vessel. Half of it was still buried in sand and broken rock, while the rest of it reached up to the sky, supported by crumbling stone walls. Its metal hull caught the piercing desert sun and threw it into their eyes. The section they could see was larger than any vehicle Brand had ever seen, easily dwarfing the *Polaris.* An enormous gun had fallen off and lay nearby. Long black scorch marks streaked the hull near the gaping hole the gun had left in the hull.

"That's the *Muspell's Sons*?" Brand said.

"What's left of it, anyway," Finn said. "Marie, get us a scan to make sure the *Dauntless* isn't waiting for us. There's our entry point," he said, pointing at the gaping hole. "Need a spot to park where Marie will be left alone."

"Area clear, Finn," Marie's crisp voice said.

Loren examined a monitor in front of him. "A video feed from a camera mounted on one of Marie's drones," Loren explained to Brand.

"It looks like we're actually flying," the gladiator said, amazed. He leaned over the gunslinger's shoulder to get a better look.

"A bit of dvergen tech we salvaged," Finn said. "Blasted useful."

As the drone circled the *Muspell's Sons*, Brand could make out a tiny *Polaris* perched on its dune above the wreck.

"How about there?" Loren twisted a knob and the video stood still. "There's a gap between the other gun and the sand, inside the ruin. We could wedge ourselves in there and burrow down."

Finn nodded. "Make it happen, Marie."

The Venator crept around to the other side of the wreck. As the drone had shown, there was a shaded pocket of air underneath the intact gun that the *Polaris* could just fit into. The deck wavered under Brand's feet as the trawler crouched down and shimmied into the hole. The cockpit was plunged into shadow.

"What's the plan, boss?" Loren asked.

Finn stood. "Loren, Brand, and I will gear up and be ready to go in fifteen minutes. Wren, hold down the fort."

"You still want me, even with my leg?" Brand asked.

"We might need a mechanic. Besides, you're still an excellent fighter," Finn pointed out. "If your leg has slowed you down, I can't wait to see what you can do once it's healed."

As Brand pulled on his armor, Me'von said, <A second pill might be worth it right now. Just in case we meet someone you have to fight in there.>

Brand balked at the idea. He'd already taken his pill for the day. <I'll pass out.>

<Go into the sleeping quarters so no one sees you. I'll wake you up.>

Brand's stomach twisted at the thought, but he did as Me'von suggested and limped into the bunk room. He sat down on Finn's bunk and quickly swallowed a blood-red pill.

As had happened the previous time, Brand was out in a matter of minutes. Me'von shocked him awake again.

Brand's muscles contracted, arching his back painfully, and then relaxed. Heart pounding, Brand cursed fiercely under his breath. He raked his graying hair with his fingers, squeezing his eyes shut and taking deep, steadying breaths.

"I hate you," he muttered. Once his pulse had evened out, he stood and limped back to the others.

The three men walked down the gangplank and into the sand. Loren slowed slightly so that he was the last down the ramp. He spun and tipped his hat to Wren, a twinkle in his eye and a roguish grin upon his lips.

"Wish us luck."

Then, as fast as he'd done it, they were gone.

The Wreck

1 October 1062 P.E.
Wreck of the *Muspell's Sons*
Border between the Badlands and Aeolian Dunes

Brand clomped down the gangplank after the other two scavengers into the shade of the ruin's walls. Here, he could see how the stones had been cut to fit exactly together with no mortar so that errant sand couldn't wear away the mortar. Just like the walls around Darnan, he mused. The ruin was rounded, as well, to turn aside the scouring winds of the dunes. The gladiator wondered who had built this place, and how long ago they had lived.

<They were your ancestors,> Me'von said. <Humans. These were some of their first settlements. They retreated to their other settlements on the other side of the mountains when the water dried up here.>

<Why did it dry up?>

Me'von didn't respond, so Brand sighed and started trudging through the sand toward the open wound in the side of the *Muspell's Sons*.

Below the hulking wreck, strange oblong cylinders were scattered in the sand. Twisted chunks of metal girders stuck out of the sand around them like jagged rocks.

The three men climbed up into the wreck through the ragged hole in the hull. Loren and Finn grabbed hold of Brand's arms and hauled him up with a collective groan.

"Good thing you're a lightweight," Finn wheezed.

Loren snorted. "I've seen runnerbeasts that didn't weigh as much as him."

Brand chuckled as he got his feet under himself. "Should have seen me at my last fight. I lost a lot of weight when I was in a coma for three weeks."

The other two men stared at Brand.

"Coma?" Loren said.

Brand tapped the pink scar on his scalp.

Finn whistled. "Bet you're glad to be away from that world. Seems they made beating on you a sport of its own."

Brand shrugged. "Yeah," he said quietly. He turned his attention to the *Muspell's Sons. I'm not free of it yet,* he thought.

<Soon,> Me'von said.

Inside the wreck, it was almost pitch black. Brand lit his lamp and held it aloft. The room they were in was filled with rows of the same strange, oblong cylinders they'd seen outside. Some were stacked along one wall while others were scattered across the floor. Sand piled up around them, holding them in place.

Brand brushed the fine, dusty sand off the side of one, revealing a flowing script in faded yellow that curled around the cylinder. A long, narrow window ran the length of the cylinder. Tick marks were etched in regular intervals into the glass. Brand couldn't see anything inside.

"Empty tanks," Loren said.

"Empty tanks for what?" Brand asked.

"No idea," Finn said. "Ammo, maybe."

Brand looked dubiously at the tanks. "Like spent cartridges?"

Loren nodded.

"One of the tank rounds we scavenged for the *Polaris* is liquid-filled," Finn said. "Solidifies on impact. Might have been something like that." He beckoned for them to move towards a doorway. There was no door in sight. "Loren, take point."

The gunslinger strode forward, flicking a switch on the side of a small box he'd mounted to the brim of his hat. Gears started clicking softly within the box and a tiny beam of yellow light splashed out into the darkness. He glanced through the doorway with revolver drawn and ready, then cautiously stepped through. As soon as he did, dim red lights flickered on throughout the ship.

Loren grunted and flicked his little hat light off, then held his revolver aloft and silently swept in across the hallway. After a moment, he motioned for the others to follow. Finn stepped into the hallway after him.

Brand hesitated. Something about this ship felt…different. It was almost like he could hear something, but not with his ears. It was an unfamiliar sense, somewhere between a touch and an emotion. He'd never felt this way before, not even while using his pharmakon abilities.

It felt hostile. Desperate. Cornered.

<An echo of the last emotions of those who died here,> Me'von said quietly. Brand could sense the kashmari's unease. <You shouldn't be able to feel them.>

<Because it's a kashmari ability? Maybe we're bonding more than you thought.>

There was a long pause.

<That's not a kashmari ability.>

<What? What is it?>

"Brand?" Finn called.

Brand still hesitated. <Well?>

"Brand!"

With a sigh, Brand followed the others.

"You alright?" Finn asked.

Brand nodded. "Just needed a moment. For my leg. Sorry. Won't happen again."

"Looks like we're alone, boss. Where to?" Loren said.

The red light flickered weakly. The long hallway tilted away from them, fading from dull red-soaked metal into complete blackness down in the depths of the ship. The opposite direction led up a short way and ended in a dead end. A little bit of light leaked in from a crack somewhere up ahead.

"Not that way," Finn said, turning away from the sliver of light to stare down into the darkness.

"How big of a device are we looking for?" Brand asked.

"No idea."

"And we don't know what it does."

"Nope."

"How are we going to recognize it when we see it?"

Loren chuckled and took a few steps into the red light. "We'll know it when we find something we've never seen before."

"Not the most foolproof plan," Brand murmured.

Loren shrugged. "You got a better idea?"

"Why didn't Sahure tell you what we're looking for?" Loren asked Finn. The scavenger shrugged.

"Fafnir didn't even tell him, or any of the other kashmari."

"Why not? If he wants the device so badly, why wouldn't he make it easier for someone to find?"

"Maybe he doesn't know what it is either," Brand said.

<Something tells me that Fafnir knows exactly what it is but is trying to keep that from the other kashmari,> Me'von said.

<Sounds like him, alright.>

Finn was saying, "I've been through enough wrecks that I can tell what's onboard just by looking at the shape of the debris. We might just have to trust our instincts on this one."

Brand followed the gunslinger down the hallway. They passed door after door, pausing for Finn to read the script and shake his head. Brand felt the strange hostility increase the deeper into the ship they went. It made his skin crawl.

<Me'von, why can I feel the last emotions of the dead crew?> Brand asked silently.

The kashmari seemed uneasy at the question. <Maybe you were right. Maybe we are bonding. But still…I thought that part of me was lost a long time ago…>

<What part?>

<Never mind for now. It'll keep.>

After several more minutes, they reached the end of the hallway. A single wide door remained.

"Cargo," Finn read. He paused. He shook his head and turned around to walk back up the hallway. The others followed him.

"Don't you want to take a quick look in there on the off chance it's in there?" Brand asked.

Finn kept walking, turned down a narrow side hall, then stopped in front of a different door.

"Only if we can't find it elsewhere. We don't have the time to waste and I'm fairly certain he wouldn't have hidden it there." Finn tapped on a metal panel beside the door. "Brand, you should be able to rewire it and get it open."

Brand looked at the door. It had no handles and no visible control panel. He looked over at the flat metal wall panel Finn had indicated. Brand pulled out a screwdriver and pulled off the panel. Behind were a series of wires.

"This door hasn't had power for a thousand years," he said. "Don't expect any miracles."

Finn smiled. "Just hot-wire the door."

Brand fiddled with the wires, pulling back casings, and twisting the bare metal off its grounding. He tapped two wires together. They sparked, and the door hissed open. Brand's jaw fell open.

"In all my years of scavenging, I've never had a door fail to open due to power loss," Finn said.

Brand arched an eyebrow at the older man. "You could have done that?"

"Yep. A good lesson about wrecks, though."

Brand rolled his eyes.

They filed into what looked like some kind of meeting room, with a long table surrounded by high-backed chairs. A small black dome sat in the center of the table, a tiny red light blinked on and off at its base. Finn moved to it and tapped on the black glass.

A miniature image of a heavy-set man appeared in midair over the dome, pale and flickering slightly. The image wore chainmail under a heavy leather tabard and a thick cloak over one shoulder, but the gigantic kashmari's face was unmistakable.

Brand's jaw dropped. "High Lord Fafnir. He looks exactly the same as he did when I saw him the other day, but this must be from…"

"A thousand years ago." Finn nodded.

The high lord's image snarled at them. "So help me, if you close that portal, Baldur, I will destroy you and every last dverger in this forsaken realm. I will—"

A flash of light flickered across the high lord's image from something that hadn't been in view of the recording. The high lord's face fell, eyes wide, mouth wide in stunned silence. It took him several minutes to compose himself enough to turn back to whatever device had recorded this.

Fafnir found his voice again at last. His voice was laced with sorrow and disbelief.

"How…how could you? You've doomed us all, Baldur. You've doomed Midgard and all the other realms as well." He drew himself up to his full height and with renewed determination, glared with bared teeth at the recorder. His voice, even across the centuries, rumbled with hatred as it shook the table. "I swear to you that I will destroy every last dverger, and then I will escape Muspelheim. I will return to Midgard, and I will complete my mission, no matter if it takes me until the end of time."

The image flickered and vanished. The crew of the *Polaris* stared at the empty air where the high lord's image had been.

<How old are you, Me'von?> Brand asked.

The kashmari sighed. <I've forgotten exactly how old. I stopped counting at two thousand years a few centuries ago, I believe.>

Brand was stunned.

<Do all kashmari live that long?>

<We have no bodies, only immortal souls. Yes, we exist for that long and longer. But do we really live?> The kashmari asked philosophically. <I don't tend to think so. It's more a crude approximation of life if you ask me.>

"Maybe I should have paid better attention to those dvergen books," Loren said slowly, "because I didn't get any of that. What's Midgard? What portal was he talking about?"

Finn shook his head, clearly baffled himself.

"No idea. Maybe someplace across the sea? Let's see if there's another recording—"

He tapped the dome again, and a new image appeared. This time, a glowing image of a smaller man appeared where Fafnir's image had just been. He looked petite like a Duati, but had nearly black hair, a beard braided and strung with metal beads, pointed ears, and piercing blue eyes. He was wearing a tunic unlike any Brand had ever seen, a rich burgundy that went to his knees with a slit at the neckline. A brooch of three interlocking triangles perched on his shoulder. Boots that wrapped his calves in soft leather. It was a simple outfit, but he stood stiffly, as though he were a man of authority. The image began to speak, the words clear despite some static.

"General, those of us who remain in Midgard salute you for the sacrifice of the crew of the *Muspell's Sons*. The exile you are about to embark upon will forever be remembered."

The figure glanced around, then slumped a little.

"You will be missed, Father," the man said softly. "May we meet again in Valhalla."

The image flickered one last time and then vanished like the first recording.

"General Baldur's son, just before this ship's final mission and Baldur's death," Finn said.

"Is there another?" Loren asked.

"We don't have time," Brand said. "We have to find Fafnir's device."

"Hold on," Finn said, holding up a hand. "No one's ever found anything like this before. Give me a minute."

He tapped the dome once more and it showed what looked like the bridge of a ship. A diminutive officer who looked like an older version of the man in the previous recording stood beside a woman, barking out orders.

"That's General Baldur himself," Finn breathed.

"Shields up."

"Forward gun battery: Stand by."

"Standing by, sir."

"Countermeasures?"

"Ready, sir."

"Bombardier?"

"Triple-checked and ready to go, sir."

General Baldur glanced back at the row of hulking men and women standing at attention behind him.

"Captain Sanders?" Baldur said.

One of the largest stepped forward. His flowing blond hair had been plaited along the top and shaved along the sides, and his beard had beads twisted into the braids.

Brand gasped. It was Alastair.

"Are your people ready?" the general asked.

Brand watched as Captain Sanders stared at something outside the viewport. Brand clenched his eyes tight, shook his head, and opened his eyes again. The tiny image of Alastair was still there.

That's impossible, Brand thought. *This was a thousand years ago.* Fafnir had been there, but he was a kashmari. Who knew what else they were capable of? But Alastair? Brand swallowed hard, trying to reason away the implication of that tiny image. Alastair was just an old man, part shopkeeper, part storyteller, part thief. This man in the recording must be someone who merely looked remarkably like a young, spry Alastair.

They bore the same surname, Brand thought. It must have been an ancestor.

Then someone started chanting and the image fizzled, then winked out of existence.

"Wait!" Brand reached out and tapped on the dome. Nothing happened. "Get it back!"

Finn frowned but tried tapping on the dome. Nothing happened. "Did you see something?"

Brand ran his fingers through his greying hair. "I…I thought I knew one of those men. But…that's impossible." He frowned. "What happened at the end of the recording?"

Finn shrugged. "Dunno. Just cut out." He reached forward and managed to pry the dome device off of the table and stuffed it into his pack. "I'll have a look at this later with Marie."

There was nothing else of interest in the room, so they exited the room and moved on down the hall. Brand reluctantly turned his thoughts away from the strange recording.

Finn led them down another hallway further into the ship. The red lights flickered above them. Loren crept along ahead as Finn examined the door plaques.

"This one," the old scavenger finally said. "Baldur's lab."

"Baldur had a laboratory?" Brand asked, surprised.

"As near as Wren and I can tell, dvergen lived for hundreds of years and picked up a lot of different vocations. I guess they got bored after several decades. Baldur joined the dvergen military as a youth and rose to prominence, but then left to study something called thaum. Then when the kashmari showed up, he felt obligated to return to fight them. Looks like he never gave up his studies, though."

The room beyond looked eerily like Brand's alchemy lab back in Darnan, but at least twice as spacious. The walls were lined with shelves of dust-covered jars, books, and instruments. Several long work benches with smooth black granite tops took up the majority of the room. A large desk stood in one corner, covered in thin sheets of metal about the size of a piece of paper.

Finn moved over to the desk and picked up one of the sheets. He shook it and it wobbled slightly. "Amazing. Not quite paper, not quite metal. Loren, hand me that pack."

Loren handed him his pack and Finn began to sort through the sheets, sticking one in the pack every so often.

"Here, take a look at this one," Finn said, handing a sheet to Loren. "Looks like a full schematic of the *Muspell's Sons*."

Brand limped over to the shelves and peered into each of the jars. Some only held dust, their contents dried out and disintegrated over the long years. Others held perfectly preserved specimens of dried-out plants and small animals the likes of which Brand had never seen. One large terrarium held several beetles as large as a small melon. Their empty carapaces glittered iridescently. One flickered like flames of red and gold. Another rippled in blues and greens like water. A third was a rich green and gold, like sunlight flitting through the canopy of a jungle.

Brand tripped over something on the floor and slammed his hip into the counter. He bit back a curse as his eyes watered. Once the pain had subsided, he looked down.

It was a skeleton.

Brand took a step back in surprise, then knelt carefully to take a closer look. He groaned a little at the strain this put on his leg. With a grunt, he shifted into an awkward sitting position on the metal deck, bad leg stuck out at an odd angle. He turned his attention back to the skeleton.

Ribbons of desiccated clothing hung around the skeleton. On its wrist, he found a bracelet made of a stone the same color as red clay.

<Redstone,> Me'von purred. <Very valuable. Very rare. He must have been someone special. Might come in handy.>

<You want me to steal it?>

<He's not going to miss it. He's dead.>

<I'm not a grave robber.>

<Why not? Are you worried you'll be cursed?> The kashmari chuckled darkly. <I'm afraid you're well past that with me in your head, my friend.>

Brand sighed. With a grimace, he pulled the bracelet off the skeleton's wrist and pocketed it.

He continued his search of the skeleton. At the skeleton's waist, he found a long narrow scabbard. He unbuckled and gently pulled the brittle leather belt off the white pelvic bone and unsheathed the blade. It was a long dagger made of the same polished reddish stone as the bracelet.

<A redstone dagger,> Me'von breathed. <That's it. That's what Sahure is looking for. It's the only weapon that can kill a kashmari.>

Brand paused. <Fafnir killed Mirane with a redstone blade, but she didn't die.>

<True. That was a steel blade, simply colored red; he carries that around to unnerve the other kashmari. He has a redstone sword, but he keeps it locked away to prevent thefts. Hold onto that dagger, and keep it safe. And secret. It's the only other redstone weapon I've seen in centuries.>

<Don't touch the blade,> the kashmari snapped. Brand's fingers froze millimeters away from the redstone. Brand felt Me'von's awe and visceral fear as though they were his own.

<Are you sure that you, a kashmari, want me to keep it?>

<This blade evens the odds against Fafnir, so yes. I'll take any advantage we can get. Let's not hand it over to Sahure, though.>

Brand glanced back at Finn and Loren. Neither paid him any attention, so he quickly slipped the dagger into its scabbard and into his boot.

<What about the bracelet? What does it do?>

<The same thing as the dagger, in a different way. Redstone interrupts all magic fields. The dagger will destroy magical beings, while the bracelet will render the wearer invisible to a kashmari or any other magic-wielder.>

<This man was hiding here,> Brand thought. <Why?>

<Who on earth was this creature?> Me'von mused in wonder. <Redstone dagger, redstone bangle—it's almost as though this was Baldur himself.>

"Well, what do you know," Finn said in wonder, perusing another semi-metal sheet, "it seems that the *Muspell's Sons* was a research ship, not a warship."

"What about those massive guns though?" Loren asked. "Those weren't just for self-defense."

Finn's eyes were shining.

"It was repurposed when the kashmari showed up. Look at this."

Brand used the edge of a work table to haul himself up, then limped over to the other two. Finn held out the sheet for Brand and Loren to see. On it was a detailed etching of a winged beast. Some kind of luminescent pigment had been rubbed into the grooves, making the beast glow eerily around its chest. A reference picture of a man was etched below its outspread wings, a mere fraction of the size of the hulking beast.

"I think this was one of the creatures they studied," Finn said. "They called it a ravener. It came from someplace I've never heard of…Alfheim? Either of you heard of Alfheim?"

Brand and Loren shook their heads.

"Sounds foreign," Finn said. "Maybe it's out past Gresh, on the eastern continent…"

"Anything on those sheets about the device we're looking for?" Brand asked.

Finn sifted through the sheets, then paused and pulled one out. It had a diagram of a long tube on it. As he read the runes etched on it, a frown creased his brow, then deepened with every word he read.

"This is a blueprint for a bomb. Says the *Muspell's Sons* was outfitted with four such bombs, as were eight other ships. Baldur wrote something in the margin: 'This device has but one purpose—to eradicate all thaumium within a given area. The effects are immediate and devastating. All thaum-dependent life is extinguished, and all rifts are immediately and permanently collapsed. Last resort. Cannot fall into Kashmari hands as it could be used as a weapon against all dvergen."

The little room was silent as the words sunk in.

Loren was the first to break it. "So that's how Fafnir did it. He used one of these to kill off all the dvergen."

<Is this true?> Brand asked.

<Yes.>

Brand's eyes unfocused as Me'von shared a memory of his own.

Lush grasslands spread in every direction. Grazing beasts with stripes of glowing bronze across their backs mingled with wolf-like creatures with shining silver manes. Among them, hovering vehicles howled as they streaked across the plains. Thick clouds clumped up by the mountains, which were covered in a thick, verdant forest.

With a start, Brand realized he knew that mountain range. He'd grown up staring at that very same silhouette across the horizon. He was standing in knee-high grass right where Darnan now stood.

And then an expanding black cloud crackling with violet energy boiled over the grasslands, consuming everything in its wake, leaving a desolate desert in its wake. Clouds heavy with water twisted into a familiar lightning-streaked sandstorm. The creatures of the plains collapsed where they stood and writhed in their death throes on grasses that wilted, dried up, and were blown away. The hovering vehicles crashed violently to the dusty earth, tossing their dead across the rocks.

Brand turned to his right and saw that he was standing shoulder-to-shoulder with Fafnir. The high lord looked just as brutish and impassive as he had the last time Brand had seen him at the shrine.

The memory faded, returning Brand to the cold laboratory.

<He used all of the remaining thaumium bombs,> Me'von continued. <Or so we thought. He deceived the dvergen captains with talk of peace, stole the bombs, and turned them on their creators. The thaum in their blood was destroyed, and without it, they all died.>

<Why did he do it? What did the dvergen do to him?>

Me'von sighed. <They tried to stop him and the rest of the kashmari.>

<From doing what?>

Me'von seemed to turn his thoughts aside, a bitterness rising from him. <From being kashmari.>

Frustrated at this sudden reticence, Brand pressed the kashmari for a little more information.

<If that last device—the last bomb—still exists, what could Fafnir possibly want with it? There's no one else for him to kill.>

Me'von thought for a long moment while Finn went over the last of the sheets.

<I'm not sure. And that worries me.> The kashmari paused. <The only way to find that out is to ask him, and that's not a prospect I'd like to think about.>

"So Fafnir thinks that Baldur had one last bomb on board when the *Muspell's Sons* crashed," Brand mused aloud, "but the storms buried the wreck before Fafnir could retrieve the bomb."

Brand took the diagram from Finn. "It's the same size as those tanks we saw in the turret. Same width, as well, suggesting it was designed to be ejected from that gun in some way."

Loren unclipped his holster, then clipped it closed again. "But all those torpedoes were empty."

"The schematic shows another turret on the opposite side of the ship," Brand said. "In that case, we'd need to look in the other turret. If Baldur intended to deploy it but couldn't, it might still be there."

"Good thinking." Finn grinned. "Let me pack up a few more of these research notes. They're incredible. Then we can be on our way."

Brand frowned. What if the skeleton really was Baldur? He limped back over and got back down on the floor beside it, this time shoving the tunic aside. A glint of metal caught Brand's eye. With a gauntleted hand, he pulled aside a skeletal arm to reveal what would have been the man's gut long ago. He reached in with a grimace and pulled out a short rod with several tiny protrusions.

Brand examined it. Loren came over to see what the gladiator was looking at.

"He swallowed it just before he died," Brand mused. "What is it?"

"Maybe a key?" Loren said from behind him. "But to what?"

They looked around the laboratory, shoving aside jars and books and tables. A very faint seam in the wall underneath a work table caught Brand's eye. He knelt and crawled stiffly over to it, dragging his bad leg behind him. The seam was covered in dust and old plaster paint that flaked off when Brand's hand brushed it. He scraped away the plaster, revealing a tiny hole the same size and shape as the key. He inserted and twisted it. There was an audible click, and a section of wall jutted out a few centimeters.

Brand used his fingers to pry the box out of the wall. The back of it was open. Brand reached into the open container and pulled out a single tarnished chain holding a glowing blue crystal.

<Thaumium,> Me'von hissed. <Do not touch it with your bare hand.>

<Why? What is it?>

<It is a powerful and deadly substance. Dvergen used it, worshiped it. Trace amounts flowed through their veins. They even used it to power their machines. That's what Baldur was studying here before he was called to war.>

Brand held up the chain, mesmerized by the glowing shard.

"What is it?" Loren breathed behind him.

"No idea," Brand lied. He carefully wrapped the chain around the crystal and put it in one of his empty belt pouches. "We can take a closer look at it on the way back. We need to get to that other turret."

As they turned to the door, a shadowy figure stepped into the laboratory. It turned to Finn.

The scavenger froze. "Rhamnus."

It was the scavenger Brand had seen outside the *Dauntless* the night Kushchai had abandoned him in the desert.

"Finn. Not as dead as I'd hoped, I see. Thanks for the location of the bomb." He swung a hammer at the panel that Brand had hotwired the door, then took a step backwards out into the hall. Brand, not stopping to think, stood and barreled to the doorway in four huge steps. Rhamnus looked up just in time to see Brand as he collided with him. Both men went down in a heap in the hallway.

The door slammed shut behind them.

Possession

"No!" Finn ran at the door as it closed. Brand heard him slam into it and swear.

Just as Brand grabbed at Rhamnus's wrists to pin him down, the man mashed a button on a metal bracer wrapped around his wrist. He vanished into thin air.

"What in the blazes?" Brand spun, searching up and down the hall; but there was no sign of Rhamnus. No sound of footsteps, no sounds of breathing, nothing. It was as if Rhamnus had been no more than a dream.

<Was that a kashmari trick?> Brand growled at Me'von.

<Partially. What you saw, at least,> the kashmari replied. <The door is real, though, so he must have locked it from the bridge.>

"Scorching door." Finn slammed his hand uselessly against the metal door.

The old scavenger grumbled under his breath as he ripped off the interior door control panel and fiddled with the wires as Brand had.

Nothing happened. Finn slammed his hand on the door again.

Brand took a step forward to the wires. "Hang on, I'll see what I can do."

"No," Finn growled. "I need you to get to that turret now, Brand. I'll figure out the door. If you don't get there before Rhamnus takes off with that bomb, we'll never see it again until Fafnir sets it off. Go!"

A chuckle echoed in all of their minds, chilling them all to the bone.

<By the time you figure out how to get out of there,> Rhamnus's taunting voice said, <Lord Kushchai will have that bomb in hand. Goodbye, Finn.>

Finn's voice from the other side of the door was frantic. "Hurry, Brand! And be careful! He'll know you're on your way!"

Brand turned and hurried back up the hallway. His leg started burning from the climb despite the double dose of prophylactic. He stumbled and fell against the wall.

Me'von sighed in irritation. <It's a pain that originates in your mind, not your leg, genius. I already told you this. You can only use the drug to trick yourself for so long before stress barges in and makes you feel the pain anyways.>

Brand straightened and started down the hall again at a much slower pace. "If it's in my mind, why don't you fix it?"

<I'm no better than the drug. I can't fix it. I can only dim it for a while, like what I do for your memories of Mirane. You'll eventually have to deal with both.>

Brand snorted. "Quick fixes sound like a great idea at the moment."

<They always do until they don't,> Me'von said, clearly exasperated.

Brand came to an intersection and stopped, leaning against the wall to take the weight off his bad leg. The pain eased somewhat.

"I have no idea where I'm going."

He glanced left, then right. Right was the direction of the turret they'd entered in by, so left would be the direction he needed to go. But did he risk taking the intersection, or continue up and risk there being no way across the ship from further up?

Suddenly, the reddish light flickered, then went out, plunging Brand into complete darkness. He froze.

<Too good to last,> Me'von said dryly.

Brand pulled his lantern off of his belt and twisted the little crank on the side until it stopped. Then he released it. The mechanism inside the lantern started clicking and the light bulb inside started to glow a warm, honey color. He held it up to light up the intersection.

<Better just pick one. Better to backtrack than stand like a statue forever.>

Brand wasn't so sure about that logic, but limped down the hall to the left anyway, the lantern swinging and spraying warm light on the bulkhead walls as he went.

He pressed on through the darkness and the eerie silence. His skin prickled in the cold as the same odd feeling of desperation and fear seeped into his mind. Brand shivered.

Brand heard a clang behind him and spun.

Nothing.

The hall was empty.

Brand took several deep breaths to still his heart, then continued on.

Again, he came to an intersection. He continued straight, figuring that when this hallway ended, it meant he'd gotten to the other side of the ship.

After another few minutes of limping, he saw the end of the hallway ahead.

Something very real and very solid crashed into him from the side and rammed him into the wall. His lantern was knocked to the floor.

Several more shadowy figures descended upon Brand like a mob of hungry pterns, all grabbing at him at the same time. He lashed out with his good foot, connecting with a groin and making the man double over. Another's nose met his fist and spun away, blood streaming from between shadowed fingers.

The others managed to grab Brand and wrestle him to the ground.

<Get the bomb,> Me'von said.

<What?>

Me'von vanished.

Brand gasped at the gaping hole in his mind where the kashmari had just been.

Me'von was gone.

Brand looked up into the eyes of one of his attackers and saw the man grin evilly at him. Before Brand realized what had happened, the man had released Brand and turned on the other two, catching them unawares and flattening them with swift blows just behind the ear.

"Go! I'm right behind you!" Me'von said from his new host's body.

Brand limped down the hallway and up the corridor. He passed by an open doorway and had to double back as he saw Rhamnus searching through rows of tanks like the ones Brand had seen in the other turret.

Beyond the *Dauntless's* chief, Brand could make out the seat and controls of the intact gun.

Brand slipped into the turret quietly, keeping to the shadows outside the ring of Rhamnus's lantern. He crept behind a row of tanks. Unlike the ones in the other turret, these emitted a soft bluish light from their narrow windows. Brand peered through the glass window of one nearby him and saw a strange blue liquid inside. It swirled like glowing ocean waves caught in a miniature maelstrom streaked with lightning, brilliant and bright and in constant motion.

<What is it?> he asked, and then he remembered with a pang that Me'von wasn't with him. He glanced at the door but didn't see Me'von.

It's got to be one of these tanks, he thought, glancing at the mountains of tubes. *But which one?*

Brand looked down at his feet and was surprised to see a softly glowing rectangle underneath his boots. He crouched down and brushed his fingers over the glowing seam. It was glowing a soft, dark violet, almost black, and seemed to pulse. Brand thought of the hidden compartment where he'd found the thaum crystal and wondered if Baldur had hidden the bomb in the same way.

Brand scratched at his beard and glanced around the tanks at Rhamnus. The scavenger was still sifting through tanks on the other side of the turret. He looked down again.

This floor panel was considerably larger than the box in the lab, and there was no spot for a key. How was he going to get it open, and without Rhamnus noticing?

Brand dug his nails into the seam and heaved backwards. He lost his grip and lurched back into a pile of tanks that clattered and slammed into the deck around him.

Rhamnus sprinted over to Brand and lifted up the larger man up by the front of his armor. Brand yelped in surprise, then gaped.

Rhamnus was a kashmari. That was the only explanation for his incredible strength. Brand's heart sank as he caught sight of the faint tendrils of darkness wrapped around the scavenger's wrists. There was no way Brand could match Rhamnus right now, not injured like this.

"Me'von," Rhamnus hissed. Brand's heart gave a little leap. Rhamnus didn't know Me'von wasn't with Brand. Maybe he could stall for time until the kashmari showed up in his new body.

Brand adopted Me'von's cultured tones and haughty attitude. "Rhamnus. I know where the device is. I'm sure we can come to an agreement if you would just let me down."

Rhamnus sneered. "Why should I do that when I can just take what I want? Hold still, gladiator."

The tendrils of darkness thickened and plunged into Brand's chest. He felt the kashmari enter his mind like bitter poison being forced down his throat. His whole body started to tingle, and then it went numb. And then Brand wasn't in control anymore.

The kashmari chuckled evilly through Brand's lips. "What, no Me'von here after all? I can't blame him, really. Your mind stinks of self-righteousness and guilt."

<NO!> Brand screamed.

The kashmari laughed, a harsh, bitter laugh. <You all scream, but in the end, you'll like it.>

Brand's mind turned of its own accord to the floor panel. Brand desperately tried to think of something else, but he completely failed as he had when Kushchai had accessed his memories.

The kashmari turned to his former host, Rhamnus, who was watching Brand intently with a spark of jealousy in his eyes.

"Help me lift that floor panel," the kashmari said through Brand's lips. He pointed at the seam glowing beneath their feet.

The two men walked over to the floor panel, then crouched and dug their fingernails in along the edges. Though they hauled with all their might, the panel didn't budge.

Rhamnus knelt and ran his fingers along the seam. "There's a thaum locking mechanism holding it in place."

The kashmari growled. "And no thaum."

"We can try blasting it open," Rhamnus said.

"We can't risk blowing up the device," the kashmari said. He turned his attention on Brand, who shrunk back into a corner of his own mind.

<What do you know?> the kashmari purred. He reached out and stroked Brand's memories. The gladiator cringed at his touch, but there was nothing he could do to stop his thoughts from turning to the thaum crystal tucked away in his belt pouch.

<See, that wasn't so hard.>

Brand felt sick and violated.

The kashmari reached into the pocket and carefully withdrew the crystal. Then, careful not to touch it, he held it by the chain over the seam and let the crystal drag along the edge of the floor panel. The panel popped up with a faint hiss.

<Who are you?> Brand asked while Rhamnus hauled the floor panel up and braced it against some glowing tanks.

<You don't recognize me?> The kashmari leered at Brand. <After all the years I protected you, sponsored you, cared for you like a son? I'm hurt, Brand.>

Brand felt sick. <Kushchai.>

The city lord chuckled as he replaced the thaum crystal in its pouch. <Yes. Very fortunate of me to have run into you like this. It might have taken hours to sort through all these tanks. I suppose that makes it worth it that you didn't die out in the desert.>

Kushchai leaned Brand forward to peer down into the recessed compartment at the bomb.

* * *

Finn pulled his gauntlet off with his teeth and grumbled under his breath as he picked at the various wires, trying to remember which one controlled the lock.

A spark flew at him and landed on his exposed finger. He drew in a sharp breath and shook his stung hand. "Slag," he growled. "Let your guard down…idiot…you were so caught up in learning about the dvergen…going to die because of it…How did he even get here this fast? He was nowhere in sight, and he just appears out of nowhere?"

Loren eyed the wall of jars. "There's got to be something around here that could burn a hole in that door."

"Good luck figuring out which one'll do that without killing us," Finn grumbled.

"You could come read the labels," Loren suggested.

Finn snorted. "My dvergen chemistry vocabulary is a little rusty. Besides, I doubt I'd recognize the chemical names. Been awhile since university."

There was an explosion that rocked the entire ship. Finn's blood ran cold.

"What was that?" Loren asked.

"Nothing good, I'm sure," Finn said from between gritted teeth. He turned back to his work, willing his fingers to move faster; but they were getting a bit arthritic these days.

"Can you go any faster?" Loren asked.

Finn's fingers shook from the effort. "I'm trying."

* * *

In the recessed compartment at their feet, another tube was hidden, glowing a dark violet. Instead of the familiar cylindrical tanks around them, though, this one was shaped like a torpedo with a pointed nose cone on one end and delicate fins on the other end. Inside, an oily black liquid twisted, its iridescent colors rippling as it flowed around the cavity. Electrical pulses pierced the darkness, starting from one corner of the tube and cascading throughout the liquid with an eerily regular frequency.

Like a heartbeat, Brand thought.

Kushchai's response surprised Brand. He felt the city lord's triumph mingle with hatred of this device, but also an almost unbearable yearning to smash it and consume that darkness. Only a bone-deep fear kept him from doing so.

Brand caught a glimpse from Kushchai's mind of a strange world with an endless night sky, a great massive tree reaching glowing white bows to the stars. A liquid just like the one within the bomb surged just under its translucent bark. Above, its delicate crystalline leaves glowed softly in pale lavenders and teals.

The tree's beauty belied an insatiable, all-consuming hunger that emanated from the tree, a hunger that could devour worlds. And every kashmari stood below it, reaching out to it with starving lips even as its sap already dripped from their fangs.

"Kushchai?" A female voice broke the kashmari's trance and the image of the tree vanished.

Kushchai turned and saw a female outlined in the doorway. She strode in, glancing around at the tanks. She whistled.

"Too bad we haven't been able to figure out their weapons, huh? This is a treasure trove."

She looked at Rhamnus. The scavenger tilted his head at Brand. The woman turned to Brand, looking him up and down appreciatively with a slight smile.

"You called for me?" she said.

"Ah, yes," Kushchai said. "One moment."

Kushchai knelt, picking up the tank. Brand felt the kashmari's smile spread across his face. He then held out the bomb to Rhamnus.

"Take this out to the *Dauntless*," Brand heard himself say. It was the strangest thing to hear the words come out of his mouth. He felt…violated. Completely powerless.

The scavenger hesitated. "My lord, let me deal with Finn. He and I have a score to settle."

Kushchai shook Brand's head.

"Finn is mine," he growled. "Return to the *Dauntless*. Now."

Rhamnus bowed his head, then carefully strapped the bomb onto a pack and slung the pack onto his back. He turned and strode out of the turret.

Brand felt his feet carry him to the door, then turn down the hallway he'd come from. The woman followed.

<Why do they need to die?> Brand asked from the corner of his mind. <They've lost. There's nothing they can do to you now.>

Kushchai snorted. <You don't know them very well, do you? Finn and his crew are some of the most tenacious and dangerous of these anarchic scavengers. He will stop at nothing to bring down all of society, kashmari and humans alike.>

<Doesn't seem like such a bad idea,> Brand retorted.

<You are such an impressionable dolt, aren't you?> Kushchai sneered. <Anyone can seed an idea in your head, and off you go. Mirane made you think she loved you, and you threw yourself at her feet. Finn makes you think he's the good guy and all of a sudden you're ready to overthrow civilization?

<Has it ever occurred to you in the last week that maybe overthrowing civilization might have dire consequences for other humans? That perhaps your friends, the other gladiators, or your de facto mother, Mrs. James, might want to eat, or not freeze to death during winter, or have access to modern hospitals? All of these were built by kashmari. Thieves and miscreants and murderers would roam the streets if it weren't for the law and order I provide. Every man, woman, and

child would die in an instant when a sufficiently powerful storm flattens Darnan without my atmomancers. All this will happen if Finn has his way and he overthrows the kashmari.>

<Is that what you want? Is it worth it?> he spat in a mocking tone.

Each word made Brand feel stupider and stupider. He knew he'd been manipulated by the kashmari. Had he been manipulated by Finn as well? Had Finn taken advantage of him the same way the kashmari had?

Suddenly, Brand felt a deep and unexpected longing for Me'von's voice. The kashmari hadn't been kind or forthcoming on many things, but he'd understood Brand. He really was more like Brand than either of them probably would wish to admit.

Kushchai laughed his harsh grating laugh. <You miss that pathetic excuse for a kashmari? Me'von is perhaps the most spectacular failure of any kashmari in existence. He's nothing more than a bottom-feeder, fit only to beg at the feet of greater kashmari than he.>

Brand cringed away from the kashmari. He tried to ignore Kushchai's words, but it was impossible. They bored into his soul and left him feeling hollowed out and desperately alone.

"What a pathetic thing you are," Kushchai sneered. "Just like the pathetic kashmari who's been inside your head."

Kushchai turned Brand to face the woman.

"Yes, my lord?" she said.

Brand felt the same pulling sensation that he'd felt the night Me'von had tortured the pale creature and shuddered. The woman's eyes grew wide, but she was as powerless to stop the kashmari as Brand was. He felt Kushchai sucking at the woman and watched the darkness swirl out of her and up his own forearms. Her whole body twisted, a silent scream contorting her face. And then she crumpled, lifeless, to the deck.

Unlike Me'von, though, Kushchai had no remorse, no self-hatred. He grinned and relished the putrid darkness consuming him, savored it, luxuriated in its foul embrace. And somehow this intensified the strength of that dark energy, distilling it like one of Brand's elixirs, until Brand felt Kushchai's unfettered greed creep into his own soul, polluting him, violating him. He shrank further back into the corner of his mind and tried to block out the filthy stain of that stolen life force, but he couldn't escape. It gnawed at him, smothered him, and left him in complete darkness.

Kushchai, swathed in crackling shadow, strode away down the hall.

Run

Finn followed Loren as the gunslinger crept down the dark hallway. The red emergency lights had gone out, so Loren had pulled the light from off the brim of his hat and held it with his fingers covering the lens so that only a tiny sliver of light escaped to light the way. He held the revolver at eye level as he crept, periodically pausing to listen. He stopped at an intersection and glanced both ways, then gestured with the gun for Finn to follow him.

Finn came up beside the gunslinger. "How much further, do you think?"

Loren pulled out the metal sheet etched with the map.

"Two more sections, then up."

Behind them, they heard footsteps. Loren clamped a hand over his light and pulled Finn into a shadowy doorway.

Down the hall, Finn saw beams of light sweeping from side to side. He turned and peered at the nameplate on the wall next to the door they were flattened against.

"Loren, shine your light on that plate."

Loren did as he was told, letting only the tiniest speck of light out.

"Armory," Finn breathed.

Loren quickly moved out of the way so that Finn could access the wall panel. Within moments, the scavenger had the door open. They ducked inside. The door hissed shut behind them.

"Did you see that?" a male voice called from out in the hallway.

"Yeah. Someone's here."

Boots clomped down the hall.

"They went into one of these rooms."

"Did you see which one?"

"No."

"Alright. Check them all."

Finn glanced around at the armory. Rows of empty upright lockers filled the room. A few long guns hung here and there. A bandoleer hanging on a peg next to one such rifle held tiny torpedo-shaped replicas of the much larger tanks they'd seen in the turret. Their tiny windows were dark and empty.

Outside, Finn could hear the men slam open a door, pause, and yell, "Clear." They were making their way down the hall, one door at a time.

Finn turned back to the door and pried off its control panel. He reached in and grabbed two wires that sparked when he touched them together. He then used them to melt the delicate circuitry, essentially locking the door. Then he ran behind a locker and crouched, pistol trained on the door. Loren vanished towards the back of the armory. They waited, listening for the footsteps outside. They came closer, then stopped outside the door. There was a light tapping, and then silence.

"This one's locked."

"On the count of three. One, two…"

Finn heard a soft click behind him as Loren pulled back the hammer on his revolver.

"Three!"

A massive bang resonated through the armory as three boots slammed into the door at the same time. The door caved, then fell off its hinges.

Three figures stepped through the doorway. In the dark, Finn could only see that the first through was tall and bulky like Brand, while the other two figures were short.

Finn held up a hand where Loren could see it. *Wait.*

The taller figure vanished into the shadows of the room while the other two moved forward slowly. A moment later, someone grabbed hold of the back of Finn's coat and slammed the old scavenger into the locker.

"Thought you were dead, old man," Rhamnus's voice hissed next to Finn's ear.

A shot rang out from behind him. Loren. Finn heard one of the other two strangers grunt and fall to the deck. The second yelled.

Rhamnus slammed Finn into the locker again. Finn rammed his head backwards and felt a crunch as he smashed into Rhamnus's nose, then slid down to the cold metal deck. He rolled past the bigger man, then stood and struck at the man's head from behind. His fist connected, thrusting Rhamnus's head forward into the metal wall.

Rhamnus growled and spun, backhanding Finn, then brought his other fist around to slam into Finn's nose. Finn's eyes watered. Rhamnus seized the opportunity to grab the front of Finn's shirt and slam the older man into a locker. Finn's head collided with an ancient gun. Blood dripped from a cut just above his eye.

Rhamnus hissed in Finn's ear. "No matter. I'll kill you however many times it takes."

Finn grunted as Rhamnus slammed him into the locker a third time.

Loren's pale arms locked around Rhamnus's shoulders from behind. The Duati heaved Rhamnus backwards into a wall. Just as the *Dauntless's* chief spun to face his new attacker, Loren brought up his revolver and shot Rhamnus in the chest. Rhamnus grunted and slid down to the deck.

Loren loaded his revolver with more bullets, spun the cylinder closed, then pulled back the hammer and aimed the barrel at Rhamnus's head.

"No," Finn said.

Loren cocked an eyebrow at the older scavenger but lowered his gun. He sighed. "Please. I may be Forsaken, but I still follow the Way when I can."

Finn glared at Rhamnus. His shirt was soaked in blood now and his breaths came out in ragged gasps. Finn shook his head. "No. He doesn't deserve it. It won't be long now anyway."

Finn looked around the room but only saw one body on the floor. A bullet wound bloodied the front of his shirt.

"What happened to the other one?" Finn asked.

"Took off down the hall. Here." The gunslinger hefted a large, oblong torpedo and handed it to Finn. "I grabbed this out in the hall just before the other guy took off. I guess he figured his life was worth more than this."

Finn snorted. "I'm not sure the kashmari will agree."

Finn turned the object over, revealing a long window. Both scavenger and gunslinger watched the pulsating dark liquid swirling inside, mesmerized. Neither man had ever seen anything like it.

"These aren't dvergen runes," Finn said, pointing at the script running the length of the torpedo.

"Looks more like decoration than words, doesn't it?" Loren said.

Finn grunted his agreement.

"What is that stuff?" Loren asked.

"No idea. Maybe Wren will know. Let's get this to the *Polaris*. Can you carry it?"

Loren nodded, taking the bomb back and using the dead man's pack to rig a makeshift sling across his back.

Satisfied, Finn left the armory. Several steps down the hall, though, he realized that Loren and his hat light weren't following him. He turned and saw Loren standing in the doorway, looking down the hall in the opposite direction.

"What about Brand?" the gunslinger asked.

Finn hesitated. A week ago, the Duati had been so suspicious of Brant that Loren had hardly slept. But somehow the earnest old gladiator had won the stoic gunslinger over. Finn slowly shook his head and took a few steps back toward the younger man. "That explosion we heard, the fact that Rhamnus had the bomb—I don't think he made it. "

Loren's pale face creased. "He could still be alive."

Finn placed a hand on Loren's shoulder. "If he's alive, he'd find a way out. Brand's a force of nature." He chuckled softly. He glanced back into the armory at Rhamnus, who was shivering in a pool of blood on the floor, and sobered. "But we're not. We need to get out of here so we don't meet the same fate."

Loren nodded slowly. Finn turned and headed down the hallway, Loren right behind him. The two men hurried back down the passage to the broken turret.

* * *

A shadowy figure followed the little bobbing light sitting atop the gunslinger's hat. He kept far enough back that Finn and Loren couldn't hear his footfalls, but close enough that when the two scavengers reentered the armored trawler, he was able to drop from the exposed turret onto the hull of the *Polaris* and ensconce himself in one of the recessed wells.

The Venator crept out of its hiding place and climbed up onto a ridge of sand overlooking the undulating dune sea.

* * *

Kushchai ran down to the lab where Finn and Loren were imprisoned. Brand's leg felt like it would snap in half, but the kashmari easily ignored the pain.

Brand knew what Kushchai had in store for his friends. The kashmari's excitement made Brand sick. But with the kashmari invader in his mind, every desperately futile idea he had to free Finn and Loren was immediately known to Kushchai. Brand screamed in frustration.

The kashmari lord laughed.

But when they got to the lab, the door was open and the two men were gone.

Kushchai swore and spun, sprinting up the long hallway to the front of the ship. Though every muscle in Brand's legs were burning and his thigh felt as though it were falling apart, the kashmari's rage pushed Brand forward at a punishing pace. Despite Kushchai's stranglehold on the gladiator's body, tears of pain fell down his cheeks.

Kushchai pushed the gladiator to the wrecked turret and made him leap out of the ragged hole in the hull. Even Kushchai couldn't keep Brand's leg from buckling under him when he hit the ground, and he collapsed in a puff of sand. Kushchai pulled the gladiator to his feet. Brand was trembling violently from head to toe.

To his right, Brand saw the *Polaris* running to the top of the nearest dune, metallic clawed feet kicking up sand in its wake. He couldn't see the *Dauntless*, but Kushchai apparently knew where it was because he sent Brand sprinting in the opposite direction, away from the *Polaris* and out of the ruins. He stopped in front of a short sand dune.

Then the dune stood up. A main gun swung around and pointed directly at Brand.

Brand's eyes adjusted to the various shades of tan and brown painted on the *Dauntless's* hull to match the surrounding sand and saw the same Titan-class trawler he'd seen when Kushchai had dragged him out into the desert—short-limbed and wide, like a crab with two rotary guns instead of claws and a long main gun sprouting from between its eyes. There was no sign of the damage it had sustained during the rebel kashmari attack.

Kushchai raised Brand's arms to the sky.

"I am Kushchai," Brand said, darkness crackling across his skin. His words echoed strangely, and Brand instinctively knew that those aboard the *Dauntless* could hear Kushchai's words in their minds.

A ramp lowered. Kushchai sent the gladiator charging up the gangplank into the gullet of the enormous trawler. Inside, he was met by a rifleman who saluted smartly. Kushchai brushed past him and headed for the cockpit, which was at the end of a short walk down a barren metal hallway.

"Lord Kushchai," the pilot and copilot chorused.

Kushchai strapped Brand into a chair. "The crew of the *Polaris* has the device. After them!"

The pilot flipped several switches, angling the *Dauntless* toward the nearest sand dune. The Titan lumbered forward, then walked straight into the dune.

* * *

Finn strode through the *Polaris* to the kitchen, Loren right behind him with the strange bomb strapped to his back. Finn grabbed at the underside of the dining table and depressed a small button there. With a *thunk*, the whole table released from the floor. Finn grunted as he hauled the table out into the ready area and set it down in front of the weapons lockers.

He then returned to the kitchen and knelt beside where the table had just been. He ran his fingers along the edge of the exposed metal plate, then pushed. The plate popped up. Finn pulled the plate up, revealing a hidden compartment large enough to hide two men in.

"In here," he muttered to Loren. Together, the two men wrestled the bomb into the hidden compartment. When they were finished, Finn hurried to the cockpit while Loren replaced the metal plate and the table.

Finn dropped into the captain's chair and leaned over the command console with a deep furrow in his brow. When the *Polaris* reached the ridge of a sand dune, Finn turned the trawler around in a circle, searching.

But as the Venator turned, Finn was met by only an empty, blinding white horizon.

The *Dauntless* was nowhere to be found.

"Of all the blasted infernals! Marie! Scan for the *Dauntless*. How in the blazes is he doing this?"

The clicking started as Marie began her scan.

"He can't have gone far," Finn muttered.

Behind him, Loren and Wren entered the cockpit.

"Where's Brand?" Wren asked.

Finn shook his head. "We'll discuss it later."

Loren gave Finn a long, indecipherable look but didn't contradict his chief.

"What does that mean?" Wren demanded.

Finn didn't answer. Instead, he squinted out at the brilliant white sand dunes.

Wren took a step forward to stand in front of Finn, arms crossed over her chest.

"Where is Brand?"

"We don't have time for this," Finn growled.

"Yes, we do. Is he dead?"

"Marie, get us out of here." Looking up at Wren helplessly, Finn slumped. "I don't know. Loren and I were trapped. I sent Brand out to go find the bomb. There was an explosion, we got out, and ran into Rhamnus and his goons. Killed Rhamnus, grabbed the bomb, and ran out of there as fast as we could. I figured Brand was dead."

"You didn't even go look for him?"

"We got what we came for!" Finn stood, took off his fedora, and scrubbed at his face in exasperation and exhaustion. "Look, we needed to get that bomb before someone else so that Fafnir couldn't get it, right? I couldn't risk going back for Brand because I'd risk losing the bomb to whoever else was in the wreck."

Now Wren looked deflated.

"I'm sorry," Finn said, grabbing her by the shoulders and looking into her brown eyes. "I would have gone back if I could."

Wren turned away and stepped to the back of the cockpit. Frustrated, Finn sat again. He glanced at the displays. Nothing.

"Where's the *Dauntless*?" Loren asked, peering out the viewport.

"Can't see it," Finn growled.

"Where did it go?" Loren asked. "It had to have just been here."

"No idea." Finn glared out through the viewport at nothing in particular. "I should have nailed Rhamnus to the wall and asked him how the *Dauntless* is doing this."

Wren asked, "You ran into Rhamnus on board the *Muspell's Sons*?"

"He's dead too."

"Good."

Again, Loren gave Finn a sidelong look. The irritated old scavenger was about to say something to the younger man when he was interrupted by the A.I.

"Scan complete," Marie said. "The *Dauntless* is two klicks to the northeast. Heading: thirty-four degrees."

"Pull us east, at seventy degrees, then once we're past the *Dauntless*, swing around to heading twelve degrees." Finn drummed his fingers on the chair's armrest. Then it hit him. He swore.

"Our infrared scanner can't pick up specific heat signatures under the burning sands," he said. "Idiot," he muttered. "Should have seen that coming."

* * *

The cockpit went dark save for the feeble light given off by blinking buttons. The rushing sound of sand paused every few moments as the trawler stopped, turned, then started forward again. Brand couldn't tell how fast they were traveling, but when the *Dauntless* finally emerged from the sand, Brand saw the *Muspell's Sons* in the distance, much further away than he'd thought possible.

The *Polaris* was skittering across the sand right in front of the *Dauntless* like a distressed armored caterpillar.

"Fire when ready," Kushchai said.

* * *

The first round from the *Dauntless* crashed into a nearby dune and threw a wave of sand over the *Polaris*. All the same, it made it clear that running past the Titan wasn't going to work.

Finn yelled, "Get to the guns!"

Wren and Loren dashed off down the hallway to the ladder that led up to the top hatch. Before he ascended, though, Loren grabbed Wren's arm.

"Good luck," he said. He flashed her a grin that lit up his whole face. "Drinks on me after?"

They were only inches apart in the cramped corridor. Wren felt her face grow hot. All she could manage was a wordless nod.

"I'll take the top, you take bottom," Loren said. He jumped on the ladder and disappeared onto the same deck as the main gun.

Wren kicked herself mentally. Why couldn't she have said something? Anything? She must have looked like a complete idiot. She sighed. Cursing the knot in her gut, she hopped on the ladder and slid all the way down into a glass bubble that protruded out from the underbelly of the *Polaris*. She sat in the single seat, a bare metal chair connected to a long rotary cannon muzzle mounted on the outside of the bubble. She sat and buckled the harness over her shoulders, then grabbed hold of the yoke protruding out at her. Her fingers found the firing triggers on the back of each handle.

Wren gave the yoke an experimental twist to the left. The whole bubble spun around to face the rear of the *Polaris*. She twisted the handles back. The bubble returned to its former position.

On every side of Wren, the clawed feet of the *Polaris* threw sand behind them as the trawler scurried away from its attacker. They rounded a dune. Her hands tightened on her targeting yoke. But all she could see was sand.

She squinted.

And then she saw it.

An outline of a behemoth of an armored trawler, easily twice the size of the *Polaris*, and more angular, the *Dauntless* was painted the same soft white and tan as the surrounding sand in a haphazard, blotchy pattern that let it blend in perfectly.

"Starboard!" Finn's voice rang out over the grate. Wren twisted the yoke to aim the rotary cannon at the *Dauntless's* viewport and mashed the triggers. The cannon started spinning rapidly. A steady stream of bullets flew from the barrel, zinging harmlessly off the armored glass.

"Aim at the guns on top," Loren's voice said.

Wren aimed the barrel of the cannon at a nearly invisible bubble shimmering slightly in the bright desert sun on top of the *Dauntless* and pulled the triggers. This time, the roar of the gun was echoed by the gun perched atop the Venator as twin streams of metal lanced the enemy's gun emplacement. The bubble exploded in a shower of sparkling shards.

"If you get a good shot at the viewport, blast it," Loren instructed.

"I already tried," Wrenn said. "It's armored glass."

Finn swore. "We'll have to use the main gun if we want to get through that. Marie, give the *Dauntless* a love tap on the side, would you?"

"With pleasure," Marie purred.

The *Polaris* lurched back as a projectile shot out of the main gun with a *whoomph* toward the *Dauntless.* Caught in the broadside volley, the *Dauntless* lurched sideways, its crab legs staggering.

Wren could just see the bottom of the *Dauntless's* main gun spinning around to point at the *Polaris.* The more nimble Venator dodged out of the line of fire just as the Titan let loose its projectile. The heavy artillery round collided with the sand several meters to the side of the *Polaris,* sending up a spray of flash-molten sand that hit Wren's bubble with a dry swishing sound.

* * *

"Too close for comfort, Marie," Finn said. "Double back around and get us in behind her."

Marie whipped the *Polaris* around fast enough that Finn's gut was rammed by the armrest of his chair. He grunted.

Rotary cannon fire erupted from the *Dauntless,* peppering the Venator's hull, pinging off it, and sinking into the nearby dune.

"Bolts!" Loran swore. "I'm hit. One of those chain gun rounds got through the glass and I got a shard in the shoulder."

"How bad?"

"Eh, who needs an arm anyways? I'll be fine."

Finn rolled his eyes. Loren's bravado was almost certainly for Wren's sake, but the old scavenger knew that if the gunslinger had truly been in danger, he would have said as much. "Ok. Marie, where's the *Dauntless*?"

The viewport spun to center on the *Dauntless*. The Titan had managed to turn its bulk around and was carefully lining up its main gun.

"Run and dive!" Finn yelled.

Finn gave his harness one more sharp tug to ensure it was secure.

Marie sent the *Polaris* sprinting straight at the nearest dune. Finn grabbed the arms of his command chair as emergency lights flashed. The *Polaris* leapt forward and buried its head in the sand with a jolt that slammed through the whole trawler.

And not a moment too soon. The *Dauntless's* round exploded in the sand right where the *Polaris* had been moments before.

Finn heard a steady stream of soft but vibrant swearing coming over the grate in Wren's voice and chuckled. The linguist must be in the bottom turret. She was safe, Finn knew, but the shock of hitting the sand so close in what was essentially a glass bubble would have shaken just about anyone.

"Can't keep dodging him like this, boss," Loren's voice said over the grate. His voice was taut. "Sooner or later, he'll catch us."

"I know. Dig us out, Marie." Finn wracked his memory of the Titan's blueprints. If the viewport had been reinforced, then the only weak point left was on its rear end, right where the exhaust was.

"Get us behind a dune Marie."

The *Polaris* scrambled out of the sand and rushed around the nearest dune, bullets skittering across the hull and zinging into the sand.

"Now out and around that one there…"

Finn guided Marie around the dunes until finally, he brought them around back to where the *Dauntless* stood.

The *Polaris* was almost directly behind the *Dauntless*.

"Armor piercing round, Marie. Right up his tailpipe, if you please."

The *Polaris* fell in behind the larger Titan. Finn hung onto his chair as the *Polaris* leapt backwards with the effort of tossing the round at the *Dauntless*. The round managed to pierce the thick armored rear, but then nothing happened.

"Marie, talk to me. Why didn't it detonate?"

"It appears the round had a damaged fuse."

Finn swore softly, but he didn't have time to ruminate on it. The *Dauntless* had pulled ahead and was swinging around, bringing his main gun into line again.

The only way that shot would kill the *Dauntless* now was if Finn could get the Titan to chase the *Polaris* for an extended amount of time. Unable to vent its exhaust due to the hunk of metal lodged in its exhaust pipe, the overheated engine would slag itself.

But whoever was captaining the *Dauntless* would know that.

"He'll catch us before that happens," Finn said quietly. He thought for a moment, then started flicking switches. "Alright, Marie. Here's what we're going to do…"

Shattered

Kushchai swore at the pilot and copilot. He leaned forward and smashed Brand's huge fists into their helmets. The metal caved slightly.

"Idiots. Bring the *Dauntless* beside that dune over there, then bury it. Wait until you see their faces before you fire."

"Yes, Lord Kushchai," the pilot murmured.

Kushchai dragged Brand down the hall and up a ladder, shoulder and leg screaming with every step.

Brand seethed. He had no way of coping with the pain, no way of screaming or crying or crumpling to the floor. Instead, the pain just built, like the tectonic pressures below a volcano. Brand could feel the cracks in his mind already, fissures held together by desperation and stubbornness. But the threat of insanity bubbled just under the surface.

On the outer hull of the *Dauntless*, Kushchai glanced around. Finn had pulled the *Polaris* around behind a sand dune again.

The *Dauntless* halted beside the dune Kushchai had indicated. The city lord ran toward the edge of the hull and hurled Brand over to the sand dune. The gladiator landed heavily and slid a bit before his boots sunk deep enough into the sand to stop him.

The Titan turned slightly so that Brand could see through the viewport to the pilot sitting inside the cockpit. The pilot gave Kushchai a double thumbs up, then guided the *Dauntless* away around the other side of the sand dune. A flurry of dust and sand flew up as the Titan buried itself in the dune.

Then all was still. Brand could only faintly hear the mechanical sounds of the *Polaris* somewhere nearby.

Kushchai faced the dune. Pulling Brand's duster up around him, the city lord began burrowing into the sand until Brand's large frame was almost completely covered in sand. Only a small space below the wide brim of his hat remained clear for him to breathe.

<Maybe you can hire the crew of the *Polaris*,> Brand said. <You don't have to kill them. Finn is an excellent scavenger. You never know when you might need someone with his skills.>

Kushchai scoffed. <I suppose he didn't tell you that he used to work for me as my head scavenger?>

Brand was stunned into silence.

Kushchai gave a bitter chuckle. <Threw my Marauder off a cliff to fake his own death. Managed to kill the rest of the crew in the process. Did he tell you that? I thought not. No, no matter how good he is at finding junk, I don't need a murderer under my employ.>

<Don't like the competition?> Brand growled.

Kushchai laughed again.

<What are you going to do with me?> Brand asked.

<You've proven yourself useful,> Kushchai mused. <I might consider making this arrangement permanent. Kashmari women seem to throw themselves at you, after all, and what's not to like about having a giant warrior body? I'm beginning to understand why Fafnir is so attached to his.>

The prospect of being enslaved for the next thousand years, unable to move or speak of his own accord, always at the mercy of Kushchai filled Brand with revulsion. Sensing Brand's horror, Kushchai sneered.

<Yes,> the kashmari's cold voice continued. <I think that will do nicely.>

Something occurred to Brand. <Fafnir might not appreciate you taking me over. He said he had plans for me.>

Kushchai's laugh echoed through Brand's head.

<He wanted you for himself, idiot! His body is old. He'll need a new

one soon. He saw you and how tough you were and thought that of all the weakling humans around, you might be a suitable replacement for him. Did you really think that he wanted you to join him?>

Brand went silent.

Brand tried to remain calm, but between Kushchai's insufferable words and the suffocating press of sand all around him, he finally cracked. He unleashed all the pent-up anger and frustration and pain and directed it straight at Kushchai, a mental blast of searing fury and hatred.

The kashmari's answering rage was far more terrible. A tremendous weight pressed down on Brand, snuffing out every thought and emotion, crushing the man's mind until he was silent and numb.

Satisfied, Kushchai turned his attention back outward.

Soon Brand heard the ponderous steps of the *Polaris*. The Venator crept by, gears whirring as it searched for the *Dauntless*. Then, as it passed, Kushchai stood. Sand cascaded off of him as he ran across the face of the dune. He leapt over to a massive leg as it passed close by.

Kushchai climbed up the mechanical limb, hand over hand, until he was standing on top of the *Polaris*.

Brand could see ahead where the *Dauntless* had buried itself in the sand not five meters from where the *Polaris* now stood. The pilot of the *Dauntless* swung the main gun around and pointed it straight at the viewport of the *Polaris*. Finn must have seen it too because he brought the Venator's main gun around. But he wasn't fast enough.

Kushchai dropped prone on the hull just as the *Dauntless's* main gun fired at point-blank range straight into the cockpit of the *Polaris*. The Venator shuddered violently below Brand. The whole front cockpit of the *Polaris* was a smoldering blackened wreck that Brand could see even from his perch on the outer hull.

<No,> Brand whispered. He felt like he was going to vomit, but of course, Kushchai had too tight a reign on his body.

Kushchai grinned and headed for the hatch.

The *Dauntless* shook the sand off and took a step.

The whole Venator around Brand lurched and bellowed, sending Brand crashing to his knees. His ears stopped working. Smoke curled from the end of the *Polaris's* main gun.

The *Dauntless's* viewport was charred and empty.

"No," Kushchai said. He stared, frozen in shock.

Something exploded deep within the *Dauntless*, then another and another.

"The *Dauntless* gunnery deck," Kushchai breathed in horror.

With a great rolling, thunderous explosion, the middle of the Titan seemed to suddenly bow out, then sink in on itself. The shock wave rocketed into the *Polaris*. Kushchai staggered back and fell, steadying himself with one hand on the hull of the Venator.

There was a metallic creaking from under Brand's feet. With an ear-splitting screech, the *Polaris* keeled forward into the sand. Brand slid across the deck. Kushchai managed to hook Brand's bad arm around a rung to stop the fall. The gladiator's full weight jerked on his bad shoulder. Brand let out a gasp.

They hung there as the *Polaris* settled into the sand. Brand's heart ached. Finn was gone. *What about Wren? And Loren? Had they been in the cockpit too?*

Kushchai got Brand's boots onto another rung and carefully climbed down the rest of the way across the hull to the hatch. He carefully opened the hatch and crept down the crazily tilted passage, murderous hatred guiding every movement.

Brand knew one thing: If Wren and Loren were still alive, Brand was about to kill them.

* * *

Finn pried his sore fingers off the main gun's control handles and stood stiffly, ears ringing from the blast despite the wax he'd stuffed in them. He hung onto Marie's robotic arm as he picked his way around upended ammo crates and various balls and cartridges strewn about the tilted gun deck. He slid down the passageway to the main deck, mildly amused by the ladder hanging off to the side by his shoulder. At the base of the ladder, Wren met him with a hug.

"We did it!" she exclaimed.

Finn held her for a long moment, letting the adrenaline ebb.

"Let's see how bad the cockpit is," he said. With no small amount of dread, he clambered over boxes of tinned vegetables strewn about the dining area, Wren close behind.

The cockpit was a charred, melted mess that radiated heat. Acrid smoke filled the cockpit. Finn put a hand up to shield his face and pulled his bandana up over his mouth and nose. The *Dauntless* hadn't just sent a cannonball through the viewport; it had lobbed an electrical bomb into the electrical nexus of the trawler. All of the circuits had overloaded, exploded, and caught fire.

Finn grabbed a bucket of sand just outside the cockpit and started dumping it on the fires. One by one, they went out. He dropped the empty bucket with a clang.

"At least Marie's brain should be safe," Finn muttered, "though she can't control the *Polaris* any better than we can at the moment."

"What do we do now?" Wren asked from behind her own bandana, looking at the slagged metal. Her eyes were red from the smoke.

Finn shook his head slowly. He stared at it too, partially in shock, partially in exhaustion. He squeezed past Wren into the kitchen and pulled a glove out from a drawer that had been dislodged from its rails. Then, pulling on the glove as he returned to the cockpit, he reached forward under the charred console, not even daring to hope.

His gloved fingers came away holding nothing but soot. The compartment where he'd hidden the acrostic ring had been incinerated. Finn's shoulders slumped.

"You put the ring on your shelf beside your bunk," Wren reminded him with a smile.

With a sigh of relief, Finn patted her on the shoulder. She was right. After Brand had shown them his strange pharmakon abilities, Finn had indeed placed the ring next to his books beside his bunk. Finn grinned and wrapped an arm around Wren.

"Thanks, kid."

"Where's Loren?" Wren asked. "He should have come down already."

Finn sighed. "I'm sure he's just taking a moment for target practice or something. He's fine. We won and we're alive, which is the most important thing right now, right?"

Finn looked at the charred cockpit. The thought of Brand still lost on the wreck of the *Muspell's Sons* somehow made that victory seem a bit hollow. Maybe now that the *Dauntless* was taken care of, the crew of the *Polaris* could stash the bomb someplace safe and double back to search for the gladiator.

* * *

As Loren picked his way down from his rotary gun, a dark figure dropped down behind Loren onto the deck of the *Polaris*.

The gunslinger spun and yelled, "Hey!"

The intruder turned and tried to run away, but Loren tackled the man and they both slammed to the deck and rolled down the deck. The intruder kicked Loren off, sending the Duati sprawling into the lockers. The intruder staggered to his feet and clawed his way up the deck to the hallway, but Loren managed to scramble after him and pin him against the deck.

"Who are you?" the gunslinger demanded.

The intruder answered by throwing his weight backwards into the opposite wall of the hall. They bounced and crumpled against the wall.

The two men rolled down the hallway into the bunk room, yanking and grabbing at each other. Loren pulled out his revolver, but the intruder grabbed at Loren's wounded shoulder, making the Duati scream and loosen his grip on the revolver. The intruder managed to twist the gun out of Loren's hand. Before the intruder could turn it on Loren, though, the Duati slapped at the weapon with his other hand, sending it skidding under one of the bunks.

The intruder kicked Loren in the groin, then reached under the bed and retrieved the gun. Loren looked up at the intruder, paralyzed. He squeezed his eyes shut and turned his last thoughts to lovely, sweet Wren.

* * *

Brand dropped down into the belly of the *Polaris*. To the right, he could hear the sounds of a scuffle in the bunk room, but Kushchai moved him in the opposite direction, towards the cockpit.

Brand crept up to the doorway into the cockpit. Wren stood beside Finn, both distracted by the shattered viewport, the blackened console scattered with piles of sand, all of it smoking. Relief filled Brand at the sight of both of them, healthy and alive.

But it was short-lived. Kushchai pulled a knife from Brand's belt.

Just then, something heavy collided with Brand and sent him flying forward, knocking over Finn.

"Thief! He's mine! Get out of his head!" Me'von snarled in Brand's ear.

* * *

The sound of boots running away from the bunk room made Loren's eyes pop open. He was alone on the floor, alone and very alive. He breathed out and laughed shakily, then ran his trembling hand through his sweat-soaked hair.

After several long, shocked minutes curled around himself, the pain in his groin ebbed enough for him to stand.

Why had the intruder let him live? Who was he, anyway?

The pale gunslinger limped down the hallway, determined to find the intruder and interrogate him. As he did, Loren looked up toward the cockpit and saw Brand, locked in combat with the intruder in the cockpit. Now that he could get a better look at the intruder, Loren realized he didn't recognize the man. Was he from the *Dauntless*, or had a third trawler finally shown up?

Loren hurried over to a storage locker and grabbed a long-handled shovel with a heavy steel head, then rushed to join the gladiator.

* * *

Kushchai tossed Me'von off Brand's back and into a cabinet. Wood splinters flew in all directions as Me'von's weight dislodged the screws keeping the cabinet secured to the bulkhead. With a crash, the cabinet fell over the doorway to the cockpit. Loren's pearl-handled revolver flew out of the intruder's pocket and skittered under the cabinet to rest at Finn's feet.

"You're a persistent pest, Me'von, I'll give you that," Kushchai snarled. He lunged at Me'von, fists flying. As he did, Brand caught a glimpse of Finn and Wren trying to shove the cabinet aside; but the corner had gotten lodged under the table. Despite their combined efforts, it wasn't moving.

Me'von brought his arms up to defend his face and lashed out with his feet, catching Brand in the gut and sending the bigger man stumbling back. Me'von then swept his boot around Brand's ankles, bringing the gladiator crashing down. The knife Brand had been holding clattered away under a cabinet.

Brand let out a hearty mental whoop that got an answering vicious snarl from Kushchai.

Just then, Loren ran into the fray brandishing a heavy steel shovel. The gunslinger swung it one-handed at Me'von. The kashmari ducked, the shovel missing him by a hair's breadth.

Kushchai reached out, grabbed the haft of the shovel, and easily ripped it from the Duati's hands. Kushchai took two steps forward and swung the shovel hard at the shocked gunslinger's face.

Loren spun and slid across the deck, then lay still. Brand could see the wicked cut that ran across the Duati's skull and down over his brow and cheekbone. Blood poured over exposed bone and the young man's pale face. Wren cried out and shoved at the cabinet. From the corner of his mind, Brand fumed helplessly.

Me'von stooped and scooped up an armful of tin cans, which he pelted Kushchai with relentlessly. Kushchai brought Brand's arms up to shield his face from the onslaught of vegetables.

Taking advantage of the distraction, Brand tried once again to wrest control from Kushchai, but to no avail. The kashmari lord held tight.

Once the tin cans were gone, Me'von was on top of Brand again in a flash. His arms snaked around Brand's throat and squeezed, pinching off the blood flow to the gladiator's brain. Spots appeared in Brand's vision.

Brand felt Kushchai's hold on him weakening. The kashmari lord rallied the dark energy within him that he'd stolen from that woman on the *Muspell's Sons*. Hatred and fury pulsed through his veins as he reached out with that darkness to lash out at Me'von.

Desperate, Brand dug down deep through the darkness and managed to find that tiny spark in his heart. It was faint, fainter than even when Me'von had been in his head; but it was there. He managed to touch it for only a moment, but that was enough.

Brand *shoved* Kushchai out of his head.

The swirling black fog that was Kushchai lurched out of Brand and hung motionless, stunned, in front of the gladiator. A heartbeat later, a similar dark fog of paler gray streamed out of Me'von's host and was sucked into Brand.

Me'von's triumph flowed into every corner of Brand's body like a breath of fresh spring air chasing away the cold of winter. The dark energy remained, however. Noticing this, Me'von hesitated for a long moment, desire warring with hatred.

<It's already here,> Me'von whispered. <We could use it against him.>

The memory of Kushchai's iron-fisted control and the feeling of having his soul violated made Brand shrink away from Me'von. This seemed to startle the kashmari out of his reverie. With a flash of disgust, Me'von did as Brand had done before and forced the darkness out through Brand's fingertips, dissipating it with a last feeble crackle.

Brand breathed deeply. He held up his own hands in front of his face and nearly cried in relief.

Beside the gladiator, Kushchai disappeared into the body of the man Me'von had just left and turned to Brand with a leer.

"What was that!" Wren yelled from behind the cabinet, horror etched all over her face.

"He's a kashmari!" Finn yelled. "They both are! Did you see that?"

Brand dove at Kushchai, grabbing the kashmari by the front of his shirt as they crashed into the wall. Brand yanked his second knife from his belt and buried it in the throat of the kashmari. Kushchai's fingers went to his throat, blood spurting from between them. He slumped to the floor.

<He's not dead,> Me'von warned. <You've only killed the host.>

Wren tackled Brand from behind, flattening him. She shoved Loren's revolver in Brand's ear and rammed her knee into the small of his back. Brand grunted and winced.

"Don't move!" she yelled in his ear. With one hand, Wren grabbed one of the ropes they'd used in the cave and lassoed it around Brand's ankle. She then tossed the end to Finn, who secured it around the base of a locker.

They must have gotten the cabinet out of the way, Brand thought. Out of the corner of his eye, he saw Finn lean over the blood-soaked dead man.

"Finn! No! No!" Brand thrashed, using his superior strength to throw Wren off. He got his feet under him and rushed at Finn. But Wren's rope brought the gladiator crashing down to the deck with a solid thud. Wren was on top of him again in a flash.

Brand groaned.

The mist of Kushchai lurched out of the body of the dead man. Finn, eyes wide, staggered back; but Kushchai was too fast. In the blink of an eye, the kashmari lord overpowered Finn.

"Kushchai is in Finn! He's in Finn!" Brand yelled to Wren. "Let me go! We have to help him!"

Finn crouched down so that Brand could see his face, then gestured at the dead body. "That kashmari's dead. We all saw the other one go into you, Brand." He shook his head sadly. "Or whoever you are now."

Out of desperation, Brand said to Wren, "You can't kill kashmari just by killing the host. Kuschai is still alive. He's taken over Finn! You've got to believe me!"

Wren pressed Loren's revolver harder into Brand's temple. "I saw it go into you. You're the kashmari."

<No! Brand! Don't! If you try to explain, you'll only dig us into a deeper hole! Just shut up!>

<I'm not a liar like you!> Brand shot at Me'von. <The truth is the only way out of this!>

Brand turned his head to look at Wren behind him, pleading with his eyes. "I've been hosting Me'von since you picked me up. He lets me…I'm in charge, not him. He's not like the other, like Kushchai, in Finn. You've got to believe me."

"This whole time?" Kushchai snarled in a fair imitation of Finn. He picked Brand's head up by his hair. "You've been a lying kashmari this whole time?"

Brand's heart sank. Me'von fumed.

Wren said, "He hasn't used his alchemy since that night…Finn, didn't you say that alchemy will kill a kashmari?"

Finn froze as the significance of that question dawned on Kushchai. His grip tightened on Brand's scalp and a mad light sparked in his eyes. "Alchemy," he breathed.

Brand felt a new terror settle in his gut.

<You idiot,> Me'von said shakily. <He knows everything now.>

Finn leered at Brand and nodded. "Yes, alchemy can kill a kashmari. Truss him up and put him in one of the wells on the outer hull. Hopefully, he won't be able to do any more damage up there while we figure out a way to get back to Darnan."

Wren went pale. "We can't go back to Darnan, Finn."

Finn sneered at her. "We can with a pharmakon in hand. Even old Kushchai would forgive the murder of his own mother if we deliver this wretch to him. And he'll take care of the others for us, too."

"No!" Brand brought his feet up to his hands to kick off the rope, but the butt of Loren's revolver crashed into Brand's temple and the world went dark.

Flashback #7: Rescue

20 May 1030 P.E.
4:00 P.M.
Northeastern Quarter, Darnan

Brand walked into the empty kitchen and grabbed a soft, green sabor fruit. He took a bite of the crisp flesh and chewed, careful not to get any of the juice on his white shirt.

He glanced over at the doorway to the room William shared with Mrs. James. Brand still hadn't told William about his excursion to the Northwestern Quarter or Alastair's imprisonment. For the entire time Brand had lived with the pharmakon, William had insisted that Brand would put Alastair in danger if he sought out the old shopkeeper. Brand was sure he wouldn't approve of Brand's desire to find Alastair.

Brand hadn't heard anything more from Ilye since the night he'd first met her. He'd thought she'd have heard something about Alastair by now. Should he go back to her? Send her a message? Would he look like an impatient fool if he did so?

The thing was, he was impatient. It bothered Brand to think of Alastair in a dirty prison, the jovial smile gone from his round face. But even if he could find out where they were holding Alastair or what his crime had been, what else could Brand do about it? He had the elixirs that William had shown him how to brew and use. He could fight now, more or less. But he hadn't been tested in a real fight yet, and breaking into a prison in another city across the desert seemed a far greater challenge than any Brand had ever attempted.

Brand tried to put Alastair out of his thoughts, to focus on the crunch and sweet tang of the greenish fruit in his hand. It smelled a bit floral, reminding Brand of the flowers William had bought Mrs. James for their anniversary last year. Their twentieth anniversary was coming up next month, Brand mused. He wondered what it would be like to be married for twenty years. Brand imagined himself holding a beautiful woman, smiling as children chased each other around their parents' knees. Mrs. James held a baby beside William, who was cooing at the little one. Alastair might sit at the table showing Brand's son how to pick apart a machine.

Brand tossed the pit of the sabor fruit into the wastebasket a little too forcefully. It hit the bottom of the basket and bounced out. Brand cursed, leaned down to scoop it up, and dropped it back into the basket. He grabbed another fruit.

Just then, William walked in, wearing a simple white linen shirt and brown trousers.

Brand stared at William's clothes. "We have to leave. Why aren't you dressed?"

William poured himself a glass of water and chugged it.

"William! What's going on?"

William set the glass down, then hurried over to the cabinet by the door. He pulled out his pharmakon glove and bandana. "I need you to cover for me tonight."

"Why? Are you going somewhere?"

William nodded. "Remember I told you about that prisoner transfer? I just got word that it's happening tonight. This may be my only chance to rescue this man."

"You said he's a rebel?"

William kept his eyes down on his glove as he carefully checked each vial. "He's been known to help the rebels, yes."

Brand stood and stepped over to the older pharmakon.

"Let me come with," he said. "I need the practice."

William shook his head. "It'll look too suspicious and we'll both lose our jobs if we both go. I need you to tell them I'm sick and that you'll do my work tonight."

Brand knew his friend was right. But the idea of staying behind and doing two servers' worth of waiting tables while William was out saving people set Brand's teeth on edge.

William grabbed Brand's shoulder with his bare hand. "I wish I could bring you with me. I could use another pharmakon out there tonight.

He sighed. Brand noticed that the skin around the older man's eyes and mouth was tight with worry. "It's going to be a challenge to break this man out, that's for sure. But I need you here."

Brand drew in a slow breath, then let it out slowly, imagining the anger seeping out of him. The visualization left him calmer, though still disgruntled.

"Alright. Good luck." He clapped William on his shoulder with a thin smile.

"Thanks."

With that, William left.

Brand knitted his fingers behind his head and looked around at the empty apartment. Then he shook his head. There wasn't anything to do but go to work and do as William had asked. He grabbed a small shoulder bag, slung it over his shoulder, and left the apartment.

Outside, Brand took the metal stairs three at a time down to street level, then hopped onto a trolley car that was ambling by, drawn by a team of four painted red and gold mechanohorses. Looping his arm around a pole to steady himself, he clutched his bag to his stomach. He could feel the outline of his pharmakon glove inside. He kept it near him at all times now on the off chance that he would hear back from Ilye at any moment.

Even if she sends a message, what are you going to do? his mind taunted him. The self-doubt and helplessness gnawed at his insides. He held the bag tighter, defensively. He hadn't heard from Ilye for two weeks, though, and Brand was half sure she'd forgotten him.

Brand let his mind wander as the trolley trundled along the streets, passing rows of apartment buildings that stretched into the sky. Bougainvilleas streamed from every windowsill. The spring wind ripped off their bracts and scattered them across the street, creating a pink desert shower to replace the rains that so seldom came.

Alastair had told him about a place where it rained every day in the summer, where the trees grew taller than the buildings here, and when you walked in the shade of those trees, you couldn't even see the sun. Brand had stolen a map and plopped it down in front of the shopkeeper, demanding that Alastair show him exactly where this place was.

Alastair had chuckled and patted the boy on the back.

"This map doesn't go that far, my boy," he'd said. "You won't find it on any map of the kashmari city-states. It's a lot farther than that."

Brand had folded his little arms over his chest and glared at Alastair. "I don't think it's real. You just made it up. Trees don't grow that big."

Alastair had given Brand a long look, pensive and withdrawn, until the boy Brand had worried he'd offended the shopkeeper.

"It's as real as you or I, Cadmus. I've been there." Alastair had said quietly. He had taken his hazel eyes off Brand and stared into the air as though he could see the jungle there on the other side of the room, but just out of reach. "But it's so far away that it might as well be made up."

Standing now, hand clasping the pole of the trolley and feeling the dry desert air whip at his face, Brand wondered if he'd ever see the strange old shopkeeper again.

* * *

7:45 P.M.
Crimson Boar, Restaurant District, Darnan

Brand was polishing glasses with a soft white cloth at the bar of the Crimson Boar, listening to an old drunk ramble on.

"—Seventeen years, y'know? That's a long time. You don't just walk out on a guy after seventeen years. Am I right?"

Brand smiled reassuringly. "Yes, you're right, Rodger."

Rodger continued on his tirade. He came in a couple of times a week to drink and rant about his ex-wife. According to William, the old drunk had been moaning about her for the last twenty years. Listening was part of the job, though, so Brand did his best to look interested in a story he'd heard a thousand times before.

"Took the apartment, took my bed. Had to sleep on the doorstep that first night, you know, until I got a place of my own."

Brand couldn't help himself. He set aside the glass and leaned forward on his elbows. "Rodger, why don't you go find a new wife?"

Rodger blinked at the young man. "A new wife? What for? The last one made me miserable."

Brand threw up his hands.

Rodger said, "Where was I...Oh yeah. Poisoned the kids against me, says I'm a drunk...what does she know, the ol' harpy—"

A commotion near the front of the restaurant interrupted Rodger and drew the attention of all the patrons. From his taller vantage point, Brand could just make out a stocky man with roughly cropped hair arguing with the seating server.

Brand nearly dropped the glass he was holding from surprise. Ilye. He placed the glass down gingerly with a shaking hand and slapped the cloth over his shoulder. He hurried over, pressing through the servers blocking the way.

"—you can't just come barging in here, dressed like that—"

"We have standards, ma'am!"

"It'll only take a moment," Ilye was saying. She caught sight of Brand and smiled in relief. "Brand! I need to talk to you!"

The other servers looked suspiciously from Brand to the coarsely dressed smith, then grudgingly parted for the big man. Brand gently caught Ilye's elbow and steered her out the door. A few catcalls and whistles followed them out onto the street.

Brand blushed crimson as he led the stocky smith around the corner to the same alley where William had first spotted Brand a decade ago.

The sun had dropped down behind the buildings, leaving the alley in shadow. It was a welcome relief from the piercing rays of the summer sun, but the alley was still hot and stuffy despite the purple sky. The only other occupant of the alley was Rodger, who'd come out behind the pair and was urinating against the wall.

"I'm so sorry," Ilye said, seeing Brand's red face. "I needed to talk to you and couldn't wait. I'm sorry I embarrassed you."

Brand smiled reassuringly. "You didn't embarrass me; they did." He waved a large hand dismissively. "They're just a bunch of oafs. What's going on? Are you alright?"

"Yes, I'm fine; thank you," Ilye said. "It's about Sanders. He's being transferred from New Braunen to the Reaches prison tonight. He's to be interrogated."

A chill ran down Brand's spine. Set on top of a mountain peak and surrounded by steep cliffs, the Reaches was an impenetrable fortress. No ordinary thieves or murderers called the Reaches home; it was a political prison and dungeon where Lord Fafnir's foes were taken to be tortured, then left to rot.

Brand shook his head. "I don't understand. Interrogated? For what? He's just a shopkeeper!"

Ilye pulled out a piece of wrinkled paper. "Apparently, he's been helping a gang of rebel kashmari. Fafnir wants their heads and he thinks Sanders can give them to him. But that's not the half of it. None of what I heard makes sense." She shoved the paper into Brand's hand.

> *It has come to my attention that you have in your custody a unique prisoner. Alastair Sanders may go by any number of aliases, but he is easily identifiable to those familiar with him. He is a man of far larger stature than is common among humans and has many tattoos of waves and scale patterns on his arms and chest.*
>
> *This prisoner is of great interest to me. It is with this in mind that I request you send this prisoner to the Reaches forthwith to undergo interrogation. I advise you to take every precaution with his transportation. His rebel compatriots will seek to liberate him en route.*
>
> *Do not take this task lightly. Alastair Sanders is the most dangerous and highly connected criminal the kashmari have ever seen. His knowledge of the rebels could help us snuff them out for good, while the loss of him could spell disaster for all.*
>
> *Sincerely,*
> *High Lord Fafnir*

Brand stared at the letter and read it over and over.

"He's just a shopkeeper," Brand muttered, trying to square his memory of the kindly man with Fafnir's dire warning.

Ilye shook her head and handed Brand another piece of paper, a form filled out in a tidy hand.

> PRISONER TRANSFER REQUEST FROM: *High Lord Fafnir*
> DATE OF TRANSFER: *Second* DAY OF THE *Fourth* Month of the Year *1023*.
> *New Braunen* TO *Darnan*
> PRISONER NAME: *Alastair Sanders, alias John Reuel*
> IDENTIFYING FEATURES: *Wave/scale tattoo on chest/arms, long scar on abdomen*
>
> AUTHORIZED BY: *Captain Richard L. Gend*

"That's tonight," Brand said. "The prisoner William intended to liberate must be Alastair. He's already on his way," he murmured. He handed the form back. Anger rose in Brand's chest. He gritted his teeth. William was going to rescue Alastair from Fafnir and he hadn't even had the decency to tell Brand?

Brand slammed his fist into the brick wall, then cursed.

Unperturbed by the young man's sudden outburst, Ilye folded up the letter and pocketed it. "Well, whoever this William is, I doubt he'll succeed."

Brand brushed red flakes of brick off his knuckles and wiped away a speck of blood. "What do you mean?"

"My cousin's a footman for High Lord Fafnir. He told me that there will actually be two transfers tonight—one with the real Alastair, and the other with a fake. The fake will be by the east gate, carried into Darnan by camelid caravan. The real Alastair was delivered this morning by train at the Southern Depot. The pod he's in is disguised as a shipment of bricks from New Braunen. It's supposed to be picked up later this evening."

Brand grimaced.

"And William won't know that."

"Exactly." Ilye pulled out a small golden pocket watch. The shine had been rubbed off over the years. "The pickup is supposed to happen at 8:30."

Brand shook his head. "We don't have enough time to find William and make it back to the Southern Depot in time for the pickup."

Ilye snapped the watch closed and pocketed it. "Then we'll just have to try and break Alastair out on our own."

The nonchalant way she said it shocked Brand.

"Just like that?" he asked. "Break out Fafnir's most wanted criminal on the way to dinner?"

Ilye leaned in close and lowered her voice. Her brow was furrowed with consternation. "If we don't, Fafnir will torture him. I've known people who've been tortured by that monster. He breaks their minds. I don't know you very well, but could you let him do that to Alastair?"

Brand did want to help. He had to help. But his doubt was stronger than his eagerness.

"I can't just leave my job," Brand said. "William asked me to cover for him tonight. If I leave, neither of us will have a job to come back to."

Ilye's face fell, disappointment evident from the way she shifted her weight onto her back foot and frowned at the young man Brand.

"The way Sanders talked about you…I really did think you must have been his son. But he doesn't mean as much to you as you did to him, huh? You don't care what that blasted high lord does to Alastair?"

Brand clenched his teeth and balled his fists. "That's not true. I just…William's counting on me tonight. He'll figure it out and rescue Alastair. He knows what he's doing. I…I don't."

Ilye leaned in close enough that he could smell the lingering lavender scent of her soap.

"William can't get there in time." She placed a hand on his forearm. His skin tingled where she touched him.

"If we don't save Alastair, they'll strip him down, whip him until his back looks like raw meat, then throw him in a dark dungeon full of rotting dead bodies and their excrement. The rats will eat his flesh and Fafnir will twist his thoughts into nightmares, until he begs for mercy and tells them whatever they want to hear. He'll tell them anything just so they let him die. So what if you and William have to look for a new job? Is it not more important to save a kind old man from that horrible fate?"

She patted his arm. "If your friend William is trying to save Sanders, wouldn't he agree?"

Brand nodded slowly.

"Alright, then let's go." Ilye let go of Brand's arm.

Brand took a deep breath to steady himself and nodded. "Alright."

The young pharmakon dodged back into the restaurant to grab his bag. He kept his head down and ducked behind some patrons so the other servers wouldn't question him, then returned to the alley where Ilye was waiting for him. Brand pulled out his glove and put it on, then stashed the shoulder bag behind a pile of wooden crates. He gestured for Ilye to lead the way.

Ilye led him out of the alley and down the street a couple of blocks until she turned down another side street where a somewhat rusty mechanohorse stood waiting patiently. The carriage it was harnessed to looked like little more than a thin metal box balanced precariously on two frail wheels.

"Get in," Ilye said, opening the door with a squeal of protesting metal.

Brand hopped into the box. Ilye followed. The carriage had no windows and was lit by a single, bare bulb that flickered slightly every time one of them moved. The interior of the carriage was bare metal, with only two simple metal planks for seats. It would have been cramped with two normal-sized people; the long-limbed pharmakon found himself twisting awkwardly to avoid crushing his companion.

Ilye patted his knee with a laugh in her eyes.

"It's no use. Just relax."

The carriage started moving without a word from either of its passengers. Brand held as still as possible, worried that one wrong move might topple the rickety contraption.

"What's the plan when we get there?" Brand asked.

"Impersonate the guards who are supposed to pick up the shipment."

"What if they show up though?"

"They won't. We'll have to take them out to get their uniforms..." Ilye looked Brand up and down, realizing the problem with this plan at the same time the young man's eyebrows shot up. She thought for a moment. "You can't be seen in that uniform or else they might assume your kashmari lord was behind it all, and I'd rather not start a war tonight. We're going to have to find you some other clothes before we get there."

* * *

7:45 P.M.
Northwestern Depot, Darnan

William swung and leapt, sliding across the rooftops with the ease and grace of a pinwheeling songbird on the wind. He dropped down into an alley and crept forward within the relative safety of the shadows cast by the setting sun. He stopped beside a shop cart and peered out, surveying the street.

The wide, packed-earth boulevard was sparsely shaded by thin trees. A caravan of camelids strained under the weight of heavy sleds laden with egg-shaped metal cargo pods. The smell of their sweaty fur and the puddles of urine they left in the dirt made William's eyes water.

William frowned. Why had they sent such an important prisoner via a camelid caravan, when they could have easily put Alastair on a train from New Braunen? The trains were run by kashmari lords, whereas the camelid caravans were used by human traders. As such, the slower caravans were considered far less safe and trustworthy through the desert.

William watched the caravan for a moment. Something else was wrong: no guards. He shifted his weight uneasily from one foot to the other. This wasn't right at all.

His fingers itched. He wanted a smoke, he realized. He pulled out his pipe and looked at it. He ran his fingers over the smooth wood, trying to remember where he'd even gotten the thing. He'd give away his location to the guards if he lit it now.

As the sun vanished behind the mountains, William squinted in the dimming light so that he could read the lettering stenciled on the sides of the pods. He didn't see the one he was waiting for. It must be further down.

He squatted down to wait.

He put the pipe between his teeth, empty. Then it hit him.

My father gave this to me on my wedding day, William realized. *It reminds me of him, and of Moira. That's why I carry it around. How could I forget that?*

The pharmakon ran his fingers fondly over the wood once more, his mind drifting to that beautiful day. His late father had danced with William's bride and made her laugh. He pocketed the pipe. *Well, I guess that's one mystery solved. But how did I forget that?*

He shoved the unsettling thought away and turned his attention back to the caravan. More of the camelids plodded by, dragging their heavy metal pods.

Alpha 22-7S, he thought as he searched. *There.*

He hesitated. It could be a trap. He glanced around, trying to peer through the growing gloom, trying to pick out the shapes of guards hidden in the shadows.

I can take out a few guards if need be, William decided. *Alastair is worth the trouble.*

He was about to step out from his hiding place when behind him, someone tugged on his shirt. He turned and found Rodger, the old drunk from the bar, standing behind him.

"Rodger," William hissed, pressing the old drunk backwards into the shadows. "What are you doing here? How did you find me?"

The old man's words were slurred together. "I saw you weren't at work, and neither was Brand."

That brought William up short. "Brand wasn't at work?"

The drunk shook his head. "He ran off with a…looked like a Navari. They were in a big, fired rush, the both of them. I saw him leave the alley. I was, you know…there, and so was he, and they said, they were saying something about someone needing to be rescued…"

William let out an exasperated sigh. He should have known Brand would have been keeping tabs on his old friend. William should have just let the young man join him.

The old drunk was still rambling on. William glanced over at the caravan. Its progress was painfully slow, but he could now see a trader whipping the hind quarter of the last moaning camelid. William only had a few minutes before the whole caravan disappeared into one of these warehouses.

William shook the drunk by the shoulders. "Did Brand say where he was going? Was he coming here? Is that why you're here? You followed Brand?"

The drunk stared dumbly at William, brought a large flask up to his cracked lips, tipped his head back, and drank sloppily. As the smell of the alcohol punched through the camelid stench, the pharmakon felt the hope drain away. Rodger dropped the flask, wiped his wet face with the back of his hand, and blinked slowly.

"I had to follow him. Girl like that…'s not right for a bright young fellow." Rodger screwed his face up, trying to gather the shreds of his thoughts into something coherent. "He said he'd be…there'd be a south gate and an east gate. Bricks, and…not bricks. Camelid caravan didn't seem right, I think. So I came here. East gate."

The drunk leaned to the side and nearly fell over, but pointed past William. "Those camelids." He burped. "Whoops. I guess I got it backwards. Should have been south. That's ok. I found you."

William shoved the old drunk to the ground against the wall of the alley. 'Just stay here, will you? I'll be right back." To himself, he muttered, "I don't have time for this."

The pharmakon snuck back to the mouth of the alley and quickly scanned the pods once more for Alpha 22-7S. It was quite a ways down the street now, so William had to sprint, dodging from shadow to shadow and staying out of sight of the merchants pacing alongside their beasts.

Keeping to the shadows of various large crates, he slipped in beside Alastair's cargo pod. He glanced at the camelid driver walking ahead and the driver behind him. When both turned away, William leapt up onto the pod.

The pod was a stubby metal cylinder held in place on the sled by thick leather ties. Once on top, William knelt and found the simple metal grate that allowed air into the pod.

"Alastair," he whispered hoarsely. No answer. "Alastair!"

He glanced around. No one had seen him yet, but the gloom of dusk was not so deep as to give him any real cover. It was only a matter of time before someone looked up and saw the pharmakon perched atop the pod.

William pulled out a tiny match and lit it, shielding its flame from the wind and prying eyes with his hand. He looked down through the grate.

The pod was empty.

"For the love of dawn," William swore softly. He glanced forwards and back along the caravan. Had he gotten the wrong pod?

Someone shouted, "Hey! There's someone up there!"

He was out of time. William vaulted off the pod and vanished into the shadows, leaving the caravan drivers to inspect thin air.

Huddled behind a large crate, William took out his pipe and sucked on the mouthpiece, overcome for a moment by frustration. Had he gotten the wrong pod? His doubts from earlier resurfaced. What if Alastair hadn't been entrusted to the caravan at all? Had he been fooled?

He watched the camelids turn a corner. He couldn't inspect any more of the pods with the drivers on alert, but soon they'd be out of reach in a well-guarded warehouse.

William stood frozen in indecision. If he went after them and continued his search, he might waste valuable time better spent searching for the real caravan.

Then he remembered that there weren't any guards in this caravan beside the camelid drivers. The guards must have left as soon as the caravan entered the city, which would never happen with a prison transport. He swore.

The pharmakon shoved his pipe in his pocket and let out a heavy sigh. He'd better check back in with Rodger. William found the drunk right where he left him.

"No Brand, huh?" the drunk mused. "Yeah, he's not at the caravan. He went south."

Realization dawned on William. Rodger had heard Brand's plans, heard Brand discard the camelid caravan as a distraction. That must mean that the younger pharmakon knew Alastair's real location.

How had Brand figured that out? William pushed that thought aside. It didn't matter right now. He needed to get to Brand and Alastair as fast as possible and all he had to go off of was a drunk's scattered ramblings.

William crouched down on his haunches next to Rodger.

"What was that about south you said?"

The drunk's head lolled forward a bit, drool dripping down the side of his mouth. William shook him. He started awake with a grunt.

"What did you say about Brand going south?"

"South? A gate? Bricks." Rodger's head lolled forward again, but shaking him didn't wake him this time.

"Full of ale and hot air," William grumbled.

The south gate, and bricks? The pharmakon fiddled with the pipe in his pocket, running his fingers along the wooden stem. After several thoughtful moments, he stood.

He'd just have to head to the south gate and hope he could puzzle out what the drunk had meant. Hopefully Brand wouldn't get himself into too much trouble in the half hour it would take William to get there.

William set off down the boulevard at a trot.

* * *

8:13 P.M.
Southern Depot, Darnan

Brand glanced down at his watch for the third time in five minutes. Ilye said she'd be back in just a moment, but that was ten minutes ago. What was taking so long?

He leaned back against the metal of the carriage, making it squeal under his weight. He ran his fingers over his short, bristly hair and clean-shaven face. Then he leaned forward, elbows on knees, head in hands.

What if they didn't get to Alastair in time? What if Fafnir got ahold of the big shopkeeper?

Brand rubbed his eyes. Was Alastair really a rebel? Had he been a rebel when Brand had known the man?

Another several minutes went by with no sign of Ilye. Brand considered opening the door and poking his head out to see if she was near, but decided against it. She'd be here any moment now.

Brand rubbed his hands together, becoming more and more fidgety.

Where was Ilye?

A thought struck Brand. Had something happened to her? Should Brand have gone with the Navari woman to help her? What if she'd been attacked? The street gangs wouldn't think anything of kidnapping a lone woman.

No, she can handle herself, Brand thought. He paused. She could, couldn't she?

The young man realized he barely knew the woman. He had no idea what she was capable of, or even if she was honest. Had she just left him here in this carriage with no intention of returning?

Just as these thoughts began to spin doubt around Brand's mind, someone rapped on the metal of the carriage door. It opened, and Ilye climbed back into the carriage. She handed Brand a package covered in brown paper and tied closed with a string and a small box.

"A set of new clothes and boots," she said.

"Took you a while," Brand said as he untied the package. Inside was a soft blue linen shirt and a pair of simple but sturdy trousers. "I thought something might have happened to you."

Ilye chuckled. "That's sweet of you to worry. No, it was just a bit harder to find something in your size than I was expecting. I hope they fit," Ilye said. She backed out of the carriage once more and closed the door.

Brand dressed as quickly as a man could when asked to maneuver in a tin can barely larger than himself. He whacked his elbows and head several times while trying to pull the trousers on. Finally, he settled back down, pulled the boots on, and opened the door to let Ilye back in. She was wearing a new set of clothes herself, consisting of a crisp white blouse, a thin necktie, a dark blue pleated skirt, and sensible black shoes.

"Where'd you get the uniform?" Brand asked as she settled in. The carriage lurched forward and resumed rattling down the street.

"At the same shop. Now we won't have to accost any innocent guards." She adjusted her skirt. "We'll just have to make sure we get Alastair and get out before the real ones show up. I think we'll make it, if just barely."

"How much farther do we have to go?" he asked. He drummed his fingers impatiently on his knee.

"Not long," Ilye replied.

When the carriage finally stopped and Brand got out, the sky was black and studded with the first stars of the evening. They were just outside the tall city walls of the southern end of Darnan. The Southern Train Depot stood nearby, belching clouds of smoke and goods from across the Wastes, then sucking up great quantities of coal to fuel its return journey. Its tall clock tower reached to the eternal stars above, keeping time for the tiny humans chained to the ticking of its great mechanical heart. Clear, cold air from the desert wrapped its icy tendrils around the young pharmakon and leeched the warmth from his skin. He shivered.

To the side was a caravan staging area protected by shorter stone walls and a wrinkled metal roof. The floor was bare rock, roughly hewn and etched by the constant rubbing of wheels and sled runners. A camelid stood at its entrance, hitched to a round metal sled pod, its owner shouting something about missed deadlines and an irate kashmari lord.

Ilye picked up a clipboard off a crate. "Follow my lead," she said.

The Navari led Brand inside the staging area and over to a pile of wooden crates piled up against one wall. Several armored city guards stood in front of the pile, long pikes glinting in the lantern light. She stepped up to one of the guards.

"I'm here to pick up a shipment of brick from New Braunen," Ilye said in a bored voice, leafing through the pages on her clipboard. She seemed to find the one she wanted and looked up expectantly at the guard. "Three cargo pods' worth."

The guard pointed his free hand to the left at a woman sitting at a table groaning under the weight of piles of paper stacked high upon it. Ilye walked over and stood in front of the clerk.

The woman didn't so much as glance in the newcomers' direction. She kept scribbling away, her pen scritching along the paper. Ilye cleared her throat.

The clerk still didn't look up. "I'll be with you in a moment."

Ilye pulled out the form from her clipboard she'd been looking at and put it down on top of the paper the woman was scribbling on. The clerk froze as her eyes poured over the words.

"You're early," she said slowly. "I wasn't expecting you for another hour."

"An hour?" Ilye said, incredulous. "Pickup was at 8:30. We're early, but not that early."

"The pickup time was changed," the clerk said. "You didn't hear?"

Ilye shook her head. "The messenger must not have found me in time."

"No matter. This way." The clerk stood and led Ilye and Brand to the mountain of crates, then off to the side. There was a cylindrical pod there, painted a dusty brown with yellow letters stenciled on the sides.

"A pod for bricks?" Ilye rolled her eyes. "I know I'm not supposed to nitpick other people, but rust me if that isn't the oddest container for them."

The other woman shrugged. "You have a way to haul it out of here?"

Ilye nodded and turned to Brand. "Come on, let's go get the sled."

Brand nodded and followed her out, puzzled. "We're fresh out of sleds," he muttered once they were out of earshot. "How were you planning on getting him out of there?"

Ilye walked around the outside of the structure, gesturing for Brand to follow. There weren't any guards here between the staging structure and the darkness of the desert beyond. After a moment, she stopped at a small gap in the stone wall, barely large enough for a person to squeeze through. Ilye handed Brand a heavy crowbar.

"That pod should be about five steps to the left here," she whispered. "Go in, pry open the pod, and run for it like a rocksaber's on your tail."

Brand wasn't impressed with the lack of detail, but he nodded anyway. If everything went sideways, he could always try punching his way out.

"What about you?"

"I'm going to go back in to stall her. Try to be quick about it, please."

Ilye slipped back around to the front of the building. Brand watched her go, then turned back to the crack in the wall. Being such a large man, he had to blow out all of the air in his lungs to fit through. On the other side, he crouched down in the shadows.

To the side stood the brown pod. Up close, Brand could see thousands of tiny scores etched along the metal.

Brand climbed up on top of a nearby crate, then scrambled up the side of the pod and looked down through a grated door. Inside, Alastair's mouth hung open.

"It's me, Alastair," Brand whispered. "You remember me? Brand? I'm here to get you out."

"Cadmus?"

Brand's face split into a grin. Alastair's eyes lit up for just a moment before clouding over. The old shopkeeper stood, stuck a meaty hand through the grate, and grabbed Brand by the wrist.

"You shouldn't be here," the older man whispered. "You need to get out of here now, Cadmus. It's not safe."

"I'll get out of here once you're out." Brand patted Alastair's hand and gingerly placed the crowbar's end under the bars of the grate. He made a motion with his hand and felt strength pour into his veins, then heaved on the crowbar. The door resisted, then gave way with a resounding clank that echoed around the building.

Twenty voices around Brand started shouting.

Brand flung open the grate and reached down, then hauled the giant shopkeeper up as though he were no heavier than a regular-sized man. Brand turned and cast about for Ilye. She was standing beside the clerk's desk still, staring at him. Brand motioned for her to run, but Ilye just stood there, jaw set and arms crossed over her chest.

"We need to go now," Brand yelled at her. Brand and Alastair jumped down to the ground.

"You're not going anywhere," Ilye called back to th pharmakon. "Guards!"

Brand heard heavy boots on the rock behind him. He spun just in time to see a wall of sword points materialize around him and Alastair. The guards watched the pair of giants with determination.

Through the bristling steel, Brand could see Ilye reach out her hands to the clerk and grab hold of the front of the woman's shirt. The clerk collapsed face-first onto the desk, eyes vacant.

Ilye turned to Brand and Alastair and stalked towards the two men.

* * *

William dropped softly down on top of the pile of crates just as the whole room erupted in shouts. Adrenaline shot through him like an electric shock. How had they seen him?

But a moment later, he saw the bulky outline of a huge man standing atop a pod at the far end of the building. The man reached down into the pod and hauled out another enormous man from the pod. The second man had shoulder-length white hair and quite a bit more mass than just muscle could account for.

"Brand," William breathed. He watched as his protégé beckoned to a woman. She shouted something at him. A line of guards materialized and encircled both Brand and Alastair, blocking the young man's way out through the front of the warehouse.

William frowned. The two men were just standing there. The aging, storm-battered wall had numerous cracks a man could fit through, which was presumably how Brand had gotten in. But neither made a move towards the wall.

William ran his fingers over his mustache, smoothing out the stray whiskers as he thought. It must have something to do with the woman. He couldn't see her from here due to the press of guards between him and her.

What was going on? Who was that woman?

One of the guards stepped forward and grabbed Brand by the arms and kicked the big man's feet out from under him. Even from his perch, William could hear Brand's grunt as he hit the rock floor. Alastair stepped over the fallen man and rose to his full height, yelling something at the guard. The guard backed off, but another charged at the white-haired giant.

With a primordial growl that rumbled through the warehouse, Alastair flung his enormous fist at the man's head. The man dropped to the ground like a rock. In seconds, a dozen other guards had pounced on Alastair and pinned him down to the hard earth.

But now William could see the woman Brand had beckoned to.

Ilye Grahm, the newest member of the kashmari, dressed in Navari blacksmithing clothes. He groaned inwardly. She'd sold her soul last week in exchange for protection for her family in Navar.

William ground his teeth. Brand had bumbled straight into a mess of kashmari politics. As a new kashmari, Grahm would try to impress High Lord Fafnir at all costs. She must have set this trap to draw out Alastair's companions and caught a pharmakon instead.

William bit his lip. Grahm now knew about Brand's connection to Alastair, but she didn't know that Brand was a pharmakon. The young man's worst crime at the moment was trying to spring a convicted criminal from prison. That relatively modest crime would be punishable by several years in prison, but not death. Maybe the boy would learn not to be so trusting of strangers.

But Alastair...Alastair still needed to get out of here. He knew too much. If the high lord got his claws in the old mechanic, a lot of people would die.

What a mess you've made, boy. If you'd only let me handle it, Alastair would be free by now.

William cursed silently. That wasn't true, though, was it? The feint with the camelid caravan had duped William. If it weren't for Rodger overhearing Brand's conversation, William would never have even known where to look for the old shopkeeper. The last piece of the puzzle fell into place. Grahm must have been the woman that Rodger had seen Brand speaking with at the Crimson Boar.

William groaned. Tonight was not going well at all.

The pharmakon shook himself. This was no time for wallowing in his frustrations. He needed to distract the guards and Grahm long enough for Alastair—and Brand—to get away before the younger pharmakon used his powers and revealed himself.

William glanced at Alastair uneasily. Or worse.

The pharmakon crouched down low, then surged forward in a great leap. He landed on top of Grahm, sending her sprawling.

"Run!" he hollered at Brand and Alastair.

Then he flung himself at the mass of guards, whirling and punching and kicking for all he was worth. He landed several blows and downed a handful of the guards. But the guards far outnumbered him and their relentless attacks soon overwhelmed him. A lucky strike from a spear sliced through William's sleeve. Another knocked him to his knees. He glanced up and saw that Grahm and a handful of guards were chasing Brand and Alastair. The older man tripped, and the guards fell upon him.

It was all or nothing now. William made a final motion with his gloved hand, the Omega sign, and felt all of the vials at his wrist pour into his veins, including the Augmenting elixir. His whole body exploded with light, making the guards around him stagger away. He surged forward and batted them away, rushed over to the guards assaulting Alastair, and shoved them aside. He then turned and placed himself protectively between Brand and Alastair on one side, and the guards and Grahm on the other.

"Get out of here!" William bellowed. His augmented hearing made Brand's and Alastair's footfalls sound like thunder as they rushed away.

* * *

The blazing light from William lit up the desert around Brand. He turned to look at his glowing mentor in awe. William looked like a pillar of fire blazing in the dark warehouse. Brand grinned as he saw Ilye stalking towards the mustached beacon. She had no chance against William.

Then Ilye reached out her hands and the light began to stream away from William in long glowing ribbons that curled around Ilye's arms and vanished. William staggered to his knees, the light fading fast. Then the light was gone. His skin took on a pale grey cast. He was shaking violently.

Ilye reached down and wrapped her fingers around William's throat. William screamed.

Brand lurched forward, panic and anger coursing through him. But Alastair's heavy frame blocked the young man like a solid wall. Brand gathered his enhanced strength and shoved his old friend away, but Alastair only staggered back a pace. His eyes glowed softly for just a second. And then the big man surged forward to grab Brand by the shoulders. Alastair shook the younger man.

"Cadmus! Cadmus! Look at me!" Alastair shook Brand again until the young man glared into Alastair's hazel eyes. "He's gone, and you'll only get yourself killed if you try to go after him. He sacrificed himself for us—now run!"

Alastair wrenched Brand up to his feet and shoved Brand forward. Brand took one glance back at William as Ilye released him. The pharmakon collapsed in a heap and lay prone and motionless on the rock.

Ilye spoke to one of the guards and pointed out into the darkness. A moment later, the guards thundered after Brand and Alastair.

Brand turned back around and saw Alastair running into the desert. He swallowed hard at the lump in his throat and followed. He caught up to the older man just as Alastair reached the city wall. He led Brand back into Darnan and down an alley, then yanked the young man down into a recessed stairway in the dusty ground. He threw open a door at the bottom and pushed Brand into the dark cellar. A moment later, Brand could hear the rumble of the guards' boots clomping overhead.

The basement Brand found himself in was completely black, with no light source. The sickly, dry sweet smells of dust and rotten potatoes assaulted Brand's nose. He felt Alastair's thick fingers close around his arm and tug him through the darkness. Brand could hear the heavy shopkeeper's breath coming in heavy pants. Judging from the sounds their boots made as they walked, the floor soon changed from a somewhat uneven concrete surface to a smooth, polished stone floor.

Finally, they stopped, though in the darkness, Brand wouldn't have known if they had ended up right back where they'd started. The scream of a steam engine's whistle pierced the ground above them, startling Brand. The darkness around Brand rumbled and vibrated for several minutes. Alastair's hands drew Brand forward. He felt the shopkeeper's arms wrap around him.

Still in shock, Brand returned the embrace. The sharp tang of machine oil mingled with sweat brought back memories of the old junk shop. The roar of the train finally passed into the distance. After a moment, Alastair released Brand and cleared his throat.

"Storming way to meet again after all these years. Whose plan was that, anyway?" Alastair asked. "Worst plan in the history of plans."

"Ilye's," Brand mumbled.

Alastair let out an exasperated sigh. "Didn't William teach you to never trust a kashmari?"

"A kashmari? She's a Navari!" Brand growled at the dark spot where Alastair's voice was coming from.

"No, she's a kashmari. You can tell by the murderous dark magic she was wielding."

The image of William's glowing light being sucked up by Ilye came back to Brand. He sagged and closed his eyes, willing the image away. But it stayed, burned onto the insides of his eyelids.

Brand felt a heavy hand on his shoulder, just like when he was a boy.

"I can't say I don't appreciate the rescue, Cadmus. I do. Truly. I just…" Alastair sighed heavily. "You screwed it up pretty well and got one of the best men I know killed. The world will be a darker place without William. That's not going to be an easy thing to live with."

Brand felt like Alastair had punched him in the face. They stood in the darkness together, the silence between them as thick as mud.

"You've been working with kashmari," Brand said, his tone laden with accusation.

Alastair snorted. "They're a different sort. Swore off blood magic, the lot of them. But it doesn't matter now. I need to get as far away from Darnan as possible and vanish."

"Why?" Brand mumbled. "What's going on? William said you've been helping the rebels."

Alastair sighed. "I can't tell you. It would put you in terrible danger."

Brand snorted. "William said I'd put you in danger if I ever went looking for you."

That prompted a slight grunt from Alastair. "I suppose the lesson is that we must stay away from each other, at least for now."

Brand slumped at those words. Alastair seemed to sense the young man's sadness.

"I don't like it any more than you do," the shopkeeper said softly. "But for now, we need to remain apart. You need to keep your head down and reinvent yourself somehow, so that that kashmari, whatever her name is, doesn't come looking for you. Maybe try the arenas. They don't pay much, but most kashmari don't frequent the fights. You'll be able to stay out of sight there."

"I need to go back and get William's body," Brand said, his voice cracking.

Alastair's irritation crackled through the air and made the hair on Brand's neck stand up.

"Haven't you been listening? You need to stay low, make yourself invisible. You can't go back for his body."

"It's my fault he's dead," Brand said, miserable. "I was trying to help, even though he told me to stay behind. I didn't listen. If I'd just listened, he'd be alive. I owe him…I can't bring him back, but I can do this for him. I can take him back to his wife for a proper burial."

Alastair growled, a deep guttural sound that belonged more to a beast than a man.

"William sacrificed his life to let us get away! And now because you're feeling sorry for yourself, you're going to just throw that away?"

Brand's face flushed, and he was glad it was so dark.

"I thought you had more sense than that." Alastair's sigh was heavy and slow. "They'll do to you exactly what they did to him if they find you. And then Fafnir will parade both your bodies through the streets."

His voice went quiet. "I thought that if William could teach you to fight, you'd have a better chance at surviving than your mother. But I was wrong. You need to hide and survive, Cadmus."

Behind them, Brand heard the muffled echoes of voices. The heavy hand lifted from his shoulder and guided Brand's hand to a wall. Then Brand heard the older man's footsteps leaving him, echoing on the stone floor, leaving the young man alone in the dark.

RISE

1 October 1062 P.E.
Aeolian Dunes

Brand woke suddenly as his arm banged into the hard metal side of one of the wells in the *Polaris's* outer hull. Looking down, he saw his wrists and ankles tied securely with thick ropes to a steel loop welded to the side of the well. His leg brace had been removed. Even if he could get out of here, it'd be impossible for him to walk. He groaned.

The sun was retreating behind the dunes, turning them the burnt orange color of autumn leaves. The smoking wrecks of the *Polaris* and the *Dauntless* huddled together in the sand, the *Muspell's Sons* barely visible in the distance. The wind was churning sand up into the air, obscuring the dunes, rocks, and crumbling ruins.

The gladiator rested his forehead on the rim of the well, thoughts running through his head like the howling wind that ripped at his exposed face and hands.

Kushchai had Finn. Wren and Loren knew about Me'von and now didn't trust Brand. And Brand was tied to the hull like a piece of scrap. He banged his head against the metal and growled.

"You've really done it now," he muttered to himself. A feeling of utter helplessness sunk into him. He squeezed his eyes shut, trying to block it out.

What did Kushchai have planned once they got back to Darnan? Brand dreaded to think what the vengeful kashmari would do. Even if Brand managed to escape, Fafnir had promised to torture Brand for returning to any city-state. He'd be doomed to wander the Wastes until a storm killed him.

Brand twisted his hands around until he was able to reach inside a belt pouch, pulling out a thin leather cord and the four beads he'd carved over the last few days. He carefully strung them, then knotted the leather cord and hung it around his neck. The smooth wood was cool against his throat. He ran his fingers along the four different designs, each carved with a single unique word: Child, Mentor, Lover, Rival. The unborn baby, William, Mirane, and Percy. Four beads for four people who had changed his life. Four beads to remind him to never forget the life that was stolen from him and every other human.

<Mirane used kashmari magic to seduce you,> Me'von said quietly. <I've been debating whether to tell you, but I think you deserve to know. I think it may help to know.>

Brand's thumb froze on Mirane's carved bead.

<Every time she touched you, she twisted your mind, made you lust for her more than any other woman alive. She took away your free will.>

Brand gripped the bead tightly and squeezed his eyes shut. He felt sick.

"Why would she do that?"

<To conceive your child, a hybrid child who would one day challenge Fafnir and put her on the throne in Valin. It was a good plan, but poorly executed.>

As the rising wind drew thick clouds of sand over the sun, the frustration and rage and unfairness of it all finally boiled over. Brand lashed out at the demon lodged in his brain.

"If it wasn't for you, I wouldn't have been stuck here like this!" Brand shouted into the sky. "All of you! All of your kind! Every kashmari I've ever met!"

Me'von shrank to the back of Brand's mind and cowered.

But Brand knew that Me'von's words weren't why he was angry. He knew that he was merely lashing out to avoid the truth.

Brand closed his eyes tight and turned his face to the hard cold metal of the hull as the first drops of rain pelted down from the sky. A spike of lightning drove into a dune nearby, its thunder momentarily deafening Brand.

He jammed his fists against his forehead as the feeling of helplessness took over, drawing out a long, anguished cry that mingled with the wailing of the wind.

He was a worthless pawn in the devil's game.

Every time he'd tried to do anything of value, it ended in ruin. When he'd first become a pharmakon as a youth, his overzealousness had gotten William, his friend and mentor, killed. He'd been tricked into thinking he'd fallen in love and watched his life fall apart because of it. He'd thought he could help the crew of the *Polaris*, and he'd ended up screwing that up and losing their trust in the process. And now, they were in danger and he couldn't even lift a finger to help them.

No one trusted him, nor should they. He had no mind of his own. He was a fool. A mere kashmari puppet.

He was a failure.

It wasn't an empty feeling. It was an active pain, inescapable and horrible, that ate at his heart. He cringed in on himself, as though folding over into a fetal position would protect him; but this danger came from within, sneering, gnawing, cutting, prodding at his heart.

Tears flowed freely down his face but gave no relief. He cried out, but the storm swallowed his voice.

Finally, exhausted, Brand leaned limply against the side of the well and turned his face upward. He wished the storm would simply end it all.

The storm tried. It razed his face with sharp jets of sand and pummeled him with rocks until his armor and shirt hung in ribbons from his shoulders. Lightning snapped nearby, blinding and deafening him as it lit a nearby desert bush on fire. The wind grabbed him out of the well and tried to shove him over the edge to the sands below, but the ropes biting into his wrists held him too tightly.

After an eternal hour, the storm finally relented. The sands settled, the rains ceased, and the clouds dispersed to reveal a crystalline night sky.

Brand hung there, sobbing, for a long time.

What a pathetic thing you are, the words echoed in his mind. *Just like the pathetic kashmari who's been in your head.*

Brand could feel Me'von cringe and retreat further.

Then another voice he hadn't heard for almost four decades, rose in his mind.

You'll never save them all, William's voice said, calm, steady, patient. *Sometimes you'll fail. You may even die trying to save them. But if you try, you also risk succeeding. And for whomever you are trying to save, that's a risk worth taking.*

<Who was that?> Me'von asked quietly.

"My mentor, William James."

The kashmari seemed to mull William's words over.

The cold was sinking quickly into Brand's skin as the wind bit into his soaked clothes and hair. His whole body ached. His heart was worn and beaten. He didn't even have the brace on his leg, and without it, he couldn't even walk. How could he do anything?

I'm not even my own person. I'm a kashmari puppet with no thoughts of my own. What if Kushchai wants me to try to save the others so he can have an excuse to kill me?

Brand recalled the first time he met Finn, who took him in without question and gave him another chance at life. And then he thought of a few moments ago, the anger and fury and hatred that had boiled out of those same eyes from a kashmari who had stolen Finn's right to ever make a choice again.

The injustice of it gnawed at Brand. He tried to pull himself up the hull to the well; but his muscles were too battered, too weak. His boots slipped on the wet metal. His arms gave out, and he collapsed against the hull with a heavy clang.

Brand groaned. "I can't," he whispered.

A spark of realization flickered from Me'von. The kashmari's words came slowly, uncertainly. <But what if we could? What if I could help you use your elixirs? Would you try?>

"It'll be torture for you. You won't survive."

Me'von grunted. <It's not like my life in this forsaken desert is all that fulfilling anyway. There may be something I can do to help, though. Will you try?>

The kashmari's words held the barest hint of hope in them. Brand clung to that hope and nodded. With a deep breath, he closed his eyes and searched in his heart for the little spark. He found it. It seemed so elusive…

Brand became aware of Me'von there somehow. The kashmari seemed to be between Brand and the spark, blocking the pharmakon's access to the light. Me'von turned away, then back to Brand, holding the spark out to the pharmakon. Brand reached out and touched the spark and felt Me'von wrapping Brand's mental fingers around it and holding them tight.

Warmth and light exploded from Brand. If the kashmari had had teeth, he would have been gritting them.

<Now!> Me'von yelled.

Brand opened his eyes and reached down into his boot and pulled out the last two vials, Armor and Stamina. He uncorked and downed them both, then quickly formed the two hand signals, Delta and Sigma, to release the elixirs into his blood. Strength surged through his limbs, shedding all the exhaustion and pain like an old, tattered skin. The full-strength elixirs made his eyes glow a brilliant amber as the strange swirling patterns of golden light exploded like rivers of fire across his skin.

Me'von grunted in surprise but didn't comment.

Even augmented so, Brand could tell that the effects of the potions were still somewhat muted; but he didn't care. He felt alive.

"Me'von?"

<Get going, you idiot! I can't do this forever!>

Whatever Me'von was doing, Brand's mind was blessedly clear. He yanked at the ropes, hauling himself up onto the top of the *Polaris's* slick hull with a great heave. He then pulled the ropes over to the sharp edge of the well's lip and began to saw, back and forth, fraying them until they snapped. He slid over to the hatch, not even bothering with the rungs. He hauled the hatch open and dropped straight down. As his boots hit the deck, he sunk into a crouch.

"What was that?" Finn's voice said from the cockpit.

Brand glanced into the bunk room and saw Loren laying on one of the bunks, dried blood caking one whole side of his face.

<Looks like Wren didn't have a chance to patch him up properly,> Me'von grunted. Then, <Look out!>

The kashmari-controlled Finn strode into the hall. As soon as he saw the glowing pharmakon, shirt shredded, arms and face dripping with blood, face determined, Finn's eyes went wide. He lunged towards Brand.

Brand leapt forward to meet the scavenger, grabbed Finn by the shoulders, and tossed him backwards. The scavenger fell onto his back, but as soon as he hit the floor, he rolled out of the way of Brand's fist. The scavenger rolled up to his feet and kicked out at Brand's gut. The big pharmakon hit the floor with a heavy thud. Finn pounced on Brand and immediately began pummeling the bigger man in the face.

Wren came in and saw the two men on the floor. She grabbed Brand around the throat to pull him off of Finn.

No no no, Brand thought. He pried Wren's hands off, twisted around, and pinned the woman against the bulkhead. "I don't want to fight you. That's not Finn! It's Kuschai!"

Wren grunted as the air was shoved out of her lungs. "You've got that the wrong way around, Brand. You're the bad guy, remember?"

Finn's fist connected with the back of Brand's head, giving Wren enough of a distraction to shove herself away from the wall and into Brand, sending the pharmakon staggering.

Finn followed his punch with another kick to Brand's gut, but Brand grabbed the scavenger's boot and wrenched it hard to the left. Finn cried out as his knee snapped. He crumpled to his other knee. Brand glanced around, searching for the dagger he had dropped earlier.

<Steel won't work!> Me'von growled. <Only redstone will kill a kashmari, remember? Use the dagger in your boot!>

Before Brand could pull the knife out, Wren launched herself onto Brand's back and grabbed him around the neck again, this time wrapping her legs around him. Brand grunted and staggered backward into the bulkhead.

Finn stalked toward them, murder in his eyes. He began to *pull* at Wren. Darkness started to stream off of her.

DÉTENTE

<No!> Me'von yelled.

Brand yelled incoherently and slammed Wren against the wall again. Weakened, she let go and fell to the floor. Brand hurled himself at Finn. As he surged forward, he slipped the redstone dagger out of his boot. He brought the dagger up and shoved it straight into Finn's chest.

The stream of darkness connecting Finn and Wren broke off. Finn staggered back into the bulkhead.

A kashmari scream threatened to rip Brand's head in half. But this time, the horrific sound didn't come from Me'von.

Me'von seemed to recoil as Kushchai's screams echoed around Brand's skull, then faded.

Unlike with Mirane, no cloudy apparition rose from Finn's body. Instead, he twitched painfully for several moments and then slumped.

After a moment, Finn straightened up and with a relieved grin, said hoarsely, "He is gone." The scavenger's smile twisted into a grimace as he doubled over and started hacking. Droplets of blood spewed from his mouth onto the deck.

Brand hurried forward and caught Finn. The scavenger gasped for air. Brand ripped a piece of cloth off of Finn's shirt and jammed it into the wound.

As he waited for Finn to catch his breath, Brand realized the strange glowing patterns on his skin had faded. That was odd. The elixirs had worn off much faster than usual.

<My fault,> Me'von admitted tiredly. <I couldn't hang on any longer. I had to get rid of the elixirs.>

Brand blinked. <How?>

<Same way you dispersed my magic. Out through your fingertips.>

<Huh.>

"Thanks," Finn croaked.

"Hang in there," Brand said.

Finn coughed again. "I think my scavenging days are over," he said.

"You're not dying," Brand said. "I made sure to puncture a lung, not your heart."

The glare Finn gave Brand could have melted a glacier.

"You're alive, you idiot," Brand said with a grin.

<Hm. Sounds like something I'd say.>

<You're rubbing off on me.>

Me'von chuckled smugly.

Finn grabbed Brand's forearm.

"Thanks," he said. He hesitated, then said, "I'm sorry for doubting you. Both of you."

<Understandable, if irritating. Apology accepted.>

Brand smiled. "Let's just get you healed."

Wren hurried over with their first aid kit and helped Brand pack and wrap Finn's wound.

Once he was certain Finn was stable, Brand turned to head down the hall to the bunk room and Loren; but Wren was already ahead of him, cradling the gunslinger's head in her lap, a rag pressed against his wicked facial wound. Brand checked to make sure Loren was breathing steadily and that Wren had all the bandages she needed, then walked back to Finn and sat beside him, back up against the wall.

Finn watched Wren carefully cleaning Loren's shattered face, his expression riddled with worry and exhaustion. Brand leaned his back up against the bulkhead and closed his eyes.

"Now what?" Brand asked, completely and utterly spent.

<Well, we won. Barely. Your crew chief is nearly dead and your

sidekick is badly wounded. Your girlfriend seems ok.>

<She's Loren's, not mine,> Brand thought softly with a pang at the thought of Mirane.

<You're the proud owner of two useless armored trawlers and a doomsday bomb that Lord Fafnir will kill for. Oh, and your limp is gone.>

Brand thought back to the last several minutes. Me'von was right. The pains in his hip and shoulder were gone.

<How did that happen?> Brand asked.

<The pain was from Kuschai. He destroyed your belief in yourself.>

<The night he tortured me?>

<No. Well, not entirely. Over decades, he imprisoned you by making you believe that you were nothing without him. When he tortured you, you finally broke under the onslaught. Your mind attached that emotional pain to the physical pain. But once you decided to help Finn and the others, you finally believed that you could be something more. And the pain went away.>

<Did you know that would happen?>

Me'von smirked. <I'd guessed.>

Wren walked back over to Finn and Brand, then sat between them.

"He's talking to the kashmari in his head, isn't he?" Finn asked.

Wren smiled. "Looks like it."

"That's going to take some getting used to," the scavenger said.

Brand smiled ruefully. "If it weren't for this kashmari, we'd be dead."

"I know," Finn said. "That's also going to take some getting used to." He turned to Wren. "How's Loren?"

"The bleeding has stopped," Wren said. She had a rag in her hands that she scrubbed across her bloodied fingers. "He's out cold, though."

"Yeah, rung his bell good, didn't I?"

"That wasn't you," Brand said firmly. "It was Kushchai."

Finn shook his head and coughed a little. He spat a wad of blood onto the deck. "I hated the kashmari before, but I dunno how I'm going to sleep at night now knowing exactly what those monsters can do."

The scavenger glanced at Brand. "No offense."

<None taken. I tend to agree.>

Brand frowned. "What happened to the bomb? Is it still on the *Dauntless*?"

"Never made it there," Finn said. He pointed to the panel under the kitchen table. "Loren picked it up off one of Rhamnus's thugs. We stashed it over there in a hidden compartment before the fight started."

Brand stood and walked over to the table.

<There's just one thing I don't understand,> Brand said to Me'von as he inspected the table and the panel underneath. <How did you survive me using my abilities?>

Me'von didn't answer immediately. After a long moment, he said, <You know, I'm not really sure. I have an idea, but…well, I might have to investigate this further.>

<So you'll be sticking around?> Brand lifted the table and hauled it aside.

<You're growing on me, kid.>

Brand let out an exasperated sigh as he returned to the kitchen. <I'm not a kid.>

Me'von laughed long and loudly.

<Yeah, you are. You're almost a baby. Don't worry; it's kind of cute.>

<Oh, shut up.>

Brand pried open the panel. There, tucked between two metal struts, was the torpedo-shaped bomb. The inky liquid inside swirled and pulsed its strange light.

Shock radiated from Me'von like the concussive blast from an explosion, making Brand stagger back and bump into the cabinetry behind him.

"What in blazes!" Brand growled. "What is it? What's wrong?"

The kashmari didn't say anything. Irritated, Brand rubbed at his temples. Me'von's sudden unexplained outburst was giving him a headache.

With a groan, Brand lowered the panel back into place and hauled the table back into the kitchen. That bomb could buy his freedom back from Fafnir. All he needed to do was hijack one of the other approaching trawlers, load up the bomb, and head for Darnan. He thought of Mrs. James. He could get his life back.

But it just felt…wrong. Whatever Fafnir had planned for the bomb, it couldn't be good.

Me'von finally spoke, and when he did, his words were harsher than Brand had ever heard him. <Fafnir can go suck on a sea cucumber for all I

care. Let's get rid of it one way or another, and tell the old brute he's been wrong all these years, that there was no device. I'd love to see the look on his face when we tell him that.>

<What is it?> the pharmakon asked.

<A thaumium bomb,> Me'von spat. A wave of horror and hatred rolled off the kashmari.

<To use against kashmari?>

<No,> Me'von growled. <To use against…well, beings like you.>

<Like the dvergen? I thought they were all killed.>

<The dvergen, and…others. Yes, Fafnir wiped them all out. But there was one being he couldn't kill.> Me'von shuddered. <I have no idea why Fafnir would want to kill *him*, though. There are just some things you don't do, not even as a kashmari.>

Brand walked back over to Wren and Finn and joined them on the deck once more.

"Amazing, isn't it?" Finn said hoarsely.

Brand nodded.

"So what now, Finn?" Wren asked. "What do we do?"

Finn snorted. "I'm half dead, and the *Polaris* is completely dead. Beats me."

Brand ran a blood-streaked hand through his salt and pepper hair, then scratched at his tangled beard. A shower sounded amazing, but it might be a while before he got one. He dropped his hand to his side.

"I could maybe find enough parts between the two command consoles to build a new one, given time," Brand said. "And if we can limp over to where that Marauder wreck was out in the dunes, I should be able to fix the rest of the trawler."

Finn nodded slowly. Wren said, "Could be a bit of a challenge with the other scavengers around."

"I think I can keep them off our backs," Brand said.

Finn chuckled, giving himself another coughing fit.

Wren put an arm around the older scavenger. "Let's get you to bed. You need rest."

Brand watched Wren steer Finn into a bunk. Anthea darted out of the room between their feet, then crouched down and cautiously tip-toed forward, bat ears erect. She crept over to Brand, stuck her little wet nose under his hand, and shoved his hand upward onto her head.

The pharmakon smiled fondly and stroked the velvety fur on the zerda's striped head.

Brand remembered the thaum crystal he still carried in his belt pouch. He carefully removed it and held it up to his face so that he could see it better.

Inside, blue mist swirled around like the blue tanks had, a watery storm laced with delicate lightning.

Anthea watched it swinging from its chain with enormous eyes. She sat back on her haunches and batted at it with a paw. Brand held it aloft so that she couldn't touch it.

"Don't touch."

<She won't be harmed by it.>

<You said I would be if I touched it.>

<It's more accurate to say that I'll be injured if you touch it, as a kashmari. But…I'm not entirely sure about that anymore. You used your elixirs and I didn't die.>

<Are they made out of the same stuff?>

<No. They amplify the thaumium within you. You call it a spark. Either way, your zerda doesn't have a kashmari in her head. She can touch the crystal.>

Brand cocked his head at the little fox. Then he carefully wrapped the chain around Anthea's neck a couple of times so that the crystal hung down her front like a glowing necklace pendant. She immediately curled up next to Brand and nuzzled under his hand again.

His hand drifted up to his throat where the carved wooden beads hung and heaved a great sigh.

The life he once knew was gone. It was time to forge a new one.

Lies

2 December 1062 P.E.
Southern Depot, Darnan

Two months later, the *Polaris* ambled up to the gate of Darnan, scarred but newly functional. Brand steered it up next to the Southern Train Depot and settled it down beside a sand-scarred engine awaiting new cargo.

Brand stood where Finn's old chair used to be. Around him, the cobbled-together command console bore long gashes and blackened burn marks that butted up against relatively clean metal. The viewport was completely missing save for a few jagged glass teeth around the edges. Brand had spent the last two months battling the ever-present sand getting into every nook and cranny, often making buttons or knobs stick.

Now, errant wisps of steam from the adjacent engine curled into the cockpit, leaving droplets here and there on every surface. Brand considered moving the *Polaris*, but realized it was futile until he repaired that viewport.

Wren and Loren stood behind him. The Duati gunslinger now sported a wicked purple scar that stretched from above his hairline down to his mouth. All three were somber.

When they got to the bottom of the gangplank, a mechanohorse-drawn carriage rolled in front of them. It stopped and a tall, slender kashmari stepped out.

Loren whispered, "What's he doing here?"

Brand swallowed and said, "I'll take care of it."

He stepped toward the group. The kashmari's bald, blue-grey head was free of any adornments or ordyeni. Fierce silver eyes locked onto the battered pharmakon. The kashmari stopped in front of Brand.

"Where's Finn?" the kashmari asked. His voice was crisp, his gaze sharp and incisive. It was clear that this lord had no interest in extraneous emotions.

<That's Sahure,> Me'von said.

"Finn's dead," Brand lied. He looked the kashmari lord up and down. "I've taken over command of the *Polaris.*"

"And you are Cadmus Brand, correct? Finn sent a message to me from Zabete telling me you'd joined them as a mechanic." He gestured one slender grey hand at the *Polaris.* "I presume you are also the one who put my Venator back together."

"That's right."

The kashmari nodded approvingly. "You have my thanks. I heard that the device was accidentally set off at the wreck?"

Brand nodded.

Sahure sighed. "I have heard third hand what happened at the wreck of the *Muspell's Sons*, but I'd like to hear it from you. These sorts of tales get sensationalized the further removed you are from the truth. Come, we can talk at my manor."

Brand glanced back at the other two.

"If they are anything like Finn, they'll want to stay as far away from the city as possible," Sahure noted with a hint of amusement in his voice. "That won't be necessary, but tell them I'll send a team of mechanics out to assist in the rest of the repairs. They may remain with the *Polaris* for now."

Brand relayed the information to the two recalcitrant scavengers, who both looked relieved and reentered the Venator. Brand followed Sahure into the mechanocarriage. They settled into their seats opposite each other. The carriage was simple yet elegant, with smooth oak benches and straightforward black curtains which Sahure kept tied back to let in the pale winter light.

"You'll excuse me a moment," Sahure said, turning his attention to a notebook he balanced on one knee. He seemed to be working out some numbers. Finally, he set the notebook aside with a sigh.

"This is going to be an expensive venture, putting the *Polaris* back together," the kashmari said. "Without Finn scavenging parts, I'm not sure how much I can afford."

"We found quite a lot of scrap in the hold of the *Dauntless*," Brand said. "Several dvergen artifacts, as well. I used some of the scrap to fix up the *Polaris* enough to get us back, but a lot of it can still be sold to pay for the other parts we need."

Sahure cocked his head, his eyes filled with curiosity, a smile creeping onto his lean face. "Interesting. I've never worked directly with a mechanic before. You seem like you'll be an excellent addition to the crew."

The kashmari continued, mostly talking to himself. "Finn will be nearly impossible to replace, of course, but I suppose I'll have to find someone. I wonder if they'd accept a kashmari now that Finn is gone..."

Brand snorted. "No, they won't. There's only one kashmari they put up with, and he's already in here." Brand tapped his temple.

Sahure blinked. "You...what? I don't understand."

"His name is Me'von."

Sahure's jaw dropped. "Me'von of Gresh? You are hosting him?" He let out a short bark of laughter and shook his head in amazement. "Of all the kashmari...I've never had the pleasure of meeting you, Me'von, but if half of what I know of you is true, I'm sure our ambitions ought to line up quite nicely."

That prompted a wave of curiosity from Me'von.

Sahure's eyes narrowed. "I take it Me'von is not in control?"

Brand shook his head. "He doesn't really need to. We have an understanding."

Me'von chuckled.

The corner of Sahure's mouth twitched up. "He always was an odd one. Well, Me'von, if you're willing to keep an eye on the crew, and if the crew will follow Brand, I am willing to give you both a chance."

Brand folded his arms over his chest. He'd long since shed his tattered armor, and now only wore his leather duster over his linen shirt.

"Your message assured me that Fafnir's warrant for my arrest would be taken care of if I returned to Darnan. Does that hold true for Me'von as well?"

Sahure hesitated. "Ah, yes, that would be an issue, wouldn't it?"

The kashmari lord's next words were careful. "I had no idea that Me'von had any part of the affair and thus had no thought to ask Lord Fafnir if Me'von was welcome in Darnan. Me'von's exploits in the past were…severe. It may behoove him to vacate this host until after we meet with the high lord."

Me'von mulled over the kashmari lord's words for a moment. Then he spoke through Brand.

"That won't be necessary," he said. "I think it's in the best interests of Brand if I stick around."

Sahure shrugged. "So be it."

Brand wasn't so sure. <What if Fafnir kills me trying to get to you?>

<Well, you'll be dead so you won't care,> Me'von said with a smirk. <Anyway, I don't think it'll come to that. He needs you alive.>

<So I'm your guarantee that he won't kill you?> Brand asked sourly.

<Basically.>

Unaware of Brand and Me'von's internal dialogue, Sahure was speaking. "Provided Fafnir doesn't incinerate the both of you, I'd like you to move back into your house on Gladiator Row. It's as good a base of operations as any for when you visit Darnan between scavenging runs." He flicked through his notebook, looking for something. "Now that the crew of the *Polaris* has earned a certain grudging respect among the highest circles of the elites, you can assure the others that their debts and…other affairs…in the city of Darnan have been handled. I cannot at present do the same for their affairs in other cities, but this one can serve as a safe haven for them."

"We weren't planning on staying long."

"No, I expect not. But still. I will have need of you all here in Darnan for a time."

Brand's eyes narrowed.

"I'm not about to be someone else's tool," he growled. "And neither are they."

Sahure smiled tightly.

"Of course. I misspoke. I don't know how much Finn told you about our relationship, but it was a partnership. After a period of getting to know each other, I dare say you and I should be able to establish a similar relationship. And as such, there are things in Darnan that you could attend to that we both could benefit from."

"Such as?"

"You were there the night that High Lord Fafnir killed Mirane. That situation and its repercussions are still developing. Fafnir might have unwittingly bitten off more than he can chew." The lord paused as though selecting his next words carefully. "I appreciate your and Me'von's recalcitrance towards working with other kashmari, especially those with ties to the high lord; but I assure you that our goals are more closely aligned than you realize."

The kashmari gave Brand a meaningful look, but it was Me'von who puzzled out the meaning behind Sahure's words.

<He wants to take down Fafnir,> Me'von said, a little amazed.

<How can you be sure?>

<Trust me. I know.>

Brand had to admit that his curiosity was piqued. Fafnir was having trouble because of Mirane's murder? The pharmakon wouldn't mind staying if it meant helping Fafnir's enemies shove the high lord into a grave. Brand let understanding slide onto his face.

"What do you need me to do?"

Sahure smiled.

"There are rumors that Lord Fafnir intends to hold a gladiatorial tournament of his own soon." Sahure held up a hand to stop Brand's interjection. "I wouldn't dream of asking you to participate. However, when the high lord calls for an event such as this, every able kashmari noble attends. Such events are prime hunting grounds for anyone seeking alliances, and I believe you could do much to win me some valuable friendships indeed. As a matter of fact, I doubt we will have any hope of success in our mutual cause should we fail to forge these alliances."

Sahure waved an unadorned hand. "But the date is not set. We will speak of these things later when I know more."

The mechanocarriage halted in front of a large rectangular house with five or six rows of windows and a perfectly manicured topiary garden. Where Fafnir's estate had been massive and regal, Sahure's manor seemed traditional and precise, like a well-tailored suit.

"Come in," the kashmari lord said. "We have more to discuss before meeting with Lord Fafnir tomorrow."

Sahure led Brand inside and into a study. Again, unlike the other kashmari studies Brand had found himself in, this one seemed less interested in impressing through artwork and more interested in knowledge. The walls were covered in massive bookcases overflowing with books. Brand couldn't help but smile. It felt like home.

But once the door closed, Brand became aware of two others who had been standing in a corner of the room. He turned and came face to face with High Lord Fafnir and Lord Jinn.

"My lords," Sahure said in surprise. "I apologize—I had no idea you were here. I was under the impression our meeting wasn't until tomorrow."

"It wasn't," Fafnir said, his deep voice rumbling. The giant high lord seemed to have a dark halo of gently crackling energy around him that Brand hadn't noticed before. It made the hairs on the back of Brand's neck stand on end. "I decided there was little point in waiting and indeed potential harm in putting it off. I'd like to hear your crew chief's version of events at the wreck now."

"Of course," Sahure said. He gestured at the chairs and the four men sat.

All three kashmari turned to look at the pharmakon.

Brand glared at Fafnir. The last thing Brand wanted to do was act civilized right now. He thought of the redstone knife in his boot and the three beads hanging at his throat.

<He needs to die.>

Me'von snorted. <You'll be dead before you realize what happened.>

<I killed Kushchai, didn't I?> Brand spat.

Me'von brushed that thought aside. <We need to know what he's up to. He said this world is about to die. We need to know how he plans on avoiding that.>

Brand stared at the hulking figure of Fafnir, his teeth clenching together. The Dragon met Brand's gaze with a cold, intelligent stare. Patient, lethal, eternal.

<He's killed gods, Brand,> Me'von said. <You can't win in an honest fight. Just tell him the story we agreed on. He will fall. But not today.>

And so Brand told them. He told them the truth, mostly, of how the

Polaris had journeyed to the wreck of the *Muspell's Sons*, how Finn had figured out where the bomb was, the fights, the destruction of the Titan and Venator, and Brand's final fight with Kushchai. He made it sound as though Finn had died of his wounds.

He also told them the lie of how Kushchai had taken the bomb and set it off by accident.

Brand watched Fafnir for his reaction to the news, but the giant kashmari seemed as impassive as ever.

<Does he believe me?> Brand asked.

<Hard to say. My guess is no. He won't say so, though.>

Brand continued with his story, telling them that Kushchai had never intended to give the bomb to Fafnir, but rather wanted to use it against him to take over the kashmari.

Fafnir nodded slowly. "Yes, I was aware of this. Had he managed to return to Darnan alive, Kushchai would not have remained so for long."

"Thank you, Cadmus Brand," Sahure said. "I will be in contact shortly for your next assignment."

Taking this as a dismissal, Brand bowed his head and left the room.

Behind him, Fafnir followed him into the hallway, closing the door to the study behind them.

"I would like to speak with Me'von," the high lord said.

Every muscle in Brand's body wanted to lash out and turn that impassive face to a pulp.

<Not today,> Me'von repeated firmly.

Reluctantly, Brand nodded and relinquished control.

Brand turned to face the giant, voluntarily stepping aside so that Me'von could assume control. It felt so different from when Kushchai had taken over.

"Yes?" Me'von said. Brand could feel Me'von stiffen.

"You've been hiding from me for a century," Fafnir rumbled, "for the fiasco in New Braunen. I ought to kill you for that."

Me'von sent Brand's hand to the knife on his belt.

Brand said, <You said we couldn't kill him now.>

<If he tries to kill me, I'm not going quietly.>

Fafnir watched the flicker in Brand's eyes with interest, seemingly understanding that there was a conversation going on behind them. He waited, making no move at all. Just watching.

"But you're not going to kill me," Me'von said slowly. "Why not? Why not make an example of me?"

Fafnir took a step closer so that Brand could smell the thin layer of desert dust on the high lord's shirt. Fafnir's eyes glittered with amusement. "I've never been one to waste a valuable resource. I can replace Kushchai and a hundred others like him. But not you. I suppose if that means quelling a rebellion every so often from you, then so be it."

Me'von's fingers didn't leave the knife hilt, but his muscles relaxed.

"You did well out there," Fafnir said, changing the subject. "You managed to not make a complete mess of things. If you want it, your position as my right hand is available to you."

Me'von was speechless. He finally let Brand's hand drop away from the dagger's sheath.

<You were his right-hand man?> Brand blurted.

<Long story,> Me'von muttered. <It would make it a lot easier to find out what he's up to…>

Brand began to feel uneasy. The thought of being so close to Fafnir and being at his beck and call…

Me'von shook Brand's head. "No, I'd rather work with Sahure, I think. But if you could call off your dogs, I'd appreciate that."

Fafnir folded his arms. "Fine. Keep that bomb safe, Me'von. I don't want it falling into any other kashmari's hands. Do you understand?"

"Not really," Me'von said. "I figured you wanted to set it off, kill a guardian perhaps."

"No. The guardian needs to stay alive. If someone gets ahold of that bomb…well, it won't be good."

Me'von frowned. "Does it have to do with the world dying?"

Fafnir hesitated, then nodded.

"And you think Brand can save the world?"

Fafnir shook his head. "I think he can get us off this world before it collapses. He could save a lot of people."

Me'von's eyes widened in shock.

"Besides, our mission has never been rescinded, Me'von," the high lord continued. "We cannot carry it out here."

Me'von cringed. "Your mission, not mine."

Fafnir sighed heavily. "You and Phoenix never could see, could never really understand. Perhaps one day you will."

Me'von shook his head. "No. The day I understand is the day I become you, and I will never let that happen."

Fafnir shook his head and prodded Me'von in the chest. "No matter. Just take care of that boy, Me'von. If you let anything happen to him, we're all dead."

"Death doesn't seem so bad. I'm not terribly impressed with eternity."

Fafnir snorted. "You'd resign millions of humans to a fiery death just like that?"

"It'd be better than letting you loose."

"Would it?"

Me'von wavered. A smile spread across Fafnir's dark face.

"Supposing I came around to your way of thinking," Me'von said, shoulders slumping. "How is Brand supposed to help?"

Fafnir shook his head. "I don't trust you that far, Me'von. I'll let you know when the time comes."

Me'von grabbed Fafnir by the front of his waistcoat, bringing the two enormous men nose to nose. Fafnir's expression darkened.

"Secrets and lies and infighting are what landed us here on this blasted world," Me'von snarled.

Fire blazed in the high lord's eyes, an unearthly flame crackling dangerously at the heart of his pupils. In a barely controlled hiss, Fafnir said, "You forget yourself."

He wrenched himself out of Me'von's grip and shoved the smaller man back.

The giant turned and reentered the study.

Me'von, shaking, relinquished control to Brand.

Brand felt like Me'von was about to be sick.

<You ok?> he asked the kashmari.

<No,> Me'von replied miserably.

Brand tried to quiet his mind to let Me'von have a moment to compose himself while they left Sahure's manor. Outside, the cold winter air bit at Brand's nose and ears. He shivered. He'd need to pick up a new duster somewhere.

Gravel crunched under the pharmakon's boots as he strode down the drive. He passed Sahure's mechanocarriage and paused. No, he needed to stretch his legs a bit. He'd been cooped up in the *Polaris* for too long these past couple of months. He set off for the Southern Depot, shoving his chilled hands into his trouser pockets.

As Brand walked down the streets of Darnan, he was amazed at how odd the familiar city looked to him now. It was just as he'd left it, and yet now he saw it with new eyes. Whereas before he'd seen the tall, stately buildings, the grand fountains, and the bustling shops, now he saw the grubby urchins huddled in doorways, the gangsters huddled together, passing a cigar around and glaring at passersby, and the threadbare skirts of the women selling flowers.

These people were hurting, Brand realized now. All those years, he could have done something, anything, to help; but he hadn't. He'd been content to hide in his ivory tower and pretend the rest of the world didn't need him.

"Do you really think the world is going to collapse?" Brand asked under his breath.

Me'von didn't answer for a moment. Then, <I'm not convinced that it is. Fafnir is a champion liar, after all. But he might be telling the truth. We need to find out for ourselves. Either way, though, Fafnir is going to try to escape, and he thinks you'll help him. We can't allow that.>

"What happens if the kashmari escape this world?" *Whatever 'this world' means.*

A deep sorrow, far deeper and more ancient than Brand could understand, suffused Me'von's emotions. His words were anguished. <They can't, Brand. I hate this world as much as they do. I'd gladly trade eternity for five minutes back home. But this is their prison. It's my prison. And we can never, ever leave it. Billions of lives depend on it.>

Brand was silent as they walked along for a couple of miles. The pharmakon was beginning to understand why Me'von felt sick. He passed a woman wrapped in a thin cloak clutching her shivering daughter. He paused, fished out a couple of coins, and gave them to the woman.

"Bless you," she said. She gathered up her child and hurried away down the street. Brand watched them vanish into a warm hotel.

"So either we all die here, or billions of others die somewhere else?" Brand whispered.

The kashmari's silence was answer enough.

"Do you think Fafnir can figure out a way to escape?"

Me'von thought for a moment. <Yes,> he said slowly. <I think he's

finally figured out a way to do it.>

Epilogue

Mrs. James gave the stew a stir, mouth watering at the rich aroma wafting around the kitchen. She'd left the window open to the cool evening air to let some of the moisture out.

She heard the knock on the door and hurriedly set aside the spoon and went to the door to unlock it. She opened the door with a smile.

A huge hulking stranger stood in the darkened doorway. Two other dark shapes waited beyond the stranger. Mrs. James's smile melted into worry.

The stranger reached forward. Heart pounding, Mrs. James hurriedly tried to close the door, but the stranger stuck out a boot. He grunted as the heavy door slammed on his foot.

"Mrs. James, it's me."

Mrs. James froze.

She knew that deep voice, as gentle and strong as the roots of a mountain. Slowly, she pulled the door open. He stepped forward into the light from the house, revealing a scarred, unkempt hairy face and hands, a long duster coat, and a sun-faded blue linen shirt covered in soot and desert dust. He pulled off a stained, wide-brimmed fedora and placed it on the little table beside the door. The stranger smiled gently at the old woman with laughing amber eyes.

"Brand?" Mrs. James breathed.

Brand's face broke into a warm smile that lit up his disaster of a face. He spread his arms wide open, and Mrs. James fell into his arms with relief.

"You're back!" she sobbed. After a moment, she pulled back and pulled out a handkerchief to dab at her eyes. "Come in, come in!"

Brand stepped into the foyer after Mrs. James, followed by two others: a Duati man as pale as the moon and a slender woman with bright eyes.

"Are you going to introduce me?" Mrs. James prompted.

"This is Loren, and Wren," Brand gestured. He paused as if listening to something. He frowned, then shook his head ever so slightly. "They'll be staying with us." To the newcomers, he said, "This is Mrs. James, my housekeeper and surrogate mother."

"It's a pleasure to meet you," the woman named Wren said. She held out a hand, which Mrs. James happily accepted.

The Duati man didn't say anything, but removed his hat and nodded cordially.

The big pharmakon breathed in deeply, his eyes closing and his smile deepening. "I don't suppose you have something to eat, do you? Maybe stew…? With meat that I didn't have to kill?"

Mrs. James laughed and swatted him on his arm. "You never change! Yes, it's been cooking all day. It's made with a tough hunk of runnerbeast, I'll warn you. This way."

Mrs. James led the trio into the kitchen and ladled out a bowl of stew for each of them. There was silence and plenty of smiles to go around, and each of the newcomers kept asking for more, as though they hadn't eaten a proper meal in years. After their taut, hungry faces had relaxed a bit, Mrs. James unleashed her curiosity.

"Alright. Brand, where have you been? What have you been up to?"

Brand sighed heavily. "I'll tell you tomorrow. Tonight, I just want to hear how you've fared here on your own."

"Oh, you needn't worry. I was fine. Tell me about your adventures."

Brand pulled the guitar out from behind his chair and set it gingerly on the table between the bowls. "Did you take up the guitar while I was gone? Or does this being down here have something to do with the extra pair of boots in the hallway that are a few sizes too small to be mine?"

Mrs. James smiled fondly at her pharmakon. "Worried that someone's been sleeping in your bed while you were gone?"

Brand's eyes twinkled. "I wouldn't normally pry, Mrs. James, but it is my house and I'd at least like the courtesy of meeting your new gentleman friend."

Mrs. James laughed. "Alright, I admit. I haven't exactly been alone."

"Oh?" Brand couldn't quite keep the grin off his face.

She sighed and straightened her shawl around her shoulders. "How I wish I could tell you that I've found true love once more at my age. Then you wouldn't have any excuse! But unfortunately, I have only been nursing a poor young man back to health."

Mrs. James explained about Erekir's sudden arrival and Kushchai's request, which prompted Brand to utter a few foul curses.

"Whatever Kushchai's designs, Erekir has been a respectable enough houseguest," Mrs. James said defensively.

"Well, at least we won't have to deal with Kushchai's antics anymore," Brand said.

"Why not?" Mrs. James asked.

"He's dead."

Mrs. James's jaw dropped. "How?"

Brand hesitated just long enough for Mrs. James to deduce that the pharmakon must have done it. She raised her eyebrows.

"Well, I can't say I'm sorry to hear that. Bread, anyone?"

She sliced a fresh loaf of bread and handed a piece to each of them.

The Duati mumbled, "Thank ye, ma'am. This stew is excellent."

"I'm glad you like it. It's my mother's recipe."

"She was a Duati?" the man asked, surprised.

Mrs. James nodded with a smile. "Been some time since you've been back, is it? I only ask because you don't seem to have the accent."

He shrugged. "Got rid of it. Took some doing, but I don't intend to ever go back."

"So where exactly is this respectable houseguest?" Brand rumbled.

"Out. He's been spending most of his evenings touring as many of the drinking establishments around the city as he can find. He usually comes back somewhat sober in the morning."

"Respectable, my foot," Brand growled.

"He's had something terrible happen to him," Mrs. James said. "I'm not sure what. I think that's why he drinks."

Brand grunted. "Well, when this young idiot of yours shows up, you can tell him he's free to go his own way since Kushchai won't be bothering him anymore."

Mrs. James relented. "Alright. You all must be tired. Mr. Brand, your room is still tidied and ready for you. I'll take your friends to rooms."

"Thank you, Mrs. James."

* * *

Erekir had wandered away from Gladiator Row, not really caring where his feet took him. The buildings around him went from crisp, tall stone edifices to rough-hewn sandstone blocks and then to hovels made from tarps propped up on long poles. The people changed too: at first, the men wore tailored suits and top hats, while the women wore long gowns, and kashmari intermingled with their bluish faces dotted and lined with white paint; then the kashmari faded along with the colors of the men's suits and ladies' dresses, giving way to simpler cotton that had lost its sheen; and finally, suits and dresses alike gave way to rough canvas trousers and simple linen shirts, often threadbare and translucent in the summer sun.

Erekir found the local pub by the stink of sweat and sour ale and the sounds of laughter and clanking glasses. Like the rest of the buildings of the northwestern quarter, it was more of a sun shelter made of tarps draped between poles that barely shaded the barrels that served as tables. He stood beside one barrel and raised a hand to get the attention of the waiter, a metal humanoid machine. Its cogs clinked rhythmically. Erekir saw its brain blinking from behind the metal filigree: a small, smooth black box that looked nothing like the clockwork person it was set in. it was probably worth more than this entire establishment. Salvage from a wreck of the Ancestors somewhere, no doubt.

"Cujar whisky," he said. The metal waiter nodded and retreated behind the bar.

Erekir didn't bother to look around. He didn't care where he was, only that he could drink himself out of this nightmare.

The waiter brought him a medium-sized glass etched by sand and filled with liquid the color of urine. Erekir downed the drink in one shot. Tasted like it, too. "Another," he barked at the waiter. He downed two more just as quickly. His body started to go numb and the pain, a deep and agonizing empty ache that sliced to the center of his soul, started to fade. The tension in his muscles started to ebb.

He closed his eyes. He was so tired. So drained. So tired of living. Why hadn't they just let him die of that blasted plague?

The kashmari lord. He wanted Erekir, to trade for something, Erekir knew. Trade him like cattle. That's all he was to them now. Cattle. That's why they hadn't let him die. Couldn't let their prized cow die.

But what did it matter what they did to him, anyway? There wasn't anything they could do to him that those pirates hadn't already done. The ache came back, rearing its ugly head as the memory of the smell of charred flesh and the sight of—

No.

Erekir shoved that memory away, shoved it down as deep as it would go. He downed another whiskey and winced, then relaxed and let the alcohol soothe the pain. His vision started to blur a bit at the edges.

"You look like a man who's trying to forget something," a voice from Erekir's elbow said.

Erekir snorted but didn't look up. "Yeah. Sharp one, you are. You wanna help me? Buy me a drink."

He turned and his jaw dropped.

Erekir's brain sluggishly kicked into gear, accepting what he saw before him. Memories tore through the drunken haze, clambering and snarling, the same pain roaring forward and stoking a fire in his brain unfettered by the whiskey. Pain and fear solidified into a white-hot rage and Erekir lunged at the man, grabbing him by the throat and shoving him down to the sand. The other man's feet kicked against Erekir, but rage had turned his hands into vices. He could feel the pulse in the man's throat under his fingers as he felt his own pulse thundering through his skull.

"Stop," the man wheezed. "I didn't kill your sister. But I know who did."

Erekir froze, then slowly let go of the man and rocked back on his heels, but remained poised to pounce again.

"You were one of the pirates that attacked our sand skiff," he said from between gritted teeth.

The other man rubbed at his throat and eyed Erekir warily. He nodded.

"Yeah, I was. But I swear, I didn't kill anyone. There weren't even supposed to be passengers on that skiff."

"Why should I believe you?" Erekir snarled, fingers itching to grab the man again.

The man pulled up his sleeve, revealing a tattoo of a dragon wrapped around his forearm. At the sight of it, Erekir relaxed. He nodded slowly.

"Who killed my sister, then?"

"His name is Junko. He's in Navar."

"Take me to him."

THE MAMMOTH BOOK OF HALLOWEEN STORIES

FROM THE SAME EDITOR

The Mammoth Book of Vampire Stories by Women

THE MAMMOTH BOOK OF HALLOWEEN STORIES

TERRIFYING TALES SET ON THE SCARIEST NIGHT OF THE YEAR!

EDITED BY

STEPHEN JONES

Skyhorse Publishing
A Herman Graf Book

Skyhorse Publishing books may be purchased in bulk at special discounts for sales promotion, corporate gifts, fund-raising, or educational purposes. Special editions can also be created to specifications. For details, contact the Special Sales Department, Skyhorse Publishing, 307 West 36th Street, 11th Floor, New York, NY 10018 or info@skyhorsepublishing.com.

Visit our website at www.skyhorsepublishing.com.

10 9 8 7 6 5 4 3 2

Library of Congress Cataloging-in-Publication Data is available on file.

Cover design by Brian Peterson
Cover illustration credit: iStockphoto

Print ISBN: 978-1-5107-3643-6
Ebook ISBN: 978-1-5107-3645-0

Printed in the United States of America

CONTENTS

For Herman Graf,
with respect and gratitude.

THE MAMMOTH BOOK OF HALLOWEEN STORIES

INTRODUCTION
WHEN CHURCHYARDS YAWN

By goblins of the cornfield stark
By witches dancing on the green
By pumpkins grinning in the dark
I wish you luck this Hallowe'en.

—Early 1900s Halloween Postcard

ALL HALLOWS' EVE . . . Samhain . . . *Día de los Muertos* . . . all names for when the barriers between the worlds are at their weakest, and ghosts and grisly things can cross over into our existence. For a short period each year, the natural becomes the supernatural, and nobody is safe from their most intimate and terrifying fears.

The history of Hallowe'en, or Halloween (a more contemporary spelling), dates back to the ancient Celts, whose Druid priests celebrated the changing of the seasons on Samhain (pronounced "sow-in"). It was believed to be a time when the veil between the worlds was at its thinnest, and the fairy-folk, or sidhe, could cross over and cause havoc in our world, while the souls of the dead returned to their homes seeking hospitality.

The Catholic missionaries embraced the festival as a method of converting the Celts, changing its name to All Hallows' Eve and moving it from its original date of May 13th to October 31st, the night before All Saints' Day.

After the Church of England broke away from Catholicism, Hallowe'en was banned for a time in Britain, but it continued to be celebrated in countries such as Scotland and Ireland, who still adhered to their Celtic heritage.

In 1785, the renowned Scottish poet and author Sir Robert Burns (1759–96) penned the verse "Hallowe'en," which described how young people playing fortune-telling games were likely to encounter the Devil.

With the great migration of the Scots-Irish to America in the mid-1800s, Hallowe'en traveled with them and was soon claimed by the Victorians as a celebration of their own. The first book devoted to the holiday, Martha Russell Orne's *Hallowe'en: How to Celebrate It*, was published in 1898, and it was not long before it became an established tradition in the United States.

The festival had always been linked with mischievous children (and perhaps less wholesome beings) playing pranks, and by the 1930s the practice of "trick-or-treating" had become an annual event every October 31st.

In the early part of the twentieth century, companies such as John O. Winsch of Stapleton, New York, were producing whole ranges of colorful and imaginative postcards—mostly printed in Germany—wishing people "A Happy Halloween." These beautifully printed cards also helped establish the associated image of witches, black cats, and grinning carved pumpkins (or jack-o'-lanterns) into the conscience of the general public.

Following World War II, manufacturers and retailers began to seriously capitalize upon the holiday, producing cheap, mass-produced toys, masks and costumes for children—and later adults—to celebrate all things grim and gruesome on one night of the year. Little did they realize that they were simply recreating a festival that those Druid priests of so long ago celebrated to mark the beginning of winter.

In 1978, John's Carpenter's low-budget "slasher" movie *Halloween*—about a group of teenagers menaced by a white-masked serial killer—forever reinvented the day for moviegoers and horror fans, and helped spawn a worldwide industry that is now worth billions of dollars a year.

The Latin American *Día de los Muertos*, or Day of the Dead, is celebrated from October 31st through to November 2nd and shares some of the same traits as Halloween while using colorful makeup and pageantry to honor friends and family members who have died.

There is no doubt that Halloween is now Big Business, but the literary tradition of the holiday dates back to the early nineteenth century and such short stories as Washington Irving's "The Legend of Sleepy Hollow" (1820) and Nathaniel Hawthorne's "Young Goodman Browne" (1835).

There have, of course, been numerous anthologies devoted to Halloween before, and so I wanted to make sure that I presented as wide a range of stories and themes as possible in this latest addition to the canon.

Over the following pages you will discover some remarkable writers—both well-established and relative newcomers—and a breadth of creative ideas that hopefully tap into all the many aspects—supernatural and psychological—that make Halloween such a memorable festival. Not all of them are horror stories, but then the holiday itself is many things to different people and continues to evolve and reinvent itself as we move further into the twenty-first century.

So relax and enjoy these stories and one poem inspired by the spookiest night of the year. And if you're disturbed by a knock at the door, and open it to find a gaggle of guisers on the doorstep demanding "trick-or-treat," then make sure you have enough candy to hand . . . and that there really is something recognizable lurking behind that mask or beneath that sheet. . . .

STEPHEN JONES
LONDON, ENGLAND

OCTOBER IN THE CHAIR

Neil Gaiman

Neil Gaiman is the author of the bestselling 2013 Book of the Year, *The Ocean at the End of the Lane*, the Carnegie Award–winning *The Graveyard Book*, as well as *Coraline*, *Neverwhere*, the essay collection *The View from the Cheap Seats*, and The Sandman series of graphic novels, among many other works.

His fiction has received many awards, including the Carnegie and Newbery medals, and the Hugo, Nebula, World Fantasy, and Eisner awards.

Originally from England, he now divides his time between the UK, where he recently turned *Good Omens*—originally a novel he wrote with Terry Pratchett—into a television series, and the US, where he is professor in the arts at Bard College.

"I began this story several years ago," explains Gaiman, "when Harlan Ellison and I were at a convention, and we were meant to be writing a story together in a roped-off area. But Harlan was late on a deadline for an introduction, so he was typing that.

"I wrote the first few hundred words of this story then and showed it to Harlan. He read it through, suggested I clean up April's language, and said no—he thought that this really was the beginning of one of my stories. So I began a different story, which Harlan called 'Shoot Day for Night' when he continued it. One day, at some other convention, behind some other ropes, I have no doubt that it will be finished.

"So the months sat around the fire on my hard disk for several years, haunting me but unwritten. Then Peter Straub asked me for a story, and I got to find out what happened next."

OCTOBER WAS IN the chair, so it was chilly that evening, and the leaves were red and orange and tumbled from the trees that circled the grove. The twelve of them sat around a campfire roasting huge sausages on sticks, which spat and crackled as the fat dripped onto the burning applewood, and drinking fresh apple cider, tangy and tart in their mouths.

April took a dainty bite from her sausage, which burst open as she bit into it, spilling hot juice down her chin. "Beshrew and suck-ordure on it," she said.

Squat March, sitting next to her, laughed, low and dirty, and then pulled out a huge, filthy handkerchief. "Here you go," he said.

April wiped her chin. "Thanks," she said. "The cursed bag-of-innards burned me. I'll have a blister there tomorrow."

September yawned. "You are *such* a hypochondriac," he said, across the fire. "And such *language*." He had a pencil-thin mustache, and was balding in the front, which made his forehead seem high and wise.

"Lay off her," said May. Her dark hair was cropped short against her skull, and she wore sensible boots. She smoked a small, brown cigarillo which smelled heavily of cloves. "She's sensitive."

"Oh puh-*lease*," said September. "Spare me."

October, conscious of his position in the chair, sipped his apple cider, cleared his throat, and said, "Okay. Who wants to begin?" The chair he sat in was carved from one large block of oakwood, inlaid with ash, with cedar, and with cherrywood. The other eleven sat on tree stumps equally spaced about the small bonfire. The tree stumps had been worn smooth and comfortable by years of use.

"What about the minutes?" asked January. "We always do minutes when I'm in the chair."

"But you aren't in the chair now, are you, dear?" said September, an elegant creature of mock solicitude.

"What about the minutes?" repeated January. "You can't ignore them."

"Let the little buggers take care of themselves," said April, one hand running through her long blonde hair. "And I think September should go first."

September preened and nodded. "Delighted," he said.

"Hey," said February. "Hey-hey-hey-hey-hey-hey-hey. I didn't hear the chairman ratify that. Nobody starts till October says who starts, and then nobody else talks. Can we have maybe the tiniest semblance of order here?" He peered at them, small, pale, dressed entirely in blues and grays.

"It's fine," said October. His beard was all colors, a grove of trees in autumn, deep brown and fire-orange and wine-red, an untrimmed tangle across the lower half of his face. His cheeks were apple-red. He looked like a friend; like someone you had known all your life. "September can go first. Let's just get it rolling."

September placed the end of his sausage into his mouth, chewed daintily, and drained his cider mug. Then he stood up and bowed to the company and began to speak.

"Laurent DeLisle was the finest chef in all of Seattle, at least, Laurent

DeLisle thought so, and the Michelin stars on his door confirmed him in his opinion. He was a remarkable chef, it is true—his minced lamb brioche had won several awards; his smoked quail and white truffle ravioli had been described in *The Gastronome* as 'the tenth wonder of the world.' But it was his wine cellar . . . ah, his wine cellar . . . that was his source of pride and his passion.

"I understand that. The last of the white grapes are harvested in me, and the bulk of the reds: I appreciate fine wines, the aroma, the taste, the aftertaste as well.

"Laurent DeLisle bought his wines at auctions, from private wine-lovers, from reputable dealers: he would insist on a pedigree for each wine, for wine frauds are, alas, too common when the bottle is selling for perhaps five, ten, a hundred thousand dollars, or pounds, or euros.

"The treasure—the jewel—the rarest of the rare and the ne plus ultra of his temperature-controlled wine cellar was a bottle of 1902 Château Lafite. It was on the wine list at $120,000, although it was, in true terms, priceless, for it was the last bottle of its kind."

"Excuse me," said August, politely. He was the fattest of them all, his thin hair combed in golden wisps across his pink pate.

September glared down at his neighbor. "Yes?"

"Is this the one where some rich dude buys the wine to go with the dinner, and the chef decides that the dinner the rich dude ordered isn't good enough for the wine, so he sends out a different dinner, and the guy takes one mouthful, and he's got, like, some rare allergy and he just dies like that, and the wine never gets drunk after all?"

September said nothing. He looked a great deal.

"Because if it is, you told it before. Years ago. Dumb story then. Dumb story now." August smiled. His pink cheeks shone in the firelight.

September said, "Obviously pathos and culture are not to everyone's taste. Some people prefer their barbecues and beer, and some of us like—"

February said, "Well, I hate to say this, but he kind of does have a point. It has to be a new story."

September raised an eyebrow and pursed his lips. "I'm done," he said, abruptly. He sat down on his stump.

They looked at each other across the fire, the months of the year.

June, hesitant and clean, raised her hand and said, "I have one about a guard on the X-ray machines at LaGuardia Airport, who could read all about people from the outlines of their luggage on the screen, and one day she saw a luggage X-ray so beautiful that she fell in love with the person, and she had to figure out which person in the line it was, and she couldn't, and she pined for months and months. And when the person came through again she knew it this time, and it was the man, and he was a wizened old Indian man and she was pretty and black and, like, twenty-five, and she knew it would never work out and she let him go, because she could also see from the shapes of his bags on the screen that he was going to die soon."

October said, "Fair enough, young June. Tell that one."

June stared at him, like a spooked animal. "I just did," she said.

October nodded. "So you did," he said, before any of the others could say anything. And then he said, "Shall we proceed to my story, then?"

February sniffed. "Out of order there, big fella. The man in the chair only tells his story when the rest of us are through. Can't go straight to the main event."

May was placing a dozen chestnuts on the grate above the fire, deploying them into patterns with her tongs. "Let him tell his story if he wants to," she said. "God knows it can't be worse than the one about the wine. And I have things to be getting back to. Flowers don't bloom by themselves. All in favor?"

"You're taking this to a formal vote?" February said. "I cannot believe this. I cannot believe this is happening." He mopped his brow with a handful of tissues, which he pulled from his sleeve.

Seven hands were raised. Four people kept their hands down—February, September, January, and July. ("I don't have anything personal on this," said July, apologetically. "It's purely procedural. We shouldn't be setting precedents.")

"It's settled then," said October. "Is there anything anyone would like to say before I begin?"

"Um. Yes. Sometimes," said June, "Sometimes I think somebody's watching us from the woods and then I look and there isn't anybody there. But I still think it."

April said, "That's because you're crazy."

"Mm," said September, to everybody. "That's our April. She's sensitive but she's still the cruelest."

"Enough," said October. He stretched in his chair. He cracked a cobnut with his teeth, pulled out the kernel, and threw the fragments of shell into the fire, where they hissed and spat and popped, and he began.

There was a boy, *October said*, who was miserable at home, although they did not beat him. He did not fit well, not his family, his town, nor even his life. He had two older brothers who were twins, older than he was, and who hurt him or ignored him, and were popular. They played football: some games one twin would score more and be the hero, and some games the other would. Their little brother did not play football. They had a name for their brother. They called him the Runt.

They had called him the Runt since he was a baby, and at first their mother and father had chided them for it.

The twins said, "But he *is* the runt of the litter. Look at *him*. Look at *us*." The boys were six when they said this. Their parents thought it was cute. A name like the Runt can be infectious, so pretty soon the only person who called him Donald was his grandmother, when she telephoned him on his birthday, and people who did not know him.

Now, perhaps because names have power, he was a runt: skinny and small and nervous. He had been born with a runny nose, and it had not stopped running in a decade. At mealtimes, if the twins liked the food they would steal his; if they did not, they would contrive to place their food on his plate and he would find himself in trouble for leaving good food uneaten.

Their father never missed a football game, and would buy an ice-cream afterward for the twin who had scored the most, and a consolation ice-cream for the other twin who hadn't. Their mother described herself as a newspaperwoman, although she mostly sold advertising space and subscriptions: she had gone back to work full-time once the twins were capable of taking care of themselves.

The other kids in the boy's class admired the twins. They had called him Donald for several weeks in first grade, until the word trickled down that his brothers called him the Runt. His teachers rarely called him anything at all, although among themselves they could sometimes be heard to say that it was a pity that the youngest Covay boy didn't have the pluck or the imagination or the life of his brothers.

The Runt could not have told you when he first decided to run away, nor when his daydreams crossed the border and became plans. By the time that he admitted to himself that he was leaving, he had a large Tupperware container hidden beneath a plastic sheet behind the garage containing three Mars bars, two Milky Ways, a bag of nuts, a small bag of licorice, a flashlight, several comics, an unopened packet of beef jerky, and thirty-seven dollars, most of it in quarters. He did not like the taste of beef jerky, but he had read that explorers had survived for weeks on nothing else; and it was when he put the packet of beef jerky into the Tupperware box and pressed the lid down with a pop that he knew he was going to have to run away.

He had read books, newspapers, and magazines. He knew that if you ran away you sometimes met bad people who did bad things to you; but he had also read fairy tales, so he knew that there were kind people out there, side by side with the monsters.

The Runt was a thin ten-year-old, small, with a runny nose, and a blank expression. If you were to try and pick him out of a group of boys, you'd be wrong. He'd be the other one. Over at the side. The one your eye slipped over.

All through September he put off leaving. It took a really bad Friday, during the course of which both of his brothers sat on him (and the one who sat on his face broke wind and laughed uproariously) to decide that whatever monsters were waiting out in the world would be bearable, perhaps even preferable.

Saturday, his brothers were meant to be looking after him, but soon they went into town to see a girl they liked. The Runt went around the back of the garage and took the Tupperware container out from beneath the plastic sheeting. He took it up to his bedroom. He emptied his schoolbag onto his bed, filled it with his candies and comics and quarters and the beef jerky. He filled an empty soda bottle with water.

The Runt walked into the town and got on the bus. He rode west, ten-dollars-in-quarters-worth of west, to a place he didn't know, which he thought was a good start, then he got off the bus and walked. There was no sidewalk now, so when cars came past he would edge over into the ditch, to safety.

The sun was high. He was hungry, so he rummaged in his bag and pulled out a Mars bar. After he ate it he found he was thirsty, and he drank almost half of the water from his soda bottle before he realized he was going to have to ration it. He had thought that once he got out of the town he would see springs of fresh water everywhere, but there were none to be found. There was a river, though, that ran beneath a wide bridge.

The Runt stopped halfway across the bridge to stare down at the brown water. He remembered something he had been told in school: that, in the end, all rivers flowed into the sea. He had never been to the seashore. He clambered down the bank and followed the river. There was a muddy path along the side of the riverbank, and an occasional beer can or plastic snack packet to show that people had been that way before, but he saw no one as he walked.

He finished his water.

He wondered if they were looking for him yet. He imagined police cars and helicopters and dogs, all trying to find him. He would evade them. He would make it to the sea.

The river ran over some rocks, and it splashed. He saw a blue heron, its wings wide, glide past him, and he saw solitary end-of-season dragonflies, and sometimes small clusters of midges, enjoying the Indian summer. The blue sky became dusk-gray, and a bat swung down to snatch insects from the air. The Runt wondered where he would sleep that night.

Soon the path divided, and he took the branch that led away from the river, hoping it would lead to a house, or to a farm with an empty barn. He walked for some time, as the dusk deepened, until, at the end of the path, he found a farmhouse, half tumbled down and unpleasant-looking. The Runt walked around it, becoming increasingly certain as he walked that nothing could make him go inside, and then he climbed over a broken fence to an abandoned pasture, and settled down to sleep in the long grass with his schoolbag for his pillow.

He lay on his back, fully dressed, staring up at the sky. He was not in the slightest bit sleepy.

"They'll be missing me by now," he told himself. "They'll be worried."

He imagined himself coming home in a few years' time. The delight on his family's faces as he walked up the path to home. Their welcome. Their love. . . .

He woke some hours later, with the bright moonlight in his face. He could see the whole world—as bright as day, like in the nursery rhyme, but pale and without colors. Above him, the moon was full, or almost, and he imagined a face looking down at him, not unkindly, in the shadows and shapes of the moon's surface.

A voice said, "Where do you come from?"

He sat up, not scared, not yet, and looked around him. Trees. Long grass. "Where are you? I don't see you?"

Something he had taken for a shadow moved, beside a tree on the edge of the pasture, and he saw a boy of his own age.

"I'm running away from home," said the Runt.

"Whoa," said the boy. "That must have taken a whole lot of guts."

The Runt grinned with pride. He didn't know what to say.

"You want to walk a bit?" said the boy.

"Sure," said the Runt. He moved his schoolbag so it was next to the fence-post, so he could always find it again.

They walked down the slope, giving a wide berth to the old farmhouse.

"Does anyone live there?" asked the Runt.

"Not really," said the other boy. He had fair, fine hair that was almost white in the moonlight. "Some people tried a long time back, but they didn't like it, and they left. Then other folk moved in. But nobody lives there now. What's your name?"

"Donald," said the Runt. And then, "But they call me the Runt. What do they call you?"

The boy hesitated. "Dearly," he said.

"That's a cool name."

Dearly said, "I used to have another name, but I can't read it anymore."

They squeezed through a huge iron gateway, rusted part open, part closed, into position, and they were in the little meadow at the bottom of the slope.

"This place is cool," said the Runt.

There were dozens of stones of all sizes in the small meadow. Tall stones, bigger than either of the boys, and small ones, just the right size for sitting on. There were some broken stones. The Runt knew what sort of a place this was, but it did not scare him. It was a loved place.

"Who's buried here?" he asked.

"Mostly okay people," said Dearly. "There used to be a town over there. Past those trees. Then the railroad came and they built a stop in the next town over, and our town sort of dried up and fell in and blew away. There's bushes and trees now, where the town was. You can hide in the trees and go into the old houses and jump out."

The Runt said, "Are they like that farmhouse up there? The houses?" He didn't want to go in them, if they were.

"No," said Dearly. "Nobody goes in them, except for me. And some animals, sometimes. I'm the only kid around here."

"I figured," said The Runt.

"Maybe we can go down and play in them," said Dearly.

"That would be pretty cool," said the Runt.

It was a perfect early October night: almost as warm as summer, and the harvest moon dominated the sky. You could see everything.

"Which one of these is yours?" asked the Runt.

Dearly straightened up proudly and took the Runt by the hand. He pulled him over to an overgrown corner of the field. The two boys pushed aside the long grass. The stone was set flat into the ground, and it had dates carved into it from a hundred years before. Much of it was worn away, but beneath the dates it was possible to make out the words

DEARLY DEPARTED
WILL NEVER BE FORG

"Forgotten, I'd wager," said Dearly.

"Yeah, that's what I'd say too," said the Runt.

They went out of the gate, down a gully and into what remained of the old town. Trees grew through houses, and buildings had fallen in on themselves, but it wasn't scary. They played hide and seek. They explored. Dearly showed the Runt some pretty cool places, including a one-room cottage that he said was the oldest building in that whole part of the county. It was in pretty good shape, too, considering how old it was.

"I can see pretty good by moonlight," said the Runt. "Even inside. I didn't know that it was so easy."

"Yeah," said Dearly. "And after a while you get good at seeing even when there ain't any moonlight."

The Runt was envious.

"I got to go to the bathroom," said the Runt. "Is there somewhere around here?"

Dearly thought for a moment. “I don’t know,” he admitted. “I don’t do that stuff anymore. There are a few outhouses still standing, but they may not be safe. Best just to do it in the woods.”

“Like a bear,” said the Runt.

He went out the back, into the woods which pushed up against the wall of the cottage, and went behind a tree. He’d never done that before, in the open air. He felt like a wild animal. When he was done he wiped himself off with fallen leaves. Then he went back out the front. Dearly was sitting in a pool of moonlight, waiting for him.

“How did you die?” asked the Runt.

“I got sick,” said Dearly. “My maw cried and carried on something fierce. Then I died.”

“If I stayed here with you,” said the Runt. “Would I have to be dead too?”

“Maybe,” said Dearly. “Well, yeah. I guess.”

“What’s it like? Being dead?”

“I don’t mind it,” admitted Dearly. “Worst thing is not having anyone to play with.”

“But there must be lots of people up in that meadow,” said the Runt. “Don’t they ever play with you?”

“Nope,” said Dearly. “Mostly, they sleep. And even when they walk, they can’t be bothered to just go and see stuff and do things. They can’t be bothered with me. You see that tree?”

It was a beech tree, its smooth gray bark cracked with age. It sat in what must once have been the town square, ninety years before.

“Yeah,” said the Runt.

“You want to climb it?”

“It looks kind of high.”

“It is. Real high. But it’s easy to climb. I’ll show you.”

It was easy to climb. There were handholds in the bark, and the boys went up the big beech tree like a couple of monkeys, or pirates, or warriors. From the top of the tree one could see the whole world. The sky was starting to lighten, just a hair, in the east.

Everything waited. The night was ending. The world was holding its breath, preparing to begin again.

"This was the best day I ever had," said the Runt.

"Me too," said Dearly. "What you going to do now?"

"I don't know," said the Runt.

He imagined himself going on across the world, all the way to the sea. He imagined himself growing up and growing older, bringing himself up by his bootstraps. Somewhere in there he would become fabulously wealthy. And then he would go back to the house with the twins in it, and he would drive up to their door in his wonderful car, or perhaps he would turn up at a football game (in his imagination the twins had neither aged nor grown) and look down at them, in a kindly way. He would buy them all, the twins, his parents, a meal at the finest restaurant in the city, and they would tell him how badly they had misunderstood him and mistreated him. They apologized and wept, and through it all he said nothing. He let their apologies wash over him. And then he would give each of them a gift, and afterwards he would leave their lives once more, this time for good.

It was a fine dream.

In reality, he knew, he would keep walking and be found tomorrow, or the day after that, and go home and be yelled at and everything would be the same as it ever was; and day after day, hour after hour until the end of time, he'd still be the Runt, only they'd be mad at him for having dared to walk away.

"I have to go to bed soon," said Dearly. He started to climb down the big beech tree.

Climbing down the tree was harder, the Runt found. You couldn't see where you were putting your feet and had to feel around for somewhere to put them. Several times he slipped and slid, but Dearly went down ahead of him, and would say things like, "Just a little to the right, now," and they both made it down just fine.

The sky continued to lighten, and the moon was fading, and it was harder to see. They clambered back through the gully. Sometimes the Runt wasn't sure that Dearly was there at all, but when he got to the top, he saw the boy waiting for him.

They didn't say much as they walked up to the meadow filled with stones. The Runt put his arm over Dearly's shoulder, and they walked in step up the hill.

"Well," said Dearly. "Thanks for coming over."

"I had a good time," said the Runt.

"Yeah," said Dearly. "Me too."

Down in the woods somewhere a bird began to sing.

"If I wanted to stay—?" said the Runt, all in a burst. Then he stopped. *I might never get another chance to change it*, thought the Runt. He'd never get to the sea. They'd never let him.

Dearly didn't say anything, not for a long time. The world was gray. More birds joined the first.

"I can't do it," said Dearly, eventually. "But they might."

"Who?"

"The ones in there." The fair boy pointed up the slope to the tumble-down farmhouse with the jagged broken windows, silhouetted against the dawn. The gray light had not changed it.

The Runt shivered. "There's people in there?" he said. "I thought you said it was empty."

"It ain't empty," said Dearly. "I said nobody lives there. Different things." He looked up at the sky. "I got to go now," he added. He squeezed the Runt's hand. And then he just wasn't there any longer.

The Runt stood in the little graveyard all on his own, listening to the birdsong on the morning air. Then he made his way up the hill. It was harder by himself.

He picked up his schoolbag from the place he had left it. He ate his last Milky Way and stared at the tumbledown building. The empty windows of the farmhouse were like eyes, watching him.

It was darker inside there. Darker than anything.

He pushed his way through the weed-choked yard. The door to the farmhouse was mostly crumbled away. He stopped at the doorway, hesitating, wondering if this was wise. He could smell damp, and rot, and something else underneath. He thought he heard something move, deep in the house, in the cellar, maybe, or the attic. A shuffle, maybe. Or a hop. It was hard to tell.

Eventually, he went inside.

Nobody said anything. October filled his wooden mug with apple cider when he was done, and drained it, and filled it again.

"It was a story," said December. "I'll say that for it." He rubbed his pale blue eyes with a fist. The fire was almost out.

"What happened next?" asked June, nervously. "After he went into the house?"

May, sitting next to her, put her hand on June's arm. "Better not to think about it," she said.

"Anyone else want a turn?" asked August. There was silence. "Then I think we're done."

"That needs to be an official motion," pointed out February.

"All in favor?" said October. There was a chorus of "ayes." "All against?" Silence. "Then I declare this meeting adjourned."

They got up from the fireside, stretching and yawning, and walked away into the wood, in ones and twos and threes, until only October and his neighbor remained.

"Your turn in the chair next time," said October.

"I know," said November. He was pale, and thin-lipped. He helped October out of the wooden chair. "I like your stories. Mine are always too dark."

"I don't think so," said October. "It's just that your nights are longer. And you aren't as warm."

"Put it like that," said November, "and I feel better. I suppose we can't help who we are."

"That's the spirit," said his brother. And they touched hands as they walked away from the fire's orange embers, taking their stories with them back into the dark.

For Ray Bradbury

REFLECTIONS IN BLACK

Steve Rasnic Tem

Steve Rasnic Tem is a past winner of the Bram Stoker, World Fantasy, and British Fantasy Awards. His last novel, *UBO*, is a dark science fictional tale about violence and its origins, featuring such historical viewpoint characters as Jack the Ripper, Stalin, and Heinrich Himmler.

Valancourt Books has recently published *Figures Unseen*, a volume of his selected stories, while *The Mask Shop of Doctor Blaack*, a middle-grade novel about Halloween, is out from Hex Publishers. With his late wife Melanie, he has also authored a handbook on writing, *Yours To Tell: Dialogues on the Art & Practice of Writing*, published by Apex Books.

"Two impulses drove the creation of this story," recalls Tem. "One was my participation in 'prophecy' games when I was young. They have them around Halloween, but also around most of the major holidays. When will I die? Will I find true love? Who will I marry? You never believe in their validity—at least I never did—but you're drawn to them anyway. In my case I was hungry for even fake assurance that I would have a normal life and get the things I imagined so-called 'normal' people get in their lives.

"The other impulse was a dissatisfaction I've always had with a perfectly ordinary state of affairs: you encounter people in the course of your life who seem quite important, who have a significant impact, and yet over the years you lose touch, and eventually they're completely lost to you. It happens to everybody, and yet it has always aggravated me, especially in this age of the Internet and social media. But many people of my generation do not participate in social media—a Google search doesn't find them. That's why various paid services exist, to find those people lost to you. But when you do find them, sometimes you wish you'd left well enough alone."

RANDALL LEFT WORK early again, feeling ill. Nothing definitive, a general fatigue, a general *malaise*—that was the word, although he'd never used it before. If he'd stayed in his chair another minute it would have required an army to get him out. He didn't know where he belonged, but he didn't belong *there.*

The bus was unusually crowded for the time of day. He wondered if there might be a concert or some such event. He found a seat quickly and hunched forward, trying to shut out the pack. But there were just too many of them, jostling about, not exactly noisy, but murmuring. That constant murmur. And they smelled: rank body odor and cigarettes, and things left out in the rain. But it had been a dry fall, so that stench had to be from something else.

He glanced around. Had they all been fighting? Their faces were discolored, bruised. That fellow's nose had gone scarlet, swollen. The woman next to him appeared caked in blue, turning black around her eyes. Another woman's lipstick smeared from both ends of her lips, as if a razor had widened her mouth. Some of their clothing was torn. He studied the women, seeking exposed flesh. It was an old habit, but he didn't mean any harm. He simply liked women. Was that an exposed breast or an elbow? He felt vaguely ashamed, but he looked anyway. Another word he'd never used occurred to him: *voyeur.*

Their outfits were unusually colorful, some of the clothing beyond outlandish. They were in costume, he suddenly realized, but they'd been wearing their costumes too long, and now their costumes stank, and their makeup had deteriorated.

Halloween wasn't until tomorrow—were people partying early? He'd never liked the holiday himself. It seemed such a sad and desperate celebration, poking at your fears for some supposed fun.

"Paula!" A female's voice from the back of the bus. Maybe an objection. Maybe a warning. Randall couldn't get the tone, the intent, or even the age of the speaker from just a single word. He turned around in his seat to see if he could tell who had said her name. Maybe, he thought, he might even see Paula herself. Would he even recognize her after so many years? He'd certainly had plenty of practice trying to imagine her older face, her body. Of course it was unlikely to be her, but what did they say? A small world.

His cell went off. One ring. He looked at the screen. NOT AVAILABLE was all it said.

"Paula!" He jerked his head up, looking for the speaker. No one looked at him. No one looked eager to speak. Each huddled to him- or herself, nursing their poorly-disguised injuries, murmuring softly.

He'd always thought of her as the one who got away, although arguably he never had her in the first place. She'd been pleasant enough, and consented to his kisses. But never further, no matter how he'd suggested it, although he'd never been that direct. They'd gone to dinners and movies, and he'd felt cowed by her quiet beauty. She was taller than him, and had that beautiful voice, especially when she laughed or whispered into his ear. Those were early college days, and he had lacked confidence. He never told her how he felt, and he had no idea how she felt about him. It was ridiculous to be thinking about her now, but someone had said her name, and he hadn't had sex in a long time. If he could find that person he would tell them to shut up.

His cell went off again. NOT AVAILABLE flashed on the screen. He answered anyway. There was nothing but static on the line, and perhaps under that a distorted murmuring.

At his stop he pushed his way through the stinking crowd. Everything he touched left his hands feeling greasy. Climbing off, he looked back to see if anyone watched him as the bus pulled away. It was hard to tell. The one face turned in his direction appeared to be sleeping.

As he walked home it occurred to him how the homeless who huddled under steps and in alleys appeared to be in costume, but for them it was constant and involuntary. But he was romanticizing things again—it had always been his problem. After the break-up Miranda said he'd always expected too much—he had too much imagination—that was why they'd ended up hating each other. She'd been the last of many.

Randall had been furious at that comment. It was as if Miranda had broken the rules—it was over, she had no reason to say anything. That night he'd tried to track Paula down. Maybe she was still unattached. Of course it was just a fantasy that they might reconnect, but such things did happen in the real world.

But he couldn't find a "Paula Jenks" on any of the social media. A general Internet search turned up very few possibilities of the right age. She might have married, of course, and had a new last name. Women were difficult that way—it made it more complicated to track them down. The websites wanted a credit card number to delve further. It felt a bit too desperate to pursue things that far, however. He would have felt like some sort of stalker. So Randall had let it go.

He felt deflated as soon as he entered his apartment. He hated the familiarity of it. No matter how much he rearranged things it always felt the same, and nothing at all like where he should live. Perhaps if he had more room, or even a house, he could turn his environment into some sort of sanctuary. But that required more money, and although he was in a job he couldn't stand, he couldn't imagine another.

He went into the dingy bathroom and washed his face. In the dim light his reflection looked darkened, bruised, and mottled as if makeup had been applied to unsuccessfully hide the damage. He was only forty, but aging poorly. Tomorrow he would wear dark glasses for his commute. He thought he had a pair large enough to disguise things.

Revelers outside his windows were breaking things. What had gotten into people? If it was this bad the night before Halloween, what could he expect on the actual night? He vaguely remembered a name for this night from when he was a kid. "Malice Night" or "Prank Night"? No, *Mischief Night* was what they had called it, but he didn't remember it being anything like this.

He thought he'd successfully put Paula out of his mind until he'd heard her name on the bus. It seemed possible the experience had ruined him. A month after he'd given up searching for her he'd been drinking and thought he'd try again. Who cared how it looked? Maybe Paula would be pleased to hear from him. Maybe she'd been thinking of him too. He chose one of those "lost loves" websites and entered his credit card information. He felt relieved that he didn't have to talk to a live person. The website just asked him a series of questions and he typed in all he could remember. He remembered she was a year younger, so he knew the year she was born, and he remembered she had lived in Georgia all her life, so she had probably been born there as well. He knew where her mother had lived, but he couldn't remember the exact address, but he thought he might recognize it if he saw it. He might have even visited Paula there, or had he?

He'd been excited when her social security number came up. There were flashing screens and PROGRESS bars—all for show he presumed—with intermittent results. Randall had been much less excited when a married name came up, PAULA DUNCAN. Husband named Frank and an address where both of them lived. Then, after an agonizing period of more so-called "processing," there was an obituary notice for Paula Duncan from a mortuary in the town where Frank and Paula Duncan lived. A vague disappointment consumed him. He did some more checking with the social security number he had. In one of the online records, that number came up DECEASED.

And that was that. The service charged his credit card and didn't even offer condolences. Why should it? He hadn't been the husband. It made him feel vaguely dirty, as if he'd been peeping through the bedroom window of Mr. and Mrs. Frank Duncan.

Randall couldn't say he was heartbroken. He was saddened, certainly, to think someone so vibrant, so beautiful, someone he might have *loved* was gone. But he hadn't seen Paula in years. It had been merely a pitiful fantasy.

Then today happened. Whoever the Paula had been on the bus, she hadn't been *his* Paula, and he needed to stop thinking *his*, because she never had been.

Randall's cell phone rang. He picked it up off the coffee table, expecting to see "Not Available" again. But this time the screen said PAULA JENKS. He frantically hit the button and fumbled it to his ear. "Hello?"

No one spoke. There was a hollow, liquid sort of background noise, a soft echoing effect, as if the phone were at the bottom of a well. "Hello?"

A clicking noise. Then, "Hello, is this Randall?" He didn't recognize the voice, and as had become his habit when dealing with telephone solicitors and scammers, he avoided saying 'yes.' "This is Randall."

"Randall, this is Alice Jenks. Paula's mother."

"Oh. Oh, Mrs. Jenks. I'm sorry. I heard. . . ."

"The reason I'm calling is because Paula has been trying to get in touch with you."

His eyes filled with tears. "I'm sorry. I heard that Paula died. I'm just so relieved. . . ."

"Died? Who would say such a thing?"

He could tell her the truth, but it was embarrassing. He couldn't think of a way to say it without sounding creepy. "I'm sorry, it was on social media. You know how that goes, rumors and half-truths. Obviously it was a different Paula."

"Well, I don't have the Internet, but I know how people are."

"Could I speak to Paula?"

There was a pause, with more liquid clicking. Randall thought they'd lost the connection. "I'm afraid not. She's lying down, feeling poorly I'm afraid, poor dear. She's been trying and trying to contact you, with no luck at all. She became quite worked up over it, actually. I told her to rest. But I had to promise I would make the attempt for her. If I hadn't I didn't think she would fall asleep."

"How did she try to contact me? I've moved a few times, but I've always left a forwarding address. And I have email, social media . . ."

"Oh, my daughter doesn't own a computer. I believe she may have written you a few times over the years and you never answered. She gave me this phone number. She wrote it on this pad by the phone, several times in fact. The same number, but several times so she wouldn't forget. But she couldn't reach you."

"I didn't get her letters. If I had gotten one of her letters I absolutely would have written her back. And I don't have any phone messages from her."

"Oh, I don't think she would have left a message. She hates speaking to those machines. But Randall, she would absolutely love to see you, she really would. She's been in poor health for years, but I think seeing you would make all the difference."

Would it be rude to ask what was wrong with Paula? He wasn't sure, and he didn't want this woman to think it would make some crucial difference to him. "Of course I can come sometime. Where do you live?"

"Might you come right away? She feels so badly, I frankly worry about her. Could you come for Halloween? She dreads the holiday, all those costumes and masks, that morbid preoccupation. We're in the same house, a few miles from the old campus. Are you very far away?"

"Not at all. Give me the address. I have to take care of a few things, but I'll be there tomorrow night."

He was at least twenty hours away by car, probably more, and he didn't own an automobile. Randall left a phone message for his boss telling him he was much sicker than he thought. He threw some clothes into a bag and left the apartment.

The rental was much too high, but he had little choice. He hadn't driven in a while, but his initial nervousness passed once he got out of the city and onto the highway. He kept his cell phone on, lying on the passenger seat beside him. He expected the woman to call back, confessing that it had all been some tasteless Mischief Night prank, but she never did.

Once he crossed over into Maryland he could see that a large number of people were out—teenagers mostly, running around in the dark, yelling and breaking things, screaming in pain or excitement. At one point he had to veer around two figures in clown suits in the middle of the road. He couldn't be sure, but his impression was they had been copulating. They howled as he passed.

He'd never liked driving at night. As it was he had no idea if he would make it to Paula's house by Halloween night, or what it might mean if he didn't. Perhaps nothing, or perhaps everything. Timing mattered in life, and his timing had always been mediocre at best. He was bound to lose his job, but it certainly wouldn't break his heart.

Paula would be much older than the woman he remembered, the woman he might have loved, but then so was he. She probably still had the eyes, those high cheekbones, that beautiful voice. He hoped she still had the smile.

Randall's night vision wasn't what it used to be. That was clear now that he was out here, the lights from the oncoming cars stabbing his eyes. The reflections off his windshield felt dangerous, confusing.

It nagged at him that he was traveling all this way without actually having talked to Paula. Her mother had sounded sincere, but here he was driving hundreds of miles with no sleep because of a phone call from a woman he might or might not have met.

About 2:00 a.m. in a rural area beyond Richmond he ran over something. He didn't see it until he was about to hit it, and he still had no idea what it was. A mound of clothes, seemingly, but there was hair, or fur, in a streak along the top. And it screamed when he ran over it.

He stopped a few yards ahead of the object and glanced in his rear-view mirror. He couldn't see very much with his taillights, but whatever it was, it didn't appear to be moving. The responsible thing to do, of course, was to walk back there and check. What if that was a human being?

But he hesitated. He hadn't seen any other vehicles the past half-hour or so. The area was poorly lit, and although there was a building just off the roadway, some sort of maintenance shed, it was dark, and there were no other structures in view, no one to call out to if he needed help.

He grabbed his cell phone. No bars, but a 9-1-1 call might still go through. Something flashed by the car. He looked up. Several dancing ragged figures—perhaps they were meant to be scarecrows—shouted at him nonsensically.

Something slapped his driver's-side window. He stared into the bloody red face. "Watch where you're driving!" it shouted, moving its lips in exaggerated fashion. What he thought was blood was actually some sort of paint, garish and dripping. He drove the car slowly through a growing crowd of garishly dressed revelers, who sprawled on and off the hood, daring him to hurt one of them. He was tempted to hit the gas pedal a few times, but what if he actually hurt someone? He would be charged—he might even go to prison. This went on for two or three miles before, seemingly bored, they let him go.

After a few more hours his cell phone rang. He jumped, almost running off the road. Paula's name flashed on the screen. When he picked it up her mother got straight to the point. "So are you coming?"

"Yes, yes. Like I said, I'm coming. It might just take me awhile."

"I just wanted to make sure. She's been asking."

"Tell her I'll be there. But I have to hang up now."

"All right, but please come." She hung up. They were up late, but then so was he. He wasn't sure why, but he felt as if she thought he'd somehow wronged Paula. But it was such a long time ago, and they'd been so young, babies practically.

He made a few wrong turns, and became lost more than once. He drove part of the next day in the completely wrong direction. He was going to be late, he supposed, but was now too tired to care. By the next evening, Halloween night, he stopped paying attention to all the people in disguise. It seemed somehow normal, as if they were at last displaying their true selves, however deplorable. Once or twice someone spit at the car, or struck it with something. Randall didn't stop.

Somewhere in Alabama both headlights went out. Randall was so tired he almost didn't notice, and when he did realize he simply stared straight ahead, counting on the moonlight and occasional streetlight and the luminous paint on the edges of the road to show him the way. Eventually they came back on as suddenly as they had gone out.

It began to rain about an hour from his destination. Randall turned the wipers on but they weren't making good contact with the windshield and left a thin skim of water after each swipe of the blades. He had to lean over the steering wheel and gaze intently through a confusing array of fragmented street lights in order to stay safely on the road. Eventually the rain let up as he entered a series of narrow neighborhood streets. Leaves were down everywhere, making a dark and nasty mess in the gutters. Water pooled in spots on the uneven pavement, shimmering with yellowish reflections. The only signs of trick-or-treaters were some scattered candy wrappers and a few soggy remnants of costume, scarves, gloves, random bits of cloth, and what looked to be a cheap mask torn in half, dropped in the hurry to get home.

He pulled up in front of the address a little past eleven. He sat for a few minutes, thinking it looked vaguely familiar. He remembered coming here with Paula, but he wasn't positive it actually happened. The house was a typical Victorian: sash windows, stained glass, and a finial on the roof, a canted bay-window in front, geometric tiled walk, and a round tower at one corner. It was hard to tell how big it was, or even the exact color. Tall, unkempt evergreen bushes and trees hugging it so closely kept it dark and secretive, in contrast to the neighboring properties and their denuded trees. He'd barely been aware of the change of seasons when he left the city. Here it appeared full-blown, almost past.

He hadn't yet decided what to say to her. He trotted up the walk before he could lose his nerve. Several windows were lit, so he assumed they were waiting for him.

The door opened before he could ring the bell. A woman's pale face: could this be Paula, aged so harshly? No, surely too old and too short.

"I presume you're Randall?" Her voice surprised him with its strength. She sounded almost angry.

"Yes. I'm sorry it's so late, but I got here as soon as I could."

"It will do."

She guided him through a short hall and into some sort of sitting room. Although there were lights on in the house, the rooms were dim. Perhaps the darkness of the wallpaper and the overdone decor were too much to overcome. This room was relatively tidy except for tall stacks of women's magazines piled sloppily by each chair. There were a number of pictures on the side tables. All of them were of Paula around the age Randall had known her, but none newer than that.

"Paula will be joining you soon. She requires a little time to get ready."

"Do you have a more recent photograph of her somewhere?" Maybe it was rude to ask so quickly, but that was what was on his mind.

"My daughter doesn't like to get her picture taken. I approve of that. I've always thought there was too much vanity in the world."

He sat down in a chair by the window. It was low, and he had bad knees. He worried that it might be a struggle to get out of it. "I think you're right. I hate getting my picture taken myself. I don't, usually. I think the last time was when I renewed my license."

"My daughter doesn't drive. She doesn't feel the need to."

"I see." Although he didn't, really. The Paula he'd known had loved touring around, driving to new places.

The old woman sat down and stared at him with an expression that was almost a smile, but not quite. Calculated interest, perhaps. Because of the lowness of his chair he had to look up at her. He felt as if he were under observation.

"It's been years since you've seen my daughter. Have you thought about her very much?"

He squirmed. "Yes, yes I have. I have many fond memories. And sometimes I wondered how she was doing."

"And yet you never called."

"I . . . think I called. I'm pretty sure I tried. But you know how it is. People move around, their lives get complicated. Before you know it, years have passed."

"My daughter has never moved. She has been here all these years." Paula's mother leaned forward slightly. Randall had the uneasy feeling she might leap on him and he wouldn't be able to get out of the chair in time.

"I'm s-sorry," he said. "I should have tried harder."

"You became involved in your own concerns, your own . . . passions. I imagine you only thought of her when you were between women, when your appetites made you remember how beautiful she was. That is often the way with you men, I think."

Surely it was more complicated than that, Randall thought. He really had cared for her. But he thought about the timing she suggested, and saw the truth in it. But still he said, "No. It wasn't like that. I never stopped caring for her. Please, can I see her now?"

She didn't answer right away. She turned her head and raised an eyebrow, as if listening for something. There was another open door on the other side of the room leading somewhere else in the house. Randall leaned slightly and tried to look through it. It was a hallway, and very dark, but he thought he saw a glimmer of something, and movement.

"She'll be down soon, I promise." He straightened up quickly, unaccountably nervous that she had seen him looking. "She just wants to look her best for you. She was always a pretty girl, but the years, they do things to the best of us, and shallow people, they sometimes judge us harshly."

"She was always beautiful. I'm sure she still is. A few wrinkles, a few extra pounds—that doesn't bother me, I promise. Look at me, I'm not perfect."

"No, you are not," she replied. He guessed she wasn't going to let him get away with anything. "You have to look past the surface to see the person inside. Tell me, if I were able to look inside you, Randall, what would I see?"

"I . . . I don't know how to answer that." But some words came readily to mind. *Petty*, *bitter*, *impatient*, *disappointed.* So he was dishonest as well. "I guess you'd be disappointed."

"Only if I had misjudged you, Randall. Only then." She turned her head and looked back through the entrance hall from which they'd entered this room. "I see it is only a few minutes before midnight." Had there been a clock in the hall? He certainly hadn't seen one. "Do you like Halloween, Randall? Are you familiar with its customs?"

"I dressed up and went trick-or-treating as a child. I guess I haven't thought much about it since then. I was never into scary stuff. I never could understand why anyone would want to be scared, frankly."

"For some, it is evidence that they are still alive. You are alive, aren't you Randall?"

He forced out an awkward laugh. In truth, he felt as if he could hardly breathe in this house. "As far . . . as far as I know." The forced laugh he repeated made him feel a bit crazed.

"You are a lucky man, certainly. The approaching hour provides us with a unique opportunity." She smiled widely, exposing several broken and missing teeth. "There is a traditional Halloween ritual. I recall it very well from when I was a young woman of marrying age. I remember being so eager to participate in this ritual, as were many of my friends. Do you want to hear about it?"

Of course he didn't want to hear about it, but he couldn't imagine saying no with her looking at him like that. "Of course. Please tell me."

"It's quite a lot of fun, actually. When you're young you're always wondering what is going to happen to you, what you might be in for in your life. More so than when you're older, I think. When you're older you already know what's going to happen to you."

"I guess. I guess that's true."

"Very good. We are on the same page, then, Randall. The ritual is simply this. At midnight on Halloween a young man or young woman turns off all the lights and stares into a mirror. Eventually, according to this ritual, you will see the face of your future spouse standing behind you, looking over your shoulder. Isn't that *delightful*? Doesn't that sound like *fun*?"

"I guess. I guess I can see how that would be fun, if you were young enough."

"Oh, don't be such a stick-in-the-mud, Randall! Do you think my lovely daughter would be interested in a stick-in-the-mud? Play along, why don't you? It's something to do until she comes down. And let's just say you see *her* face in the mirror, looking over your shoulder. Think of her reaction if you told her that! It would likely make her very pleased, don't you think?"

"It might." It was an interesting idea. It gave him something to open with when he finally saw Paula. And he could tell her anything—it didn't matter what he actually saw in the mirror. He didn't expect to see anything. But he could tell Paula he saw her in the mirror, and how beautiful she was, but not nearly as beautiful as she was actually standing there in front of him. "I'll do it. Where's the mirror?"

"We only have the one. In this entire house, only the one mirror. It's hanging on the wall at the end of that hall." She gestured to that other open door and the darkness beyond. "But you must hurry. It's almost midnight. Soon it will be too late."

Randall struggled out of his chair with some effort. It felt as if the air in the room was so heavy he could hardly move against it. He staggered a bit as he made his way to the open door. "Could you turn the light on in there? I can hardly see."

"Oh, but Randall," she said sternly behind him. "Weren't you listening? The lights have to be out, or the game won't work at all!"

Game, ritual, he wished she would make up her mind. He peered down the hall, his eyes struggling to adjust. There was that slight glimmer again. It must be the mirror, he thought. But no signs of movement. "Okay. Okay."

He stepped forward a few steps. The lights in the sitting room went off behind him. "Hurry!" she said from the dark. Her voice rose. "There isn't much time!"

He quickened his pace. The glimmer at the end of the hall appeared to change. Of course, he thought, because of his own movement. There was a sound behind him. Was the old woman following him in? He stared into the darkness, trying to concentrate, attempting to force his eyes to adjust.

"One more thing," she said behind him, but her voice had subtly changed. "*Voyeur.*" Had he understood what she said? "If the viewer were destined to die before getting married, he or she would see something else entirely." Her voice was completely different now, completely changed, reminding him of that voice he had heard, and been captivated by, that beautiful voice so many years ago.

"Midnight," the voice said.

He was looking into the darkness so determinedly his head was splitting. But at last he was beginning to see his reflection in the black, his features distorted, melting, disappearing in patches, moving, rotating. A woman's face rushed out of the darkness behind him and stopped above his shoulder. Paula was as beautiful as ever, unaged, until she too began to distort, the flesh melting from her bones, until that moment when they were exactly alike, two naked skulls, staring.

THE HALLOWEEN MONSTER

ALISON LITTLEWOOD

Alison Littlewood's latest novel is *The Crow Garden,* the tale of a Victorian mad doctor so obsessed with his patient he follows her into the darkened rooms of mesmerism and séances. Her other novels include *The Hidden People*, *A Cold Season*, *A Cold Silence*, *Path of Needles*, *The Unquiet House*, and *Zombie Apocalypse!: Acapulcalypse Now.*

A winner of the Shirley Jackson Award for Short Fiction, the author's stories have been selected for several "Year's Best" anthology series and are gathered together in her collections *Quieter Paths* and in *Five Feathered Tales*, the latter a collaboration with award-winning illustrator Daniele Serra.

"Halloween is the perfect time to reflect on the masks we wear," she explains, "not just on the one night we get to wear costumes, but all year round. It's also a time to consider real monsters as well as the imaginary kind—those that are truly terrifying, rather than the ones we dress up as for fun.

"My character is navigating all the tribulations of school and a new home, stepping carefully and playing his part, until Halloween forces him to confront his own nature. Though perhaps having done so, it will also make him evolve into something else. . . ."

IT WAS A dead night, not like the ones I remembered. We had no pumpkins, no apples to duck for, no candies in a bowl. It was Dad who did all that, though I hadn't realized it at the time. I'd thought then it was just the way things were.

This Halloween Dad was gone and I knew Mum wouldn't open the door, not for anyone. She had that hollow look about her, her eyes focused too far away. It was only four o'clock but it was getting dark outside, and she'd already started walking past the drinks cupboard, back and forth, running her fingers over the wood. She didn't like to start before five. Not like *him*, she always said, as if Dad didn't have a name any longer.

I wondered where he was now. Somewhere better than this, I supposed.

Halloween used to be good. Dad would dress up as a monster—all kinds, it didn't seem to matter. He'd have a bolt through his neck or a mask or a sheet to make him look like a ghost, and he'd throw apples into a bowl of water, light candles, whatever it was that occurred to him. And he'd drink too, but he wasn't scary, not that night. On Halloween, everything was funny instead.

I slumped onto the sofa, picking the cushion with the broken springs underneath so it wouldn't annoy Mum when she sat down. She had her back to me, looking out of the window, seeing whatever it was she saw. But it seemed she wasn't so far away after all because she said, "Isn't it time you went?"

Her voice had that shaky edge it took on as the clock edged toward five. I didn't answer; I didn't know what she meant. I wasn't going anywhere. I was too old for trick-or-treating, too old for costumes.

She turned around. I saw that she was crying and I caught my breath. I remembered the way we'd laughed once, laughed as we decided what to carve into the pumpkin's face, and I wondered if I knew what she'd been staring at all along: not the dark, but memories.

She shook her head. "Out," she said. "Out!"

I fought my way up from the sagging sofa, wishing I'd picked the better cushion after all, and grabbed my coat. When Mum said something in that voice, it was best not to say anything at all. Best just to get as far away as possible.

Outside, the sky looked dirty, and the air was cold and sharp and smelling of the main road that ran past the end of our street. That was where ex-council houses with peeling window frames gave way to rows of terraces with narrow lanes and narrower back alleys; we'd moved here after Dad left. I zipped my coat to the neck. I didn't think I'd ever been out on Halloween night alone, and for a second I imagined zombies and ghouls and mad axe-men, real ones, hiding in full view among all the costumes and masks. I forced out a huff of laughter and started walking toward town.

A group of blonde and blue-eyed girls dressed as fairies emerged from someone's gate, their mum giving me a funny look as she herded them past me. The shop over the road had a strand of orange and black bunting in the window, but the shutter was down over the door. The next house had two carved pumpkins on the step, shuddering candles revealing matching grins. From somewhere down the road I heard kids' voices, raised in the old chant: *Trick or treeaaat!*

Some fucking trick, I thought, pulling sharp air into my lungs and coughing, and I heard, "Oi, Connor—here!"

At first I couldn't place it, didn't even think the shout was aimed at me, then it came again and I recognized Gary Turner's voice from school. I didn't see him much—he spent most of his time smoking behind the gym, or in detention, or not showing up at all. I wasn't hard enough or soft enough to attract his notice; I was surprised he even knew my name. But then, it seemed he didn't.

"It's Cam," I said, as I approached. He was standing farther along the road, next to an alley that ran behind the terraces. "My name's Cam. Not Connor." I stopped a few yards short of him. I'd rather have ignored him and walked away, but it wasn't worth pushing it with Gary Turner.

"Don't care." He cast his eyes down to my cheap knockoff trainers and back up again. "Give us a hand, will you?"

He nodded toward the alleyway and I realized he wasn't alone; two others were standing there. I knew them from school too. Everybody did. James Poole and Dale Harris; they didn't grin or wave or nod.

"In there," Gary said.

I froze. There was no way I was stepping into the alley with those three waiting to close off the exit.

"We don't want you, dickhead," he said. Maybe he'd read my thoughts, or maybe he could smell fear. "We're after the cat."

I frowned, peering into the narrow, piss-stinking place. At first I couldn't see any cat, and then I did; it was pitch-black, difficult to make out against the rot-streaked wall. It knew we were there, though. Its back was arched, its legs stiff and tail raised, its yellow eyes unblinking. I also made out a thin red collar. I recognized it at once.

"Little fucker doesn't want to be caught," Gary said. "Need another pair of hands, innit? Nearly scratched Dale's arm off."

"What do you want it for?" I asked.

He didn't answer, and then I realized he had after all. He had fished in his pocket and was showing it to me: a length of twine dangled from his fingers. It looked like he'd picked it up off the floor, frayed and filthy, but made of strong blue nylon. It wouldn't break easily. It looked strong enough for whatever he planned to do. I thought I might just be able to imagine what that was.

I looked at the cat. It didn't look scared. It looked straight back at me, as if it didn't quite know what I was.

"Come on." Gary laughed. "It's cold as a witch's tit. Haven't got all night."

Dale and James laughed, as if he'd told a joke.

"Why?" I said.

Gary stilled. He turned and looked at me. He looked at me as if he wasn't used to being questioned. Then he shrugged and grinned, as if I was his mate.

"Let me tell you a story, Connor me lad," he said.

Cam, I thought, but didn't bother to say.

"Tonight is Halloween, if you hadn't noticed. And tonight's the night when witches—real witches, mind, not pretend ones—can turn themselves into cats. Black cats, specifically, like this one. And if you catch the cat, if you *hurt* the cat, you hurt the witch too. Geddit?" He patted me on the shoulder, as if I were a little kid, as if I was just a bit slow. I stared at him. I had no idea what he was on about.

"You can tell 'em because they make weird noises—not like a normal cat. Like this 'ere cat did when it nearly took your arm off, isn't that right Dale? And because they won't let you catch 'em—they fight like devils. Devils and *witches*, yeah? Ain't you seen *Supernatural*?"

"I—" I hadn't a clue what to say. I hadn't believed in that stuff since—well, forever. I didn't remember ever believing in it, not really. Halloween was fun. The monsters were only Dad dressing up. He'd jump out at me and shout *Rahrrr!* and I'd laugh. It was the other nights when the real monster came out. The nights he was bored, out of work, pissed off with Mum and me and life. The nights when the only answers he could find were at the bottom of the next bottle, and the next. And the next.

"Look, you don't have to believe it. All you have to do is help us catch the fucking cat."

I turned and looked at Gary. It was hard to believe he was asking me for a favor, even if he had got my name wrong. Even if he really believed in some stupid story, if he was completely nuts. And he *was* nuts.

I knew he was nuts because of the things he'd done at school, to lads who were harder or softer than me. I could hear it in the edge that was in his voice, sense it in the words he didn't say but that hung in the air between us: *Do it—or else*.

I took a deep breath. "All right," I said, "I'll help you catch it. But that's it." I thought maybe I could get hold of that twine somehow, get it away from him and lose it as quietly as I could. At least, that's what I told myself.

We lined up, the four of us, at the mouth of the alley. It smelled worse when I stepped inside it. It reeked like the watery stuff that dripped from bin-bags that were overdue emptying. Slimy brick walls rose all around us, high over our heads. There were doors set into it at intervals, but they were all blank, all closed. I knew cats could jump, but I didn't think they could jump that high. The thing was trapped.

"Stop it getting out," Gary said. "It nearly did, before. There weren't enough of us. I'll go first and chuck my coat over it."

The cat, as if it knew what we were doing, pushed its back into an even higher arch. It opened its mouth—I saw a flash of red—and hissed. There did look to be something demonic about it, but cats were like that, weren't they? They were claws and spitting and teeth. I wondered for a moment if Gary had really seen its true nature, and pushed the thought away. The cat was just a cat. He belonged to the woman who lived on the corner of our street, the one with the big garden where it liked to hide in the long grass. My mum stopped to talk to her sometimes. They'd call the cat to them with silly clicking noises, calling his name. It had a stupid name—*Whirligig*, that was it.

That gave me an idea. "Wait," I told them.

Gary shot me a dirty look and I shrugged. Then I crept forward, bending low to the ground, reaching out and rubbing my fingers together. I made clicking noises with my tongue. The cat didn't relax, not really, but it closed its mouth and watched me, its eyes wide.

I took another step and it didn't move. It didn't run. There wasn't really anywhere to go but I didn't think that was the reason. I thought that maybe the possibility of finding a friend meant a whole lot more when you were stuck, on your own, in a place like this; even if you were a cat.

I was within a couple of feet of it now. It started to relax its back a little. It didn't hiss or spit or do anything. It just followed me with those yellow eyes.

And then I bent and scooped it up.

It went rigid for a second before I felt its face nudging my cheek, the softness of fur as it rubbed itself against me.

I heard Gary's laugh as I turned. "All *right*," he said, and I don't think he just meant the result. I thought he also meant me.

He held out the rope. "It needs to go over its head."

I didn't move. He surely couldn't think I'd do that. But then—I'd known what he intended, didn't I? He'd pretty much told me, and I'd still done what I'd done. I was still holding the cat. It didn't squirm. It was surprisingly heavy for its size, its back end hanging loosely over my arm. It seemed quite happy there, and I wondered why that was.

Gary twitched the rope, as if enticing me like I'd enticed the cat. "Come on, do it then. Show us what you're made of—*Cam*."

I shifted my grip on Whirligig, holding him more firmly. Gary couldn't really mean to hurt it. He was daring me—testing me. I wondered what would happen to me on Monday if I failed. And what might happen if I succeeded. . . .

I reached out, without quite touching the rope. He'd already knotted one end into a loop, or maybe he'd found it that way, because the knot looked drawn as tight as it would go. I didn't think it could be pulled tighter still—but maybe I was wrong.

I looked down and saw Whirligig's red collar, softer and wider than the rope. I imagined the cord sinking into his neck. From a long way away I heard kids' voices, the chants of Halloween followed by laughter: someone getting a treat maybe—or playing a trick.

"The cat isn't a witch," I said. My words didn't come out clearly, clogging in my throat. "It's only a cat. It's only a story. I don't believe in stuff like that anymore."

For a second I saw my dad, the year he'd dressed like a vampire. He'd been passed out on the sofa, the pointed teeth half-slipped from his mouth, drool running down his chin. I knew there were no monsters. Those were just pretend. They were masks people wore to hide what lay beneath, if only for one night.

Gary stared at me for what felt like a long time. Then he let out a sharp splutter. That turned into laughter and he hooted with it, doubling over. I turned and James's and Dale's faces were distorted with amusement as they all laughed and laughed.

Then Gary straightened. No trace of humor remained. His eyes were cold. His didn't look like a face that had ever laughed, that *could* laugh. And I knew then that there was no room for stories behind that look, not even nasty ones. There was no room for anything but this—brick walls, concrete, rot; and a rope.

I found myself stepping away. I felt cold now too. It was like ice in the pit of my stomach, and it was spreading, slowly, along each vein. I knew the reason why. It was not the thought that he believed in some old tale and would do terrible things because of it. It was knowing that he *didn't* believe. He never had. It was just some story he'd told because he *wanted* to hang the cat. He wanted to watch it struggle and spin and flex. He wanted to hear it choke. He wanted to see the yellow light fade from its eyes, because he would be bigger then, wouldn't he? More powerful. Something more than he had been.

I stepped away from him again.

"You don't want to mess with me, *Connor*." Gary's hands curled into fists and I stared at him. I realized I'd done what my gut had warned me against after all. I'd gone into the alley. Now the three of them were lined up, just as we had been with the cat, only now it was me that was trapped.

All three of them had the same eyes, a row of pinprick lights shining. Their faces were as blank as Halloween masks. He held out the rope again and I wondered if he still meant it for the cat. Slowly, I reached out and touched it, but Whirligig—such an odd name—wriggled in my arms and I grasped him tighter.

"Christ. I'll do it," Gary said, and he stepped toward me, looking taller than ever; like someone I wouldn't want to mess with, someone I wouldn't want holding a grudge come Monday morning, or lunch break, or the way home.

And I knew that I was a coward.

Another flashback. My dad's fist, driving deep into Mum's stomach. Her face crumpling. And her screaming—*Get out*—because she'd rather take any number of punches than have him turn on me. And I *had* got out. I'd grabbed my coat then too and run out of the door, and I'd thought at the time that I'd done the right thing, done what I was supposed to do. Now, I wondered.

Gary held the loop out wide and he started to slip the twine over Whirligig's head. I pictured the woman who owned the cat. She had gray hair and flowery dresses. The last time I'd seen her, she'd been smiling; smiling at the cat.

And I threw it at him.

Whirligig exploded from my arms in a ball of hair and claw and tooth, yowling his rage. Gary jerked away. I saw fragments: a red line scratched into his hand; Dale barging in, almost knocking him over; the cat, falling; Gary snapping out his hand and grabbing hold of its leg. I saw the way Whirligig twisted in the air but couldn't fall, couldn't right himself, and I heard the snap of a bone breaking.

Then he was on the ground, his legs spread, fur standing on end. And he ran, but not how he had used to run. He ran in a jaggedy, spiky way, his right foreleg held in the air, the paw sticking out at an odd angle.

"Fucker." Gary caught hold of my coat, shoving me up against the wall. My head banged against the bricks but I didn't cry out.

He stared into my face. He looked at me as if he hadn't yet worked out what I was. Then he said, emphasizing each word, "You're—not—worth it."

He let go of my coat. When he turned away his cronies flanked him again, and they walked away, leaving me in the dark. I hoped they wouldn't find the cat again. I could still hear the echo of the sound of its leg breaking. I didn't know what its owner would do; I didn't know what she'd say to me if she found out, or if my mother did. I didn't know how they'd look at me.

I put my hand to my face. It felt cold, like a mask, but I didn't have a mask, not this year. I was too old for them.

I stayed there for a while. Then I pushed myself away from the wall and turned to start the walk home.

The next day, the sky was a solid gray, like cigarette ash, and I pulled on my coat as I stepped out of the door. I noticed something white against the fabric and I realized the stuffing was coming out where it had been slashed by sharp claws.

It was a good job Mum hadn't noticed. She was still sleeping, passed out on the sofa, where she'd spent the night. I knew she'd say sorry, later. She'd say it in a voice quiet enough not to hurt her own hangover-ridden head. I found I didn't care.

I could smell the fumes of passing buses and the grimier hint of rubbish clogging the gutters, and I saw all the after-effects of Halloween. The road was littered with candy wrappers, abandoned treat bags, empty beer bottles, spent matches. The fruitier smell of charred pumpkins came from doorsteps where the rotting things leered. There were a couple of gates off their hinges, leaning against the wall—an old trick, played on any who hadn't enough treats to pacify Halloween's goblins.

I was planning to walk into town, but when I glanced ahead I saw the house on the corner, the one with the large and tangled garden. I hadn't allowed myself to think about what happened last night, but the sight of it brought it all back—the cat's sharp hiss; Gary Turner's narrowed eyes; its willingness to come to me, the warm weight in my arms; the snap of a bone breaking.

My own limbs felt heavy as I went closer, heavier, in fact, with every step. I imagined standing by while my Mum chatted with the woman about the awful thing that had happened to her cat. Of course, she wouldn't know it was me—she'd never know. Whirligig could have fallen off a wall that was too high, or been hit by a car. But I could still hear Mum exclaiming over the cruelty, how she couldn't understand it.

I found my eyes stinging and rubbed at them. I couldn't avoid walking past the place; I'd just have to get used to it. I hadn't even *done* anything.

I reached the edge of a fence that was once painted blue, probably a long time ago. And I saw the woman who owned the cat. She was standing outside her door, not chatting to anybody, not doing anything at all. She was just standing there, staring into space.

I didn't look directly at her. I looked from the corner of my eye, but I couldn't see her face anyway because her hair was hanging down over it in long, straggly clumps. I forced myself to keep walking. She didn't move an inch.

Then, as I drew level, she did.

Every sound suddenly seemed very loud. I could hear my own breathing, and her footsteps, irregular and uneven, scattering thin gravel as she came down the path. No: as she *lurched*.

The woman was limping.

If you catch the cat, if you hurt *the cat, you hurt the witch too.*

Slowly, I turned and looked at her, opening my mouth to say a friendly "Hello," just as Mum would have; just as anyone would have who hadn't tempted her cat into its enemies' hands, who hadn't broken its leg. And it *was* her—but of course it was; I think I'd even seen her wearing that same dress before, flowery but ill-fitting, hanging off her bony frame. It was her, but her face was different. Older. Her skin had grayed, looking stretched where her beak nose poked between strands of hair, sunken into dark hollows at the cheeks. Still, her eyes shone out—they were no-color, but very bright. She was looking straight at me.

She *knew*.

I froze. She didn't stop, though. She kept on lurching down the path, that weed-choked path where Mum and her and me—yes, me too—had all bent and made clucking noises at her cat. There was no cat now, not a trace of him.

I could see her loss, the pain of it, under the blank shine of her eyes. It was awful, and it was fascinating, and I couldn't look away from it.

I realized I didn't even know her name.

I couldn't see which leg she was limping on. Was it her right? It was impossible to tell. She moved more as if she'd been winded, punched in the stomach, maybe. An image rose: Dad driving his fist into Mum's belly. I saw again the way she crumpled and went down. She hadn't got up again. She hadn't lurched after me, like this; like a monster.

And I looked harder, and I saw that the woman hadn't seen me at all. Her eyes still stared straight ahead. I didn't know what she was looking at. I wasn't sure she saw what was around her, or anything at all.

I found I could move again. I looked toward the main road and saw Gary Turner, standing alone on the opposite corner, leaning against the wall. He looked like he was waiting for something, and as I watched his head swiveled toward me—*us*—and I made out the slightest twitch of his lips. Did he think I was here to chat to my neighbor? I could already imagine what he'd say.

The woman sank to her knees. She reached out, grasping at something lying on the path, and I thought of the cat but saw only pieces of wet, shattered pumpkin that someone must have thrown into her garden. She caught up the pieces and threw them back over the fence. Another memory: my Dad carving jagged teeth into a pumpkin. I could see it perfectly, never could forget it. He was taking me trick-or-treating. We'd told each other silly stories we didn't believe with torches shining under our faces, and we'd laughed. We'd laughed all night, and Dad hadn't got mad, not once. Had he known, then, that it would be the last time?

The spell was broken. I walked up to the woman's gate and looked down at her. I watched as she raked her long nails through the gravel. It didn't matter that I didn't know her name. I knew now what she was. I saw her knotted, colorless hair, her dull eyes, her hollow cheeks. I saw that there was no beauty left in her, nothing anyone could want, no one left to care what happened to her.

Witches didn't have names. They didn't need them.

In my mind's eye, I saw again the way she'd walked down the path. It *had* been her right leg she was limping on: yes, definitely. And she'd aged since yesterday. That wasn't right, was it? It was as if her younger self had been the illusion and now her true age was revealed, now that I'd unmasked her—now that I *knew*. She was a witch. We'd done right to hurt the cat after all. It was nothing more than she'd deserved. We'd *had* to hurt the cat.

I stooped slowly and picked up a stone. It was a stone from her own garden, poking between the slats of that badly painted fence. I felt its texture, dry and caked with earth, turning it in my hand. Then I drew my arm back and threw it as hard as I could.

It struck her head. The sound of it was sharp and shocking but I wasn't shocked, not really. I was something else, though I didn't know what; not yet.

A moment's silence and a darker line appeared in her dirty hair.

She raised her head and saw me at last. She stared at me. Fixed me with her witch's eye. And she started to shriek.

I walked away, ignoring her cackles. I wondered if I should be afraid—anyone might hear, anyone might come running, but somehow I knew they wouldn't. Dad had hit Mum many times. Anyone could have heard that, but no one had ever come.

I drew myself taller as I went. Gary Turner had pushed himself away from the wall, was standing looking at me, his mouth slightly open. I remembered the way I'd felt when I'd last seen him. I'd been afraid to be alone in the dark, afraid of stepping into an alley. I'd been frightened, just for an instant, that zombies and ghouls and axe-men would get me; that the monsters would appear.

But it wasn't Halloween when scary things happened; it was anytime and all the time.

I sauntered over to Gary Turner. "All right?" I said, and I kept on walking, heading toward town, and I heard the scuffing of his feet as he started to follow.

I didn't need a costume any longer, didn't need a mask. I was too old for trick-or-treating; I had gone beyond all that. I was something more powerful, something more than I had been.

I was the monster now.

THE PHÉNAKISTICOPE OF DECAY

James Ebersole

James Ebersole's stories and poems have appeared in such publications as *The Horror Writers Association Poetry Showcase* (Volumes I and IV), *Folk Horror Revival: Corpse Roads*, *Richmond Macabre*, *Werkloos*, and *Broken Worlds*.

"At the time I wrote this story," he explains, "it was late summer and I had just moved to Atlanta, Georgia. I felt lost in a new place, sick of the heat and strangeness. I set about writing my way out of that sense of displacement.

"What began as a notion for a cursed-object story ultimately became a meditation on resistance to change, and the desire for familiarity and repetition in the face of entropy. The upstate New York setting came naturally—with its crimson leaves and crumbling Main Streets, I could think of no better place to fit the mournful and autumnal mood I desired."

Halloween, 1989

"IT'S SO DARK now," Andrew said, breaking a silence the other children hadn't noticed setting in. "It's so dark," he repeated, "and I need to get home."

"We can't stop now," Elliot replied.

"Yeah, there's one more house. Let's do that first," Carly said, her mouth full of gummy bears.

"Nobody lives there," Takiyah said.

"Then why is there music coming from it?" Heather asked.

"I don't hear any music," Andrew mumbled from behind his rubber mask.

The children argued, shouting over each other. Carly said it wasn't fair that they all had to go home because Andrew's parents were such hard-asses. As she spoke, she flung her arms around wildly, candy spilling all over the damp pavement.

Elliot turned away from the group, and looked to that final house at the end of the lane. It was a thin, crooked building. Victorian-style, the pale facade shrouded in a green veil of Camperdown Elm.

He walked down the weed-covered cobble path in the front yard. He didn't care about winning some argument with his friends. He didn't care about the candy. He just felt an urge, the tug of an impulse to get closer to this building, to listen to its secrets.

The wooden stairs creaked beneath his feet. The paint on the porch was peeling. Termites crawled. The smell of wood-rot and mildew filled his nostrils, blocking out the chocolate aroma of the night's haul.

For all the disrepair of the rest of the deck, the front door was perfect, and shining red with a fresh coat of paint. There was no doorbell. Only a brass knocker that felt heavy and cold in Elliot's hands.

The knock reverberated like a drum. And there was some other noise as well, from beyond the door. Was it music? Elliot wasn't sure.

The floorboards creaked beneath his feet as he inched away from the door, which loomed blindingly red before him. He looked back to his friends in the street, still disputing their next move, unaware of his absence from their ranks. He was contemplating returning to them.

And then the red door opened.

Elliot turned to face an empty doorway. The light from the street outside illuminated a few inches of wooden floor at the threshold, crooked and carved with swirling symbols.

"Hello?" Elliot called into the darkness.

A flickering bulb switched on. The shadowed figure of a man stood at the far end of the hall. He walked toward Elliot, his fists opening and closing around the dusty air.

The man wore a wrinkled blue blazer and track pants. Silver stubble framed a pale mouth, a thick mustache dangling over his dry lips like moss. He was oldish, but in the "older than parents and younger than grandparents" sort of way that was hard for Elliot to really understand.

"Trick-or-treat," Elliot said, holding out his candy bag.

The man squinted out into the street, where Elliot's friends were. "Halloween. Right. I've slept in again." He scratched at his stubbled cheek with jagged, discolored fingernails. "Where are my manners? Would you like to come in for a cup of tea? Wait. No. That's not it. Not tea. Candy. I must offer candy. Yes. Candy." The man looked around the empty hallway. "I'm afraid I don't have any candy."

Elliot heard the stairs creak behind him. His friends had joined him on the front porch, just as he was thinking it was time to leave.

The man in the doorway shuddered and grinned. His teeth were nearly perfect, all but one—a rotten and shriveled canine that looked as if decay had filed it to a needle-sharp point.

The man must have seen Elliot staring at his mouth. But he only grinned wider.

"I have just the thing. Five treats for five tricksters, yes."

The man went down the hall, moving much faster than before. He disappeared around the corner, out of sight. The noise that may have been music resumed, and it didn't sound any less strange than before.

"We should go," Elliot said to the others.

"What? You were the one who said we had to stay out," Takiyah reminded him.

"Yeah, but what about Andrew? He's late."

Andrew shrugged. "I'm already late either way. May as well add to the loot."

"What, are you scared?" Heather asked.

"No. It's just, the guy who lives here is really weird. He said he didn't have any candy."

"He just said he had a treat for us."

"Maybe he'll give us money. Even better."

The music abruptly stopped. The man reappeared at the end of the hall, a tattered leather briefcase in his hands. He held it away from his body, as if whatever was inside would do him harm if it got too close. He moved toward the children with trudging steps, then knelt down at the threshold, placing the briefcase on the floor. He craned his neck and grinned at the children, his rotten tooth gleaming purple-green in the moonlight.

The briefcase had a six-digit combination lock.

The man's knotty hands spun the numbers around, until they read:

102918

Elliot felt a twinge of familiarity at the number. Like he had seen it before. And not just familiar like a phone number you dial often enough, but like it should mean something *big*.

The lock clicked open. The man undid the clasps with a dramatic flourish of fingers. The lid popped open, revealing five objects nestled in the moth-bitten lining that looked sort of like old pinwheels, or lollipops made of wood and stiff paper.

It appeared that there were markings painted on the discs, but Elliot couldn't quite see what they were.

"Do you kids like cartoons?" the man asked.

"Yeah, I guess so," Andrew mumbled.

"But not the shit for babies," Takiyah added.

Elliot grimaced, expecting the man to scold Takiyah, but he didn't seem to mind the swearing.

"These are the original cartoons, you could say. Well, not these particular ones, though they are still very old. Older than me. Older than any of you for sure."

"What? How does it work?" Carly asked.

"Hold it up, to a mirror, facing this way, so the images are reflected. Look through here, this notch. Spin it, like this. That's all—you'll see the beauty of movement revealing itself. So simple. No batteries required."

He passed the objects out to the children as he spoke.

"But this part is very important. Do not look at the mirror itself. When you are finished, please leave the room for two hours at least, and do not, do not, *do not* look at the mirror."

Elliot was only half-listening to this warning. Instead, he was looking down the hall, toward where the music came from. His eyes had, by that point, adjusted to the dark interior of the house. He saw a staircase, and beside the staircase, a gray-metal door. The door rattled, as if reverberating from some unheard sound on the other side.

"Come on, Elliot, let's get out of here," Heather said, tugging on his shirtsleeve.

Had they seen it too? he wondered, as he was practically dragged down the creaking front steps of the house. If they did, none of them gave any indication. They all seemed bored, tired, ready to go home.

They were already halfway out of the dead-end street when Elliot realized the sack of candy wasn't the only thing he was carrying.

He had no recollection of taking the object from the man, but there it was, in his hand. He inspected it by streetlight as he walked. He saw painted on the disk a progression of cartoon skeletons, positioned like the numbers of a clock, each one standing in a slightly different position.

"Do you think what he was saying about the mirror is real?" Heather asked.

"Don't be stupid. He was just trying to scare us," Carly replied.

It started to rain, and the children picked up the pace.

Andrew's house was the first they passed. His mom was waiting for him on the porch, her arms crossed beneath the rain poncho draped over her shoulders.

"Busted," he whispered, as he left their ranks.

Takiyah's place was next, then Carly's. By then, the rain had let up a little. Elliot and Heather walked in silence for two whole blocks. The streets were empty, quiet.

Elliot thought it was strange that there was no one else out, now that the rain was over. It was dark, sure, but not *that* late.

When they got to his house, Elliot mumbled goodbye.

"Happy Halloween," Heather whispered back. She hesitated, as if she wanted to say something else to him. "You too," he said back to her, and turned away, walking toward the jack-o'-lanterns that lined his front porch.

Up in his bedroom, he began to sort out his candy, but was quickly bored by the task. The skeleton disc sat on the floor, and as much as he didn't like the thing, he was tempted to see what its story was.

He took it to the shared bathroom in the hall, and locked the door behind him. He held it up to the mirror, and with a flick of his hand, the disc began to spin.

The image was of a skeleton, dancing with a cane and top hat, its movements harsh and jerky, like a puppet's. The whole effect reminded Elliot immediately of a flip-book, except, with its circular motion, it never ended. The image repeated itself, the same dance, over and over. It was hypnotic.

Then, there was a change in the figure. Skin began to fill out over the bones, blooming like a peach-colored fungus. The cane transformed into a rope. The rope came into focus, coiling into a noose, slithering up the skeleton-man's arm, around his neck. The man kicked once, and stopped dancing. His hat fell off, his skin fell with it, and he was a skeleton again, dangling in the squiggly lines of a paper-wind.

Elliot turned away from the image, and tried not to look in the mirror as he left the room. He went straight to bed, but slept fitfully, dreaming of the trembling gray door.

"November," he mouthed into the dim morning light of his room. "November," he repeated. He didn't know why, but it was his favorite word ever. It just sounded like so much magic.

But he hated the month itself.

It was cold out in the park. He sat on the swing set, waiting for the school bus to come. He hated going to school the day after Halloween.

He just wanted a Saturday morning candy-breakfast in front of the TV, but the weekend was still so far away.

A breeze picked up, swirling the fallen leaves around his feet. The swing next to him creaked in metallic song. Somewhere behind him, something else creaked—it was the sound of the strained fibers of a rope.

He turned to look.

A man was hanging from the oak tree where the tire swing used to be, a man he didn't know but who looked familiar all the same.

Maybe it was the top hat that gave him away.

He was hanging there, feet kicking, a noose around his neck. His eyes turned down to look at Elliot. They were wide with fright, or confusion, seeming to ask, "How did I get here?" The top hat fell from his head, obscuring his face as it drifted down. As the hat passed, the eyes followed it until the man's stare remained fixed to the ground. The mouth hung open, limp, breathless.

And though the face went still, the feet seemed to dance in the breeze.

Elliot ran all the way back home. He passed Andrew and Carly, walking on the other side of the street. They stared at him in confusion as he ignored their waves.

His parents were still at the breakfast table drinking coffee when he got home. He told them he was sick, and they didn't believe him until he threw up all over the floor.

He didn't tell his parents about what he had seen. He couldn't find the words. He went up to his room with nervous footsteps. He felt light-headed.

The object was still sitting on the bathroom shelf where he had left it. He reached for it with his head turned away, not daring to look at what gruesome image it might show him this time. He took it and hid it deep under his bed, way past his stack of board games and shoeboxes full of trinkets and treasures.

He went back to school the next day, and tried to tell his friends what had happened. But he couldn't find the words. They didn't have many words for him either. Everything seemed changed. None of them talked about the things they received on Halloween night, and the images they contained.

Halloween 1990 was the last time Elliot ever trick-or-treated. That year, everything was different. Where once five children walked the cold upstate streets, now there were only four of them.

Over summer vacation, Carly and her entire family disappeared. The children discovered this when school started, and she never showed up. None of the adults would tell them where she went. Soon they stopped asking and just accepted it—that she had simply vanished from their lives.

But they all agreed to stay well away from the creepy man in the crumbling Victorian house.

The years passed, like the herky-jerky movements of a cartoon skeleton in a mirror.

Halloween, 2018

Elliot left New York City the morning after a sleepless night. The bus was full at first, but by the time he arrived at the Trailways Bus terminal, he was the last person on board. As soon as he stepped off the bus, the doors shut and the driver pulled away, leaving him standing among the autumn leaves and broken glass of a small lot tucked behind Main Street.

He stopped for lunch at the Yellow Deli. It was crowded, with children running around in papier-mâché masks. He had to remind himself it was Halloween. That this was normal. But then, this place had always seemed a bit odd to him any day of the year. And all the things he'd seen in the big city didn't change that one bit.

After four cups of black coffee, he knew he couldn't stall any longer. He left the desolate Main Street, where so many of his teenage haunts were now boarded-up, and made his way through the quiet residential back streets. As he walked, the clouds occasionally parted to blinding sunlight. A cat stared out at him from an abandoned field. The cat's mouth parted in a muted *meow*, and a pair of worms fell out, writhing to the dirt, entwined in some slithering dance.

The house was just as he remembered it. The Halloween decorations were up in the yard. The same cardboard gravestones, the same scarecrow he and his mom made when he was nine. The mailbox was full of junk mail that would never be read by its intended recipient. He let himself in with the hide-a-key under the welcome mat. The plastic mummy candy bowl sat empty on the kitchen counter. He looked through the pantry, but couldn't find candy to fill the bowl anywhere. It seemed Mom and Dad never made it to the store for that. He had found the cooking sherry, the only alcohol his parents ever kept in the house, and poured some into one of Mom's tea saucers. He took a long pull. It tasted dusty and harsh.

He went up to his childhood bedroom. Mom and Dad said they had converted it into an office, but he was surprised to see that, other than the addition of Grandpa's antique roll-top desk and a filing cabinet from IKEA, the room was very much how he had left it in a previous millennium.

He noticed a foul, acidic scent tingling his nostrils. He raised the sherry to his nose, but no, that wasn't it at all. It smelled like something fermenting, something rotting. It was coming from under the bed. He lifted the duvet, bracing himself for what he'd see.

It was still there. Right where he had stashed it. The phénakisticope. Over the years, he had convinced himself he had dreamt the whole thing up, that he had never seen that terrible thing in the park.

But no, the object that foretold that horror was in his hand now.

And the image was different.

Where once there was one dancing skeleton, now there were two. They seemed to be beckoning to him, urging him to set them in motion, to witness their horrible dance.

He would do no such thing. He threw the object onto the bed, and went down to the kitchen to pull out his laptop.

The others. He had to talk to them, to the ones that remained. Of the four friends who were with him that night, two were still alive. At least, he assumed Carly wasn't alive at this point. Sometimes, late at night, he would try to Google her name, to search pages and pages of results for any hint of what had happened to her. But there was no obituary, nothing. She had really just disappeared, back when the Internet was in its infancy. Andrew's demise was more recent, more definite—a heroin overdose at that cursed age of twenty-seven. His funeral was the closest Elliot ever got to returning to his hometown, but a job interview at the last minute kept him in Manhattan (he never got that job anyway).

He drank the last of the sherry he had poured earlier, and called the number he had listed in his contacts for Heather. It rang and rang and rang. No voice mail or anything. He finally gave up, and focused his attention on his laptop. He pulled up an old email thread with Takiyah. It was from three years ago, when she was working on some Off-Broadway production and wanted to meet up with him for a drink (they never did).

Her email signature contained her contact information from that time. He knew for certain the mailing address was no good anymore, but he tried the phone number anyway.

It went straight to voice mail: Takiyah's voice, stating she was out of the country for the foreseeable future, and that she could be reached at. . . .

He typed the number into an international calling service on his laptop, and received the connecting call on his cell phone.

"Hello?" Takiyah answered.

"Hi. Takiyah. It's me, Elliot."

"Oh shit. Hey, what's up?"

"I'm at my parents' place. In Oneonta." He didn't explain why he was there. It felt too hard. He was relieved when she didn't ask him how his parents were, and instead talked about herself, informing him that she was living in Thailand now, teaching English, and that she was currently at a bonfire party on the beach and that, she was sorry, but she really couldn't hear him very well.

"Do you remember that Halloween before Carly disappeared?"

"What?" she asked.

"Do you remem—"

"Hello?"

The call dropped.

He started to type the number in again, when his phone rang.

"Hey," he answered.

"Hi. This is Elliot, right?" a voice that wasn't Takiyah's replied.

"Uh, yeah."

"Sorry, I'm at work and saw you called. What's up?"

"Heather. Hey. I'm in town."

"Really?"

"Yeah, I'm at my parents' house. I wanted—"

"Sorry, Elliot, I've got to get back to it, the cashiers need help. Last minute Halloween shoppers and all."

"Yeah, of course. When do you get off?"

"Four, Four-thirty. Depends. Your parents still live on Linden Avenue?"

"Yeah," he said. He wondered if there was a quick and painless way to say to Heather that, yes, his parents' house was still in the same place as ever, but they no longer lived there, that they no longer lived at all.

"Cool. I'll stop by when I get off."

"Okay, I'll be here."

The line went dead, and he was alone in the silence of the house again. He tried not to think about the thing upstairs. He refilled his sherry saucer and took a sip.

He was about to try to call Takiyah back when the doorbell rang.

He drained the saucer in one long pull and went to the door. There, a very young vampire mumbled "Trick-or-treat" through a crooked maw of baby teeth.

He looked out past the child. Midafternoon sun filled the yard. He saw the kid's parents standing in the street, watching somnolently with arms crossed.

"I haven't got any candy I'm afraid," he said, tasting the vapor of sherry trailing out of his mouth. "Not just yet, anyway. Come back later when it's dark out."

"My parents don't let me out when it's dark," the child replied. Then added: "What about your parents?"

Elliot's hand tightened around the door handle. "My parents?"

"Do they let you out at night?"

Out in the street, the child's parents turned to face each other. They raised their hands to the other's cheeks, as if both were racing to pull the other into a kiss. But they did not kiss. Instead, with thin fingers probing at the edge of each jaw, the couple, in perfect synchronization with each another, removed their partner's faces, like they were masks.

The faces hit the ground with a wet smack. Underneath the skin was not the bone or muscle or blood that Elliot had anticipated. There was nothing so human as that left in their faces. The space beneath their hairlines was filled with mildewed decay, all brilliant colors and strange shapes, like bowls of fruit left in a cold, dark place for far too long. The child on the porch laughed. Hand-in-hand, the faceless lovers danced the do-si-do, their skin falling away in sheets with each shuddering movement.

The child's laughter cadenced. From nearby, Elliot heard the sound of some unseen crowd clapping.

Elliot stumbled back through the threshold of his parents' home, and slammed the door shut.

His vision darkened, blurred, then came back into focus.

Next to the coatrack was a puddle of vomit. It smelled like sherry. Elliot didn't remember throwing up, but the back of his throat burned as if he had.

It was quiet now. But he didn't dare look out through the peephole in the door.

He thought about calling the police, but he never wanted to call them under any circumstance. A boyfriend back in Brooklyn had left him in the middle of the night just because he wouldn't call the cops on his noisy neighbors. He liked the boy and he liked his neighbors, and he didn't know which to betray, so in the end he stuck with inaction.

But he didn't like what he had just seen on the porch.

And what did I see? he thought.

Maybe this was a new thing that wasn't feasible in the big city. Trick-or-treaters bringing the haunted houses *with* them, showing off spooky effects to the whole neighborhood.

Just a magic trick.

Just an illusion.

Just a thing that looked too real to possibly be true.

The doorbell rang again.

He looked through the peephole and saw a woman about his own age. For a second, he expected her skin to fall away like the flesh of the dancers, for some child to leer out from the bushes. But she just stood there, arms crossed, tapping the toes of her Doc Martens.

She wore khakis, a superstore polo, a thick black sweater, aviator sunglasses. Her cropped hair was dyed a purple-tinged black. But the way she looked around, surveying her surroundings, so patient and alert, was unmistakable.

He opened the door for Heather.

"Come in, come in, so good to see you," he said as he pulled her into an awkward, one-armed hug. He hurriedly beckoned her into the kitchen, hoping she wouldn't see or smell the pool of vomit beside them. If she did, she gave no indication.

"Cup of tea?" He asked.

She shrugged, removing her sunglasses. "Do you have anything stronger?"

Elliot thought of the cooking sherry, the acidic burn of it at the back of his throat, the bile, the laugh of a child, the skin falling away, all the skin in the world. . . .

"Just tea, I'm afraid."

"Sure, tea's fine. Just no caffeine please, it's bad for my anxiety."

He put the kettle on and found a packet of store-brand sandwich cremes in the cupboard, which he arranged on a dinner plate.

"I know why you're in town. Sorry for your loss."

"Thanks."

He didn't want to talk about his loss, so he fixated on the simple fact that he was there, not the reason. "It's weird being back. It's been so long, and it seems so different here, but also . . . also the same really."

"Why didn't you ever come back? To visit your parents? To visit me?" She whispered the last part.

He shrugged. "Mom and Dad always liked coming to the city. Every Christmas, more or less. They liked walking around, seeing the Rockefeller tree lit up, sitting in coffee shops to meet whatever new person I was seeing at the time. And no matter how short any of those relationships were, they always had a Christmas present for whoever that might be. They visited a lot in winter, said it got so lonely out here. And what about you?"

"What about me?"

"Why did you stay?"

"Because I can't leave." She said it so definitively, like some unseen force had kept her in the same place her whole life. "Oneonta is my home," she added.

They sipped their tea in silence.

"I talked to Takiyah."

"What did she say? Is she still living in LA?"

"No. She's in Thailand now. Teaching English, it sounds like. It was pretty late, and she was at some bonfire party."

"Can you call her back?"

"What, right now?"

"Yes."

"It's like four in the morning there."

"I'd like to speak to her."

He redialed the number, and listened to the ringing as he sipped his tea.

He was about to hang up, when the connection went through.

A masculine voice answered in what Elliot assumed was Thai. There was a lot of noise on the other end.

"Uh, hello. I'm calling for Takiyah. This is her phone, yes?"

"Are you family?"

"No, just a friend. From the States."

"Do you know her family?"

"Not really. Not lately. What's this about?"

"I am talking to you from hospital. Your friend was in a motorbike crash, very bad. She's in, what is it. . . ." The man paused, and Elliot could hear a woman shouting on the other end of the line. "Not sleep. Coma. Yes, she's in coma."

The man gave Elliot the number of the hospital's main line, telling him if he could find her family, to have them call that number. Elliot said "Thank you" and, just before the line went dead, he heard some strange and familiar music echoing through the halls of a hospital halfway across the world.

Heather watched expectantly for an explanation, her teacup cradled in nail-bitten hands.

"Takiyah was in an accident, she's in a hospital. They wanted me to have her folks give them a call."

Heather gulped the last of her tea.

"Well, let's go then."

"Go? What, to Thailand?"

"Back to the house where all this started."

"Where what started?"

"You looked in the mirror. Even when he said not to. I know. I can tell. I did it too."

Elliot felt like he had a thousand questions, but he didn't know what to say.

"Let's go. Takiyah's house is on the way," Heather said.

They walked through the streets, so familiar yet so strange. Everything was washed in golden-hour light, and the trick-or-treaters were coming out in force. Elliot couldn't remember the last time he spent Halloween in such a suburban place. All the costumes looked so cheap and plastic and boring. He felt so fucking old, so far removed from these children, living out their early years in the same place he once did.

He was starting to sweat. Was he nervous? *No, it's just the heat. Way too hot to be October.* Even the leaves on the trees had hardly changed as much as they should. Everything was too green—the trees, the lawns of so many abandoned houses, too many abandoned houses.

Others had left this place. Not just him. The streets did seem so very empty.

"Oh. . . ." Heather stopped suddenly.

"What's up?" Elliot asked. And then he saw it. The ruined rubble of a house fire, on the lot where Takiyah once lived.

"Fuck, man. I had heard there was a fire around here in August, but I didn't realize. . . ."

"What do we do now?"

"We can deal with Takiyah back at your place. She's safe where she is, and we're almost where we need to be."

This was his chance—face his past, or go home and pretend none of this ever happened. He nodded, and Heather led the way.

They turned down the dead-end street, and walked to the very end.

The house looked just as he remembered. It appeared to be locked in a timeless state of decay, neither renovated nor more rundown than all those years ago.

But there was one difference.

The For Sale sign out front.

He felt the pull of the house, the same irresistible urge he felt all those years ago.

"It's locked," Heather said in a tone of defeat.

"I think I know the code."

"What the fuck are you talking about?"

He stood before the red door, the realtor's lockbox off to the side. There were six blank spaces on the screen. Six numbers. Six numbers he saw at this very place. He punched them in, with a precise and deliberate jab.

1 0 2 9 1 8

And this time he knew why it should be familiar. This was a date, a date that, first glimpsed in his childhood, had come to pass a few days ago. This was the date that his father, newly a widower, took his own life.

The screen of the lockbox flashed green. Elliot slid open the case, revealing a single skeleton key.

He slid it into the lock of the red door, slowly turning it. The door swung inwards, revealing the same hall, just as he saw it one Halloween, as a child.

Elliot and Heather entered the house, side by side. He flicked on the light switch, and a bulb above them flickered to life.

Heather led the way down the hall. She seemed at ease, almost familiar with the space. The only thing he could hear was the sound of their creaking footsteps and his own breath.

After a small eternity, they were at the end of the hall, standing before the metal door.

"I know how he died. The man who lived here," Heather said, her face turned away from Elliot.

The gray door shook.

"I saw it happen. In the phénakisticope he gave me."

"What did you see?" Elliot asked.

The knob of the gray door turned. The door swung outwards. Heather ran inside. Elliot hesitated for a moment, and then followed her into the darkness.

There were stairs in the dark. He couldn't see very much, but he heard something from below. A sound from his childhood. That strange music. Definitely music. He was closer to it now than he had ever been that night. He descended the stairs with slow, probing footsteps, trusting the music to lead him on.

The stairs abruptly leveled off into a cool, packed-earth basement. Elliot didn't know what a tomb smelled like, not really, but he figured this would be it. The odor was oddly comforting.

The space was illuminated by a dim light he couldn't account for.

"Heather?" he called out. His voice echoed amid the sound of music. Other voices answered. What they said he wasn't sure, but he followed them deeper into the subterranean space.

As he crossed the dimly lit basement, passing a multitude of folding-chairs stacked haphazardly along a wall, he realized that he could no longer hear the music or the voices anymore. Instead he heard another sound—it was like sheets of paper, flapping in a wind.

It sounded so familiar.

And then he saw the source of both the light and the sound before him.

There was a long mirror set across the entire back wall of the basement, running parallel to a row of metal chairs. Between each chair and the mirror was a phénakisticope. Many of the chairs were occupied, those seated facing the mirror with their backs to Elliot. He moved closer, and saw the faces in profile. Their bodies were stiff with rigor mortis, but their eyes were bright, and shining, and watching the images in the mirror before them.

Elliot saw the man from the park, the first person he ever saw die, watching the spinning disk set before him, depicting himself hanging from a tree.

He saw Andrew, watching himself slipping the lethal needle into his arm.

He saw Takiyah's parents sitting side by side, watching themselves burn.

There was an empty chair beside them. In front of that chair was a spinning disc with a cartoon Takiyah, crashing her motorbike over and over again.

The man who answered the door of this house all those years ago sat there as well. He was watching himself dying of cancer in a hospital bed.

And the real estate agent. He recognized her from the sign out front. She was watching herself fall down the stairs of this very house.

There were others too.

His fifth-grade math teacher.

The creepy barber.

His high school crush that he thought had moved away just like him, but who came back here to die in a car crash on Christmas Eve.

And there was Heather. Her phénakisticope showed her gunned down during a botched robbery attempt. She was wearing the same clothes in the spinning disc as she had on now.

There was an empty chair at the end of the row, beside Heather. His own phénakisticope sat before the chair, with the happy dancing skeletons. He wanted so badly to sit down.

Heather turned toward him and smiled.

He realized then that all the watchers looked so contented, and not a single one appeared a day older than the day they died. They had achieved some kind of immortality down here, their souls spinning on and on and on and . . . Heather gestured toward the empty seat. In that moment, he wanted nothing more than to sit and join her. It seemed so simple. For his whole life, he felt like a spectator. Why not go all the way?

But then he realized that there were some people missing. Carly, gone as always. But not just her. There was something else.

"Where are my parents?" he asked.

The side of Heather's eyes twitched. Not so much like a muscle spasming, more akin to a bug crawling beneath the skin.

"I'm sorry Elliot. Your parents had ordinary deaths," Heather replied. The words came out garbled, barely decipherable. When she opened her mouth to speak, all her teeth were gone.

He looked back toward the mirror. His phénakisticope was spinning. The image began to change. There was one skeleton now. Skin began to bloom on its face.

It was his face.

He lifted the empty folding-chair, and threw it as hard as he could at the mirror.

The glass shattered, from end to end.

The watchers screamed in unison. The sound was like that strange music transposed into the wrong key.

Heather's skin began to fall away, a shimmering layer of mold sprouting in its place. She decayed before Elliot's eyes. All the watchers did. Everything was replaced by an armor of rot, everything but their eyes, still gazing at the spinning of the disks, still seeing their lives reflected back at them in the fragmented remains of the mirror. Only this time, they didn't look so content with what they were seeing. In fact, the eyes gazing out through all that corruption looked so very frightened.

Elliot ran through the basement, not daring to look back. He ran up the stairs, to the hall. He was surprised to find the front door was still open, that escape was still possible.

He ran all the way home, past the burnt-out remains of Takiyah's home, past the superstore where Heather had been gunned down in a robbery. He entered his parents' house, and pulled the car keys out from the side table, next to the puddle of his own drying vomit. He quickly climbed into his parents' car and drove away, out past the last lights of town.

He never made it back to the city. Instead, he ditched the car in the JFK parking lot and bought a one-way ticket bound to Kuala Lumpur. He left that night, and throughout the whole flight he imagined his own phénakisticope depicting a plane crash. He watched a film that made him think about his mom. The plane landed. *A runway crash, then*, he thought.

But no disaster occurred. Instead, the plane landed safely, and a sleepless layover in Beijing followed.

He tried to read a paperback thriller from the newspaper kiosk, but couldn't focus. He drank Tsingtao beer for five hours straight as he continuously refreshed his email, looking at the barrage of angry messages from relatives stuck at his Mom and Dad's funeral, wondering where he was and when he'd be getting there. He boarded the final flight not exactly drunk, just vaguely bloated and dehydrated.

He spent two weeks intoxicated on the beach before he got the nerve to face what he had come here for. He tracked down the hospital in Phuket where Takiyah was supposed to be a patient. No one there could tell him anything about what happened to her. They had no record she was ever there.

So he was the last one, then. He thought about going back to New York only briefly. Memories of that basement with its spinning phénakisticopes quickly snubbed out the notion, and he decided he was far enough away already. Not like there was really such thing as a "far enough" from fate anyway.

He fell in with the local community quickly enough, and took a part-time job as a scuba instructor to supplement the slowly dwindling inheritance from his mom and dad. Every day he spent out on the water, he wondered if this was where he would die. If, somewhere across the world, someone was spinning a disk with his image on it. If they saw him devoured by sharks, or getting in a boating accident, or drowning.

Once, in a café in Bangkok, he thought he saw Takiyah through the window. It was monsoon season, and she was the only person out on the street, walking through the downpour as if she didn't notice it. She glanced back through the window at him, and he thought there was a hint of recognition, a sense of fear. She ran from view, and by the time he threw some money onto the table and hurried out into the street, she was gone.

He smoked a stale Marlboro knockoff under the café awning, and listened to the rain. Somewhere in the distance, he heard the sound of a motorbike revving its engine, the squeal of tires, and a collision. He threw his cigarette, burned down all too quickly, out into the water streaming through the cracks in the road.

He wondered if Takiyah, despite escaping the fate of rotting in that basement, had found herself trapped in an image foretold, in a glitch of repetition, a cycle of collision, always trying to ride away and survive, always crashing, always dying, and doing it all again. Stuck in a loop, stuck in a foreign land, spinning around and around and around and. . . .

MEMORIES OF *DÍA DE LOS MUERTOS*

Nancy Kilpatrick

Award-winning author Nancy Kilpatrick has published more than twenty novels, seven collections of stories, and fifteen anthologies. Recent short fiction has appeared in such volumes as *Nightmare's Realm*, *Black Wings V* and *VI*, *Searchers After Horror*, *The Darke Phantastique*, *Zombie Apocalypse: Endgame!*, *The Madness of Cthulhu 2*, and *Innsmouth Nightmares*. The graphic novel *Nancy Kilpatrick's Vampyre Theater* was based on her work, and her story "Heart of Stone" was adapted for another graphic collection, *Tales from the Acker-Mansion*.

Thrones of Blood, her new six-novel series from Crossroad Press, so far comprises *Revenge of the Vampir King*, *Sacrifice of the Hybrid Princess*, and *Abduction of Two Rulers*, while a new collection of her short stories is forthcoming from Hippocampus Press.

"'Memories of *Día de los Muertos*' was written from a dream I had almost thirty years ago," she reveals. "I awoke, knowing nothing at that time about the Mexican Day of the Dead, and sat down at my computer. This story came out of me full-blown, and I think I subsequently changed only two words.

"Years later, when I visited Mexico for the celebrations over November 1st and 2nd, I was astonished that so much of what I'd written was a reality during these colorful, annual events where people connect with their ancestors.

"Several Spanish teachers have used this story in their classroom to give students a taste of what the holiday is about. I've always loved this story because it feels like it came to me as a gift."

YOU CALL ME "death-bringer," as though ancient words can wound me. When I was mortal, as you are still, that name filled me with loathing. Now, because I live forever, because I have seen your grandparents rot and will watch *los gusanos* devour your children, your words fade like the ghosts of memories.

This eve of the Day of the Dead—my day, although you do not yet realize there are many ways to be dead—I watch you enter the cemetery just after sunset. The crude wooden crosses as well as those of fine marble are draped with fragrant bougainvillea and gardenia, and you add your flowers to the stones you stop beside. I see your wife spread a colorful blanket over the graves of your ancestors and open jars and boxes for the long night of sharing. A night when the dead will consume the spirit of the food you offer. Food you expect to devour.

Your son and two daughters pulse with life. Life I no longer possess. They skip along the dusty paths eating sugar skulls and clutching papier-mâché skeletons until the sky blackens and the few fires scattered throughout the graveyard become the only light under a moonless sky. The children fall silent and huddle near you, fearful, expectant. You tell them a story. Of how the dead, on this day, return to converse with the living. To fulfil promises and offer guidance. To bring good fortune. As you strum your guitar and sing a song, your eyes are sad and fearful.

Years have passed since you have visited the dead. Few still come here to spend the night.

By the flickering embers you stare at the worn oval photograph of your mother and imagine her returning. You want this, yet fear it. To speak with her again, to feel her bless you and the ones you love. . . .

Your son and daughters have fallen asleep. Your wife is drowsy. She leans back and closes her eyes, her long black hair and the crucifix she wears falling away from her throat. You are alone.

Outside the cemetery walls the mariachi band has stopped playing. A cool wind caresses you, blowing hair up the back of your head, exposing your neck. You shiver. I laugh, and you turn abruptly at the sound. Familiar. Alien. Darkness presses in on you and the dead beneath you struggle to call a warning, but their voices were silenced long ago by the worms. You look again to the picture of your mother, then to the sky, and cross yourself, sensing she can no longer help you.

Something flies through the night air, beyond the illumination of the fire. A bat, you hope. Wings flap and you listen as though to a voice. The tequila bottle is less than half full; you take another swallow and I can see you are wondering how you will endure this night.

Once, long ago, when your ancestors and I walked in daylight together, I sat where you sit now. Honoring the dead. Singing sad and joyous songs to them. Telling their tales of grief and bitterness and of how they loved. Of how they lived, and died. Memories stir in me like petals rustled by a breeze.

At last you see me, a shadow among shadows. The guitar slips from your hands. I have come for you. Your eyes are red-rimmed with the knowledge. You plead. Your wife, you say, and your children. There are things you have not yet done. You beg me to spare you until morning, imagining I do not know my powers will wane with the sun. I laugh as tears spill down your weathered face. I am incapable of pity. When I reach out to stroke your cheek, to feel the warmth pushing against your flesh, salty wetness coats my dead fingers. Astonished, I remember.

On a Day of the Dead such as this, when I sat where you sit now, my loved ones beside me, music floating on the cool breezes drifting down from the mountains, I, too, wept. My vulnerable tears betrayed me then, as yours betray you now. My tears did not save me.

What warms your body will soon warm mine. I nod at the boy child, the youngest. A substitute. You decline, as I knew you must. I do not see this as heroism or bravery, simply what you would do.

You turn to the picture of your mother. She will intercede, you think. You pray to her. To anyone. A small iguana springs onto the tombstone next to the melting candle you have placed there. He pauses to stare at you; he is a sign, you believe, good or ill, how can you be certain? I step into the firelight. Neither the dead nor the living can help you now.

"Why?" you ask me. This question I have heard many times over the years. Many times. It is a question for which there is no answer. Your life does not mean to me what it means to you. I feel no love or sympathy, no pity; I no longer understand remorse. All I can tell you is that I long for your hot blood to swirl through my cold body. Your eyes are the only reflection I am capable of seeing and in them I find myself as I once was but am no longer. This image cannot sway me. What I need I must have.

You suddenly understand a horror that all your life you have avoided. You find this incomprehensible: dead exist to whom you mean nothing. And yet even you must know that blood is all that matters on this day when *los muertos* are honored.

Across the graveyard another calls his ghosts and I listen, intrigued by the bittersweet song. The night is long; there are many here with offerings. Many. To one such as myself, all are equal.

Before I turn away, I glimpse disbelief in your eyes. Gratitude. You cross yourself and fall on your knees before your mother. Before me.

I drift between the worn stones toward new warmth. You are a memory already fading. A memory that will die. A memory of the dead.

FRAGILE MASKS

Richard Gavin

Richard Gavin's fiction is described as "exploring the realm where fear and the sublime intersect." His horror stories have been collected in five volumes, including *At Fear's Altar* and *Sylvan Dread: Tales of Pastoral Darkness*, and have been selected for several volumes of the annual *Best New Horror* anthology. The author has also published numerous works of esoteric nonfiction.

"The impetus for 'Fragile Masks' was my desire to write a contemporary story that conveyed the timeless undercurrent of Halloween," explains Gavin, "yet did not rely on the holiday's familiar modern tropes (children trick-or-treating along leaf-carpeted streets, etc.). Mine needed to be an adult tale, in part because I wanted characters who could not dispel their glimpse through Samhain's thinned veil as simply childish imaginings.

"There is a rarefied atmosphere that arises whenever one is in the proximity of an authentic spirit, and it is not at all like the foggy, half-realized images of reverie. It is a sheer mental clarity, an overwhelming awareness of some ineffable form whose presence eclipses conventional logic.

"I believe that the finest ghost stories can evoke something of this sensation."

"WOOLF."

The word caused Paige to flinch in the passenger seat. She scanned the leaf-carpeted banks of the road, looking for signs of movement.

"It was Virginia Woolf who took her life that way, not Brontë," Jon explained, "my mistake. Wait, did you think I saw an actual. . . ."

"You gave me a start," she said brusquely.

Jon's mouth hitched into a grin, which made him look more pained than amused. "Maybe you have some Halloween spirit after all."

Paige made a noise with her throat then stared out at the drabness that surrounded them. The road was all clay and ugly stones, and the trees that flanked it had lost their foliage. They passed a pumpkin patch, a cornfield, both of which had been gleaned of their growth. Even the sunlight was filtered through strips of gray clouds that reduced it to a vague glimmer, the way the features of the dead grow indistinct beneath the shroud.

"Any of this look familiar?" asked Jon.

"The country all looks the same to me."

"Oh. Well, according to my phone we're less than three miles from the bed-and-breakfast."

The final bend was riddled with potholes, forcing Jon to slow the car to a crawl. The phone app instructed him to turn left.

"Hmm," he muttered, "that doesn't seem correct."

"Why not?"

"Take a look down there, honey. That lane looks like a footpath. I doubt I could even get the car down there without getting the sides all scratched up by those trees. I'd hate to damage my new present." He patted the dashboard gently, then touched Paige's hair. "I know you said these places all look the same to you, but do you remember turning down a little lane like this when you were last here?"

"Teddy and I didn't stay at this *particular* place," Paige explained, "but it was near here."

Jon rubbed the back of his neck. The rush of blood had made him feel hot. "*Teddy*. . . ." he mumbled, though not so softly as to go unheard.

She reached to the steering wheel, placed her hand over his. "This can be our place."

They made the turn.

He'd been correct about the narrowness of the lane but had underestimated its length, for by the time they came upon the white two-story house the main road was no longer visible. It was obvious that the photos they'd seen of the establishment online had been taken in fairer weather and during better times. The sloping lawn that had appeared so rich and manicured was now a sparse, brownish mat, interspersed with mud puddles and a broken stone birdbath. Jon did his best to mask his feelings of having been swindled.

"I guess we just park over there." He indicated an ovular patch of the yard that was inlaid with white gravel. They drove up alongside the beige jeep that was parked there, and Jon switched off the engine.

He gave the car, which Paige had given him as a spontaneous gift over the summer, an inspection for scratches.

"The paint is fine," said Paige.

Jon nodded, collected their bags. The only detail that distinguished the house as a business was a small placard beside the doorframe: GUESTS—PLEASE RING DOORBELL FOR SERVICE.

"This doesn't look very. . . ."

"Very what?" Paige asked.

Jon shrugged. "All I mean is, you can afford to holiday in places much nicer than this."

"I think it's perfect."

Paige obeyed the sign and pressed the button. They stood in wait on the covered porch and Jon whispered to her that he hoped they would have enough privacy.

The woman who drew back the inner door was genial, energetic, and, Jon felt, very well put together for someone her age. Her hair, obviously dyed, was the color of rusted tin. She extended her hand, introduced herself as Imogene, and then plucked both suitcases from Jon's hands.

"Oh, that's not necessary," he said.

"Nonsense," replied Imogene, "come, come."

The couple followed the wake of perfume that smelled of clean linen. Imogene led them to a handsome Edwardian desk and bade them to sit. Stationing herself behind the desk, she deftly collected file folders and confirmed the details of their stay.

"Just one night it is then?"

"Yes," Paige said.

"It's refreshing to have guests here on a Tuesday, especially during the off-season. Both of my rooms are booked for tonight in fact. Are you here for the Halloween Ball over in Durham?"

"There's a Ball?" Jon asked.

At this same instant Paige uttered, "No."

"Oh, that's too bad," said Imogene. "The other couple that's here said they're not going either. You really should reconsider. It's a good deal of fun. I'm going there myself after supper tonight. You did know that here we offer both dinner and breakfast to all guests?"

"Yes, that's excellent, thank you," said Paige.

"Can I ask if that scent from the kitchen is tonight's dinner?" Jon said.

"It is—Irish stew and homemade bread."

"Good Celtic faire. That's fitting."

Imogene looked confused.

Jon felt himself blushing. "Halloween . . . it was a Celtic holiday . . . way back, I mean."

"A fountain of information, this one," she said, winking at Paige.

They signed the registration forms and were shown to their room, which was slight but stylish.

"The tub is really something," Paige said as she emerged from the washroom, "I could practically swim in it." She found Jon standing between the bed and the nightstand. He had a finger pressed to his mouth. Warbled voices, one deep and the other bright, were audible from the adjoining room.

"Just as I'd feared," grumbled Jon as he maneuvered out of the awkward space. "These walls are like tissue paper. We'll not have any privacy at all. I can practically hear them breathing next door."

"Well there's nothing we can do about it now."

"I suppose. Why don't we go for a walk before dinner?"

"I'd rather not."

The woman beyond the wall laughed shrilly.

Jon sighed. "What would you like to do?"

"I think I'm going to soak in that tub for a while."

He was hoping for some indication that Paige wanted company. When none came, he proceeded to unpack and then went to appreciate the view, such as it was, from the upper story window. The landscape that surrounded them looked as dull as the piled clouds. Their room was facing the lane. Even from this higher vantage, the main road remained obscured by bends in the lane and by the unkempt verge.

"Pretty?"

Paige's voice startled him. He spun around and asked, "How was your bath?"

"Lovely, but now I'm famished. I'll get dressed and we can go downstairs."

Soon after, they were about to venture down when Paige decided to change shoes. While Jon was waiting in the hallway, the other couple emerged from their room. Jon experienced a pang of social anxiety. The three of them nodded and offered vague greetings.

The other man then said, "Hello, Paige."

Jon snapped his head back to the doorway of his room.

"Teddy."

"Did you say?" Jon uttered hoarsely.

"I'd like you to meet Alicia, my fiancée. Alicia, this is Paige and . . . ?"

Jon shook hands but did not think to introduce himself. The four of them casually forged a circle. Three of them conversed. Jon, however, scarcely spoke and heard even less of the discussion. His brain was oscillating between disbelief and rage.

"Well," Teddy said, checking his watch, "shall we go down?"

He wrapped his arm around Alicia's waist and the two of them descended the stairs. Paige was about to follow when Jon gripped her wrist.

"I need to talk to you," he rasped. "In here." He opened the door to their room. Paige was reluctant to close it once she saw the expression on her lover's face. "What do you take me for?"

"I'm sorry?" she said.

"Is this your idea of a sick joke, dragging me here to spend the night with your ex-husband? What, are you two comparing your new paramours?"

"I didn't know he would be here!"

"Right."

"I *didn't*. Last year we stayed near here, yes, but how could I have known that he would pick this exact place on the same night as we did?"

"An amazing coincidence, no?"

"That's just what it is." She pressed herself against him, kissed his neck. "I swear. I'm not thrilled with this either, but let's not let it ruin our trip. Let's just go have some dinner, be civil for an hour or so, and then I'm going to prove to you that I'm yours and only yours."

Paige's whispered words and the gestures that followed caused Jon's anatomy to reflexively awaken even though his take on the situation hadn't changed. Paige took his hand and together they slipped down to the dining room.

Four settings had been placed upon a large tortoise-shell table that sat beneath a hanging lamp with a golden dome. Teddy and Alicia were already seated, their hands clasped in a churlish show of their bond. Jon forewent his habit of pulling out Paige's chair. One wall of the dining room was covered in gold-veined mirror panels. Jon moved in front of this and sat down heavily. He poured himself some ice water from the crystal pitcher. He could feel Teddy seeking eye contact, perhaps to start a conversation, perhaps to assess how deeply his presence was troubling him. Jon refused to look up from his glass, at least until the kitchen door swung open and he caught sight of Imogene wheeling in a serving cart. It took all his resolve to keep from laughing in the woman's face.

Imogene's costume, if it was that, was a hybrid of Hollywood witch and low-rate prostitute. Her reddish hair was now capped with a conical hat and her eyes were heavily laden with kohl. The dress she wore revealed too much of her flesh, which in turn betrayed far too much of her age, or so Jon felt. Her breasts, plumped by a push-up bra, were creased and freckled, and her legs sat lumpy inside their stockings.

Jon's sense of disgust was suddenly replaced by a powerful lash of shame. Had his inner self always been this judgmental, this ugly, he wondered?

The other guests proceeded to heap praise on their hostess's appearance, which only increased Jon's bout of self-loathing.

"I'm off to the dance just as soon as I see that you good people have been fed," said Imogene. "Now, please don't even trouble yourself once you're finished. I'll clean everything once I'm back, and then the dining room will be all ready for your breakfast feast tomorrow."

As she ladled out the stew, Teddy questioned her about it containing eye of newt. Other jokes, equally dreadful, were offered. With the main course served, Imogene then made several trips back to the kitchen, returning each time with a platter of desserts, which she laid out in a row on a stout hutch that stood against the dining room wall.

"Here is my cell phone number," she said, snapping a business card onto the table. "Don't hesitate to call if you need anything, but I won't be late at all. Happy Halloween!"

Her heels click-clacked along the hardwood floor and she was gone.

Jon spooned up more of the stew, which was nowhere as succulent as its aroma. Teddy, Alicia, and Paige had no difficulty finding topics of conversation. When Jon emptied the last drop from the pitcher, Teddy clapped his hands and announced that he'd brought something much finer than ice water. He rose from the table and darted upstairs, returning a moment later with a bottle of twenty-year-old scotch. Glasses were filled, including Jon's. They drank and chatted and switched off the overhead light to bask in the cold moonlight.

Jon cleared his throat. "Alicia, can I ask you something?"

In the bluish light, her startled expression appeared ghastly. "I . . . suppose so."

"Did you know that Teddy here was married to Paige?"

Alicia's eyes fell to her finger of scotch. "Yes, of course I did. Teddy told me."

"*When* did Teddy tell you? Before you came up here? After?"

Paige gripped Jon's forearm, mouthed the word 'stop.'

Alicia shrugged and said, "I think the important thing is that we all managed to get away, tonight especially."

"Why? Because of Halloween?" asked Jon.

"Because of Paige's father," Teddy said in a steely, final-sounding tone.

Jon felt his brow furrowing.

"This is the anniversary of his passing."

The fact that it was Paige who provided this information refreshed Jon's overall annoyance. The fact that he was ignorant of today's underlying significance to Paige made him feel wilted.

Alicia reached over and began to rub her paramour's back. Teddy's eyes were fixed on Jon. Shadows obscured the nature of his gaze, but Jon could sense that it was withering.

"I'm sorry, I didn't realize." Jon was overcome with regret the instant he uttered the apology. Why should he offer comfort to this man who should by all rights be a relic in his lover's past? But Teddy was no memory, no skeleton in Paige's closet. He was here, right alongside them, shadowing their every moment together.

"I take it that you were close to your late and *former* father-in-law?" asked Jon.

"Teddy and I tended to him during his last year," Paige explained. "It was an awful time. Daddy was so sick, so frail. He required around-the-clock care."

Jon didn't care at all for the way Paige's expression changed while she recalled this ordeal, of which he had known nothing. Her face was a mask of admiration, respect.

"If he was so sick," Jon began, "his death must have been something of a blessing then, yes?"

"I'm sure it was no less painful." This time it was Alicia doing the judging.

Jon had to resist the urge to let out a primal scream.

"That's why Paige and I, together or separately, always try to get away every October 31st and go somewhere new."

"Somewhere we've never been."

This last phrase was uttered by Paige and Teddy in unison. Jon turned to her, saw the tears sparkling beneath her black lashes. Alicia reached across the table and handed Paige a napkin.

"I'll be in the room," Jon said plainly. His ascent of the stairs was noiseless. Once inside their room he found he was without energy. He flopped onto the bed and switched on the television, which was ludicrously large for a room of this size.

A news station was recapping its main stories. Jon gazed absentmindedly at this for a few minutes before deciding that discussions of the Dow Jones and fuel-tax hikes were much too vulgar. A changing of the channel flung him into a séance. The Classic Movie channel, like most stations, was marking the holiday with a horror marathon. This particular scene was unfamiliar to Jon, which did not surprise him as he'd never been much of a film buff. It was in black-and-white. A lone violin provided the reedy, spectral score. A foursome of well-to-do-looking adults was seated around a circular table. They appeared to be meeting in a seaside mansion. A lone white candle guttered in the foreground. The camera was positioned to give the viewer the impression that they too were part of this circle.

One of the women at the table began to groan. The camera spun to face her. ". . . *Laughing Lady, is that you?*" gasped one of the others at the table. "*Laughing Lady, come back. Join us in this circle, gathered here in your honor. In life, your powers condemned you to the bedlam. In death, you found freedom. Share your wisdom with us!*"

Cackling suddenly blasted from the speakers. Jon was surprised to feel the hair on his arms lifting. A howling wind extinguished the on-screen candle. Jon took up the remote and pressed the Information button:

HAUNT OF THE LAUGHING LADY / 1958 /
CAST: JAYNE VANCE, CYRIL DONNELLY. DIR: JACQUES PEPPET.

Jon had never so much as heard of the film or any of its talents. He switched off the set and reposed for a few moments in the unlit stillness.

His trance was broken when a pair of headlights brightened his window. He listened intently but heard no car moving down the lane. The lights dimmed then dissipated. Jon went to the pane and peered out. The moon was now masked by clouds, so only hints of the environment were visible: the skeletal trees, the vague lay of the path, his and Teddy's vehicles reposing side-by-side. Had Teddy's jeep also been a gift from Paige, Jon wondered?

"We need to talk."

He hadn't even noticed Paige entering the room, so her voice startled him. He had to squint just to pick up her reflection in the glass.

"I don't feel like talking."

He returned to the bed and lay down again. Paige continued to speak, even lecture, but Jon did not listen.

What he did listen to were Teddy's and Alicia's voices as they leaked through. The exact words were instantly interred in the dividing wall, but Jon could tell that their conversation was, if not heated, then certainly emotional. At one point he heard their door close, then heavy footsteps on the stairs. He strained to pick up any further sounds; the closing of the house's main door, the sound of Teddy's jeep engine, but the only noises were those of Paige readying herself for bed and, later, the faint rumble of her snore. Jon knew that for him sleep was far off, if not altogether impossible.

Another pair of lights suddenly brightened the window. Though these lights were somewhat murkier than the first, their hue was unusual—red-tinged, like two signal-lanterns glowing wanly by some rustic stretch of railway. Again, these lights arrived noiselessly, but this time they lingered.

Jon rose and moved to the glass.

The light radiated from two small orbs the size and hue of fresh embers. Jon watched them as they bobbed before the main floor window. The sensation that overcame him as he studied the orbs was something Jon could not identify. Though the lights dazzled him, he felt no joy. While their sheer strangeness frightened him, he would not have called this feeling horror.

The lights began to waver, brightening and fading in turn.

It was crucial that he see them, that he bask in their presence as intimately and for as long as possible. He mustn't let them vanish. Even the act of closing the door behind him felt like an interminable delay.

Jon took the stairs two at a time, but by the time his feet hit the foyer the glowing orbs were gone.

Disappointment weighted him like a millstone. He imagined himself as the figure in some Expressionist painting—all shadow and low-hanging head, stewing in his own ennui.

"Is she taking care of you?"

Jon spun around and saw that he was not the sole figure in this grim setting. Teddy was seated at the dining table. The bottle of scotch before him was visibly emptier than it had been at dinner. Judging by the slur of his speech, much of it had gone down Teddy's throat.

"Did you see them," Jon asked, "the lights?"

"I'm sure she is," Teddy continued. "Paige takes care of all her men. For a while. That's the way it goes . . . Paige's father took care of her, then we took care of him . . . That long final year . . . we took care . . . we just had to add a little bit in his food . . . just a touch . . . meal after meal after meal . . . even the coroner couldn't tell . . . Paige saw to everything . . . And then the windfall was all hers . . . she told me it'd be ours . . . but it was hers . . . or hers and yours now maybe. . . ."

"What are you saying?"

Teddy refilled his glass. The silence that hung between the two men was made even more tedious by the grandfather clock, whose ticking emphasized just how long the pause truly was.

"I don't like this place." Teddy's voice had now assumed the grating whine of the self-pitying drunk. "Don't like it at all . . . too close to last year's . . . we should have gone farther away . . . you should have gone farther, too. . . ."

The light returned. Or perhaps this was the emergence of a different light altogether, for its color and its intensity were different. No longer the scarlet orbs, this new light was bluish and painfully bright. It pressed in on the entire front of the house, brightening the foyer like some close, ferocious moon. Jon hurried to the living room's picture window.

Without, the entire property was awash in the livid shimmer. All shadow had been purged.

This queer new illumination made the figure that was moving down the lane plainly visible. It was human, or had once been, but its form was devious in shape and each shambling step it took toward the house looked painful. The figure's right arm swung wildly as it moved, yet its left seemed almost fossilized in place. The head was cocked at an impossible angle. Jon hoped that it was merely the wind pressing against the boards, for he could hear the unmistakable sound of moaning.

"What is it?" Teddy had moved up behind Jon and was squinting through the hanging sheers. ". . . Why. . . ." This was the only word Teddy managed before his breathing was reduced to a series of sharp, frantic gasps. He backed away from the window, moving into the dining room where he upset one of the high-backed chairs before crumpling down onto to the carpet. "*We didn't hide well enough . . . he's found us . . . he's found. . . .*"

Teddy's voice was muted. What silenced it was the presence that had miraculously managed to go from shambling down the winding lane to standing inside the foyer of the house.

Jon stood in the living room, staring at the apparition. It was the first time he'd ever doubted his mind and all his senses. For even though he was wholly present, his every sense engaged by what was now before him, his rational brain refused to accept it. Like a spoiled child, his reason ranted against the sight of this crooked guest.

The interior of the house had become stilled, as if the hands of time were being held in place by some greater force. Everything seemed to be stretching, crackling with the cold, stifling power of impossibility.

The figure was that of an old man. Jon's nostrils were impacted by a waxy stench of illness and unwashed skin.

For an instant Jon thought of bursting through the picture window and tearing down the lane. What prevented him from doing this was a genuine uncertainty that he would even find a world out there, at the lane's end.

The figure advanced to the staircase. It appeared to be using the banister to pull its frame up the steps. When it was halfway up, Jon discovered that the revenant was footless.

By now the bluish glow had faded, leaving the main floor in a terrible darkness. Paige's face flashed in Jon's mind, breaking his trance. He took a step forward and was instantly overwhelmed with vertigo. Swallowing back the bile in this throat, he staggered to the stairs.

Teddy was visible in his periphery, huddled like an animal under the dining room table, his large frame quaking, his sobs sounding like cat mewls.

Jon found himself no better equipped to scale the stairs than the specter had been. Even the idea of touching that banister repulsed him. Instead of using it, he crawled up the carpeted steps before frantically moving down the hall. He turned the handle to their room, tumbled inside, and immediately shut and locked the door.

"*Paige!*" he hissed, again and again. Her snoring was louder now. Not even his violent shaking of her body managed to rouse Paige from sleep.

The walls here were so very thin, every sound seeped through from the opposite room. Jon sat on the floor beside the bed. He listened helplessly, or, if he was being honest, feebly, to every awful noise that stabbed at his psyche; the thuds, the feminine screams muted by . . . what? A pillow? A foul hand? There was low grunting and creaking springs. The headboard thumped against the wall again and again, in a rhythm that should only ever be made by lovers. One of the room's hanging pictures was knocked from its hook.

When Jon heard Alicia struggling to call out Teddy's name, he dragged himself into the bathroom and shut the door. Not daring to switch on the light, or even to breathe too loudly, he crawled into the tub that was still damp from Paige's luxurious bath.

Jon shifted, his limbs aching. Though he was sure he hadn't slept, he was groggy nonetheless. He sat up in the tub and, against his better judgment, he strained to listen.

There were noises in the house, but not the kind he was expecting. Through the floor he could hear the chink of dishes and women's voices. He recognized Paige's laugh.

He climbed out of the tub and, with held breath, pulled back the door. Clear autumnal sunlight filled the bedroom. His and Paige's suitcases were sitting atop the made bed.

Stepping into the upper hall, Jon had no trouble avoiding the closed door to Teddy's and Alicia's room. He descended the stairs, keeping his hands in his pockets.

Paige was the only guest in the dining room. When she saw Jon in the foyer, her only greeting was a lift of her eyebrows. She bit into a pastry, then reached for her coffee cup.

The hutch by the mirrored wall was heaped with a variety of cakes and pastries. The silver coffee urn needed polishing.

Imogene entered through the swinging kitchen door. Her outfit was in such contrast to yesterday's attire that it took Jon a moment to identify her.

"Good morning," she said. She was dressed in slacks and an oversized cable-knit sweater that was the color of yellow sugar. Imogene placed another tray of delicacies on the serving table.

Jon pulled out a chair and sat down.

"Imogene was telling me that she's thinking of only staying open for the summer from now on," Paige said.

"I'm considering it," said Imogene. "It would be nice to just let people see the place in full-bloom. I might close it up once the leaves begin to turn." She was not wearing any makeup.

The sound of movement drew Jon's eyes from his hostess to the foyer. Teddy was patiently leading Alicia down the stairs, whispering lovingly to her the entire time. When Jon saw Alicia's appearance, last night's potent vertigo once again pressed through him. Her flesh was as bloodless as the revenant's. Jon couldn't help but wonder if she was now somehow infected, if she shared in whatever affliction kept creatures like that in their half-life. Her manner was catatonic.

The couple exited the house without a word. Through the picture window Jon watched their jeep driving down the sunlit lane.

Imogene went back into the kitchen, at which time Paige expressed how disappointed she would be if the bed-and-breakfast wasn't open next fall. She said this could be the beginning of a new Halloween tradition for the two of them.

Jon was unsure which two she meant. He stared at his reflection in the mirrored wall, whose gold veins marred his face like cracks in a fragile mask. This image bored into him, caused his hands to tremble. Halloween's masquerade was now over and fate, it seemed, was forcing him out of his cherished disguise. The last twenty-four hours, with all their ugly spite, antagonism, and above all cowardice, raced through Jon's mind. Everything was coming undone. His precious mask was slipping. Jon lowered his head, partly in shame and partly to avoid looking at the marbled glass. He knew it was only a question of time before he'd have to look upon the long-hidden face of his true self.

BONE FIRE

Storm Constantine

Storm Constantine is the creator of the Wraeththu Mythos, the first trilogy of which was published in the 1980s. She has written more than thirty books, including full-length novels (such as *Hermetech* and *Burying the Shadow*), novellas, short story collections, and nonfiction titles.

Her latest book is the Wraeththu story collection *A Raven Bound with Lilies*, and she has recently edited two anthologies—*The Darkest Midnight in December*, supernatural tales connected with Yuletide, and *Songs to Earth and Sky*, an anthology of seasonal stories. She is also the founder of the independent publishing house Immanion Press.

"For this tale I delved into the origins of various Halloween customs," reveals the author, "the traditions that were allegedly taken over to America by Irish settlers. I incorporated some of this fascinating folklore into my story.

"Two ideas particularly intrigued me: children being dressed up as ghosts and imps to confuse malevolent spirits and demons, who would mistake them for their own kind and leave them be, and that the term 'bonfire' is derived from 'bone fire'—the rest of the story grew from these two ideas.

"Jenna's chant to Hekkate is adapted from a quote by George Carlin: 'There are nights when the wolves are silent and only the moon howls.'"

WHEN THE SUN threatens to die at the end of the year, it's up to us to keep it alive during the long dark. When it's weak, the rule of light weakens too, and the dark may slip through a veil we cannot see. Here, far away from the world of the blind, we do what we must. We make our own light.

Our village, Door's Dale, lies in a hollow, surrounded on two sides by ancient forest. A road pours down from Heron's Cop, to the east, and wanders through the village to the setting sun and the slow rise of Acre's Hill, in the west. At Hallow's Eve, in the fields, where once the wheat and barley blew, we raise the bone fire. Its flames mimic the sun in summer, and through our intent, keeps the solar eye alive throughout the long darkness. You wonder what we burn upon the fire? Must be bones, mustn't it? Do you want to hear?

Summer had been good that year; the Kindly Ones had turned smiles to us rather than blades: they who live in the trees, in the clear cold brooks, and beneath the fields. We knew, however, that winter would be harsh, for in August the fields had been hidden often by thick fog, and the geese and ducks had left early, heading south. Woodpeckers had been spied, in their green and red coats, sharing a tree—always a sign. Among the hedgerows, I'd noticed spiders had spun their webs larger than usual, and the house-walker kind was heading indoors in crowds, to scuttle about in the evenings and be eaten by cats. So, as a precaution, the bone fire would be bigger than usual too this year.

Jenna Harne was my friend. We were fourteen years old, tugging at the leash of childhood, knowing it must eventually snap; if we tugged hard enough perhaps that would be soon. We loved Hallow's Eve, but who didn't? It was a time for games and celebration, feasting and dancing and dressing up. I would guise as a Kindly Woman that year, with a face of green and a robe of leaves, with bees in my hair, albeit made of wire and sheep's wool rather than real ones. Jenna's costume was that of a demoness, of red and black rags with a crown of late roses she'd dyed almost to soot by standing them in ink. Her face was painted red, with gouts of black around the eyes and mouth. She looked wickedly lovely.

In the early evening, we'd walk the lanes between the farms, each carrying a basket and a lantern. At the crossroads we passed over, we would place an apple and a gobbet of raw meat for She of the Four Faces, but when we came to a house or farm where a turnip lamp was lit upon the step, we'd knock at the door and ask for gifts for Those Unseen. At the end of our journey, we'd eat what we'd been given—small sweetmeats—and say, "This for you, dear ghost, enjoy its taste through me." If we carry out this task every year, then the ghosts and demons themselves do not have to, and it's safer for everyone. We dress up to fool the real spirits, for they are partial to children, especially at Hallow's Eve, for then the Kindly Ones and their friends from beyond the veil are full of tricks and mischief, as we are. If we wear a guise, they take us for one of their own and pass us by.

Jenna and I set out as usual, with apples and wrapped meat in our baskets and our lanterns on sticks. I wore a cloak of green, and Jenna one of crimson. We sang songs to warn people of our approach. As younger children, we'd loved this part of the event the most, but now, with that leash tethering us to innocence wearing thin, we were eager to return to the village for the main celebration. On this night, we'd be allowed to drink cider. Jenna wanted to flirt with boys and show how well she could dance. At the end of the evening, she'd allow someone to kiss her. I hadn't quite caught up in that respect and was looking forward to the feast more than anything, and being able to pretend I was an adult, but in a different way. I'd walk around as if I had property and animals, my head held high, my gown trailing in the grass.

At the first crossroads, we placed our offerings at the stone cross—me the apple, Jenna the meat—and Jenna chanted:

"Hekkate, Hekkate, bring me tonight
sweet love in the light of the bone-fire,
when your dogs hold their tongues
and only the moon may howl."

I rolled my eyes and sighed. Even I knew Hekkate was not a goddess interested in love, since she was the four faces of the moon, from light to dark, and was friendly with Death. "Maybe she'll give you a corpse to love," I said.

"Don't be stupid, Emlie," Jenna snapped. "I want one of her sons, for she lends them sometimes and puts them in the body of a boy. Tonight, I want something better than a sweaty, snotty barn-boy."

"Idiot," I said, and we linked arms and walked away.

We called at six farms and, after the seventh, intended to return to Door's Dale. Earlier, we'd passed many other guiser groups on their rounds of the farms, but now, on our way to Kettle Farm, the lanes felt empty and desolate. A snowy owl swept across our path and Jenna said, "There's winter's sentinel." Anything could be keeping pace with us behind the high hedges on either side of the lane. We shivered and hugged each other, laughing in delicious fear.

A lamp burned upon the porch step of Kettle Farm, but when we knocked the door there was no answer. Jenna put her hands in a funnel against the kitchen window and peered through. "No one here," she said.

"Maybe they've gone to the feast already," I said.

"Perhaps, although there are two pies on the table. They wouldn't forget those."

"Maybe they're for later. Shall we go?" I was beginning to feel more than mildly frightened. The night felt so still, watchful, and we were alone out here. Would our guises hold? I adjusted my crown of bees.

Jenna picked up her basket and lamp, but before we could go back down the track, someone came around the side of the house. We both shrieked and jumped, then began to laugh. It was a boy, probably a son of the house, dressed in a costume of black, with the white bones of a skeleton painted over it. He was tall and had long black hair that was grayed with ash. His face was painted white like a skull. He might be beautiful or hideous, it was impossible to tell, but struck me as graceful. He bowed to us extravagantly and said, "Ladies!"

"This house has no gift for us?" Jenna said archly. "Would you scorn a Kindly Lady and her friend from Hell?"

"My bones can't hold a gift," said the boy.

"What about those pies in there?" Jenna insisted.

"You must know I can't go in and steal those without being invited."

"Oh well . . ." Jenna's banter faltered. "Let's go, Emlie."

I felt that boy standing there behind us all the while we walked down the farm driveway. I didn't think he was a son of Kettle Farm, but more likely a guiser, like us. They had a lot of boys there, true, but he'd felt different somehow.

"What a fool," Jenna grumbled, once we'd reached the lane.

"Could have been Hekkate's son," I said.

"Her sons aren't idiots."

For a moment, I wondered why she was so grumpy, but then she began to sing, and I joined in, and the spirits kept their distance.

We reached the field just as the bone fire was being lit. It was built of branches and unwanted lumber, but there were bones in its heart—those of the first lambs eaten in the spring and kept for this time, as well as the flayed bones of beloved old dogs who had died, because the dog was Hekkate's sacred animal. Fiddlers were playing and capering about, and the air smelled of burned sugar, apples, and turned soil. Torches on tall poles blazed wildly, providing the traditional hellish light. A large crowd had gathered, people from the village and all the outlying farms. Jack of the Lantern had been brought from the church, where he was kept all year in a box under the floor stones, and was being paraded around by Farmer Docken, he who owns the most land in our parish. The lantern was an ancient human skull, in which a candle burned; the sun caught in bone. Jack grinned at the fire, his eyes alight with the writhe of captured flame. He was, for that night, lord of the land, our lord, who protected us. The priest had come to join us, as he always did, although he'd left his saints at home.

Jenna and I joined a group of our friends, and began to dance and sing. Jenna indulged herself in some mild but apparently unsatisfactory flirting. "They're all so dull," she confided to me. Hekkate's son was yet to materialize.

Then I nudged her arm. "Look, the skeleton."

On the other side of the fire, close to the trees of Tedder's Wood, stood the tall boy we'd met at Kettle Farm. He was drinking from a cup and appeared to be eyeing up the revelers. "I think he's a stranger," Jenna said. "What's he doing here?"

"Perhaps the answer to your prayer," I said.

"Let up on that!" Jenna snapped. "He must be a relative of the Kettles. Hekkate's son would be different."

"Can't we just pretend he is?"

Jenna sighed. "Don't be silly. Come on." She took my arm and we went over to him.

"Hello," Jenna said boldly. "Are you with the Kettles? We met you at their farm earlier."

"Yes, I'm from that farm," said the boy, somewhat unconvincingly, I thought.

Close up, you could see his wide dark eyes and the fine shape of his lips, even though they were caked in white paint. He smelled like burning, like a hearth fire in winter. Once again, he bowed to us, "Lady of Hell, will you walk with me around the fire?"

Jenna took his arm. "All right."

I was about to protest, "What about me?" then realized the folly of it. The time had come to let Jenna make her own entertainment. Somewhat downhearted, I began to walk back to our friends, but then another boy stepped into my path. It was the night for it, of course. He didn't smell of burning, nor was he very tall, but his eyes were pale without being blue, and his teeth when he smiled looked sharp. "Why aren't you in costume?" I said.

"I am," he replied. "I'm a spirit of the hedgerows."

"I see." I noticed then, as if it had just appeared, he wore a wreath of berries and twigs on his head. But he felt comfortable to me, as if I'd known him as a kind friend for a while.

"What's your name?" he asked me.

I told him.

He offered me a berry sprig, and his arm, which I took hold of, and suddenly Jenna was forgotten. Skipping along beside this unexpected prince of the night, I rejoined the party, and danced till my shoes were blood, as the saying goes.

Eventually, the flames burned lower and people were yawning. Only the stalwart few were left to dance and sing till dawn. And dawn is a long way away at Hallow's Eve. I'd drunk enough cider to be tipsy and was wondering if I wanted to kiss my prince or not. He was certainly handsome, a little older than me, and my friends were all clearly fascinated by him. His name, he'd told us, was Tom, and he was the son of a traveling woman, who was visiting several parties that night and would eventually come to fetch him. He had his arm about my shoulder now. I'd lost my crown somewhere and my hair hung loose. I felt beautiful and grown up, and didn't want this magical night to end.

Jenna's mother came up to me. She was wearing her cloak, as if she was about to go home, and I saw that Jenna's red cloak hung over her arm. "Where is the little strumpet?" Jenna's mother asked, but not angrily. "I found this dropped on the ground near the woods, and it's all muddy. You know where she's gone off to and who with?"

I said I really didn't know, but imagined she was somewhere with her bony boy, perhaps being initiated into mysteries of life I didn't yet care for.

"Well, I can't just leave her out here and let her come home alone, at the Kindlies know what hour," said the mother. "Help me find her, children."

So we split up into pairs to search the fields and the nearby woods. I hoped I wouldn't be the one to find her and her boy. I didn't want to see what they were doing.

Tom came with me and asked me what was going on. I told him what had happened at the farm and by the fire. "He said he's with the Kettles," I said.

"Then you should have told her mother."

I spluttered a laugh. "No! I couldn't!"

Tom stopped me, put his hands upon my arms. "Remember what night it is."

"What do take me for? I know it's a night of spirits. But I also know that boy wasn't Hekkate's son."

Tom blinked. "What?"

I told him the rest, Jenna's prayer.

"She asked for that?" he said.

"Yes. Why?"

"You should be careful what you ask for on Hallow's Eve. You know why you wear the costumes. People you meet in the smoke might not be who they say they are, and they can hear the words inside you."

The atmosphere between us had dampened, and I felt I'd offended Tom in some way, and now he saw me as silly and frivolous.

"She's only larking about," I said, peevishly. "He wasn't a spirit, or a goddess's son. Simply a boy visiting the Kettles. It's just a party."

Tom's voice was sour and cold. "Which is, of course, why your priest leaves his collar on the altar this night, and Jack surveys the land."

"Tom, don't be like this. We were having fun."

He paused, looked at me for some moments, then smiled. "Of course. Shall I kiss you now?"

"I suppose so."

It was the kind of kiss you remember for the rest of your life, so you can tell of it in detail to your great grandchildren. Perhaps the memory has grown better than the reality, but to a young girl that night, in the dying smokes of a Hallow's Eve bone fire, and the scents of the land strong in witcheries, it was the kiss of a king of Faery.

When he had done with enchanting me, Tom held my face in his hands and said, "What do you want for the future, Emlie? Make a wish."

"I will, but surely I mustn't speak it."

"You can tell me."

So I told him my heart's desire, for my own land, and a long, low house, and a high-stepping mare, and three black-haired daughters who looked like witches.

"It's yours," he said, and kissed me again. "Now, I must go, because my mother is calling."

"I can't hear anything."

"Sometimes calls are from the heart, not the mouth," he said.

Then he ran away and left me alone among the trees. I wasn't very pleased about that, but found my way back all right. No one had found Jenna, though.

By this time, her family were panicking and there was talk of kidnapping and murder. I had to tell them what had happened at Kettle Farm and that we'd seen the boy by the fire. My mother slapped my head for not mentioning it earlier. The Kettles were approached and—to no one's surprise—didn't know who the bone boy was. All their relatives were accounted for.

We searched all night and found nothing, but in the wan, mist-haunted morning, the Docken twins found Jenna by Bride's Mere. She was wandering as if blind, her hair like a thatch and her costume torn to tatters. She was muttering a weird song, and didn't seem aware of other people around her. Rob and Lily Docken brought her to her family. The priest was called from wading in the nearest pond, where he and other men had been dredging. He put his hands on Jenna's head and said she'd been assailed, although, when she was later examined by the women, there were no marks to be seen upon her. She didn't seem frightened or hurt, only dreaming. Her song, when we could understand it, was a song of love.

As for the bone boy, he'd vanished, having no doubt had his fun, though why Jenna's mind had gone away with him, I've no idea.

In the copse beside the mere, Amy Proudtoe found a pile of human bones—old, brown ones, as if unearthed from a grave—with a skull on top, laughing as skulls always must. We knew then that that had been his costume. The priest confirmed it. Jenna had dressed too well. Her disguise hadn't failed, it had succeeded, or so people said. The bony boy had taken her for one of his own. If he hadn't, they'd have found *her* bones, her cold flesh, not his discarded costume.

The women carried the old brown bones to the embers of our Hallow's Eve fire and found its dying yet still-beating, blistering heart. Here, they placed the demon's guise, and the priest said a few words he'd never speak on a Sunday in his pulpit.

"Hide your children well, in costumes of ghosts and witches. Or a denizen of Hell might come to them, dressed in human skin and bones to make a human guise."

He kept Jenna's mind, that boy. It never came back and neither did he.

As for me, Tom had known who and what I was, and that I'd never made a prayer at the crossroads, at least out loud. His mother had heard my heart, not Jenna's demand, perhaps, and had preferred my desires to hers.

Even to this day, I leave offerings to She of the Four Faces at the crossroads, and I work always in her name, doing her business. But she never sent him back to me, even when I earned my land and house, and bought my high-stepping mare, and gave birth to the first of my black-haired daughters who look like witches.

Jenna had a child too, nine months from that Hallow's Eve. It looked healthy and normal enough, but it only lived a day.

QUEEN OF THE HUNT

ADRIAN COLE

Adrian Cole's first published work was a ghost story for IPC magazines in 1972, followed soon after by The Dream Lords trilogy of sword and planet novels from Zebra Books. Since then he has gone on to have more than two dozen books published, including the Omaran Saga and Star Requiem fantasy quartets, and the young adult novels *Moorstones* and *The Sleep of Giants*. His most recent novel is *The Shadow Academy* from Canada's Edge Science Fiction and Fantasy Publishing.

His collection *Nick Nightmare Investigates*, which featured a number of stories about the eponymous hard-boiled occult private eye battling the minions of H. P. Lovecraft's Cthulhu Mythos, won the British Fantasy Award, while more recent collections include *Tough Guys* and *Elak King of Atlantis*, the latter continuing the exploits of Henry Kuttner's sword and sorcery hero.

"I've always been fascinated by Hecate," explains Cole, "since I first discovered her as a teenager (in *Macbeth*, not in reality). This 'close contriver of all harms' is well-established across Europe, and as a focal point for my story is clearly intent on living up to her reputation.

"I'm equally inspired by all things elemental—probably attributable to my country background (rural Devonshire in England)—and my fiction often reflects its living landscape's relationship with the inner world of its inhabitants. Who could fail to be moved by Dartmoor, the sea or the deep forests, and the powers inherent in them? They will always be here as metaphors—or perhaps something even more tangible?"

LATE OCTOBER. TOO cold, as if November had arrived early.

Craig's back was visible through the stand of trees, his head bowed in characteristic manner, his hands shoved deep into his pockets. Several uniformed policemen stood around, motionless, waiting for further instructions from him. Otherwise the copse was silent, an odd moment frozen in time.

Coming toward them, Phillips gripped the leash of his German Shepherd tighter, the big dog straining forward as it led the way across the open field. Initially it had shied away from this place, and although its hackles were up, it had changed tack, eager to get into the dell. The smell of blood came unmistakably on the stiff breeze. To the dog it would have been potent.

Craig turned, fixing the dog and its handler with a sour look. "Sorry to drag you out," he said. He wasn't, of course. "But I think you can help with this one." His bulk—he was tall and broad—momentarily blotted out the scene beyond him.

Phillips had been told it wasn't pretty. The dog pulled its lips back in a feral snarl, not at Craig, but at what was beyond. It was properly spooked, inquisitive, but highly nervous. Phillips tugged the chain hard and brought the dog to heel. It took all his strength. He glanced beyond Craig into the dip. There were a lot of leaves, churned up and scattered as though a storm had blustered its way through here. The air was calm within the trees, though the breeze wasn't enough to remove the smell of blood and opened flesh.

"Christ," said Phillips when he saw the body. It was lying at an awkward angle as if it had been dropped from a great height, arms and legs twisted under it. The clothes had been ripped from it in places, the exposed flesh blotched with mud. Where the head joined the shoulders there was an open wound, the blood glistening as it coagulated. There was so much of it, clotting the leaves. The throat had been torn out and half the face was missing, as if someone had pulled it off clumsily, removing a mask.

Craig sucked in air through his teeth and exhaled. "Been here a day or two. I'm thinking this isn't the work of a person. Not even a madman. Any thoughts?"

Again Phillips had to restrain the dog. It wanted to sniff at the corpse, but at the same time its nervousness—no, *fear*, the handler realized—held it back. He tried to soothe it. Phillips felt its thick hide trembling. Something weird was going on here.

"He's been savaged, sir," he said, bending down to look more closely, in spite of his revulsion.

"I reckon a dog, or dogs," said Craig. "You'd know more about these things than me."

Phillips nodded, studying the body and several places where the flesh had been torn and peeled away. "I was down in Cornwall a while back, when they had the last lot of sightings of the so-called Beast."

"Wasn't that a big cat?"

Phillips shook his head. "No, sir, not by my reckoning. Everyone thought so and it suited the media to play up to the big cat story."

"What did you think?"

"Dog. I've seen enough sheep-worrying incidents and what dogs can do. A cat has teeth like needles, even the bigger ones. The teeth used on those sheep were canine. People may have seen big cats lurking about the fields—may even be some throwbacks to the old zoos from years ago. I'm sure they're around. But all the dead animals I saw were killed by dogs."

Craig studied the mangled body. "So I was right. This was a dog?"

"Maybe a pack of them."

Craig frowned. "A pack? You mean, wild? Domestic dogs don't usually hunt in packs, do they?"

Phillips stood up. He'd been told Craig was astute. For a Detective Inspector, he had the brains to move up in the system, but the word was he was a bit of a loner and liked his own way of doing things. Didn't always fit in with the bosses. "You're right, sir. Dogs can be organized in packs—like in a fox hunt. I guess you know it still goes on around these parts, never mind the ban."

Craig grunted. It was both an acknowledgement and a sound of disapproval.

"Foxhounds didn't do this. If you had a wild pack of dogs loose," Phillips added, "you'd know it. Is this an isolated incident, sir?"

"As far as I know. No one else has been attacked, never mind killed. I'll find out about the sheep. The local farmers will provide us with that."

"You might find, sir, that if any of them have shot any dogs lately, they might not want to own up to it. Probably buried the evidence. It's how things work."

Craig made no comment. "Okay. Can you see if your dog can pick up a trail? If this is a dog, or dogs, we ought to be able to track them down."

"Right. Mind you, we never did nail the sheep-killer on Bodmin Moor. There's so much terrain. Same around here. A lot of forest. Wild dogs will go to ground."

Craig looked at him for a moment as if he'd rebuke him. "Well, see what you can do, eh?"

By the end of the day, the body had been removed, and Craig met up with Phillips at the edge of a field, where it dipped down into a fast-flowing stream.

"We tracked something to this stream," said Phillips. The big Alsatian sat beside him, tongue lolling, the dog apparently relaxed.

"You think it went into it?"

"Can't find any tracks either upstream or down. We went a good mile or more in both directions. There's a farm one way and a road the other. Whatever came here used the water to cover its tracks."

"How about the other side?"

"Same, sir. Nothing."

Craig scowled. "So we have a pack of dogs, possibly one dog, and they went into the stream and—what? Disappeared?"

"If the dogs had a handler, they could have gone down to the road, to wait."

"And a van? Bundled the dogs in and drove away?"

"Seems a bit far-fetched, sir."

Craig sucked in a breath. "If it's a stray, or a pack, someone will be aware."

"Do you know who the dead man is, sir?"

Craig nodded. "Yes, he's a local guy. Owns a small company, making saddles and gear for horses. Riding is popular hereabouts. Roger Poulter-Evans. Fifty-five. Married, two kids, both working in London."

"Does the wife know?"

Craig grunted. "No. I have the dubious pleasure of telling her." He looked at his watch. "God knows what I'm supposed to say."

"What was he doing out here, sir? It's a bit off the beaten track. Did he have his own dog? Taking it for a walk?"

"Would you say he was attacked and killed in that wood? Or was he taken there and dumped?"

"It was done there. Too much mess for anyone to have disguised it. And Rex would have found traces of anyone else, if people were involved in the wood."

"Okay. Thanks for coming over. I may need to contact you later. I'll have my sergeant correlate any dog attacks. Let me know if you hear of anything."

Mrs. Poulter-Evans was a slender woman whom Craig took to be about fifty. Her dress was expensive but plain, her home immaculate, and he imagined it being vacuumed and dusted several times a week. It was bright, everything meticulously set out, permanently ready for any visitor. The air smelled clean, the lounge suite was comfortable, cushions plumped, fresh flowers from an equally immaculate garden on display. A few pieces of sculpture, some modern, some older, like the oddly pot-bellied figurine in a glass case. *Earth Mother, or something*, Craig surmised.

None of this sanitized organization made it any easier to impart his news. He'd been ushered politely into the living room, along with the young policewoman, Anders, for whom this was going to be a new experience, and almost as harrowing as it would be for Mrs. Poulter-Evans he imagined. Their hostess sat opposite them, made smaller by the armchair, her white, frail hands gently clasped in her lap. She avoided looking Craig in the eye.

"I'm afraid it's very bad news, ma'am," he said. He was just going to have to be direct. "There's been an accident." He glanced at Anders. He'd told her how he wanted to play this.

Mrs. Poulter-Evans shuddered, raising a hand to her mouth. "It's Roger, isn't it?"

"Yes. I'm afraid he's been killed." What the hell else was he supposed to say?

She held her hand tightly to her face, tears squeezing from her eyes. She shook her head. "How? How could it have happened?"

"It was a dog, or dogs. Do you have a dog of your own?"

She shook her head, frowning. "Roger hated dogs. I would have liked one, but he wouldn't hear of it." There was a brief flash of anger in her eyes.

"No. Well, he was crossing a nearby field, near a wood, walking. Do you know why he was doing that? Recreation, perhaps?"

"Yes, he did like to walk, to clear his mind."

"When did you last see him?" Craig made a brief gesture to Anders and she went into the kitchen.

The dead man's wife seemed to be struggling to pull the memory from her mind. "Two days ago. Thursday. Yes, he went out that evening."

"And you haven't seen him since?" Craig spoke flatly, his personal views concealed.

"Well, no, I—I'm used to him going off. I just assumed he'd come back and gone out to see friends, or to see work colleagues. He does that sometimes, works late. Or spends time away. He's—was—on the Council, you know. I went out as well, to see some friends of my own. When I got back, Roger wasn't here."

"What about his car?"

"No, it's in the garage. But I thought someone had picked him up. I know it sounds strange—Inspector Craig, did you say?—but we aren't very close. We haven't been for a long time. Not since the children left. We tend to leave each other to our own devices." She looked distant, maybe scanning something in the past. "I thought he'd just come back when he'd finished whatever he'd gone out to do. In fact, when you rang the bell, I wondered if it was him. He's always misplacing his keys."

Anders came in with a tray of tea. "I thought you'd appreciate this."

Mrs. Poulter-Evans looked up at her in surprise. "Thank you, that's very kind." She poured a little milk into a cup and poured herself tea before the policewoman could do it for her. She stirred it for a long time.

"I'm going to have to ask you to come and identify him," said Craig. "Will you feel up to that tomorrow?"

"Of course."

"In the meantime, have you got anyone, family or friends, who can stay with you?"

"What?" she said, even more distantly. "Oh yes, yes, of course. I can ring them."

"I'll stay with you until they arrive," said Anders.

Mrs. Poulter-Evans nodded, sipping her tea.

Craig got up. "Again, I'm very sorry about this, ma'am. I'll see you tomorrow."

Anders escorted him to the door. "It's never easy," he said to her. "Keep an eye on her." He wasn't sure what else he could say, but she'd handle this better than he could, he supposed.

Craig felt himself dozing off. Back at home, late as usual, he'd hung up his jacket and slumped into the welcoming sofa. Maud had called out from the kitchen, and he'd responded with a grunt. For a moment he'd superimposed the Poulter-Evans couple over himself and his wife, their tired relationship, the quiet distance.

Craig opened his eyes and rubbed them. He'd need to question the woman further, so she'd need to be up to it. Did her husband have enemies? Rivals, maybe? If the dogs had been deliberately set on him, why?

And where the hell were the dogs now? Maybe he'd know more in the morning.

"You look exhausted, darling," said Maud, suddenly breaking into his thoughts.

She's still an attractive woman, he thought. It would be nice to get up and wrap himself around her, hugging her close. But, she wouldn't have approved. *When did she last let me do that?* He wondered. *A long time ago*. There was a barrier there now, and he didn't know how to remove it. He'd tried, but she wasn't prepared to let him. She liked things as they were.

"A difficult case. The media will be all over it soon."

She sat down opposite him. She never sat beside him on the sofa these days. "Shall I put the news channel on?"

"If you like. I need a shower."

"I'll warm up a pie and veg."

He left her to it. In the shower, under the piping hot stream, he saw again the ripped-up body of the dead man. For a moment the steam around him was a pink mist. Dogs. Big dogs. Someone would know about them. Heard them, if not seen.

When he returned downstairs, Maud was engrossed in the television. "My God," she said. "That's terrible. They say he was torn apart. It's monstrous."

"Yes, for once they're not exaggerating." *Impossible to keep these things quiet*. He saw the look of horror on her face. "No need for you to worry about it, though—"

"Roger Poulter-Evans. But I know his wife, Phoebe. Oh, not very well. We've only met a couple of times. More to say hello to."

"Fragile creature. Yes, I saw her earlier. I had to break the bad news."

"God, she must be devastated."

"In shock. What do you know about her—and her husband?"

"She hardly mentions him. Typical middle-class marriage, I suppose. I got the impression they live their own lives. Pretty well off. She seemed content with things. Not very demanding of life."

He didn't comment. Instead he moved to the kitchen, where the pie was simmering in the oven and vegetables were boiling in a couple of pans. He got a plate and helped himself.

"Roger Poulter-Evans was killed by dogs?" Maud said, watching him eat slowly. "That's weird. Dogs. How could that have happened?"

"It's a lonely spot, so I don't suppose anyone heard it."

"What were they—strays?"

"Either that, or someone let them loose. Someone who didn't much care for him."

"Deliberate? My God, wouldn't that be murder?"

"It's a possibility. But keep it to yourself." Craig knew she would. Whatever else, she'd always been loyal to him where his job was concerned. She had a quick brain and sometimes he was glad of her shared thoughts when he was puzzling something over.

"Why would anyone want to murder Phoebe's husband? He was just a local businessman. I doubt if he had any rivals. Oh, he was on the Council, but I can't see any of their squabbles escalating to something like this."

"How do you know her?"

"She's a friend of Mavis. I think we first met in Mavis's shop. You know, the bric-a-brac place she's opened in the Arcade."

Craig looked at the various pieces of colored stone and sculpture on display in an adjacent glass cabinet. There was a new one, a female figure that looked vaguely Roman. "Is that where you got that?"

Maud glanced across. "Minerva, yes. Or Sulis, if you prefer the British name of the goddess."

"Ah, the Roman city of Bath. Aquae Sulis. Mother goddess. Fertility and all that." There was a slightly caustic edge to his voice.

Maud seemed to ignore it. "Rebirth and regeneration. Rather a nice idea."

It was another cold, gray morning, with a threat of rain, or worse. Craig was at his desk at the station when Anders came in.

"How'd it go?" He'd assigned her to accompany Phoebe Poulter-Evans to identify her husband's body.

"So-so. She took it quite calmly, although the body's a mess. I think if anyone I knew ended up like that, I'd have thrown up."

"What do you make of the woman?"

"I think she's a bit out of it, sir. Probably the sedatives. She doesn't seem to have much idea about what's going on. She wasn't that close to her husband."

Craig grunted. "No, so I gather. Anyway, I'm off to interview one of the dead man's colleagues. Get hold of Phillips, will you. See what's he's found out about any local dogs."

He followed her out into an annex and reached for his overcoat. Something dark and musty hung next to it. He drew back. *What the hell?* It looked like a mangy pelt, maybe a bearskin. Unaccountably he felt his own skin crawling, as if he'd reached into a dark place and almost touched something revolting.

Anders saw his expression. "Sorry, sir. That's mine. It's part of my costume."

"Christ, you're going to *wear* that?"

"It needs cleaning. It's for Halloween. Friday." She looked at him as if to say, *everyone knows that.*

He'd forgotten. There'd be a Festival, and no doubt Maud would want to be involved. "Halloween. That's the last bloody thing we need." He grabbed his coat and left before she had a chance to call him a miserable old sod.

Terrance Moore took Craig into his living room, an expansive area with a dramatic view of the countryside that seemed to go on forever into the distance, fields broken by small stands of trees and low hedges.

"When did you last see Roger Poulter-Evans?" asked Craig, once they'd dispensed with the pleasantries.

Moore appeared relaxed, though tired. He was in his fifties and uncomfortably overweight, his shirt bulging, his face sagging, his eyes darkly rimmed. Craig imagined he lived well—too well—and he noticed the nicotine stains on the fingers of his right hand. Maybe the death of his friend had come as a shock. That or something else.

"Four days ago, at the factory," Moore replied.

"You didn't arrange to meet him, off the beaten track?"

Moore snorted. "You mean in that field? No. He liked to walk, burn up a bit of energy. He told me to do the same often enough, but I'm a slob, Inspector. I like my home comforts."

Craig went through the process of extracting information almost mechanically. He wasn't getting anywhere. Instinct implied Moore had nothing to do with his colleague's death. No motive suggested itself. The detective scribbled a few notes.

"How about enemies?" he said, watching for a reaction.

"Roger? He was pretty well liked. Those who didn't like him steered clear of him. Good God, you don't think his death was more than an accident? I thought it was a pack of dogs?"

"What about his wife?"

"Phoebe? What, as an enemy? No, she was comfortable. They may not have been a happy couple, but they lived life pretty much as they chose to."

"Yes, I got that impression. Is there anything about him I ought to know?" Craig looked directly at Moore, who appeared to be turning something over in his mind, something slightly unsavory.

"Well, it's nothing, really, inspector. Roger was having an affair. It was a minor thing, a passing fancy. Rita's a bit loose, to be honest. She's had a few flings since her old man died. Roger was just another. It wouldn't have lasted."

"Did Mrs. Poulter-Evans know about it?"

"Almost certainly. It wasn't the first time he'd played away. Nothing serious." He said it as though it was a normal part of working lives.

"How do you think she felt about it?"

Moore was starting to look uneasy. "Well, it's ironic, really. Roger told me he thought *she* was having an affair. I mean, he wasn't bothered. It kind of evened things out. You're probably wondering why they stayed together."

"Something like that."

"Convenience, especially given Phoebe's situation." He gave a little, odd laugh. "Wanted to keep things quiet, I daresay."

"Things?"

"Phoebe's partner was another woman. So Roger believed. He had no idea who she was. It could have been embarrassing."

Craig's expression never changed. He pictured Phoebe Poulter-Evans when he'd told her about her husband's brutal death. She'd been horrified, but she'd handled it remarkably coolly. Maybe it had been a mixture of shock and relief.

"I don't know who it was, Inspector," Moore was saying. "As I said, it was not something Phoebe wanted to advertise. Not in a small town like this."

Craig sat in the car and punched his cell's keypad, cursing as his fingers botched the numbers. Why did they always make these things too small?

"Anders? It's me. Anything on the dogs?"

"Phillips got back, sir. There've been no reports anywhere in the region about escaped dogs or related incidents. One of the farmers said there'd been sheep-worrying back in the summer, but it had to do with holidaymakers. They'd let their dog off its lead. Other than that, nothing."

"How about the farms? That one near the stream."

"Phillips went there, sir. They've got dogs, but they're not allowed to roam. Phillips saw them and said they weren't hostile. He didn't think they were likely to have attacked the victim. Seems as if our dogs were from away."

"Which brings us back to a possible van."

"I had that road checked, sir. It's a bit muddy, but no tire tracks of any significance."

"So where the hell did they go?"

"We're still searching the surrounding fields. Nothing yet."

"Okay, keep at it, will you?"

Craig checked his cell phone and saw he had a message waiting. It was from Hawkins, the pathologist. Craig rang him back.

"Hello, David." Hawkins's voice was flat, unexcitable. "Something rather odd has cropped up. I've started a preliminary postmortem on Poulter-Evans. Phillips was right. Dogs killed him. No other signs of attack. They would have been very large dogs, something like wolfhounds, so they'd stand out in an area like this."

"Unless they were brought here and removed in a van."

"Right. What baffles me, though, is what I found in the blood around the wounds. There's a lot of saliva mixed in with the blood. You'd expect that in this sort of killing. There's dog slaver, but also something else. Saliva, but I can't isolate it. It's mingled in, almost inseparable. I'm not sure what it is."

"Wouldn't you expect the victim's saliva in the throat area?"

"I don't mean the victim's."

Craig stared out at the fields. A small flock of crows argued noisily in a solitary tree. "Other saliva? What exactly does that mean?"

"I don't have the specialized equipment here to test the stuff. In fact, I've had to send it away for examination. There are experts who can make better-informed decisions than I can. Frankly, David, I'm baffled."

"Okay. Look, get back to me when you know more, okay?"

Craig switched off the phone and sat back. The more he thought about it, the more he felt this was no simple dog attack. *Saliva? Not dog saliva. What the hell did that mean?*

Phoebe poured the sparkling wine into four glasses on the draining board. Her hand shook slightly. She looked out of the kitchen window at the early evening shadows on the lawn. The shrubs on either side of it looked like distorted figures, about to move every time she took her eyes off them. She felt the soft touch on her waist and jumped.

"Sorry," said Clara, her lips close to Phoebe's neck. "You're a bit edgy. You okay?"

"The last couple of days have been a bit harrowing."

Clara slid her arm tighter and gave Phoebe a soft hug. "That bloody man from the local rag was a pain. Hoping to make a name for himself."

"I'll be fine. Let's take the wine through." She gently disentangled herself. The others knew about her and Clara, but it was too soon to be this public. Phoebe knew she was old-fashioned. The world was a different place these days, but even so, she wasn't ready to be so open. "I want to enjoy tonight."

"Good." Clara stood back and let Phoebe carry the tray carefully into the living room. Maud and Mavis were sitting on the sofa, chattering animatedly. Phoebe admired Maud's calmness—nothing ever seemed to faze her. Maybe it was something to do with being married to the taciturn, stoic detective, David. And Mavis always seemed to be in control of her life, even if she lived it breathlessly. *You couldn't get two more opposite people*, Phoebe thought, and yet they were in perfect sync.

"Lovely," said Maud, taking a glass. She was dressed smartly but not in a showy way, nothing out of place. For her age she was very attractive, a natural thing. Mavis on the other hand was about as showy as you got, with her amazing explosion of strawberry ginger hair, very Pre-Raphaelite, and her painted nails and crazy bling. She'd been a beauty when she was younger, and although she'd aged well, there was no disguising its signs. At times Phoebe found her a little too exuberant.

Phoebe finished delivering the wine and sat down with her own glass. She glanced at Clara. Like the others, she was in her early fifties. I got the best deal, Phoebe told herself. Clara is the one who thinks more of others than herself. Me, especially. She'd rather sit in the background and watch, or encourage.

"Here's to the Festival!" said Maud, raising her glass and the others chimed in, clinking their glasses.

"The vicar wanted to scrap the whole thing," said Mavis, screwing her face up with disapproval.

"Out of respect for Roger, I suppose," said Clara.

Phoebe put her glass down. "Roger never went to church. He wasn't a practicing Christian."

"Quite the reverse," said Clara and they all knew what she meant. If anyone else had said it, Phoebe might have been offended.

"The vicar," said Maud, with a mirthless smile, "can go and screw himself tonight. It's time to let the pagans loose!"

They all laughed, although Phoebe felt uneasy. As the newest member of the circle, she wasn't quite used to its independence, its assertiveness. She was determined to master it, though.

Maud appeared to have read her thoughts. "Roger doesn't control you any more, Phoebe. You'll get used to making your own choices."

Phoebe blanched. She knew what Maud meant.

"Enjoy tonight. Let your hair down. After that, it'll be a new start," said Maud.

"Yes, I tell myself that every Halloween," said Mavis. "A new year starts! Maybe a new romance!"

"Mavis, don't be ridiculous," said Maud, but she was laughing again. They all were.

The television was on, but Craig wasn't paying attention. He sat back in the armchair, contemplating having a stiff glass or two of whiskey. Earlier he thought Maud was going to insist he join her at the Halloween festivities. If she'd insisted, he'd have given in and gone with her to the center of the town, where there'd be the usual furor, but mercifully she hadn't pressed him. She'd known he was preoccupied and had left him to it.

He couldn't free his mind of Roger Poulter-Evans's killing. The twisted, bloodied body kept materializing before his eyes, a mangled version of Banquo's ghost. Frustration gnawed at him. So far they had nothing. His men had scoured the land, widening their net. The dogs responsible had not been traced, only to the stream. No spoor, no hint of the animals. Craig kept coming back to the idea of a van. Yet if it *was* murder—why? He'd talked to everyone he could think of locally who knew or worked with Poulter-Evans. He was generally either well liked or avoided. Craig had even spoken to the woman he was fooling around with. She was clearly distraught. There was no reason for her to have wanted him dead, and besides, she'd not have organized the setting on of the dogs.

He was about to get himself that whiskey when his cell beeped.

"Craig."

"Darling, it's me." Maud, sounding anxious. "I'm at Clara's. You know? Willowfield Close."

"Yes. Readying the troops for tonight's festivities. Everything okay?"

"Well, I don't know. We were getting ready to leave, when Clara said something about a dog howling. This afternoon. I know you've been hunting high and low—"

Craig cut her short. "Where was this?"

"There's a barn beyond the fields at the end of her garden. Almost derelict. Clara thought she heard a dog. I went outside with her just now and we heard it."

"You're sure?"

"Yes. Actually there could have been more than one. It's getting very windy."

"Listen, Maud, I don't want to spoil your evening, but for Christ's sake, don't leave the house. Not yet. I need to have this checked out. You and the other women, stay in the house. Lock yourselves in."

"David, that's a bit over the top, isn't it? We're about to dress up for the Festival."

"If it's the dog or dogs that killed Poulter-Evans, you must keep inside. Do it now. Lock yourselves in. I'll ring you when it's clear."

"What are you going to do?"

"I'll have the barn checked out."

"Not on your own. David, you mustn't—"

"Don't worry, I'll bring in as many of my people as I can. Just stay put. Right?"

"Well, okay. Ring me as soon as you can."

He rang off and checked his watch. 9:45 p.m. Anders was on duty until ten, when she'd be off to join the Halloween festivities herself. He remembered she had a boyfriend in the town, so she'd likely get away promptly. He rang her phone and she answered at once.

"Before you go, get the word around," he told her. "I want as many people as we've got out at Willowfield Close. There's an old barn at the back of the fields there. I'll be waiting. Have the men armed."

"Is it the dogs, sir?"

"I think so. Make it fast. Ring-fence the place." He'd have gone in to the station and issued the instructions himself, but he knew the young policewoman was dependable.

She rang off and Craig grabbed his coat. Outside the wind was cold, the atmosphere freshening. The threat of sleet or snow of earlier remained in the air. *That's all I need*, he thought, yanking the car door open and ducking inside. Moments later he was heading along the streets, night's shadows crowding in as if they, too, were eager to get on with the business.

Willowfield Close was no more than a couple of miles away, on the outskirts of the town. He knew the roads and took a turning that would bring him around the fields. He pulled up halfway down the lane and went to a gate. Standing on its bottom bar, he craned his neck and looked out into the gathering night. He could see the lights of the bungalows to his right. To his left, a hundred yards away, there were a few trees and the gray smudges of what could have been the barn. If he wanted to get closer, it would have to be on foot.

He waited impatiently for a few minutes, time dragging. The wind had dropped and he listened out for any sounds from the barn area, but the place was silent. Finally he clambered awkwardly over the gate, cursing his age, and dropped down into the thick grass. The field was overgrown, uncultivated for a long time, its vegetation almost waist high. Craig pushed through it, keeping low down. It was wet and clung to him, but he was glad of its cover.

Near the edge of the field, under the shelter of the trees along its border, he crouched down, again listening. The night was silent, the sky clear. The air was cold and his breath clouded in front of him. Where the hell was his support team? He looked back toward the road, but there was no sign of life. Beyond the gate the sky glowed faintly yellow with the lights of the town and there was a hum, traffic in the distance, but not yet coming this way.

Ahead of him, the grasses parted, startling him, but it was a cat, darker than the shadows. It saw him and, obviously used to people, approached to where he was squatting. He reached down and ruffled its fur. He could feel it purring. It fussed about him for a while, then wandered back the way it had come. Suddenly it froze, its relaxed attitude changing into one of defense. It rose up on all fours, its back arched, its tail bushing.

Craig couldn't see what had frightened it. It crouched down, teeth bared, and gave a strangled cry, a challenge to something beyond the hedge. Craig edged forward, but as he did so, the cat leapt up and spun around, racing away into the field, ears flattened to its head, body low. Whatever had terrified it was in or very near the barn. A dog?

There was still no sound of approaching vehicles. Craig moved to a break in the hedgerow. He could see a wall of the barn beyond. It was not as derelict as he'd thought, and was much larger.

He looked at his watch. It was gone 9:00 p.m. His support should be here by now.

He moved quietly through the gap and stood by the wall of the barn. The trees thickened further along the wall, a copse obscured by darkness. Somewhere beyond them he heard the sound of a horn. A hunting horn. It wouldn't be a fox hunt, but maybe the revelers were using it as part of their festivities, which would be well under way in the town by now.

The sound repeated itself. It was an odd, mournful note, and Craig felt himself stiffen. What had Maud said to him? She'd been enthusing about Halloween and its rituals, and he'd been listening with one ear. Something about a Wild Hunt. Among her daft curios and oddments relating to the past was a painting. Hecate, Queen of the Witches and leader of the Wild Hunt. It was a dramatic affair, vaguely Germanic, he thought, although he knew these traditions were often as much European as home grown. Personally he'd never been one for Wagner and the like.

As he listened for the horn again, he heard a less familiar sound beyond the trees. A rumbling, as though from underground. It was muffled by the surrounding foliage and then the barn itself. Horses? Yes, that was it. So the revelers were riding tonight. He heard the procession pass, voices and shouts mingling with the growing thunder of hooves. Abruptly it all stopped, muffled by the mass of the building next to him.

Moving quickly, Craig came to an open doorway in the wall, the wooden door long since rotted away. He'd brought a small flashlight and flicked it on. Inside, the barn appeared to be immense, a series of rooms, or stables.

Beyond one of the walls, he thought he heard soft movement, a twig snapping. A low growl. He flattened himself against the wall and dipped his flashlight beam. If there was a dog in here, it could be chained up. It was unlikely it would have remained here, especially if it had seen the cat.

He noticed an old stone stairway leading upwards and climbed it very slowly. On the floor above, he tested the wooden floor gingerly. If these floorboards were rotten, he could crash through them all too easily. There were gaps in them. He crawled along on his hands and knees and peered through, but below him was only darkness, like a thick, oily pit.

Something moved in it, and again he heard the low growl.

He felt his cell phone vibrate and he sat back, the dust swirling around him. He looked at the phone's screen. Text message. From Hawkins. Typically he'd been working late, his personal world centered on his lab and its mysteries.

> *Word back from the experts. That saliva-stuff. It deteriorated and dissolved. They managed a few tests first, but can't identify it. Except they think it's partly human. Not the victim's. Drop in tomorrow.*

Craig stared at the words, reading and re-reading them. *Partly human? What in hell did that mean?*

And where were those cars? He tried to call the station, but he couldn't get a signal. Below him there was another, very distinct growl, as though whatever was down there had heard him.

He crawled over to a gap in the boards and shone the flashlight downwards. Something snarled, shifting out of the light—a humped shape, its size indefinable. Craig tried to find it with the flashlight beam, but it had taken cover. He told himself it must be chained, otherwise it would have come up here after him.

I hope to God Maud and her pals haven't ignored my warning. As long as they stay indoors, they'll be okay. He decided to try and ring her. No reason to think he'd get a signal over this side of the barn, given his failure with the station, but he had to try. He pressed the shortcut key on his phone and waited.

Something in the nearby darkness chimed, the sound crystal clear. It made him start. He swung around, probing with the flashlight. The chiming repeated. *A cell phone.* There were several shapes against the far wall, thick, blurred shadow-forms. He eased forward, avoiding the worst of the floorboards, realizing some of them had rotted through.

The shapes resolved themselves into clothing. *Coats, five of them.* Below them, on a bench, five sets of clothes had been neatly folded, with five pairs of shoes under the bench below each set of garments. Craig shone the flashlight on them, examining them. Four of the coats were women's coats, in good condition. Christ, had these people changed into costumes for the Halloween Festival and left their clothes here?

He realized his cell phone was still trying to contact Maud. The chiming came from one of the coats. It was only now that he recognized it.

It was one of Maud's. The chiming came from inside it. Her phone. *Maud was here? After he'd warned her?*

He studied the other coats. The last of them made him draw back in shock. It was a heavy-duty police coat. The clothing on the bench beneath it was a policewoman's uniform. That could only be Anders. But surely she knew how dangerous this place would be?

Behind him he heard a low growl, from the far wall, where the stone stairs emerged. He swung around, face bathed in the chilling sweat of fear.

For a moment there was only a misshapen cloud of sheer darkness—it shuddered and there was a big dog standing at the top of the stairs, partially cloaked in writhing shadows. Big? No, it was huge. A hound. He directed the flashlight beam at it, revealing a distorted snout, sharp teeth gleaming, strings of saliva dripping. The thing was monstrous, its eyes fixed on him, unblinking and savage. There was something about those eyes, their color, their bizarre expression.

He had nowhere to run. The hound blocked his only retreat. It came forward, almost in slow motion, then crouched. He felt his throat drying up. If he tried to shout, nothing would come out. Christ, but it was so big! Like a small horse. Its breath hovered around it in a white steam and he heard the continuing growl deep in its throat. He wanted to look for something, anything, to use in his defense, but he couldn't take his eyes off that face. This thing had ripped open Roger Poulter-Evans's neck as if it had been wet paper.

Without warning, it leapt, its spring powerful. Sliding backwards, Craig felt himself strike the bench and he floundered among the clothes, both arms raised against the attack. The beast landed a few feet in front of him, and as it struck the floor there was a dull snapping sound, wood breaking apart. A cloud of dust billowed around the hound as the floorboards collapsed under its weight. Its rear end disappeared as its front paws clawed at the floor in front of it, trying to gain purchase. Several lengths of floorboard had sprung loose, the end of one jutting up in front of Craig.

He acted from instinct. No time to think. He bent down and tried to twist the board loose. Nails groaned, but the wooden plank remained stubbornly fixed. Its far end, where the collapse had taken place, was wormy and crumbling like a biscuit. As the hound frantically dragged itself up from the drop, Craig used both feet to kick his end of the floorboard, which had remained solid, unaffected by the rot. The ferocity of his desperate kick tore it loose and its far end rammed into the face of the hound, partially disintegrating in another cloud of dust. But it was enough to dislodge the grip of the beast. It snarled, tossing its head this way and that, flinging out a shower of spittle and blood.

Craig watched as it made one final effort to avoid being swallowed by the drop. Then it was gone. He heard it hit the ground below. Quickly, but very carefully, he stood up and made his way to the edge of the hole, keeping off any damaged boards. He pointed his flashlight downward. The inert form of the hound was lying there, twelve feet below.

He skirted the hole and made for the stairs, descending as quietly as he could. At ground level he paused, listening, his flashlight off for a moment. In the darkness he could barely discern the fallen shape of the hound. It seemed smaller now, still motionless. *Had he killed it? The chances were it was injured, dazed, but dead? Probably not.*

He had to get out of here, and fast. If that thing came to, there'd be no second chance. He was about to dash for the doorway, when other shapes moved in the deep shadows around the chamber.

My God, it's the women! They don't realize. He flicked on the flashlight and used its beam in a brief sweep. He was right—four figures were converging on the fallen hound. He was about to shout a warning, but something stopped him.

He gaped at them. They ignored him, their attentions fixed on the beast. It was four women and he saw Maud's face—and that of Anders—as they studied the hound. All of them were wearing some sort of shaggy coats, part of their paraphernalia for the Festival. Witches, or servants of Hecate, whatever it was Maud had told him earlier.

Maud crouched down and actually *touched* the hound. She lifted her head and gave a cry. An *animal* cry. And yet he recognized in it the sound of mourning. The fallen hound was dead.

Then all four women turned, looking directly at Craig. He dropped his flashlight in horror. They were partially obscured by the darkness, but he could see they'd dropped to all fours. Now they seemed somehow larger than they should have been.

He sprang for the door and out into the colder air. His sweat felt like ice on his face. He ran along the hedgerow to the opening into the field. Behind him he heard the baying of the pack, for that's what it had become, he knew for sure.

Desperately he ran on toward the gate, flinging himself over it, almost crashing to his knees as he landed. He got to the car and fumbled with the keys. He could hear the pursuit coming across the field, the sound like the pounding of hooves. Christ, how many of them were there?

Finally he got the door open and swung into the seat, slamming the door and jabbing the key into the starter, twisting it and yanking the gear stick. The engine revved obligingly and, as the first huge shapes swarmed over the gate, he accelerated away. Something thumped on the roof, although his velocity must have quickly flung it off. The hedgerows closed in as he buffeted his way down the confines of the lane. Nearer to town, the road widened and the hedges dropped lower. He was aware of something, a cloud of shapes, pouring along behind him. There was a din, a horn, and the beating of huge wings.

He glanced out of the side window and almost swerved off the road in terror. A huge figure had appeared, astride a beast that was impossible to define; an armored warrior, the face distorted with fury, a fiery resolve to bring the car to a shuddering halt. A woman's face, distorted with hellish fury. Craig had seen it before. In that painting of Maud's. Hecate, Queen of the Wild Hunt.

He crouched over the steering wheel and fixed his eyes on the road ahead, ignoring the frightful baying of the hounds, the shriek of a hundred wild voices, and the thundering of the hooves as whatever nightmare the darkness had spewed forth boiled after him. Miraculously, he reached the outskirts of town. Apart from a few parked cars, the streets were quiet, so his erratic, high-speed driving got him through. The lights brightened, and he knew he was finally outpacing the tide of horrors.

With a jolt, he realized he had dropped his cell phone as well as his flashlight. His home was a lot closer than the station, so he made for that. As he pulled in to the drive, he heard a distant baying, fading. *Maybe they'd been called off? What in the name of hell had they been?*

He crashed open his front door as he stumbled in, shutting it behind him and sliding two sets of bolts. As quickly as he could, he checked the back door and did a brief tour of the windows. They were all closed, of course they were. It was October. They weren't opened at this time of year. He switched on every light in the place and looked around for a weapon, his chest heaving. Finally he sat in an armchair, realizing his entire body was shaking.

The station—I must ring the station, he thought and got up. As he did so, his eyes were drawn by the small painting opposite him on the wall. The Wild Hunt, led by the towering figure of Hecate. Her face was now turned, her eyes looking directly at him. He staggered back as if he had been punched by a fist.

Must phone! Behind him, he heard the sound of footsteps. He gripped the back of the armchair for support.

Maud stood in the doorway. She had discarded her Festival coat and looked quite serene in her usual clothes, as though she'd never left the house.

"What are you?" he gasped.

She smiled. "Darling, what on earth do you mean? I'm your wife, what else?"

He'd bolted the front door. *How had she got in?* "Keep back," he said.

"Don't be ridiculous."

"I need to phone the station."

She shook her head. "No. Not now. Later this morning, when they find Phoebe's body."

How could she possibly be so calm?

"Another tragedy," she said. "Her husband's death was too much for her. So she committed suicide, out there in that deserted barn. They'll find her, hanging up, her neck broken."

"No—I saw what happened—"

"Don't be a fool, David. No one's going to believe that."

He opened his mouth to protest, but realized she was right. Supernatural hounds? The Wild Hunt? Hecate?

"Well, it's been a harrowing night. I'm going to bed." She turned away insouciantly, then back, saying, as an afterthought. "Are you coming?"

For a moment he was tempted, oh how he was tempted. He shook his head. "No. Tonight I'll sleep down here."

Outside, the wind gusted, a momentary howl of capitulation.

THE OCTOBER WIDOW

ANGELA SLATTER

Angela Slatter is the author of the urban fantasy trilogy *Vigil*, *Corpselight*, and *Restoration*, as well as eight short story collections, including *Sourdough and Other Stories*, *The Bitterwood Bible and Other Recountings*, *Winter Children and Other Chilling Tales*, and *A Feast of Sorrows: Stories*.

She has won a World Fantasy Award, a British Fantasy Award, a Ditmar Award, and six Aurealis Awards. A graduate of Clarion South and the Tin House Summer Writers Workshop, her work has been adapted for the screen, and translated into Japanese, Russian, Chinese, French, Spanish, and Bulgarian.

"I'd been thinking about how Halloween today is very different to Halloween of times past," recalls the author. "How the idea of 'soul cakes' is maintained in the echo of 'candy.' I was thinking sacrifices—who makes them, what they are worth, how much we take out of the world, and how little we put back.

"And I began to think of the cyclical nature of life, of how someone like the October Widow might be fighting to keep balance even though what she does could seem horrific to some."

MIRABEL MORGAN SUSPECTED herself hunted, though she'd caught no trace of whoever pursued her.

She was careful when she left the house, keeping a weather eye on the rearview mirror, but able to discern no particular vehicle standing out from those sharing the road with her. At night, she made sure to close the curtains well before darkness fell, when lights might pick her out as a target against the evening gloom. Yet no one appeared on the pavement or stoop, there were no raps at the door, no envelopes in the mailbox. No sign that she should flee. She watched the calendar tick over with inexorable certainty and, as the day paced closer, the grid of nerves inside her chest tightened like wires pulled by circus strongmen.

Tendrils of white had appeared at her temples regular as clockwork, and her face, though still handsome, had crow's feet radiating from the corners of her eyes, and lines formed parentheses from nose to mouth. The chin was less firm than it had been, but her cheekbones still soared high, kept her profile patrician. Her knuckles were swollen, like dough sewn with yeast and carelessly kneaded, furrows left embedded. They'd been aching since the temperatures had lowered, the same gnawing pain that afflicted her at this time. Made it harder to do things when she most needed to be agile if not sprightly. Every cycle she told herself that the next would be different, that she'd be better prepared. Yet each turning she did the bare minimum, ensuring the new abode was livable, then went off to enjoy her annual youth while it lasted.

In the garden, the leaves changed colors, swapped out their green for amber and yellow, ochre, and sepia. Those so inclined fell and were carried off on the biting breeze. The sky, perpetually iron-gray at this point, was occasionally lightened by white clouds, however more often darkened to thunderous black. The vegetables and flowers had died, turned dry and shriveled. She didn't plant fruit trees anymore for she moved so often, and hated to watch them wither prematurely as they inevitably synched with her eternal, truncated rhythm. The small town of Ashdown had served her well, and she in turn had served it, bringing all the boons attendant upon the October Widow's tenure. The secret tithes she took seemed, to her, rather insignificant. The tiny offerings that staved off the moment when a larger one had to be made.

Henry did as he usually did and went straight around the back of the house, to the little shed where Mrs. Morgan kept her hand mower. He was late, but he knew the older woman wouldn't mind. "As long as it's done by nightfall on Friday, Henry, I don't care what part of Friday you do it!" she'd said. But he liked to be reliable. He liked her to know that she could count on him. This morning his pickup had a punctured tire; it looked as though a knife had been stuck into the tread, but he couldn't for the life of him figure out who want to do him an ill-turn. He'd taken his brother's battered VW instead of wasting time changing the flat.

He began where he always did, out the front, with its tiny patches of grass broken up by flowerbeds filled with dead plants. The rosebushes looked especially sad, bare but for their thorns and the crinkled brown remains of red and pink blooms. The mower was stubborn, though he'd oiled it only last week, and took more than a few enthusiastic shoves before the blades loosened and did their job. He hated the thing, but enjoyed the workout it gave. If it were a bit warmer he'd have his hoodie and T-shirt off, so the three teenage girls who lived next door could peek out and watch him sweat and glisten in the afternoon sun. But that time was done, the season passed. Too cold now for such exhibitionism; he had to keep his peacock preening to the public bar in the evenings until next summer.

He moved into the back, which was the easier spot, the vegetable beds running along the side-fences, out of the way, leaving the rest a clear run right up to the edge of the property where lawn met woods in a hard line. The garden did not gradually grow wild and blend into a creeping foliage that led to full-blown forest. Just ended in a stern demarcation line between the tame and the uncultivated. A creak and a tumbling sound snapped his head up to see three crows flapping and finding new perches; their previous branch had broken and hit the ground just as he looked. Black eyes regarded him, curiously, somehow fondly. There must have been something dead in the undergrowth he decided, or dying. They were waiting until it was weak enough.

He reached the boundary and turned the recalcitrant machine. The curtains on the kitchen window twitched aside. Mrs. Morgan stood at the sink, giving him a wide smile. She made the usual hand gestures: *Come inside when you're finished, I'll make you a hot drink.* And there'd be buns too, freshly baked, warm enough to melt the butter and run the thick raspberry jam thin. She'd put a little whiskey in his coffee: *Irish it up*, she'd say like she always did. And she'd smile and he'd smile back, watch her as she moved around the small kitchen, never still, but never hurried, always assured, seemingly always in the spot where she was meant to be. And he'd watch how her hips swayed, how her breath made the breasts covered by her lilac blouse shift up and down, how shapely her calves were beneath the hem of the black skirt. How her face was shaped just like a sweetheart, her lips full, her skin creamy, her eyes not quite blue and not quite green but caught somewhere between. How any wrinkles were shallow and made by laughter not loss. How graceful her hands, her wrists, her fingers were as they reached toward him to lead him upstairs so he might see to Mirabel Morgan's other needs.

Cecil Davis, despite his grief and rage, had not become sloppy in anything but his personal hygiene. If the woman had gotten wind of his presence, she'd have fled, he was certain, no matter how invested she was in remaining in Ashdown. He'd tracked her for so long and, having found her, rented a house two doors down and on the opposite side of the street. It gave him an uninterrupted view of her property. He kept the curtains closed, but affixed cameras under the eaves, trained them on the woman's cottage. The place had come furnished, which was convenient, but hadn't mattered one way or the other to him. He'd have happily brought along the sleeping bag and air mattress he'd once used for camping and then, later still, for surveillance after. . . .

He'd even managed to plant a GPS tracking device on her car, something impossible to notice unless you were actively looking for it. He didn't have to leave his four walls, just stared at the monitors he had rigged up so he could keep an eye on her comings and goings while he still managed to run his software support business from a separate laptop. The business he'd hoped to pass on now had as its sole purpose keeping the money coming in to fund his mission.

She was going by *Mrs. Morgan* now, though his researches showed she recycled her names as she went, different ones each time, no discernable pattern, but he'd learned them, if not all, then many. Knowing what to look for meant he had found her at last, though it took him seven years. Seven years of hacking utilities records, bank records, seeing patterns, recognizing names, catching the scent. As much as anything it was his willingness to believe in strange things when no one else would.

It had taken all his determination, all the internal resources that had made him a successful businessman, to keep him focused. To keep him going after. . . .

Of course, he could only watch the exterior of the house. He'd not gone into her home, couldn't bring himself to do that, though he'd never admit it was fear. It was caution, pure and simple. *Caution*, he'd have said if there'd been anyone to talk to about it; if the police in Ottery St. Mary had listened with anything but pity, or the parents in the other small villages he'd gone to after. . . .

The young man who did the gardening was there again, in spite of the penknife Cecil had stuck in the back tire of his vehicle, trying to put an obstacle in his way. Cecil had to admit it hadn't been a very effective obstacle. He was aware that if he approached the man, tried to tell him what he knew, he'd come across as a nutter; that the lad would back away, go straight to the woman and warn her. Though he'd let things like bathing and general grooming fall by the wayside, Cecil knew there were some illusions he needed to keep intact.

He'd do what he could to protect the lad, within reason. He was someone's son after all, and Cecil had no wish for another father, another mother, to go through what he had; to wake and find their boy gone forever, become no more than motes of dust on the wind. He blinked as thoughts of Gil, tall and strong, young and vital, made heated tears rise, made the tendons of his heart thrum deep and discordant.

Cecil looked away from the screens, to the corner of the sitting room, where his gear lay in a pile. He still wasn't sure what to take with him. He knew where she would be, where she'd been going these past weeks, the place she had been preparing. But he didn't know what to take, what would work, he didn't really know *what* she was.

He only knew that when he confronted her there would be no words, no recriminations, no time wasting that might give her a moment's chance to escape. He doubted she remembered Gil. He doubted she remembered any, certainly not by name. He suspected there had been so many she couldn't keep track of them all.

No. No words. Whatever he might say didn't matter. Wouldn't matter. It was only what he *did* tomorrow evening that mattered.

She lay back, listening to Henry's heavy footsteps retreating down the stairs, the rattling of the pipes as he ran a shower. The smell of him was strong in her nostrils, the sweat from manual labor ever an aphrodisiac. He'd been worried, when they first started this, that she'd become pregnant. She'd laughed so hard at the idea he'd been offended, thought she was impugning his fertility, his god-given right to get her up the duff. He'd required stroking, reassuring, promises that it wasn't him but *her.* In their months together he'd had no more cause for complaint; his time might be brief but she gave him the best of herself, helped him live full. He got what he wanted and she took pleasure in it too; taught him a few things that had made his eyes grow round. Taught him a few more things she didn't mind if he tried out on others, younger women. She was not jealous, did not need his singular adoration; considered her lessons a gift. *You're welcome.*

The mattress beneath her was soft and she gave it a fond pat. A fine thing that had done good service. She wasn't always so lucky when she rented a new house: fully furnished was essential for her lifestyle. Having to pick up and pack everything once a year was a burden she'd long ago dispensed with. Only ever own what you can't do without. Only ever have essential things that you can fit in a single small bag. Travel lightly, live deeply, serve faithfully.

And she had done that. Done it for so long she could barely remember when she hadn't been what she'd become. What she was. Could barely remember a time before that first fire, that first night, before she took the mantle from the one before her. She saw no time in front of her, either, when she might relinquish the position. It was her duty, her obligation, her keeping of faith. She would not let it go easily. Besides, where might she find someone to replace her?

Sometimes it was hard, she admitted, to maintain such single-minded devotion when the world around her changed quickly, quickly. Much more so than before. Difficult to be a fixed point in a whirling universe, holding to an idea, a certainty, an allegiance, a moral obligation. She took some comfort when the core of things stayed true: soul cakes had become candy, but the idea of *benefaction* was still there.

And the fires.

The fires were always lit.

The fires remained.

And the sacrifices could still be made, though the ideas underpinning them drew cries and condemnations in this soft society. Still they were needful things; if only people appreciated that something had to be given back in order for the wheel to spin, for the earth to bloom anew. A child lost here, a pet taken there; the tiny sacrifices that kept the world going until the larger giving might happen.

She did not like to take small girls, little cauldrons of life that they were, so much potential lost when their flame guttered. An unhelpful sacrifice that almost lost more than it gained. But the wee boys . . . ah, the boys were like tadpoles, only good for Mischief Night pranks, and so many of them spawned . . . how could one or three be missed? How could they be seen as anything but small coin in return for the greatest gift?

But no one thought like her anymore. Or no one worthwhile. Murderers, cultists, wasters, and nihilists, who neither knew nor cared what they did. Whose killings and leavings brought no benefit, just the brief satisfaction of destruction for the individual.

No, no one thought like her anymore. That was why she'd had to prepare the glade on the wooded tor herself, prepare the fire alone; there were no acolytes nowadays, no pretty maids to do the grunt work; her only handmaidens were black and feathered, sharp-eyed and beaked.

She grinned. Just her, lugging branches, oak and larch and yew, collecting the smaller tinder, and constructing it all into something that resembled a bed, a bier, a pyre. Threading it with mistletoe, mandrake, mugwort, and rue. Doing what was required for when the doors between life and un-life opened and the dead danced through, to visit loved ones or to exact vengeance on rivals and enemies.

Downstairs the closing of the front door sounded. Henry was gone. Strangely, she felt bereft. She rolled onto her side, curled into a ball and closed her eyes, slowed her breathing, commanding her body to sleep deep and late. Soon the changes would come and she would need all her energy for the next night.

The day began deathly gray and did not improve. The afternoon light into which Henry stepped was so weak and ineffectual that he almost missed the crouched man. If he'd not been heading toward the pickup he'd spent part of the morning changing the tire of, he'd not have seen the man at all. As he got closer Henry saw the dull gleam of a blade, not terribly big, but big enough to do damage. The man was about to puncture the tire yet again.

A red veil covered Henry's eyes. His temper wasn't short, not by a long shot, but nor was he inclined to forgive this kind of spiteful vandalism. He didn't know who the bloke was or why he was targeting Henry, and at that point he didn't care. The youth took swift steps, got close enough for the other to hear him and begin to turn and rise.

Henry threw himself forward.

Henry stopped.

The rank body odor hit him first, then the man's fist punched him in the stomach. Henry caught a glimpse of a frightened weary face, rumpled as if someone had slept in it too long, mud-green eyes swimming in fear and guilt, and a mouth that kept saying something over and over. Henry's hearing had deserted him, the world fallen silent, and his belly flared both hot and cold.

He looked down.

The knife was protruding from his hard-earned six pack.

He didn't think the man had meant to do it; it was just the angle, Henry's momentum, the man's fright. He wanted to say *It's okay*, that he knew it hadn't been on purpose. Noise began to seep back to him, and he heard the man yelling *Help! Help!* as he caught at Henry and laid him down on the footpath. *Help! Help!* as he ran away so he wouldn't get caught. As if he had something better to do.

Chills rushed through him, up and down. Henry hoped someone would let Mrs. Morgan know he wouldn't make it tonight. He hoped he wouldn't feel worse. He hoped someone would come soon.

Cecil ran like he'd never done before. He wasn't a runner. He was a short, fat, middle-aged man burdened by grief and junk food. After Gil had gone, after Cecil's wife had left him, no one cared for him, not even Cecil. He just kept going, knowing he needed nourishment and nothing more. He didn't eat for taste or enjoyment or health, just to exist. It meant he wasn't fussy with portions or calories; it meant things fried deeply and provided quickly formed a major part of his diet. He couldn't remember the last time he'd eaten a piece of fruit, or there'd been something in his fridge that was green because it was meant to be, rather than green because it was going off and Cecil's refrigerator was the place things went to die. He ran, though he knew he couldn't be as fast as he felt, as if things sped by in the gray dusk. As if he flew along the deserted streets as he fled the terrible mistake he'd made.

He'd stopped shouting soon after he'd let the boy down, pressing the lad's large hands to the wound. He'd pulled out the knife, knowing it would make the lad bleed all the worse, but Cecil couldn't leave it behind. There were his prints—a drunk driving conviction fifteen years ago meant he'd be on file—and he didn't want to let the thing go because it had been Gil's. He hoped someone had gone to the boy's aid, hoped it wasn't the sort of neighborhood where shouting caused people to secure their doors and huddle inside until everything seemed quiet again. But he couldn't stay. He couldn't get caught. He was so close.

He stumbled over the threshold of his rented house and slammed the door, pressed his forehead against it, then turned, rested his back on the wood, waited until the breath shooting from his lungs didn't feel like fire, until the shaking of his limbs had calmed. And then he bent over and vomited hard on the tenant-resistant, slate-colored carpet. He huddled, hands wrapped around his head, ragged nails biting through his thinning hair into the pale scalp beneath. The pain brought him back to himself.

He had to focus.

He had to go on.

This was his chance.

He couldn't let it—her—slip away again.

He forced himself upwards. He had hours yet; he should clean the mess he'd made, watch the monitors. But somehow he knew he couldn't wait them out here. He should go. He should go before the streets began to hold traces of random trick-or-treaters. What if someone had seen? What if he'd left some trace, though he couldn't image what it might be. What if, what if what if? What if the police were already speeding toward this place?

That thought galvanized him. He picked through the gear in the sitting room, extracted the sleeping bag for warmth and the ghillie suit for camouflage. In the end he took only the Swiss Army knife, wiping its blade as clean as he could, stuffing it in a trouser pocket.

He knew where she would go.

He knew where he would meet her.

The air was brisk, lacing her lungs as she breathed deeply, taking long strides up the incline. Once she'd have carried a burning brand to illuminate her track, to ignite the pyre, but that might have caught attention. So, it was a Maglite in her hand, providing a bright circle to follow, but giving off no warmth the way an old torch would. It was enough that the *form* of things be honored in spirit, not slavish mimicry.

Around her foxes yipped and badgers snuffled; other things she couldn't identify made noise too, but Mirabel had no fear of the dark, no fear of the forest. She'd walked across the fields, then taken the path around the base of the tor, traversing rills and ditches, stiles and fallen trees, marking the way with light, the way that must lead ever upwards. When she passed under the canopy of trees that would take her to the glade, where Henry would be waiting, she sighed contentedly. In her long years she had never been let down by any of her chosen. All things had their time, their natural conclusion.

Everything she directed her existence toward was coming to fruition.

Cecil almost gasped as she moved past him in the darkness. Her face was shadowed, but he knew it was her, knew her shape; he'd watched her enough from the first time they'd met. From when she'd moved in across the street from his family home in Ottery St. Mary and lived there for a year. The lovely, gracious woman who'd asked politely if their son, their only child, just turned nineteen, might be kind enough to do some gardening for her. Effortlessly attractive, effortlessly desirable.

The woman who'd come and gone like a storm, like a flood, stealing something so precious he'd not cared to see what she'd left behind, the benefits she'd given to a village that had been foundering, its crops poor and stunted, its children pale and sickly, its businesses and farms dying a slow death. A village that, after Gil had gone, began to breathe, to produce, to be *fertile* again, though that benevolence gladdened Cecil's heart not a jot.

She walked slowly, he noticed, slower than seemed normal. He wondered if she'd injured herself crossing dark fields, then reminded himself it didn't matter. He waited until she was well ahead, then rolled from the sleeping bag, left it and the ghillie suit behind, and began to follow.

She reached the top of the slope, stepped into the clearing. The bulk of the woven bed was there, picked out by the beam of the Maglite. On top lay the torch she'd made, a branch of yew, one end wrapped around with dried henbane and belladonna and other lesser kindling. She lit it with the matches in her coat pocket and switched off the flashlight. The burning brand gave better light and she nodded with satisfaction, feeling her blood warmed by the leaping blue-orange flame. She held it high and looked around.

No sign of Henry.

She frowned.

Called his name and received no reply.

Looked at the cheap watch on her wrist, though she didn't need to; the tides in her veins kept track of the hours. Fifteen minutes. He still had fifteen minutes.

She threw the brand onto the pyre; that at least could be started. She felt the heat and smiled, welcoming it like an old friend to warm her ancient bones. Once the blaze was settled, she turned her back to it as she always did, knowing the bright amber light made of her a silhouette so Henry, as he came up the bridal path, could not see the change in her. Could not see how, on Halloween Eve, age had rushed in upon her, how all the seasons' endings had converged where she stood, rendering her old, weakened, vulnerable.

Tension was beginning to take a hold on Mirabel when she at last saw the blurred shape appear at the mouth of the path; her eyes aged too, let her down. A man, yes. Henry, she thought and relaxed into a smile. He wouldn't see her face, not until the last moment and by then it wouldn't matter.

She raised her hands, stretched out her arms to welcome him, though it caused an ache in her hoary joints, a popping she feared was audible. Her smile would not be dimmed, however, as she felt the ebbing that was essential for a new beginning.

Henry came toward her, faster now, faster, and as he got closer she knew something was wrong.

Her face was a blank, black oval to Cecil, his eyes burned by the glare of the bonfire behind her, but he saw in the way she shifted that she *knew*. She knew somehow.

That something was not right.

And Cecil was filled with an unreasoning terror, that she would get away. That she would turn into a puff of smoke, sprout wings and fly, become airy in the extreme and sink into the earth's arms, away from his. He put on a burst of speed, the last he'd ever make, propelling his fat little self forward until his soft body met her bony one, and he heard bones break with the impact, heard her gasp turn into a shriek as they both plummeted back, against the pyre, then into its heart as flames reached up and around to envelop them.

And in that moment, that final moment, Cecil experienced with startling clarity a rare self-awareness. He knew, at last, that his question for the October Widow was not and had never been *Why my son?* but rather *Why not me?*

When she woke she sensed an earth changed and not for the better, and that she had changed, also not for the better. She ached, not as badly as on her last night, but still a dull throb of pain ran through her. Where was the spring in her step, the strength in her form that renewal had always promised and ever delivered?

The October Widow had slept for two solid days in the ashes and bones, the dirt and cinders, while the land and her body re-knitted themselves, made themselves anew, the debt called in with the blood of the young king.

She shook her head. Her memories were loose, scrambled, rattling around in her head as though her skull were too big for her brain. Lying back in her cold charcoal bed, Mirabel closed her eyes, breathed deep, trying to center herself, to pull the core together.

No. Not the young king. Not her consort, *not* her sacrifice.

Someone else. A man, yes, but not Henry. A man, older, soft and lost, barely holding on to his life. A man weak and whimpering, clasping her as if she were a mother who'd failed to love him.

A man who didn't know what he'd done.

Slowly she raised her hands, examined them. Brown-spotted, dry, fingers twigs, nails broken and brittle, joints swollen. She put them to her face and felt the damage there: skin corrugated, furrowed like a field before planting. The eyebrows bushy, the dips beneath the eyes so soft they felt like decayed fruit, and the chin—oh, the chin! Raised lumps . . . not moles, nothing so benign, but *warts*. With stiff sharp hairs growing from them.

Slowly she rolled to one side, drew her legs toward her chest, then rolled onto hands and knees, as if to search for something in the cinders, as if to beg. When at last she found her feet, she dug them through the clinkers and soot, ignoring the sharp bits of broken, unconsumed bone, until she found the ground proper. Looked down at her naked body as she waited, saw first-hand the damage done by an inappropriate forfeit: stretch-marked skin, empty dugs for breasts, scrawny arms, a hollow pelvis, thighs destined never to meet, knees like knucklebones, calves no more than long ankles. The October Widow shuddered. She closed her eyes again, concentrated. Listened. Felt.

She'd always known where to travel next for the pulse of the world directed her. But now . . . now it was weak, so weak she could barely feel it beneath the soles of her feet. She had to kneel once more, press her ear and her palms to the dirt, heedless of the gray-black that coated her flesh, to try and find it. To hear its voice more clearly.

She straightened. There was a message, yes, but it wasn't a location, not yet. The world wasn't strong enough to know, for everywhere the slow decline that a lesser offering brought was beginning. That man, she thought, that stupid sad little man had dumped all his grieving, all his pain into the sacred fire, into her, into the earth. Left his mark behind and it would not be easily erased.

But it *could* be done.

She *would* do it.

In that renewal would be her own, the little man's stain washed away with a tide of young blood.

BEFORE THE PARADE PASSES BY

MARIE O'REGAN

Marie O'Regan is a British Fantasy Award–nominated author and editor. Her first collection, *Mirror Mere*, was published in 2006 and followed a decade later by *In Times of Want*, while her short fiction has appeared in a number of genre magazines and anthologies, including *Best British Horror* and *Great British Horror: Dark Satanic Mills*.

She is coeditor of the bestselling anthology *Hellbound Hearts*, *The Mammoth Book of Body Horror*, and *A Carnivàle of Horror: Dark Tales from the Fairground* (all with Paul Kane), and she also edited *The Mammoth Book of Ghost Stories by Women* and *Phantoms*.

"When I first considered submitting a story to this anthology," reveals the author, "I was a bit lost—I'd only just written a Halloween story and couldn't come up with anything. Then I saw a picture of early Halloween 'pumpkins,' except they used turnips, and they were terrifying. You may have seen the same images cropping up on your own Twitter feed.

"That seemed to cross with the idea of a haunted house, and with the image of kids having fun on Halloween. Then there was the idea of a parade, except now it wasn't fun, and all the children were scared. After that the story seemed to gel quite quickly, and at a certain point Hannah seemed to take over.

"And all the while I was writing, I had that old song 'Before the Parade Passes By' in my head—as if it were telling me it should be the story title. I think it was right."

HANNAH WATCHED AGHAST as she saw her daughter flying toward her across the playground while she stood waiting at the school gates. Her blonde hair was whipping around her head as if she were Medusa, its fine strands caught and toyed with by the wind that was seeping in through Hannah's coat.

Tilly's cheeks were rosy, her eyes bright—she was delighted about something, that was plain. As Hannah waited, she started to take in details: Tilly was carrying something that looked quite heavy, wrapped in a creased and well-used Bag for Life. She was running leaning slightly to one side, balancing whatever it was in the bag, and the excitement on her face showed Hannah she couldn't wait to show it to her mother.

She smiled and leaned down, arms opening wide to scoop Tilly up and contain her excitement.

"What have you got there?" Hannah asked as the mini-dynamo hurtled into her arms, knocking her backward.

"It's for Halloween!" the child shouted, and then there was a barrage of words that Hannah could barely make out, too many for such a small child to release in one breath.

Hannah waited for her daughter to wind down. At this speed that wouldn't take long at all, and then she could find out what this was all about. Sure enough, less than a minute later Tilly was staring at her expectantly, gasping for breath, her face blazing with excitement.

"Well?" she asked. "Can I?"

"Can you what?"

Tilly pouted, her eyebrows drawing down into that familiar thundercloud. "I knew you weren't listening!" she shouted. "You never listen!"

"That's enough, Tilly," Hannah snapped. "I was trying to listen, but you were going too fast. Tell me again, but slower this time."

Tilly sighed, and started to repeat everything as Hannah took her hand and they began to walk home.

By the time Hannah unlocked the front door and eased it open, following the whirlwind that was forever Tilly down the hall to the kitchen, she knew all about the school's (and Tilly's) plan for Halloween. There was going to be a Halloween Parade, and a party, and it was in a haunted house, and . . . the list went on.

Tilly slammed the fridge door shut and barreled past her mother, clutching a juice and trying to force the straw into the carton while running.

"Tilly, slow down!"

Too late; she was gone. And if Hannah knew her daughter there'd be a purple stain on the tastefully neutral hall carpet outside her bedroom when she went upstairs to check on her later. She sighed. Tilly was lovely; she was kind, funny, interested in absolutely everything—but she was exhausting. Hannah had often been called "a force of nature" by people who admired her efficiency and drive, but she knew she had nothing on her daughter.

"Shit!" She tripped over something and righted herself quickly, glancing over her shoulder as she did so, hoping she hadn't been caught out swearing by Tilly. The stairs were empty, and Tilly started singing something tunelessly above her head, still caught up in the day's events.

Hannah grinned. So far, so good. Now what had she tripped over? Looking down, she saw the heavy-looking Bag for Life Tilly had been lugging as she left the school building, unwilling to let her mum help with carrying it or even putting it in the car. Hannah nudged it with a toe and stepped back when it appeared to shift, as if something inside were moving.

The bag stared back at her, motionless, and after a few moments Hannah chided herself for her fears. She prodded it once more, just in case, and then bent down and eased the edges apart, revealing what was inside.

It was just some black cloth, surely, nothing that could shift like that. Hannah shook the bag, and was relieved to hear something knock against the floor—so it wasn't just cloth, then. She reached in, careful not to disturb anything, and pulled the material out. Examining the length of what looked like black velvet she was holding, she saw it was a cloak of some kind—rich, black velvet, with black satin ribbons hanging from an embroidered fold-over collar.

Hannah buried her face in its warmth and inhaled; it smelt of smoke, and something else she couldn't identify—something unpleasant. She put it down, sniffing, wondering why she felt scared, suddenly. Something tickled at the back of her mind, some fragment of a memory, and she shivered.

She remembered then that there was something else in the bag, and almost reluctantly she leaned forward and felt inside it again, rummaging around (surely it was bigger than she remembered?) until she found it. Something hard was lurking at the bottom of the bag: its surface was uneven, and appeared to have holes or some kind of shapes cut into it.

She got her fingers around it and pulled, surprised by how heavy it was. Then she saw what it was, and sat down hard with a shriek.

It was a *face*. Hannah stared at it, shocked. It was pale and wizened, with hollows for eyes and mouth that somehow showed pain and fear, and even tiny teeth. Who'd make such a thing?

"You found it!"

Hannah jumped visibly, then forced a smile and stood up, wiping her hands on her jeans as she did so. "What is it?"

Tilly grinned. "It's for Halloween. I have to make a mask, but that's my cloak and Jack."

"Jack?"

Tilly gestured at the pale head on the floor. "It's a jack-o'-lantern. The teacher said to call it 'Jack.'"

Hannah stared down at the thing, wondering what to say. It was hideous. She tried for humor, and thought she almost pulled it off. "Ugly, isn't it?" she said, her tone bright and cheery—or as near as she could manage.

Tilly moved forward and picked it up, brushing her hand over the top as if dusting it, her face thoughtful. "I suppose so. I think he looks sad."

"He?"

"Jack." Tilly placed the head carefully on the kitchen table and pushed it forward, away from the edge. "See?"

Hannah looked, wondering what her daughter saw. She didn't think Jack looked sad; she thought he looked angry. And ready to get even. She could see now that he'd been fashioned from some kind of vegetable, but was off-white rather than the flashier orange of a pumpkin.

"He's made from turnip," Tilly said, as if she'd heard what her mother was thinking.

"I see," Hannah answered, stepping forward and reaching out to touch the vile thing again. Its surface wasn't quite smooth, there were ridges here and there, and even tiny holes that looked like pockmarks. And it smelled stale, almost rotten, although it looked dry enough.

"His head's hollow, see?" Tilly was in front of her mother now, and lifted the top of the turnip's head to reveal the hollowed-out inside. The inner walls of the thing were blackened, presumably by candles, which probably accounted for the faint whiff of old smoke.

"Why did the teacher give you this, Tilly?"

Tilly replaced the lid and whirled round, smiling up at her mother. "So I can wear it in the Parade, silly. Before the party, there's a parade. We go from the school, through the village, to the haunted house."

"Where's the haunted house?" Hannah asked, frowning. "I've not heard of that since we've been here."

"Amy says it's at the back of the church," Tilly answered, absorbed now in tracing the contours of Jack's "face" with her fingertips. She appeared to be trying to force its mouth to grin. "You know—up the hill from here."

And Hannah found she *did* know. They'd been here three months now, and settled in pretty well, she thought. But she could never forget the massive, decrepit old house at the top of the hill their cottage stood on, looming over them like some kind of threat. The shadow it cast on bright days was immense, and Hannah always felt like it was trying hard to reach them. To reach *her*.

"They're having a party in that?" she asked, aghast.

Tilly nodded, oblivious to her mother's anxiety, absorbed in tracing Jack's features. "Fun, eh?"

"I hope so," Hannah muttered, going to the window and staring up at the broken-down house her daughter would be playing in in just a few short weeks. "Do the teachers need any help, do you think?"

"Maybe. Want me to ask?"

"Please."

Tilly nodded and, picking up the head, skipped over to the window, where she placed it reverently on the window-ledge. "There. He can get the sun, now." She turned to her mother, grinned, and said, "Can I go play till dinner?"

Hannah nodded dumbly, unable to tear her gaze away from Jack—who stared back at her, in turn, with blank eyes that seemed to see straight through her. It was going to be a long two weeks.

The rest of the evening passed slowly. Tilly was quiet during dinner, and Hannah found herself getting terse in response—it didn't make for a relaxed meal. After they'd eaten, Tilly excused herself and wandered into the living room, where she switched on the TV. Within moments, Hannah could hear the sounds of Tilly's favorite Disney movie—her version of comfort food. She was upset, and it was Hannah's fault: she'd been far more cross than the situation warranted—being quiet wasn't being naughty. She went to the living room door and looked in at her daughter. Tilly was lying on the sofa with a blanket over her, and she was sucking her thumb, a sure sign she was upset.

"Room for me?" she asked, and was rewarded with a smile as Tilly scrambled to one side of the sofa, taking her blanket with her. Hannah smiled back, and went to sit beside her, hauling Tilly and her blanket onto her lap. "Sorry, button," she whispered into the child's ear, "I guess I'm tired too."

Tilly didn't answer, but as she nestled against her mother and buried her head in her shoulder to watch the movie, Hannah had her reply anyway. All was forgiven. Hannah kissed the top of her head and relaxed, let the movie wash over them both. Peace restored.

It was dark. Hannah opened her eyes slowly, groaning at the ache in the back of her neck. The television had long ago gone into standby mode, and Tilly was a dead weight across her lap, snuffling gently as she breathed.

Something creaked in the darkness, and Hannah froze in the act of trying to ease Tilly sideways onto the sofa so she could get up and carry her to bed.

There it was again, a scraping sound off to the side of the living room. Was someone tapping at the window? The sound stopped, and Hannah waited for almost a minute before finishing her repositioning of Tilly and easing herself upward without disturbing the child. She looked down at her daughter, a bundle of blankets with a tuft of white-blonde hair poking out of it, and smiled. It didn't matter how bad things got, at least she had Tilly.

The scraping came again, and Hannah shifted position without even thinking, standing between her daughter and the direction she judged the sounds to be coming from. Tilly sighed behind her, and Hannah felt the hairs on the back of her neck prickle as they stood proud.

Slowly, Hannah moved toward the window, wishing she had some means of protecting herself if there should be an intruder. *Don't be stupid*, she told herself, *it's probably Mrs. Evans's bloody cat again*. When she reached the window, she pulled the curtain open, fast, hoping to surprise whoever it was scraping on the glass. A shaky laugh escaped her when she realized the window had come open, or hadn't been latched properly—the metal rod that held the frame shut when pushed down over a peg was loose, scraping against the window-ledge as the soft breeze pushed the window back and forth.

She quickly pulled the window shut and pushed the latch firmly down. It wouldn't move again tonight. Then she reached up to grab the curtains, ready to pull them closed for the night—only to stop when she noticed that the jack-o'-lantern had moved.

It hadn't moved far, only an inch or so, but now it seemed to be gazing out at the night beyond, its expression slightly darker than the crazed grin it had held initially. Now its mouth seemed to hang a little straighter, its eyes a little narrower, as it stared into the blackness outside.

Hannah shivered, and pulled the curtains firmly together. It was too late to be this stupid—she was just going to spook herself and if that happened, it was going to be a very long night, on her own in that big bedroom staring at the ceiling, alone with her thoughts and fears.

"Stop it," she told herself. "It's just a lantern, for God's sake."

As she turned away from the window and went to pick up her daughter so she could put her to bed, she tried not to listen to the little voice in her head whispering that God had very little to do with the horrible thing on the window-ledge.

Hannah frowned at the kitchen clock—they were going to have to hurry now.

"Tilly!" she called. "It's eight o'clock, we'll be late!"

She was rewarded with the sound of a door slamming over her head, and feet clomping to the bathroom. Tilly was not happy, that much was clear, but Hannah wisely refrained from yelling up that she shouldn't stamp her feet like that; now was not the time. Ten minutes later a bedraggled-looking Tilly appeared in the doorway, frowning up at her mother.

"Why didn't you wake me up?"

Hannah blinked. "I did, at half-seven. Don't you remember?"

Tilly's frown deepened, staring at her mother. "I didn't hear you."

"You did, love," Hannah said. "You spoke to me."

Big blue eyes stared up at Hannah in disbelief. "No, I never."

"It's 'no I didn't,' not 'no I never,'" Hannah corrected absently, searching her daughter's expression for signs of illness. Or perhaps she'd banged her head? She ruffled the child's hair with affection, but couldn't feel any bumps.

"Whatever."

As her mother stared at this unexpectedly adult response from an eight-year-old, Tilly stomped forward and scraped a chair backward.

Hannah clenched her teeth at the screech and chose to ignore the attitude for now. Anyone could have a bad morning—perhaps Tilly hadn't slept well. Thoughts of her own inability to escape the feeling something was watching her from the shadows came back to her, and she shook her head. *Enough.* All they needed was a good breakfast.

She busied herself dishing up cereal and buttering toast, making tea. Tilly said nothing, just ate whatever was put in front of her without a sound.

As Tilly put the last crust down on her plate and pushed her chair back, Hannah whisked plates away as she glanced at the clock again. Eight-twenty, and Tilly was dressed. Maybe they'd make it on time after all.

"Ready?" she asked.

Tilly smiled and nodded, her mood much lighter now. She went and got her coat and book-bag, and stood by the front door. As Hannah joined her and started digging in her coat pocket for her keys, Tilly exclaimed "Jack!" and ran back to the living room.

"Not now, Tilly!" Hannah shouted. "We'll be late!"

Tilly came hurtling out of the living room, sobbing. She collided with her mother and wrapped her little arms around Hannah's waist.

"What is it? What's wrong?" Hannah asked, bending to try and see the child's face.

Tilly raised her eyes to her mother's, stormy blue to puzzled green, and sobbed, "He's gone!"

"What?" Hannah stood and stared toward the living room, trying to see the window-ledge. Tilly had left the curtains half-drawn, but even so Hannah could see the lantern was still there, peeking out from behind the right-hand one. "It's there, love. Look!"

Tilly looked back over her shoulder, hiccuping as her sobs died away. "But . . . he wasn't, honest!"

Hannah delved into her pocket for a tissue and wiped her daughter's face dry. "You must have just missed it, love. That's all. Now come on, we'll be late!" She grabbed Tilly's hand and led her out of the house. There wasn't a lot of time for talk on the hurried walk to school, but Hannah had managed to cheer the child up by the time they reached the gates. She bent down to kiss Tilly goodbye, and smiled at her warmly. "Have a good day," she whispered. "I'll see you tonight."

Tilly wouldn't let go of her hand. She grabbed her coat with the other hand and pulled Hannah forward so she could whisper to her. "It moved," she said. "I know it did. *It wasn't there, Mum.*"

Hannah slowly straightened up, frowning. She stroked Tilly's cheek as she tried to reassure her. "It must have been," she said. "It can't move on its own, can it?"

"Morning, Tilly!"

Mrs. Smythe, Tilly's teacher, was descending on them like a ship in full sail. Her floaty, overly floral dress was billowing about her in the wind, and the smile on her rosy face looked as if it was about to split it in half. She looked down at Tilly and her smile faltered. She turned to Hannah, her expression worried. "Anything wrong, Mrs. Lytton?"

Hannah forced a smile. "Oh no," she said. "Not really. Tilly managed to spook herself with the jack-o'-lantern this morning—thought it was gone from the window-ledge and then it was there."

Mrs. Smythe stared at her for what felt like minutes, her eyes serious. Finally, she looked down at Tilly, and when she saw the child staring back up at her, scared, she smiled at her. "You must have made a mistake, lovely."

Tilly shook her head. "No, I didn't, Miss."

Mrs. Smythe laughed, a jagged, nervous sound that didn't hold a hint of humor. "It can't move, Tilly," she said as she took the girl's hand and ushered her toward the school's entrance.

Hannah could have sworn that, just before they were swallowed by the building's interior, she heard Mrs. Smythe say, "Not yet."

At 3:30 in the afternoon, Hannah was standing outside the gates once more, waiting eagerly for the school to disgorge her daughter. She didn't have to wait long. The bell rang and suddenly there were dozens of children appearing in the entrance, chattering excitedly and waving when they saw parents and started to run toward them. Tilly didn't keep her waiting long. As she exited the building she was whispering to another little girl, one Hannah didn't recognize. The child had red hair, that copper shade that appears almost polished in the sunlight, and a mass of freckles over an upturned nose that made her look as if she was constantly about to grin.

"Mummy, this is Annie," she said, and Hannah fought not to smile. Annie's parents had clearly shown a sense of humor when naming their offspring.

Annie was frowning at her, an expression that didn't seem to sit right on a face built for cheerier expressions. "What's funny?" she said.

Hannah smiled at her and Tilly, eager to be friendly. "I'm sorry," she said, "you just reminded me of someone, that's all."

"As long as it's not that bloody musical," Annie muttered as she stalked off toward a woman with flame-red hair who was standing, scowling, at the gates.

Hannah stared after her, open-mouthed. She was what, eight? And already swearing. Silently, she resolved to try and minimize the time Tilly spent with this girl. She was a bad influence, that much was obvious. She felt Tilly tugging at her sleeve, and looked down. "What?"

"She doesn't swear much," Tilly said, her face sad. "I haven't heard her do it before."

"She shouldn't do it all," Hannah answered stiffly. "How good a friend is she?"

"I don't know her that well," Tilly admitted, "we got talking in class today."

"What about?"

"Halloween," Tilly whispered, and something about her voice made Hannah lean down, bending so that she was face-to-face with her daughter.

"What about it, love?" she asked.

Tilly smiled, and it nearly broke Hannah's heart. It was Tilly's biggest smile, the one reserved for things like Christmas, birthdays, and surprises (a serious girl, Tilly wasn't given to laughing often, but when she did, she was delighted—and so was Hannah). Yet now her eyes were welling up with tears, and her face was so pale. . . .

"Tell me," Hannah whispered, stroking Tilly's cheek.

"Annie said that the Halloween Parade is when you get taken," she said, and now tears were falling quickly down her cheeks, leaving grubby marks when she wiped them away.

"Taken where?" Hannah asked.

Tilly shrugged. "Don't know. Just taken." She was in her mother's arms, then, crying. "I didn't like it," she whispered, "it sounds scary, Mum. Do I have to go?"

Hannah squeezed her daughter tight, alarmed at the speed of the child's heart thumping against her chest. "No, love, you don't."

"Promise?"

"Promise." With that, Hannah hauled herself upright with Tilly still in her arms, a feat that was much harder these days than when Tilly was smaller. She turned and walked away from the gates, shushing Tilly as she went and rubbing her back. She had seen Mrs. Smythe approaching with a frown on her face, clearly wanting to engage in some discussion about what was wrong, but now wasn't the time. She had to get Tilly home. She lengthened her stride, and was halfway down the street when Tilly whispered, "She's gone back in now," and Hannah relaxed but didn't slow her pace.

"Let's go home," she said, "get you in the warm."

Tilly's arms tightened around her neck and she felt the child nod, making her hold her daughter just a little tighter as she walked.

Ten minutes later she was fumbling in her coat pocket for her keys, having shifted Tilly's weight onto one hip. Tilly seemed to have nodded off, her body limp in her mother's arms, her breath puffing warm into Hannah's neck. She found them, unlocked the door, and pushed it open with her foot, then walked into the living room and laid the sleeping girl down on the sofa.

She wondered whether to rouse her enough to take her coat off, but one look at her daughter's peaceful expression decided that. Time enough when she woke up—let her rest. She eased Tilly's shoes off, one by one, and laid them on the floor beside her. Then she made sure Tilly was comfortable, and pulled the girl's favorite soft gray blanket over her before heading back into the hall to take her own coat off and hang it on the hook by the door. She peeped back at Tilly to check she was still sleeping, then went into the kitchen to put the kettle on.

Ten minutes later she was sitting in the armchair, sipping thoughtfully at her tea, staring at her sleeping child. Tilly had burrowed down under the blanket, and all Hannah could see, once more, was her hair. Hannah sighed. Tilly would be so hot when she woke up, but better that than upset and shocked, as she had been when she got out of school. Hannah's thoughts wandered to Annie and her sullen-looking mother, and she wondered where they lived. Hopefully nowhere near them.

The shadows made their way across the room as the sun went down, and still Tilly slept. Hannah didn't have the heart to wake her, even though she knew it would probably mean a sleepless night ahead for both of them.

Finally, at almost seven o'clock, Hannah heard a deep sigh coming from the depths of the gray blanket. She leaned forward, placing her now-empty cup on the coffee table beside her.

Tilly sat up. Sleepy-eyed, she yawned, stretching her arms above her head.

Hannah's heart melted—she looked about three when she did that.

Then Tilly turned to her mother, and the smile was back—that bright, shining light that only showed when Tilly was really happy. "Mum!"

"Evening, poppet," Hannah answered. "Feel better?"

Tilly nodded, swinging her legs down so she was sitting upright. Her thumb found its way to her mouth, and with her other hand she started twirling her hair as she gazed at her mother.

Hannah's smile faded, just a little. Tilly hadn't sucked her thumb since she was three, although she did still play with her hair sometimes, when she was especially tired or upset. She cleared her throat, and asked, "Hungry?"

Again the nod. Hannah thought for a moment—they were both tired, and Tilly was obviously still bothered by the incident at school. She didn't want to leave her daughter unattended while she cooked, and it was getting late. There was one thing guaranteed to bring a smile to Tilly's face, and her next words did the trick. "Shall I order pizza?"

Tilly lit up, nodding as she ran for the menu.

Half an hour later they were back on the sofa, feet up on the coffee table (permission granted especially for pizza, so long as shoes were off), with big glasses of milk and slices of Tilly's favorite pizza. Another Disney movie was on TV, and Hannah found she was almost word-perfect as they watched together.

Gradually, Hannah felt herself beginning to relax. Tilly seemed to have forgotten the upset at the gates, and she didn't want to open that can of worms again—she wanted her daughter to sleep tonight.

As the film ended, Tilly was beginning to nod, drowsily hanging on to her now-empty plate, her hair falling perilously close to the tomato sauce smeared across it.

"Bedtime, Tilly," Hannah whispered, easing the plate out of her daughter's hands and smoothing her hair back.

"'Kay," the girl muttered, and she leaned across to kiss her mother before heading upstairs unbidden to get into her pajamas and brush her teeth.

Hannah watched her go, and was surprised to feel a pang of sadness at the sight of her little girl traipsing up the stairs, yawning as she went. *She'll be too big for kisses soon*, she thought, and then told herself not to be stupid. Kisses weren't defined by age—they were there when wanted or needed. She wasn't like her parents, confined by the norms of their day and not able to show affection as easily as she and Tilly could. Still, the thought persisted, and her mood was spoiled as she cleared up the evening meal and washed up the plates and glasses. The movie was over, and once Tilly was in bed the rest of the evening was hers.

Tilly was sitting up in bed, knees drawn up to her chest with her chin resting on them when Hannah made it upstairs to say goodnight some ten minutes later. She smiled as her mother entered the room, her expression a little wistful.

"Okay, button?" Hannah asked, worried that the afternoon's upset might have returned.

Tilly nodded. "I'm fine, just thinking about Daddy."

Hannah sighed, and went to sit next to her daughter, who shuffled across to make room. "Me too," she confessed, and stroked Tilly's cheek. "Especially this time of year."

Her daughter nodded. "Do you want to know something?" she asked.

"Of course."

"I *hate* Halloween!" The words were spat out, real passion behind them, and Hannah realized that for Tilly nothing had faded, as it hadn't for her. Adam's loss still burned deep, even though it was almost three years past now.

"Me too, in some ways," Hannah said, a little surprised at how shaky her voice was. "But there are fun things too—like this parade? The party? And we can watch movies and cartoons and eat all the candy. You like that, remember?"

Tilly nodded, her face a little less sad. Her eyes, though, were still haunted. "That's true," she said, "but I wish Daddy could be here too."

"I know, love," Hannah said, and leaned forward to hug her daughter, smiling through the tears that threatened as the child hugged her back tightly, holding on as if she'd never let her go. *Too old for kisses*, she thought, and smiled a little wider. *Yeah, right.* "But you know Daddy, he wouldn't want you to be sad. And he's always with you, inside."

Tilly didn't say anything, but Hannah recognized the wry look she gave her mother as she plumped herself down on the pillow and pulled the duvet up over her. It was a look that her father would have given.

Hannah bent down to kiss Tilly goodnight. "Don't forget to say your prayers, love."

"I won't."

Tilly's voice was small and already on the verge of sleep—the day's events had tired her out, and yet it seemed they were already mostly forgotten. Hannah envied her that.

Downstairs once more, she found herself staring at the photo taken three years before, just before Adam had died—mown down by a drunk-driver dressed as Freddy Krueger, on his way home from celebrating a little too enthusiastically at a local Halloween party. Adam hadn't stood a chance—his head had hit the curb as he fell, after being thrown high into the air on impact; his skull was shattered, and the resulting bleed on his brain had finished the job.

There he was, smiling back at her, a grinning Tilly in his arms, her arms around his neck. She'd adored him—the two of them had been frequent partners in crime, and Hannah had loved to watch them. Now she had to be both mother and father, and at times she thought the weight of it might be the death of her, but not tonight. Tonight she'd successfully fended off the descent into maudlin that usually followed when Tilly mentioned Daddy, and Tilly was probably already asleep.

Thoughts of Adam inevitably led to thoughts of the pain she'd gone through as Tilly tried to adjust to the news. She'd taken it hard, and for months Hannah had wondered if they'd ever be able to cope. Slowly, week by week, the tantrums and nightmares had first slowed, then stopped, until finally it was only during the weeks leading up to Halloween that trouble flared. Hannah had hoped that this year the school celebrations would have averted that.

She went to the fridge and got out the remains of a bottle of wine, poured herself a glass, and went through to the living room and sank down on the sofa, remote in one hand, wine in the other. Hopefully there'd be a movie or something she could lose herself in until it was time for bed. Two hours and a lot of channel-hopping later, plus the rest of the wine, Hannah gave up and went up to bed. She had a feeling it was going to be a long night.

She was awakened by high-pitched laughter, and the sound of furniture scraping in the kitchen underneath her. Groaning at the jolt of pain in her head as she leapt out of bed, Hannah pulled on her dressing gown and dashed down the stairs two at a time, wondering what on earth Tilly was up to this time.

Tilly was standing in the living room, all wide eyes and innocence, staring at her mother as she crashed through the door.

"What was that noise?" Hannah panted.

"What noise?"

Hannah frowned. "Don't give me that, something scraped along the floor."

Tilly sighed. "Oh that. It was just the chair, Mum." She indicated one of the kitchen chairs, now parked beside the sofa in front of the TV.

"What's it doing there?" Hannah asked.

Now Tilly started to look evasive, an expression Hannah wasn't used to seeing on her daughter's face.

"I said, what's it doing there?" Hannah insisted.

"I thought Jack could sit on it," Tilly said, and indicated the kitchen chair's seat.

The jack-o'-lantern now occupied the middle of the seat, and to Hannah's eyes it looked bigger. It was just as ugly as ever, but the mouth was drawn down and someone had cut a frown line in between the eyes. That hadn't been there before, had it?

"What did you do to its face?" Hannah asked, as she picked it up and deposited it back on the window-ledge—wiping her hands on her dressing gown after doing so.

"Nothing, why?"

Hannah turned it around to face the street, almost smiling when an elderly lady passing by flinched away from it. Turning back to her daughter, she shook her head. "Oh nothing, I just thought it looked a bit grubby, that's all."

Tilly stared at her, her expression doubtful. "Well I didn't do anything."

"Okay." Hannah picked up the chair and used it to prod Tilly into the kitchen. "Let's have breakfast, eh?"

Tilly got to school on time and without further incident, and for a week or more things carried on as normal. As the Halloween Parade and party got nearer, though, Hannah started to be concerned. There was nothing ostensibly wrong: Tilly went to school, came home, ate and did her homework, went to bed. Her brief resistance at going to the Parade had gone, Annie's words forgotten. But her sleep was becoming increasingly disturbed, although she claimed never to remember why, and she was losing weight.

Again, Hannah couldn't put her finger on what was different—Tilly ate her meals, and when Hannah asked the staff at school if they'd noticed her not eating lunch she was told that everything was fine: Tilly was happy and productive, and eating well with her friends in the canteen at lunchtime.

And yet the weight was falling off her. Her fingers were long and bony, the knuckles large protuberances dotted along pale stalks; she complained of being cold, and her cheekbones had actual hollows underneath. What healthy eight-year-old had hollow cheeks?

A few days after Tilly had tried to sit Jack by the TV she'd had to take him and the cloak back to school, ready for "dress rehearsal" for the Parade. She'd come home that night with no appetite, looking as if she were about to cry. Hannah had tried to find out what was wrong, but all she'd say was that she was tired. No amount of wheedling or coercing had got anything more out of her than that, and Hannah had given up before risking seriously upsetting Tilly.

Then, on the Monday before the Parade (Halloween was on a Friday this year, a fact Hannah had noted with some disquiet), Hannah was approached by Annie's mum as she waved Tilly goodbye. She had her coat pulled tight around her against the biting wind, and her hair looked as if it never saw a brush. She also looked scared.

"Can I talk to you?" she said, and looked as if she expected the answer to be no.

"Of course," Hannah said, and forced a smile. "It's nice to meet you. I'm Hannah."

The woman smiled, and put out her hand. "I'm Sarah, Annie's mum."

"Hello," Hannah said, and shook her hand. It was like shaking a wet fish. "How's Annie?"

"She's fine, worrying a bit about the Parade on Friday. I'm sure Tilly is, too."

"She seems to be, not quite sure why."

Sarah stared into Hannah's eyes, her own brown eyes serious. "Aren't you?"

Taken aback, Hannah shook her head, trying to laugh it off. "Well no, there's no reason she should be, is there?"

"I wanted to warn you," Sarah said, placing her hand on Hannah's arm. "Before Friday."

Hannah opened her mouth to answer but was interrupted by Mrs. Smythe, as ever busily patrolling the playground before closing the gates until home time.

"Is there a problem, ladies?" Her tone was icy, her expression stern as she saw the two women standing close together.

"No," Sarah shot back quickly, "of course not. We were just . . . getting to know each other—the girls are friends, after all."

Mrs. Smythe flashed a smile, gone in an instant. Hannah just had time to notice how white her tiny teeth were. How pointed. "Well yes, they are," she agreed. "Lovely girls, the pair of them. Now if I could just close the gates?"

She was ushering them out of the playground, moving forward relentlessly and giving them no option but to step back until they were outside the school grounds. The gates clanged shut behind them, and Mrs. Smythe turned a heavy key in the lock. "Right then," she said, "see you tonight, ladies! Don't do anything I wouldn't do!" With a laugh, she directed that last at Sarah, then turned and marched briskly back toward the school entrance. The doors slammed shut behind her, leaving the two women standing alone on the outside, wondering what had just happened.

Sarah was leaving. Whatever she'd wanted to say, Mrs. Smythe had made her think better of it.

"Wait," Hannah said. "I thought you wanted to warn me about something?"

Sarah stopped then, her expression pained. "I did. It's just . . . she knew, didn't she? She knew what I was doing. And I don't want. . . ."

Hannah was alarmed now. "Don't want what?" she asked. "What did she know?"

Sarah shook her head, turning around to stare at the windows. "She'll see. I have to go."

She turned away and started to move off, and Hannah only just caught the whispered: "Walk behind me, I'll tell you when we're out of sight."

The two women started to walk away from the school, Hannah crossing over to the other side of the road so that no one could think they were chatting. She wondered what Sarah was so scared of, and what was wrong with them talking anyway. As she turned the corner, she stopped and leaned against the wall, watching to see what Sarah would do.

Annie's mother looked both ways, then crossed the road at an angle that would take her away from the view of anyone looking out of the school. When she was sure the street was empty, she crossed again and stood by Hannah. "You live near here, don't you?"

"Just up the road," Hannah answered, and gestured toward her house. "The one with the red front door, see?"

Sarah nodded. "I'll go round the block first, then knock on your door."

Then she was gone, walking swiftly down the street, head down in case anyone spoke to her. Hannah watched for a few seconds, then made her way home, shutting the front door loudly behind her and leaning against it.

She was in the kitchen making tea when the knock came, less than five minutes later. Sarah was inside the house almost as soon as Hannah had got the front door open, slamming it shut behind her.

"Tea?" Hannah asked.

Sarah shook her head. "I can't stay. If anyone finds out I told you, I'll lose her anyway."

"Lose who?" Hannah asked, shocked at the fear evident in the woman's eyes.

"Annie. I've already lost her brother. I won't lose her too."

"What do you mean, you lost her brother? How?" Hannah was starting to wonder whether the woman was seriously deranged, and thinking about ways to get her out of the house without incident, or who she could call for help.

Sarah laughed. "I know. I look mad, and sound worse. But I did, I promise." She turned around and stared through the front door's peephole, scanning the street outside. "Your kitchen's at the back, isn't it?"

Hannah nodded.

"Should be safe there," the woman answered, and Hannah could only follow as she scurried down the hall and into the warmth of the kitchen. Once there, she pulled the blinds down and shut the door behind them before sinking onto a kitchen chair and resting her head in her hands as she leaned on the table.

Hannah inched forward, reluctant to touch her even though she was clearly in distress. "Are you sure I can't get you anything?" she asked, her voice gentle, but was rewarded with a shake of the head and a muffled sob. She left the woman alone, then, and sat on a chair at the end of the table, watching as Sarah pulled herself together. She didn't think she was dangerous, but you could never be sure.

Finally, Sarah pulled a dirty white cotton handkerchief out of a pocket and blew her nose loudly, sniffing as she crumpled it up and put it back. She wiped her eyes on her sleeve, still sniffing furiously, and finally stared at Hannah as if daring her to make fun.

"What's the matter?" Hannah asked. "You can't just give hints of something awful and then not say anything, you have to tell me!"

Sarah glared at her. "Wasn't hinting," she said. "Told you the truth."

"You told me some of it, maybe. Barely anything, really."

"All right!" Sarah gathered herself up, frowning, and whispered, "Halloween's different here. It's because of the house."

Hannah flinched and turned involuntarily to stare in the direction she knew the "haunted house" to be. "The house?"

"They say it's haunted, and it is, but it's only the ghosts of the children it's taken. They don't mean any harm."

Hannah was horrified. "Children?"

"They go missing every year," Sarah whispered, as if afraid she was going to be overheard and reported. "It's the Halloween Parade."

"The Parade?" Part of Hannah was aware she was simply parroting what Sarah was saying, and that she sounded like an idiot, but she was lost for words. What did you say to something so crazy? Did you humor the speaker, go for help, what?

Sarah sighed. "I know you think I'm mad. Perhaps I am mad, I don't know anymore. But it's true. The kids do the Parade every year, and one always goes missing."

"Missing?" There she went again, repeating what the other woman had said.

"Tell me," Sarah said urgently, leaning forward to grasp Hannah's hands. "Does she have the jack-o'-lantern? The old turnip thing?"

Hannah nodded, feeling all the warmth drain out of her as she did so.

"Has it moved yet?"

Hannah shook her head, and now she could feel the tears welling up. She was sitting here, listening to some lunatic and, to cap it all, now she was going to cry. Finally she got herself together enough to get out, "I . . . I'm not sure!"

"Then maybe it'll miss Tilly out. I hope so." Sarah glanced around, as if suddenly fearful that it was here, listening to them. "Where is it?"

"School," Hannah answered. "They wanted it back for a dress rehearsal."

"Oh, God."

Neither woman spoke for a time, each staring at the other in dread. Hannah wondered which of them were mad, or if perhaps they both were.

"I have to go," Sarah said finally. She looked visibly lighter now that she'd unburdened herself, whereas Hannah was sure she looked a million years older. "Maybe it'll be all right."

"They need helpers for the Halloween Parade, don't they? I asked Tilly, but she never said any more," Hannah asked suddenly, gripping Sarah's sleeve as she stood up. "I could help?"

Sarah nodded. "That's right, they do. If you can keep her close. . . ."

Then she turned and was gone. "Good luck," she said, over her shoulder. "I hope I'm wrong."

Hannah stared after her as the front door slammed once more. The house seemed immeasurably colder all of a sudden, and she shivered. She stood and went back to the living room, wanting to look out of the window, and stopped short in the doorway as a scream caught in her throat.

The jack-o'-lantern smiled at her agreeably from the coffee table, not frowning now. It was happy.

When Hannah collected Tilly from school that evening she tried to find Mrs. Smythe, dragging the girl along with her while she looked.

"But why do you want to see her?" Tilly asked, worried. "Am I in trouble?"

"No, love. I just want to volunteer, that's all." It was starting to rain, and the sky was iron-gray, whipped into scudding clouds by the rising wind. Hannah shivered, and bent to pull up Tilly's hood.

Mrs. Smythe appeared out of nowhere, frowning. "Goodness, Tilly looks freezing! Shouldn't you be taking her home?"

"I . . . I wanted to volunteer," Hannah stammered. "For the Halloween Parade."

"For the Parade?" Mrs. Smythe looked stunned.

"To help," Hannah went on. "You know, be a helper." She stared down at her daughter and inspiration struck. "Tilly gets nervous. I could walk with her."

"Mu-*um*!" Tilly was dragging on her hand, eager to get her away from school and stop the embarrassment.

Mrs. Smythe smiled, an unpleasant expression on that vapid face. It lent her a malignancy that Hannah hadn't noticed before—that smile said she knew what Hannah was doing, and it wouldn't do any good. "Of course," she said. "If you'd like to walk with Tilly that's absolutely fine. I'll see you on Friday, at home-time," she said, ushering them both toward the gates. "Get out of the cold now," she said. "Take Tilly home."

Hannah nodded and muttered a "thank you," but Mrs. Smythe had already got them outside the gates and locked them out. She stared out at them and grinned, suddenly, and Hannah was forcibly reminded of the way a snake could spread its mouth wide when it wanted to swallow something.

"Come on, Mum!" Tilly was dragging her homeward, obviously mortified at her mother's actions.

Hannah said nothing more, just took Tilly home and started dinner in a lonely kitchen. Tilly had stormed upstairs and slammed her bedroom door shut as soon as they were inside. The rain was still hammering down, running down the windows in sheets; it made the sullen atmosphere inside the house even gloomier.

As she stood at the stove, mindlessly stirring a pan of beans, Hannah found herself wondering if all this was real, or if she was locked in a padded room somewhere, howling her loss in vain at the walls. She heard Tilly moving across the hall upstairs, followed by the slam of the bathroom door, and wiped her eyes. It was only a few days until Friday. She'd find out soon enough.

Friday dawned bright and clear, but cold. The blue sky held the promise of ice later on, and Tilly had moaned loudly at the bright red hat and scarf her mother had made her wear. Hannah had brooked no argument, confident Tilly would be easily recognizable in the dark. She waved her daughter off with a smile, and nodded a greeting to Mrs. Smythe in return to her own, then she went home to prepare.

She didn't mean to be separated from her child—not tonight, not ever. She went through the items laid out on the kitchen table and nodded her satisfaction. There was a torch, small enough to fit in her coat pocket but still powerful; spare batteries, and a knife—its blade maybe three inches long but slim, sharpened to within an inch of its life. Hannah was pretty confident that, should someone try and take Tilly, she wouldn't hesitate to use it. Tilly was all she had left, and no one was going to hurt her.

The day passed slowly, but finally it was time to leave for the Halloween Parade. Hannah locked the door behind her, hoping they'd both be back later, the Parade over for another year.

The school was eerily quiet as she approached, its windows dark as they watched. Mrs. Smythe was waiting for her at the gate, a look on her face Hannah couldn't decipher.

"Come along," she said, "Tilly's waiting for you." She turned on her heel, her footsteps echoing her way up the corridor, disappearing through a door most of the way down on the right. Hannah hesitated before walking into the room after her, wondering why it was so quiet. Then she stepped inside, and understood.

The room was empty save for Tilly and Mrs. Smythe, the latter holding Tilly firmly by the wrist as she stared expectantly at Hannah.

"Where are the other children?" Hannah whispered.

"They're outside, waiting. Here you are." With that, she pushed a silent Tilly forward, proffering the child's hand.

Hannah grasped her daughter's hand, shocked by how cold it was.

"Tilly?"

The child said nothing, but Hannah was relieved to feel her grip tighten on her mother's hand.

Hannah looked up at Mrs. Smythe. "Why isn't she talking?"

The teacher smiled. "All part of the Parade, my dear. She's under strict instructions not to utter a word until she reaches the house and hands over the jack-o'-lantern."

"Hands it over?"

Again, that nod, impatient this time. "To the Keeper of the Flame." Then she was gone, as if that answered everything.

Hannah straightened up, adjusting the black cloak Tilly was wearing to try and keep her warm. Was she wearing makeup? Her face was bone-white, her eyes sunken into dark hollows. Her mouth was turned down, and Hannah didn't know if that was makeup or Tilly was just scared. "C'mon, kiddo," she whispered, "let's get this over with so we can go home."

Tilly followed her without argument, holding her hand tightly. Hannah found herself impressed at how far she was taking the role. Then they were outside, following a straggly line of kids in Halloween costumes, all eerily silent.

At least the rain had stopped. The night was as cold as Hannah had feared, and she shivered, but was surprised to see that none of the children seemed to be affected. They walked for what felt like miles, and Hannah realized that she didn't know where they were anymore. These streets were narrower than the ones she was familiar with, their surfaces slick with something darker than rain, the buildings old and ramshackle, and there was a smell, thick and dank, as if something dead were nearby.

Hannah held tightly on to Tilly, who still hadn't said a word. She leaned down, suddenly desperate to see her daughter's face, and recoiled when the thing holding her hand stared back.

It wasn't Tilly. The creature walking beside her had no flesh that she could see—its eyes were nothing more than hollows that somehow managed to be empty and threatening at the same time. Its face was a sickly off-white, marked in places as if its features had been hewn, not grown. The black cloak flapped over a body that was barely more than suggested, clad all in black that hid any identifiable detail, rather than Tilly's familiar school uniform.

Hannah tried to free her hand, but the creature just kept walking and wouldn't let go. She was forced to maintain her pace and stay in the procession, her mind racing. This couldn't be real. She was holding Tilly, not some monster, and when the procession was over she'd get her daughter to take off that damn costume and they could go home.

Hannah staggered blindly on, and at some point the roads became the ones she knew again. When she looked down, she saw that now she walked alone, and in her hand she held a stick with the jack-o'-lantern attached, nothing more. She groaned, praying that she was hallucinating, and recognized Tilly's teacher, Mrs. Smythe, when she turned around and started to laugh.

Finally, their destination came into view—the "haunted house." Its windows were ablaze with light, and the street leading up to it was lined with people. Hannah recognized several of the parents from Tilly's class, and standing alone apart was Sarah, an arm held protectively around a terrified Annie as she held her back from the front of the crowd. Sarah couldn't meet her eyes.

Then the children ahead of her started to enter the house, and Hannah began to cry. When it was her turn, finally, she stood in the open doorway and saw . . . nothing. The children that had gone before were nowhere to be seen, and Mrs. Smythe was sitting halfway up the rotting staircase, a robe of some kind covering her considerable bulk.

"What?" she said, in response to Hannah's incomprehension. "Surely you knew this was where it ended?"

"Where *what* ended?" Hannah asked hesitantly. "I don't understand. This is supposed to be a Parade!"

"And it is," the woman answered. "A Parade to honor this night."

"Halloween?" Hannah felt numb. Tilly was nowhere to be seen, and everyone seemed to know what was happening except her.

"More properly, the Celtic festival of Samhain," Mrs. Smythe corrected her, "the night the veil lifts, and we can see what the Other Side holds for us. This house stands on both sides, and if we want the doors to remain closed for another year something must be sacrificed." She eyed the jack-o'-lantern Hannah held, and Hannah cried out in relief when she saw Tilly standing there once more, the stick holding the lantern grasped tightly in her hand. Tilly shook her other hand free, her face solemn, and moved forward to present the lantern to her teacher.

The teacher shifted the lantern-stick into her right hand, and Hannah watched as the woman raised it aloft and held it over her head.

The jack-o'-lantern was on fire. Scarlet flames had sparked inside it, and were licking up its sides in an effort to escape. Gradually the flames spilled out of the lantern and spread down her arm to cover her completely, yet she remained unharmed. "I am the Keeper," she intoned, her words somehow filling the air. "I must close the door."

She pointed at Tilly, and Hannah screamed as her daughter faded from view once more, her eyes pleading with Hannah until she was gone. The jack-o'-lantern was ablaze now, a scarlet flame that guttered and flared.

"What is that?" Hannah cried, on her knees now. Tilly was gone, she had nothing left to lose. She wanted her daughter back, could still feel her, smell her. The air around the teacher was shimmering, insubstantial, and Hannah glimpsed motion on the Other Side.

"This holds the flame, which burns for a year until it demands another soul. Tilly was strong, like you." She smiled down at Hannah as if she were bestowing a blessing. "She—both of you—*nearly* thwarted us."

Was that supposed to be a comfort, Hannah wondered? She'd almost managed to save her daughter? She got to her feet, and started to walk toward her tormentor.

"Fuck you," she said, and rejoiced when she saw the other woman take a step backward.

The veil was thinning now, and she could almost see through it. Something small was standing there, waiting for her, and as she walked toward the thinnest part of the veil she saw something—*someone?*—move closer, to stand behind that forlorn shape. Was it beckoning to her?

The teacher raised an arm, moved as if to stop her, and Hannah gathered all her strength and shoved her out of the way.

The woman stumbled and fell backward, the lantern falling from her hands and onto the floor. Flames licked across the rotten wooden floorboards and caught the hem of Mrs. Smythe's robe. She screamed as she really caught fire this time, her screeching quickly silenced as she inhaled the searing heat. She fell writhing to the ground, and soon stopped moving after that.

The air was growing unbearably hot, and the veil was once more closing for another year. It was becoming impenetrable again, Hannah could tell. She stared at the flames now licking around her as the old house was consumed and wished she could take it all back—wished that she and Tilly could go home and Adam would be there, waiting with candy and a Disney movie cued up for them to watch.

It was too late for that. With one last sob, Hannah took a deep breath and stepped through the dwindling veil, smiling as she finally saw what awaited her on the Other Side.

She was home.

HER FACE

Ramsey Campbell

The *Oxford Companion to English Literature* describes Ramsey Campbell as "Britain's most respected living horror writer." He has received more awards than any other writer in the field, including the Grand Master Award of the World Horror Convention, the Lifetime Achievement Award of the Horror Writers Association, the Living Legend Award of the International Horror Guild, and the World Fantasy Lifetime Achievement Award. In 2015 he was made an Honorary Fellow of Liverpool John Moores University for outstanding services to literature.

Among his novels are *The Face That Must Die*, *Incarnate*, *Midnight Sun*, *The Count of Eleven*, *Silent Children*, *The Darkest Part of the Woods*, *The Overnight*, *Secret Story*, *The Grin of the Dark*, *Thieving Fear*, *Creatures of the Pool*, *The Seven Days of Cain*, *Ghosts Know*, *The Kind Folk*, *Think Yourself Lucky*, and *Thirteen Days by Sunset Beach*. His most recent title, *The Way of the Worm*, concludes The Three Births of Daoloth trilogy, which also comprises *The Searching Dead* and *Born to the Dark*.

Campbell's short fiction is collected in *Waking Nightmares*, *Alone with the Horrors*, *Ghosts and Grisly Things*, *Told by the Dead*, *Just*

Behind You, and *Holes for Faces*, while *Needing Ghosts*, *The Last Revelation of Gla'aki*, *The Pretence*, and *The Booking* are novellas.

His novels *The Nameless* and *Pact of the Fathers* have been filmed in Spain, where a movie of *The Influence* is in production.

"'Her Face' was written to commission," explains the author, "to be about three thousand words long. I find that kind of requirement productive of discipline, though I wouldn't yield to it too often.

"I searched my notebooks for an idea that could be developed at such a length, and here's the result, using an aspect of Halloween I hadn't previously turned into a tale. Surprising, really, since the mask is one of the lasting icons of horror."

JOE KNEW HE shouldn't, but he did. When he saw the corner shop on his way home from school he felt glad Mrs Dillard was in hospital. It wasn't as if he'd said so to anyone; he was alone in the side street except for the murmur of traffic on the motorway behind the houses beyond the shop. He was making for his house, which was diagonally opposite Dillard's Provisions, when he saw Mrs Dillard watching him. She was pretending to be one of the Halloween masks in the window.

Her face always looked as though it had been squeezed pale and dry—as though someone had gripped it until the wrinkled mouth shrank small and the nose poked out thin and sharp. As Joe told himself she couldn't know his thoughts he realised he was only seeing one of the masks, which owed some of its pallor to the white glare of the streetlamp on the corner. He forgot about it as he stepped off the pavement into the house.

The narrow hall bisected by the stairs smelled of tonight's kebab and chips, which his mother would have bought on her way home. As Joe hung his coat from one of the shaky bunch of hooks beside the stairs, his mother came out of the kitchen, extracting ten pounds from her glittery handbag. "Just run across and get some ciggies, Joe. Hurry up so your dinner won't go cold."

Joe wished she'd asked before he'd started struggling to free a frayed edge of his coat from the zip, but she misunderstood his hesitation. "Don't worry, June will sell you them. Mrs D won't be there." When he headed for the door his mother cried "Don't go out without your coat. We don't want anybody saying I don't look after you."

Joe shoved his arms into the lumpy sleeves as he hurried across the road. Presumably someone had bought the mask, since it was no longer in the window. How could Joe have thought it was Mrs Dillard? She would have had to clamber on all fours into the window to poke her face between the stand that held the masks and the one displaying magazines. As he went into the shop the bell above the door pinged like the microwave to which he owed most of his meals at home. June Dillard was behind the counter, talking to a customer. "I'm sorry, June," the woman said.

"It was a relief as much as anything, Mrs Allen. Right to the end she was hanging on like grim death."

Joe felt like an intruder. While June's face—a chubby version of her mother's, with a nose as long but broader and blunter—was its usual amiable self, the eyes were wetter than he cared for. She dabbed at them and donned a smile for him. "What can I get you, Joe?"

Embarrassment made him blurt "Were you talking about Mrs Dillard?"

"She left us this morning. Let's hope she found some peace." As Joe wondered why June should think otherwise she said "So what's your pleasure, sir?" like a joke she was sharing with the grown-up customer.

"My mam sent me for cigarettes."

He saw June glance at the room behind her and remembered her mother telling her off when he'd come on the same errand. The shrill voice had felt like spikes in his ears. Mrs Dillard had disagreed just as much with his calling her daughter by her first name, though June encouraged everyone to do so. In a moment June shook her head at herself and found a pack of Joe's mother's brand. "Just be sure and take those straight home to her," she said.

As soon as Joe handed his mother the cigarettes and change she tore off the cellophane so eagerly that he couldn't help saying "They said at school those are bad for you, mam."

"They want to get on with their own job and let the rest of us alone. Have they been up working since four? Maybe if they had to do two jobs to make ends meet they wouldn't be so keen on telling other people how to relax." She crumpled the cellophane and tramped just as fiercely on the pedal of the bin before stalking into the back yard to light a cigarette. "But don't you ever start," she called through the door.

She was behaving as every adult seemed to, telling him not to do what they did themselves. Had Mrs Dillard treated June that way? One summer night not long before she had been taken into hospital he'd heard her berating her daughter. Even if his bedroom window had been shut he might have been able to make out every word: how June left too many lights on in the shop, how she needed to stay open later because the Pakis up the road did, how she ought to ask the customers what the shop should carry as long as she couldn't be trusted to choose only items that would sell . . . "And you couldn't even get yourself a man," Joe had heard Mrs Dillard screech, "he'd have looked after both of us," and despite the distance he'd felt as though her voice was scraping his eardrums. How her daughter must have felt, he didn't want to think.

When he went up to bed that night he saw that the shop lights were still on, though the sign said Dillard's was closed. Was June wasting electricity as a declaration of defiance now that she could do as she liked? The idea made him uneasier than he quite understood. Perhaps realising that a grown-up could act that way did. He lay waiting for the traffic on the motorway to lull him to sleep—he always thought it sounded like waves on a seashore, though he'd never been.

The next night all the shop lights were lit when his mother sent him to buy lemonade. The masks in the window watched him cross the road, except they couldn't without eyes. He didn't think Mrs Dillard would have approved of them—last year he'd heard her telling June that Halloween was an ungodly evil business—or would she have tolerated them if people bought them? More than one of them looked like rubbery old women, and he could almost have imagined June had them in the shop for company if not to remind her of her mother. "What is it this time, Joe?" she said.

She seemed distracted, glancing into the back room again. "I only want some lemonade," Joe said.

"You get whichever you like and don't mind me. Late hours and having to do all the work, not that that's anything new." As if she'd said too much she added quickly "Maybe you'd like to give me a hand at the weekend."

She seemed so anxious that Joe said "I could."

"There'd be a bit of pocket money in it for you. See what your mother says."

"You go and help June tomorrow. Don't ever start thinking women should do all the work," his mother said, which was one of the reasons she'd fallen out with Joe's father. As Joe went back to tell June the decision he saw that she hadn't sold the mask he'd seen yesterday after all; it was on a hook in the darkest corner of the room behind the counter. At least, he thought so until he reached the counter, across which he couldn't even see a hook on the wall of the room. He must have glimpsed some kind of reflection, and he forgot about it upon seeing how much happier June looked because she wouldn't be alone in the shop.

At first he didn't know why. On his way to bed he noticed that the shop was lit, and so was June's flat above it. They still were when he made his breakfast, his mother having left to clean wards at the hospital hours ago. As he crossed the street the glare of the lamp on the corner seemed to deepen the holes that the masks had for eyes. He was early enough for Dillard's to be shut, but he'd barely tried the door when June flustered out of the room behind the counter. "Who is it?" she demanded and was visibly grateful to see Joe's face once it wasn't hidden by the placard hanging on the glass. "Here's our new assistant. Let's see what jobs we can find."

Of course she wasn't really discussing him with someone else. She looked as though she hadn't slept too well, and Joe hadn't previously observed the traces of grey in her hair. As she turned the placard to show the shop was open it must have caused a draught, because a mask in the window shifted like a head that was starting to waken. "Will you check all the dates for me?" June said. "Find out what's so old it should be gone."

"Where?"

"On the tins and in the fridge. I know I should know what's out of date. One more thing I couldn't be trusted to look after," June complained and then clearly wished she'd said less.

The task occupied much of the day. Well before Joe finished taking items to show June that they were past their dates he saw her trying to hide her dismay that the articles were so numerous. She dumped them all in cartons in the back room, and Joe thought she was anxious not to let customers see them, not that too many people came into the shop. Whenever any did he thought he could help June best by pretending he was a customer.

The door kept disturbing a mask in the window. Joe saw its pale reflection shift on the glass as if drawing a breath or stretching to accommodate a face. He didn't care for the sight, however blurred the features were, and he took to staying well clear of the window, especially whenever June retired upstairs yet again. She was in her flat when he heard movement in the shop.

Had some of the out-of-date produce attracted a mouse or a rat? The scraping on the bare floorboards beyond the sets of shelves between him and the window didn't sound as he imagined either creature would. He was about to venture to look when a voice so shrill it made him flinch demanded "What is it, Joe?"

June strode past him before he could answer. He heard her gasp, perhaps only with exertion, as she stooped beyond the shelves. She straightened up, crumpling a mask in her fist. "No use to anybody when it's been down there," she said more fiercely than Joe understood. "Too grubby to live." She marched out of the back door, and Joe heard the clang of a bin lid.

Dinnertime was imminent when Joe began to wonder if she meant to keep him in the shop until it shut. Perhaps his face gave his thoughts away, because she said "I'll see you in the morning. Or do you go to church?" When Joe shook his head she muttered "I don't suppose it'd do any good."

His mother had Chinese fish and chips waiting. "How was your first day at work?"

"I liked helping June," Joe said but wondered how he had.

"So long as it doesn't get in the way of your schoolwork. You'll want a better job than that and mine."

Joe tried to think it was only the shop that kept June up so late. In the middle of the night he stumbled to the bedroom window to see that all her lights were on. At first he hadn't been able to sleep for the noise of whatever she had on television or the radio, a thin shrill muffled voice. Eyeless faces met his gaze, and he didn't care to look too closely at them, however many there were. He retreated to bed and did his best to slumber.

When he went over after breakfast the shop was already open. Presumably June didn't want to risk losing any customers. He wondered which mask she'd thrown in the bin; more than one of those left in the window looked like an old woman. He was more disconcerted to see June, whose face was thinner and increasingly lined, while her greying hair looked as if she'd forgotten to brush it after a restless night. "What can you do for me today, Joe?" she said.

This sounded not so much like musing aloud as a question if not a plea. "Can I help you serve people?" Joe suggested.

"I shouldn't really be employing you at all at your age. They could shut me down if they found out. I know," she added and plainly hoped. "Can you count all the stock on the shelves and write it down for me?"

She found him a clipboard and a chewed ballpoint along with several sheets of paper blank on one side, all of which made Joe feel more like a child given a diversion than an assistant. He started at the window, where he counted a dozen masks. He'd hardly begun listing tins of food on the shelves when he had to ask "Aren't these some of the ones we took off?"

"I've put some back. The dates are just a guide. We can't afford to throw away that much. Besides, it's a sin how much some people waste."

Joe wondered if she was repeating complaints she'd heard from her mother, especially since she was reviving some of that shrillness. By the time he finished his task he suspected that June had returned all the merchandise to the shelves overnight. He would have preferred her not to keep leaving the shop so often today, as if there was something she wanted to find or else to avoid. Being left alone made him feel watched, not least while listing the packets of cigarettes behind the counter. He could have imagined one of the masks was facing him. Of course all the reflections on the window were, and he needn't look more closely at them.

He saw June consult her watch several times—it kept slipping down her wrist—before she said "I expect you'll want your dinner. I don't suppose I'll see you till the weekend."

She thanked him for his help and released ten pounds from the till, gazing at the note on the way to handing it to him. When his mother asked about his day Joe said "I think she just wants someone to be there with her."

"She must be missing her mother."

Joe wasn't so sure. Each night when he went to bed, and whenever the thin shrill distant voice made him restless enough to get up, he saw that June had all the lights on. Perhaps she wasn't being defiant; perhaps she simply didn't like the dark. He couldn't bring himself to ask his mother if she'd heard what June was listening to; his mother needed a good night's sleep—she'd told him often enough. She needed her cigarettes as well, and on Tuesday she sent him over the road.

June's face was thinner and more lined, and her hair was so unkempt it mightn't have been brushed for days, although surely it couldn't be greyer. "Please don't make a habit of this, Joseph," she said.

Was she calling him that as an extra rebuke? "I'll tell my mam," he said, which sounded too much like a childish threat. "I'll say June said."

June's voice rose higher. "You can tell her Miss Dillard did."

Joe felt worse than unwelcome. He snatched the packet and blundered out of the shop. Shutting the door disturbed a mask in the window, and he could have thought the scrawny whitish face was making an effort to turn towards him. At least it would soon be Halloween, and then all the masks would be gone from the window. Presumably June would store any unsold ones for next year.

He didn't like to imagine them lurking somewhere nearby in the dark. He had to look out of his bedroom window to convince himself they weren't worth any loss of sleep. He was doing his best to count them when someone out of sight behind the display took hold of a mask. It had to be June who was inserting her fingertips into the eyeholes of the sharp pale wizened face and her thumb between the thin lips. Certainly an object was poking the lips apart and squirming from side to side. Joe seemed unable to look away or move, and he couldn't help thinking that the spectacle was meant just for him. He fell back from the window and huddled in bed, but it took him quite a while to stop seeing the mask.

In the morning he couldn't tell which mask he'd seen. He was glad his mother didn't need him to go over to Dillard's when he came home from school. That night he went to bed without looking out of the window. He wasn't expecting to sleep too well, but exhaustion caught up with him until a sound roused him. It wasn't the alarm, although that was imminent. The small harsh noise was somewhere outside. It reminded him of digging, but that wasn't right; somebody was shuffling across the street, except that the sound was too hollow. Whatever was inching towards him halted close to the house.

His mother had already left for work. Joe stayed away from the front windows while he used the bathroom and got dressed, all the while listening for activity in the street. All he could hear was traffic on the motorway and his own thumping pulse. He managed to hope that the street was deserted, and it almost was. When he ventured out to be dazzled by the lights in Dillard's, just a face on the pavement was waiting for him.

It was an old woman's pinched wrinkled face. The streetlamp made it paler and stuffed the eyeholes with shadows that could have been lumps of earth. Though it was just a mask, Joe couldn't avoid thinking it had crawled across the road like a shell with a denizen underneath, or had it humped grub-like over the kerb onto the pavement outside his house? He needn't fancy it had any life, although weren't the contents of the eyeholes a little too lively for shadows? Wasn't there some movement within the white slit of a mouth? Joe made to lift the mask with his foot, but was daunted by thinking it was like turning over a stone to see what lived underneath. Instead he trampled on it. He wasn't sure if he felt something inside it give way, but the sensation filled him with such loathing that he kicked the mask into the nearest drain and stamped on it until the last fragment had dropped through the grid.

While he was at school it wouldn't stay out of his mind. At least when he came home the street was empty. All the masks in Dillard's window reminded him how many hours of Halloween were left. He was glad his mother was already home, and more grateful that she didn't send him to the shop. But he was washing up after dinner when she said "Just go over to June's, will you?"

"I didn't tell you. She doesn't like me buying cigarettes."

"You shouldn't really. I'll get them myself in future."

"That's not all," Joe said in desperation. "She isn't like June any more."

"It'll be losing her mother, Joe. We don't want anyone trying to scare her or trick her tonight, do we? Not when she's in that state. Go on," Joe's mother said when he looked for an excuse to linger. "I've had a hard day at work. See how she is and stay with her for a bit if she needs company."

Joe couldn't help wondering if June already had some. At least when he trudged out of the house Dillard's was as bright as it could be. The street was empty, not even a mask to be seen except for the crowd in the window. As he opened the shop door the bell went off like a timer. He just had time to see that the shop was unoccupied before it went dark.

Had the bell fused the lights? Joe wavered on the threshold while his eyes adjusted to the pallid dimness. The streetlamp left too much of the interior unlit, especially the doorway behind the counter. The lights were off in the rest of the premises, then, but why couldn't he hear any reaction? "June?" he called, not very loud.

"No."

The voice was piercing and yet muffled. He couldn't tell whether the word was a denial or a warning. In a moment a thin figure darted out of the back room, jerking up its hands. It had the face he'd trampled on, as sharp and bloodless as ever. The eyes might have been no more than shadows, but a tongue was struggling to part the pinched lips. As the figure lurched forward through the shadows Joe slammed the door hard enough to crack the pane and fled across the road. "June's, there's something wrong with her," he cried. "Get someone, mam. Call the police. Call an ambulance."

The emergency services seemed to think the call could be a Halloween prank, especially since Joe was unable to convey what was wrong at the shop. At last his mother persuaded the operator that a woman on her own had experienced some kind of breakdown, and Joe retreated upstairs to watch from the safest distance he could find. He heard worse than a commotion in the shop or in June's flat—the voice screeching "Go away" and a smash of glass. He didn't know if he would rather think that June was telling him and any other aid to go away or someone he preferred not to bring to mind.

At last he heard the ambulance. The siren drowned out her cries, though not by any means immediately. The flashing lights came to rest outside Dillard's, and two paramedics hurried in. The shop lit up almost at once, and soon the upstairs rooms did, which only made the voice rise higher. It was still repeating its plea when the man and woman ushered their charge to the ambulance, and Joe saw the hands jerk up again to drag at the stiff white dried-up face until the attendants recaptured the arms. As the vehicle sped away Joe heard a shriller sound in the midst of the siren. Soon the deserted street grew quiet, but he was left with yet another thought he didn't want to have: that the glass he'd heard breaking had been a mirror.

A MAN TOTALLY ALONE

Robert Hood

Robert Hood has been writing in various genres for many years, especially in the areas of horror, crime, and weird fiction. Once described as "Aussie horror's wicked godfather," his work has gained him various Australian award nominations and publication worldwide, mostly for short stories.

His epic fantasy novel, *Fragments of a Broken Land: Valarl Undead*, won the Australian Ditmar Award for Best Novel, and his most recent collection is the award-winning *Peripheral Visions: The Collected Ghost Stories*—complete, that is, except for the new story that follows. He is currently completing a supernatural crime novel entitled *Scavengers*.

"Though Halloween itself is a relatively low-key event in Australia," Hood explains, "it has picked up some momentum in recent times, spurred on by increased commercial interests.

"It's the traditional supernatural meaning that lies behind Halloween that interests me most—the ancient pagan celebrations of the end of summer and the harvest seasons, and the beginning of the darker half of the year, celebrations for which some find connections going as far back as the Roman Parentalia, the nine-day festival of the dead, and (more commonly) the Celtic ritual of Samhain. When Christianity reworked the ritual it became All Hallows' Eve, and was followed by All Hallows' Day. Yet Halloween as a supernatural celebration of the dead lives on, even if it has gradually lost its religious and supernatural meanings.

"Before I decided to write the following story, I'd read an article about the ruins of an ancient Viking village found in Australia, seeming to confirm a long-held belief that the Norsemen had 'discovered' the island continent long before those more traditionally recorded as doing so had arrived on the shores of the Great Southern Land. The idea of combining this with a Halloween scenario appealed to me for obvious reasons—not least of which was the title, a phrase taken from the well-known Nordic epic *Hervarar saga ok Heiðreks konungs*. Connecting Vikings and the theme of loneliness to this popular festival of the dead seemed to me like a perfect fit, and made for an interestingly appropriate conflation of ideas.

"Incidentally, the Vikings had their own version of Halloween, some say—Álfablót, or the Sacrifice to the Elves—the 'elves' in Old Norse referring to spirits that are both earth-creatures and the souls of departed men."

SAND AND SCATTERED rocks crunched under the wheels. Salinger could feel heat eating its way up through the chassis as the 4WD shook and rattled. He squinted toward the outlying crags of the Coolangamar hills, the sun's glare squeezing in through his eyeballs like a headache.

"Is it far?" he growled.

"Far from what?" his passenger said.

Salinger had picked up Doogan at the main road as requested, and so far, hadn't been able to get any sensible information out of him.

The older man laughed. "Sorry it's so hard on ya vehicle. Ground's pretty rough, eh?"

"The quake?"

Doogan ignored his question. "The body's over there." He pointed. Salinger could just make out through the heat-haze what might have been a vehicle. Doogan added, "Poor bugger was in a hole opened up by the tremors, we think."

"Any sign how he got here?"

"Na. There's bugger-all for a hundred kilometers."

"Except the mine."

"And it's twenty kays that way." Doogan pointed toward where the sun would set in five or six hours. "Couldn't have walked from there. Couldn't've walked from anywhere. Not in his state." He grinned. "Someone dumped him, probably. Or he was buried somewhere there and got spewed up by the quake."

Salinger grunted. This whole thing would have been a hell of a lot easier if HQ had let him use the chopper instead of a four-wheel drive. But the pilot wasn't available. Salinger could fly the damn thing. Just because his license had been taken from him. . . .

He felt a memory twinge and pushed it away. He didn't need to go to bad places right now.

"There they are. See 'em?"

He could hardly see anything through the glare and the dust on the windscreen. The heat was fierce, despite the 4WD's air-con. The arse-end of October was always a killer out here. *At least I could've remembered to bring sunglasses*, he thought bitterly.

He braked to a stop near the Land Rover. It was even more battered than his own. He let the engine die.

"Come on," said Doogan, getting out of the vehicle. Salinger followed.

Two men—an Aboriginal, twenty, twenty-five maybe, and a white bloke some years on from that—materialized through the haze. Doogan said, "Denny and Wal."

Salinger nodded toward them, but his eyes were scanning the area. The two men were standing just outside the shadow of a rock outcrop, beneath which the ground had split open to create an overhang. He could barely make out the body sprawled there.

"You sure he's dead?"

Wal grunted. "Woulda called the Flying Docs if we weren't. Instead we got you."

"Yeah. Lucky me."

Denny said nothing. Eyes bright against the darkness of his skin evaluated Salinger without comment.

"So how'd he die?"

"Bugger if I know. That's your job, ain't it?" Salinger found Wal's antagonism annoying, but he didn't take it personally. There'd been a fair bit of trouble at the Tyanerong mine over the past decade—what with issues of indigenous land rights, low-paid illegal immigrant workers, variable pay conditions, and environmental irresponsibility provoking all sorts of argy-bargy—and police action hadn't always gone the way the miners wanted.

"It's my job to ask questions," Salinger said flatly.

"Don't mind him." Doogan shot Wal a snarly look, which Salinger wasn't supposed to see. He did, though, and it made him wonder what was going on under the surface. Not that he cared. There was *always* something going on beneath Doogan's surface. He stepped past both of them and knelt next to the body.

As his eyes readjusted to the shadow's comparative gloom, what he saw didn't fill him with confidence that he'd be able to come up with answers any better than these blokes had. The corpse was that of a man whose age was as indeterminate as where he'd come from. Walking hadn't been an issue. Even at a glance, the state of the dead man's skin made it obvious he'd been dead for a long time. Its texture was dark—not indigenous dark, but old, dried-out dark—and wrinkled, without fat reserves so that it had shrunk around his bones like gauze. Looked singed, too. His head was more like a skull than a head. Clothes were rags, linen pants hand-sewn and coat baggy and torn. Parts of it seemed to have rotted right through. What remained was well on the way. His feet were bare.

"Has he been moved since you found him?"

"Na," snapped Wal. Too quickly.

"Didn't touch him," Doogan added. "Besides, just lookin' at him you can see he's dead."

Salinger placed his fingers on the man's neck to check for an impossible pulse. The skin felt cold, totally arctic, despite the heat, with little meat or muscle underneath.

"He's been dead for months, I'd say." He glanced back at Doogan. "Probably longer."

"Ya reckon?" Wal smirked.

Salinger gestured toward the surrounding ground. Obvious marks in the dirt led up to where the dead man's hands with their long, cracked fingernails and his desiccated, shoeless feet were spread out at random angles. "Who made all these tracks?"

Doogan grunted. "Guess *we* did."

"Could any of them belong to someone who put the corpse here?"

"Ask Denny. He's the expert."

Salinger turned his gaze back toward the Aboriginal bloke, who shrugged. "Them's ours all right," Denny muttered. "No others. No tire marks 'round here either . . . 'cept the ones we made."

"No animal tracks?"

"Bloody big windstorm bugger three nights ago woulda wiped 'em all."

Salinger nodded skeptically. "A big storm that covered all traces, yet the body's not covered in sand or any other debris?"

Denny shrugged. "No other fella's trail that I can see."

Salinger turned his attention back to the corpse. On closer inspection, this thing had to have been dead for years, not just months. Yet here it was, ragged and dried out, but no sign of windblown exposure. Tentatively he felt the clothes it was wearing, what there was left of them. The texture was rough and brittle. Old. Very old. Rotten in places. His fingers brushed against a hard object. Not bones.

"There's something here."

He reached under the corpse, fingers closing around the object. It felt wooden—flat and round. It was the size of a Vegemite lid, slightly smaller than his palm, with a decorated surface. He pulled. The object moved a few centimeters, partly appearing from under the man's clothing. Something held it back. He pulled harder and the corpse shifted. It took a moment for Salinger to realize the round object was held by a chain that circled the dead man's neck.

"He's wearin' a medallion," Wal said. "Looks like snakes or somethin'."

Two-headed snakes. Four of them, evenly spaced around the raised outer rim of the medallion, each bent in half and crossed over themselves, their heads facing in opposite directions. The curve of their "middle" part touched the solid center of the medallion. Each head was looking at the head of another snake, but none looked at their own "second" head.

"It ain't some Abo thing." Wal glanced at Denny as though expecting him to say something.

Denny ignored him. Salinger could tell he didn't like either Wal or his comment. Probably both.

Suddenly, irrationally, as he knelt there next to the desiccated cadaver, holding the medallion in his fingers and wondering at the odd feeling he was getting from these men, Salinger felt a wave of utter loneliness wash over him. Desolation ached in his chest, pounding like a second heart, one long dead but struggling to return to life, and in so doing filling him with sorrow. His mind was swept by a chilly wind that carried images of his wife, Leslie, dead now for near seven years, and his daughter, Nat, both killed in a freak storm that caused him to lose control of the chopper they were flying in that November night. If only he hadn't brought them with him! He had survived, barely—the only remnant of his family—and the thought once again filled him with grief. Tears welled in his eyes, as hadn't happened for years now, carrying with them a misery as potent as ever. He had never felt more alone.

He exhaled a deep sobbing groan.

The medallion fell from his fingers. As it tumbled back into the folds of the corpse's clothes, the feelings of despair that throbbed in his gut diminished, leaving an emptiness filled with distant sounds echoing not just from a few years ago, but over centuries.

A hand grabbed his shoulder. He turned, a stab of terror sweeping through him.

"What's up with you, mate?"

It was only Doogan. But for a moment the man had looked like some sort of demon.

"Nothing," Salinger gasped out, too forcefully, as the emotions retreated. "Tomorrow. It's the anniversary. Of when she died. . . ." He fumbled through his mind for a memory that had already retreated back into his subconscious.

"When who died?"

He paused, stilling his nerves. Then, "Forget it," he said. "It doesn't matter. I don't know what I'm saying. A dizzy spell."

He pushed himself up, tried to gather his strength, to gain some equilibrium.

"You got a problem?" growled Doogan.

"I do, as a matter of fact," Salinger said. "This isn't a crime scene." He gestured at the corpse. "And that's not a job for the police."

"Not the cops' job? It's an unexplained dead body, ain't it? Who else should deal with it?"

"An archeologist maybe."

Doogan's weather-beaten face scrunched up even more than normal. "You're bullshitting me, right?"

For a moment Salinger said nothing, staring blankly into Doogan's eyes.

"Look," he said finally, forcing a patient tone to cover his annoyance, "It's obvious this is a very old corpse. That's all I'm saying."

Wal sneered. "So, we shoulda just ignored it then?"

"I didn't say that."

"What's ya beef then?" growled Wal.

Salinger directed his attention to Doogan. "Can I speak to you, Sam . . . alone?"

Doogan obviously didn't like the idea, but shrugged and followed Salinger away from the others. When they were far enough out of earshot, Salinger stared Doogan in the eyes for a few moments. Doogan shifted uneasily.

"Well?" he muttered.

Salinger sighed. "You do realize this whole thing is as suspicious as hell, right?"

"What'd you—?"

"You know what I mean. I'm surprised you expect me to buy it."

"What's ya problem, mate?"

"For a start, tell me this: How did you bastards happen to stumble on this desiccated corpse way out here in the middle of nowhere? Having a little stroll through the desert, were you? On a workday?"

"We were heading back to town . . . for supplies. . . ."

"And saw it from the highway even though it's in a hole overshadowed by a rock at least a kilometer away? Need I point out a dozen other unlikely aspects to this . . . whatever it is?"

Doogan sighed. "Look, mate—" He glanced toward his underlings, "—let's just say it's dumb chance, eh? Seriously, getting to the truth'd be a pain in the arse. Not 'cause there's anything illegal goin' on. Just 'cause it'd be bloody inconvenient."

"Inconvenient?"

"Yeah. Hypothetically speaking."

"Well, hypothetically, how about you come clean, Sam, and tell me all about the inconveniences."

Doogan sighed, finally raising his head to look at Salinger with an air of resignation.

"We *might've* found the bloody thing in a new part of the mine, in a pocket opened up by the 'quake. You're right, it's real old. It couldn'ta been put there any time in the past coupla hundred years 'cause the space was completely sealed off 'til we came along. But look at it! It might be pretty wasted and dried out, but there's still some meat on its bones. How the fuck could it be there, in a hole in the ground that no one's seen since before us white bastards turned up to pinch this land off the natives?"

"You tell me."

"I can't. But we knew straightaway there was something weird about it. It freaked a lot of the men out. Even the local Abos wanted nothin' to do with it. Wasn't an ancestor of theirs or anythin', so they wanted it off their land. And at any rate turning the mine into a huntin' ground for feral academics woulda meant suspending current operations—and we can't bloody afford to do that. The company's already close to bankruptcy, Jimbo, what with the Greenie's war on coal and all that eco-shit. And. . . ."

His diatribe morphed into a political rant. Salinger listened patiently until he got bored with it, then gestured for Doogan to stop.

"Yeah, yeah, I get your point, Sam." Doogan adopted an air of puppy-dog misery. "You really didn't think this through though, did you?" Salinger continued. "You *hypothetically* dump the body out here where it's unlikely to have been unearthed and then you tell me you stumbled across it. Why? Maybe because you reckon I'm just a dumb cop and won't notice the illogic of it all?"

"Mate, I just—"

"Why did you even call me? If you'd dumped it, covered it over, who would've known?"

"Thought it might be . . . you know . . . important. Seemed like the right thing to do." His face adopted an expression of confusion. "Shit, I don't know. I just felt . . . I had to. The others weren't keen but. . . ." He tapered off. Then: "There's something I should tell you, something . . . about this thing."

"Oh?"

"It's crazy, but . . . since we found it, everyone's been antsy. Weird shit has been happening—"

"Weird shit?"

"Reports of . . . the men seeing . . . you know. . . ."

"What?"

"Ghosts or somethin'."

"Really?"

"And voices . . . well, one voice. . . ."

"Saying what?"

"No one could tell. But Frank Napper . . . remember him? He went nuts and tried to kill himself. Kept yelling he couldn't stand being alone anymore. That the shadows had told him he'd be better off dead."

Salinger stared at him in amazement.

Doogan looked embarrassed. "I want to get rid of it, okay, but I couldn't just toss it."

"Why?"

"It wouldn't let me."

"Wouldn't let you? The corpse wouldn't let you? Are you kidding me?"

Doogan shrugged.

"This sounds like complete bullshit."

"Yeah? Well, think what ya bloody like. What're ya gonna do? Arrest us?"

Salinger sighed. "Sounds like you're all going nuts. Just clean up the site and get rid of your own presence here. I'm tired of this crap. I'll take some pictures of the location, because I'm supposed to. You can help me put the bloody thing in the jeep. I'll take it back with me and—"

"We really can't have the mine turned into an archeological dig, Jim. It'd be the last straw. That's fair dinkum. I swear there was nothin' else of interest in the grotto where we found the bloody thing. Nothin'."

Salinger gestured for silence. "I'll make up some shit about a tourist who stumbled onto the body while they were wandering around looking for somewhere to piss."

"But your boss'll want to interview someone. . . ."

"Yeah, yeah. I'll deal with it. Okay?"

Doogan looked doubtful.

"Okay?" Salinger growled insistently.

Doogan nodded.

As he drove back to town, Salinger found himself becoming more uncertain than ever about this whole business. What a load of shit! And it was one hell of a drive, too. The heat played games with his skull, making him feel light-headed, and disturbingly dizzy. About a half-hour into it, memories of Leslie and Nataly and the horrendous aftermath of the accident that took them from him began leaking back into his consciousness. He remembered how he'd struggled with his feelings of loss and guilt at the time, and began to relive the sorrow that had nearly driven him to suicide. Sudden awareness of just how lost and isolated he still felt after all these years caused him to lose focus, and he only snapped out of it when he found himself veering off the road toward a dry riverbed. He slammed on the brakes at the last moment and sat clutching the steering wheel until his fingers ached. He swore at the car, at fate, at the God that had thrown his 'copter into an irresistible dive . . . but mostly at himself.

Einn Saman, Myrkvar Grímur.

These words, sounding like the tail end of a failing radio broadcast, snapped him out of his melancholic paralysis. Strange, unfamiliar words they were, yet seeming to resonate with his thoughts. He glanced up compulsively. Something was in the rearview mirror. A grim, skeletal shadow stared out at him. A face.

"Who the hell—?"

He turned, but there was no one behind him. All he could see was the body bag containing the long-dead corpse that had drawn him out here in the first place.

A shiver ran through his muscles. He breathed out, and in again, with calm determination. He had to keep himself together. Had to. This was his job. And he couldn't let this particular case, though undoubtedly bizarre, propel him into a state of self-pitying and superstitious delusion. Best it was just forgotten. Doogan's bullshit was getting to him.

But the feeling that something was happening didn't go away. The shadow-face in the mirror had no doubt been his own, but he'd for sure heard the words. From the radio maybe? He checked it, but it was definitely off. He tried to repeat the words then, and even though they were foreign and meaningless he found he could remember them. *Einn Saman, Myrkvar Grímur.* How could he possibly recite that? His memory wasn't good enough to recall a nonsensical sentence he'd heard once—and not very clearly—when he couldn't even remember his own address half the time. Maybe he'd merely dreamed he heard the words and, in hindsight, any sequence of sounds would have been recalled as accurate.

"Bugger it!" he muttered and gave up, dismissing the whole episode as a dream.

It was late afternoon by the time he got back to the station. As luck would have it, the only person in attendance was Constable Hurley, who was on front desk duty. The way she stared at her computer, with a sort of sardonic intensity, suggested it was Facebook that was keeping her busy.

"Hey, Flo," Salinger said.

She glanced up. "You took your time." She grinned. "A three-beer problem was it, eh?"

"Just a body," he said.

"Anyone I know?"

"Doubt it. It's old and way past its use-by date."

"Older than you?"

"Very funny." He gestured toward the back. "Is the cold room open?"

"It will be if you use a key." She tossed it to him.

"Thanks."

"Shouldn't you have left the victim where it was and called for the ME?"

"It's very old, Flo. Ancient. Pretty much just skin and bone. Been in the ground for quite a while. Coughed up by the quake last week, I'd say. I took site pics." He paused. "Besides, it was way out in the middle of nowhere."

Hurley looked doubtful. "The Chief won't be happy."

"Is he around?"

"Took the arvo off. Something about his son and prepping for a Halloween party."

"Halloween?"

"Yeah. You know, trick-or-treat. It's tonight. The 31st. Haven't you been paying attention?"

"Do the kids still do that shit these days?"

"Sure. Kids like getting free sugar highs. Not as obsessively as in the States, but some of the shops hereabouts've been pushing it. Business, you know?"

Salinger huffed. "Is Jen still around?"

"She's staying over."

"Well, let her know there's a corpse waiting for her, please?" Jen was the itinerant pathologist and medical examiner. She'd been called in to deal with the forensic aftermath of a multi-vehicle incident that had taken place a bit further north the day before. "Tell her it's a Halloween treat from me," he added. "She should take a look."

"I don't think she's due back in 'til later tonight."

"No hurry. The dead bloke's not going anywhere. Been lying around since colonial times by the look of him."

"Really?"

"Something like that. I'd like her opinion at any rate. The whole thing's pretty weird. Meanwhile, I'm going home. I'll talk to her in the morning."

Flo grinned mischievously. "Okay, but you really should do the paperwork first."

"It can wait," he growled, and headed for the door.

By the time he'd deposited the corpse in a fridge-drawer in their on-site morgue, such as it was, dusk was starting to settle in. Salinger's head felt like it was about to explode. As a result, he drove through town slowly and carefully, noticing the general lack of Halloween pumpkins, dancing plastic skeletons, and other decorations so prominent in seasonal American horror flicks. As he said, the tradition hadn't really caught on here—probably because it wasn't the depth of winter. One house, just one, had a skull-shaped candleholder flickering in its front window. The Dahlman house. Dahlman was from Scandinavia or one of those places, wasn't he?

Only once did Salinger pass a hopeful group of kids, most of them done up like Spider-Man or fairy princesses. The arachnid superheroes in particular looked rather uncomfortable in their all-encompassing costumes. The temperature was too extreme, even as the sun headed for the horizon.

A few kids had given themselves over more thoroughly, if unknowingly, to the spirit of the day and were masquerading as zombies or skeletons or ghosts—and that's really what Halloween was about, wasn't it? All Hallows' Eve, Samhain, Day of the Dead: the night when the deceased, good and bad, returned to walk the Earth, demanding appeasement or atonement, before being sent back into oblivion. Manifesting as the walking dead, hockey-masked killers, spooky clowns—spirits that returned to plague humanity year after year—they knock on your door and demand recognition (in the form of treats) to send them on their way.

That's why Salinger hated it. Mortality was, had never been, something he wanted to be reminded of. Not right now, and not so close to the anniversary of the day his family had been taken from him—no, don't think about that! He wouldn't go there. He suppressed the thought, refusing to ponder on it further.

One of the "zombies" waved at him. Salinger pretended not to notice. At least these particular restless spirits were accompanied by parental guardians who would stop them from grabbing the souls of ungenerous residents and hopefully limit the noise. As a cop, he approved of that. As himself, too. With a bit of luck, none of them would get to his part of town before darkness descended—and his personal demons began screaming even more loudly in his head.

His road, which lacked streetlights and was unsealed, remained typically devoid of activity, showing no sign of trick-or-treaters. Thanking whatever deity was responsible for that, Salinger parked the Rover on the tire-worn grass next to the house. As he climbed out and slammed the car door, he sensed a movement behind him, and glanced around, reacting with a twinge of uncertainty, a touch of dread.

But it was only Stan Grundy from the dilapidated graveyard of dead cars that formed a peripheral eyesore at the far end of the street. He didn't acknowledge Salinger's presence, so Salinger gratefully reciprocated the man's lack of neighborly camaraderie by turning away and trudging toward his own front door.

Once inside, he fetched a beer from the fridge, and took a few desperate swigs to wash down some paracetamol tablets he'd scrounged from his medicine cabinet. Afterwards, he sat in the gloomy lounge, curtains drawn, and tried to forget the day's craziness. He needed to clear his mind of both Doogan's nonsense and the painful memories that were still knocking against the back of his skull.

The first was easy enough, the second less so. At some point his phone rang, several times perhaps, but he ignored it. Gradually consciousness drifted away along with the few threads of sunlight leaking in through gaps in his curtains.

Persistent banging on the door dragged him awake again. For how long he'd been asleep, he didn't know. He was sitting in almost complete darkness now, but though his headache had faded, he still felt numb and disorientated. Whoever was at the door knocked again.

Should he get up? Could be important. But he really didn't want to. A bleak weariness of spirit drained him of any real motivation. Anyway, maybe it was those damn Halloween kids. "Piss off!" he muttered beneath his breath.

"Jim, are you in there?" called a female voice through the wood and frosted-glass of the door. For a moment, his pulses raced.

"Leslie?" he whispered. The voice sounded like it could have been his wife's.

"Jim?"

A rush of shock and desire convinced him it was her. Ghost or living victim of misidentification, he didn't care. He pushed himself up and stumbled toward the door.

"Jim?" said the voice once more.

"I'm here, Les," he yelled. "Hang on! I'm here!"

He flung open the door, and there she was—Leslie. Looking just as she looked in what was left of his visual memories of her. Elation swept through his body, overriding any rational doubts he might have had.

"Trick-or-treat!" the apparition said, grinning.

He blinked, stifling a cry as the figure's face morphed into the wretched, rotting visage of a supernatural vagrant. Dark eye-sockets, though empty, stared back at him.

He gasped and felt the energy drain from his legs. He began to collapse. But before he hit the floor, the undead horror stepped forward with a cry, grabbing him under his arms. He felt his attacker's skeletal fingers pressing into his flesh.

"Leslie!" he groaned.

"It's me, Jim," the figure said. "Jennifer . . . Jennifer Eastbridge."

Jen?

His eyes cleared then, and the vision he'd awoken to swept away into the night.

"Are you okay?" she asked.

Salinger considered the question. Pushing himself from her grip, he shrugged. "Sorry." He wiped his hands over his face. "I was asleep. I think I was dreaming."

"No, *I* apologize." Jen gently aimed him toward his chair. "I didn't mean to startle you."

He sank into the cushions and reached for his half-empty beer bottle, noting that there were two other bottles there as well, both empty—and he didn't recall getting up at any point to fetch them from the fridge.

"It's okay," he managed. "I had a tough day."

"Yes," she said, "that's what I wanted to talk to you about. But maybe you'd rather not—"

"No, it's okay." He gestured toward the kitchen. "Go make yourself some tea or something. Or there's beer and wine in the fridge. Whatever. I'll be more . . . um, coherent . . . by the time you get back."

"If you're sure."

He nodded.

Salinger watched her as she walked down the corridor to the kitchen, turning the lights on as she did. Jen and he were friends now, though there had been a time, back in their early twenties, when a more romantic friendship had come to an end and they'd drifted apart with some bad feelings. Jen had gone off to study medicine at the University of Western Australia, while he had been doomed to stay where they'd grown up, later to be trained more locally to join the police force.

She had returned, still single, but by then Salinger had married Leslie and had started to build a family. Things had been awkward for a while, though they'd gotten over it and embraced a more platonic relationship, given time. Yet even after Leslie's death, the romance had not returned.

Sometimes he looked at her, though, and her familiar beauty, unaggressive intelligence and kind, altruistic nature would nudge him to pursue a more passionate intimacy. But he couldn't do it. Something in him resisted. Something in him had died with Leslie and Nataly that day. He had survived the crash, but not intact.

By the time Jen returned with a cup of tea, Salinger had managed to at least partially rebuild the wall he mentally constructed to keep the dark emotions contained. He didn't want to forget the sorrows of his past, but he didn't want to relive them on a daily basis either. Of course, the wall had holes in it and dark leakage would seep through eventually. Especially tonight.

"You okay?" asked Jen, sinking into the nearest chair. *"Nataly's chair," the dark wind hissed.*

"I guess the Halloween gag was a bit insensitive, eh?" she continued, with a sympathetic frown. "My bad. I forgot for a moment. Sorry."

He nodded and silently waved away the apology.

Jen continued. "Doing Halloween seems to be on the rise—a bunch of kids were trick-or-treating along Lawson Street. I haven't seen that before around here."

"Yeah. I noticed them earlier. They haven't made it out this far, have they?"

"Relax. They were heading back into town." She paused. "Actually, Halloween has come to the morgue, too, as you suggested."

"What?"

"That corpse you wanted me to look at. . . ."

"What about it?"

"It doesn't make sense—and is positively creepy, even for me. Nothing about it is normal."

"What do you mean?"

Her light hazel eyes had a strange intensity to them. "Just tell me where it came from. I noticed you didn't write a report."

"I had a headache."

"Sure, but I need to know the details."

"Now?"

"Yes, now."

He grumbled, but emptied the beer bottle into his mouth, got up to fetch another and returned to drop onto the sofa again. Jen scowled at him. "You're drinking too much."

"Not enough, if you ask me," he said, and downed another mouthful.

"So are you going to tell me?"

He gave her a rundown of the day's events, leaving out the mine, Doogan's fairy tales, and his own emotional reactions to it all—which, to be fair, were where the real issues lay. In the end, he could tell from the look on her face that she knew there was much more to it than that.

"So what's your problem?" he asked.

"My problem," she said in a serious tone, "is that it doesn't make sense. From a forensic point of view, that corpse is a completely impossible anomaly. Some indicators suggest death occurred in the past few weeks, others that it is ancient. Was the corpse placed in a coffin immediately upon death? Perhaps, though from what you say there was no evidence of that—but even so, it's not right. It shows no signs of having gone through the normal bloating stages nor has it decayed, except for some external patches. It *has* dried out and shrunk somewhat, but minimally—the shrinkage is what gives it the skeletal appearance. Likewise, there's no sign of embalming of any kind. Other indicators—including the lack of moisture and active decay in its remaining flesh and skin—would suggest it was chemically embalmed or some other preservation method was used, though there's no other sign of it. Has it been underground for decades? Even longer? Maybe. Probably. Yes and no. It's all contradictory. I would have to guess it has not been exposed to bacteria or insects at all during that time, though once again, how could that be?"

"It is pretty dry out here—and if it was originally buried deep in the bedrock—"

"What'd you mean in the bedrock? You said it was more or less out in the open."

He had to back off. "Anyway, from the look of it, I thought it was more a job for an archeologist than us."

"I'd agree. But at the same time. . . ." She shrugged, then looked at him intently, her eyes pinning him to his seat. "Where did it really come from, Jim?"

Salinger had been hoping the whole thing could be filed under "weird shit" and left at that. But of course, Jen was much less of an emotional coward than he was. Sighing, he gave in without fuss and told her about the mine in which the corpse had been entombed (according to Doogan), even the motive behind Doogan's attempts to distance it from that location.

"It'll have to be investigated," Jen said.

"Why? What does it matter? The body has obviously been dead for longer than we could possibly investigate. Did you find any indication of cause of death? A knife wound maybe? Indented skull?"

"Nothing. Closer investigation might reveal something. But there's more to it—"

"I'm for burying it again and forgetting about it."

"It could have considerable historic importance, Jim. There may be a lot more evidence to be found."

"Doogan says there's nothing."

"How deeply has he investigated?"

"I don't know." He took another swig and discovered the bottle was empty. "But I still don't see why it matters. My gut tells me we should leave it alone."

Jen reached for her handbag and pulled out a sealed forensic specimen bag. "Did you notice this?" she said, holding it up. Inside the bag was the medallion he'd held for long enough to be overwhelmed by the bleak emotions that seemed to emanate from it. Once again he felt echoes of a distant, but profound despair. He took it from her grip.

"Can you feel it?" he whispered staring intently at the object.

"Feel what?"

He looked into her eyes, but saw only curiosity.

"Nothing. So, what about it?" he said.

"I'm pretty sure it's an ancient, very early Old Norse artifact—a Viking pendant or talisman of some kind. As far as I can tell, it's genuine. If what Doogan told you is true, it might date from . . . God knows how long ago, well before Australia was visited by Captain Cook and even before either the Portuguese or Dutch stumbled upon the place—"

"A Viking pendant? You mean the Vikings got to Australia first?"

"Long after the Aboriginal People, of course, but ahead the others, yes. Could be. Various scholars have been speculating about the possibility for a good many years. And a team of archeologists from the University of Sydney recently excavated what seems to be a Viking settlement on the northern coast near Derby. Not too far from here, really. It dates from the eleventh century, they reckon."

"And this—" Salinger held up the medallion in its forensic bag. "This proves the dead man was a Viking?"

"Maybe. Both that and the corpse will have to be subjected to a more sophisticated examination than I can manage. DNA tests, for one thing, but historical stuff, too. The pendant and its design for another. And I suspect what's left of the man's clothing will prove to be important, too. But I'm a pathologist, not a historian."

"Sure, though—"

"God knows what's still in the mine. And none of it can explain the contradictory state of the body."

Salinger gave her a tired, even despairing look, placing the artifact on the table next to his chair.

"You know, just to make things weirder," Jen added, "I'm convinced that pendant was actually embedded into the surface layers of the dead man's chest."

"What?"

"There's an indentation just over his heart, the exact size of the medallion. It fits into the skin and muscles there, right down to the ribcage, which was dented, with some cracking."

"Is that what killed him?"

"I don't think so. Looks like it settled into him over time, as though it was much heavier than it actually is. Another oddity. From what you told me, you would have pulled it out of the indent when—"

"—I yanked on it."

"Yep. I think it may be some sort of magical charm, probably intended to keep the corpse from rising."

"Who the hell was this guy? What did he do to deserve this?"

"We'll probably never know. Something pretty bad, I'd guess, given the effort they went to. Incidentally, did I mention his heart is still there, not beating, of course, but neither decayed nor damaged?"

"Surely that's impossible."

"That's what I've been saying." She shook her head, noticed that her red-tinged hair had come loose from the bun it had been forced into to accommodate her work-cap, and flicked it aside. "I think I might need a beer after all."

Salinger watched her stand.

"Jen?" he said. "Am I right in remembering that you studied some ancient languages in uni?"

"Only as an aside, as part of my undergrad work. Mostly Latin and Greek."

"Old Norse?"

She shrugged, with a faraway look, as though remembering. "A short course on Old Norse sagas. A nice diversion from all the body-horror of forensic studies."

"So, do you know what '*Einn Saman, Myrkvar Grímur*' means? Is it Old Norse?"

A puzzled look spread over her face. "Well, normally I wouldn't, but that's a famous one. Yes, it's Old Norse. It's from *The Saga of King Heidrek the Wise*. It's often quoted."

"So what's it mean?"

"Translates as 'a man totally alone' or 'a man all alone,' depending on which version you read. The whole sentence goes '*Foolish he seems to me, who goes there, a man totally alone, through dark night*.'" She shrugged. "Once upon a time, I knew the entire sequence. In Old Norse. Used it in a psych paper I wrote."

"I'm amazed you knew as much as you did."

"So where did *you* come across it? Been reading Nordic sagas in your spare time?"

"Just something I heard on the radio. Go get your beer."

Salinger watched as she strode off into the kitchen. "Hey, bring me one, too, will you?"

"Haven't you had enough?" her voice echoed along the short corridor.

"Define 'enough.'"

She didn't reply.

"Jen?"

Salinger waited for a few minutes, but she neither replied nor reappeared.

"Jen? What are you doing in there?"

Again, no response. He looked down at the pendant, reached out against his better judgement, and picked it up. A strange chill settled over the room, the sort of feeling he had experienced earlier—a debilitating emptiness that nearly overpowered his ability to breath, to move. Unnerved, Salinger tried to cry out, to stand, to do anything. But it felt as though his legs were paralyzed and the room was collapsing inwards. Lights appeared to dim, threatening to flicker out completely. Shadows gathered around the walls.

A movement sensed out of the corner of his eye made him jerk around. Two areas of darkness were forming as the gray shadows that were engulfing the room became denser, darker. Heart racing, he stared, trying to focus his eyes. The blurred patches of shadow gradually solidified. Took the form of human figures. Two women, one shorter than the other. They slid toward him and as they did, they clarified further, uncertain edges becoming clearer, features becoming three-dimensional. He recognized who they were.

But it was impossible.

"No," he whispered, "You're not here."

The taller of the two reached out to him.

Don't let it engulf you. He didn't so much hear the words as feel them resonate, fully formed, in his mind. *It's all tricks. Only tricks. Don't feed it.*

"I don't know what you mean. You're not real. This is all in my head."

Just don't give it what it wants.

"Leave me alone. Go! Please. I can't believe you're real."

A heavy pounding sound echoed through the house.

Salinger blinked, startled, glanced toward the door where the pounding had come from, then looked back. The human shadows of Leslie and his daughter were gone.

Another knock thudded into his head.

Now what? he thought. *Those trick-or-treating kids, I bet. Just what I need.*

Knock. Knock.

"Get lost!" he yelled. The effort made the headache he hadn't been able to shift flare up and pound against his temples.

Knock. Knock.

He cursed and staggered toward the door. Another heavy pounding vibrated through him as he reached for the doorknob. He paused, swore again, then finished the movement, gripping the knob and flinging open the door.

"There's nothing here for you lot—" he began.

"*Einn Saman, Myrkvar Grímur,*" whispered a skeletal shape that stepped out of the darkness. Its withered hand moved toward him.

Only then did Salinger realize what it was he was still holding in his left hand.

"*Einn Saman, Myrkvar Grímur.*"

He felt the empty spaces within expand to engulf him completely.

"Was that someone at the door?" Jen said as she walked back into the lounge, carrying two beers. A strange haziness hung around the edges of the space, though the lighting was as strong as ever. When she looked to where she expected Salinger to be, she realized he wasn't on the sofa where she'd left him only a few minutes before. A quick glance toward the open front door told her where he'd gone.

He was lying sprawled there, unmoving.

"Jim!" she cried, nearly dropping the bottles. She put them down on the nearest table with exaggerated care, and rushed toward him. "Jim! Are you all right?"

He didn't respond. She checked for a pulse and found one, though it was barely detectable. As she lowered his hand she realized he was still holding the forensic specimen bag that had contained the pendant. It was torn and empty, and she couldn't find the artifact itself anywhere around him.

She glanced out the open door into the darkness of the street, vaguely afraid of what might be there. But she saw nothing. Nothing unusual. No trick-or-treaters. No phantoms.

She glanced back at her comatose friend. "Jim," she whispered, "What did you do?"

His eyes were open, staring into a world that lay far distant from this one, a dark world inhabited only by himself.

"Jim, can you hear me?"

No response. She felt for his heart, but if it was still beating, it was too weak for her to detect.

Forcing her emotions aside, she closed the door. Then, feeling no safer, she fetched her phone to ring for help.

BLEED

Richard Christian Matheson

Richard Christian Matheson is an author, screenwriter, and producer. He has created, written, and produced acclaimed television series, movies, and mini-series, including an adaptation of Stephen King's *Battleground*, which won two Emmy Awards. He has had fifteen movies produced, and has worked with Steven Spielberg, Dean Koontz, Roger Corman, Tobe Hooper, and many others.

Matheson's dark, psychological stories have been collected in *Scars and Other Distinguishing Marks*, *Dystopia*, and *Zoopraxis*, and his work has been featured in more than one hundred anthologies, including many "Year's Best" volumes. He is also the author of the suspense novel *Created By* and the Hollywood novella *The Ritual of Illusion*.

Most recently, Joe Dante directed Matheson's "Mirari" for the anthology movie *Nightmare Cinema*. A professional drummer, he studied privately with Cream's Ginger Baker and has two blues/rock albums forthcoming.

About the following story, the author observes:

"Children are always the first to suffer.

"And Halloween is the perfect time to make them hurt.

"It's like giving candy to a baby."

I

BIG MOON. LOUD wind.

Pumpkins growl. Flames for brains.

Mommy said trick-or-treaters will be here. I'm too sick to go out. Mommy says it's the flu. My tummy is mad at me and wants to throw everything out.

My Daddy is dead. One year.

They put him in the ground and sent him away. Mommy said God has a subway down there. He waits till all the people in black leave.

Then, the box revs like a car and leaves and keeps going until it gets to Heaven.

When the children came tonight, I saw them from my window. They all had on costumes and I liked the astronaut best with silver skin and glass head. Then, I started to throw up. And the big tree outside scraped the house like it wanted it to bleed.

I fell asleep.

When I wake up, Mommy is next to me. Sitting on my bed. My tummy aches and burns. She smiles. Dabs blood from my mouth.

"How was your first Halloween?" she asks.

I smile and she strokes my forehead, tucks me in more.

She is happier now. She was sad until she met the new man. I like when Mommy is happy.

II

"Good boy," she says, turning off the light.

My room is dark. It starts to rain and I close my eyes. I think about Daddy. I miss him. My stomach hurts more. I hear Mommy in the kitchen. She sings softly, making sure not to wake me. She is on the phone with the new man. They whisper.

The apple Mommy gave me is on my plate. I could only eat half. Mommy says apples are good for me. Says candy wrecks my teeth. Says Daddy always ate apples. But it feels like something is cutting me inside.

I try to call Mommy but can't make words. I feel cold, like I'm snowing inside. All I hear is my breathing. Blood soaks my pillow.

I imagine Daddy sitting in his big car, grinning up at me, in my room. He beeps the horn and I run down and we drive away into the big white clouds that turn apple-red.

And the sky starts to bleed.

THE ULTIMATE HALLOWEEN PARTY APP

LISA MORTON

Lisa Morton is a screenwriter, author of nonfiction books, award-winning novelist, and Halloween expert whose work was described by the American Library Association's *Readers' Advisory Guide to Horror* as "consistently dark, unsettling, and frightening."

Recently, she has coedited the anthology *Haunted Nights* (with Ellen Datlow) and published the nonfiction book *Ghosts: A Haunted History*. She has also coedited an annotated anthology of classic ghost stories (with Leslie R. Klinger) and has written for the mosaic novel series *The Lovecraft Squad*.

"As a Halloween expert, an editor of Halloween-themed anthologies, and an author who has written a great deal of Halloween fiction, the challenge for me with this piece was to come up with something completely new," explains the author, "something I hadn't read (or written) before about Halloween.

"One of the recent innovations appearing in a lot of Halloween haunted house attractions is the idea that you go through a maze with your phone, which has downloaded an app that reveals specters and clues you wouldn't see otherwise, so I pushed that concept into the near-future. Sadly, I see violence and terrorism becoming an increasingly important part of our daily lives, so I integrated that into the story as well."

MARCUS WATCHED AS his friend Jet dissolved, head first, skin and hair turning into a blood-colored liquid that burned away his clothing as it gushed down his body. Within seconds Jet was little more than dripping bones, the jaws still clacking up and down although his voice now sounded hollow.

". . . If you think *this* is freq, then you don't want to miss the party. Fuck the terrorists with Halloween horrors! Halloween night, my place, with apps that may literally destroy your head."

The skull laughed and blew up.

Marcus flinched to avoid flying chips, then had to laugh at himself. "Pretty good, Jet," he said, as the image in his oculars was replaced with date (*October 31st*), time (*9:00 p.m.*), and address. "End," Marcus muttered. The invitation left his field of vision, replaced by a transparent screen showing the usual status alerts for parts of the city currently under attack.

Marcus envied Jet's ability to always be a step ahead of everyone else, although as a team leader in development at WhApp, he of course had an unfair advantage. Two years ago at a Christmas party, Jet had let his guests sample the first feelie three months before the release; although of course they had become common since then, the idea that an app downloaded into your implant could make you experience physical sensations had been revolutionary. Whatever he had for Halloween would be special.

Special . . . just what Marcus had been waiting for, the thing he needed to invite Olivia out.

Two months ago she'd arrived in the accounting department of the implant manufacturing company Marcus worked for; she'd had to leave her last company when the headquarters were bombed by the UWF. Marcus was smitten immediately. The way her glossy, black hair fell across the dark skin of her back, the way she moved, her smile, her soft voice . . . he knew he wasn't the only one at the company taken with the new arrival—he'd already watched two crash-and-burn attempts from coworkers asking her out—so he waited. It had to be right. It had to be special. It had to be mind-blowing.

To his (happy) surprise, she accepted immediately. She said she really liked Halloween, and was a fan of the stuff WhApp put out, had even already purchased a preorder download of their next release, The Ultimate Halloween Party App. She wanted a night of magic, she said; her brother had been injured fighting the Alabaster Militia recently, and she needed a distraction. Marcus preferred to think it had more to do with the way she looked back at *him*.

Plans were made, the date set. Halloween was still weeks away.

But Marcus had a feeling that it would be worth the wait.

On the evening of the 31st, Marcus picked her up just before 9:00 p.m. The evite had specified that costumes weren't necessary, but Olivia had dressed in a deliciously bold orange-and-black one-piece that suggested "costume" without actually being one. Marcus regretted his simple light shirt and dark slacks.

As his car took them to Jet's address, they talked about meaningless things: coworkers, a new restaurant near work that served only synthfood, the gossip about Hamid Malouf, governor of Sagantown on Mars. When the car abruptly chose a new route to avoid fighting taking place on Broadway, they barely noticed; when the sky to their left lit with an orange glow, Marcus felt a small stab of concern, but mainly because he wanted to protect her. They talked about how The Ultimate Halloween Party App had been brilliantly marketed and broke preorder records, even though WhApp had been enigmatic in saying what it actually was. It was easy talking to her; Marcus never felt uncomfortable, at a loss for words, as he sometimes had on other first dates. He'd had one date with a coding star that had been so uncomfortable he'd actually been searching the web for conversation topics and clever lines while they were talking, and had been glad when they'd been ordered to clear the restaurant.

After the car parked, they left and walked from the garage to the front door of Jet's home, an old three-story office building he'd bought after nailing his first big contract with WhApp. Marcus was slightly surprised to see that Jet hadn't decorated the exterior of the building, but he thought maybe his friend had chosen not to draw attention to it on a night many security experts had predicted would offer "elevated risk levels." After they reached the front door and were scanned, a message notification popped up in their oculars.

Marcus and Olivia both directed, "Open."

Jet appeared in the message, speaking to them. "Welcome, foolish mortals, to my first annual Halloween party! However, before you may enter my humble abode, you must make a choice. Tonight, you will participate in the unveiling of WhApp's latest and greatest release—The Ultimate Halloween Party App. At the end of this message, you'll be given a choice between three themes, but choose carefully, because your selection will dictate what you'll experience for the rest of the evening.

So, without further delay, I herewith present to you The Ultimate Halloween Party App from WhApp!"

The door before them opened, and at first Marcus wasn't sure if he was seeing something in his oculars or if the door had really opened, but then he heard voices and laughter and music. A menu appeared, hanging in the air before the door, as a voice in his head intoned: "Before you can experience The Ultimate Halloween Party App, you must choose between three themes. Number one: Classic Monsters."

The Frankenstein Monster and Dracula both burst out of the house. Marcus laughed at his own involuntary step back before the creatures dissolved into pixels.

"Number two: Haunted House."

A startling shriek filled Marcus's hearing as translucent, skull-faced specters rushed through the doorway and out into the night before vanishing.

"Or number three: Gore Factory."

A hockey-masked maniac with a machete in one hand and a dripping, freshly-severed head in the other thrust out of the house and disappeared.

"Whoa," Olivia said softly, beside Marcus. "That is *intense*."

Marcus grinned when he saw her astonishment and delight. "So which one are you going to pick? I've always been a fan of the old movies myself, so I think I'll go with Classic Monsters."

Olivia gave him a playful shove, a touch that, even small, left him buzzing. "That's for kids. I'm going with Gore Factory."

Staring at her in surprise, Marcus said, "Really?"

"Yeah. That's more like what *I* grew up with."

They made their choices. Bela Lugosi as Dracula appeared before Marcus, framed in Jet's doorway. "Welcome to my castle. Enter freely and of your own will." He held a candelabrum in his left hand while his right gestured elegantly toward the interior.

"Oh my God," Olivia said, with a nervous giggle. Marcus had been about to step into the house when he realized she was holding back. "What?"

"Oh, I forgot—you're not seeing what I am. There's a guy standing in the doorway cradling his own guts in his hands."

"Do you want to try to end the app?"

"No. It's fun when you know it's not real." She grabbed his hand and headed up the steps.

A short hallway brought them to a huge central space; the bottom floor had once held offices and storerooms, but Jet had knocked down the walls. It was filled now with partygoers, some chatting, some eating, some dancing. The lights—which Marcus knew were real—flickered in carefully-programmed shades of blue and green. Marcus heard a loud shriek, and then laughter.

"Do you see your friend?" Olivia asked.

Marcus scanned the crowd—there had to be two hundred people present—and wondered how he'd find Jet. He was about shake his head when he noticed a man pushing through the crowd toward them. He was tall, wearing an antiquated suit and cape, with a black skullcap and a featureless white mask. He strode purposefully toward Marcus and Olivia, who waited, intrigued.

"What do you see coming toward us?" Marcus asked.

"A killer in overalls and a pig's head. The resolution is *amazing*."

The figure stopped a few feet away, and abruptly tore away the mask, revealing a grimacing face with jutting cheekbones, wide eyes, irregular teeth, and a few strands of hair draped over skin the color of a toxic fungus.

Marcus couldn't restrain a gasp, followed by an exclamation. "The Phantom!"

The Phantom executed a courtly bow, but when he rose again Marcus saw his friend Jet. Marcus put out a hand to shake or bump, but put it back at his side when he realized Jet wasn't doing the same. "Good to see you, man," Jet said, grinning. "Thanks for coming out in all the chaos."

"Wouldn't miss it. Jet, this is Olivia."

Jet turned to her and asked, "Which option did you choose?"

"Gore Factory."

"So you just met the Pig Man, right?"

She laughed. "I did. This app is *freq*! You worked on it?"

"It's kind of my baby."

"It's so *real*! I mean, even the best feelies still have that sort of translucent look. . . ."

Jet nodded, obviously pleased. "We found some interesting new ways to make your 'plant stimulate the retinal ganglion cells. Of course that's not what I do—I'm more of a design guy than a neurotech."

"Well, whatever you do, it's brilliant."

Marcus didn't need an app to know that the grin Jet turned on him said, *You got a winner here, brother.*

Jet looked up sharply. "More guests arriving. Catch you two later. Forget the outside world and dive in!"

He rushed off. Marcus turned to Olivia. "Hey, I could use some food."

She nodded. "Let's go."

They pushed through the crowd. Marcus saw a few faces he knew, offered some waves and greetings. He paused to chat with a friend, Cho, whom he hadn't seen in a year, and whose face was now badly scarred from a bomb explosion ("Hey, I got lucky—the dude next to me lost both eyes and an arm"). They spotted tables arrayed along a wall with more food than Marcus had ever seen in one place, including slices of what he guessed was real meat, not the usual vat-grown synthfood. He wondered how Jet had gotten so much of it; even with serious black market connections, it'd been hard to come by since the Animal Liberation Army had disrupted so many of the transport lines out of agricultural areas.

"Wow," Olivia muttered.

Marcus agreed. "Jet knows how to throw parties. And he's made enough money to do it right."

Olivia picked up a narrow cracker spread with a creamy cheese. "I'm betting this doesn't look like a severed finger to you."

"No—" Marcus broke off as the food array shimmered, changing into heavy wooden banquet tables of long-decayed rot covered in thick, dust-sprinkled cobwebs and crawling with rats. "Oh, wait—I got Dracula's banquet hall, I think."

The food changed back, leaving Marcus smiling.

They took plates of exotic fruits, hors d'oeuvres that were each miniature works of art, imported cheeses, beef and (real) smoked salmon, macarons, and tiny crème brûlées. They made their way through the party, juggling the plates, until they came to a less-cramped area where they could chat as they ate. At one point the nearby walls transformed into the shadowy, hieroglyph-scrawled interior of an Egyptian tomb. Olivia saw Marcus react, asking, "What?"

"The walls just turned into a set from *The Mummy*."

"Oh. Maybe I should've picked 'Classic Monsters,' because I'm looking at walls that are gushing blood."

The building rocked, causing the lights to dim. Marcus knew this wasn't part of the app.

He and Olivia stopped eating to look at each other. In the wavering light, they held each other's gaze. In that moment Marcus knew that if he died here—if his luck finally ran out tonight, on Halloween, if fate determined that he'd sidestepped one too many attacks—he would die with Olivia, and that thought brought peace.

But then the shaking stopped, the power stabilized, and they both looked away, nervously, not because of the explosion outside but because of what had happened *here*, between them.

They didn't speak for a few seconds. Both set their half-eaten plates down, and they reached out, clasping hands. Marcus leaned in and kissed her, gently. When they separated, he was relieved to see her smiling.

She uttered a small cry and leapt back. At first Marcus feared something had gone terribly wrong, but she was looking past him. "What?"

"A deformed man with a chain saw just popped up behind you. It's okay, he's gone now."

Marcus didn't like the shadow he saw on her face. "Are you sure you don't want to delete the app?"

"I'm not sure we can. Does yours have a delete or even a pause function? I can't find one in mine."

Scanning across his visual field, Marcus realized there were no function keys or icons at all. "That's weird—it's got to have them." He thought for a second, then said, "Pause app."

Olivia turned into Frankenstein's Bride and shrieked at him.

Marcus pushed down a rising alarm—his friend had designed this thing, of *course* there had to be a way to disable it, turn it off. "Return to main menu."

Nothing happened.

The Bride asked, "Remember what it said when we first loaded the apps? Something about how we wouldn't be able to change for the rest of the evening?"

"Yeah, but that was just about which theme we chose. . . ." Marcus broke off, realizing he wasn't sure at *all* what that had meant. "Jet will know. Let's ask him."

Olivia nodded. Marcus led her through the party.

They didn't find Jet in the main room. Marcus walked her toward the rear of the main floor, where Jet had installed an indoor pool. There were fewer people here; occasionally one would glance at the pool and point or cry out.

Marcus was about to walk around the side of the pool when Olivia resisted. "I don't want to go this way."

"Why not?"

"Because the pool is full of rotting bodies."

Marcus glanced down—and stumbled back as the Creature from the Black Lagoon leapt out of the pool, reaching for his ankle. He knew it wasn't real—that it was just a collection of pixels projected into his retina from the app—but knowing that didn't quell his unease. "Yeah, let's go another way." He deliberately turned his back on the green monster hauling itself up out of the murky waters of the pool, although he heard its clawed web feet slapping the floor behind him, its labored breath as gills struggled with air. . . .

The building shook again. The sounds of the Creature behind Marcus vanished. Jet's voice replaced the music over the speakers.

"Hey, everybody, we've got some action going on in the street right outside. Don't worry—the building's protected with half-inch reinforced plasteel—but I have to ask everyone to stay where you are until it's safe. Shouldn't be long. Thanks, and party on!"

The music came back, but the mood of those around them was considerably less festive. Now the revelers chatted together in hushed, fearful tones, glancing around anxiously. Marcus turned to Olivia. "Looks like we're stuck here for a while."

"Just not near that pool, please."

They found an empty couch in the main room and claimed it. After sitting quietly together for a few seconds, Olivia said, "Marcus, I hate to ask you this, but . . . how well do you know your friend Jet?"

"What do you mean?"

She leaned toward him. "I mean . . . this guy's supposed to be a top app designer, right? So what designer designs an app you can't easily remove? Or even turn off?"

"Are you suggesting it's deliberate?"

Olivia just looked at him.

Marcus turned away, considering. He'd met Jet three years ago when his company had contracted to work with WhApp on implants modified for gaming. They'd hit it off, spent several nights bar-hopping around battle zones. What *did* he know about his friend beyond that, and his fame as an app creator? He realized he didn't know Jet's views on politics, religion, or any of the other things that fired up recruits to terrorist organizations (although he guessed that extreme veganism was out, given the amount of meat laid out with the party food).

Olivia stroked his shoulder. "Hey," she said, softly, "I'm sorry, I don't mean to make him sound like the villain, but. . . ."

"No, you're right—I *don't* know him that well."

After that, they spent an hour together, mostly not talking, finding comfort in just being together, in knowing that whatever happened they might go forward . . . *together*. The party picked back up, surging around them like some great, amorphous beast. Occasionally a monster popped into Marcus's view, and when he saw Olivia flinch or grimace, he knew her app had haunted her as well.

They were sharing glasses of wine and laughing at the conversation of a nearby man who was clumsily hitting on a much younger man when a huge, gong-like sound silenced everything. At first Marcus thought it was only in his app, but when he saw the looks on all the other faces, saw their heads tilt up as chatter ceased, he knew it was something played over the speakers.

DONG . . . DONG . . . DONG . . .

"Oh," Olivia said, "it's midnight."

Dread blossomed in Marcus's gut.

He found himself counting the sounds—*six, seven, eight, nine, ten, eleven . . .*

At twelve, a handsome man in a tuxedo appeared before Marcus. It took Marcus a few minutes to identify him: he couldn't remember the actor's name, but he knew the character was Dr. Jekyll, from an old black-and-white movie.

"Midnight has arrived, dear friends," Dr. Jekyll said, "and so it's time to reveal the secret behind The Ultimate Halloween Party App. Some of you have wondered how to turn the app off or remove it. The truth is: *You can't.* The app is now coded permanently into your 'plants."

Marcus heard two hundred gasps, cries, and mutters. Beside him, he felt Olivia tense.

Dr. Jekyll continued. "Over thirty million of you downloaded and installed the app. We hope you're enjoying it, because you'll be living with it now for the rest of your lives. Victory to the Walden Movement!"

Dr. Jekyll shook, shimmied, doubled over—and rose up as the animalistic Mr. Hyde, who lunged at Marcus. Marcus drew back, and saw that the app had transformed everyone in the party into a monster. Nearby, Olivia cried softly, her eyes closed tightly. "No . . . no . . . no. . . ." she murmured.

Marcus sat by her, taking her hands. "Olivia, just remember: it's not real. None of it is real."

She didn't open her eyes, or stop crying. "I know, but—*I still see them even with my eyes closed.*"

Marcus shut his own eyes. The room went away, but the monsters were still there, clawing and hissing and snarling at him. "Oh my God," he said. There would be no shutting them out.

Screams sounded around them; he knew everyone else had discovered the app's real abilities as well. Somebody shouted, "Maybe it'll stop when we're away from this house." The party-goers rushed for the front entrance.

Marcus turned to Olivia. "That could be right—surely you can't write an app that takes complete control of vision. Maybe he's beaming something through the party. Once we get out of here—"

Olivia didn't answer, but she did open her eyes and allow Marcus to pull her along with the crowd.

It took five minutes of pushing and elbowing, but the front door was open, the street outside was clear, and they were free of the house.

But the monsters were still there. A glowing red blob slid down over the side of the building across the street; Marcus could see half-digested bodies within it. He heard a gigantic scream resonate through the night sky, and knew that any second a giant reptilian foot might smash down beside him.

"Let's get to the car," he said.

They made it to the garage. Marcus found that he could at least access his other apps, so he called the car. It arrived and they fell in, numb, drained.

On the ride home, they talked. "I wonder how long your friend's been part of the Walden Movement. I think they usually recruit pretty young."

Marcus felt shame, as if *he* had committed the act of terrorism tonight. "Probably the whole time I knew him." He reminded himself that Olivia had already preordered the app anyway, but he still felt guilty.

"Do you think he was even at the party tonight?"

Marcus started to protest, but then remembered: Jet had refused their usual handshake when they'd arrived. "God. Probably not. He's somewhere safe, where they can't get to him."

Olivia stayed with Marcus that night, but they clutched at each other out of horror, not desire. The last thing Marcus said to her just before dawn was, "Don't forget who we work for—a 'plant company. By twelve noon we can have these 'plants out of our heads."

She gave him a half-nod, but then flinched at another gruesome offering from The Ultimate Halloween Party App.

Fuck this shit.

They told me to try writing about all this in third person, that it would help me "gain distance" and "separate truth from fantasy." They said it would help me "process Olivia's death" and prepare me for the next step.

It didn't. All it did was make me remember it all over again.

After that Halloween, people all over the world tried to have their 'plants replaced. Most neuroclinics were reporting six-month-long wait times.

I did manage to pull strings at my company so that Olivia and I were among the first to get our 'plants pulled.

It didn't work.

Jet and his team had taken the next step forward with apps: they'd figured out a way to use one to permanently rewire the brain. It was theoretical . . . until Halloween, when thirty million people thought they were installing an innocent party game, but the trick was that the treat was permanent.

A lot of them couldn't take a life of monsters, or ghosts. The ones who chose Gore Factory had it the worst. Suicide rates skyrocketed.

It was ironic that Halloween became the source of so much real terror, wasn't it?

Two weeks after Jet's party, Olivia drove a steak knife through each of her eyes. She bled to death alone on the floor of my apartment while I was at work. I found her when I got home. Now, thanks to my new brain, I see her as a shroud-draped vampire, or a tattered, shuffling zombie. They tell me it's not real, but it grabs my heart and hurts every time.

I don't even know for sure who "they" are. Government, or a rival terrorist gang, it seems all the same to me.

They came a week after Olivia's self-mercy-killing. They said they couldn't reverse the damage the Halloween app had done to my brain, but they could put it to use. Did I want to fight terrorists?

No, not really, I told them.

Then they asked me the better question: Did I want to fight *monsters*?

Yes. God, yes.

So I let them give me a new 'plant. It at least lets me know if a monster is real or not, and who it is. I can now identify friend from foe, flesh from phantom. They taught me how to use weapons. They're ready now to send me out into the field.

I may not be able to get to Jet for what he's done, but I can take out some of his friends.

I'm coming for you, monsters. I've got a stake sharpened for you, Count. Igor, I'll take that tiki torch and douse it in gasoline. Im-ho-tep, what will rockets do to your wrappings?

Let's find out.

THE FOLDING MAN

Joe R. Lansdale

Joe R. Lansdale has published more than forty-five novels, dozens of novellas, and over four hundred short stories and articles. He has written for *Batman: The Animated Series* and *Superman: The Animated Series*; his novella *Bubba Ho-Tep* was filmed by director Don Coscarelli and starred Bruce Campbell, and his novel *Cold in July* was made into a movie starring Michael C. Hall, Don Johnson, and the late Sam Shepard. More recently, his series of books about the eponymous oddball couple has been adapted for the Sundance Channel as *Hap and Leonard*, featuring James Purefoy and Michael Kenneth Williams.

Lansdale has been named a Grand Master by the World Horror Convention and has received the Lifetime Achievement Award from the Horror Writers Association. His other awards include ten Bram Stoker Awards from the HWA, an Edgar Award from the Mystery Writers of America for his novel *The Bottoms*, and a Spur Award from The Western Writers of America for his novel *Paradise Sky*.

"Growing up," recalls the author, "I heard the story now and again about the black car, or the old black buggy, that would come to pick people up and take them away to some place darker than here.

"I thought about that old tale, and tried to put a modern spin on it. The result was 'The Folding Man,' which came to me quickly and was written quickly. Once the story arrived, it had to be told."

THEY HAD COME from a Halloween party, having long shed the masks they'd worn. No one but Harold had been drinking, and he wasn't driving, and he wasn't so drunk he was blind. Just drunk enough he couldn't sit up straight and was lying on the back seat, trying, for some unknown reason, to recite the Pledge of Allegiance, which he didn't accurately recall. He was mixing in verses from "The Star-Spangled Banner" and the Boy Scout oath, which he vaguely remembered from his time in the organization before they drove him out for setting fires.

Even though William, who was driving, and Jim who was riding shotgun, were sober as Baptists claimed to be, they were fired up and happy and yelling and hooting, and Jim pulled down his pants and literally mooned a black bug of a car carrying a load of nuns.

The car wasn't something that looked as if it had come off the lot. Didn't have the look of any carmaker Jim could identify. It had a cobbled look. It reminded him of something in old movies, the ones with gangsters who were always squealing their tires around corners. Only it seemed bigger, with broader windows through which he could see the nuns, or at least glimpse them in their habits; it was a regular penguin convention inside that car.

Way it happened, when they came up on the nuns, Jim said to William at the wheel, "Man, move over close, I'm gonna show them some butt."

"They're nuns, man."

"That's what makes it funny," Jim said.

William eased the wheel to the right, and Harold in the back said, "Grand Canyon. Grand Canyon. Show them the Grand Canyon . . . Oh, say can you see. . . ."

Jim got his pants down, swiveled on his knees in the seat, twisted so that his ass was against the glass, and just as they passed the nuns, William hit the electric window switch and slid the glass down. Jim's ass jumped out at the night, like a vibrating moon.

"They lookin'?" Jim asked.

"Oh, yeah," William said, "and they are not amused."

Jim jerked his pants up, shifted in the seat, and turned for a look, and sure enough, they were not amused. Then a funny thing happened, one of the nuns shot him the finger, and then others followed. Jim said, "Man, those nuns are rowdy."

And now he got a good look at them, even though it was night, because there was enough light from the headlights as they passed for him to see faces hard as wardens and ugly as death warmed over. The driver was especially homely, face like that could stop a clock and run it backward or make shit crawl uphill.

"Did you see that they shot me the finger?" Jim said.

"I did see it," William said.

Harold had finally gotten "The Star-Spangled Banner" straight, and he kept singing it over and over.

"For Christ's sake," William said. "Shut up, Harold."

"You know what," Jim said, studying the rearview mirror, "I think they're speeding up. They're trying to catch us. Oh, hell. What if they get the license plate? Maybe they already have. They call the law, my dad will have my mooning ass."

"Well, if they haven't got the plate," William said, "they won't. This baby can get on up and get on out."

He put his foot on the gas. The car hummed as if it had just had an orgasm, and seemed to leap. Harold was flung off the back seat, onto the floorboard. "Hey, goddammit," he said.

"Put on your seat belt, jackass," Jim said.

William's car was eating up the road. It jumped over a hill and dove down the other side like a porpoise negotiating a wave, and Jim thought: *Goodbye, penguins*, and then he looked back. At the top of the hill were the lights from the nun's car, and the car was gaining speed and it moved in a jerky manner, as if it were stealing space between blinks of the eye.

"Damn," William said. "They got some juice in that thing, and the driver has her foot down."

"What kind of car is that?" Jim said.

"Black," William said.

"Ha! Mr. Detroit."

"Then you name it."

Jim couldn't. He turned to look back. The nun's car had already caught up—the big automotive beast was cruising in tight as a coat of varnish, the headlights making the interior of William's machine bright as a Vegas act.

"What the hell they got under the hood?" William said. "Hyper-drive?"

"These nuns," Jim said, "they mean business."

"I can't believe it, they're riding my bumper."

"Slam on your brakes. That'll show them."

"Not this close," William said. "Do that, what it'll show them is the inside of our butts."

"Do nuns do this?"

"These do."

"Oh," Jim said. "I get it. Halloween. They aren't real nuns."

"Then we give them hell," Harold said, and just as the nuns were passing on the right, he crawled out of the floorboard and onto his seat and rolled the window down. The back window of the nun's car went down and Jim turned to get a look, and the nun, well, she was ugly all right, but uglier than he had first imagined. She looked like something dead, and the nun's outfit she wore was not actually black and white, but purple and white, or so it appeared in the light from head-beams and moonlight. The nun's lips pulled back from her teeth and the teeth were long and brown, as if tobacco-stained. One of her eyes looked like a spoiled meatball, and her nostrils flared like a pig's.

Jim said, "That ain't no mask."

Harold leaned way out of the window and flailed his hands and said, "You are so goddamn ugly you have to creep up on your underwear."

Harold kept on with this kind of thing, some of it almost making sense, and then one of the nuns in the back, the one closest to the window, bent over in the seat and came up and leaned out of the window, a two-by-four in her hands. Jim noted that her arms, where the nun outfit had fallen back to the elbows, were as thin as sticks and white as the underbelly of a fish, and the elbows were knotty and bent in the wrong direction.

"Get back in," Jim said to Harold.

Harold waved his arms and made another crack, and then the nun swung the two-by-four, the oddness of her elbows causing it to arrive at a weird angle, and the board made a crack of its own, or rather Harold's skull did, and he fell forward, the lower-half of his body hanging from the window, bouncing against the door, his knuckles losing meat on the highway, his ass hanging inside, one foot on the floorboard, the other waggling in the air.

"The nun hit him," Jim said. "With a board."

"What?" William said.

"You deaf? She hit him."

Jim snapped lose his seat belt and leaned over and grabbed Harold by the back of the shirt and yanked him inside. Harold's head looked like it had been in a vice. There was blood everywhere. Jim said, "Oh, man, I think he's dead."

BLAM!

The noise made Jim jump. He slid back in his seat and looked toward the nuns. They were riding close enough to slam the two-by-four into Williams's car; the driver was pressing that black monster toward them.

Another swing of the board and the side-mirror shattered.

William tried to gun forward, but the nun's car was even with him, pushing him to the left. They went across the highway and into a ditch and the car did an acrobatic twist and tumbled down an embankment and rolled into the woods tossing up mud and leaves and pine straw.

Jim found himself outside the car, and when he moved, everything seemed to whirl for a moment, then gathered up slowly and became solid. He had been thrown free, and so had William, who was lying nearby. The car was a wreck, lying on its roof, spinning still, steam easing out from under the hood in little cotton-white clouds. Gradually, the car quit spinning, like an old-time watch that had wound down. The windshield was gone and three of the four doors lay scattered about.

The nuns were parked up on the road, and the car doors opened and the nuns got out. Four of them. They were unusually tall, and when they walked, like their elbows, their knees bent in the wrong direction. It was impossible to tell this for sure, because of the robes they wore, but it certainly looked that way, and considering the elbows, it fit. There in the moonlight, they were as white and pasty as pot stickers, their jaws seeming to have grown longer than when Jim had last looked at them, their noses witch-like, except for those pig-flair nostrils, their backs bent like longbows. One of them still held the two-by-four.

Jim slid over to William, who was trying to sit up.

"You okay?" Jim asked.

"I think so," William said, patting his fingers at a blood spot on his forehead. "Just before they hit, I stupidly unsnapped my seat belt. I don't know why. I just wanted out I guess. Brain not working right."

"Look up there," Jim said.

They both looked up the hill. One of the nuns was moving down from the highway, toward the wrecked car.

"If you can move," Jim said, "I think we oughta."

William worked himself to his feet. Jim grabbed his arm and half-pulled him into the woods, where they leaned against a tree. William said. "Everything's spinning."

"It stops soon enough," Jim said.

"I got to chill, I'm about to faint."

"A moment," Jim said.

The nun who had gone down by herself, bent down out of sight behind William's car, then they saw her going back up the hill, dragging Harold by his ankle, his body flopping all over as if all the bones had been broken.

"My God, see that?" William said. "We got to help."

"He's dead," Jim said. "They crushed his head with a board."

"Oh, hell, man. That can't be. They're nuns."

"I don't think they are," Jim said. "Least not the kind of nuns you're thinking."

The nun dragged Harold up the hill and dropped his leg when she reached the big black car. Another of the nuns opened the trunk and reached in and got hold of something. It looked like some kind of folded-up lawn chair, only more awkward in shape. The nun jerked it out and dropped it on the ground and gave it a swift kick. The folded-up thing began to unfold with a clatter and a squeak.

A perfectly round head rose up from it, and the head spun on what appeared to be a silver hinge. When it quit whirling, it was upright and in place, though cocked slightly to the left. The eyes and mouth and nostrils were merely holes. Moonlight could be seen through them. The head rose as coatrack style shoulders pushed it up, and a cage of a chest rose under that. The chest looked almost like an old frame on which dresses were placed to be sewn, or perhaps a cage designed to contain something you wouldn't want to get out. With more squeaks and clatters, skeletal hips appeared, and beneath that, long, bony, legs with bent-back knees and big metal-framed feet. Stick-like arms swung below its knees, clattering against its legs like tree limbs bumping against a windowpane. It stood at least seven feet tall. Like the nuns, its knees and elbows fit backward.

The nun by the car trunk reached inside and pulled out something fairly large that beat its wings against the night air. She held it in one hand by its clawed feet, and its beak snapped wildly, looking for something to peck.

Using her free hand, she opened up the folding-man's chest by use of a hinge, and when the cage flung open, she put the black, winged thing inside. It fluttered about like a heart shot full of adrenaline. The holes that were the folding-man's eyes filled with a red glow and the mouth-hole grew wormy lips, and a tongue—long as a garden snake, dark as dirt—licked out at the night, and there was a loud sniff as its nostrils sucked air.

One of the nuns reached down and grabbed up a handful of clay, and pressed it against the folding-man's arms; the clay spread fast as a lie, went all over, filling the thing with flesh of the earth until the entire folding man's body was covered.

The nun, who had taken the folding man out of the car, picked Harold up by the ankle, and as if he were nothing more than a blow-up doll, swung him over her head and slammed him into the darkness of the trunk, shut the lid, and looked out to where Jim and William stood recovering by the tree.

The nun said something, a noise between a word and a cough, and the folding man began to move down the hill at a stumble. As he moved, his joints made an unoiled hinge sound, and the rest of him made a clatter like lug bolts being knocked together, accompanied by a noise akin to wire hangers being twisted by strong hands.

"Run," Jim said.

Jim began to feel pain, knew he was more banged up than he thought. His neck hurt. His back hurt. One of his legs really hurt. He must have jammed his knee against something. William, who ran alongside him, dodging trees, said, "My ribs. I think they're cracked."

Jim looked back. In the distance, just entering the trees, framed in the moonlight behind him, was the folding man. He moved in strange leaps, as if there were springs inside him, and he was making good time.

Jim said, "We can't stop. It's coming."

It was low-down in the woods and water had gathered there and the leaves had mucked up with it, and as they ran, they sloshed and splashed, and behind them, they could hear it, the folding man, coming, cracking limbs, squeaking hinges, splashing his way after them.

When they had the nerve to look back, they could see him darting between the trees like a piece of the forest itself, and he, or it, was coming quite briskly for a thing its size until it reached the lower-down parts of the bottom-land. There, its big feet slowed it some as they buried deep in the mud and were pulled free again with a sound like the universe sucking wind. Within moments, however, the thing got its stride, its movements becoming more fluid and its pace faster.

Finally, Jim and William came to a tree-thickened rise in the land, and were able to get out of the muck, scramble upward and move more freely, even though there was something of a climb ahead, and they had to use trees growing out from the side of the rise to pull themselves upward. When they reached the top of the climb, they were surprised when they looked back to see they had actually gained some space on the thing. It was some distance away, speckled by the moonlight, negotiating its way through the ever-thickening trees and undergrowth. But still it came, ever onward, never tiring. Jim and William bent over and put their hands on their knees and took some deep breaths.

"There's an old graveyard on the far side of this stretch," Jim said. "Near the wrecking yard."

"Where you worked last summer?"

"Yeah, that's the one. It gets clearer in the graveyard, and we can make good time. Get to the wrecking yard, Old Man Gordon lives there. He always has a gun and he has that dog, Chomps. It knows me. It will eat that thing up."

"What about me?"

"You'll be all right. You're with me. Come on. I kinda know where we are now. Used to play in the graveyard, and in this end of the woods. Got to move."

They moved along more swiftly as Jim became more and more familiar with the terrain. It was close to where he had lived when he was a kid, and he had spent a lot of time out here. They came to a place where there was a clearing in the woods, a place where lightning had made a fire. The ground was black, and there were no trees, and in that spot silver moonlight was falling down into it, like mercury filling a cup.

In the center of the clearing they stopped and got their breath again, and William said, "My head feels like it's going to explode . . . hey, I don't hear it now."

"It's there. Whatever it is, I don't think it gives up."

"Oh, Jesus," William said, and gasped deep once. "I don't know how much I got left in me."

"You got plenty. We got to have plenty."

"What can it be, Jimbo? What in the hell can it be?"

Jim shook his head. "You know that old story about the black car?"

William shook his head.

"My grandmother used to tell me about a black car that roams the highways and the back-roads of the South. It isn't in one area all the time, but it's out there somewhere all the time. Halloween is its peak night. It's always after somebody for whatever reason."

"Bullshit."

Jim, hands still on his knees, lifted his head. "You go down there and tell that clatter-clap thing it's all bullshit. See where that gets you."

"It just doesn't make sense."

"Grandma said before it was a black car, it was a black buggy, and before that a figure dressed in black on a black horse, and that before that, it was just a shadow that clicked and clacked and squeaked. There's people go missing, she said, and it's the black car, the black buggy, the thing on the horse, or the walkin' shadow that gets them. But, it's all the same thing, just a different appearance."

"The nuns? What about them?"

Jim shook his head, stood up, tested his ability to breathe. "Those weren't nuns. They were like . . . I don't know . . . anti-nuns. This thing, if Grandma was right, can take a lot of different forms. Come on. We can't stay here anymore."

"Just another moment, I'm so tired. And I think we've lost it. I don't hear it anymore."

As if on cue, there came a clanking and a squeaking and cracking of limbs. William glanced at Jim, and without a word, they moved across the lightning-made space and into the trees. Jim looked back, and there it was, crossing the clearing, silver-flooded in the moonlight, still coming, not tiring.

They ran. White stones rose up in front of them. Most of the stones were heaved to the side, or completely pushed out of the ground by growing trees and expanding roots. It was the old graveyard, and Jim knew that meant the wrecking yard was nearby, and so was Gordon's shotgun, and so was one mean dog.

Again the land sloped upward, and this time William fell forward on his hands and knees, throwing up a mess of blackness. "Oh, God. Don't leave me, Jim . . . I'm tuckered . . . can hardly . . . breathe."

Jim had moved slightly ahead of William. He turned back to help. As he grabbed William's arm to pull him up, the folding man squeaked and clattered forward and grabbed William's ankle, jerked him back, out of Jim's grasp.

The folding man swung William around easily, slammed his body against a tree, then the thing whirled, and as if William were a bullwhip, snapped him so hard his neck popped and an eyeball flew out of his skull. The folding man brought William whipping down across a standing gravestone. There was a cracking sound, like someone had dropped a glass coffee cup, then the folding man whirled and slung

William from one tree to another, hitting the trees so hard bark flew off of them and clothes and meat flew off William.

Jim bolted. He ran faster than he had ever run. Finally he broke free of the woods and came to a stretch of ground that was rough with gravel. Behind him, breaking free of the woods, was the folding man, making good time with great strides, dragging William's much-abused body behind it by the ankle.

Jim could dimly see the wrecking yard from where he was, and he thought he could make it. Still, there was the aluminum fence all the way around the yard, seven feet high. No little barrier.

Then he remembered the sycamore tree on the edge of the fence, on the right side. Old Man Gordon was always talking about cutting it down because he thought someone could use it to climb over and into the yard, steal one of his precious car parts—though if they did, they had Gordon's shotgun waiting along with the sizeable teeth of his dog.

It had been six months since he had seen the old man, and he hoped he hadn't gotten ambitious, that the tree was still there.

Running closer, Jim could see the sycamore tree remained, tight against the long run of shiny wrecking-yard fence. Looking back over his shoulder, Jim saw the folding man was springing forward, like some kind of electronic rabbit, William's body being pulled along by the ankle, bouncing on the ground as the thing came ever onward. At this rate, it would be only a few seconds before the thing caught up with him.

Jim felt a pain like a knife in his side, and it seemed as if his heart was going to explode. He reached down deep for everything he had, hoping like hell he didn't stumble.

He made the fence and the tree, went up it like a squirrel, dropped over onto the roof of an old car, sprang off of that and ran toward a dim light shining in the small window of a wood-and-aluminum shack nestled in the midst of old cars and piles of junk.

As he neared the shack, Chomps, part-pit bull, part-just plain big ole dog, came loping out toward him, growling. It was a hard thing to do, but Jim forced himself to stop, bent down, stuck out his hand, and called the dog's name.

"Chomps. Hey, buddy. It's me."

The dog slowed and lowered its head and wagged its tail.

"That's right. Your pal, Jim."

The dog came close and Jim gave it a pat. "Good, boy."

Jim looked over his shoulder. Nothing.

"Come on, Chomps."

Jim moved quickly toward the shack and hammered on the door. A moment later the door flew open, and standing there in overalls, one strap dangling from a naked arm, was Mr. Gordon. He was old and near-toothless, squat and greasy as the insides of the cars in the yard.

"Jim? What the hell you doing in here? You look like hell."

"Something's after me."

"Something?"

"It's outside the fence. It killed two of my friends. . . ."

"What?"

"It killed two of my friends."

"It? Some kind of animal?"

"No . . . It."

"We'll call some law."

Jim shook his head. "No use calling the law now, time they arrive it'll be too late."

Gordon leaned inside the shack and pulled a twelve-gauge into view, pumped it once. He stepped outside and looked around.

"You sure?"

"Oh, yeah. Yes, sir. I'm sure."

"Then I guess you and me and Pump-Twelve will check it out."

Gordon moved out into the yard, looking left and right. Jim stayed close to Gordon's left elbow. Chomps trotted nearby. They walked about a bit. They stopped between a row of wrecked cars, looked around. Other than the moon-shimmering fence at either end of the row where they stood, there was nothing to see.

"Maybe whatever, or whoever it is, is gone," Gordon said. "Otherwise, Chomps would be all over it."

"I don't think it smells like humans or animals."

"Are you joshin' an old man? Is this a Halloween prank?"

"No, sir. Two of my friends are dead. This thing killed them. It's real."

"What the hell is it then?"

As if in answer, there was the sound like a huge can opener going to work, and then the long, thin arm of the folding man poked through the fence and there was more ripping as the arm slid upward, tearing at the metal. A big chunk of the fence was torn away, revealing the thing, bathed in moonlight, still holding what was left of William's ragged body by the ankle.

Jim and Gordon both stood locked in amazement.

"Sonofabitch," Gordon said.

Chomps growled, ran toward it.

"Chomps will fix him," Gordon said.

The folding man dropped William's ankle and bent forward, and just as the dog leaped, caught it and twisted it and ran its long arm down the snapping dog's throat, and began to pull its insides out. It flung the dog's parts in all directions, like someone pulling confetti from a sack. Then it turned the dog inside out.

When the sack was empty, the folding man bent down and fastened the dead, deflated dog to a hook on the back of what passed for its ankle.

"My God," Gordon said.

The thing picked up William by the ankle, stepped forward a step, and paused.

Gordon lifted the shotgun. "Come and get you some, asshole."

The thing cocked its head as if to consider the suggestion, and then it began to lope toward them, bringing along its clanks and squeaks, the dead dog flopping at the folding man's heel. For the first time, its mouth, which had been nothing but a hole with wormy lips, twisted into the shape of a smile.

Gordon said, "You run, boy. I got this."

Jim didn't hesitate. He turned and darted between a row of cars and found a gap between a couple of Fords with grass grown up around their flattened tires, ducked down behind one, and hid. He lay down on his belly to see if he could see anything. There was a little bit of space down there, and he could look under the car, and under several others, and he could see Gordon's feet. They had shifted into a firm stance, and Jim could imagine the old man pulling the shotgun to his shoulder.

And even as he imagined, the gun boomed, and then it boomed again. Silence, followed by a noise like someone ripping a piece of thick cardboard in half, and then there were screams and more rips. Jim felt light-headed, realized he hadn't been breathing. He gasped for air, feared that he had gasped too loudly.

Oh, my God, he thought. I ran and left it to Mr. Gordon, and now . . . he was uncertain. Maybe the screams had come from . . . It, the folding man? But so far it hadn't so much as made breathing sounds, let alone anything that might be thought of as a vocalization.

Crawling like a soldier under fire, Jim worked his way to the edge of the car, and took a look. Stalking down the row between the cars was the folding man, and he was dragging behind him by one ankle what was left of William's body. In his other hand, if you could call it a hand, he had Mr. Gordon, who looked thin now because so much had been pulled out of him. Chomps's body was still fastened to the wire hook at the back of the thing's foot. As the folding man came forward, Chomps dragged in the dirt.

Jim pushed back between the cars, and kept pushing, crawling backward. When he was far enough back, he raised to a squat and started between narrower rows that he thought would be harder for the folding man to navigate; they were just spaces really, not rows, and if he could go where it couldn't go, then—

There was a loud creaking sound, and Jim, still at a squat, turned to discover its source. The folding man was looking at him. It had grabbed an old car and lifted it up by the front and was holding it so that the back end rested on the ground. Being as close as he was now, Jim realized the folding man was bigger than he had thought, and he saw too that just below where the monster's thick torso ended there were springs, huge springs, silver in the moonlight, vibrating. He had stretched to accommodate the lifting of the car, and where his knees bent backward, springs could be seen as well—he was a garage-sale collection of parts and pieces.

For a moment, Jim froze. The folding man opened his mouth wide, wider than Jim had seen before, and inside he could glimpse a turning of gears and a smattering of sparks. Jim broke suddenly, running between cars, leaping on hoods, scrambling across roofs, and behind him came the folding man, picking up cars and flipping them aside as easily as if they had been toys.

Jim could see the fence at the back, and he made for that, and when he got close to it, he thought he had it figured. He could see a Chevy parked next to the fence, and he felt certain he could climb onto the roof, spring off of it, grab the top of the fence, and scramble over. That wouldn't stop the thing behind him, but it would perhaps give him a few moments to gain ground.

The squeaking and clanking behind him was growing louder.

There was a row of cars ahead, he had to leap onto the hood of the first, then spring from hood to hood, drop off, turn slightly right, and go for the Chevy by the fence.

He was knocked forward, hard, and his breath leaped out of him.

He was hit again, painfully in the chest.

It took a moment to process, but he was lying between two cars, and there, standing above him, was the folding man, snapping at him with the two dead bodies like they were wet towels. That's what had hit him, the bodies, used like whips.

Jim found strength he didn't know he had, made it to his feet as Mr. Gordon's body slammed the ground near him. Then, as William's body snapped by his ear, just missing him, he was once more at a run.

The Chevy loomed before him. He made its hood by scrambling up on hands and knees, and then he jumped to the roof. He felt something tug at him, but he jerked loose, didn't stop moving. He sprang off the car-top, grabbed at the fence, latching his arms over it. The fence cut into the undersides of his arms, but he couldn't let that stop him, so he kept pulling himself forward, and the next thing he knew, he was over the fence, dropping to the ground.

It seemed as if a bullet had gone up through his right foot, which he now realized was bare, and that the tug he had felt was the folding man grabbing at his foot, only to come away with a shoe. But of more immediate concern was his foot, the pain. There hadn't been any bullet. He had landed crooked coming over the fence, and his foot had broken. It felt like hell, but he moved on it anyway, and within a few steps he had a limp, a bad limp.

He could see the highway ahead, and he could hear the fence coming down behind him, and he knew it was over, all over, because he was out of gas and had blown a tire and his engine was about to blow too. His breath came in chops and blood was pounding in his skull like a thug wanting out.

He saw lights. They were moving very quickly down the highway. A big truck, a Mac, was balling the jack in his direction. If he could get it to stop, maybe there would be help, maybe.

Jim stumbled to the middle of the highway, directly into the lights, waved his arms, glanced to his left—

—and there it was. The folding man. It was only six feet away.

The truck was only a little farther away, but moving faster, and then the folding man was reaching for him, and the truck was a sure hit, and Jim, pushing off his good foot, leaped sideways and there was a sound like a box of dishes falling downstairs.

Jim felt the wind from the truck, but he had moved just in time. The folding man had not. As Jim had leaped aside, his body turned, through no plan of his own, and he saw the folding man take the hit.

Wood and springs and hinges went everywhere.

The truck bumped right over the folding man and started sliding as the driver tried to put on brakes that weren't designed for fast stops. Tires smoked, brakes squealed, the truck fishtailed.

Jim fell to the side of the highway, got up and limped into the brush there, and tripped on something and went down. He rolled onto his back. His butt was in a ditch and his back was against one side of it, and he could see above it on the other side, and through some little bushes that grew there. The highway had a few lights on either side of it, so it was lit-up good, and Jim could see the folding man lying in the highway, or rather he could see parts of it everywhere. It looked like a dirty hardware store had come to pieces. William, Gordon, and Chomps, lay in the middle of the highway.

The folding man's big torso, which had somehow survived the impact of the truck, vibrated and burst open, and Jim saw the bird-like thing rise up with a squawk. It snatched up the body of Mr. Gordon and William, one in either claw, used its beak to nab the dog, and ignoring the fact that its size was not enough to lift all that weight, it did just that, took hold of them and went up into the night sky, abruptly became one with the dark.

Jim turned his head. He could see down the highway, could see the driver of the truck getting out, walking briskly toward the scene of the accident. He walked faster as he got closer, and when he arrived, he bent over the pieces of the folding man. He picked up a spring, examined it, tossed it aside. He looked out where Jim lay in the ditch, but Jim figured, lying as he was, brush in front of him, he couldn't be seen.

He was about to call out to the driver when, the truck driver yelled, "You nearly got me killed. You nearly got you killed. Maybe you are killed. I catch you, might as well be, you stupid shit. I'll beat the hell out of you."

Jim didn't move.

"Come on out so I can finish you off."

Great, Jim thought, *first the folding man, and now a truck driver wants to kill me. To hell with him, to hell with everything*, and he laid his head back against the ditch and closed his eyes and went to sleep.

The truck driver didn't come out and find him, and when he awoke the truck was gone and the sky was starting to lighten. His ankle hurt like hell. He bent over and looked at it. He couldn't tell much in the dark, but it looked as big as a sewer pipe. He thought when he got some strength back, he might be able to limp, or crawl out to the edge of the highway, flag down some help. Surely, someone would stop. But for the moment, he was too weak. He laid back again, and was about to close his eyes, when he heard a humming sound.

Looking out at the highway, he saw lights coming from the same direction the trucker had come from. Fear crawled up his back like a spider. It was the black car.

The car pulled to the side of the road and stopped. The nuns got out. They sniffed and extended long tongues and licked at the fading night. With speed and agility that seemed impossible, they gathered up the parts of the folding man and put them in a sack they had placed in the middle of the highway.

When the sack was full of parts, one nun stuck a long leg into the sack and stomped about, then jerked her leg out, pulled the sack together at the top and swung it over her head and slammed it onto the road a few times. Then she dropped the sack and moved back, and one of the nuns kicked it. Another nun opened it up and reached inside the sack and took out the folding man. Jim lost a breath. It appeared to be put back together. The nun didn't unfold the folding man. She opened the trunk of the car and flung it inside.

And then she turned and looked in his direction, held out one arm and waited. The bird-thing came flapping out of the last of the dark and landed on her arm. The bodies of William and Gordon were still in its talons, the dog in its beak, the three of them hanging as if they were nothing heavier than rags.

The nun took hold of the bird's legs and tossed it and what it held into the trunk as well. She closed the lid of the trunk. She looked directly where Jim lay. She looked up at the sky, turned to face the rising sun. She turned quickly back in Jim's direction and stuck out her long arm, the robe folding back from it. She pointed a stick-like finger right at him, leaned slightly forward. She held that pose until the others joined her and pointed in Jim's direction.

My God, Jim thought, *they know I'm here. They see me. Or smell me. Or sense me. But they know I'm here.*

The sky brightened and outlined them like that for a moment and they stopped pointing.

They got quickly into the car. The last of the darkness seemed to seep into the ground and give way to a rising pink—Halloween night had ended. The car gunned and went away fast. Jim watched it go a few feet, and then it wasn't there anymore. It faded like fog.

All that was left now was the sunrise and the day turning bright.

I WAIT FOR YOU

Eygló Karlsdóttir

Eygló Karlsdóttir is the author of the short story collection *Things the Devil Wouldn't Dream Of and Other Stories* and *All the Dark Places: A Novella*. She is also the creator of the experimental zine *The Chestnut*, where she publishes one short story each month.

"I had in my head the silhouette image of a woman walking up a hill toward a house that looked rather spooky," explains the author, "and I attempted to write about her several times before a little bird whispered to me that her story might be related to Halloween.

"After that it all fell into place."

"IS THERE LIFE after death?"

The words echoed constantly in her head, a never-ending repetition that always took center stage. His thin face looking up at her, with his big, blue, questioning eyes. "Is there life after death, Mom?"

The sky was quietly on fire, bejeweled with an intense orange color. The hollow oak could be seen as a dark silhouette up on the hill beside the house. It had been such a long time since she visited. She brushed dust off her jeans before she continued, careful not to step in the horse manure on the road.

There was smoke in the air, quietly ascending from the chimneys, whisked away in the easy breeze. The smell of yew wood so familiar that she halted again, putting her burlap knapsack down. She pulled out a water bottle and drank from it. Then she took a deep breath, inhaling old memories with the familiar smell before she moved forward again.

When she got up to the top of the hill, she walked toward the tree and slapped the bark lightly with the palm of her hand. The sound of the dead wood echoed back at her. She found the hole and looked inside. An old fire truck lay on its side inside the tree trunk, a beheaded Barbie doll lay beside it, indicating the atrocious incident that had transpired in the children's games earlier in the day.

She smiled and walked up to the house. There was a glowing pumpkin in front of the porch. The demon carved in its flesh startled her at first. The light inside flickering madly as a gust of wind blew past her. She held her hand momentarily above the pumpkin and instantly the demon died as the light flickered out.

She sighed with relief and walked up the wooden steps.

There was nothing but an old rocking chair on the porch. A wool quilt had been carelessly thrown over it and the chair swayed as if someone had been sitting there, but decided moments ago to get up and go inside. There was light in the kitchen and the wind chimes hanging beside the window played a soft melody. It made her feel at home.

She sighed, put her knapsack on the chair and went to the door, hesitating before knocking.

"Trick-or-treat," she whispered and smiled to herself.

She heard the footsteps inside, the floorboards creaking. A man opened the door. He was wearing a T-shirt and a pair of faded jeans. There was a tattoo of a mean-looking skull on his shoulder. She wished she could flick that off as easily as the demon. It made her ill at ease.

"Can I help you?" the man asked.

"I'm sorry to bother you," she said, trying hard to remain calm. "I used to live here, long ago, and I was wondering if I could take a look. I haven't been in the neighborhood for ages." She didn't really know why she was lying to him, it just came naturally and the truth was far more difficult.

"You used to live here? Really?" he asked, but opened the door wide so she could enter.

She stood still, hesitating on the threshold.

"Oh damn," the man suddenly exclaimed. "The light's gone out." He went inside and came back almost instantly with something in his hand. Then he ran down the steps and opened the lid on the pumpkin, lighting the candle quickly before he replaced the lid and ran back up the steps again. "Come on in," he said.

She walked inside, closing the door behind her.

"Thank you," she said. "I appreciate it. Have you lived here long? Do you know what happened to the family that lived here before? There was a little boy—" her voice faded away as she realized she wasn't sure what the facts were.

The man looked at her and shrugged. "I've lived here all my life, actually. When did you say you lived here?"

She sat down on a chair in the hallway and tried desperately to still her hands. She looked up at the man and sighed. "It was a while ago. How old are you?"

"Not quite as old as I look, I hope," he said. "You can't be much older though," he smiled. "Are you sure you have the right house?"

She didn't have an answer to that. Instead she stood up and walked into the kitchen.

It was just as she remembered it, except the stove had been replaced with something modern. She put her finger on the countertop and stroked it lightly. The dent in the wood was still there. She remembered that day vividly.

The autumn winds had been howling about the roof. It always made her ill at ease that sound, especially around this time of the year. It had frozen early, ruined the remainder of the crops that they hadn't managed to get inside. Winter would be harsh.

The boy had been particularly difficult that day. She had given him some pancakes, but that hadn't helped much. When the knock came on the door she had been so deep in thought that the knife slipped in her hand, slicing her finger and chipping the wood. She hissed and started sucking on her finger while rushing to the door to greet whoever was there.

The woman at the door had been the bearer of bad news.

She looked back at the man who had been observing her tour of the kitchen. His hair was light brown; vigilant, steel-gray eyes, and he bore a striking resemblance to her father she realized. She staggered when she understood who the man was.

"Do you live here alone?" she asked calmly.

"Well," he hesitated and looked to the floor as if the answer was standing there, staring at him. Meanwhile, she examined the skull on his shoulder and a shiver ran through her.

"The kids are out trick-or-treating with their mom somewhere," he mumbled.

"With your wife?" she asked.

He nodded his head and looked at her. "Well, we're not actually married," he added.

"You're not?" she walked toward him, felt like stroking the lock of hair that had fallen into his eyes, but refrained.

"Nah. Do you want the grand tour?" he said, changing the subject.

"I sure would," she said. "Is the old bed still in the master bedroom? The one with the iron frame?"

"Oh yeah," he said. "I painted it white, bought a new mattress too. Come on, I'll show you," he said.

She noticed his hands were trembling.

"You know," he said. "My mother loved that bed. She said it was an heirloom, that it had seen countless births and countless deaths and that it was sacred. That it was the one thing in the family that always survived."

"Sounds like a wise woman your mother," she mused.

He opened the master bedroom door and pointed toward the bed.

It was the same one, but he had painted the frame and, to her surprise, it was properly made with beautiful pillows and a fluffy quilt. She had never been able to get him to make his bed when he was a child. His wife had to be a neat woman.

"That's beautiful," she said.

"Thank you," he smiled. "I'm glad you're here to see it," he added in a low voice.

"So you do recognize me?" she asked, suddenly on the verge of tears.

"Of course, Mom," he whispered. "I always do."

She took his hand and drew him to her, hugged him tightly, the way she used to do when he was a boy, then she held her hands on his cheeks and kissed him lightly. He was so different, her baby boy.

"It's so good to see you," she said. "I just wanted to know how you were doing. I came to—"

He didn't let her finish. "I know, Mom," he replied. "You've come to let me know that there really is an afterlife," he sighed. "I know."

She looked at him, hands falling to her sides. "You do?" she whispered.

"Let's go downstairs," he said. His eyes shifting.

She followed him down the stairs, wondering what his words meant. It had been so hard to make the journey, and now that she was here he looked nothing like she had expected. In fact, none of this was anything like she had expected. It wasn't exactly disappointment that she felt, but the lack of enthusiasm puzzled her.

"Can we go to the living room? I'd like to see the portraits before I have to go," she whispered.

"Of course," he said and led the way.

The living room was different from what she recalled. The old couch was gone and instead there was a giant leather sofa filling a corner of the room. A big television took up an entire wall, and her mother's chair was gone. The carpet was also missing, and instead there was a wooden floor that had seen better days.

The picture wall was still untouched, although she could see that a few portraits had been added. She walked to the wall and stared at them. In the sea of family photos she found the one she was looking for. Her husband, standing in the back wearing his worker's overalls. She remembered how angry she had been at him that day, because he didn't have the time to change before the photographer came. She had told him how important it was to her, but he had sneered and told her that she was old-fashioned: "What would be more perfect than having a photograph of me in the overalls I wear all day, every day?" he had asked her.

Now she understood what he meant. He wouldn't have looked right wearing the suit he only wore to weddings and funerals. And then there were the children, looking clean and well-dressed, all except Johnny who had spilled jam over himself and hid it from her so that she only realized when she saw the stain in the photograph.

"Johnny," she said. "You don't seem too happy to see me." She turned to face him, "I thought you—"

"I am happy to see you, Mom," he smiled, but it was weak and didn't reach his eyes. "It's just that I never know what to expect," he added.

"What do you mean?" she asked. She walked to the window. The crescent moon was wading in clouds, showing itself for just a moment before it hid behind the veil again. There were new houses in the valley now, houses halfway up the hill. It had all been farmland when she lived here.

He was silent.

"What do you mean?" she repeated and turned around again to face him. "I don't understand."

"You are a bit unpredictable," he said.

She saw him blushing and wondered why her little boy was so awkward around her. Her boy that had stuck with her through thick and thin when the others had turned and left because her illness had been too hard to deal with.

"You don't remember?" he asked.

"I don't know what you're talking about."

"You come here every year, Mom," he told her. "Every Halloween I wait for you." He looked her directly in the eyes as if that would somehow confirm that he was telling her the truth.

"Every year? But I only just made the journey, I only just made it. . . ." she whispered.

"Every year," he said. "But it's not always this easy," he sighed. "Sometimes it's—" his voice failed him and she could see him struggling to continue. "Sometimes it's a bit scary, to be honest."

"Scary?" she whispered.

He smiled and took her hand. "Come with me," he said and pulled her away from the living room and into the hallway again. There was a big mirror at the end of the passage. It had been there since before she was born, had been bought and paid for by her own father.

"Stand in front of the mirror," her son said, "and tell me what you see."

She looked at him and then she moved slowly toward the mirror, touching the wooden frame that was so beautifully carved with flowers and little birds. She kept her hand on the frame, fondling it lightly.

"Mom," he whispered. "Focus."

She looked at him again and smiled. He hadn't outgrown his impatience, he was still the little boy she knew. She nodded her head, bewildered. Then she turned and stared at her mirror image. There was nothing particularly strange in the reflection. She had brown hair, like his. She had wrinkles at the edges of her blue eyes and dark bags underneath, which wasn't unusual considering the journey she'd been on. Her clothes were a bit worn—a white blouse and dark jeans. She looked his age, and it wasn't until she turned back to her son that she realized the significance of that.

"What am I looking for?" she asked.

"Just look closer," he whispered, and she did as he told her.

At first she saw nothing. She was just a woman standing in front of a mirror in a house that was very familiar. It was home. She looked at him again, but he just nodded encouragingly.

Then she started to see something strange. It was as if her image in the mirror was dissolving, as if her body wasn't tangible anymore. It flickered out of existence, came back and faded again. Her hair was suddenly silvery and her fingernails long. There was fire in her eyes—not enthusiasm, but real burning fire—and then she saw the teeth, sharp and pointy. It was like looking into the gape of a shark.

She fell backward, only then noticing the lightness of her body, the way she seemed to float without touching the ground. There was no thud as she fell to the floor, just the deadly silence. She looked up at him, but he just smiled at her.

"I wanted to—" she whispered.

"Sometimes you don't remember why you're here," he said. "You rage through the house looking for something and never seem to find it. When I was nineteen you spent the entire night shaking the mirror in my room so violently that it shattered into a thousand pieces."

"The entire night?"

"Always Halloween," he added.

"All Hallow's Eve," she whispered. "When the souls of the dead go roaming."

"We thought of moving, but—" he went silent for a moment "—but it wasn't your fault."

She saw tears in his eyes. She got up from the floor. She wanted to embrace him, but then she remembered what she looked like now. "How long?" she asked.

"Since the year you died," he said. "It's been terrifying at times, and of course Dad never believed me."

She stood there, hands hanging by her sides, feeling the embers of her enthusiasm dying out as she listened to him.

"I was scared, but that wasn't your fault." He looked at her. "I won't sell the house, I won't," he looked down, fighting the tears.

She tried to put her hand on his shoulder, but now that she'd seen herself, she couldn't touch him—her hand just went through him. A feeling of violent disgust and anger passed through her but she pushed it down, had to listen to what he had to say.

"My wife wants to sell the house," he sighed. "But you will keep coming here and—" he sighed again. "It's not fair to you, not fair to the people who possibly buy the house and—" he raised his hand in a gesture she didn't understand "—and I'd miss seeing you. It's a reminder."

"There's life after death," she whispered. "But I guess that doesn't seem very comforting to you."

He smiled. "It's fine, Mom. We're good. I just wish you were this communicative every year. Last year the kids weren't out of the house when you came. Little Lina saw you like this. She had nightmares for months."

"Little Lina?" *Her* name, she recognized it now that he said it.

"Your grandchild. She looks just like you," he laughed. "It's sometimes a bit disconcerting, to be honest."

She laughed along with him, and with the laughter she seemed to release the tension that had built up inside her. She walked to the mirror again and tried to see herself and not the hideous image that was being portrayed. Slowly her features returned to what she was used to, calm settled again into her bones.

"Once you told me that if I didn't want you to come, that I shouldn't leave a lighted pumpkin outside the house. That you'd never find your way," he said.

"I did? Does it work? Oh, you have such talent carving."

"I always keep a pumpkin lit outside on this night, but I haven't forgotten."

"You keep doing that even though I scared your daughter?"

"You scared me more when I was a child. It's hard having your mother haunt you, you know. Most mother's cause their teenage sons grief in other ways, but not you. You haunted me on Halloween so grimly, I sometimes thought I must have done something horrible to deserve it."

She stared at him.

"It's fine," he said, and gave a little laugh. "At least I'm unique, eh?"

It wasn't rage she felt, but grief.

"You had such big eyes," she recalled. "You asked me so sincerely if there was life after death. I always remember that, even when I forget everything else."

"I know, Mom."

"I just wanted you to know that—"

"I know, Mom," he said.

"I'm sorry, Johnny."

"I know, Mom. It's fine."

"Why do you keep the pumpkin?"

"Because it's better than the alternative," he said.

"Is it?"

"Thinking of you roaming out there, lost and bewildered. Maybe when I die you can come with me to some other place. Until then, I'll see you on Halloween. No matter what."

"You were so young," she suddenly remembered. "Your father was always working. Couldn't face what was happening to me. You were here, listened to my every word, ran when I needed you to run errands. Did everything I asked you. Brought me my medicine. Remembered where I put my glasses when I could hardly remember my own name anymore."

She walked to the door and opened it. It was an easy maneuver. She didn't even have to touch the handle. "And this is how I repay you?" she looked at the pumpkin burning outside. The demon was spectacularly carved, a terrifying creation.

"Well, maybe I deserve it," he said.

She turned and looked at him. He was standing by the mirror, the light behind him casting a long shadow. She wanted to ask, but couldn't bring herself to say the words.

"You see," he continued, as he walked toward her. "It may be my fault that you're in this predicament."

"How? *No!*" she said loudly. She could hear the floorboards trembling underneath her, though she couldn't feel it.

"You were in such bad shape at the end," he said. "All I had to do was give you your dose twice, and then three times. You couldn't remember that you had already taken your pills. You took them and that was that."

"*You?*" she whispered.

"So I guess in the twisted way of the world, it was actually a blessing." He moved closer to her and, at that moment, his presence overwhelmed her. As she rose up from the floor, the howling she heard wasn't from the wind but from her own throat.

"It was my fault though, so it's only fair."

"It's not your fault," she said.

"It is," he said. "I did something terrible and I deserve this, you—" suddenly he smashed his fist to the wall. "I was just a kid, and I didn't think it was fair and—"

She felt her hair standing on end. The door slammed behind her, opened and slammed again as if a defiant child was making a point. She could hear herself screeching, but couldn't bring herself to stop making the sound, didn't even know how she was making it. It just was, like she was—she had no control over that either.

"Mom, it's all right," he said.

"Have you told anyone?" she asked.

"No," he said. "I'll take the knowledge with me to the grave and then we can haunt this house together, you and I." He laughed.

She didn't like hearing him so bitter. She settled on the floor again, the air calmed around her. "I forgive you," she said. "It wasn't your fault. I'm sorry you had to go through all that."

He stepped toward her and tried touching her arm, but it was phantasmal again. She felt an eerie draft, it chilled her to the bone. A shimmering sensation went through her as a hint of something entered her mind. A sense of the past, a glimpse into a realization she'd had previously, but her memory wasn't what it used to be. She couldn't easily recall, and she had no way of refreshing her memory, no way of triggering what it was that was gnawing at her. She looked at him and shook her head. Involuntarily she hissed, her teeth protruding in a gesture she could see reflecting back at her in the mirror.

"Of course, once I had got the taste for it, I couldn't stop. I rarely do it, but sometimes I just can't stop myself. I remember you and the peaceful look on your face and I just have to experience that again. The peaceful look on the women's faces."

She didn't want to comprehend, didn't want to hear any more. She rose up into the air, put her hands over her ears and flew up into the ceiling, then through the floorboards and up to the top floor. She saw the children's room, small made-up beds and stuffed animals. She rose up further, through the attic, and suddenly she was hovering above the house, floating as she looked out over the village and over the acres that had once belonged to them so long ago.

She heard his voice echoing in her head again and again, remembered hearing him say these words before. She just wanted to forget. She just wanted to forget everything.

"I sometimes confess to you," he had told her countless times. "They look so peaceful, and life is so hard."

She screamed at the top of her lungs, she screamed and, before oblivion and forgetfulness came and started the cycle once more, she remembered everything. Remembered every complaint, every sigh and every whisper. Remembered the sorrow in his eyes, the ache as he saw his mother wither away. It was her fault, what he was—it was *her* fault. She screamed, and this time every window in the house shattered into a thousand pieces, along with the mirror in the hallway.

"Another seven years of bad luck," she heard him say from inside the house as she was whisked away with the breeze.

"Is there life after death, Mom?" he cried.

She remembered his beautiful blue eyes, so big and questioning, so innocent.

"Is there?"

Soothingly, she had put her hand on his head and whispered, "There is and we'll meet there, you and I, we'll meet again."

The sky was dark, had long since lost its colorful, orange hue. The pumpkin illuminated the front porch, the demon flickering silently toward anyone who happened by. The shards of the windows lay scattered on the ground all around the house, glimmering like stars in the sky. The crescent moon cast its pallid light on the villa for a moment, before it shied away again.

The man inside sighed, went to the kitchen and retrieved a bucket and a shovel and proceeded to clean up the mess. He would have to board up the windows too and contact someone in the morning. It would be fine. The air was wintry, but the cold never bothered him, so he started his work.

His footfalls were heavy as he descended the porch steps and started gathering up slivers of glass from beneath the kitchen window. The demon flickered silently in the pumpkin as if it was anxious to escape. But there would be no escape for it. . . .

Not tonight.

DUST UPON A PAPER EYE

Cate Gardner

Cate Gardner has published more than one hundred short stories. Most recently, her work has appeared in *The Dark*, *Black Static*, *Postscripts*, *Sherlock Holmes's School for Detection*, and *The Year's Best Dark Fantasy & Horror 2017*. She has been twice nominated for the British Fantasy Award.

"In 'Dust upon a Paper Eye,' Hen jokes that she is half-a-minute from living on the streets," says the author. "Early in 2017, I attended a talk run by an aid-worker from the The Whitechapel Centre, a homeless charity in Liverpool. She told us how anyone can end up on the streets—they deal with solicitors, bank managers, secretaries, shop workers, etc.—and that we are all two or three months from living on the streets depending on our savings.

"Although, Hen's story wouldn't emerge for another few months, it festered in the background."

STILLNESS.

Henrietta danced between the frozen people, tickling their skin with a feather duster, enchanted until she noted a shock of short blonde hairs rise on the arms of the ruby-red girl. She brushed her finger over them, to flatten. They lay for a moment and then sprang up again. Why go to so much detail when the audience wouldn't note them? A cough caused her to fall against ruby-red and together they toppled to the boards. Like dominoes, others began to tumble. The owner of the cough saved the final doll from falling into the orchestra pit.

Untangling herself from the dolls, Hen asked, "Who are you?" of the boy in the torn jeans, dirty shirt, and month-grown beard.

"Just a fan."

There were no fans of this show. It hadn't opened yet and wouldn't do so for a week. There were faded posters outside the theater and a list of invited guests, of which he would not be among, and there would be only one performance. She didn't understand the whys of it, but she was paid to first dust the exhibits, then apply stage makeup. Her employment thanks to a City & Guilds course in the late 1980s.

"Sure. Help me pick them up and then scoot. You can't be found here. How did you get in?"

"Stage door was open. Thought the place abandoned to be truthful, thought I'd catch a nice dry sleep with the company of a few pigeons. Thought there may even be others here from the street, like. Dominic."

"Hen. Henrietta. But, just Hen."

She couldn't lift a doll alone, nor could he. Between them, they settled them into place, if not the right place. Hopefully, the theater owner and director, Herr Smithton, wouldn't notice. *Of course, he would.* Scratches ran down ruby-red's arm, where it had caught against the splintered boards. She'd have to paint over them. Hen traced the outline of the scars. *So realistic.*

"I live in the alley behind The Bridge, cardboard box number two, if you fancy a cuppa. Have to bring your own though. One for me would be good too." With that, he disappeared among the frozen crowd.

A door opened at the top of the auditorium followed by steel-capped footsteps and the bark of Herr Smithton, "Are we finished up there? Are we done? Can we bugger off now?"

Then she, too, was gone from the theater and the dolls were alone with their creator.

The streets were dark. The day scurried behind thick gray clouds that offered downpour. She rushed to her home, the flat above a chippy with its greasy windows and permanent stink. Still, it had a roof and it would be warmer than a cardboard box in an alley behind a pub. She should invite Dominic around for a hot meal, but she could only afford one portion of chips and she'd made that mistake before with others. A blanket offered her warmth and the kettle whistled on the one hob that worked. The three-bar fire might provide heat, but she couldn't afford to try it. She ate a chip, chewing it around her mouth as if it were made to poison her. She'd lived on the streets; she knew you couldn't afford to be fussy about what you ate if you wanted to survive. This was surviving. The chip caught in her throat.

"And action," Herr Smithton said, as she entered from stage right. "What, what are you doing girl? This is a rehearsal. Can't you see they are preparing to dance?"

If the audience had paid for tickets, they were going to demand a refund.

"Sorry, I thought you'd finished. I'll come back later, start applying the makeup."

"Oh yes, you are that girl. I forgot. You are such a mouse. Mousey girl creeping about the ghosts. Do your thing. Make my beauties stand out, their eyes, their lips; they are to engage our audience. Oh yes, oh yes, oh yes. I forget your name."

"Hen."

"There, it is gone again. You would like tickets for the show? Work hard and I'll give you a front-row seat, hell, you could be center-stage if you so wished. Can you dance?"

Hen shook her head. "No, sir."

"Probably for the best. You have family, no doubt. A drunken father and a dead mother. An aunt who cares but just doesn't have the space to take you in because the third bedroom belongs to the cats. I will need your help on the night. Take tickets, offer champagne. Try not to piss yourself. You are available. Halloween, yes."

"Yes, sir."

"Maybe we'll make a star of you yet."

When he'd left, Hen dragged a stool to the mannequin standing next to ruby-red and began applying his face. His pupils seemed to dilate, but that would be her imagination. Either way, he stared. Instead of hardening her, the streets had left her unnerved. It would be that she wasn't used to being seen. Stepped over, kicked, spat on, but not looked at, and certainly not with such intensity. These dolls were magnificent. A shame they were set for one brief show. As the hours passed, she constructed five faces, the instructions as to makeup were specific and she had to keep reapplying, mainly because her skills were at least two decades out of date. She would leave ruby-red until last. She was the centerpiece, the leading lady. Before packing the makeup kit away, Hen reached out, held ruby-red's hand. Her warmth radiated into the doll until it seemed they were both alive. When Hen let go, they both returned to nothing.

Dominic waited in the alley. He'd seen her go in and hoped she'd invite him for lunch. Hen bought him a bacon bap and a pumpkin-spiced latte, and another bap and sweet tea for herself. Her belly rumbled. On the radio, "Monster Mash" boomed. The chef danced along to it. Halloween would be a riot here, more fun than the theater at any rate.

"Strange goings-on," Dominic said.

"What? Where?" Did he mean the theater? Theaters were always full of oddness and oddities, of prima donnas, of the desperate, the winning, the lost. "It's just one show."

"Exactly. Who goes to all that trouble for one performance? And they never actually do anything. I mean they can't. Maybe he'll attach string to them, make them marionettes, but where are the puppeteers?"

She hadn't looked for answers, just a paycheck. What harm if an eccentric wanted to put on a show for his friends? Even if she would like to slap his horrid smirk. "Sometimes I imagine they're alive."

"You too? I swear I recognize a few from the streets."

Ridiculous.

"When I kissed her, the red-haired girl, I swear her lips moved beneath mine. They felt like skin. Too pursed to find a tongue though."

He kissed her. "You kissed her?"

"I've hit a jealousy nerve. Sorry."

"No." She wasn't interested in him. Not because he was on the street, she'd spent a short time there herself.

"Well that's me told." He laughed. "Ever think of sneaking in there when he's out, steal the dolls?"

"Drag them along the streets like corpses? That'd be fun. Not."

"We could set them up on street corners, a bit like 'penny for the guy' and get some extra cash. Maybe even enjoy a slap-up meal or get some tickets for this whacko show."

"I'm working the show, and for us this *is* a slap-up meal."

He swallowed the remainder of the bap. Stealing ruby-red, now there was an idea. *He kissed her.*

"Dominic, who were you?"

"Worked in an office, admittedly a dead-end job, made redundant, couldn't find another job, landlord didn't want benefit-scum, his words, living in his flats, so I was out and couldn't get on the housing list. I hope to trip over the turd's corpse one day. An aid-worker from a homeless shelter came into the office once to give a talk and persuade the company to sponsor the charity. She said that we were all two or three months from living on the streets, dependent on our savings. I joked I was half-a-minute from. Not so funny now."

The waitress cleaned the cups away. She wanted them gone.

Dominic slept on the floor of the flat, a threadbare towel rolled up to provide a pillow, his coat providing a blanket. He couldn't stay permanently, this was a one-off, although she'd said he could use the address for job application purposes. His snores filled the flat as Hen headed for the theater. October 30th. One day until the show, and only one face to make up. Ruby-red.

Herr Smithton waited in the auditorium. This time he didn't object to her company.

"Rehearsal tonight. I want my shining beauty to eclipse them all. You can do it? Yes, yes. This one needs hardly any work at all. They will all want her. As, I suspect, do you."

Herr Smithton grabbed Hen's chin. She balled her fists but didn't strike him. Yet. Job would be over in two days and he was hardly the sort you'd offer up as a reference.

"You tell me about yourself. I want to know what I employ. And your friend who sneaks around backstage. I want to know about him too. Oh, don't look so shocked. I have eyes and ears and not just on the stage. Little birds tell me things. We all have hopes, dreams, desires. Even them. Perhaps them most of all."

"He's not my friend. I mean he wasn't my friend. I thought he worked here."

"No you didn't, but I'll ignore the lie. We are all allowed one lie."

Ruby-red's skin proved softer, more pliable than the others. Careful not to smudge the makeup, she pressed her finger to the cheek of the man beside her. It, too, offered a softness. She pinched the man's arm. Did he wince? Herr Smithton had unnerved her as he always did. One more day and then it was back on job seeker's allowance until she found other employment. Unlike Dominic's previous landlord, hers would take money from anyone for that rat hole; of which he had several such dives in the city center.

Herr Smithton joined her on stage, moving among the dolls to adjust clothing and realign their arms so they were in a position that suggested dance. He couldn't expect they would move tomorrow night. Halloween might allow the dead to walk, but not mannequins. Unless said dead needed bodies to inhabit. Now she was growing fanciful and idiotic. The dead were dead and if they weren't, they would have come back long ago to help her. Still, ruby-red's lips were pliable. She tried to poke a finger between them, to find the tongue. Lips shot open. Teeth. A tongue traced the tip of her finger. She drew back, trying not to catch Herr Smithton's attention.

"Are you done? Are you going now?"

Without realizing, she'd moved a good few inches from ruby-red, almost to the edge of the stage and in danger of dropping into the cob-webbed orchestra pit. She shuffled the chair closer.

"Almost done."

She couldn't close the mouth. Would he notice? All the other dolls were tight-lipped. *Did I wake you?* You cannot wake that which is inanimate, but then neither can it lick your finger. She would come back later to save this one doll.

"I've finished, Herr . . . Mr. Smithton."

"Let me see. Let me check my beauty."

This was the time for Hen to not only leave but to run.

"What have you done? Her mouth, her teeth. Oh, it's exquisite. It's as if she is about to burst into chorus and she will prove to be such a little songbird. Oh yes, she will sing for us tomorrow night and the audience will want to carry her away."

That's if Hen and Dominic didn't carry her away first.

"Before you go." He grabbed her arm, fingers digging into skin, perhaps to check she wasn't an escaping doll. "I have a new addition to the chorus line."

He pulled her through the crowd to the dark of the stage. Against a faded backdrop of a chandelier stooped a figure she'd left dreaming on her bedroom floor. Dominic.

"I don't understand."

She tried to pull away. Herr Smithton's fingers dug harder, sharp fingernails drawing blood. The stage spun or she spun, projectile vomit would ruin her work. Any moment now Dominic would move and they'd laugh and it would prove a joke. Only Herr Smithton wasn't the joking type, certainly not with the likes of her.

"Paint."

Hen shook her head.

"Paint or lie with the spiders in the pit."

She took out her kit. *Sorry.* Dominic's blank-eyed stare didn't note her. His skin pliable, as soft as ruby-red's. These weren't dolls. What madness had she descended into? There would be no rescue of ruby now, she'd only have enough strength to drag Dominic from the theater. If

Herr Smithton allowed her to leave. He waited at her shoulder. He watched the work of her fingers, of the skill she'd developed over the past week. She'd thought ruby-red would be her masterpiece.

"He likes pumpkin-spiced latte and bacon sandwiches. He had hope despite a sodden cardboard box for a home, and he was kind and funny and so much more than the streets claimed."

"I can't allow you to leave."

"You can't make me stay."

She needed an advantage. There had to be an advantage. He twirled her chair around, brought herself to face not him but a mirror. A sharp jab in the arm caught her unawares.

"What?"

The stage, Herr Smithton, her image in the mirror blurred. She was here and she was a thousand miles away. He began to apply her makeup, turning her into a circus freak. She would not shine. She was no ruby-red.

Who would carry them out now?

She must have passed out, for next she woke to music and chatter; to a theater alive with an audience. The mirror remained in place. She sat at the edge of the stage, staring at her reflection, while behind her the others began to dance around ruby-red. Everyone waited for the star to awake. If only she could break the glass. Shatter this illusion, shatter that of the audience. *We are not dolls.* Hen jerked forward. She would fall from this seat, even if the orchestra pit proved her destination. She would show them she was flesh, blood, and stolen.

Numbers were being shouted from the audience. Dancers dragged to the front of the stage. Bartered for. Who would want a doll that only danced on Halloween? This was kidnap, this was . . . Herr Smithton dragged her to the front of the stage, the chair clattered to the boards. The audience laughed. She did not dance, she did not sing. Tiny balled fists fought against the fugue. The prices shot up at that. They liked her spunk. This wasn't spunk.

She teetered at the edge of the stage. Ruby-red twirled forward. She was to be the star, not Hen. Never meant to be Hen. Did she even know who she was anymore? Teeth bared, ruby-red leaned forward to kiss Hen. The audience gasped and clapped and proclaimed for them both. Instead, she bit Hen's lip and pushed her over the edge.

Cymbals clashed. Drumskin didn't so much break her fall as break her back. A few faces peered over into the pit from the audience side. Above, Herr Smithton tried to bring his show under control.

"That doll is bleeding," a woman said, her voice shrill. "Dolls do not . . . Henry. Henry dear, I think I may faint." She wasn't the only one. "Someone call an ambulance."

On stage, Herr Smithton attempted to regain his audience, "Ladies and Gentlemen, this is our Halloween extravaganza. These beauties were brought here for your delight, but you, I'm afraid, were brought here for them."

The great doors leading into the auditorium slammed, the drawing of bolts echoed across the expanse. The screams didn't die for some time, perhaps a little after the end of Hen.

NOT OUR BROTHER

Robert Silverberg

Robert Silverberg has been a professional writer since 1955, the year before he graduated from Columbia University, and has published more than one hundred books and close to one thousand short stories.

His books and stories have been translated into forty languages, and among his best-known novels are *Lord Valentine's Castle*, *Dying Inside*, *The Book of Skulls*, *Nightwings*, *The World Inside*, and *Downward to the Earth*. He has also edited dozens of science fiction and fantasy anthologies, including *The Science Fiction Hall of Fame*. His collaboration with Isaac Asimov, *The Positronic Man*, was made into the movie *Bicentennial Man* starring Robin Williams.

More recent titles include *First-Person Singularities*, a collection of stories entirely written in the first person; *Rough Trade*, a collection of crime fiction dating back to the 1950s; and *Living in the Future*, a collection of essays about science fiction from NESFA Press.

Silverberg is a multiple winner of the Hugo and Nebula awards. He was inducted into to the Science Fiction Hall of Fame in 1999, and in 2004 was named a Grand Master by the Science Fiction Writers of America, of which he is a past president.

"In the autumn of 1981 short stories were emanating from me with a swiftness that I had not experienced in several decades," recalls the author. "'Not Our Brother,' grew out of my fascination with Mexico and Mexican dance masks, which I had begun to collect. It was not science fiction but horrific fantasy, and I thought *Playboy* might like it.

"Fiction editor Alice K. Turner replied on November 25: 'I hate to do this, but I'm turning it down. It is very similar in both structure and content to "Via Dolorosa," and I think it had the same problems. I won't go into detail unless you want it, for I know you will easily sell the story elsewhere, but what it comes down to is that I don't love this the way I love "Gianni" and "Conglomeroid." So I'm going to wait for the next one. The way you're going, I expect to see it in a week or two.'

"I thought that the resemblances between 'Not Our Brother' and 'Via Dolorosa' were fairly superficial ones. Perhaps they ran deeper than that, though, because when I sent it to T. E. D. Klein of the *Twilight Zone Magazine*, who had published 'Via Dolorosa' and 'How They Pass the Time in Pelpel,' he commented that it seemed 'awfully similar to both of them in theme and other elements.' Well, all three were stories about Americans experiencing strange events in Third World countries, I suppose.

"Despite his qualms, T. E. D. accepted the story gladly, and *Twilight Zone* published it in the July 1982 issue."

HALPERIN CAME INTO San Simón Zuluaga in late October, a couple of days before the fiesta of the local patron saint, when the men of the town would dance in masks. He wanted to see that. This part of Mexico was famous for its masks, grotesque and terrifying ones portraying devils and monsters and fiends. Halperin had been collecting them for three years. But masks on a wall are one thing, and masks on dancers in the town plaza quite another.

San Simón was a mountain town about halfway between Acapulco and Taxco. "Tourists don't go there," Guzmán López had told him. "The road is terrible and the only hotel is a Cucaracha Hilton—five rooms, straw mattresses." Guzmán ran a gallery in Acapulco where Halperin had bought a great many masks. He was a suave, cosmopolitan man from Mexico City, with smooth dark skin and a bald head that gleamed as if it had been polished. "But they still do the Bat Dance there, the Lord of the Animals Dance. It is the only place left that performs it. This is from San Simón Zuluaga," said Guzmán, and pointed to an intricate and astonishing mask in purple and yellow depicting a bat with outspread leathery wings that was at the same time somehow also a human skull and a jaguar. Halperin would have paid ten thousand pesos for it, but Guzmán was not interested in selling. "Go to San Simón," he said. "You'll see others like this."

"For sale?"

Guzman laughed and crossed himself. "Don't suggest it. In Rome, would you make an offer for the Pope's robes? These masks are sacred."

"I want one. How did you get this one?"

"Sometimes favors are done. But not for strangers. Perhaps I'll be able to work something out for you."

"You'll be there, then?"

"I go every year for the Bat Dance," said Guzmán. "It's important to me. To touch the real Mexico, the old Mexico. I am too much a Spaniard, not enough an Aztec; so I go back and drink from the source. Do you understand?"

"I think so," Halperin said. "Yes."

"You want to see the true Mexico?"

"Do they still slice out hearts with an obsidian dagger?"

Guzmán said, chuckling, "If they do, they don't tell me about it. But they know the old gods there. You should go. You would learn much. You might even experience interesting dangers."

"Danger doesn't interest me a whole lot," said Halperin.

"Mexico interests you. If you wish to swallow Mexico, you must swallow some danger with it, like the salt with the tequila. If you want sunlight, you must have a little darkness. You should go to San Simón." Guzmán's eyes sparkled. "No one will harm you. They are very polite there. Stay away from demons and you will be fine. You should go."

Halperin arranged to keep his hotel room in Acapulco and rented a car with four-wheel drive. He invited Guzmán to ride with him, but the dealer was leaving for San Simón that afternoon, with stops en route to pick up artifacts at Chacalapa and Hueycantenango. Halperin could not go that soon. "I will reserve a room for you at the hotel," Guzmán promised, and drew a precise road map for him.

The road was rugged and winding and barely paved, and turned into a chaotic dirt-and-gravel track beyond Chichihualco. The last four kilometers were studded with boulders like the bed of a mountain stream. Halperin drove most of the way in first gear, gripping the wheel desperately, taking every jolt and jounce in his spine and kidneys. To come out of the pink-and-manicured Disneyland of plush Acapulco into this primitive wilderness was to make a journey five hundred years back in time. But the air up here was fresh and cool and clean, and the jungle was lush from recent rains, and now and then Halperin saw a mysterious little town half-buried in the heavy greenery: dogs barked, naked children ran out and waved, leathery old Nahua folk peered gravely at him and called incomprehensible greetings. Once he heard a tremendous thump against his undercarriage and was sure he had ripped out his oil pan on a rock, but when he peered below everything seemed to be intact. Two kilometers later, he veered into a giant rut and thought he had cracked an axle, but he had not. He hunched down over the wheel, aching, tense, and imagined that splendid bat mask, or its twin, spotlighted against a stark white wall in his study. Would Guzmán be able to get him one? Probably. His talk of the difficulties involved was just a way of hyping the price. But even if Halperin came back empty-handed from San Simón, it would be reward enough simply to have witnessed the dance, that bizarre, alien rite of a lost pagan civilization. There was more to collecting Mexican masks, he knew, than simply acquiring objects for the wall.

In late afternoon he entered the town just as he was beginning to think he had misread Guzmán's map. To his surprise it was quite imposing, the largest village he had seen since turning off the main highway—a great bare plaza ringed by stone benches, marketplace on one side, vast heavy-walled old church on the other, giant gnarled trees, chickens, dogs, children about everywhere, and houses of crumbling adobe spreading up the slope of a gray flat-faced mountain to the right and down into the dense darkness of a barranca thick with ferns and elephant-ears to the left. For the last hundred meters into town an impenetrable living palisade of cactus lined the road on both sides, unbranched spiny green columns that had been planted one flush against the next. Bougainvillea in many shades of red and purple and orange cascaded like gaudy draperies over walls and rooftops.

Halperin saw a few old Volkswagens and an ancient ramshackle bus parked on the far side of the plaza and pulled his car up beside them. Everyone stared at him as he got out. Well, why not? He was big news here, maybe the first stranger in six months. But the pressure of those scores of dark amphibian eyes unnerved him. These people were all

Indians, Nahuas, untouched in any important way not only by the twentieth century but by the nineteenth, the eighteenth, all the centuries back to Moctezuma. They had nice Christian names like Santiago and Francisco and Jesús, and they went obligingly to the *iglesia* for mass whenever they thought they should, and they knew about cars and transistor radios and Coca-Cola. But all that was on the surface. They were still Aztecs at heart, Halperin thought. Time-travelers. As alien as Martians.

He shrugged off his discomfort. Here he was the Martian, dropping in from a distant planet for a quick visit. Let them stare: he deserved it. They meant no harm. Halperin walked toward them and said, "*Por favor, donde está el hotel del pueblo?*"

Blank faces. "*El hotel?*" he asked, wandering around the plaza. "*Por favor. Donde?*" No one answered. That irritated him. Sure, Nahuatl was their language, but it was inconceivable that Spanish would be unknown here. Even in the most remote towns someone spoke Spanish. "*Por favor!*" he said, exasperated. They melted back at his approach as though he were ablaze. Halperin peered into dark cluttered shops. "*Habla usted Español?*" he asked again and again, and met only silence. He was at the edge of the marketplace, looking into a chaos of fruit stands, taco stands, piles of brilliant serapes and flimsy sandals and stacked sombreros, and booths where vendors were selling the toys of next week's Day of the Dead holiday, candy skeletons and green banners emblazoned with grinning red skulls. "*Por favor?*" he said loudly, feeling very foolish.

A woman in jodhpurs and an Eisenhower jacket materialized suddenly in front of him and said in English, "They don't mean to be rude. They're just very shy with strangers."

Halperin was taken aback. He realized that he had begun to think of himself as an intrepid explorer, making his way with difficulty through a mysterious primitive land. In an instant she had snatched all that from him, both the intrepidity and the difficulties.

She was about thirty, with close-cut dark hair and bright, alert eyes; attractive, obviously American. He struggled to hide the sense of letdown her advent had created in him and said, "I've been trying to find the hotel."

"Just off the plaza, three blocks behind the market. Let's go to your car and I'll ride over there with you."

"I'm from San Francisco," he said. "Tom Halperin."

"That's such a pretty city. I love San Francisco."

"And you?"

"Miami," she said. "Ellen Chambers." She seemed to be measuring him with her eyes. He noticed that she was carrying a couple of Day of the Dead trinkets—a crudely carved wooden skeleton with big eyeglasses, and a rubber snake with a gleaming human skull of white plastic, like a cue-ball, for a head. As they reached his car she said, "You came here alone?"

Halperin nodded. "Did you?"

"Yes," she said. "Come down from Taxco. How did you find this place?"

"Antiquities dealer in Acapulco told me about it. Antonio Guzmán López. I collect Mexican masks."

"Ah."

"But I've never actually seen one of the dances."

"They do an unusual one here," she said as he drove down a street of high, ragged, mud-colored walls, patched and plastered, that looked a thousand years old. "Lord of the Animals, it's called. Died out everywhere else. Pre-Hispanic shamanistic rite, invoking protective deities, fertility spirits."

"Guzmán told me a little about it. Not much. Are you an anthropologist?"

"Strictly amateur. Turn left here." There was a little street, an open wrought-iron gateway, a driveway of large white gravel. Set back a considerable distance was a squat, dispiriting hovel of a hotel, one story, roof of chipped red tiles in which weeds were growing. Not even the ubiquitous bougainvillea and the great clay urns overflowing with dazzling geraniums diminished its ugliness. Cucaracha Hilton indeed, Halperin thought dourly. She said, "This is the place. You can park on the side."

The parking lot was empty. "Are you and I the only guests?" he asked.

"So it seems."

"Guzmán was supposed to be here. Smooth-looking man, bald shiny head, dresses like a financier."

"I haven't seen him," she said. "Maybe his car broke down."

They got out, and a slouching fourteen-year-old *mozo* came to get Halperin's luggage. He indicated his single bag and followed Ellen into the hotel. She moved in a sleek, graceful way that kindled in him the idea that she and he might get something going in this forlorn place. But as soon as the notion arose, he felt it fizzling: she was friendly, she was good-looking, but she radiated an off-putting vibe, a noli me tangere sort of thing, that was unmistakable and made any approach from him inappropriate. Too bad. Halperin liked the company of women and fell easily and uncomplicatedly into liaisons with them wherever he traveled, but this one puzzled him. Was she a lesbian? Usually he could tell, but he had no reading on her except that she meant him to keep his distance. At least for the time being.

The hotel was grim, a string of lopsided rooms arranged around a weedy courtyard that served as a sort of lobby. Some hens and a rooster were marching about, and a startling green iguana, enormous, like a miniature dinosaur, was sleeping on a branch of a huge yellow-flowered hibiscus just to the left of the entrance. Everything was falling apart in the usual haphazard tropical way. Nobody seemed to be in charge. The *mozo* put Halperin's suitcase down in front of a room on the far side of the courtyard and went away without a word. "You've got the one next to mine," Ellen said. "That's the dining room over there and the cantina next to it. There's a shower out in back and a latrine a little further into the jungle."

"Wonderful."

"The food isn't bad. You know enough to watch out for the water. There are bugs but no mosquitoes."

"How long have you been here?" Halperin asked.

"Centuries," she said. "I'll see you in an hour and we'll have dinner, okay?"

His room was a whitewashed irregular box, smelling faintly of disinfectant, that contained a lumpy narrow bed, a sink, a massive mahogany chest of drawers that could have come over with the Spaniards, and an ornate candlestick. The slatted door did not lock and the tile-rimmed window that gave him an unsettling view of thick jungle close outside was without glass, an open hole to the wall. But there was a breathtaking mask mounted above the bed, an armadillo-faced man with a great gaping mouth; and next to the chest of drawers was a weather-beaten but extraordinary helmet mask, a long-nosed man with an owl for one ear and a coyote for another; and over the bed was a double mask, owl and pig, that was finer than anything he had seen in any museum. Halperin felt such a rush of possessive zeal that he began to sweat. The sour acrid scent of it filled the room. Could he buy these masks? From whom? The dull-eyed *mozo*? He had done all his collecting through galleries; he had no idea how to go about acquiring masks from natives. He remembered Guzmán's warning about not trying to buy from them. But these masks must no longer be sacred if they were mere hotel decorations.

Suppose, he thought, I just *take* that owl-pig when I check out, and leave three thousand pesos on the sink. That must be a fortune here. Five thousand, maybe. Could they find me? Would there be trouble when I was leaving the country? Probably. He put the idea out of his mind. He was a collector, not a thief. But these masks were gorgeous.

He unpacked and found his way outside to the shower—a cubicle of braided ropes, a creaking pipe, yellowish tepid water—and then he put on clean clothes and knocked at Ellen's door. She was ready for dinner. "How do you like your room?" she asked.

"The masks make up for any little shortcomings. Do they have them in every room?"

"They have them all over," she said.

He peered past her shoulder into her room, which was oddly bare, no luggage or discarded clothes lying around, and saw two masks on the wall, not as fine as his but fine enough. But she did not invite him to take a close look, and closed the door behind her. She led him to the dining room. Night had fallen some time ago, and the jungle was alive with sounds, chirpings and rachetings and low thunking booms and something that sounded the way the laughter of a jaguar might sound. The dining room, oblong and lit by candles, had three tables and more masks on the wall, a devil face with a lizard for a nose, a crudely carved mermaid, and a garish tiger-hunter mask. He wandered around studying them in awe, and said to her, "These aren't local. They've been collected from all over Guerrero."

"Maybe your friend Guzmán sold them to the owner," she suggested. "Do you own many?"

"Dozens. I could bore you with them for hours. Do you know San Francisco at all? I've got a big old three-story Victorian in Noe Valley and there are masks in every room. I've collected all sorts of primitive art, but once I discovered Mexican masks they pushed everything else aside, even the Northwest Indian stuff. You collect too, don't you?"

"Not really. I'm not an acquirer. Of things, at any rate. I travel, I look, I learn, I move on. What do you do when you aren't collecting things?"

"Real estate," he said. "I buy and sell houses. And you?"

"Nothing worth talking about," she said.

The *mozo* appeared, silently set their table, brought them, unbidden, a bottle of red wine. Then a tureen of albóndigas soup, and afterward tortillas, tacos, a decent turkey molé. Without a word, without a change of expression.

"Is that kid the whole staff?" Halperin asked.

"His sister is the chambermaid. I guess his mother is the cook. The *patrón* is Filiberto, the father, but he's busy getting the fiesta set up. He's one of the important dancers. You'll meet him. Shall we get more wine?"

"I've had plenty," he said.

They went for a stroll after dinner, skirting the jungle's edge and wandering through a dilapidated residential area. He heard music and hand-clapping coming from the plaza but felt too tired to see what was happening there. In the darkness of the tropical night he might easily have reached for Ellen and drawn her against him, but he was too tired for that, too, and she was still managing to be amiable, courteous, but distant. She was a mystery to him. Moneyed, obviously. Divorced, widowed young, gay, what? He did not precisely mistrust her, but nothing about her seemed quite to connect with anything else.

About nine-thirty he went back to his room, toppled down on the ghastly bed, and dropped at once into a deep sleep that carried him well past dawn. When he woke, the hotel was deserted except for the boy. "*Cómo se llama?*" Halperin asked, and got an odd smoldering look, probably for mocking a mere *mozo* by employing the formal construction.

"*Elustesio*," the boy muttered. Had Elustesio seen the *Norteamericano señorita?* Elustesio hadn't seen anyone. He brought Halperin some fruit and cold tortillas for breakfast and disappeared. Afterward Halperin set out on a slow stroll into town.

Though it was early, the plaza and surrounding marketplace were already crowded. Again Halperin got the visiting-Martian treatment from the townsfolk—fishy stares, surreptitious whispers, the occasional shy and tentative grin. He did not see Ellen. Alone among these people once more, he felt awkward, intrusive, vulnerable; yet he preferred that, he realized, to the curiously unsettling companionship of the Florida woman.

The shops now seemed to be stocking little except Day of the Dead merchandise, charming and playful artifacts that Halperin found irresistible. He had long been attracted to the imagery of brave defiance of death that this Mexican version of Halloween, so powerful in the inner life of the country, called forth. Halperin bought a yellow papier-mâché skull with brilliant flower-eyes and huge teeth, an elegant little guitar-playing skeleton and a bag of grisly, morbid marzipan candies. He stared at the loaves of bread decorated with skulls and saints in a bakery window. He smiled at a row of sugar coffins with nimble skeletons clambering out of them. There was some extraordinary lacquer work on sale too, trays and gourds decorated with gleaming red-and-black patterns. By midmorning he had bought so much that carrying it was a problem, and he returned to the hotel to drop off his purchases.

A blue Toyota van was parked next to his car and Guzmán, looking just as dapper in khakis as he always did in his charcoal gray suits, was rearranging a mound of bundles in it. "Are you enjoying yourself?" he called to Halperin.

"Very much. I thought I'd find you in town when I got here yesterday."

"I came and went again, to Tlacotepec, and I returned. I have bought good things for the gallery." He nodded toward Halperin's armload of toy skulls and skeletons. "I see you are buying too. Good. Mexico needs your help."

"I'd rather buy one of the masks that's hanging in my room," Halperin said. "Have you seen it? Pig and owl, and carved like—"

"Patience. We will get masks for you. But think of this trip as an experience, not as a collecting expedition, and you will be happier. Acquisitions will happen of their own accord if you don't try to force them, and if you enjoy the favor of *amo tokinwan* while you are here."

Halperin was staring at some straw-wrapped wooden statuettes in the back of the van. "*Amo tokinwan?* Who's that?"

"The Lords of the Animals," said Guzmán. "The protectors of the village. Perhaps *protectors* is not quite the right word, for protectors are benevolent, and *amo tokinwan* often are not. Quite dangerous sometimes, indeed."

Halperin could not decide how serious Guzmán was. "How so?"

"Sometimes at fiesta time they enter the village and mingle. They look like anyone else and attract no special attention, and they have a way of making the villagers think that they belong here. Can you imagine that, seeing a stranger and believing you have known him all your life? Beyond doubt they are magical."

"And they are what? Guardians of the village?"

"In a sense. They bring the rain; they ward off the lightning; they guard the crops. But sometimes they do harm. No one can predict their whims. And so the dancing, to propitiate them. Beyond doubt they are magical. Beyond doubt they are something very other. *Amo tokinwan*."

"What does that mean?" Halperin asked.

"In Nahuatl it means, 'Not our brother,' of different substance. Alien. Supernatural. I think I have met them, do you know? You stand in the plaza watching the dancers, and there is a little old woman at your elbow or a boy or a pregnant woman wearing a fine *rebozo*, and everything seems all right, but you get a little too close and you feel the chill coming from them, as though they are statues of ice. So you back away and try to think good thoughts." Guzmán laughed. "Mexico! You think I am civilized because I have a Rolex on my wrist? Even I am not civilized, my friend. If you are wise you will not be too civilized while you are here, either. They are not our brother, and they do harm. I told you you will see the real Mexico here, eh?"

"I have a hard time believing in spirits," Halperin said. "Good ones and evil ones alike."

"These are both at once. But perhaps they will not bother you." Guzmán slammed shut the door of the van. "In town they are getting ready to unlock the masks and dust them and arrange them for the fiesta. Would you like to be there when that is done? The *mayordomo* is my friend. He will admit you."

"I'd like that very much. When?"

"After lunch." Guzmán touched his hand lightly to Halperin's wrist. "One word, first. Control your desire to collect. Where we go today is not a gallery."

The masks of San Simón were kept in a locked storeroom of the municipal building. Unlocking them turned out to be a solemn and formal occasion. All the town's officials were there, Guzmán whispered: the *alcalde*, the five *alguaciles*, the *regidores*, and Don Luis Gutierrez, the *mayordomo*, an immense mustachioed man whose responsibility it was to maintain the masks from year to year, to rehearse the dancers and to stage the fiesta. There was much bowing and embracing. Most of the conversation was in Nahuatl, which Halperin did not understand at all, and he was able to follow very little of the quick, idiosyncratic Spanish they spoke either, though he heard Guzmán introduce him as an important *Norteamericano* scholar and tried thereafter to look important and scholarly. Don Luis produced an enormous old-fashioned key, thrust it with a flourish into the door and led the way down a narrow, musty corridor to a large white-walled storeroom with a ceiling of heavy black beams. Masks were stacked everywhere, on the floor, on shelves, in cupboards. The place was a museum. Halperin, who could claim a certain legitimate scholarly expertise by now in this field, recognized many of the masks as elements in familiar dances of the region, the ghastly faces of the Diablo Macho Dance, the heavy-bearded elongated Dance of the Moors and Christians masks, the ferocious cat-faces of the Tigre Dance. But there were many that were new and astounding to him, the Bat Dance masks—terrifying bat-winged heads that all were minglings of bat characters and other animals, bat-fish, bat-coyote, bat-owl, bat-squirrel, and some that were unidentifiable except for the weird outspread rubbery wings, bats hybridized with creatures of another world, perhaps. One by one the masks were lifted, blown clean of dust, admired, and passed around, though not to Halperin. He trembled with amazement at the power and beauty of these bizarre wooden effigies. Don Luis drew a bottle of mescal from a niche and handed it to the *alcalde*, who took a swig and passed it on; the bottle came in time to Halperin, and without a thought for the caterpillar coiled in the bottom of the bottle he gulped the fiery liquor. Things were less formal now. The high officials of the town were laughing, shuffling about in clumsy little dance steps, picking up gourd rattles from the shelves and shaking them. They called out in Nahuatl, all of it lost on Halperin, though the words *amo tokinwan* at one point suddenly stood out in an unintelligible sentence, and someone shook rattles with curious vehemence. Halperin stared at the masks but did not dare go close to them or try to touch them. This is not a gallery, he reminded himself. Even when things got so uninhibited that Don Luis and a couple of the others put masks on and began to lurch about the room in a weird lumbering polka, Halperin remained tense and controlled. The mescal bottle came to him again. He drank, and this time his discipline eased; he allowed himself to pick up a wondrous bat mask, phallic and with great staring eyes. The carving was far finer than on the superb one he had seen at Guzmán's gallery. He ran his fingers lovingly over the gleaming wood, the delicately outlined ribbed wings. Guzmán said, "In some villages the Bat Dance was a Christmas dance, the animals paying homage to little Jesus. But here it is a fertility rite, and therefore the bat is phallic. You would like that mask, no?" He grinned broadly. "So would I, my friend. But it will never leave San Simón."

Just as the ceremony appeared to be getting rowdy, it came to an end: the laughter ceased, the mescal bottle went back to its niche, the officials grew solemn again and started to file out. Halperin, in schoolboy Spanish, thanked Don Luis for permitting him to attend, thanked the *alcalde*, thanked the *alguaciles* and the *regidores*. He felt flushed and excited as he left the building. The cache of masks mercilessly stirred his acquisitive lust. That they were unattainable made them all the more desirable, of course. It was as though the storeroom were a gallery in which the smallest trifle cost a million dollars.

Halperin caught sight of Ellen Chambers on the far side of the plaza, sitting outside a small café. He waved to her and she acknowledged it with a smile.

Guzmán said, "Your traveling companion?"

"No. She's a tourist down from Taxco. I met her yesterday."

"I did not know any other Americans were here for the fiesta. It surprises me." He was frowning. "Sometimes they come, but very rarely. I thought you would be the only *extranjero* here this year."

"It's all right," said Halperin. "We *gringos* get lonely for our own sort sometimes. Come on over and I'll introduce you."

Guzmán shook his head. "Another time. I have business to attend to. Commend me to your charming friend and offer my regrets."

He walked away. Halperin shrugged and crossed the plaza to Ellen, who beckoned him to the seat opposite her. He signaled the waiter. "Two margaritas," he said.

She smiled. "Thank you, no."

"All right. One."

"Have you been busy today?" she asked.

"Seeing masks. I salivate for some of the things they have in this town. I find myself actually thinking of stealing some if they won't sell to me. That's shocking. I've never stolen anything in my life. I've always paid my own way."

"This would be a bad place to begin, then."

"I know that. They'd put the curse of the mummy on me, or the black hand, or God knows what. The sign of Moctezuma. I'm not serious about stealing masks. But I do want them. Some of them."

"I can understand that," she said. "But I'm less interested in the masks than in what they represent. The magic character, the transformative power. When they put the masks on, they *become* the otherworldly beings they represent. That fascinates me. That the mask dissolves the boundary between our world and *theirs*."

"*Theirs?*"

"The invisible world. The world the shaman knows, the world of the were-jaguars and were-bats. A carved and painted piece of wood becomes a gateway into that world and brings the benefits of the supernatural. That's why the masks are so marvelous, you know. It isn't just an aesthetic thing."

"You actually believe what you've just said?" Halperin asked.

"Oh, yes. Yes, definitely."

He chose not to press the point. People believed all sorts of things, pyramid power, yogurt as a cure for cancer, making your plants grow by playing Bach to them. That was all right with him. Just now he found her warmer, more accessible, than she had been before, and he had no wish to offend her. As they strolled back to the hotel, he asked her to have dinner with him, imagining hopefully that that might lead somewhere tonight, but she said she would not be eating at the hotel this evening. That puzzled him—where else around here could she get dinner, and with whom?—but of course he did not probe.

He dined with Guzmán. The distant sound of music could be heard, shrill, alien. "They are rehearsing for the fiesta," Guzmán explained. The hotel cook outdid herself, preparing some local freshwater flatfish in a startlingly delicate sauce that would have produced applause in Paris. Filiberto, the *patrón*, came into the dining room and greeted Guzmán with a bone-crushing *abrazo.* Guzmán introduced Halperin once again as an important *Norteamericano* scholar. Filiberto, tall and very dark-skinned, with cheekbones like blades, showered Halperin with effusive courtesies.

"I have been admiring the masks that decorate the hotel," Halperin said, and waited to be invited to buy whichever one took his fancy, but Filiberto merely offered a dignified bow of thanks. Praising individual ones, the owl-pig, the lizard-nose, also got nowhere. Filiberto presented Guzmán with a chilled bottle of a superb white wine from Michoacán, crisp and deliciously metallic on the tongue; he spoke briefly with Guzmán in Nahuatl; then, saying he was required at the rehearsal, he excused himself. The music grew more intense.

Halperin said, "Is it possible to see the rehearsal after dinner?"

"Better to wait for the actual performance," said Guzmán.

Halperin slept poorly that night. He listened for the sound of Ellen Chambers entering the room next door, but either he was asleep when she came in or she was out all night.

And now finally the fiesta was at hand. Halperin spent the day watching the preparations: the stringing of colored electric lights around the plaza, the mounting of huge papier-mâché images of monsters and gods and curious spindly-legged clowns, the closing down of the shops and the clearing away of the tables that displayed their merchandise. All day long the town grew more crowded. No doubt people were filtering in from the outlying districts, the isolated jungle farms, the little remote settlements on the crest of the sierra. Through most of the day he saw nothing of Guzmán or Ellen, but that was all right. He was quite accustomed now to being here, and the locals seemed to take him equally for granted. He drank a good deal of mescal at one cantina or another around the plaza and varied it with the occasional bottle of the excellent local beer. As the afternoon waned, the crowds in the plaza grew ever thicker and more boisterous, but nothing particular seemed to be happening, and Halperin wondered whether to go back to the hotel for dinner. He had another mescal instead. Suddenly the fiesta lights were switched on, gaudy, glaring, reds and yellows and greens, turning everything into a psychedelic arena, and then at last Halperin heard music, the skreeing bagpipy sound of bamboo flutes, the thump of drums, the whispery, dry rattle of tambourines, the harsh punctuation of little clay whistles. Into the plaza came ten or fifteen boys, leaping, dancing cartwheels, forming impromptu human pyramids that promptly collapsed, to general laughter. They wore no masks. Halperin, disappointed and puzzled, looked around as though to find an explanation and discovered Guzmán, suave and elegant in charcoal gray, almost at his elbow. "No masks?" he said. "Shouldn't they be masked?"

"This is only the beginning," said Guzmán.

Yes, just the overture. The boys cavorted until they lost all discipline and went pell-mell across the plaza and out of sight. Then a little old man, also unmasked, tugged three prancing white goats caparisoned with elaborate paper decorations into the center of the plaza and made them cavort, too. Two stilt-walkers fought a mock duel. Three trumpeters played a hideous discordant fanfare and got such cheers that they played it again and again. Guzmán was among those who cheered. Halperin, who had not eaten, was suddenly captured by the aroma from a stand across the way where an old woman was grilling tacos on a brazier and a tin griddle. He headed toward her, but paused on the way for a tequila at an improvised cantina someone had set up on the street corner, using a big wooden box as the bar. He saw Ellen Chambers in the crowd on the far side of the plaza and waved, but she did not appear to see him, and when he looked again he could not find her.

The music grew wilder and now, at last, the first masked dancers appeared. A chill ran through him at the sight of the nightmare figures marching up the main avenue, bat-faced ones, skull-faced ones, grinning devils, horned creatures, owls, jaguars. Some of the masks were two or three feet high and turned their wearers into malproportioned dwarfs. They advanced slowly, pausing often to backtrack, circling one another, kicking their legs high, madly waving their arms. Halperin, sweating, alert, aroused, realized that the dancers must have been drinking heavily, for their movements were jerky, ragged, convulsive. As they came toward the plaza he saw that they were herding four figures in white robes and pale human-faced masks before them, and were chanting something repetitively in Nahuatl. He caught that phrase again, *amo tokinwan*. Not our brother.

To Guzmán he said, "What are they saying?"

"The prayer against the *amo tokinwan*. To protect the fiesta, in case any of the Lords of the Animals actually are in the plaza tonight."

Those around Halperin had taken up the chant now.

"Tell me what it means," Halperin said.

Guzmán said, chanting the translation in a rhythm that matched the voices around them: "*They eat us! They are—not our brother. They are worms, wild beasts. Yes!*"

Halperin looked at him strangely. "'They eat us?'" he said. "Cannibal gods?"

"Not literally. Devourers of souls."

"And these are the gods of these people?"

"No, not gods. Supernatural beings. They lived here before there were people, and they naturally retain control over everything important here. But not gods as Christians understand gods. Look, here come the bats."

They eat us, Halperin thought, shivering in the warm humid night. A new phalanx of dancers was arriving now, half a dozen bat-masked ones. He thought he recognized the long legs of Filiberto in their midst. Darkness had come and the dangling lights cast an eerier, more brilliant glow. Halperin decided he wanted another tequila, a mescal, a cold *cerveza*, whatever he could find quickest. *Not our brother.* He excused himself vaguely to Guzmán and started through the crowd. *They are worms, wild beasts.* They were still chanting it. The words meant nothing to him, except *amo tokinwan,* but from the spacing, the punctuation, he knew what they were saying. *They eat us.* The crowd had become something fluid now, oozing freely from place to place; the distinction between dancers and audience was hard to discern. *Not our brother.* Halperin found one of the little curbside cantinas and asked for mescal. The proprietor splashed some in a paper cup and would not take his pesos. A gulp and Halperin felt warm again. He tried to return to Guzmán but no longer saw him in the surging, frenzied mob. The music was louder. Halperin began to dance—it was easier than walking—and found himself face-to-face with one of the bat-dancers, a short man whose elegant mask showed a bat upside down, in its resting position, ribbed wings folded like black shrouds. Halperin and the dancer, pushed close together in the press, fell into an inadvertent pas de deux. "I wish I could buy that mask," Halperin said. "What do you want for it? Five thousand pesos? Ten thousand? *Habla usted Español?* No? Come to the hotel with the mask tomorrow. You follow? *Venga mañana.*" There was no reply. Halperin was not even certain he had spoken the words aloud.

He danced his way back across the plaza. Midway he felt a hand catch his wrist. Ellen Chambers. Her khaki blouse was open almost to the waist and she had nothing beneath it. Her skin gleamed with sweat, as if it had been oiled. Her eyes were wide and rigid. She leaned close to him and said, "Dance! Everybody dances! Where's your mask?"

"He wouldn't sell it to me. I offered him ten thousand pesos, but he wouldn't—"

"Wear a different one," she said. "Any mask you like. How do you like mine?"

"Your mask?" He was baffled. She wore no mask.

"Come! Dance!" She moved wildly. Her breasts were practically bare and now and then a nipple flashed. Halperin knew that that was wrong, that the villagers were cautious about nudity and a *gringa* especially should not be exhibiting herself. Drunkenly he reached for her blouse, hoping to button one or two of the buttons, and to his chagrin his hand grazed one of her breasts. She laughed and pushed herself against him. For an instant she was glued to him from knees to chest, with his hand wedged stupidly between their bodies. Then he pulled back, confused. An avenue seemed to have opened around them. He started to walk stumblingly to some quieter part of the plaza, but she caught his wrist again and grinned a tiger-grin, all incisors and tongue. "Come on!" she said harshly.

He let her lead him. Past the tacos stands, past the cantinas, past a little brawl of drunken boys, past the church, on whose steps the dancer in the phallic bat mask was performing, juggling pale green fruits and now and then batting one out into the night with the phallus that jutted from his chin. Then they were on one of the side streets, blind crumbling walls hemming them on both sides and cold moonlight the only illumination. Two blocks, three, his heart pounding, his lungs protesting. Into an ungated courtyard of what looked like an abandoned house, shattered tumbledown heaps of masonry everywhere and a vining night-blooming cactus growing over everything like a tangle of terrible green snakes. The cactus was in bloom and its vast white trumpet-like flowers emitted a sickly sweet perfume, overpoweringly intense. He wanted to gag and throw up, but Ellen gave him no time, for she was embracing him, pressing herself fiercely against him, forcing him back against a pile of shattered adobe bricks. In the strange moonlight her skin glistened and then seemed to become transparent, so that he could see the cage of her ribs, the flat long plate of her breastbone, the throbbing purplish heart behind it. She was all teeth and bones, a Day of the Dead totem come to life. He did not understand and he could not resist. He was without will. Her hands roamed him, so cold they burned his skin, sending up puffs of steam as her icy fingers caressed him. Something was flowing from him to her, his warmth, his essence, his vitality, and that was all right. The mescal and the beer and the tequila and the thick musky fragrance of the night-blooming cereus washed through his soul and left it tranquil. From far away came the raw dissonant music, the flutes and drums, and the laughter, the shouts, the chants. *They eat us.* Her breath was smoke in his face. *They are worms, wild beasts.* As they embraced one another, he imagined that she was insubstantial, a column of mist, and he began to feel misty himself, growing thinner and less solid as his life force flowed toward her. Now for the first time he was seized by anguish and fright. As he felt himself being pulled from his body, his soul rushing forth and out and out and out, helpless, drawn, his drugged calm gave way to panic. *They are—not our brother.* He struggled, but it was useless. He was going out swiftly, the essence of him quitting his body as though she were reeling it in on a line. Bats fluttered above him, their faces streaked with painted patterns, yellow and green and brilliant ultramarine. The sky was a curtain of fiery bougainvillea. He was losing the struggle. He was too weak to resist or even to care. He could no longer hear himself breathe. He drifted freely, floating in the air, borne on the wings of the bats.

Then there was confusion, turmoil, struggle. Halperin heard voices speaking sharply in Spanish and in Nahuatl, but the words were incomprehensible to him. He rolled over on his side and drew his knees to his chest and lay shivering with his cheek against the warm wet soil. Someone was shaking him. A voice said in English, "Come back. Wake up. She is not here."

Halperin blinked and looked up. Guzmán was crouched above him, pale, stunned-looking, his teeth chattering. His eyes were wide and tensely fixed.

"Yes," Guzmán said. "Come back to us. Here. Sit up, let me help you."

The gallery-owner's arm was around his shoulders. Halperin was weak and trembling, and he realized Guzmán was trembling too. Halperin saw figures in the background—Filiberto from the hotel and his son Elustesio, the *mayordomo* Don Luis, the *alcalde*, one of the *alguaciles*.

"Ellen?" he said uncertainly.

"She is gone. *It* is gone. We have driven it away."

"It?"

"*Amo tokinwan*. Devouring your spirit."

"No," Halperin muttered. He stood up, still shaky, his knees buckling. Don Luis offered him a flask; Halperin shook it away, then changed his mind, reached for it, took a deep pull. Brandy. He walked four or five steps, getting his strength back. The reek of the cactus-flowers was nauseating. He saw the bare ribs again, the pulsating heart, the sharp white teeth. "No," he said. "It wasn't anything like that. I had too much to drink—maybe ate something that disagreed with me—the music, the scent of the flowers—"

"We saw," Guzmán said. His face was bloodless. "We were just in time. You would have been dead."

"She was from Miami—she said she knew San Francisco—"

"These days they take any form they like. The woman from Miami was here two years ago, for the fiesta. She vanished in the night, Don Luis says. And now she has come back. Perhaps next year there will be one who looks like you and talks like you and sniffs around studying the masks like you, and we will know it is not you, and we will keep watch. Eh? You should come back to the hotel now. You need to rest."

Halperin walked between them down the walled streets. The fiesta was still in full swing, masked figures capering everywhere, but Guzmán and Don Luis and Filiberto guided him around the plaza and toward the hotel. He thought about the woman from Miami, and remembered that she had had no car and there had been no luggage in her room. *They eat us.* Such things are impossible, he told himself. *They are worms, wild beasts.* And next year would there be a diabolical counterfeit Halperin haunting the fiesta? *They are—not our brother.* He did not understand.

Guzmán said, "I promised you you would see the real Mexico. I did not think you would see as much of it as this."

Halperin insisted on inspecting her hotel room. It was empty and looked as if it had not been occupied for months. He stretched out on his bed fully clothed, but he did not particularly want to be left alone in the darkness, and so Guzmán and Filiberto and the others took turns sitting up with him through the night while the sounds of the fiesta filled the air. Dawn brought a dazzling sunrise. Halperin and Guzmán stepped out into the courtyard. The world was still.

"I think I'll leave here now," Halperin said.

"Yes. That would be wise. I will stay another day, I think."

Filiberto appeared, carrying the owl-pig mask from Halperin's room. "This is for you," he said. "Because that you were troubled here, that you will think kindly of us. Please take it as our gift."

Halperin was touched by that. He made a little speech of gratitude and put the mask in his car.

Guzmán said, "Are you well enough to drive?"

"I think so. I'll be all right once I leave here." He shook hands with everyone. His fingers were quivering. At a very careful speed he drove away from the hotel, through the plaza, where sleeping figures lay sprawled like discarded dolls, and mounds of paper streamers and other trash were banked high against the curb. At an even more careful speed he negotiated the cactus-walled road out of town. When he was about a kilometer from San Simón Zuluaga he glanced to his right and saw Ellen Chambers sitting next to him in the car. If he had been traveling faster, he would have lost control of the wheel. But after the first blinding moment of terror came a rush of annoyance and anger. "No," he said. "You don't belong in here. Get the hell out of here. Leave me alone." She laughed lightly. Halperin felt like sobbing. Swiftly and unhesitatingly he seized Filiberto's owl-pig mask, which lay on the seat beside him, and scaled it with a flip of his wrist past her nose and out the open car window. Then he clung tightly to the wheel and stared forward. When he could bring himself to look to the right again, she was gone. He braked to a halt and rolled up the window and locked the car door.

It took him all day to reach Acapulco. He went to bed immediately, without eating, and slept until late the following afternoon. Then he phoned the Aeromexico office.

Two days later he was home in San Francisco. The first thing he did was call a Sacramento Street dealer and arrange for the sale of all his masks. Now he collects Japanese *netsuke*, Hopi *kachina* dolls, and Navaho rugs. He buys only through galleries and does not travel much anymore.

THE SCARIEST THING IN THE WORLD

Michael Marshall Smith

Michael Marshall Smith is a novelist and screenwriter. He has published more than ninety short stories and five novels—*Only Forward*, *Spares*, *One of Us*, *The Servants*, and *Hannah Green and her Unfeasibly Mundane Existence*—winning the Philip K. Dick, International Horror Guild, and August Derleth Awards, along with the Prix Bob-Morane in France. He has also received the British Fantasy Award for Best Short Fiction four times, more than any other author.

Writing as "Michael Marshall" he has published seven internationally bestselling thrillers, including The Straw Men series (currently in development for television), *The Intruders*—recently a BBC America series starring John Simm, Mira Sorvino, and Millie Bobby Brown—and *Killer Move*. His most recent novel under this byline is *We Are Here*.

"One of the things I value most about being a writer is the occasional opportunity to catch up with old friends during conventions," he explains, "while at the same time gaining a quick glimpse into a country; although it can also be strange—the concertinaing effect of maintaining relationships through an annual, or biannual, or every-five-years evening spent in a bar. It can make you very conscious of the passage of time, and what it's doing to you . . . and them.

"Like the narrator of the story, I walked away from Helsinki with precisely two new words at my disposal: *kiitos* and *moi* (an informal word for 'hello'). I never got the hang of pronouncing the former, but perfected the latter to the point where it became a problem, as people started to assume that I was a local, which led to me shrugging like a hapless buffoon as they launched into a stream of Finnish."

I GOT THE cab to pull up a hundred yards short and paid the guy in cash, adding a generous tip despite having been told multiple times that people didn't do that here in Finland. A few euros here or there make little difference to me, but they might to the driver. I worked as a waiter for a couple years, back in the day. What goes around comes around.

"Halloween party?"

"No," I said. "Well, sure, tonight's the night, I guess. But this is part of the Festival of the Fantastique."

"Ah, yes. I heard of this."

Hard not to. European cities tend to care a lot more openly about the arts, and the center of Helsinki was festooned with banners for this celebration of the Gothic and weird, in prose, film, and art—with big posters at most of the bus stops, and on the trams too. The venue for Greg's event was an imposing neoclassical stone frontage that looked like a museum or embassy or church, strikingly up-lit on either side of a large central doorway. I'd asked to be dropped down the street to have a private moment for a cigarette, and also to see how the land lay. The line snaked fifty feet down the cold, dark street.

"Big crowd, huh?"

"Looks like it," I said.

I climbed out, wrapping my coat around as a chill wind came whipping down the road, and used half of my grasp of the Finnish language in one sentence. "*Kiitos.*"

After the cab pulled away I blinked, stretched my mouth and eyes wide, and lit my cigarette. I was, I noticed, pretty drunk. That's unusual for me now, especially at a festival, though in the early days it was near-mandatory. We'd arrive in a chaotic flock, get our work hung or installations set up as quickly as possible, and immediately head en masse for the nearest dive-bar to talk arty bullshit and get flamboyantly wasted into the small hours. Repeat for however many nights the event lasted, ending with a wretched train ride home.

But I don't go to festivals by train any more. Or doze my hungover way home in the back of some guy's truck, buffeted by unsold prints and paintings. I fly. Actually, I am flown. If I find myself in a bar it's an invite-only party and I arrive escorted by the organizer and their assistant, the PR, sometimes a gallery owner. I am deferentially handed a glass of obligatory champagne and sip it while chatting with whoever's allowed through the cordon. I'll have a glass of wine during dinner, two at most, before switching to espressos and water. Being drunk in public is fine for enfants terribles. Not for me. Instead I'll retire to my hotel room, catch up on email, stand a while looking out the window at whatever city it happens to be. And go to bed.

Tonight the party hadn't been at a public venue, but—as sometimes happens—the home of a notable collector of my work.

And that's where the trouble started.

I dropped the cigarette butt in the trash and headed across the street.

Something of a frisson ran through the line as I walked toward the entrance. Half the crowd was in Halloween costume, thankfully all horror-related instead of the ballerinas and baseball players and other random crap you'll see at home. I considered democratically joining the end of the line, but only for about a second. That just doesn't work. People leave their positions to come say "hi," and the whole system goes to shit and it's hassle the organizers don't need when they're trying to get an event started in a timely manner.

The Festival secretary was at the front, standing with the people checking tickets. Her eyes widened as I approached: not three hours previously I'd told her I wasn't coming to this event.

"Mr. Williams," she said. She'd gotten into the spirit of the night in a low-key way, up-spraying her hair like the Bride of Frankenstein, completing the effect with curved brows and beesting lipstick. "What a pleasure to see you here."

"Figured I'd come support an old friend."

"Aha," she said. "And did you announce you might be attending, on the social media?"

"I may have mentioned it."

She smiled, and looked at the people snaking away down the sidewalk. "So that explains this."

"No, no," I said. "It's been a while since he had a show. I'm sure there's a lot of interest in what Greg's come up with."

She winked, as if we both knew that wasn't true. "Still no costume for you?"

"I am what I am. That's scary enough." I held up my hands like claws and made a deliberately lame growling sound.

She laughed, but then her face turned a little more serious. "I should warn you," she said. "Your friend . . . he's in a strange mood, I think."

"Probably nervous. It's a big crowd."

She nodded, as if reassured. "I'm sure that's all it is."

The ticket-collectors stood aside to let me pass, and the people at the front of the line nodded and grinned at me. That's the weirdest thing, the aspect I still haven't gotten used to. I mean, sure—I'm recognizable, somewhat, in certain milieux. The TV show did that, along with being laughably characterized as "the Anthony Bourdain of art," and simple self-marketing tricks like always wearing a charcoal suit. But why does that mean I get to jump the line? I don't get it.

For a moment I considered stopping, briefly joining the front of the line as a gesture of solidarity with the masses. But then realized I was being a bit drunk and in reality I needed both a piss and some more to drink and I didn't want to wait for either, and so I swanned in as God intended.

A short, dark corridor led to a large, circular room with a domed ceiling. This was crowded with a couple of hundred people, chattering and milling about and waiting for the event to start. I wrongly assumed the gents would be at the far side of the room, and found myself heading down some stone stairs into a sepulchral space beneath the building, like a crypt made of corridors. There were big bundles of straw and rolls of cotton wool piled up against the walls throughout, and large barriers of corrugated cardboard, painted black. Sound baffles, presumably. But nowhere to piss.

I went back upstairs and found the john, and as I came out a festival underling spotted me and hectically led me to one side. She was shy, her English rather more heavily accented than most of the Finns I'd encountered so far, and so it took me a moment to understand where she was taking me.

But then, there he was.

Rather more overweight than his picture in the festival program suggested, significantly more balding, standing by himself in a cordoned-off area and holding a bottle of champagne bullishly by the neck.

"Danny *boy*," he said. "As I live and breathe."

"Greg," I said. "Looking good."

"That's horseshit and you know it. You of course look exactly how you do on the TV. I guess that's what a shit-ton of money will do for you."

That, and going to the gym, and watching what I eat, I thought, *and making the effort to do all the other tiresome things required not to look like crap at our age*. Didn't say it. "You going to give me some of that drink?"

"Oh yeah." He peered around, eventually spotted the clearly visible array of glasses on the table behind him, and slopped a random amount of champagne more or less into one of them. "There were a couple of the festival people here, but I said something borderline rude to that organizer woman and they all kind of drifted off."

"Rude about what?"

"You, to be frank."

I laughed. "What did you say?"

"Just that I didn't think you were all you were cracked up to be. 'Course at that point I had no idea you'd actually be turning up. Look at 'em . . ." he gestured out at the crowds milling around the room, more than a few of whom were sneaking glances over at us. ". . . isn't that fucking weird? Them wanting to *look* at you like that? Or are you used to it now?"

"Doesn't bother me," I said, giving a little wave to a couple of people who seemed familiar. They looked delighted, and waved back.

"Having been recognized by their lord, the peasants rejoiced."

"Piss off, Greg."

"Why are you even here?"

"Dude," I said. "It's been a long time. But back in the day . . . I'd say we were friends, wouldn't you?"

"Sure," he said, reluctantly. "But I didn't mean that. I meant at this festival. It's all horror stuff. They can call it "Gothic" or "fantastique" or whatever they like, but that's what it is. Horror movies, horror books, horror art. The genre slum. You haven't done anything like that in fucking decades."

"My Dark Side series two years ago—"

"Oh fuck off. Putting in more shadows and ladling on the burnt umber does not make you a master of the macabre."

"I'm flattered you've been keeping up with my work."

"Can't fucking avoid it. Any idea what *I've* been doing?"

"To be honest, no. Not since."

I left it there. He looked away, then back. It was the first time in the entire exchange we'd had direct eye contact. He looked drunk, also tired and hurt. "Installations."

"Well, yeah, I know that. Which is what the thing tonight is, right? That's great. I always said that was your best medium in the early days."

"Are you taking the piss? These still *are* the early days for me, Danny. I am literally back where I fucking started."

"Careers can be like that."

"Not yours."

"Look, what do you want me to say? I've been lucky."

"And you sold out."

"That's unfair."

"Is it? The annoying thing, the thing that really pisses me off, is you were *good*. You painted stuff that unnerved the crap out of people. But then you figured out there was no money in it, and so you jumped into the abstractosphere."

"We all make choices."

"Meaning?"

I shook my head. He knew I was referring to his defining moment. The point where—resentful at not receiving the recognition that in all honesty he probably deserved—he spiraled off into using a genuinely remarkable level of technical skill to start forging art instead of creating it. Of course faking is an act of creation, of a kind, not least in the level of attention to detail required to convincingly replicate the techniques of others, especially old masters. But it's a road to nowhere good, especially if you have an ego as big as Greg's. They say many serial killers get to the point where they basically want to be caught, either to be put out of their misery or—more likely—finally get the attention they've always craved. It's the same with forgers. Almost none of them are in it for the money. They want to get one over on the gallery owners and collectors and other so-called experts who turn some artists into rock stars and consign others to obscurity. For a while it's enough for you alone to know you're doing this. Not for long, though. Consciously or otherwise, eventually you'll leave a clue. Greg tried to pull the same trick twice (painting a semi-obvious forgery on top of a much better one, thus getting the latter accepted as real) and was caught. And vilified.

"Fuck you," Greg said. He said it very clearly. Several people outside the cordon heard him, and quickly looked away.

"Thanks. I was the sole person from the old days who stood up for you. Literally the only one."

"And that's why fuck you. It was that which pushed me over the fucking edge. How do you think it felt, charity from somebody who gets his assistants to do all the work?"

"Yeah, I've heard that rumor," I said, knocking back the glass of wine. "It isn't true. Everything with my name on it is mine. I work long hours. And I work hard."

"With your eyes closed?"

I was saved from having to answer this by the approach of the Festival Secretary. She'd been hovering the background for a few minutes. "I'm sorry to . . . interrupt," she said. "I just wanted to remind you it's due to start in twenty minutes."

"I know," Greg said. "I can tell the fucking time."

"Thank you," I told her. She backed away.

"That's why there's a crowd here tonight, isn't it?" Greg said to me, angrily. "You fucking tweeted it. Didn't you. You couldn't even let me have *that*."

"Fuck's sake. I'm going outside for a cigarette."

"You still smoke? I'm genuinely amazed."

"We all have a dark side, Greg. I just hide mine. Whereas you get yours out like your cock, and wave it around."

"At least I'm honest."

"Maybe. But the problem is then everybody's already seen your dick and you've got nothing left to shock them with."

There was still a line at the door, though shorter. It was getting close to show time. I walked quickly past with my head down and went far enough up the street that I could stand in a doorway without being seen. Not that I give a damn about people knowing I smoke. I'm fifty-two. My parents are dead and my wife is now an ex-wife, and there's not really anybody's judgement that I have to take seriously.

Except my own, of course. I stood huddled in shadow and sucked down the first cigarette quickly, decided to have another, on the grounds I had no idea how long this event was going to take: the description merely said it was something everybody experienced together, rather than wandered through in their own time. Seeing Greg had affected me in ways I hadn't anticipated, too. Most of my reason for being here was genuinely to show support. But sure, I'll admit a portion of it was to present myself to him. To the guy who'd always had so much more flair in the old days, always attracted the lion's share of attention, who had no qualms about elbowing "friends" aside in order to get to the reviewer, gallery owner—or girl. The alpha creator, the hare, who'd burned out and let the beta male tortoise overtake on the long haul.

Being in the same physical space for the first time in probably twenty years, however, had caused that to fall away. Instead it reminded me of the days when you hung with people because of a spark, not because of their status, and you created things not because they'd be good investments, but because they touched people. Because what you did was real.

As I was lighting the second cigarette I realized someone was approaching. My heart sunk. The glass of champagne I'd thrown back had topped me up to pretty-drunk level, and I didn't want to undergo a stilted conversation with a fan.

"Can I bum one of those?"

It was Greg. I held out the pack. He took one and accepted a light. Stood for a moment, looking along the dark street. Shook his head. "Sorry I was such a cunt."

"I enjoyed it. Reminded me of the old days."

He laughed. "You win that one."

"Well, I'm a winner, to the bone."

This had been a catchphrase of Greg's, thirty years ago. He remembered. "Yeah yeah, fuck you. Look, seriously though. And this is important. Why are you actually here?"

"What difference does it make?"

"I wasn't kidding earlier. During that whole dumpster fire four years back, after I was dumb enough to try to sell a fake to a celebrity and wound up being the poster boy for pricks everywhere, it was you coming to my defense that pushed me over the edge. I spent the next three years raging drunk."

I started to speak but he rode over me. "I know, I know. I'm sure you did it with good intentions, because you've always been a good boy, but that's what happened. My shit is closer to being back together now. And so I just want to know how much charity is involved here."

"Not at all," I said. "If you want to know, it's this. Punching a hole. Remember that?"

He did, and the act of recollection made him look much younger for a moment. "Of course. What I used to say we were going to do. Or *should* do. Not just put rectangular shit on people's walls. Make things that changed the world. Things would be remembered forever."

"Right. Did you bring the champagne out with you?"

"The Finns are open-minded, but not *that* open-minded," he said. "However." He pulled a small flask out of his coat. I unscrewed it and took a long pull. "But I don't get what you're saying."

"I was at a dinner this evening," I said. The vodka felt good and warm inside me. It did what ill-advised drinks always do, which is make you want to have a dozen more. "At the home of the biggest collector of my work in Finland. Whole of Europe, in fact. Roasted boar. Appetizers with seven different types of smoked fish. Champagne that was older than the pert little things who were serving it."

"I went to McDonald's."

"Whatever, Greg. Just listen. The Festival committee was there. A couple of super-fans. The freakin' mayor. And this collector and her husband, of course. And before the food is served we were all led—with great ceremony—to a separate wing they've had built to showcase their art. One room of which, the *main* room, the reason the wing was *built*, is specifically for me. I hadn't realized how much of my stuff she had. It was like seeing my entire life nailed to the walls. And there, at the end of this gallery, is a huge space dedicated to a single painting from my Dark Side series. It's very big. I used nearly a bucket of burnt umber on that one alone. Spot-lit, in full glory, probably the best thing I've ever done. And the hostess stands there and regales everybody with how, in the nine months since the wing was built, she's made sure every guest comes and sees this work of mine, and how they all tell her how marvelous it is. And she raised her glass to me, and then to the painting, and the assembled company spontaneously broke into applause."

Greg was looking down at the sidewalk now. I knew how he'd be feeling, and also that we were running out of time.

"So what's your point?" he muttered.

"It'd been hung sideways," I said.

As we walked back to the building I saw the festival organizer waiting in the doorway. She looked relieved to see us.

"Everybody is downstairs," she said. "Waiting. It's amazing. There's over three hundred people."

"Cool," Greg said. "Let them get settled. Five minutes. You not going down?"

She shook her head apologetically. "I don't like the dark."

I followed Greg into the big antechamber room, which was now empty. "So what is this thing of yours anyway?"

"Borderline plagiarism," Greg said, looking slightly embarrassed. "Which is why you were in my mind, and probably why I dissed you to that woman earlier, if I'm honest. Actually, I'm pretty sure we talked it into shape together, some long drunken night of yesteryear. But the initial idea was yours."

"Idea for what?"

"'The Scariest Thing in the World.'"

For a second I had no idea what he was talking about. Then I remembered. "*Christ*," I said.

He rolled his eyes. "I know, right? The years go by."

I nodded, though he'd misunderstood. I hadn't meant how long it was since we'd talked about a "psychological horror" installation—though yes, it had to be a quarter of a century. I'd meant how dumb and sad it was to go ahead and actually do it.

It had seemed grown-up and cool back then, before we were real adults. Get people down into a confined space. Turn off the lights, deaden the sound, close the door so that nobody can find their way out, and make them stay there for half an hour. The idea being to demonstrate that it wasn't horror, or the fantastical, that was truly frightening. That those are merely entertainments, distractions, safe spaces, crèches for our anxieties—and the real and oldest horror, the scariest thing in the world, is being alone in the dark.

Very big, right? Very *deep*.

Back then. Now it felt woefully simplistic and juvenile, cool and edgy only before you'd had to deal with grown-up stuff like the lingering death of parents or marriages exploding into bloody shards: before you'd learned that the deepest pit is not the dark, but our own fears and doubts, regrets and wrong paths and mistakes: before you'd found yourself looking around in panic and not understanding where you are or how you got there, or in which direction—if any—a meaningful future lies. All Hallow's Eve is supposed to be when the walls of reality come down, and the dark spirits walk abroad and knock on doors.

But the truth is, they're already inside.

The idea we'd once nurtured was adolescent and naive, and I knew that when people left the venue tonight, Greg's career would be over forever.

"Well, good luck," I said, however. "And the funny thing is, I remember the idea being yours anyhow."

He looked at me with an expression I'd never seen on his face before. Or anybody's, probably. Only someone pretty close to the very end of their tether lets emotions like that out of the back of their mind, far enough to show in the eyes.

Bitter gratitude, mangled with utter desperation.

"Your stuff's okay," he said, quietly. "You know that. And I know you didn't actually sell out."

"You don't think?"

"No. You just choked."

He said this with offhand authority, and for a moment I was back to being the twenty-three-year-old I was when I first met Greg. A couple of years older than me. Far more self-assured. Better-connected, part of the scene. Already making waves. Confident he was going to carve his mark on the world.

"Of all of us," he said, "You were the one who could have punched a hole. I knew it then. Which is why I was kind of an asshole to you at times." He shrugged. "Ah well. That ship sailed, I guess. Too late for any of us now."

"Life goes on."

"For better or worse." He smiled, genuinely. And gestured with his head. "Show time."

I followed him to the big door in the corner of the room, and started down the stairs after him into the lower area. Basement, crypt, whatever it was. All the lights down there had been turned off. There was a distant rustle of all the people wandering around the corridors, in the pitch-dark, waiting for this thing to start, not yet knowing what it was, but the sound was soft, deadened. Dead.

Before we were even at the bottom of the stairs I realized Greg wasn't as dumb as I'd thought.

This felt like going somewhere unsafe.

This was a place where, like everybody else, I'd be forced to look inside. To think about a world in which I'd stuck with what I'd been doing, and turned out to be the same kind of genuinely interesting footnote to history Greg was, and possibly even remained his friend. Or where I'd parlayed the TV show into one on a bigger network, maybe even taken up one of several offers to direct a movie, instead of listening to the quiet inner voices that told me I'd screw it up. Where I'd had the courage to turn down endless commissions and instead spend sufficient time on the woman I loved, giving her enough attention to still have her, instead of losing her to a broken heart.

But I didn't. I choked each time. I got to the edge but couldn't make myself jump over. Couldn't take the risk of stretching my soul until it broke, and instead failed my way into something that only looked like success from the outside.

The scariest thing in the world is the widening gap between who you are and who you wanted to be, and the truth was that Greg wasn't the only faker here tonight.

That was a fact worth learning. But I didn't have to spend half an hour having it hammered home.

"I've got to take a piss," I said. "I'll be right back."

"Sure," Greg said, face blank. "Close the door on the way out. And keep having a great life."

He walked away into the darkness, dismissing me. He knew I wasn't coming back. I hesitated. Maybe it would be good for me to confront myself, to stumble those interior corridors for a while, trying to find a way out. But I didn't want to.

I turned and walked back up the stairs.

The festival organizer was standing outside on the street. She looked around quickly when I came out of the building, caught in the act of having a cigarette break.

"Your secret's safe with me," I said.

Surprised, and side-lit by the uplighter by the door, she actually did look kind of like Elsa Lanchester, or close enough. She smiled gratefully. "You're not staying?"

"It's been a long day. And I don't want there to be any distractions after the show. It's going to be a big success, and I want to make sure Greg gets all the credit. He's going to get what he always wanted."

"And what was that?"

I just smiled and walked away.

After a few minutes I found a cab and got in and sat in the back, not listening as a chatty driver took me to the Hilton through dark, wet streets: back to another hotel in yet another city, back to my great life.

I was glad that I had not stayed for the show, that instead of following the path of least resistance I had made a decision and done something. I was glad that I, for once, had not choked.

And I felt fine about the fact that, before securely closing the heavy door to the basement, I'd held my lighter down to the nearest bundle of straw, waited until it caught alight, and then watched as the flames started to spread.

THE NATURE OF THE BEAST

Sharon Gosling

Sharon Gosling is the author of such middle-grade children's books as *The Diamond Thief*, *The Ruby Airship*, and *The Sapphire Cutlass*, along with a number of nonfiction books about television and film (*The Art and Making of Penny Dreadful*, *Wonder Woman: The Art and Making of the Film*, and *Tomb Raider: The Art and Making of the Film*).

Her most recent titles are the Scandinavian-set young adult horror novel *FIR*, which was shortlisted for the Centurion Award and Lancashire Book of the Year, and a novel set in the world of Victorian stage magic. She is also working on a full-length horror novel set in the wild and empty borderlands between Cumbria, Northumberland, and Scotland.

For the author's first foray into adult horror writing, she recalls: "I first had the idea for a child with pitch-black eyes and saw-blades in her mouth about ten years ago, while I was standing on a dismal, packed London Underground platform waiting for a delayed train.

"Then a few years ago I wrote a short scene in which she is discovered as part of a murder investigation, although at that point the setting was a fairly standard one in the city. It wasn't until I moved to where I live now—a remote village in Northern Cumbria—that the idea really found its home.

"Our tiny village is in the foothills of the Pennines. (Incidentally, it is also home to one of the oldest vampire legends in the UK—every Halloween we still get people braving the churchyard, thinking it's the one from the legend.) There is nothing beyond us but Northumberland: wide stretches of high fell littered with abandoned dwellings, the wreckage of crashed planes, and whatever can eke out a living on rough pasture or smaller living things.

"I'd like to think that the girl and others like her have been thriving up there amid the ancient landscape since time immemorial. I just wouldn't want to meet them when they're hungry."

CASSIE SPIED THE doughy bulk of Evans, visible through the wet windscreen of his worn silver Honda. She pulled to a halt beside him, glancing at the time—barely 7:00 a.m.—then slipped on her stab vest. Swinging open the door, she stepped out, pulling her heavy wool coat along with her. Dragging it on, she turned the collar up against the rain as her skipper hefted himself out of his driving seat, clutching a radio in one hand.

It wasn't until Evans glanced at her and then did a sharp, scowling double take that Cassie remembered the need for sunglasses. She ducked back inside the car, pulling them from the cupholder between the seats and jamming them on, kicking herself. The dim world grew dimmer still.

"Christ on a bike, Wish," her DI said, as she shut the door again. "Tell me you at least punched the bugger back."

"Not really advisable, sir." At his raised eyebrow, she shrugged. "Neighbor's toddler got a bit free with a toy fire engine, that's all."

Evans grunted. "Boy's a top shot then. That's the third bullseye he's scored in a month, by my count."

"It's a girl, actually," Cassie said, blithely.

He regarded her silently with shrewd eyes. Then he turned away, jerking his chin at the farm.

"This place came out of last night's appeal," he said.

It was derelict, squatting miserably in wet fields thick with mud and empty of livestock. A farmhouse connected to two barns, forming a U shape around three sides of a courtyard. The roofs of the buildings were sagging under the weight of years, their windows smashed, their doors splintered. The open end of the courtyard was cut off by three support vans, parked in a semicircle with their riot shields up.

Ten disappearances at the rate of two a month for the past five, though it had taken a while for the police to realize what they were dealing with. There was no obvious connection between the victims other than their proximity to Carlisle and the kind of bad luck that goes with vulnerability. Drug dealers, drug addicts. Runners on the fells, old people going out for morning papers, children failing to return from games with friends: people disappearing into the uncertain light of dawn and dusk.

As the list of missing had increased, so had the media frenzy surrounding it, the sense of panic and paranoia spreading like mold across a damp wall.

Press conferences had followed, along with recreations and harrowing public appeals from distraught parents and lovers. The only common factor came in the mention of a straggly looking man with a crossbow who had been seen in the proximity of several disappearances. It was a detail that Evans had insisted on leaving out when talking to the press, seeing it as the only possible identifier that could help navigate the high tide of calls the incident room received after every public appeal.

The last disappearance had been three days ago: a twelve-year-old girl called Kelly Stevens had failed to arrive home from an after-school club. Cassie knew Evans hadn't slept since, covering his exhaustion with a nonchalant bravado she neither believed nor could find it in her heart to blame.

But then, she always had been softhearted. It made up for other, less obvious deficiencies. Not even Nick had noticed those yet, and they'd have been married two years come December.

"First team's gone in," Evans told her. "If the tip's a good 'un, we'll find him. I've got the rest of them on the perimeter in case he makes a run for it. You got your vest on under that monstrosity?"

"Yes, sir."

Evans gave a brief nod and turned to look toward the buildings. He shivered a little, a frown creasing lines across his weathered face. "This is the place, Wish. I can feel it."

Cassie silently agreed. The crumbling farm had a feel of death about it that reached beyond the obvious signs of age and neglect. There were plenty of places like this dotted about on the Cumbrian fells, returning gently to the landscape as they tumbled into themselves, but this was different. There was a pervasive sense of hopelessness to the place, a heaviness that had nothing to do with the low sky and the persistent misery of the weather as October twisted its face toward November.

A shout echoed from somewhere inside the buildings, followed by another and then a brief scuffle. A couple of minutes later, another shout, louder this time.

"Clear!"

The sodden, empty courtyard was suddenly a bustle of activity. The response team filled it, pouring like black oil from the fractured doors. In the midst of the flow of guns and uniforms was a foreign piece of flotsam, a thin figure forced forward, arms held behind his back. One of the officers holding the suspect also had a crossbow dangling from his left hand. It had no arrow fitted to its shaft.

The apprehended man had greasy gray-brown hair the length of his jaw, falling in straggly lines that half-obscured his down-turned face. He seemed emaciated—his shoulders bony, his fingers thin, tapering into grimy, broken nails bitten to the quick. His face sagged like the folds in a sack of flour, rheumy eyes sinking into etiolated skin. He was barely Cassie's height—five-three—and weighed less. She'd put him at forty if he were a day, though he looked worn down by years beyond his own.

For a monster, he was oddly pathetic.

A movement to his right drew Cassie's attention. A second officer was holding the missing arrow. It was strung with bodies: rabbits, four of them, fat little things, pinioned through their skulls like the slaughtered moles her father-in-law hung from the barbed-wire fences of the family farm.

DI Evans stepped forward, reaching out to tap the spindly bones of the crossbow with his forefinger.

"Got a license for this?"

The suspect said nothing. Cassie watched his flaccid face. He seemed so out of it that it crossed her mind that he might be high. Beside her, Evans shifted his weight to his heels, nodding at the silence. Cassie saw Evans's fist tighten around the radio.

"What's your name?"

Silence.

"Is Kelly here? The others?"

Still nothing. Just the sound of rain dabbing rhythmically into the mud at their feet. Cassie could feel it beginning to soak through her coat and onto her shoulders.

Evans jerked his chin. "Get him out of here."

The suspect seemed to wake from his slumber as he was being led away. Cassie followed Evans as he strode quickly toward the nearest barn, but the turbulence behind drew her attention back to the courtyard. The man was trying to turn in her direction, struggling against two pairs of hands. He was back from wherever he'd been, and his eyes were wild.

"Don't let her out," he croaked, as he was pushed into one of the vans. "Don't—" The rest of his warning was severed by the slamming shut of the vehicle's doors.

"Sir?" Cassie called after Evans, who was already ducking under a sagging lintel. "The B team. We should wait—"

Evans lifted the radio to his lips so quickly that she wondered if he'd simply forgotten that they weren't there alone. He spoke into the radio, a brief order sharply barked.

"B team—search the house. DS Wish and I have got the barns."

Then he was off again. Cassie followed quickly, the heavy black shadow of her coat swinging out to snag against the splintered doorframe as she passed through it. Inside, the barn was dark but mostly dry aside from shallow pools of greasy rainwater. Evans and Cassie kicked through detritus on the barn's concrete floor: dried leaves, wisps of straw, dirt, the faded silver corpses of ancient tin cans, all coated with the white spatter of bird shit, old and new, years of it, years. As they passed beneath the skeleton eaves, there came the sound of winged things in hurried flight: an exodus of feathered creatures from the cavity of the roof. Cassie looked up, saw the phantasm shapes of birds disturbing the air as they escaped into the wet sky. Faint plumes of debris tumbled down the dim shafts of light in their wake, a precipitation of brick-dust added to the incessant fall of rain.

There was nothing here. No spatters of blood, no echoing screams. No sign of murder, of torture, of pain. No sign that any had been cleared up, either.

Although . . .

Was there something?

Cassie looked around, trying to get a fix on whatever it was that had wisped across her copper's senses, but there was only emptiness. Dereliction.

She followed Evans through the first barn and on into the second. In the corner was a makeshift camp, comprised of a low-slung canvas bed on foldout metal struts, a battered camping stove, a bottle of lighter fluid, an empty pan, and a five-liter bottle of water. Cassie thought of fat rabbits strung on the shaft of an arrow and wondered if, actually, there could be more than one displaced soul with a crossbow tramping around Cumbria. As campsites went, a homeless person could do worse, especially if they were able to hunt their own food. Maybe the guy they'd just nabbed was innocent, after all.

Don't let her out. Don't.

Ahead of her, Evans uttered a frustrated curse. His radio crackled.

"The house is clear," said the voice, scratching into the dim light.

"Have you checked for a cellar?"

"There isn't one."

"A coal bunker, then. A wood store—anything."

There was a pause, another crackle. "There's nothing guv. I'm sorry."

"Search again."

Another pause, teetering on the edge of argument, then, "Guv."

Evans turned toward Cassie. "It's here," he muttered, more to himself than to her. "I know it is. I bloody know it. *Somewhere.* It must be the house—"

He took off again, back into and through the larger barn, making his way out. Cassie stopped following when she was halfway across the floor.

It was there. The wisp. It *was*.

Something.

"Sir," she said and then, when Evans didn't stop, louder: "*Sir*."

Evans turned. Cassie pointed, finger angled down. He stared.

"Bird shit," she said.

Evans grunted, impatient. "Yes. And . . . ?"

"It's everywhere," she said. "Loads of it. Except . . . *there*."

He froze for a second or two, then came back toward her. Stopped at her side. Looked again. Saw. Two square meters or so in the center of the barn, covered in exactly the same dirt as the rest of the floor. And sure, there was bird shit, too. Just not as much of it.

Evans lifted the radio to his mouth. "The barn. Get in here."

The two of them scuffed the dirt away with their feet as the B team arrived. Beneath the detritus was a wooden trapdoor, barely more than a meter square. It fitted so smoothly into the floor that Evans and Cassie could have walked across it and still not known it was there.

"Black or not, DS Wish," Evans said. "Your eyes are a bloody marvel."

It was the reek that hit them first. The copper with the crowbar almost passed out before he'd managed to lever open the hatch. The smell rolled out, rotting flesh and fly-blown corpses, snails and shit and gas-bloated innards, a paste of odor thick enough to coat the back of Cassie's throat. Around her, the team coughed and gagged, retching as they turned away, a reflex as human as the need to defecate. The stench didn't recede as the trapdoor thumped open with a dull *whump*. It got worse, so bad in fact that Cassie felt her own empty stomach heave, and

God knew it took a lot to make her gut churn. It was genetic: one of only two useful things she'd inherited from her dad.

Cassie pulled out her flashlight and flicked it on. The narrow beam of light sliced into the dark space below the trap door, and there she was, crouching in one corner: a folded-double white grub in the vague shape of a child. Her white head was either bald or shaved, and she was dressed in the incongruous shape of a nightdress that had once been white and pretty.

"Jesus Christ," Evans muttered, beside her, and it wasn't just the girl that evinced the blasphemy, nor she who was giving off the worst of the smell.

The walls and floor beneath the hatch were coated in gore, thick with it. Smears of blood in varying colors—black with age here, redder there, fresher. Rotting tissue, sinew, scraps of flesh, sections of yellowing cartilage, muscle—bodily remains plastered against the concrete like wallpaper paste. It was layered inches thick so that in places the surface undulated, grotesquely cushioned with its organic decoration. It made Cassie think of a uterus, thick tissue swollen with blood.

In the midst of this miasma nestled the girl. She lifted her naked head, trying to look up. She kept her hands over her face, peeking through half-closed fingers as if she were playing a game.

"It's all right," Cassie told her. Retrieving the kid seemed to have fallen to her, since her fellow officers were still retching and puking at the periphery. All but Evans, of course. He remained as stalwart as ever, watchful and silent. "You're safe now. We'll get you out."

Cassie shrugged out of her coat, heavy now, wet, and dropped it amid the barn's more acceptable filth. She passed the torch to Evans and knelt at the edge of the hatch, stretching down with spread hands, encouraging the girl to reach up.

The girl put up her arms just as Evans angled the light down toward her and in the same second that it swept across the child's face, the girl gave a high, inhuman squeal. She dropped her head, ducking away, but Cassie caught one wrist before she could twist back into the filth.

"The light," Cassie gasped, fighting to keep hold of the wriggling girl. "Switch it off!" She'd seen the child's eyes as the torch's beam had washed over them: pupils so huge that they were barely more than solid black orbs.

Evans took the order.

Cassie pulled the girl out, the child's sharp fingernails scrabbling at her wrists as she stumbled backward onto her arse. Cassie grabbed at her coat and hauled it over the girl, head to toe, like a cocoon. She felt the child's arms snaking around her torso, felt the press of a tiny, cold nose and mouth against the skin above the collar of her stab vest. She tightened her arms around the small body as it quivered, invisible under her coat, stinking like an abattoir. She looked up at Evans. The torch hung from his hand like a broken extra digit.

"It's not Kelly Stevens," he said.

Back at the station, they couldn't get the girl to let her go. The child had clamped herself to Cassie's body and clung there as tenaciously as a limpet.

"I can't delay the questioning," Evans told her, as Cassie sat in an interview room with the mute girl straddled across her legs, still hidden beneath the coat. "I know it's not fair on you, given the work you've done on this case, but—"

"It's all right, sir," she told him. "If there's a chance the others are out there, still alive. . . ."

She let the end of the sentence hang, and so did he. Scenes of Crime Officers were currently scraping down the walls of the girl's cell, though what good it could do the investigation as evidence was anyone's guess. The best bet was that they'd still be able to isolate DNA from the bone fragments mashed into the softer tissue, because otherwise identifying individuals from the mess of human remains would be impossible. The closer one looked, the more it seemed as if the bodies had been sucked from their bones and put through a mincer, then systematically used to coat the walls.

"There's no clue as to who she is yet," Evans told her. "There haven't been any reports of any children going missing, not since Kelly Stevens. Our best guess is that she's from a traveler family, but just getting them to talk to us will be a task in itself."

Cassie shifted in her seat. Her legs were going numb. "Maybe we should look further back. Try the national databases for missing people."

"What makes you say that?"

"You haven't seen her eyes. I only had a glimpse, but they looked as if she hadn't seen light for a long time. Her pupils are huge."

Evans grimaced. "She can't have been down there that long. She'd have died of exposure. Anyway, why would he keep her rather than kill her the way he did the others?"

Cassie thought. "Then maybe she's different, somehow. Maybe she's something else to him. A daughter?"

Evans considered. "Bit of a leap there, Wish."

Cassie shrugged, the weight of the girl rising and falling in time with the movement. "Just a thought."

He nodded. "All right. Get a DNA sample when the doctor does the works. If neither of them are going to volunteer any information, it might help us work out who she is, at least." Evans's glance drifted to her hand as Cassie lifted it. He frowned. "You're bleeding."

Cassie looked down at herself, surprised to see drying blood on her wrist. "She must have scratched me when I pulled her out. Her nails are sharp."

"You should have made cleaning those scratches up a priority," Evans told her.

"Yes, sir," Cassie said. "Sorry. Didn't notice. Adrenaline, I suppose."

The door behind them opened and the duty doctor appeared, a woman in her late forties called Mary Dixon. She'd already been in once, but the girl had coiled Cassie's coat so tightly around her that Dixon hadn't even got as far as seeing her face.

"I've called Child Services," she said. "They're having trouble getting hold of the social worker on call. It may be a while."

Evans made a sound in his throat. "What else is new?"

The doctor looked uncomfortable. "They are understaffed," she reminded him.

"Aren't we all? Wish—I'll see you later, all right? Keep you up to date. Or if you manage to get out of here, have a shower and join the interview."

"Thank you, sir."

Evans's attention dropped to the mass on her lap. Only the girl's filthy bare feet were visible, caked with dried gore where they poked from beneath the coat. For a moment Cassie thought he was going to say something else. Then he gave a nod that encompassed both Cassie and the doctor and left, pulling the door shut behind him.

It took another three hours before Dixon managed to perform the examination. The girl couldn't bear any sort of light at all. In the end they switched off the fluorescent overheads and relied on intermittent bursts of light from the flashlights on their phones, placed far enough away across the room to give only the merest hint of illumination. In the darkness Cassie managed to coax the girl off her lap and out from beneath her coat, though she retreated to it periodically, usually when Dr. Dixon tried to get her to speak.

Dixon cut off the nightdress, attempting to keep the garment as complete as possible for the evidence bag Cassie held out. Beneath it the girl's skin was mottled and filthy. Dixon used sterile wipes to clean her, slowly revealing pale but apparently healthy skin.

"She's not undernourished," the doctor said, frowning at the conundrum. "She's not been mistreated, either, or at least it doesn't look that way from a cursory visual examination. Her scalp shows no signs of abrasion or bruising. Or stubble, for that matter. Her hair hasn't been cut, or shaved. It could be stress alopecia, of course."

"What about there?" Cassie asked, pointing to thin red wheals across the girl's left cheek. "And her arms. Are they cuts?"

Dixon smiled at the girl as she lifted one of the small hands toward her to take a closer look at the pattern of short, narrow marks that feathered between her wrists and elbows.

"I don't think they're cuts," said Dixon. "They look more like scratches, though some are quite deep." Here she addressed the silent child directly. "Did you hurt yourself, sweetheart? With your nails, perhaps? We should give those a trim, shouldn't we?"

Self-harm was a reasonable line of inquiry. Cassie watched for a reaction, but none was forthcoming. The girl just hung her head, her eyes squeezed shut. She gave no indication that she understood that someone was speaking to her.

"Could she be deaf?" Cassie asked.

The doctor frowned, then held one hand a couple of inches from the child's ear and snapped her fingers. The girl instantly turned her head, though she kept her eyes shut. Her nostrils flared.

"Not deaf," the doctor said, unnecessarily. "Language or learning impaired, perhaps?"

Cassie shook her head. "I don't think she's an abductee," she said, the conviction growing. "I think this is something else."

"Well." The doctor sighed, turning away to reach for the clean pair of child's pajamas she'd brought with her. "Whatever she is, she's going to need specialist help. I don't want to have her in this room longer than necessary, but until Child Services make an appearance. . . ."

"It's all right," Cassie said, as she reached for the pajamas. "I'll stay for as long as I can."

"That's right. You used to be National Crime Agency, didn't you? With the trafficking task force?"

Cassie nodded.

Dixon gave her a quiet smile. "You'll have had some training then. More than most, anyway. I can imagine the sort of stuff you've seen builds up a tough skin. We're lucky to have you with us, DS Wish."

Cassie didn't answer that. She concentrated on getting the girl into fresh nightclothes, instead.

She drove home to Penrith along the A6 with the rain screwing itself hard into her windshield. Large yellow signs had appeared since she'd come in the opposite direction that morning, warning that the center of town would be closed to traffic the following night for The Winter Droving. Traditionally, the droving was the time the farmers brought the sheep down from the high fells to more accessible pasture in preparation for winter. In recent years one of the town's arts charities had reinvented it as a local festival, centered around an after-dark parade of huge wheeled animal lanterns formed of wicker and paper. Attendees were encouraged to join the procession wearing elaborate masks, the weirder the better.

Cassie had gone the previous year and been caught up in the strange, feral nature of the night. It was a faux-pagan circus winding slowly through the streets of the small town, accompanied by drummers and torchbearers, fire-eaters, stilt-walkers, and acrobats. It had little to do with the droving of old, all the excuse Nick needed to discard it out of hand, but it was an impressive event that helped to bring in the tourists as the season tailed off.

This year the organizers had spied a new opportunity and the droving had been pushed back a week to coincide with Halloween. The windows of the shops around the old market square had shivered with grotesquerie for weeks. They weren't hawking the standard tat of orange pumpkins and witches on broomsticks, either, but gargoyles of an entirely more Cumbrian nature. Fairies with evil in the curve of their smiles, elves with teeth as sharp as needles, demon dogs with fiery eyes, green gods of earth and water—though not the sort you'd pray to or for.

Her phone rang as she pulled off the main road and into the tangle of new streets that laced the hill overlooking the town. She glanced at the clock on the dashboard—it was gone 10:00 p.m. Cassie answered, expecting it to be Nick. She was late. He hated that.

It wasn't Nick.

"Saw you on the news just now," said a female voice, roughened by years of smoking.

"Liv," Cassie greeted. "What's up?"

"What the fuck do you think is up?" Liv said. "You, standing in the back, dark glasses on a live broadcast? Think I was born yesterday?"

Cassie tried to make light of it. "Didn't even realize I was in shot. Sharp eyes. You should have been a copper."

"Swear to god, Cass," Liv rasped. "I am going to smear that splash of shit so thin he'll think he's paint. When are you coming home?"

Cassie turned onto her street, a row of red brick houses set in squares of fenced-off patches of grass. It wasn't the quaint rural cottage she'd half-imagined when Nick had decided they were moving back to his hometown. She pulled onto the blank oblong of concrete that was their driveway and killed the engine.

"I am home," she said.

"If Dad was alive today, he'd already have sent someone up there to sort him out."

"If Dad was alive today, he'd be in prison," Cassie told her. "It's late. I just want a glass of wine and something to eat. Can we do this another time? I'm fine. I promise. I'll call you."

"Bloody pigs," was her sister's venomous parting shot.

The house was in darkness. Cassie opened the door and flicked on the hallway light. She could hear the television burbling from the front room.

"Nick?" she called, hanging her bag on the banister as she passed the stairs on the way to the darkened kitchen. "Sorry I'm late. It's been a crazy day. Have you eaten? I'm—"

The first punch blindsided her, flying out of the darkness of the kitchen where he'd been waiting. His closed fist thumped against her ribcage hard enough that she felt something give. The second sent her reeling sideways, her forehead connecting with the wall, hard.

"You fucking bitch," he snarled, face looming above her. "You did that deliberately."

Cassie pulled herself upright. "What? Nick—"

"The dark glasses. I'm going to be the butt of every joke going on the farm tomorrow."

He came at her again, aiming higher this time. Cassie intercepted his fist before it reached her jaw, her open hand clenching hard around his closed one. She saw the split-second flicker of surprise that glinted in his eye. She always had been stronger than anyone gave her credit for.

"I've told you before," Cassie said, calmly. "Not the face." She let him go, pushing him away with enough force that he took a step backward to regain his balance. "I'm too tired for this right now," she told him, then. "I am going to make something to eat. I am going to have a drink. Then I am going to go to bed."

Cassie moved farther into the kitchen, reaching for the fridge door. She couldn't remember what they had in: her head had been so full of the case for so long that it was an age since she'd been to the supermarket. She stared at the plastic box of graying diced beef on the second shelf, it's packaging slightly blown. It probably should have gone out weeks ago. An image flashed back to her, of that hell-pit below the barn floor. She opened the salad compartment and retrieved an onion, glancing at the worktop and the box of eggs there. An omelet would do.

"You're so smart, aren't you?" Nick hissed, behind her. "Always in control. Always know exactly what to do. Little Miss Perfect."

Cassie turned around to face him. She'd thought he was a nice guy, once. What a fool she'd been. As if she hadn't already seen enough evidence of what even the nice ones were capable of given half a chance. And Cassie, she'd given him all the chances he deserved, because she'd wanted her marriage to work. She'd wanted to prove that she wasn't either of her parents, that she could come from a place that bad and still have a nice, normal, law-abiding, *happy* life. But she'd picked the wrong man and this move North had been nothing but a forlorn hope. She wasn't sure, anymore, what she was trying to prove. It was almost the cliché that upset her the most. Almost.

He stepped closer, head and shoulders over her and almost twice as broad. "Don't ever try to make fool of me again. Understand?" He lifted a hand and jabbed her hard with one finger, right where he'd punched her in the ribs just a few minutes before. "We could have been happy, you know," he added. "If you weren't such a fucking cold bitch. Sometimes I wonder if you actually feel anything at all."

Cassie didn't bother to reply. There appeared to be a fundamental truth about her that he hadn't managed to grasp, not even when she took the hardest punch he could throw and still kept her feet. Did he think she was just that stubborn? She imagined him with a crossbow hanging from one hand. He seemed a far more appropriate match for the monster they'd been hunting than the pathetic bundle of bones Evans currently had in custody.

It was a truth that had always fascinated her: that so often appearances had very little to do with nature.

Cassie woke at 4:00 a.m., alone in a quiet bed. She could hear the television still on downstairs and knew Nick would be passed out on the sofa, another empty scotch bottle lying on the floor. She fantasized briefly about him going to work drunk or so hung over that he'd walk into the path of something heavy and dangerous, something that would mash him into the wet earth as surely as those remains had been mashed onto the walls of that cellar.

Thinking of the crime scene led her to the girl. She'd eventually fallen asleep and Cassie had laid her on the bench in the darkness, locking the door on the way out and posting a constable to keep an eye on her through the observation window. Cassie had hated to leave a vulnerable child in such a place, but there was nothing else to be done. She'd put in another call to Child Services, but the out-of-hours emergency number wasn't even staffed, just an answer-phone.

Now she lay awake, watching as the orange light from the streetlamp outside her window made a quavering pattern of lace on her ceiling. She felt guilty—what if the girl woke before Cassie got back to the station? She'd be afraid and alone, and surely she'd already endured more terror than anyone should have to face across a lifetime. She could still feel the cold press of the child's lips and nose against her clavicle, feel those thin little arms clasped around her waist.

Cassie got up and looked out of the window. The October moon was waning gibbous as the month died. Blencathra was just visible on the horizon, the curve of the saddle on the fell's back glinting slightly. A first spattering of snow, caught in the moon's pale glare.

Snow for Halloween, she thought. *That seems very Cumbrian.*

She drove back into Carlisle on roads that were wet, though it was no longer raining. The duty sergeant nodded to her silently as she arrived, but made no comment about the hour. Cassie went straight to the room adjoining where the girl was being held, pushing open the door onto muted light and silence.

"Morning, Cattrick," she said, quietly to the constable on duty. "How's she been?"

"Morning, Sarge. She's not moved so much as a muscle all night," said the young woman, standing and stretching her legs. "Been curled up under that coat of yours so tightly I've not seen hide nor hair. Think you might have to write that one up as 'lost in the line of duty,' ma'am—I can't see her giving it up easily."

Cassie smiled faintly and walked to the observation window.

"Why don't you go and get yourself some coffee?" Cassie suggested, peering at the huddle of coat just visible in the darkened room beyond the one-way glass. "I'm sure you could do with some. I'll keep an eye for a while."

Cattrick grinned. "Thanks, Sarge. You're a gem."

A moment later and Cattrick had gone, light footsteps echoing along the corridor and away. Cassie found herself enveloped in a silence that thickened the longer it brewed. She stood close to the window, watching the darkness, almost in darkness herself.

The mound beneath her coat began to move. It grew, heaping like a new fell erupting from the earth. The girl must have pushed herself into a crouch on the bench while the coat tented around her. Then the child's head appeared, white and smooth, pushing out like a maggot emerging from a wound. The coat slipped back to the narrow grace of the girl's neck, then slid down her shoulders, then across her back until finally it dropped in a pile around her bare feet. The girl unfolded herself from the bench. One small leg reached toward the floor, then another, her body opening up like a flick-knife until she stood upright. She stayed still for a moment. Cassie could see the child's nostrils flaring, scenting something in the air.

In the next second the child was moving, heading straight for the observation window, directly for where Cassie stood, so quickly and with such determination that despite the wall between them, Cassie took a step back. The girl didn't stop until her face was pressed against the one-way glass, small white palms flat either side of her cheeks. She stood still. Her breath puffed against the barrier, pooling and dissipating, pooling and dissipating, as she looked up with the kind of eyes that Cassie had only ever seen once, years before.

It had been in the London Aquarium, on a family outing that had constituted a rare flash of normality in an abnormal upbringing. She'd seen these eyes looking out at her from the shark tank. The girl had shark's eyes, expressionless, depthless, nothing but voids that sucked in light. The girl could see perfectly in the dark, Cassie realized, and for her the glass wasn't one-way at all. It was merely glass.

The girl parted her lips. At first Cassie thought she was smiling, but the child's mouth continued to expand, kept stretching wider and wider until it seemed her cheeks must surely split with the pressure. That little mouth opened so wide that Cassie could see the girl's pink wet tongue, the fleshy tunnels of her trachea and esophagus. The child's lips folded back until her gums were visible, except that where her gums should have been seemed to be more bone. There was a cleft in its middle, as if the bone was jointed above her central incisors.

As Cassie watched, the girl's teeth disappeared, angling back into the gaping cavern of her mouth. The joint popped, opening, not that far, just enough to create a point, like the prow of a boat. The motion made Cassie think of a snake dislocating its jaw. Then, from behind this new shape descended a fresh row of denticulation, then another inside that, and another inside that: three rows of progressively smaller pearly-white teeth, each sharper than the sharpest point of the sharpest knife. The girl had saw-blades inside her mouth.

Four fat rabbits, hanging from the shaft of an arrow.

Don't let her out. Don't.

Cassie made herself stand there, smiling, until her skin no longer crawled at the sight. In any case, it wasn't revulsion she felt. She recognized fear, had grown up with it, and had long ago decided she would no longer allow it to have any hold over her. Once its prickle had subsided, what Cassie felt most was sympathy. Understanding, too. Affinity even, perhaps, in some ways. The girl couldn't help what she was, after all.

Nature. It was such a difficult thing.

"We're getting nowhere with the suspect," Evans told her later that morning. "Can't get the bugger to say a thing."

"Anything from forensics yet?"

Cassie carried the weight of her new secret around with her the same way she did all of her others: as if they did not exist at all. There was a wisp of something on her periphery, a blip on the radar of her senses she hadn't quite worked out yet. She had learned long ago that silence was safety.

She watched as the skipper rubbed a hand over a face gray with fatigue. DI Eddie Evans was a tall man in his fifties with a round, pale face running to fat. His hair was coarse and graying, cut short to disguise a creeping bald patch. She'd not been sure of him for a few months, but Cassie now thought of him as a decent copper and a good man.

"It's too early yet," he said. "Poor buggers are still scraping down the walls. Although they did say they've found some anomalies they can't explain."

Cassie felt a cold finger worming its way into her chest to scratch against her heart. "Anomalies? Like what?"

"They think there's a possibility that the victims were killed somewhere else and predated on before their remains ended up where they did. There are teeth marks on some of the bone fragments, but no signs of animal infestation in situ. Although they can't work out what sort of animal made them, and I can't see that being right anyway. They had to have all been killed and dismembered in that cellar. There's no trace of matter anywhere outside it. I can't see our suspect having the wit to be able to clean up after himself that thoroughly."

"I don't know, sir. He hid that hatch pretty effectively."

Evans sighed. "True. Right, then. You ready to take a crack at him?"

Cassie tried, but had no more luck than her senior officer. She thought about attempting a new tactic, something that would shock the suspect out of his silence. Cassie imagined asking him a question he wasn't expecting.

It's difficult, isn't it? Caring for a child? Being a single parent? You do your best, don't you? You always do your best. Of course you do. Just like everyone else. But sometimes it's not enough. Is it?

Cassie imagined his eyes flashing up to meet hers, at the unspoken answer that would be there in the few seconds before he had a chance to cover his surprise. It would work, she knew it. The certainty was an instinct as sure as the one that had tingled against her skin in the gloom of that barn as she'd seen something at the same time as not seeing it. As sure as the one that kept her silent now.

Cassie did not ask the question. She was too busy mulling over other, more important ideas, questions she had no intention of asking anyone but herself.

Later that day she intercepted Dr. Dixon as the woman went to enter the child's room with a packet of sandwiches, a bag of crisps, and a bottle of water.

"Poor thing must be starving," Dixon said, as Cassie maneuvered herself so that she could enter the room first. "She didn't touch what we left her this morning. God only knows the last time she ate. She doesn't seem to have drunk anything, either."

The room was still mostly in darkness. From the heaped pile on the bench, Cassie could tell that the child had again retreated to the perceived safety beneath the coat. Cassie was relieved. She took the items Dixon carried and put them down on the table.

"I'll stay with her," Cassie said. "I'll try to get her to eat something. I'm sure you've got other things you could be doing."

Dixon sighed. "I'm still trying to sort out what to do about her welfare. I refuse to let her spend another night here."

"I've been thinking about that," Cassie said. "I can take temporary custody. She can come home with me. Just until Child Services get their act together, obviously."

"Oh, I don't think that's advisable," Dixon said.

From the corner of her eye, Cassie could see the dark shape moving slightly: the girl, waking. Cassie took a casual step away from the table, putting herself between the bench and Dixon.

"Why not?" Cassie asked. "You said yourself I've had the training. And she seems to have bonded with me, doesn't she?"

"Well. . . ."

Cassie saw a white foot protrude from beneath the coat's edge. Then another. The grub, emerging.

"Ah-ha, the sleeping beauty wakes," Dixon said, cheerfully. "Would you like some dinner, sweetheart?"

Cassie turned her head, watching the girl straighten up, nostrils flaring. The voids of her eyes looked past Cassie, fastening on Dixon instead. The doctor stepped forward, one hand held out in an attempt at reassurance. Cassie sensed rather than saw the girl move, just as quickly as she had that morning, a shark scything through the water to its kill.

Cassie turned, one smooth movement with her arms outstretched, stepping sideways so that the girl walked straight into her. Cassie hugged the girl to her, the child's face against her body. She felt the girl's arms fasten around her middle, heard a tiny keening noise and then, very slightly, the feeling of something being drawn lightly across her stomach.

There was a second of stillness. Cassie looked down at the child in her arms. The girl lifted her head to look up at her, and Cassie mouthed the word, *No.* The black eyes blinked, once. Then the open obscenity of her jaws began to recede, her mouth shrinking back to its normal size. Cassie felt a wave of relief. Something else, too: pride, perhaps. She held the girl tighter, then looked over her shoulder to Dixon. She gave a bright smile, a slight shrug.

"I really think she should come home with me," she said. "I'll handle Evans and the paperwork. Otherwise you know she's going to end up spending another night here. Neither of us wants that. Do we?"

The doctor watched her with a strange expression.

"Hey," Cassie said. "If you really think I'm not fit, that's fine, but—"

"No, no," Dixon said, quickly. "That's not what I meant at all, DS Wish. Your credentials are impeccable and as you say, you do have the training. It's just . . . it could be difficult. Dealing with children in trauma can be traumatizing in itself."

Cassie smiled down at the strange child in her arms. The girl was calm now, no hint of the secret she harbored behind those black, black eyes. It was extraordinary, really, how much could be hidden, how completely, and for how long.

"Believe me, Doctor Dixon," she said. "Childhood trauma is something I understand."

Dixon was still watching her. When Cassie looked up again, the doctor's focus was on the bruise still festering around her eye.

"And you can guarantee she'll be safe with you?"

Cassie smiled. "Doctor, I stake my life on it."

It was after 8:00 p.m. when Cassie began the drive home, dark enough that the girl abandoned the shelter of the coat entirely. Beyond the car's windows, the youngest trick-or-treaters were out on the streets, diminutive superheroes and miniature Disney princesses towing their parents through a persistent drizzle.

Cassie watched the adults as they huddled in clusters of twos and threes, waiting beside garden gates while their children toddled up unknown paths to unknown doors to beg for sweets from utter strangers in a city of unexplained disappearances.

The girl crouched on the back seat, her face pressed against the window, watching avidly. Occasionally someone on the pavement would look up, catch sight of her, and falter for a moment before carrying on. Even without the fangs on show she was a disturbing sight. Once or twice, Cassie glanced in the rearview mirror to see the reflection of someone shaking his or her head. *The lengths some people go to for Halloween, it's ridiculous. Pushy parent syndrome. Poor kid.* Other faces took on a sympathetic expression: *Maybe the kid has cancer. Maybe this is her last Halloween. Maybe the mother's doing her best to turn that bald scalp into something positive.*

They were waiting at a stop light on the tattered edge of Harraby when Cassie felt a small hand snaking around her waist. The girl found the small patch of drying blood on her shirt, the small tear that was neat enough to have been cut by scissors. She rested her fingers over it with another slight keening sound, as if she were trying to speak. Cassie turned her head and smiled.

"It's all right," she soothed. "I know you didn't mean to. It doesn't hurt."

The black gaze changed its focus. A moment later the girl lifted one hand to Cassie's face and traced one small finger around the edge of her glorious bruise.

"That doesn't hurt either," Cassie said.

She avoided the main road into town, taking instead the route that coasted over the golf course and on to the high vista of Beacon Edge. Pooling in the valley below, the town was a dichotomy of lights. LED gaudiness had sprung up everywhere, on houses and shops, on streetsigns and garden gates, tainting the night with cheap pound-shop explosions of purple, green, and orange, as if the commercial world had decided this night had an acceptable color scheme that consumers must be forced to observe. Amid this, though, was the orange-yellow-white glow of naked flame. It gave light of an ancient quality—raw, elemental, alive.

Cassie watched it as the car traveled through the encroaching darkness, knowing that it marked the point from which the droving procession would begin. The massed flames of the lanterns and the torchbearers that would provide its escort made the rest of the town's decoration look meager in comparison.

She glanced in the rearview mirror again. The girl was transfixed by the flames, rocking back and forth, staring out into the darkness. A small bead of thick saliva had worked its way from the corner of her mouth. Her small fingers kneaded the air, opening, closing, opening, closing, clutching at nothing, just in motion.

"Poor thing," Cassie said. "You must be starving."

The procession began as she parked the car on the drive. Cassie got out and watched for a moment as the flames began to move. A coil of fire unfurled and a heavy lone drumbeat began. The percussion echoed across the valley, loud, deep. Others joined it, one heartbeat becoming many, rising above the general noise, or perhaps forcing a tunnel beneath it.

The procession set off, a line of flame moving slowly along streets lined with masked watchers, ancient things, feral and strange: devil-dogs and evil fairies, water sprites. Elves with the sharpest of sharp teeth.

Cassie brought her gaze closer to home. There were people everywhere, noise sifting and shifting in the night, the manic laughter of sugar-drunk children, music from a party at the house next door, from another farther down the street. A tumult of paganism, old and new, as if some rift had opened up and folded the town into itself—the dark ages thrown into the drift of a purple electric light.

She opened the rear door of the car and held out hand. "Come on," she said, to the girl. "Let's get you inside."

Nick's reaction when she brought the girl in was so predictable that she almost laughed in his face.

"You must be fucking joking," he said. "I'm not having that freak under my roof. No way."

"It's just for one night, maybe two," Cassie told him. "Have a bit of compassion, why can't you?"

"Forget it," he said, crumpling his empty beer can in one fist as he got up from the sofa. "Go on, get her out of here, right now. I'm going for a piss and when I come down again, you'd better already be in the car with it *compassionately* buckled into the back. Or I swear, Cassie Wish, you'll wish you'd never been fucking *born*."

Cassie held on to the girl's hand until he'd stalked past them and out of the living room. They heard his heavy footsteps on the stairs, an echo of the drumbeat that had reached out from that procession of flames.

Cassie waited until he'd reached the landing, then crossed to the Bose speaker and turned up the volume. She didn't even know what the playlist was, some shitty pop-themed mulch. Nick's taste in music always had been terrible. She counted one second, two—enough time for him to have stumbled into their bathroom, enough time for him to pull his limp excuse for a dick out of his trousers.

Cassie turned. The girl was watching her, head cocked to one side, the black sockets of her eyes bigger than ever, nostrils flaring like a bloodhound with the Devil inside. Her fingers were curled in on themselves, her small body quivering with the effort of remaining still.

Cassie smiled.

"You're such a good girl," she said. Then: "Go for it."

The girl understood her meaning even if she didn't grasp the words themselves. A second later Cassie was alone, the living room door rocking slightly in the wake of the girl's passage through it, a soft sound on the stairs as she scampered up them, light and quick as falling rain.

Cassie heard the first scream despite the sappy crooning from the speaker, then the reverberating thump of something heavy hitting a wall, followed by some desperate scrabbling. She pumped the volume louder and found herself tapping along to the rhythm despite herself. She took off her jacket, then her shirt, leaving only the short-sleeved white T underneath. Cassie left enough time for one jaded beat to fade into another that was almost identical. Then she went upstairs.

The thumping had stopped, but there were still sounds emanating from the bathroom. They echoed along the hallway and down the stairs.

Cassie climbed slowly, deliberately, because she wasn't really in any rush. When she reached the bathroom, the door was shut. She pushed it open carefully and watched a trickle of dark red blood become a thick smear across the pale ceramic tiles.

Nick was sandwiched between the shower cubicle and the toilet, his head and neck compressed awkwardly against the wall. The rest of him trailed across the floor like roadkill. The girl had started with his stomach, ripping it open lengthways across the lower abdomen. She'd pulled out his intestines, a coiling mess of grayish-yellow organic rope, slippery enough that they kept escaping her small hands even as she tried to stuff them into her mouth.

Cassie moved farther in to the room, then dropped to a crouch at Nick's twitching feet. She was fascinated to see that her husband was still alive. He was moaning—pathetic, breathy sounds that honestly made her want to laugh. Where was the tough guy now? Where was he?

"Nick?" Cassie called, softly.

His eyes flickered open, glazed with pain and misery. They took on a new expression, though, as they saw her. She thought it was probably hope. He tried to move, his shoulders levering up, then dropping back, a dead weight.

"Does it hurt?" she asked.

He nodded, nothing more than a slight movement of his chin. His skin had turned gray. He was fading fast. He must have known it. Still, he reached out a hand, palm-up. Begging. *Trick-or-treat. Please, please, give me the treat.*

"Funny," she said. "I've always wondered what that feels like."

The girl chose that moment to dip her head into the cavity she'd torn in his gut. She bit into something new. It must have been a lung because Cassie heard the crunch of thin bones snapping and a wet, popping sound, almost like a balloon bursting.

Nick jerked, a weak scream bubbling out along with a glob of blood. His eyes clouded.

Cassie stood. The girl looked up at her, demon-teeth fully extended, covered in blood. Cassie reached out, gently touched her smeared head, and smiled.

"Be quick," she said. "I'm going to need you downstairs." Cassie mimed what she meant too, just in case. She still didn't really know how much the girl understood. Still, there was a connection, somehow. Like recognizing like, perhaps.

Cassie made sure her feet and hands were covered in Nick's blood. Then she ran down the stairs, slipping, sliding, hands gripping the banister then colliding with the walls. She stumbled into the kitchen, scrabbled against the cooker, against the drawers. She dropped to her knees as she fumbled opened the one where they kept the knives. She took out the carving knife, then slumped back to the floor, her back against the fridge door. She stayed there, waiting. Music pounded from the living room and through the wall from the neighbors' party. There was a drumbeat, too, under everything, pumping, thumping in time with her heart.

When the girl came into the kitchen, Cassie said, "You're going to have to bite me." She proffered her arm.

The girl looked at it, blankly, blood dripping from her fangs. There was human matter splattered all over her head, over the clean clothes she'd been given, over her feet. Cassie could imagine the mess she'd left on the stairs, dragging the remains of that filth in the bathroom with her.

"You have to," Cassie said, again. "Or they'll know. Do you understand?"

The girl dropped to her haunches, still staring. Weirdly, for a creature straight out of nightmare, she looked more horrified than horrifying.

Cassie lifted the knife. Clutching it, she sank in into her own outer arm, just below the shoulder. Bright blood welled up and gushed over the blade. The girl keened and cantered forward on all fours. Cassie dropped the knife, then dug her own fingers into the cut and pulled back a thick flap of skin.

"It's all right," Cassie said. "It doesn't hurt. You won't hurt me. You can't. *Please. . . .*"

The girl hesitated for another second. Then she leaned forward with her demon teeth. She nuzzled at the loose flap, tearing it deeper, then yanking. The flesh ripped in a wide strip, skin and sinew parting down to the bone. Cassie watched, fascinated by the revealed tangle of veins, the secret shapes of her own muscle.

"Okay," she said, once the girl had torn a chunk as far as her elbow. "That's enough. That'll do."

The girl sat back, teeth snapping around the fresh meat, swallowing it down. Cassie dragged out her phone with her one good hand. The other she couldn't seem to move, her arm just hung against her like a broken wing, though she felt no pain. Blood was rapidly soaking through her clothes. It was pouring out of her like a river, hot and sticky, spreading across the kitchen floor in a viscous flood. She couldn't feel a thing, but she needed help. She knew that much.

"You have to go," Cassie said and heard the slur in her words. Something was happening in her brain. More than anything, she wanted to sleep. Cassie blinked, sight blurring as she punched in the numbers, muttering all the time, hoping that the girl could understand. "I have to call this in. You have to run, *now*. No one out there will think twice about you tonight. Get out of town—go up on the fells . . . Hide. I'll find you. I promise. I will. Try to stick to sheep. Run. Please, run. . . ."

The girl's face swam toward her, snuffling at her cheek. Her breath was warm, rank. The operator's voice echoed in Cassie's ear, far away, farther, farther. Then there was nothing but a black void even deeper than the girl's eyes.

She opened her eyes into a light so bright it was blinding. Cassie turned her head away, crushing her face against a soft pillow.

"Wish?" said a familiar voice. "Well, now. There you are. There you are, lass. You're all right. Take it easy."

Cassie forced her eyes open again, blinking into thin sunlight. The room swam around her, then solidified. Everything was white and smelled of disinfectant. Hospital, then. There was a figure sitting beside her bed. It took her a moment to realize that her hand was clasped in another, larger one that on closer examination belonged to DI Eddie Evans.

She blinked at him. He came slowly into focus, an anxious face staring at her closely. He looked older than the last time she'd seen him, as if he was trying to smile with ten-ton weights attached to his lips. His brow was heavy over watery eyes.

"Sir?" she croaked. Her body was throbbing. Cassie looked down at herself. Her left arm was heavily bandaged, suspended from a crane-like apparatus that stood on the other side of the bed.

"Bloody hell, DS Wish," said Evans. "Bloody, bloody hellfire, Cassie lass, you were a lucky one."

Cassie still felt groggy, but she remembered to ask about Nick. Evans's head dropped. She shut her eyes, turned her face away again. Even faked a tear or two. Evans's hand squeezed hers. When Cassie looked at him again, she wondered what it would have been like to have him as a father. She wondered what difference it would have made, or whether it would not have changed a thing.

Nature. It was such a difficult thing.

THE BEAUTIFUL FEAST OF THE VALLEY

STEPHEN GALLAGHER

Stephen Gallagher is a Bram Stoker Award and World Fantasy Award nominee, and winner of the British Fantasy Award and International Horror Guild Award.

The author of fifteen novels, including *Valley of Lights*; *Down River*; *Rain*; and *Nightmare, with Angel*; recent TV work includes an award-winning episode of *Silent Witness* and a stint on *Stan Lee's Lucky Man*. He has also written for *Doctor Who*, *Murder Rooms*, and *Rosemary & Thyme*, and is the creator of Jerry Bruckheimer's science thriller series *Eleventh Hour*. His latest novel is *The Authentic William James*.

As the author explains: "In my *Murder Rooms* episode there's a mummy-unwrapping scene in which I had Professor William Rutherford—Arthur Conan Doyle's model for Professor Challenger—speculate on the practical nature of the Ancient Egyptian afterlife. The lines still linger in my memory, with the feel of unfinished business.

"Today we're more focused on the idea of preserving the conscious mind than resurrecting the physical body. But the obsession's not so different, and in this story I saw a way to bring ancient and modern together."

SOMETIMES I SEE her. Magdalena, late at night, in the stacks on the seventh floor where she used to work and study. I know she isn't there, and I don't believe in ghosts. This is something else.

I'm taking out my keys as I approach her carrel. At this hour there's only the night cleaning crew and me, and they're somewhere on another floor. We close the library at nine, but I have staff privileges. It's a modern building, low ceilings, open-plan. The lights are turned low but the air-conditioning is a constant; old books need a steady climate, and the bound volumes on the seventh are among the University's rarest. It's always quiet. On warm summer days our undergrads will seek out the cool air and fill the study areas but, at other times, not so much.

The carrel was Magdalena's private space, and now I suppose it's mine. It's at the end of the building with a corner view over the campus. An odd shape, thin-walled, hardly big enough to call a room—just a desk and chair, a lamp, and her boxes. The sense of her presence is strong.

But I think I've told you already, I don't believe in ghosts.

I'm working my way through Magdalena's boxes. Two were here when she died, and I retrieved the others after her mother and sisters had been through her flat. The boxes contain her work diaries, her notebooks, all the background research for her doctorate, even lecture notes and timetables from her student days. I gave the hard drives to Henrik in Computer Sciences, and he gets back to me for anything he needs explained.

Henrik claims that he's mastered classical Greek, but he's joking. With his programmer's mind he quickly grasped the alphabet, and he enjoys my show of faux-horror when he mangles the words.

I switch on the lamp and draw out the chair. The folder on the desk is open, the papers arranged as I left them.

I admit that I struggle. I used to manage with a big magnifying glass, but now I've an app on my phone that does the job almost as well. Eyesight problems apart, I found her handwriting almost impossible at first. Some of it's in a personal shorthand that no optical scanner could ever decipher. Now I know it as well as my own.

Halfway down an old shopping list, which has no relevance to the project but which fascinates me nonetheless, the phone vibrates in my hands. I still jump when that happens. I answer and it's Henrik.

He says, "Do you have a copy of the index?"

"Not to hand. Why?"

"I've some content with no attribution. Thought you might know it."

"You want to send it over?"

"I could read you the first few lines."

"Just send it."

While I'm waiting for the attachment to show up, I look out of the window. I can see; I just can't see well. The campus is deserted, though the main walk-through stays lit for student safety. I can see across to the white tower of the Computer Sciences building where I imagine Henrik alone in the basement, surrounded by his technology, while I'm here in the sky amongst my centuries-old texts. Two lonely souls in our different spheres, working on into the night.

One of us haunted by a dead spirit, the other working to recreate one.

My phone vibrates again as the attachments come in. The Greek text is accompanied by a crude machine translation, which I ignore.

From the Greek I read:

> *This story was told to me by a priest. It concerns a slave who had been one of the many prisoners of war taken by Sesostris, men of the vanquished countries who were brought home and set to work on great monuments to their conqueror's name.*

I don't recognize it but I'm thinking that it reads more like Herodotus than Plutarch. Magdalena was familiar with both. It's no more than two or three hundred words, but I save it for later when I can view it on a bigger screen.

It's after eleven when I leave. With its long rows of shelves and the whisper of hidden engines, the seventh floor has the feel of an empty aircraft on a long night's flight. Hard to believe that such shiny modern architecture can house spooks and shadows, but there it is.

No, she isn't here now. I can look for her in the stacks, but that isn't how it works. I travel down in a glass lift, I walk out across the concrete way. I suspect that architects love concrete far more than people love architects.

The roads around the University are older, tree-lined; the houses tall and Edwardian. I live only three streets from here, in two rooms and a kitchen on the second floor of a mid-terrace villa. Walking home through fallen leaves and autumn chill, I see haloes around every street lamp. Magdalena's been dead almost a year, and I should be feeling her absence by now. But she hasn't left me.

Going blind has few compensations, but I found one.

> *This story was told to me by a priest. It concerns a slave who had been one of the many prisoners of war taken by Sesostris, men of the vanquished countries who were brought home and set to work on*

great monuments to their conqueror's name. You may choose to believe or disregard these Egyptian tales, however you wish; for my part, I set them down just as they were given to me.

The name of the slave is not known, but I will call him Fahim. After capture he had been set to work on the building of a causeway. Along this causeway, mighty blocks of stone were to be hauled from the Nile to the Libyan hills. The blocks had been cut in the Arabian quarries of Fahim's homeland and ferried over to Egypt; it was an enterprise involving a hundred thousand slaves, and many would not live to see the work completed. Fahim was one such. He had risen in the hierarchy of slaves to a position of some responsibility when, despite a strong constitution and better nourishment than most, he succumbed to a fever.

Sesostris had closed all the temples and forbidden the religions of the vanquished, so Fahim was buried in the manner of the Egyptian poor; which is to say, with little preparation or ceremony in the dry desert soil where natural processes would imitate—or so it was hoped—the more elaborate preservation rituals of the high-born.

One year after his death, on the morning that followed the ceremony of The Beautiful Feast of the Valley, Fahim dug his way out of the sand.

I write up my translation of the fragment, along with alternate word choices to reflect shades of meaning. Late in the morning I receive a text from Henrik, and I call by to see him in the afternoon.

He says, "I've run a search against all the digitized material. I can't link it to anything in the dialogue corpus. Nothing even close."

"Then where did it come from?" I say.

"That's the thing. Nowhere."

"You don't mean the machine wrote it." I wait. Then, less certain, "Do you?"

"That's not how it works," he says. "Everything has to be sourced from in-domain data. Did you find any clues in the handwritten stuff?"

"That's going to take a while," I tell him.

I should explain the situation. For several months before she died, Magdalena had been providing library support for Henrik's interactive AI project. She wasn't our most senior classicist but she was a Plutarch specialist, and Henrik is building a database of literary material with the aim of creating a virtual personality based on an ancient writer's works. He chose Plutarch of Chaeronea because of the sheer volume of the philosopher's output and legacy, passing over a more obvious choice like Shakespeare—the low-hanging fruit of linguistic analysis and too well-used a figure to bring much glory to a new researcher. And Shakespeare hid behind fictions; Plutarch was chatty, personal, immensely prolific, and available.

Also, Henrik had approached the English department and they didn't want to know.

Henrik's aim is to recreate Plutarch the man, within the machine. To be able to ask a question, and have Plutarch answer, by triangulating a personality from the texts and incorporating multiple translations, along with commentaries and monographs, to eliminate linguistic bias and reach the author's bare thoughts.

Behind the gimmick lies some serious AI research but I'll be honest, from the moment we heard the pitch we all thought the idea was Gold Standard bonkers. Our Head Librarian thought so too, but Magdalena spied an opportunity to digitize the collection on another department's budget, and he was talked around.

Henrik says, "Can't we speed things up a little? I'm not having a go at you. Maybe we could put a student on it."

"There's no money for that," I say.

"For the experience?" he suggests, hopefully.

"Not at this uni," I say. "They just don't have the Greek, Henrik."

It's true. A Classics education isn't what it was.

And the fact is, I don't want anyone else let into this . . . I almost called it a relationship. When Magdalena died I volunteered to step in. Not because I'm a Plutarchian—I'm not, and I've no interest in computing. I'm doing it for her.

In case I've been giving you the wrong impression . . . no, there was nothing between us. To Magdalena I was just a colleague, no doubt an unremarkable one. I'm sure she had no feelings for me at all. Mine for her stole up on me over time, and I knew better than to declare them.

Oh Magdalena, Magdalena; name from a Hungarian father, looks from her Italian mother, an accent from the Western Isles of Scotland where she grew up. She ran, she swam, she sang, and it's fair to say that I loved her from afar. Loved her and lost her; she was killed on the way back from a climbing weekend with her similarly sporty and outgoing group of friends. Their minibus ran off the road at two in the morning and she was thrown clear. They say she died instantly.

Now I have what I often wished for, though by the most terrible means. I have her to myself. I sift through her papers, through her notes, through her stray thoughts jotted in margins; I transcribe, I upload, and every now and again Henrik bothers me for some further detail.

People say that we live on in the memories of others. I find that more sentimental than useful. Remember me all you like but if I'm to live on, I need to know about it. Henrik talks of a future when we'll be able to upload our thoughts and live forever. I don't see it. Copy what you may into a machine, I'll still be here. And when this life ends, I'm still gone. My own perception is that every one of us is a conscious mind in a private box, self-contained, looking out. Henrik's vision is a future of empty boxes, pointlessly interacting, endlessly pinging each other in a space without voices.

Naturally, he doesn't see it that way.

Fahim stood upon the hot sand and looked down at his hands, at his funeral clothes. He remembered nothing of his burial. He did, however, recall his suffering and being aware of his impending death, and he recalled the grief of those who wept at the prospect of his departure. Although a slave, Fahim had a home and a family, and friends to mourn him. On the ground around him lay evidence of their devotion in the remnants of bread and leeks and rotting fruit, all scattered by his emergence along with a spilled half-cup of wine.

He lifted his gaze to the necropolis across the plain. There, some distance away, stood the tombs and the chapels of the wealthy. Spread far and wide across the ground between were the graves of the poor, in shallow pits marked by nothing more than a reed mat or a stone. Some, like his own, bore the signs of a feast-day celebration—The Beautiful Festival of the Valley, on which day a procession bore the sacred image of Amun from city to necropolis. There its followers made music and performed rituals to honor their ancestors, while outside the necropolis those of lower birth performed their own humbler, though no less heartfelt, ceremonies. They dined, they drank, and through drinking they often fell asleep on the graves to dream of their dead.

Fahid was not alone. Others had risen, and stood looking lost. Others before them had risen and departed, leaving the ground disturbed and the grave-offerings trewn about. Fahim's one urge was to follow their example. Cramped and stiff from a year crouched in the pit, he began to make his way home.

She sits in the corner and watches me. I've never known her so close. If I turn my head, she'll be gone. So I don't turn.

I'm working on the new material from Henrik. I don't know where it's coming from but it isn't Plutarch, nor is it Herodotus as I'd thought, although it mangles Egyptian history as cheerfully as that ancient did. I do find it hard to concentrate, feeling her so near.

As my grandfather grew deaf, he began to hear music. Not to imagine it, but to hear it. He feared that it was the beginning of dementia. Doctors explained that he'd no mental impairment but as his hearing declined, his brain was replacing the missing signal by releasing stored memories into the auditory channel. Once my grandfather knew what was happening, he welcomed it.

With me it's in the eyes. Magdalena is my music.

This old Egyptian tale, it puzzles me. Nothing in any version of Plutarch's *Moralia* corresponds to it. If Henrik's program is restricted to in-domain data, where's it coming from? A machine can't create. Henrik is getting excited, of course, persuading himself that it might.

I go down to see him.

It's midafternoon, and he looks as if he hasn't slept since yesterday. Turns out that he hasn't. Around him are stacked the different components of his project, no one machine but a lash-up of many, always running, processing, crunching, rendering. At the heart of it all sits an enhanced keyboard and an ordinary monitor. Henrik's screensaver is a spinning representation of the bearded Plutarch in marble, minus most of a nose. Henrik hits a key and the bust disappears, revealing the torrent of type that's going on behind.

"I'll say it now," Henrik tells me, "I don't know what we have here. It looks like it's the same unfolding narrative but it's flipping back and forth, Greek and English."

I observe for a while. "Is it broken?"

"A glitch wouldn't explain it."

"There's nothing in the index to match the fragment."

"You're way behind. It's not just a fragment now."

"There's more?"

"It's fascinating to watch. It juggles the words and phrases until they settle and make sense. What's coming out . . . I don't know, it's not like the usual parroted stuff."

What he doesn't dare say is, it has the feel of new thought.

I say, "This is what you wanted, isn't it?"

"Early days," Henrik says. "Early days."

On the road to Karnak he saw Ahmose, son of Hekaib, whom the gods had taken at the age of nineteen; Fahim approached him with a cry of delight, but became more solemn as Ahmose told his story. Ahmose had risen some hours before and with the same desire to see his family once again. What a welcome would await him, he imagined. But it was not to be.

At first there was joy. But they brought him food and he could not eat. They brought him water and he could not drink. When the knife slipped as he sliced the fruit they offered him, he did not bleed.

His sisters fled in terror, and his uncle barred the door. When his mother could be persuaded to come out and speak to him, she wept and begged him not to stay. We mourned you, she told him, we honor you at the Beautiful Feast. We do not know how to greet you in this form, your place is no longer here with us.

As Ahmose spoke they were joined on the road by another of the risen, and a third. All had attempted to return to their homes, to be met with the same response.

Uncertain now of where to go, they returned together to the field. On every side the dead were rising in increasing numbers, spitting and clearing the dirt from their eyes. Among them Fahim recognized Khalidin, his father's cousin and a much older man, taken into slavery in the same great raid by Sesostris but fated not to survive his first year in the Black Land.

They sat on the ground together. Fahim told of events that the elder had missed in his absence from this earthly life. Fahim refused to bow to misery; if a return to the old life was not possible, he would seize the new.

At this, there came a distant roar from the direction of the necropolis, and Khalidin turned to look at the far-off site, its walls and taller structures shimmering on the horizon. Others of the risen were beginning to move in its direction, as if summoned.

And Khalidin said, as the poor rise from the ground, so do the rich emerge from their tombs. Death offers no release. The order will be preserved. Slaves we were and slaves we will remain, required always to serve.

I can see why Henrik's excited. To him it suggests a breakthrough; that his virtual philosopher is evolving a philosophy of its own. There's no Internet link, nothing in the enclosed system beside the code that he's written and the immense volume of raw material supplied by Magdalena. Has he done it? Has he created the beginnings of a conscious mind, self-contained in an actual box? Will Plutarch eventually speak to him? Or is he merely creating for himself the experience of hearing Plutarch speak?

If we raise the dead this way, can the dead ever know?

Later on, I go back to the library. No cleaning crew tonight. I swipe my pass and ride the glass elevator up to the seventh. I think she's there, but she doesn't appear. When I reach the carrel I leave the door open, and when I look back she's a small figure at the end of the row, watching me from afar. When I turn away I can feel her gaze upon my back, like a faint electric touch.

I take my seat and open the next folder.

All of her important material has been scanned or transcribed and uploaded now. I'll be surprised if there's anything here that will be of use to Henrik. It's from her undergraduate stuff, mostly timetables and reading lists. I glanced through everything when I first took over, and I'd put this folder to the bottom of the pile. After this it's mainly old bills and receipts, and then I'll have reached the end of it all. The boxes will go back to her family, and I'm not sure what I'll do with my evenings from there on. It'll be a wrench.

There's something handwritten on the back of her Year Two Classics book list. I flip it over and hold the phone where it can magnify her scrawl.

It's no more than a few lines. It begins, *Idea for Story* and offers just the bare bones of a thought:

> Idea for story—Egyptian slave revives after death—the myths are true—struggles out of the ground where he/she was buried intact for inexpensive mummification in dry hot sand.

And then underneath it, written in different ink and in what I recognize as Magdalena's more mature hand, the note-to-self comment, *NB: Think of an ending!*

Now I'm in the Computer Sciences block and Henrik's not here. They wouldn't let him bed down in the building so I expect he's given in to exhaustion and gone home to sleep. As far as I'm aware, the rendering is a hands-off process and doesn't happen any faster if you watch. I can understand his urge to be in the room as it all comes together, but adrenaline and caffeine can only do so much.

I have the paper with me. It's no more than a scribble, an idea jotted down in a spare moment, returned to once and then almost certainly forgotten. All her later creativity was channeled into academic rigor. I've seen her teenaged poetry and in the course of the project I've turned up some of her short amateur fictions, mainly written for school magazines, but this didn't become one of them.

The screensaver is up on the monitor, that noble head rotating in imaginary space. A touch anywhere on the keyboard will make it vanish and reveal what's going on behind. I don't *think* it will interfere with the running of the program, but I don't know enough to be sure.

Henrik will kill me if I'm wrong. But I have to know.

I touch the space bar.

It's revealed. The torrent of type has given way to a static page of text:

> *When Fahim and Khalidin reached the necropolis, they found themselves at the back of a vast and growing crowd of their own kind; and far from being downcast at the prospect of a return to servitude after death, those before them seemed to be in a mood of celebration. They jeered and roared as if at some sport or entertainment that Fahid could not yet see.*
>
> *He pushed through the crowd and found that, at its heart, they'd created a circle of bare ground resembling an arena. In this space several of the risen were stumbling blindly, back and forth, to the great amusement of all.*
>
> *Each stumbling figure wore gorgeous attire. Some were still bandaged. Most prominent among them was a figure in the robes of a high priest who, as Fahim watched, staggered with outstretched*

arms into the ring of spectators and was repulsed back into the circle.

The priest was trying to scream. But his screams were silent, for he was without lungs, without organs, without eyes. All had been removed in the elaborate funeral rites of the high-born. Unwisely, it now emerged. Dried onions plugged his eye sockets, peppercorns his nose. The stitches that sealed up his flank had broken, and from this wound in his side the embalmers' linen packing trailed and was causing him to trip.

In this manner the well-heeled dead lurched back and forth, colliding, causing laughter, capable of nothing other than suffering, unable to find any escape from their pain.

From a group of nearby buildings came a cheer, as a tomb was broken open and another rich official dragged out. A chant was raised to fetch the old king himself, and a party was assembled for the task. These were slaves who had built the royal tomb, and knew all its secrets. They moved off with assurance and impunity; for what punishment can be exacted on the unwanted dead?

Then a gap of a couple of lines.

And then the words, *NB: Need a closing line!*

It stops there. The cursor blinks, ready to accept—what? An instruction? A question? I look down at the paper in my hand.

I hesitate.

Then with one finger I type in, *Magdalena, is that you?*

I'm not sure how this works so I just hit ENTER.

And now I wait.

IN THE YEAR OF OMENS

Helen Marshall

Helen Marshall is a senior lecturer of Creative Writing and Publishing at Anglia Ruskin University in Cambridge, England. Her first collection of short fiction, *Hair Side, Flesh Side*, won the British Fantasy Society's Sydney J. Bounds Best Newcomer Award in 2013, and *Gifts for the One Who Comes After*, her second collection, won both the World Fantasy Award and the Shirley Jackson Award in 2015.

She edited the 2017 volume of *The Year's Best Weird Fiction*, and her debut novel *The Migration* is forthcoming from Random House Canada.

"I love the smell of woodsmoke and dying leaves," admits the author, "the crispness in the air and those clear bright skies fading into early dusk. As a teacher I still feel as if autumn offers the real beginning of the year, when the easy days of summer give way to the coming cold.

"This story was an attempt to capture the strangeness of October when I was a child, and everything felt possible yet completely baffling, as if I was on the edge of comprehending something vast and mysterious about myself.

> "But I suppose that's what growing up is—a series of revelations that bring you into a more complex world, a world sometimes beautiful and sometimes frightening."

THAT WAS THE year of omens—the year the coroner cut open the body of the girl who had thrown herself from the bridge, and discovered a bullfrog living in her right lung. The doctor, it was said by the people who told those sorts of stories (and there were many of them), let the girl's mother take the thing home in her purse—its skin wet and gleaming, its eyes like glittering gallstones—and when she set it in her daughter's bedroom it croaked out the saddest, sweetest song you ever heard in the voice of the dead girl.

Leah loved to listen to these stories. She was fourteen and almost pretty. She liked swimming and horses, sentimental poetry, certain shades of pink lipstick, and Hector Alvarez, which was no surprise at all, because *everyone* liked Hector Alvarez.

"Tell me what happened to the girl," Leah would say to her mum as she sliced potatoes at the kitchen counter, careful, always to jam the knifepoint in first so that they would break open as easily as apples. Her dad had taught her that before he had died. Everything he did was sacred now.

"No," her mum would say.

"But you know what happened to her?"

"I know what happened, Leah."

"Then why won't you tell me?"

And Leah would feel the thin weight of her mother's frame like a ghost behind her. Sometimes her mum would touch the back of her neck, just rest a hand there, or on her shoulder. Sometimes, she would check the potatoes. Leah had a white scar on her thumb where she'd sliced badly once.

"You shouldn't have to hear those things. Those things aren't for you, okay?"

"But mum—"

"Mum," Milo would mumble from his highchair. "Mum mum mum mum."

"Here, lovely girl, fetch me the rosemary and thyme. Oh, and the salt. Enough about that other thing, okay? Enough about it. Your brother is getting hungry."

And Leah would put down the knife, and would turn from the thin, round slices of potatoes. She would kiss her brother on the scalp where his hair stuck up in fine, whitish strands. Smell the sweet baby scent of him. "Shh, monkey-face, just a little bit longer. Mum's coming soon." Then Milo would let out a sharp, breathy giggle, and maybe Leah would giggle too, or maybe she wouldn't.

Her mum wouldn't speak of the things that were happening, but Leah knew—of course Leah knew.

First it was the girl. That's how they always spoke of her.

"Did you hear about *the girl*?"

"Which girl?"

"*The girl.* The one who jumped."

And then it wasn't just *the girl* anymore. It was Joanna Sinclair who always made red velvet cupcakes for the school bake sale. It was Oscar Nunez from the end of the block whose tongue shriveled up in his mouth. It was Yasmine with the black eyeliner. She used to babysit Leah when she was younger.

"Maybe it'll be, I dunno, just this one perfect note. Like a piano," Yasmine had murmured before it happened, pupils big enough to swallow the violet-circled iris of her eyes. "Or a harp. Or a, what's it, a zither. I heard one of those once. It was gorgeous."

"You think so?" Leah asked. She watched the smoke curl around the white edge of her nostrils like incense. There were only four years between them, but those four years seemed a magnificent chasm. Across it lay wisdom and secret truths. Across it lay the Hectors of the world, unattainable if you were only fourteen years old. Everything worthwhile lay across that chasm.

"Maybe. Maybe that's what it will be for me. Maybe I'll just hear that one note forever, going on and on and on, calling me to Paradise."

It hadn't been that.

When Hector found her—they were dating; of course Hector would only date someone as pretty and wise as Yasmine, Leah thought—the skin had split at her elbows and chin, peeled back like fragile paper to reveal something as bony and iridescent as the inside of an oyster shell.

Leah hadn't been allowed to go to the funeral.

Her mum had told her Yasmine had gone to college, she couldn't babysit anymore, Leah would have to take care of Milo herself. But Leah was friends with Hector's sister, Inez, and *she* knew better.

"It was like there was something inside her," Inez whispered as they both gripped the tiled edge of the pool during the Thursday swim practice, Inez's feet kicking lazily in hazy, blue-gray arcs. Inez had the same look as her brother, the same widely spaced eyes, skin the same dusty copper as a penny. Her hair clung thick, black, and slickly to her forehead where it spilled out of the swimming cap.

"What kind of thing was it?" The water was cold. Leah hated swimming, but her mum made her do it anyway.

"God, I mean, I dunno. Hector won't tell me. Just that . . . he didn't think it would be like that. He thought she'd be beautiful on the inside, you know? He thought it would be something else."

Leah had liked Yasmine—even though she had always liked Hector more, liked it when Yasmine brought him over and the two of them huddled on the deck while Leah pretended not to watch, the flame of the lighter a third eye between them. Leah had wanted it to be a zither for her. Something sweet and strange and wondrous.

"I thought so too," Leah whispered, but Inez had already taken off in a perfect backstroke toward the deep end.

It was why her mum never talked about it. The omens weren't always beautiful things.

There had always been signs in the world. Every action left its trace somewhere. There were clues. There were giveaways. The future whispered to you before you even got there, and the past, well, the past was a chatterbox, it would tell you everything if you let it go on.

The signs Leah knew best were the signs of brokenness. The sling her mum had worn after the accident that made it impossible for her to carry Milo. The twinging muscle in her jaw that popped and flexed when she moved the wrong way. It had made things difficult for a while. The pain made her mum sharp and prickly. The medication made her dozy. Sometimes she'd nod off at the table, and Leah would have to clear up the dishes herself, and then tend to Milo if he was making a fuss.

And there was the dream.

There had always been signs in the world.

But, now. Now it was different, and the differences both scared and thrilled Leah.

"Mum," she would whisper. "Please tell me, mum."

"I can't, sweetie," her mum would whisper in a strained, half-conscious voice. Leah could see the signs of pain now. The way her mum's lids fluttered. The lilt in her voice from the medication. "I just don't know. Oh, darling, why? Why? I'm scared."

But Leah wasn't scared.

A month later Leah found something in the trash: one of her mother's sheer black stockings. Inside it was the runt-body of a newborn kitten wrapped in a wrinkled dryer sheet.

"Oh, pretty baby," she cooed.

Leah turned the lifeless little lump over. She moved it gently, carefully from palm to palm. It had the kind of boneless weight that Milo had when he slept. She could do anything to him then, anything at all, and he wouldn't wake up.

One wilted paw flopped between her pinkie and ring finger. The head lolled. And there—on the belly, there it was—the silver scales of a fish. They flaked away against the calluses on her palm, decorated the thin white line of her scar.

Leah felt a strange, liquid warmth shiver its way across her belly as she held the kitten. It was not hers, she knew it was not hers. Was it her mum who had found thing? Her mum. Of course it was her mum.

"Oh," she said. "My little thing. I'm sorry for what's been done to you."

She knew she ought to be afraid then, but she wasn't. She loved the little kitten. It was gorgeous—just exactly the sort of omen that Yasmine ought to have had.

If only it had been alive. . . .

Leah didn't know what her own omen would be. She hoped like Yasmine had that it would be something beautiful. She hoped when she saw it she would know it most certainly as her own special thing. And she knew she would not discard it like the poor drowned kitten—fur fine and whitish around the thick membrane of the eyelids. Not for all the world.

She placed the kitten in an old music box her dad had brought back from Montreal. There was a crystal ballerina, but it was broken and didn't spin properly. Still, when she opened the lid, the tinny notes of 'La Vie en Rose' chimed out slow and stately. The body of the kitten fit nicely against the faded velvet inside of it.

The box felt so light it might have been empty.

Now it was October—just after the last of the September heat had begun to fade off like a cooling cooking pan. Inez and Leah were carving pumpkins together. This was the last year they were allowed to go trick-or-treating and, even so, they were only allowed to go as long as they took Milo with them. (Milo was going to dress as a little white rabbit. Her mum had already bought the costume.)

They were out on the porch, sucking in the last of the sunlight, their pumpkins squat on old newspapers empty of the stories that Leah really wanted to read.

Carving pumpkins was trickier than cutting potatoes. You had to do it with a very sharp, very small knife. It wasn't about pressure so much. It was about persistence—taking things slow, feeling your way through it so you didn't screw up. Inez was better at that. It wasn't the cutting that Leah liked anyway. She liked the way it felt to shove her hands inside the pumpkin and bring out its long, stringy guts. Pumpkins had a smell: rich and earthy, but sweet too, like underwear if you didn't change it every day.

"It's happening to me," Inez whispered to her. She wasn't looking at Leah, she was staring intensely at the jagged crook of eye she was trying to get right. Taking it slow. Inez liked to get everything just right.

"What's happening?" Leah said.

Inez wasn't looking at her, she was looking at the eye of the jack-o'-lantern-to-be, her brow scrunched as she concentrated. But her hand was trembling.

"What's happening?"

Cutting line met cutting line. The piece popped through with a faint sucking sound.

"It's happening to me. You know, Lin. What's been happening to . . . to everyone. What happened to Yasmine." Her voice quavered. Inez was still staring at the pumpkin. She started to cut again.

"Tell me," Leah said. And then, more quietly, she said, "Please."

"I don't want to."

Plop went another eye. The pumpkin looked angry. Or scared. The expressions sometimes looked the same on pumpkins.

"Then why did you even bring it up?" Leah could feel something quivering inside her as she watched Inez saw into the flesh of the thing.

"I just wanted to—I don't even know. But don't tell Hector, okay? He'd be worried about me."

Leah sneaked a look at Hector, who was raking leaves in the yard. She liked watching Hector work. She liked to think that maybe if the sun was warm enough (as it was today—more of a September sun than an October sun, really), then maybe, just maybe, he would take his shirt off.

"It's okay to tell me, Inez. Promise. I won't tell anyone. Just tell me so *someone* out there knows."

Inez was quiet. And then she said in a small, tight voice, "Okay."

She put down the knife. The mouth was only half-done. Just the teeth. But they were the trickiest part to do properly. Then, carefully, gently, Inez undid the top three buttons of her blouse. She swept away the long, black curls that hid her neck and collarbone.

"It's here. Do you see?"

Leah looked. At first she thought it was a mild discoloration, the sort of blemish you got if you sat on your hands for too long and the folds of your clothes imprinted themselves into the skin. But it wasn't that at all. There was a pattern to it, like the jack-o'-lantern, the shapes weren't meaningless. They were a face. They were the shadow of a face—eyes wide open. Staring.

"Did you tell Hector?"

"I'm telling you."

"God, Inez—"

But Inez turned white and shushed her. "Don't say that!" Inez squealed. "Don't say His name like that. We don't know! Maybe it is, I mean, do you think, maybe He . . . I mean, oh, Jesus, I don't know, Lin!" Her mouth froze in a little "oh" of horror. There were tears running down her cheeks, forming little eddies around a single, pasty splatter of pumpkin guts.

"It's okay, Inez. It's okay." And Leah put her arm around Inez. "You'll be okay," she whispered. "You'll be okay."

And they rocked together. So close. Close enough that Leah could feel her cheek pressing against Inez's neck. Just above the mark. So close she could imagine it whispering to her. There was something beautiful about it all. Something beautiful about the mark pressed against her, the wind making a rustling sound of the newspapers, Hector in the yard, and the long strings of pumpkin guts lined up like glyphs drying in the last of the summer light.

"It's okay," Leah told her, but even as their bodies were so close Leah could feel the hot, hardpan length of her girlish muscles tense and relax in turns, she knew there was a chasm splitting between them, a great divide.

"Shush," she said. "Pretty baby," she said because sometimes that quieted Milo down. Inez wasn't listening. She was holding on. So hard it hurt.

Inez was dead the next day.

Leah was allowed to attend the funeral. It was the first funeral she'd been allowed to go to since her dad's.

The funeral had a closed casket (of course, it had to) but Leah wanted to see anyway. She pressed her fingers against the dark, glossy wood of the coffin, leaving a trail of smudged fingerprints that stood out like boot-marks in fresh snow. She wanted to see what had happened to that face with the gaping eyes. She wanted to know who that face had belonged to. No one would tell her. From her mum, it was still nothing but, "Shush up, Lin."

And Hector was there.

Hector was wearing a suit. Leah wondered if it was the same suit that he had worn to Yasmine's funeral, and if he'd looked just as good wearing it then as he did now. A suit did something to a man. Leah was wearing a black dress. Not a little black dress. She didn't have a little black dress—she and Inez had decided they would wait until their breasts came in before they got little black dresses. But Inez had never gotten her breasts.

The funeral was nice. There were lots of gorgeous white flowers, roses and lilies and stuff, which looked strange because everyone was wearing black. And everyone said nice things about Inez—how she'd been on the swim team, how she'd always got good grades. But there was something tired about all the nice things they said, as if they'd worn out those expressions already.

"She was my best friend," Leah said into the microphone. She had been nervous about speaking in front of a crowd, but by the time her turn actually came she was mostly just tired too. She tried to find Hector in the audience. His seat was empty. "We grew up together. I always thought she was like my sister."

She found him outside, afterward. He was sitting on the stairs of the back entrance to the church, a plastic cup in one hand. The suit looked a little crumpled, but it still looked good. At nineteen he was about a foot taller than most of the boys she knew. They were like little mole rats compared to him.

Her mother was still inside making small talk with the reverend. All the talk anyone made was small these days.

"Hey," she said.

He looked up. "Hey."

It was strange, at that moment, to see Inez's eyes looking out from her brother's face now that she was dead. It didn't look like the same face. Leah didn't know if she should go or not.

Her black dress rustled around her as she folded herself onto the stair beside him.

"Shouldn't you be back in there?"

Hector put the plastic cup to his lips and took a swig of whatever was inside. She could almost imagine it passing through him. She was fascinated by the way his throat muscles moved as he swallowed, the tiny triangle he had missed with his razor. Wordlessly, he handed the cup to her. Leah took a tentative sniff. Whatever it was, it was strong. It burned the inside of her nostrils.

"I don't know," Hector said. "Probably. Probably you should too."

"What are you doing out here?"

Hector didn't say anything to that. He simply stared at the shiny dark surface of his dress shoes—like the coffin—scuffing the right with the left. The sun made bright hotplates of the parking lot puddles. Leah took a drink. The alcohol felt good inside her stomach. It felt warm and melting inside her. She liked being here next to Hector. The edge of her dress was almost touching his leg, spilling off her knees like a black cloud, but he didn't move. They stayed just like that. It was like being in a dream. Not *the* dream. A nice dream.

"I miss her, Lin. I can't stop it . . . you look a bit like her, you know? I mean, you don't look anything like her really, but still," he stumbled, searching out the right words. "But."

"Yeah," she said.

"I'm glad you're here."

She took a larger swallow. Her head felt light. She felt happy. She knew she shouldn't feel happy but she felt happy anyway. Did Hector feel happy? She couldn't tell. She hadn't looked at enough boys to tell exactly what they looked like when they looked happy.

Suddenly, she was leaning toward him. Their hands were touching, fingers sliding against each other, and she was kissing him.

"Lin," he said, and she liked the way he said her name, but she didn't like the way he was shaking his head. She tried again, but this time he jerked his head away from her. "No, Lin. I can't, you're . . . you're just a kid."

The happy feeling evaporated. Leah looked away.

"Please, Hector," she said. "There's something. . . ." She paused. Tried to look at him and not look at him at the same time. "It's not just Inez, okay? It's me too."

He shook his head again, but there was a glint in his eyes. Something that hadn't been there before. It made him look the way that Inez's mark had with its wide, hollow eyes. Like there could be anything in them. Anything at all.

"I've found something. On my skin. We were like sisters, you know. Really. Do you want to see it?"

"No," he said. His eyes were wide. Inez's eyes had looked like that, too, hadn't they? They both had such pretty eyes. Eyes seeded with gold and copper and bronze.

"Please," she said. "Would you kiss me? I want to know what it's like. Before."

"No," he whispered again, but he did anyway. Carefully. He tasted sweet and sharp. Like pumpkin. He tasted the way the way a summer night tastes in your mouth, heavy and wet, wanting rain but not yet ready to let in October. The kiss lingered on her lips.

Leah wondered if this was what love felt like. She wondered if Yasmine had felt like this, if Hector had made her feel like this, and if she did, how could she ever have left him?

She didn't ask for another kiss.

The world was changing around them all now, subtly, quietly at first, but it was changing.

The day after the funeral Leah cut her hair and died it black. She wore it in dark, heavy ringlets just as Inez had. She took a magic marker to the space just below the collar of her shirt, the place Inez had showed her, and she drew a face with large eyes. With a hungry mouth.

She looked at forums. They all had different sorts of advice for her.

If you say your name backwards three times and spit . . .
If you sleep in a graveyard by a headstone with your birthday . . .
If you cut yourself this *way . . .*

Those were the things you could do to stop it, they said. Those were the things you could do to pass it on to someone else.

But nothing told her what she wanted.

For Milo, it started slowly. When Leah tried to feed him, sometimes he would spit out the food. Sometimes he would slam his chubby little hands into the tray again and again and again until a splatter of pureed squash covered them both. He would stare into the empty space and burble like a trout.

"C'mon, baby," Leah whispered to him. "You gotta eat something. Please, monkey-face. Just for me? Just a bite?"

But he got thinner and thinner and thinner. Her mum stopped looking at him. When she turned in his direction her eyes passed over him as if there was a space cut out of the world where he had been before, the way strangers didn't look at each other on the subway.

"Mum," Leah said, "what's happening to him?"

"Nothing, darling. He'll quiet soon." And it was like the dream. She couldn't move. No one could hear what she was saying.

"Mum," Leah said. "He's crying for you. Can you just hold him for a bit? My arms are getting tired and he just won't quit. He wants you, mum."

"No, darling," her mum would say. Just that. And then she would lock herself in her room, and Leah would rock the baby back and forth, gently, gently, and whisper things in his ear.

"Mummy loves you," she would say to him, "c'mon, pretty baby, c'mon and smile for me. Oh, Milo. Please, Milo."

Sometimes it seemed that he weighed nothing at all, he was getting so light. Like she was carrying around a bundle of sticks, not her baby brother. His fingers poked her through her shirt, hard and sharp. The noises he made, they weren't the noises that he knew. It was a rasping sort of cough, something like a choke, and it made her scared but she was all alone. It was only her and Milo. She clung tightly to him.

"Pretty baby," she murmured as she carried him upstairs. "Pretty, little monkey-face."

It was only when she showed him the little kitten she had tucked away in her music box that he began to quiet. He touched it cautiously, fingers curving like hooks. The fur had shed into the box. It was patchy in some places, and the skin beneath was sleek and silvery and gorgeous. When Milo's fingers brushed against it, he let out a shrieking giggle.

It was the first happy sound he had made in weeks.

What were the signs of love? Were they as easy to mark out as any other sort of sign? Were they a hitch in the breath? The way that suddenly any sort of touch—the feel of your hand running over the thin cotton fibers of your sheets—was enough to make you blush? Leah thought of Hector Alvarez. She thought about the kiss, and the way he had tasted, the slight pressure of his lips, the way her bottom lip folded into his mouth, just a little, just a very little bit.

Leah checked her body every morning. Her wrists. Her neck. She used a mirror to sight out her spine, the small of her back, the back of her thighs.

Nothing. Never any change.

The stars were dancing—tra lee, tra la—and the air was heavy with the fragrant smell of pot. They passed the joint between them carelessly. First it hung in his lips. Then it touched hers.

"What are you afraid of?" Leah asked Hector.

"What do you mean, what am I afraid of?"

Leah liked the way he looked in moonlight. She liked the way she looked too. Her breasts had come in. They pushed comfortably against the whispering silk of her black dress. They were small breasts, like apples. Crab apple breasts. She hoped they weren't finished growing.

She was fifteen today.

Tonight the moon hung pregnant and fat above them, striations of clouds lit up with touches of silver and chalk-white. It had taken them a while to find the right place. A gravestone with two dates carved beneath it. His and hers. (Even though she knew it wouldn't work. Even though she knew it wouldn't do what she wanted.)

The earth made a fat mound beneath them, the dirt fresh. Moist. She had been afraid to settle down on it, afraid that it wouldn't hold her. Being in a graveyard was different now—it felt like the earth might be moving beneath you, like there might be something moving around underneath, below the sod and the six feet that came after it. Dying wasn't what it used to be.

"I mean," she said, "what scares you? This?" She touched his hand. Took the joint from him.

"No," he said.

"Me neither." The smoke hung above them. A veil. Gauzy. There were clouds above the smoke. They could have been anything in the moonlight. They could have just been clouds. "Then what?"

"I was afraid for a while," Hector said at last, "that they were happy." He was wearing his funeral suit. Even with grave dirt on it, it still made him look good. "I was afraid because they were happy when they left. That's what scared me. Yasmine was smiling when I found her. There was a look on her face. . . ." He paused, took a breath. "Inez too. They knew something. It was like they figured something out. You know what I mean?"

"No," she said. *Yes*, she thought.

Her mother had been cutting potatoes this morning. Normally Leah cut them. She cut them the way her dad had taught her, but today it was her mother who was cutting them, and when the potato split open—there it was, a tiny finger, curled into the white flesh, with her dad's wedding ring lodged just behind the knuckle.

It was happening to all of them. When she walked down the street, all she could imagine were the little black dresses she would wear to their funerals. The shade of lipstick she would pick out for them. Her closet was full of black dresses.

"I've never felt that way about anything. Felt so perfectly sure about it that I'd let it take me over. I'd give myself up to it."

"I have," she said. But Hector wasn't listening to her.

"But then," he said, "I heard it."

"What?"

"Whatever Yasmine was waiting for. That long perfect note. That sound like Heaven coming."

"When?"

"Last night." His eyes were all pupils. When had they got that way? Had they always been like that? The joint was just a stub now between her lips, a bit of pulp. She flicked it away.

"Please don't go away, Hector," she said.

"I can't help it," he said. "You'll see soon. You'll know what I mean. But I'm not scared, Lin. I'm not scared at all."

"I know," she said. She remembered the way Milo had been with the kitten. He had known it was his. Even though it was monstrous, its chest caved in, the little ear bent like a folded page. It was his. She wanted that, God, how she wanted that.

And now Hector was taking her hand, and he was pressing it against his chest. She could feel something growing out of his ribcage—the hooked, hard knobs pushing through the skin. He sighed when she touched it, and smiled like he had never smiled at her before.

"I didn't understand when Yasmine told me," he said. "I couldn't understand. But you—you, Lin, you understand, don't you? You don't need to be scared, Lin," he said. "You can be happy with me."

And when he kissed her, the length of his body drawn up beside her, she felt the shape of something cruel and mysterious hidden beneath the black wool of his suit.

That night Leah had the dream—they were on the road together, all four of them.

"Listen, George," her mother was saying. (What she said next was always different; Leah had never been able to remember what it actually was, what she'd said that had made him turn, shifted his attention for that split-second.)

Leah was in the back, and Milo—Milo who hadn't been born when her father was alive—was strapped in to his child's seat to her.

"Listen, George," her mother was saying, and that was part of it. Her mother was trying to tell him something, but he couldn't hear her properly. So he turned. He missed it—what was coming, the slight curve in the road, but it was winter, and the roads were icy and it was enough, just enough.

"Is this it?" she asked. But her mum wasn't listening. She was tapping on the window. She was trying to show him something she had spotted.

Leah knew what came next. In all the other dreams what came next was the squeal of tires, the world breaking apart underneath her, and her trying to grab onto Milo, trying to keep him safe. (Even though he wasn't there, she would think in the morning, he hadn't even been born yet!)

That's how the dream was supposed to go.

"Listen, George," her mother was saying.

The car kept moving. The tires kept spinning, whispering against the asphalt.

"Is this what it is for me?" she tried to ask her mother, but her mother was still pointing out the window. "Is this my sign?"

And it wasn't just Milo in the car. It was Inez, too. It was Oscar Nunez with his shriveled-up tongue, and Joanna Sinclair, and Yasmine with her black eyeliner, her eyes like cat's eyes. And it was Hector, he was there, he was holding Yasmine's hand, and he was kissing her gently on the neck, peeling back her skin to kiss the hard, oyster-gray thing that was growing inside of her.

"She can't come with us," her mother was saying. "Just let her off here, would you, George? Just let her off."

"No," she tried to tell her mum. "No, this is where I am supposed to be. This is supposed to be *it*."

And then Leah was standing in a doorway, not in the car at all, and it was a different dream. She was standing in a doorway that was not a doorway because there was nothing on the other side. Just an infinite space, an uncrossable chasm. It was dark, but dark like she had never seen darkness before, so thick it almost choked her. And there was something moving in the darkness. Something was coming . . . because that's what omens were, weren't they? They meant something was coming.

And they had left her behind.

When Leah woke up the house was dark. Shadows clustered around her bed. She couldn't hear Milo. She couldn't hear her mother. What she could hear, from outside, was the sound of someone screaming—or singing—she couldn't tell which one it was, but she wanted to scream along with it, oh, she wanted to be part of that, to let her voice ring out in that one perfect note. . . .

But she couldn't.

Leah turned on the light. She took out the mirror. And she began to search (again—again and again and again, it made no difference, did it? it never made a difference).

She ran her fingers over and over the flawless, pale expanse of her body (flawless except for the white scar on her thumb where she'd sliced it open chopping potatoes).

Her wrists. Her neck. Her spine. Her crab apple breasts.

But there was still nothing there.

She was still perfect.

She was still whole. Untouched and alone.

THE MILLENNIAL'S GUIDE TO DEATH

Scott Bradfield

Scott Bradfield is the author of *The People Who Watched Her Pass By*, *Dazzle Resplendent: Adventures of a Misanthropic Dog*, and *Why I Hate Toni Morrison's Beloved: Several Decades of Reading Unwisely*. He reviews regularly for the *New York Times*, the *Los Angeles Times*, and the *Los Angeles Review of Books*.

"I got the idea for this story a couple decades ago," he recalls, "when I noticed that my graduating college students were going into 'careers' that treated them like I was treated as a part-time, fifteen-year-old gas station attendant.

"Over the years, the situation only got worse, giving me the time I needed to find my first paragraph."

DEATH STILL DROVE the same 1998 Plymouth Sundance he had received from his parents for college graduation, and lived in the basement of his sister's central Connecticut marital home—a two-story colonial with dry rot and a leaky septic tank, just a few blocks from his old grammar school. He practiced safe sex with women of known backgrounds and origins, worked out at the gym three times per week, and never drank too much or too little red wine, even when attending upscale social events as part of his job. And on the advice of his broker, he invested exactly one quarter of his annual income into tax-deferred pension schemes and a Silver-Grade Health Plan. But despite these rigorously worked-out living standards, he needed at least two part-time jobs to subsidize his salary as the Prince of Hopelessness, Void, and Despair; otherwise, he wouldn't have enough left over at the end of each month to cover his share of the rent and utilities.

And no matter how many times he broached the subject of a raise, Mother Nature simply refused to budge.

"Look, Davey," she told him over brunch at the Hartford Holiday Inn, where she was attending a Heritage Foundation conference on Saving the Ecosphere through Capitalism, "if I bumped up anything—your per diem, your body commission, even mileage—that would reduce your attention to cost-efficiency and time-management. You can't just throw money at problems and think they'll get better, Davey. And anyway, if I gave *you* a raise, everyone would want one. Cupid, for instance. That horny, selfish old bitch hardly gets out of bed until three in the afternoon, and why should I be subsidizing *her* sloth and wastefulness? But look, Davey, I like you, and I know you're having trouble managing your finances lately, so maybe I could help you in other, non-remunerative ways, such as in the area of personal management advice. You could even drop by my place later this evening, and we could relax, discuss things further, and maybe try out some of this nice little pinot I brought back from Sebastopol last month. . . ."

Death was trying to disregard the long, almost prehensile-seeming toes that, under the table, were currently climbing up the inside of his pants's cuff. It was the only thing he could really count on from Mother

Nature—she was just so goddamn *natural* all the time. It could really get on his nerves.

"Look, Ms. Nature," Death said, withdrawing his leg while pretending to scratch his thigh, "I appreciate your offer, but setting up another credit card repayment plan isn't what I need right now. At the end of the day, I simply don't *make* enough to *live*. I work seventy hours a week, hardly get any sleep, and it's all starting to impair my performance. Seriously, I would do a much better and, as you say, more *cost-efficient* job, if I could first take better care of *myself*—"

Thribbbbbb-buh-buh. Thribbbb-buh-buh.

"—and while I realize there isn't any magic money tree out there—even for you, Ms. Nature—"

(The embarrassing part was that he could never tell which of his pagers was throbbing—the Eternal Contact Device or, nestled right beside it, the Uber Driver App on his iPhone.)

"—but if you could see your way to upping my commission by ten percent or so, and make it retroactive going back to, say, that school bus crash up in Truckee, well, I might actually be able to afford those new tires I've been needing. The old retreads are coming apart like vampires in a tanning salon—"

Thribbbbbb-buh-buh.

Mother Nature was sitting up sternly with the deeply unsettling look of a demigod scorned.

"Shouldn't you get that?" she said stiffly. "Our little meeting here is already over."

And of course, as always, Mother Nature was right.

Her name was Norah Littleton, and like all of Death's last-minute clients, she was certain there had been some kind of mistake.

"Look," she insisted, leaning over from the back seat and shoving her laminated driver's license in his face. "I'm only *fifty-six*, for God's sake. Don't look at the picture—that makes me look a hundred. Just look at my birthdate. This right *here*—"

If there was one thing Death didn't have time for right now, it was a talker. And one of those lost-in-her-own-world type talkers like Norah who actually believed that she carried her own private reality around everywhere she went.

"And look at me. I exercise. I'm not overweight. I keep my mind active in community groups and reading clubs at the local library. I mean, just last week I read *Anna Karenina* from cover to cover in only *one* week. Does that sound like the mind of a woman knocking on Death's door? Or, in this case—"

If Death didn't dislike Norah already, he definitely disliked her now—especially the way she looked disfavorably around at the broken side window covered with gray duct tape, and the red and yellow fast food wrappers littering the floor. Then she pursed her lips, as if she tasted the shape of her next words before she spoke them.

"—riding around in the back seat of his . . . is this a *Chevy Sundance*? I didn't even think they built those anymore."

Norah had insisted on dressing up before they left her one-bedroom apartment in Van Nuys: a frilly Easter bonnet with a big pink bow knotted under her chin, stiff cardigan that looked fresh out of a gift box, and patent leather pumps. *I guess she wants to look good when we get there*, Death thought. But if she only stopped to think about it for two seconds, nobody *ever* looks good when they get there. To themselves or to anybody else.

The road was growing longer and murkier, and even the crooked high beams couldn't penetrate the blackness coming down on them like a stage curtain. Death took a deep breath; his chest rattled with a thin, strained ache. He was pretty certain he was developing a case of asthma, but he had been postponing his visit to the doctor on account of the deductible.

"Look, Norah," he said finally, as if he were laying down the law to a gentle, attentive pet. "I don't make the rules. I just do what I'm told. And I definitely don't get paid well enough to listen to you complain. Now, if you could move over and make some room, I haveta stop by Pizza Hut and deliver several large pepperonis to some college kids in Burbank. But don't worry about us being late or anything. It's on our way."

Most mornings, Death lay alone among his cold unwashed sheets in his unheated basement apartment, gazing up at the bare-beamed wooden ceiling and preparing his fuddled energies for the long, complicated day ahead. There was a gas bill due, and the cell bill, and he still needed to pick up his dry cleaning. He was supposed to meet his girlfriend at the Westfield Mall to pick out a wedding gift for her sister, but couldn't remember which of his credit cards was still viable. Then he needed to pick up his payroll check at Dominos and send his invoice to Uber. And there was that smog inspection before he could pay the new registration fee, and something else . . . something else he kept intending to do.

Oh yeah. Call his parents.

"Hello, hon," Mom said when she picked up. It was her frosty voice, like frozen peas in a plastic bag kind of frosty, reminding him he probably hadn't returned a call since Christmas. "Are you okay? Have you spoken with your father? I'd put him on but he's taking a nap."

And something had been nagging at the back of Death's mind since the last requisition schedule came through from central processing in Peoria. . . .

After taking a moment to digest, Death asked, "How's Dad doing, anyway?"

And then another long period of static on the phone line. It might have been his mother thinking, or an echo from inside Death's own eardrums.

"He can't keep down solid foods," Mom said. "That nodule on his colon is worse than they thought. He's on so many different types of painkillers I can't tell them apart, and I'm pretty sure he's addicted to opioids, though I'm not sure if those are the ones in the red bottle or the ones in the green bottle, maybe both. I asked him to try this medicinal marijuana thing I ordered through Doctor Rosen, but you know your dad. He never tries anything new."

On Friday, Death's girlfriend, Cherie, took him to a Halloween Party at the home of a colleague, where they were greeted by the usual medley of conventional monsters (Frankenstein and Dracula), conventional superheroes (Spider-Man and Wonder Woman), and the slightly unconventional "joke" costumes, such as The National Debt (a ruptured papier-mâché pink piggy bank) and Obamacare (a twisted gray-haired Obama mask riding atop a surgical gown and stethoscope.) Costume parties always made Death feel self-conscious, since he had to either pretend he was somebody he wasn't, or deliver himself to a series of disappointed expressions.

"Who are you supposed to be?" asked a buxom Marilyn Monroe wannabe.

She wore a birthmark on the wrong cheek that resembled one of Dad's recent melanomas.

"He's Death," Cherie said, with a faint wisp of pride. "He doesn't have to wear a mask since Death always comes as who he actually is.

Right, honey? And he makes no bones about it. Get it? Makes no *bones* about it?"

Cherie had come dressed as one of her childhood heroines, Hilary Clinton, in a Mao-red pantsuit and a hard helmet of dirty blonde hair. Unlike Death, Cherie loved dressing up as somebody she wasn't. It even seemed to make her horny.

"I still don't get it," Marilyn Monroe said, sipping what smelled like gin out of a plastic party cup. "You got these ragged jeans. Your Nikes have seen better days. You still owe my boyfriend ten dollars since September for your share of the bowling fees, and suddenly you're this Master of Darkness and Despair and so forth. Next year, blow a few bucks on a Trump mask or something. It'd sure as hell be a lot scarier."

It was a terrible party. The punch was so weak you could barely taste the vodka, and the so-called "snacks" amounted to one cracked ceramic bowl of gummy bears, and another ceramic bowl of crumbly barbecue-flavored Lay's potato chips.

"I got them at the Dollar Shop for like fifty cents per liter bag," the host said. His name was Jimmy Something (a friend of Cherie's from work), and he had slapped on the usual white collar, fangs, and gooey substance that made him look as shabby and complacent as last decade's aluminum Christmas tree. "They look like somebody dropped a safe on them. So you're Cherie's boyfriend, huh? I'm Mitch." Then he dispensed the sort of manly but not-to-make-a-big-deal-of-it handshake that Death would have expected from a man named "Mitch." "And I was wondering. Do you do private contract stuff? Like snuff people out and all that? Good way to pick up a few extra bucks, right? I'm asking for a friend."

He was a bit lean, Death thought. And he had dark patches around his eyes. But he sure didn't look like a potential client. Yet.

"You see, I work like sixteen hours a day and can't make a dent in my student loan," Mitch told a green gummy bear pinched between his thumb and forefinger. "This house looks nice but it's my mom's, and when she gets back from Maui I go straight back to a hammock in the tool shed. My good-looking girlfriends keep leaving me for their bosses at work, and the only ones who stick around are like the really unattractive girlfriends, like Marilyn Monroe over there with the fake tits, and that's bad for the soul. So maybe we could make a deal. I can't pay you now, but once Mom's out of the picture, I'll take the house and you can have the car. It's a Lexus."

By this point, they were both gazing at the same pincered green gummy bear, as if only he could save them. Then, almost as a taunt, Mitch lifted the small unstruggling creature to his nose, sniffed, and popped it in his mouth.

If only they all went that easy, Death thought. Then heard a clamor at the front door, the buzzer buzzing, and a rush of loud urgent voices converging in the front hall.

Then, after another moment:

"Hey! Death, where are you? You got company!"

It was a busload of elderly men and women from the Suncrest Senior Living Complex out for an afternoon of pumping buckets of quarters into slots at the Mohegun Sun. Their bus had hit an icy patch on 84, slid down a flinty hill, and ignited against a power line. At a hundred dollars a head, Death could see those new steel-belted snow tires being ratcheted onto his rear axles already. But there was only room for six or seven passengers in his car at a time, depending on the size of their hip-replacements. He would have to make several trips.

It was almost impossible to tell them apart. They all smelled like dirty laundry. And all they did was complain, complain, *complain*. Turn up the heat! Roll down the windows! Roll *up* the windows! I can't find my medication! Can't you play anything but smooth jazz? Death thought they would never shut up.

Until, of course, they reached their Final Destination—at which point they did what all of Death's clients did when they reached their Final Destination.

They screamed and screamed and screamed and screamed.

Thribbbbb-buh-buh.

Thribbbb-buh-buh.

After the last group of screaming seniors had been sucked into the maw of Mindless Dissolution, Death was brushing the charred roaches and pretzel fragments from his seats. He took the phone between his ear and shoulder.

"Yeah?"

"Hi, hon. Me. Look, I've got some good news and some bad news, and this isn't meant to be a joke or anything, it's just that lately I can't decide which is which anymore. The ol' clock on the wall tells me your dad's time is up, but since it qualifies as both a workday *and* a personal day, I'm paying you twice the normal commission. Satisfied? Bye."

It was always the same at Mom and Dad's house. Death was actually glad to see them for about five seconds. Then they started arguing.

"Where's my razor?" Dad shouted from his private bedroom in back, where he served out every evening in solitary confinement on account of his snoring.

"You don't need a razor, Dad. You're dead."

Mom didn't look up from the vintage Samsonite brown hard leather suitcase propped open on the living room sofa. It exuded a smell of mothballs and tobacco.

"He said you don't *need* a razor, dear! You're dead!"

"I'm not deaf, for crying out loud! Where's my hearing aid?"

"You're wearing it!"

"And anyway, Dad. You don't need it. You're—"

"I know already. I'm dead. But what if somebody asks me something? And where are my good socks? Hon, did you pack my good socks?"

Mom looked at Davey with her customary "your Dad" expression—it was located somewhere between sucking on an uncrackable sourball and moistening her lipstick.

"I packed them, hon. Six pairs."

"He doesn't need his socks, Mom. In fact, I can't fit that suitcase in my trunk. He just brings what he's wearing. They'll have anything else he needs when he gets there."

After they finally lodged Dad into the cramped, crooked passenger seat, Death kissed his mother goodbye.

"Be careful on the roads. Don't let your father get too cold. And make sure he calls when you get there. You know how I worry. Oh, and another thing. I don't mean to embarrass you, but this is probably the last chance I'll ever get to say this. I know your dad can be difficult. I know your dad can be inflexible. And I'm sure your dad would have attended more of your school concerts as a child if it hadn't been for his drinking, but it's just not the way your dad was made. But however he may have behaved, your dad always loved you. And if he acted disappointed with your current, you know, occupation and all, it was just because he always expected more from you. He wanted to brag about you to his friends at the Senior Center, and, well, the opportunity to brag about you just never materialized, did it?"

Death blew his nose with some crumpled Kleenex from the dashboard, buckled up, and backed out of the driveway.

"What about *my* seat belt?"

"It's broken, and anyway—you're dead. Just help me look out for kids, will you? It's Halloween."

There were still several small, ebbing tides of children drifting through the streets in ragged, broken clouds of shiny fabric. They carried hand-worn brown grocery bags, and wore skull-slung plastic masks of Spider-Man, Thor, and Donald, and were pursued lackadaisically by minor Hell-spawned demons who were finding it hard to keep up. "Boo," they whispered, slumped over with low-swinging claws and dragging their forked tails in the littered streets like departed glory. "Ooooh-eee-oooooh!" It sounded like an evil cacophony being read out loud phonetically by drama tryouts at a primary school production of *Paradise Lost*. "This is the night when evil walks the earth. You better watch out, kids, or we'll drag your souls straight to Hell. Ooooooooooh." They clearly felt no enthusiasm for their jobs, having been hastily bumped up from low-ranking administrative positions after their superiors had been headhunted off to glitzy, six-figure salaries at places such as Blackwater, Koch Industries, and the U.S. Department of Justice.

"Is there anything to eat?" Dad said, rummaging through the glove compartment. "I didn't have dinner."

"I'm sorry, Dad. If you didn't eat, you didn't eat. I wish I could do something about it but I can't."

When they arrived at their destination, Death did something he never usually did: he parked across the street, shut off the engine, and turned on a soft rock station on the dashboard radio. Then he offered Dad a Parliament from a pack left behind by a former client, and provided him one last opportunity to apologize for all his bad deeds. Unfortunately, Dad didn't feel like apologizing for anything.

"I kept my job, even when I hated my boss and all he stood for, just so you could go to college and sleep with all those nice girls who eventually dumped you. I lived with your crazy mother for five *decades*, even while all the sensible guys from my generation were buying sports cars and sleeping with young girls. I built up a good credit score so I could buy a big house I couldn't afford so that I could help you buy a house that you couldn't afford and, hah, fat chance, you couldn't even come up with a share of the deposit, so why'd I waste my time? And then I spent almost the entirety of my old age listening to you and your mother complain about all your lousy breaks and what a tough time you were having. 'Things aren't as good for our boy as they were in our day,' your mother kept saying. 'Nobody can afford decent health care, and when they leave college, they owe tens of thousands of dollars to cutthroat corporations.' Well, *whoop-de-dooh*, as my old man used to say. That's life, kid; get used to it. Which reminds me: when I'm gone, don't even *think* of taking my Oldsmobile. Your mother's going to say, 'Hon, why don't you take your Dad's Oldsmobile,' and you're gonna say, 'Sure, why not,' and let me tell you why not. I donated that Oldsmobile to NPR, which shows just how pissed off I was when you didn't bother to call me on my birthday last year. And you know how much I hate those bastards at NPR."

It was a disused industrial road just outside Hartford, featuring a rusty mailbox, a rusty Ford Fairlane, and the rustily broken awnings of the Eternal Self-Storage warehouse. Death couldn't help noticing that things were quieter than usual. The minor functionary demons weren't standing outside the wide-panel doors, passing back and forth loosely rolled cigarettes. The high klieg lights flickered indecisively with a soft, phosphorescent glow, as if they couldn't tell whether to illuminate the scene or simply retreat into their own interior gloom. And even the faint clamor of lost souls rattling around inside the warehouse had diminished to a soft, conch-like susurration that, after a few moments, Death recognized as the sound of cars passing distantly on I-84. In the midst of these slow recognitions, Death noticed that Dad had finally stopped blathering. In fact, he seemed to have completely run out of things to say.

He called Mother Nature's office but the line had been disconnected. He called her cell and got a message.

"*Hola!*" There was always something at once sultry and parched about Mother Nature's voice, like that of a vulture on aphrodisiacs. "It's little ol' me, y'all. I've reached one of those major life-decisions that can only be achieved after several Happy Hour margaritas at Berrigan's, and here it is: I'm semiretiring *immediatamente*, and heading off to a lucrative consultancy gig at Whole Foods, where I've been offered an offer I *could* refuse—but then what would happen to all that nice money? I've done my time in public service, and let me tell you what I learned: public service sucks. Especially with people like me running things. So this is one of those 'to whom it may concern deals'; write it down. I left the keys in the top drawer of my office desk. The safe combination is written on the door, but don't bother. I stripped the pension funds, the payroll, and whatever looked halfway decent in the Lost & Found, such as a couple iPhone cases that I can probably sell on eBay, and a genuine mahogany frame umbrella. Don't bother to write and I won't bother to read it if you do. Mother Nature is off to enjoy the remainder of her life while she still can."

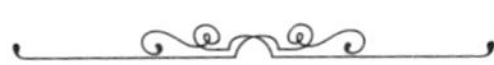

As Death quickly realized, there isn't much you can do with a company—however ancient and well-regarded—that has been asset-stripped down to the floorboards. He tried selling off the warehouse space, only to learn it had been mortgaged into the next millennium. He discussed the possibility of a merger with Big Pharma and was told he didn't have anything they didn't already own. He even tried to sell off some of his most lucrative subsidiary contracts—to the Pentagon, Blue Cross, Monsanto, and the prison-for-profit industry—but nobody was buying; they already had too much of everything. Death was no longer the only doom-merchant on the block. He wasn't even listed in the Top Ten.

In fact, it got so bad that even the lost souls were packing up their bags and vamoosing off for parts unknown.

"Toodle-ooh, toots!" shouted the senior citizens, piling onto their battered and algae-streaked yellow bus. "We got an appointment with endless rounds of Bingo in whatever Indian casino will have us! Which, by our calculation, would probably be all of them!"

And a slightly more raucous Norah Littleton chimed in, "And that goes for yours truly—truly! I told you—I'm only fifty-six!" Then, hiking up the skirt of her floral-patterned sundress, she climbed onto the back of a throbbing Harley Davidson behind a multiple murderer (and eventual murderee) in a Nazi helmet named Elroy P. James.

"At first, it all seemed pretty disconcerting," Death confessed to his former girlfriend, Cherie, at the all-you-could-eat lunchtime buffet at Round Table, where they had spent the rosier days of their romance before everything had gone sour. "But then I looked twice, and for a bunch of dead people, they didn't look much worse than they originally did. So everybody went buzzing off to their new non-lives, and at least I didn't have much cleaning up to do. I sublet the empty space as artist lofts, and then some jewelry-makers showed up, and a few falafel stands, and some vintage LP merchants, and before I knew it, the place was kind of like London's Camden Market, except for the smell. You definitely don't get that kind of smell out of the carpets with a steam-clean; believe me, I've tried. I even put Dad to work in the guardhouse, where he carries on doing the same things he did when he was still alive—shouting abuse at CNN, and falling asleep to *Wheel of Fortune*. So at the end of the day, I guess life has really been looking up, and I'm going to enjoy it while I still can. Anyway, I'm glad we could get together like this, Cherie, and sorry if I monopolized the conversation. Maybe next time you can tell me how things are working out with your new boyfriend, Bacchus. I know he drinks heavily, and finds it hard settling down with one woman, but he's got a good soul, and that's something you never saw very often in my business. A good soul, I mean."

Cherie looked puffy and slightly red-faced from either too little sleep or too much pressure at work. Against Death's advice, she had taken the position of chief administrative secretary at Mother Nature's latest start-up (it had something to do with building a pollution-free ecosphere for super-rich people on the Moon) and she was now so thin and lifeless that she resembled one of her old dresses hanging in a closet.

"That's good news, hon," Cherie said softly, addressing her half-finished slice of pepperoni. "But I've got a conference call at twelve-thirty. Maybe I should pay and get us out of here, okay?"

And sitting there on a friendly basis with his ex-partner after what had not been a very satisfactory relationship for either of them, Death couldn't help feeling that sometimes, if you keep your head up and your heart confident, life *could* get better, and often *did*. It might *seem* like this insurmountable series of obstacles, but if you persevered, and enjoyed a little luck, you could often find your way to the end of the race. You might not win the race or anything, but winning wasn't the important part. *Surviving* was the important part. And surviving long enough to enjoy the time you had left when you didn't have to run any races at all.

"Sounds like a plan, Cherie," Death said, placing his crumpled paper napkin on the middle of his tomato-sauce stained paper plate like a small tombstone memorializing several slices of veggie supreme. "But I gotta insist on one thing. You bought me enough meals in the past. This time, for once, let *me* pick up the check."

WHITE MARE

THANA NIVEAU

Thana Niveau is a Halloween bride. Originally from the United States, she now lives in the UK, in a Victorian seaside town between Bristol and Wales, where she writes horror and science fiction.

She is the author of the mini-collection Unquiet Waters, and her short fiction has appeared in such anthologies and magazines as *Best New Horror*; *Best British Horror*; *Darker Companions: A Tribute to Ramsey Campbell*; *Whispers in the Dark*; *Zombie Apocalypse!: Endgame*; *Steampunk Cthulhu*; *Terror Tales of Cornwall*; *Terror Tales of Wales*; *The Black Book of Horror*; *Love, Lust, and Zombies*; *Magic: An Anthology of the Esoteric and Arcane*; *Interzone*; and *Black Static.*

Her first novel is forthcoming from Horrific Tales, and her second short story collection is due from PS Publishing.

"The origin stories of Halloween are fascinating," observes the author, "even if no one seems to agree exactly how the modern customs evolved from their pagan Samhain roots. I've always loved the idea that the worlds of the living and dead merge on that one night, and that we must honor the demons to make them go back to their own realm.

"'Guising' is believed to have evolved from a tradition of impersonating the dead, and requesting offerings of food on their behalf. Disguising yourself as an evil spirit would supposedly hide or protect you from them. Certain other ancient customs are performed at Midwinter, and you might recognize elements of one I twisted into something far less benign.

"I wasn't stuck for ideas, but I did initially have a hard time trying to scare myself because, for me, Halloween doesn't conjure thoughts of horror. Rather, it triggers nostalgic Bradbury-ish reminiscence—in America, all those gruesome pagan traditions have evolved into what's basically just a giant cosplay party. So I approached it from a fish-out-of-water angle, to contrast the loathing so many Brits have for the holiday with my own rose-tinted memories."

APRIL WAS THE cruelest month for grown-ups, but for kids it was definitely September. The wild ride of summer came crashing to an end and the return to school was like being dragged back to prison after weeks of freedom.

Heather had never minded, though, because September gave way to October. And October was her favorite month. The air turned crisp and the leaves were at their most vibrant and colorful. And best of all, there was Halloween. It was a magical time, a time when the world transformed, putting on one last show before the long cold winter set in.

Heather had turned fourteen the month before, and her dad was letting her throw her first party, to celebrate both holidays. Together they spent a week transforming their boring little house in the Austin suburbs into a haunted palace.

They decorated it with orange and black streamers and stuck rubber blood spatters on all the windows and mirrors. They turned the kitchen into a gruesome abattoir, with peeled grape eyeballs and pasta intestines lying in dishes under low lights. A cauldron filled with dry ice bubbled ominously on the stove. The bathrooms were crawling with plastic spiders while glow-in-the-dark skulls and ghosts grinned from every shadowy nook and corner. Outside, a hideous animatronic scarecrow rose up to scream at anyone who came near enough to wake him.

It was total overkill, but it was totally worth it. Sam and Mia said it was the sickest party they'd ever seen. Word got out on Twitter and soon the house was full. You knew a party was a success when kids you didn't even know started showing up.

They gleefully drank blood punch from plastic goblets and ate zombie cake off black paper plates. And even though they were technically too old for it, the costumed teenagers went trick-or-treating up and down the block, then gorged themselves on candy and pumpkin pie when they got back to the party. Heather had dressed as Wednesday Addams (her dad's idea), but she was having such a blast it was impossible to stay in character. Her deadpan demeanor gave way to shrieking and giggling along with her friends at every manufactured scare.

Of course they also took great delight in terrifying any kids brave enough to come knocking. Heather's dad jumped out from his hiding place dressed like a medieval executioner, swinging a huge headsman's axe. One younger group of trick-or-treaters ran screaming back to their mother's car and were too afraid to return for their treats. Heather and her friends had laughed themselves into hysterical tears over that and declared that Dave Barton was the Coolest Dad Ever.

It was the best night Heather could remember in a long time. It was almost enough to make her forget that her mother had vanished without a trace the year before.

"Night, Mom," Heather whispered to the creased photo she kept tucked under her pillow. "You would have loved it."

But even as she said it, she realized that the raw, aching wound in her heart had finally begun to heal. A year ago she'd never have imagined herself capable of smiling again. Her dad either for that matter. But if the trauma had brought the two of them closer, the party had made them best friends.

She'd always secretly believed it was a magical time of year. Now she knew it for a fact. So of course she began counting down the days until they could do it all again.

"We're going *where?*"

She could remember the moment like it was yesterday. Her father had sighed and looked down at the table, where loads of important-looking papers were strewn out in front of him. "England. Just for a while. Just to get things settled."

England. The other side of the world. Where she didn't know *anybody*.

"But why do we have to go now?"

"Because otherwise the farmhouse is just sitting there abandoned. It's already been broken into twice. We can't afford to leave it and let it get trashed."

Heather hadn't been able to stop herself resenting Ruth, her dad's recently deceased maiden aunt. She'd never even met the woman who'd surfaced from the distant past just to dump her creepy old farm on them.

"Besides," her father added sheepishly, "we need the money we'll get from the sale of whatever's inside. She apparently had a lot of antiques."

"So why can't we go over Christmas?" Heather persisted. Missing out on Christmas was vastly preferable to being deprived of another awesome Halloween.

"Because it's too expensive. Everyone flies over Christmas."

"But our party—"

"Heather." For long moments her father stared down at the scattered papers, shaking his head sadly. Suddenly he wasn't Dave Barton her BFF anymore; he was just "Dad."

When he finally met her eyes again, he seemed profoundly weary. Heather knew that look. He'd worn it every day until the police told them they'd abandoned the search for her mom. And then every day after that. There had been no evidence of foul play, no suggestion that she'd run off with another man, no . . . nothing. It had broken her father.

Heather's face burned as she realized how selfish she was being. Last year's Halloween/birthday bash had been the first time they'd had fun since the nightmare began, the first time they'd been able to cut loose. But love wasn't just about the fun times. What had the school counselor told her? Two steps forward, one step back?

Her dad hadn't known his aunt well. Hadn't even seen her in twenty years. The death of a virtual stranger was nothing compared to what they'd gone through over Heather's mom. But it was still awful. Aunt Ruth was dead. Not missing. Not vanished without a trace. Stone-cold factually *dead*. And she'd left them her farm.

"Hey," Heather said, her voice catching. She moved to her father's side and flopped down on the floor, resting her head on his knee. "It's okay. I understand." It was all she could say without breaking down.

She felt her father's hand in her hair, ruffling the pixie cut. "Thanks, kiddo. I knew I could count on you. And you never know—we might actually like it there."

She'd forced a brave smile at the time, even though she knew there was no way she would.

It was raining when they landed at Heathrow, and it rained during the long drive that followed. Heather's first impression of England was that it was very green and very wet. Presumably one because of the other. Thorpe Morag was a small Somerset village nestled in a valley in the middle of wet green nowhere. It was near places with even weirder names, like Middlezoy and Huish Champflower.

Her second impression was that everything was *old*. Like straight-out-of-a-history-book old. The roads, the houses, even the trees all seemed impossibly ancient. America was all shopping malls and Starbucks and nail salons and car dealerships, all of it new and shiny and clean. Here, Heather wouldn't be surprised to see medieval peasants plowing the fields.

A battered sign finally told them they'd reached Thorpe Morag, and a winding road led them into the village. Two rows of cottages faced each other across a wide patch of grass with a little duck pond and a couple of rotting park benches. The "village green" apparently. There was a pub, the White Mare, and a shop that looked like something from an old black-and-white movie. As far as Heather could tell, its name was just "The Shop."

At the far end of the green, a cluster of trees sheltered a narrow track that led to the Barton farm. The house was a blocky stone structure that looked more like a storage building than a home. It was almost hidden in the shadows of the foliage surrounding it. The trees looked intent on consuming the upper story, and the view from at least one window was entirely obscured. Heather shuddered at the thought of branches scraping her bedroom window like bony fingers before breaking the glass and reaching in for her.

"It's, um . . . nice," she said, staring in dismay at the farmhouse. The photos emailed by the solicitor had clearly been taken on some enchanted spring morning when sunlight had conquered the gloom. Heather glanced at her father, but his expression was unreadable. They were really going to stay here? *Live* here? A glance back at the sparse village didn't reveal any alternatives. It wasn't like there was a hotel down the road or anything. But there had to be a city nearby. How far away was London? Surely they could find somewhere else to stay, *anywhere* else . . .

Her dad took the first step toward the farmhouse and Heather had her answer. She heaved a morose sigh as she trudged after him, resigned to her fate. That was when she saw it.

Her gasp must have sounded like one of pain because her dad whirled around. "Heather! Are you okay?"

"Oh my god," she breathed. She didn't so much walk as float toward the fence, where a beautiful horse stood gazing at her with huge dark eyes. Its coat was a rich deep red, its mane and tail long and black.

Without hesitation Heather reached out to stroke the animal's sleek neck, and the horse nickered softly and tossed its head. It seemed to be laughing. When Heather pulled her hand back, the horse thrust its nose underneath her palm, nudging her. It felt like velvet.

"I think she likes you," her dad said. "Or *he* likes you."

"You were right the first time," came a voice from behind them.

They both jumped and turned to see a man standing there. Wisps of white hair framed a thin but rugged face and his bright blue eyes shone with friendliness.

"Didn't mean to startle you folks," he said. His accent made him sound like Hagrid in the Harry Potter movies. "I'm Chester." He stuck out his hand for each of them to shake. His grip was so firm it made Heather wince. "You must be the new owners."

"Yes. I'm Dave Barton and this is my daughter, Heather. Ruth was my aunt."

Chester bowed his head, revealing a bald patch he made no effort to hide. "Damn shame," he said. "She was a fine woman. Always good to me, was your Ruth. I take care of her animals for her. That is, I *took* care. Still will if you'll have me."

"Well, I think . . ." Dave glanced at Heather, who could only offer a shrug. Behind her, the horse was nudging her roughly in the back, demanding attention. Dave laughed. "I'm sure that would be just fine. Just tell me what your arrangement was and I'll continue to honor it. For as long as we're here, that is."

"Fair enough," Chester said, nodding with satisfaction. He turned his attention back to the horse. "Her name's Callisto."

Heather stood on tiptoe and pressed her forehead to the horse's. "Hi, Callisto," she said softly. "I'm Heather. And I think you just made things a whole lot better for me here."

From that moment on, Heather and Callisto were inseparable. Heather had never ridden a horse before, but Callisto didn't seem to mind her inexperience. She would stand patiently while Heather clambered up onto her back from the fence. Chester had shown her how to put the saddle on, but Heather preferred the intimacy of riding without it. She loved the feel of Callisto's warm flanks beneath her and the rich animal smell she left on Heather's clothes.

Ruth had clearly loved Callisto and spoiled her with treats and attention, a responsibility Heather was happy to assume. The horse shared the pasture with a flock of six sheep, who seemed to be terrified of absolutely everything. They allowed Chester to get close, but they scattered whenever Heather went near them. The noises they made sounded like the voices of angry old men.

The farmhouse itself wasn't actually as awful as Heather had imagined, but she still spent as little time inside as possible. There was nothing good on TV and her phone wasn't set up to work overseas. And, of course, reclusive old Aunt Ruth didn't have a computer. Heather felt like she'd gone back in time. But because of Callisto, she found that wasn't so bad after all. By the end of the first week she was hardly even missing her friends back home. Sam and Mia and the others would be stuck at school while Heather had a month-long pass.

While her dad sorted out the legal headache of unloading the house and all its dusty antiques, Heather explored the outside world with Callisto. Occasionally her father went too, walking along beside them. And sometimes they both walked and took turns leading the horse.

But she was by herself the day she found out just how cut off she was from the world that she knew.

Callisto hadn't wanted to come out of her stall that morning, so Heather walked down to The Shop to see if they sold sugar lumps. Dave and Heather did all their food shopping at a supermarket on the outskirts of town and had never even been inside the little village shop.

The sugar lumps were easy enough to find, but getting a treat for herself proved more difficult.

"Hi," she said, approaching the ancient lady behind the counter. "Do you have candy bars?"

The woman blinked slowly at her, like a tortoise. She didn't speak for so long Heather began to wonder if she was deaf.

"Candy?" the woman repeated, dragging out the word as though she'd never heard of such a thing.

Just then, the bell over the door clanged and Heather turned to see three teenagers—two boys and a girl. They were laughing and shoving each other, but they stopped and stared when they noticed the stranger in their midst.

Relieved to see someone her own age, Heather smiled and gave a little wave. She expected one of them to speak first, but all three merely stood where they were, staring at her. The girl had her arms crossed over her chest and looked bored.

Unable to handle the awkward silence, Heather took a brave step closer. "I'm Heather. My dad and I—"

"We know who you are," said one of the boys. He was tall and gangly, his accent so thick Heather could barely understand him. He nudged his shorter friend, whose blank expression showed he wasn't up on current events. "They took over the Barton farm, Harry. I told you."

Heather shifted uncomfortably, not liking the way he had phrased it, as though they'd invaded and conquered the place. "We inherited it actually. It belonged to my dad's Aunt Ruth. I never even met her."

"You inherit that horse too?" This time it was the girl who spoke, her voice devoid of inflection.

The tall boy sniggered. "Chloe's jealous," he said, earning a black look from her.

"Shut it, Ian," Chloe growled, glaring at him.

"You could come see her," Heather offered, eager to keep the peace. But no one responded to her invitation.

"You want these or not, love?"

She glanced back at the old woman, who was holding up the box of sugar lumps. Heather hurried back to the counter. "Yes. And a candy bar. Chocolate or something. Anything, really."

That provoked a giggle from Chloe. Heather affected a laugh as well, assuming the joke involved the idea of her feeding candy to the horse.

The woman rummaged behind the counter and produced a bar of chocolate with an unfamiliar name. She quoted an amount and it took Heather some time to fish through the exotic coins to pay for it.

She turned to go, slightly unnerved to see that the group still hadn't moved. She wanted to believe they were just awkward around a newcomer, but she was beginning to get a darker vibe from them. She decided to make one last attempt to make friends.

"So . . . what are you all going as for Halloween?" she asked.

Ian blinked. "Going as?"

"Yeah," Heather said. "Won't there be a party somewhere? Or trick-or-treating?"

Chloe snorted. "Trick . . . or . . . treating?" She enunciated each word, as though it was the stupidest idea she'd ever heard.

Heather felt herself shrinking, her face burning as she looked down at the ground. "I guess, I just thought . . . I mean. . . ."

"I don't know what you do where *you* come from," Ian said, putting on an exaggerated American accent, "but Halloween ain't some kiddie fun fair."

Harry was the only one who didn't seem eager to make fun of her. "We have old customs," he said without elaborating. "Maybe you think they're strange."

"Oh no, I'd never—"

"Or beneath you," Chloe sneered. "Bet she thinks we're all just ignorant yokels."

Heather desperately wanted to leave, to hide her face before the shame made her cry. She decided to keep quiet and let the moment run its course.

"You Americans with your stupid costumes and parties," Ian said, now making no attempt to conceal his hostility. "What are *you* going as, Heather? A Disney princess? A unicorn? The Statue of Liberty?" At each insulting suggestion, he gave her a little shove until her back was against a shelf. Something wobbled behind her and fell to the floor with a thud.

Tears were blurring her vision but she refused to give them the satisfaction of seeing her cry. The old woman was clearly not going to intervene and the only way Heather was getting out of the shop was by pushing her way through the awful trio.

"There's things here you don't want to see," Harry said. "Things you have to . . . appease."

"Don't warn her," Ian said. "She don't care. Her and her rich daddy and her fancy horse, ridin' round like she owns the place." He edged closer, getting right in Heather's face. "She'll find out, though. When *they* come through."

Heather felt like she'd been doused with ice water. She tried not to flinch away, but his cold eyes and colder voice were too intimidating. She couldn't hold back her tears any longer and she pushed him aside and fled. Their laughter followed her all the way home.

She spent the rest of the afternoon with Callisto in her stall. She threw the chocolate away without eating it.

The woods behind the farm were ancient and obviously haunted. Callisto wasn't normally skittish, but in the woods she often shied at nothing. Nothing visible anyway. Each time Callisto jumped at a shadow, Heather would lean forward, stretching along the length of the horse's neck, stroking her and murmuring softly until she was calm. Sometimes it felt as though their souls were connected, as though they had a language all their own. She'd heard the term "horse whisperer" before and liked the way it sounded. She couldn't necessarily whisper to *all* horses. But this one understood her perfectly. Even her father could see they had a special bond.

The three of them were taking a walk one day when Dave remarked that they could throw one hell of a party in the woods, among the trees. Heather laughed, not wanting to admit that the idea made her uneasy.

There's things here you don't want to see.

When she didn't say anything in response to the suggestion, Dave swooped his hand over the top of her head.

Heather frowned. "Huh? What'd I miss?"

Her dad blinked in astonishment. "Really? Come on, kiddo. You forget the date or something? Sure you didn't fall off Callisto and hit your head?"

Suddenly she realized he'd been serious about the party. She blushed and lowered her head, stroking the lean, muscular leg of the horse walking beside her. "Oh." She shrugged. "I just . . . I don't know anyone here. I'd rather wait until we get home."

"What? No way! It'll all be over by then!"

But his enthusiasm only made her feel more uncomfortable and she pressed closer to Callisto, who leaned down to snort a burst of hot air down the back of her hoodie.

Dave sensed her discomfort and drew them all to a halt. "Hang on. I thought you met some of the other kids in the village."

Heather shrugged again. "Yeah." She didn't want to say more, didn't want to tell him how they'd made fun of her accent and her customs and hinted that something horrible was coming for her.

"That's not like you," he persisted. "You're the one who walks into a room full of strangers and leaves with ten new friends."

"Maybe back home," she said. "Here's it's just you and me and Callisto." Seeing concern in his face, she hurriedly added, "But that's fine. I'm having a great time."

But Dave didn't seem convinced. "I know you love the horse, but you've always been a pack animal. Are you sure you're okay? Sure you don't want a party? We're going to get quite a lot of money for some of the stuff in the house, you know. We can afford to 'splash out,' as they say over here."

Heather smiled. "You really are the Best Dad in the World, you know?"

He looked down at the ground, embarrassed by her praise.

"But," she continued, "no party is ever gonna top last year's. You don't have to try so hard. I'm okay. Really. We're both okay now." She wrapped her arm around him and squeezed, knowing he would take her meaning. He was often guilty of trying to fill the hole left by her mother. And if the past year had taught her anything, it was that he was all she needed.

After a while he nodded, understanding. "If you're sure," he said. "We'll set our sights on next year, then. A Halloween to remember."

"One for the ages."

She had successfully quashed the idea of a party, but her father still pressed her about Halloween. It was out of character for her not to be excited about it and planning what to wear, narrowing down costume choices.

"They don't really do Halloween over here, Dad," Heather mumbled. She picked at her dinner. Frozen pizza with the thinnest crust they'd ever seen.

But Dave persisted. "Don't be ridiculous. They had all kinds of stuff at the supermarket."

Heather shrugged. The supermarket was only two miles from Thorpe Morag, but it might as well have been another country. "I'd rather just hang out and watch TV," she said, trying to sound convincing. "Save all the real fun for when we're back home."

But even the thought of home wasn't entirely comforting. Because going home meant leaving Callisto behind. Chester had promised to take care of her in Heather's absence, but that didn't change the fact that Heather would never see her horse—and she had come to think of Callisto as *her* horse—again.

Dave didn't respond. Heather kept her head down, pretending to be absorbed in spreading the sparse toppings around on her pizza. She counted three whole pieces of pepperoni. When the silence began to feel awkward, she finally looked up, only to frown in confusion at her dad's expression. A cryptic grin had spread across his features.

"What?"

"Oh kiddo," he said with a good-natured chuckle. "Don't you think I know why you've been so moody lately?"

She froze with her pizza slice halfway to her mouth. He knew?

Now his chuckle became a full laugh. "Your face! You look like you've just seen your own tombstone." He reached across the table and pushed her pizza slice back down to her plate so he could grasp her hands. "It's Callisto, isn't it? You're upset about leaving her behind."

Heather relaxed a little, relieved that he'd only guessed half of what was eating at her. The safe half. "Yeah," she said. "I'm really gonna miss her."

"Well, maybe you don't have to miss her at all."

Her eyes widened as she waited for him to elaborate, too afraid to risk guessing and be wrong.

He didn't keep her in suspense long. "We're going to make a lot of money from the farm," he said. "A lot more than I originally thought. I didn't want to say anything until I double-checked the figures, and I was going to wait until tomorrow to tell you, but you just seemed so glum. We'll be able to afford some nice things back home. Like maybe a new house, with a big yard. And. . . ."

Heather squealed with excitement and jumped up so fast she knocked her chair over. She ran to her father and threw her arms around him, tears of joy filling her eyes. "Oh my god, I don't know what to say! Thank you!"

"Happy birthday, Heather."

She clung to him, unable to hold back the tears any longer. And now she didn't have to. Those horrible village kids could torment her all they wanted to now and it wouldn't matter one little bit because Callisto was going home with her!

That night she went out to the stable to share the good news. Callisto tossed her head and pawed the ground, expressing her own excitement at the knowledge that they weren't going to be separated.

October 31st dawned cold and foggy, just like any other day in the damp valley. It was so different from Austin. Back home all the houses would have Halloween decorations up and there would be people already wandering around in costume. Lots of kids at school would be dressed up, as would the coolest of the teachers. Even people at various jobs would be in costume. But here it might as well be any other day of the year.

Heather had taken to riding Callisto through the woods, avoiding the village, and she spent the day among the trees. At one point they encountered a deer, which froze, staring, until Callisto stretched up to nibble the few remaining leaves on a nearby tree. The deer startled and was gone in a flick of her tail.

They had both grown more comfortable in what Heather called The Haunted Woods. She supposed she had the village kids to thank for that. Their nastiness was worse than anything she and Callisto were likely to encounter out here. But she was still bothered by what Harry had said about old customs.

Things you have to . . . appease.

She shook her head to banish the memory. Her favorite holiday could come and go without fanfare, but it didn't matter because next year she and her dad would throw the most awesome party ever. She'd already decided on Callisto's costume: she would find a pair of huge white-feathered wings for the horse. The idea of riding Pegasus filled her with joy. She left the woods and returned home feeling as though she and Callisto were already flying.

They were having dinner when it happened. Someone was pounding hard on the door and there was the sound of raucous laughter outside. Heather looked at her dad with wide eyes and shook her head, silently urging him not to go.

But he frowned in confusion at her and got up from the table. "It's probably just trick-or-treaters," he said.

Heather followed him, feeling like a scared kid and wishing she'd told him the whole story, that Halloween wasn't about fun here.

We have old customs. Maybe you think they're strange.

Her father flung open the door and boldly walked out onto the step while Heather hid behind him in the porch. A group of people had gathered in front of the farmhouse, and Heather gasped as she saw what they were wearing. It looked like a gathering of demons.

They were dressed in black robes and masks. Horrible, misshapen things that looked like they'd been put together and painted in the dark. A trio at the back held torches. Not flashlights, but actual flaming torches.

"Hey there," her dad said, sounding uneasy. "I thought you guys didn't do Halloween."

That prompted a chorus of laughter and one man started up a chant.

At first Heather thought they were saying "nightmare." But as others took up the chant, she realized it was just the name of the pub. White Mare.

Dave glanced back at Heather, and his expression of concern worried her. He motioned for her to stay back, and that frightened her even more.

"Listen, fellas," her dad said, "I'm not sure what this is about, but—"

They wouldn't let him talk. The crowd shouted him down with their strange chant. Dave stepped back inside and took hold of the door, but one of the robed figures jumped across the threshold and kept him from shutting it.

There was a flash of white among the crowd and the jingle of bells. The figure moved quickly, bobbing and weaving between the revelers. Heather covered her mouth with both hands as she caught a glimpse of it. If the people in black looked like demons, this thing looked like a monster. The head was huge and white, and the jaws made a horrible clacking sound as its mouth opened and closed.

At last it broke through and stood at the entrance. It wasn't a monster. It was worse.

"White Mare! White Mare!"

A white sheet draped the person holding the awful clacking head. At least Heather *hoped* there was a person under there. What she'd first taken for a monster was only a skull. A horse's skull, long and gaunt and grinning horribly. Someone had filled the empty eye sockets with gleaming red baubles.

Her dad shouted over the noise. "Go on! Get out of here!"

But the crowd continued to chant, growing louder and louder. The horse-man capered on the step, dancing in a circle. The skull reared back, its mouth open in silent laughter, before jerking down again and appearing to look straight at Heather. She screamed.

That was when the robed people shoved her father aside and forced their way into the house. The horse-man continued its hellish dancing as it followed, with the others standing aside to let it pass. It "galloped" down the corridor and as soon as it passed, Heather ran to her father and clung to him.

"Make them stop," she sobbed. "Make them go away!"

Dave held her tight as he edged them both into the nearest room and slammed the door behind them. "Don't worry, Heather. I'm calling the cops."

An old rotary dial phone stood on the table in the corner and Dave grabbed it and dialed 9-1-1. Then he cursed and hung up, remembering to dial 9-9-9 when he tried again.

Heather listened in horror to the shouting and chanting as the group marched through the house. Some of them had musical instruments and began playing, the melodies harsh and discordant. Others sang in high screeching voices. But above the chaos, one sound was clearest of all.

Clack! Clack! Clack!

"Yes, hello? I need the police at the Barton farm in Thorpe Morag. Half the village just broke into my house!"

He was silent for a few moments as he listened to the operator. Then his expression turned incredulous.

"What the hell kind of advice is that? And they're already in, didn't you hear me? No, I don't know anything about any custom but it doesn't change the fact that they're trespassing. They scared my daughter half to death. Now send someone out here right—" He broke off and held the phone away from his face, staring at it in shock. "I don't believe it," he said. "She hung up."

Heather bit her lip as the party continued their dancing, singing invasion. The skull clacked out of time with the stamping feet and the chanting voices.

"White Mare! White Mare!"

Clack! Clack! Clack!

"What did she say?" Heather asked.

Dave shook his head. "Something about some local custom. She told me to let them in. I said they were already in!"

She'll find out, though. When they *come through.*

Heather eyed the door uneasily, but the sounds were growing faint as the group moved deeper into the house. A shudder ran through her and she hurried to her father's side. They held each other as they listened.

"Maybe they'll just go," Dave said. "It's probably some Halloween prank. The emergency operator didn't seem to think it was anything to worry about."

Heather nodded in hopeful agreement, but she couldn't stop replaying the conversation with the village kids. Were they here now, dressed like demons and dancing around with the others? She imagined pulling off one of those hideous masks only to find the same face underneath.

She hadn't wanted to tell her dad about the encounter, but now it was weighing on her. This was all her fault. Because she hadn't listened to them. In their own nasty way, they'd tried to warn her.

"Daddy? There's something I have to tell you. . ."

Her face burned with humiliation at the memory, but she managed to tell him the whole story without bursting into tears.

Dave listened without interrupting. And when she was done he wrapped his arms around her tightly. "It's not your fault, Heather. They're a bunch of insecure yahoos and they were just trying to scare you."

"Yeah, well, they did a good job."

"We'll be back home soon," Dave said, his voice calm and reassuring. "Another couple of weeks and we'll be out of here."

"Yeah."

The party lasted for almost an hour. More than once Dave reacted to the sound of breaking glass and got angrily to his feet. Heather stopped him each time, begging him not to leave her alone.

"If they've destroyed anything valuable. . . ." But he never finished the threat. What recourse did they have? Sue them? If the police weren't interested, they'd have no case anyway.

Heather's fear had given way to exhaustion and she was curled up on the floor when she heard the front door slam. Then all was silent inside. The voices and music and laughter moved like a wave down the drive and out into the night.

"Are they gone?"

Her father went to the door and pressed his ear against it, listening. "I think so." Then he took a deep breath and turned the knob.

Heather inched toward the doorway, expecting to find the house trashed. They went from room to room, but except for a couple of broken knickknacks and one picture frame, the place seemed to have been left in one piece, if a little disarranged. They sighed with relief as they moved the furniture back to where it belonged.

Heather stared in dismay at the remains of their interrupted dinner before sweeping it all into the trash. She'd lost her appetite.

Once they'd made sure the doors were locked, they trudged upstairs to bed, hoping sleep would obliterate the awful memory.

Heather slept fitfully, dreaming of monstrous figures dancing around her. They jabbed at her with spikes and called her insulting names, putting on exaggerated American accents.

Less all go tricker-treatin', y'all!

Gimme some caaandy!

She woke with a cry and bolted upright. Sunrise was just beginning to color the sky, turning the curtains a sickly yellow. A gap in the fabric allowed a pale stripe of light to creep across the floor toward the bed like a pointing finger. She felt singled out, accused. The dream had unnerved her, but she also felt nagged by a strange sense of guilt.

She slipped out of bed and padded downstairs in her pajamas. An eerie silence enveloped the house, and she realized that the same silence extended outside. There were no birds singing, no wind rattling the dead leaves, no sound of any kind.

The front door was closed and locked. But Heather still didn't feel reassured. Something was wrong. She knew it. Something had happened. Then she saw the note. It hadn't been there last night. Someone must have slipped it under the door while they slept.

She thought of waking her dad, of letting him see it first. But somehow she knew the note was for her. On the folded slip of paper was a single cryptic phrase.

THE WIGHT MARE TAKES WHEN YOU DON'T GIVE

At first she thought the word had been misspelled. But she could still hear the fanatical chanting in her head, and she realized that was what they'd been saying. Whatever it meant, it must be the name of that awful skull creature. The thing you had to *appease*.

But what were they supposed to give it? Her stomach fluttered with unease, and then swooped in a dizzying plunge.

She didn't want to open the door, didn't want to look. But it felt as if she was caught in some terrible ritual, playing a part they had forced on her. Her hand shook as she reached out to turn the key and unlock the door. The handle was like ice beneath her palm. She took a deep breath and threw it open. And when she saw what was waiting for her, she screamed.

Impaled on a spike was a huge bloody mass. In her delirium it took her a moment to realize that it was a horse's head. Callisto.

It was a long time before she stopped screaming.

There was no anger, only despair. Heather felt drained of all emotion. Her father expressed enough fury for both of them, but it made no difference. The solitary policeman who had come to the house shook his head sadly and explained that no crime had been committed. It was a local custom to allow the guisers in and offer them food and drink.

"What the hell are guisers?" Dave demanded. "Like 'disguise'? They were disguised, all right. We couldn't tell who was who but I'm pretty sure it was the whole damn village!"

"There's nothing I can do, sir," the young constable said calmly.

When Heather showed him the threatening note, he merely explained that appeasing the Wight Mare was an ancient tradition. It was an honor to don the guise of the spirit horse and perform the ritual. The community went from house to house, the Wight Mare and her demon entourage, where offerings would be made to ensure that the door between worlds would close at dawn. If entry was refused. . . .

Heather choked back another sob.

"That's insane," Dave said, shaking his head in disbelief.

"This is a very ancient part of the world, sir, with ancient traditions."

The patronizing tone only further antagonized Dave. "We're not talking about Druids here! We're talking about a group of juvenile delinquents who bullied my daughter, broke into my house and then murdered her horse! And for what? Because we didn't hand out treats?"

His hands clenched on Heather's shoulders as he spoke and she was reminded of the last time her father had confronted policemen, demanding answers to a mystery that was never to be solved. Sometimes people just disappeared and were never found.

"With all due respect, sir, the term 'murder' only applies to a person." The constable shrugged as he pocketed his notepad and made as if to leave. "I'm sorry, but all I can do is repeat that there has been no crime committed here."

"Well, that's not good enough!"

The policeman turned back to Dave, his expression hardening. "It'll have to be," he said coldly. "Maybe next time you go to another country you'll make a note of their customs and be more respectful of them."

Heather could feel the tension in her father's hands as he struggled not to lose his cool. She knew his rage was about more than the invasion and what the villagers had done to Callisto. She forced herself to take deep, calming breaths, hoping he would do the same.

Together they watched the constable amble back down the lane and drive away. As one, they turned to look at the shrouded thing sticking out of the ground. Dave had thrown a blanket over it so Heather didn't have to see it anymore, but the shape was unmistakable.

The body was too large to bury, but Heather insisted they dig a grave for the head. They'd never had a funeral for Heather's mother because they still refused to admit she was dead. But there was no gray area here, no hope that Callisto might return someday. The finality of it turned Heather's heart to stone and she stared with dry, empty eyes at the little mound of dirt when the grave was filled in.

Ian tried again to slide his hand up under Chloe's skirt, but she slapped him away. "Get off, perv," she said, laughing.

"Bloody tease is what you are," Ian complained, not for the first time. He took a swig from the bottle of lager he'd nicked and peered up into the trees. He could see the moon through the bony limbs, a fiery eye staring down at them. Something about it made him uneasy and he looked away.

Chloe made a pitying face. "Aww, poor thing. Ain't had enough fun already."

A grin spread across his features. "Yeah, the other night was brilliant. Only wish I coulda seen her face the next morning."

Chloe pawed at the bottle and he passed it to her. "Stupid twat," she sneered. "She totally deserved it."

Ian laughed, although in truth, he hadn't enjoyed killing the horse. That had been Chloe's idea. And Harry hadn't wanted any part of it, mumbling something about how it wasn't theirs to take. But it was just some stupid old custom their parents kept alive.

"It's getting cold," Ian said. "Let's go back to your house."

"Yeah, all right." Chloe finished the lager and hurled the empty bottle into the woods, where it struck a tree with a satisfying smash. She giggled and staggered to her feet. Then she froze, holding up her hand.

Ian stared at her, still grinning. "What? You about to hurl?"

"Shut up! Listen. I heard something."

He stood up and cocked his head, listening. "There's nothing. Just—" His voice trailed away. It couldn't have been what it sounded like. But one look at Chloe confirmed that she'd heard the same thing. He shook his head. No. There was no way. . . .

Clack! Clack!

They'd heard that sound plenty on Halloween, when they'd gleefully joined in the old custom, eager to teach those stupid foreigners a lesson. But now it sounded different. There was the suggestion of something wet as the jaws slapped together. And the smell. . . .

They fumbled for each other, clasping hands as they started backing away. The noise was getting louder, coming nearer. And now it was unmistakable. Hoofbeats.

A cloud must have passed across the moon because it was suddenly too dark to see. Chloe held up her phone, but the light from the screen did little to penetrate the deepening black.

"Let's get out of here," she said.

Ian didn't need any convincing. Harry had weirded him out enough with all that talk about how they'd stolen from the Wight Mare, that it would be back. He wanted to believe it was Harry now, just trying to scare them. But there was no faking those sounds. Or that smell. Something was coming toward them through the trees, crunching in the dead, dry leaves. Something that snorted heavily as it got closer.

"Which way do we go?" Ian hissed. "I can't see a bloody thing!"

Chloe kept her phone up high, shining the light around. "Fuck! I don't know! Where's the path?"

"I think it's—"

He gasped, certain that the light had swept across something.

"What?"

Chloe whirled around, brandishing the phone. A huge pale shape emerged from the gloom, draped in a ragged, filthy sheet. Light and shadow trembled over the jagged contours, gleaming where the bone showed through the strings of muscle and tendon still adhering to the skull. The huge white teeth seemed to be grinning as the jaws opened and closed, dislodging a clump of soil caked inside.

Clack!

One eye was gone. The other hung loosely from the socket, milky and deflated, but its gaze was far from blind. It was staring right at them.

Chloe screamed and dropped her phone. The light shone upward from the ground, giving the skull an even more malevolent expression.

It jolted Ian from his paralysis. He tried to pull Chloe away, but she seemed rooted to the spot.

Leaves crackled and twigs snapped as unseen hooves pawed the ground. The putrefying skull turned, tilted down toward them, and opened its mouth again.

Chloe shook her head, mumbling desperately. She reached up one trembling hand as if to stroke the long muzzle. Instead, she placed her hand inside the creature's mouth. The jaws snapped shut on her wrist and the skull jerked violently from side to side, like a dog shaking a toy.

Her screams were terrible. Wild, primal animal sounds. She flailed at the skull with her other hand, trying to pull away. But the creature pushed her down on the ground. She made a sound as if she'd been punched in the stomach, a breathy "Oof!" that might have been funny under other circumstances.

Ian could only stare in horror as something heavy pressed her down, stamping repeatedly. But there was nothing there. Only the floating shroud with the terrible skull emerging from it. Chloe's screams became guttural croaks as the powerful jaws finally snapped the bone and wrenched her hand away. Blood spurted across Ian's face but still he couldn't move.

"I'm sorry," he whispered, lowering his head. He stared at the ground beneath him, where blood was trickling between the dead leaves. Chloe's hand dropped into the detritus in front of him and he felt his stomach lurch. He couldn't bear to see any more, so he closed his eyes. "Sorry, sorry, sorry. . . ."

Strident neighing broke the silence, but Ian didn't move. He felt his bladder let go as he sank to his knees, waiting, praying for mercy he knew would not come. When he felt the hooves smash into the back of his neck, he fell forward into the bloodstained leaves. The pain was terrible, but he couldn't scream. His mouth was too full of earth.

"Are you all packed?"

Heather nodded without looking up at her dad. Her suitcases were laid out on the bed and she was ready to go, ready to leave this awful place far behind.

Dave gave her shoulders a reassuring squeeze. "I'll take those out to the car."

Once he was gone, Heather made her way slowly through the house and stood by the back door, peering out into the garden. The little wooden cross she had placed there lay on its side, and the soil was disturbed, scattered across the ground in a trail that led all the way into the woods.

Heather looked down at her hands, at the jagged, broken nails caked with dirt and dried blood. Beneath her shirt, the horsehair was beginning to itch.

As she made her way to the car, she clicked her teeth together, three times. It felt strangely reassuring.

PUMPKIN KIDS

Robert Shearman

Robert Shearman has written five short story collections, and among them they have won the World Fantasy Award, the Shirley Jackson Award, the Edge Hill Readers Prize, and three British Fantasy Awards.

He is probably best known for his work on *Doctor Who*, bringing back the Daleks for the BAFTA-winning first series in an episode nominated for a Hugo Award. His latest collection, *We All Hear Stories in the Dark*, is forthcoming from PS Publishing.

"England in the 1970s wasn't very glamorous," he remembers, "and as a kid it always felt just my rotten luck, both England and the 1970s were what I was stuck with. My parents knew it wasn't very glamorous either, and they had good reason to feel it more than most. They had lived in New York for several years, only moving back to the London suburbs just before I was born. I often rather resented them for that. I could have been a confident, wise-cracking, street-smart boy living a life around skyscrapers, movie stars, and Disney parks. And Halloween. I'd have been allowed to enjoy Halloween.

"We didn't celebrate Halloween in the UK. Of course not. That would have been impossibly fun. No trick-or-treaters, no ghosts, no pumpkins. One year I asked my mother whether we could get a pumpkin and she was appalled. She lived in England now, she said, and her taste in vegetables must reflect that. She'd feel more comfortable with a carrot, and a cabbage was as cosmopolitan as we were going to get.

"And yet I yearned for Halloween—something I really only knew about from comic strips in *Peanuts*, where Charlie Brown and the gang put sheets over their heads to get candy, where Linus sat all night in the garden waiting for the arrival of the Great Pumpkin. My parents wouldn't discuss Halloween. In all the years they'd lived in the United States, it was the one thing they'd never adjusted to. 'Why would people want to celebrate death and horror? What's the good of that? I do hope,' my father added, and looked at me sternly, 'that you'll grow up soon, and put this nasty horror thing behind you.'

"I got to visit America eventually, of course, and at Halloween too. Forty years on I carved a pumpkin, and I knew I was too old for it all now, but that didn't matter; it felt strangely like a homecoming—and I remember being so happy as I reached inside to pull out all the gloop.

"After my parents died I found a box full of old photographs taken while they'd lived in the States. They looked impossibly young and excited. And there it was: a picture of their first Halloween. My mother in a witch's hat, my father with a cape and plastic fangs—and between them a pumpkin of their own. And all three of them were laughing and seemed so very happy."

I

MY PARENTS DESPISED me, of course, and with good reason. But they didn't hate me, and I need you to understand that. They were good people. They fed me and they clothed me and they kept a roof over my head—and no, they didn't tuck me in at night, and they didn't read me bedtime stories, but I didn't need tucking and I didn't need stories; they taught me right from wrong, they instilled within me some sense of morality, and isn't that more important? In these difficult days, when everything has turned so topsy-turvy, they gave me an upbringing. And the fact that I have lived this long and have done so many Questionable Things, and yet have never been arrested or put on trial or sentenced to any sort of Christ-witnessed punishment can only be testament to the quality of that upbringing. I was lucky.

Or rather—my Da didn't hate me. He wasn't a man who had much hate within him. Momma was another matter. I like to think that what she felt for me wasn't hatred in the strictest sense—but when she got angry or frustrated or just plain fed up there was a vein in her forehead that used to bulge, and the bulge used to alarm me, and sometimes I was reading a book or playing with my toy and just minding my own business and then I'd realize she was staring at me and I didn't know why she was staring at me and I could see she had a full bulge on, and I didn't know what I had done other than just *being* there. Other than simply existing. So I tried not to be there very much, I tried not to exist when Momma was about—but the house was small, and there weren't many places to hide, and so she got angry quite a bit.

Momma only told me she hated me on two occasions, and considering I lived with her until my sixteenth year, that is hardly excessive. The first time I was five, maybe six—either way, I was old enough to have known better. And it was Momma's birthday, and I had spent *ages* making her a birthday card; well, it felt like ages, but it was probably no more than a couple of months. I'd drawn it myself, and I'd decorated it with lots of sticky sparkles, and I'd tried to draw *her*, but smiling, with a great big smiley face. And in the morning I gave it to her, and she looked at the card and she seemed bemused, I think she even seemed a little pleased, she said a thank you and everything. But that night, when I was in bed, she suddenly stormed into my room and snapped on the lights. I had never seen her so furious, her entire face was a bulge. "Can't you understand how much I hate you?" she screamed. "Why don't you just *die*?" And she tore up the birthday card and threw it at me. "I'd curse you," she said. "I'd curse you, if only curses worked, but they don't, so what's the point?" And she was right, I've tried cursing many times, I've done them proper the way the Bible tells us, and they do no good at all.

Don't you go thinking bad of Momma. The reason this is such a particular memory is because it was out of the usual. If she'd frequently screamed at me and flung birthday cards at me, I'd have nothing to remember, would I? In a way, this only shows how patient she was with me every other day of my childhood. It should only define her in your head as a strong and worthy mother. But that said, at the time my feelings were hurt and I was picking up sticky sparkles from my bed for weeks.

Just as my parents did, I spent a lot of time thinking about the Pumpkin Kids. About what I might have been. Should have been. How I'd been cheated out of my birthright—but there was no one to blame but myself, I had done the cheating: right from the moment I was born I had fucked things up royally and I would *never* be special and I would *never* be of any use. Sometimes I got angry too. They say that when I was a baby I used to lie in my cot and rant and kick and yell, and I had to be injected with a sedative the doctors had prescribed just so my poor parents could get some rest.

But the awful truth is this—some days I wouldn't mind I'd not been born a Pumpkin Kid. I'd even feel relieved. Some days, and more and more as I got older. I would always be an also-ran, and that was better. And I despised myself for that, just as my parents despised me, just as the neighbors did, and the school teachers, and Pastor Lewis. How feeble I was, that I *embraced* failure. Maybe that was the point? That I didn't feel strong enough to be a Pumpkin Kid, to be born with all that responsibility, to know that I'd have a Christ-witnessed purpose to live up to, that would justify my life and the lives of the parents who had spawned me, forever and ever and ever, amen. Oh, easier not to bother. Easier to hide in the shadows, if you can find shadows big enough to hide in—and stay still, and be quiet, and do nothing.

I guess if I *had* been born a Pumpkin Kid, I would have been born with that Pumpkin Kid strength, and I wouldn't have had these doubts. But then, I wouldn't have been me.

Half an hour after Momma left there was a knock at my bedroom door. "Are you asleep?" It was my Da. I wasn't asleep, I couldn't have slept, right at that moment I wasn't sure I'd ever be able to sleep again. Da came in and sat on my bed—which he never did—and he stroked my head—which he never did neither. "Momma was drunk," he whispered. "Or she wouldn't have said such things." He didn't tell me he was sorry, and he didn't tell me Momma hadn't meant it, and that was good, falsehoods are doorways to the Devil. He didn't say anything else for a while, and I just lay there and I closed my eyes, and I tried to keep them open too so I could enjoy my father being there—and I make-believed that for all the hate my mother felt for me my father felt the same amount of love. And he said eventually, "This day of the year, it's hard to be around you. It was on her birthday, when she'd been drinking, I got her into bed with me. It was on this day that you were conceived, and everything in our lives went wrong."

I miss my Da. He died only a short while later. I came home from school and Momma told me he was in the bathroom hanging from a rope. I asked if I could go and look, and she said no. "With Heaven's favor, we'll see him again soon." But we haven't yet.

So I gather, this is what happened.

I was expected on the last day of October, some time early afternoon. There was no reason to anticipate any problems with that—the pregnancy had gone without a hitch, my mother had been strong and healthy throughout, she hadn't even suffered so much as a twinge of morning sickness. There are never problems with Pumpkin Kid pregnancies—all other children are conceived in sin and guilt, and the struggle to bring them into the world only reflects that; Pumpkin Kids are pure. And my parents were pure too, I knew they were, and this was the pregnancy they deserved, because they loved Jesus with all their might.

They were admitted into their own private suite in the hospital, paid for by the Council. From now on, and for the rest of their lives, everything would be paid for by the Council—we honor those who create the miracles. Doctors and nurses all came in to pay their respects, and asked if there was anything they could do to make my mother more comfortable. There wasn't. She was serene.

It was only as afternoon passed into evening that Momma began to show any concern. And the doctors tried to reassure her that the timing of birth is never an exact science—little miracles must be allowed a degree of willfulness! Baby would come out when Baby was ready. But my mother was right—and as the hours ticked by she began to get so distressed there was nothing anyone could say to calm her down. "Why won't it come out?" she cried. "What's the matter with it?" And she battered at her swollen belly with her fists, clawed at it with her nails as if to prize it open. "What bloody game does it think it's playing in there?"

Past eleven o'clock, and still no sign of contractions. My mother begged the doctors to induce the birth. They refused. They couldn't intervene with a miracle, God would see. Halloween wasn't over yet, they told her. The baby could still come out in good time. And you can imagine that the doctors must have been panicking too—Pumpkin Kids were *never* born late, this wasn't how God willed it. Forty-five minutes. Thirty. Ten. At five minutes to midnight my mother let out a groan so profound that for a moment the medical staff assumed the baby must have finally given up the fight and popped out—but no, my mother could feel all she had ever wanted and all she had ever dreamed of slipping away from her and she'd given a cry of heartbroken despair: her child would be nothing, she was nothing, there was nothing to hold on to any longer. At midnight the nurses helped my mother up out of bed, and supporting her by the shoulders moved her from the luxury of her suite and into a public ward.

I was born on November 1st, a little after four o'clock in the morning. "I don't want it," my mother said. "I don't want it." But there I was.

Pastor Lewis was by her side. He'd been in attendance thinking to bless the arrival of a miracle; now he was on hand to offer good counsel. "You're still a young woman," Pastor Lewis said, "and you're still fertile. You have a Pumpkin Child in you, I know it. You mustn't be discouraged by this near-miss. Go to it again. Go to it, and breed for us all something outstanding."

But my parents didn't breed again. I remained their only child. I don't know why they didn't, Pastor Lewis was right, they were clearly capable—and the sin was mine, it wasn't on their heads, was it? Was it?—and yet all my life I remember them only sleeping in separate beds, at opposite sides of the room, as far away from each other as they could get. I never saw them kiss, or hug, or touch.

One Sunday I decided to stay after church and talk to Pastor Lewis. I liked church. I liked the way that I felt part of a community. I could sing the hymns along with everyone else, and pray, and nod my head and say "Amen"—and just for a little while I didn't stand out and nobody judged me.

And I liked the way that when we lined up before the altar, and Pastor Lewis gave us a sip of wine, how it became coppery and thick when it turned into the blood of Christ. I liked how those little wafers of bread became fat hunks of raw flesh. I felt awe that something so simple could be transformed by the grace of God, I dared to hope that through that grace I too could be transformed.

Pastor Lewis glared as I approached him. Of course he did. He raised an eyebrow as I told him I needed his help. "I want to be a Pumpkin Child."

"Indeed?"

"I'm very nearly a Pumpkin Child already. I was very close."

He sighed, and began collecting up hymn books. "You can't *nearly* be a Pumpkin Child, any more than I can nearly be Jesus Christ. You either are, or you're not."

And I started to cry, because I knew it was true, but up until that moment I had allowed myself a little hope. I didn't want to cry—I'd quickly learned that my crying just irritated people—and I expected the pastor would be irritated too. Instead he put the books down, and turned to me with an expression that seemed almost sympathetic.

"Look at me," said the pastor. "Can you guess when I was born? I was born on April 16th. More years ago than you can imagine. I could never have been born a Pumpkin Child, that was never my destiny. But I determined to do my best with the limitations I had, and I became a priest. It's all we can do. We take what God has given us, and make the best of it."

"Yes," I whispered.

"But you," he said. And he wasn't trying to be cruel, but he couldn't help it, his lip twisted into a sneer. "God offered you everything. He *chose* you. All you had to do was lie back and relax and get born. And you wouldn't do it. You decided not to. What little slice of evil was already in you, boy, so to take God's bounty and fling it in His face?"

"I'm sorry," I said. "I didn't mean to."

He reached out his hand, and cupped my chin, and stared right into me—and I flinched, because no one ever touched me, and because his fingers were bony and sharp. "I don't know," he said. "Could it be that you're not wicked at all, but clumsy and indolent?"

"Yes, that's it," I said, too eagerly, and my chin waggled in his grip. "Clumsy and indolent! I'm clumsy and indolent!"

He nodded at this. "Then it's not impossible. Maybe there's a little pumpkin inside you after all. Shall we go and see?"

I'd never been in the vestry before. It smelled of old books and pipe-smoke. He went to his desk, opened a drawer, and took out a knife. "This is my pumpkin knife," he said. I had honestly thought it would be a lot bigger.

"Now," he said, "every year, before it's Halloween, I go and visit all the little Pumpkin Children, and find out whether they're ripe or not. You've got to check! Jesus only wants the ripe ones! We can't expect much, but I could apply the same procedure to you, see if I recognize any familiar signs. . . ."

No one had ever been quite this nice to me my entire life. "Yes, please!"

"Keep your head still," he said. "This won't hurt a bit." That wasn't true. It did. He made a slice at my neck. "Now, now!" he chuckled.

"Don't cry out, that's not the way proper Pumpkin Children behave! We have to make a second notch across it, so it's the sign of the cross." And he cut at me again, and I could feel the blood running down my skin, and this time I clenched my teeth tight and it didn't hurt so much.

I asked if I were now a Pumpkin Kid, and he laughed. "I can't tell just by *looking* at the blood," he said. "What do you think I am? I tell by taste." And that's when he pressed his lips against my neck, and his tongue lapped away at the gash he'd made, and the stubble on his chin was rough and tickled but it wasn't the sort of tickle that makes you want to laugh. I wanted to pull away but didn't for fear of spoiling the magic.

"Well?" I asked when at last he stopped. I dared to hope.

Pastor Lewis frowned. He smacked his lips a few times as if he was appreciating a fine wine, then sighed, and wiped the blood from his mouth away with the back of his hand. "I'm afraid," he said gravely, "I can't taste any pumpkin in you at all. No, more than that. I'd say there was *less* pumpkin in you than an ordinary person." He passed me a paper towel. "Clean yourself up."

And I wanted to cry again, and my neck was smarting, and I felt crushed, and also betrayed somehow. Yes, betrayed—as if everything that could have made me good and decent and worthwhile was just arbitrary, and God didn't care, and Pastor Lewis didn't care either. But I didn't cry, and I wasn't going to cry, not ever again, not for anyone. I would be like a proper Pumpkin Kid, I would be patient and unfeeling and I would never say a word. I turned to leave, and then the pastor said, "Of course, it could just be that you've not ripened yet. We could try again. If you want to. If you ever feel a little riper, come back and see me." And I didn't thank him, and I didn't say yes or no, I just left the vestry and closed the door behind me.

When I got home my parents didn't notice the cuts upon my neck, or the blood upon my shirt, or maybe they did, and just didn't say anything. And every week I'd go back to church, and sometimes Pastor Lewis might catch my eye, and give a subtle nod towards the vestry door. Had I ripened? Had I turned pumpkin yet? And sometimes I stayed behind to find out, and sometimes I didn't.

II

It wasn't until Momma brought one home in the trunk of her car, gagged and all trussed-up like a turkey, that I had the chance to see an unripened Pumpkin Kid up close. They don't go to school like the rest of us, they don't need to learn the stuff we do, and they are mostly kept at home away from prying eyes—after all, we'll get to see them properly all in good time, we don't want to spoil the Halloween treat! But once in a while you might see one out on the streets, always flanked by two chaperones, and you never want to stare, that would be rude. Rude and *ungrateful*. We'll mutter a "Thank you for your service," look down, and hurry past.

I looked out of my bedroom window to see that Momma had come home from her job at the supermarket. I waited for her to get out of the car, bring in the bags of food she would cook for us. But she just sat there—she didn't move. Her hands were gripped tight upon the steering wheel, and I thought she must be very angry with me that she didn't even want to come indoors, I thought there'd be a big bulge upon her face. There wasn't. There was nothing there at all.

And I knew as I hurried down to find her that something was very wrong. I thought she might be dying, having a heart attack maybe. And I was frightened, yes—but mostly I think I was excited.

I rapped on the car window. I didn't expect Momma to look around. She did.

"What have I done?" she said.

"Momma?"

Her voice was muffled behind the glass. "I don't know," she said, "what I've done." And then it was as if she recognized me at last, her face came back to life, and hardened. "In the trunk," she said. "Open it. Carefully."

I did so. I looked inside. Then I lowered the lid, and went back to my Momma.

"Do you see it?" she said, and I nodded. "Is he still breathing?" I didn't know, so I went back to check. She had stuffed some plastic bags from the supermarket in his mouth as a gag, but his nostrils kept flaring inwards and outwards, and I took that as a sign of life. I closed the lid again, and went back to tell her the good news.

We waited until the coast was clear, and then we lifted the kid out of the trunk, taking one arm each and yanking until he was out in the open. Then we staggered with him up to the house. The kid didn't help at all, but he wasn't just being difficult, Momma had tied his legs together with tow rope, so it really wasn't his fault.

It wasn't until the front door closed behind us and we let the kid drop to the floor that either of us dared catch our breath.

"I just saw him there on the street," Momma said. "A Pumpkin Kid, large as life. And so I took him."

"Where were his chaperones?"

"He didn't have any."

"Did anyone see you?"

"I don't know."

"Someone must have seen you, Momma. His chaperones."

"I told you, he didn't have any. He was just staggering about on his own. I thought at first he was a drunk, until I realized he was wearing the orange smock. Wearing the smock, and it's not even Halloween, anyone could have seen him! He was lucky. Anyone could have seen him, anyone could have hit him over the head, and stuck him in the trunk of their car. He was lucky it was me."

I don't know whether the kid realized he was lucky. He was still lying on the floor, his head jammed against the skirting board, and he was twitching a little. We sat him up so he might be more comfortable. His eyes began to take in his new home slowly and incuriously.

"He was just *there*," said Momma. "I don't know why I did it. But if I hadn't done it, if I'd let this one chance just slip through my fingers, to get myself a real life Pumpkin Kid . . . I don't know. I would have regretted it the whole of my life. Do you understand?"

Of course I didn't. "What are you going to do with him?"

"Let's put him in your room." That wasn't quite what I had meant, but I didn't push the point further.

"We aren't going to hurt you," I said to the kid, though I didn't really know whether that were true. We laid him on the bed so he was staring right up at the ceiling.

I asked if we could take out the gag, and Momma thought about it for a bit, and then said that we could. I pulled it out from his mouth, and Momma had pushed those plastic bags in pretty deep, I'm surprised he hadn't choked. I then asked her if we could take off the ropes that were holding his arms and legs in check, and Momma thought about that too, and then said, no, best not—we'd already taken out the gag, we mustn't get carried away.

What did he look like? He didn't look much like a pumpkin, really. Maybe there was a wet sheen to his skin, and his face was a bit fat. But if he hadn't been in his orange smock, really, you wouldn't have known he was part vegetable at all. He was just a kid. Younger than me, maybe twelve or thirteen. His orange smock was dirty. His feet were bare and bruised.

I knew, of course, that what Momma had done was a Questionable Thing. I'm not sure it was even Questionable; it might even have been a proper unambiguous Crime. And I knew too that we were going to get caught. You can get away with a few Questionable Things here and there and everyone will turn a blind eye—Pastor Lewis had told me every time we'd met in his vestry. But no one was going to accept the disappearance of anything so precious as a Pumpkin Kid. They were going to hunt us down, and catch us, and then they'd be really mad.

"We could just take him back," I said. "No one would know. We could just leave him somewhere on the side of the road, what's he going to say, he isn't going to say anything."

And I think for a moment Momma may even have been considering it. We wouldn't have to destroy our lives over this. We could just sink back into the quiet misery of before. But then, as if to call me a liar, the Pumpkin Kid began to open his mouth. We heard the lips pull apart, we heard the jaws creak as they stretched like taffy.

"He's going to speak!" Momma said, and she was so excited, because the words of Pumpkin Kids are rare blessings. And we put our ears close to listen.

He didn't speak. Instead out from his mouth rolled a ball of vegetable pulp. It was wet and it was warm, and it fell upon my mattress. And then the kid closed its mouth, and smiled at us for the first time, big and wide, as if he'd done something extraordinarily clever.

"He's mine," said Momma. "And I'm not giving him back, not ever." And she smiled too, which only made the kid smile wider still, as if his only possible purpose was to please her—and there they were for a while, the two of them, grinning at each other. And I saw that vein in her face give a satisfied bulge, and I knew nothing now could dissuade her.

I'd lost my bedroom to the Pumpkin Kid, and so I tried to make the downstairs sofa as comfortable as could be.

But it was hard to sleep, knowing there was another body in the house. For so long it had just been me and Momma, and now someone else was breathing our air, and it sounds stupid but I suddenly resented that, we only had so much air to go round and here was some stranger making free with it and sucking it into his body and wasting it—and then I thought I could hear him upstairs, a third heart in the house beating away and making the night that much louder—and I knew he couldn't stay here, he didn't belong—and I thought that if I opened my eyes I would see him, he'd be in the room, he'd be looking at me. And I didn't want to open my eyes and find out it was true, I wanted to be asleep, why couldn't I just be asleep? I wasn't going to open my eyes, I refused to do it, and then I did it anyway, I opened them, and he *was* there, he *was* in the room, he was standing in the doorway and looking at me.

He didn't say anything. "What are you doing here?" I managed to get out—but no, nothing—and then as if in answer he took a step forward. And I could see his face more clearly in the moonlight. His head seemed more swollen than before, and in my terror I could see it was starting to crack, his face was splitting and juice was bubbling to the surface.

And he was smiling in that strange vacant way he had, as if the smile wasn't triggered by anything, it was just the shape into which his mouth had been carved. His teeth were jagged, his nose a cavity. And those eyes.

I closed mine. I squeezed them tight, and lay back down on the bed, and turned my body toward the wall. And I promised myself I wouldn't open them again until I had to, not until he touched me—when he touched me I would have no choice, I would have to do something, I would run or I would fight, I didn't have to decide just yet. Not until he touched me. But right now I was safe, I was safe for just a few precious moments longer and I wasn't going to spoil them by worrying. And I waited. I waited a long time. I began to feel impatient. I counted in my head, and when I reached one hundred I felt brave enough to turn around and see what the Pumpkin Kid was doing.

He was gone.

I got up from my bed. I went upstairs. I didn't want to look.

I went into my old bedroom. And there he was. Still tied up upon the mattress, face up towards the ceiling. Still nothing more frightening than an ordinary little boy. I tiptoed to his side, I didn't want to wake him—and then I realized he wasn't asleep. His eyes were wide. It made me jump—but he didn't even flinch, he looked straight through me, he didn't care, I was nothing to him.

And slumped in the chair by the bed, there was Momma. She was fast asleep, and she was smiling. I shook her gently by the shoulder; she stirred. "Come on," I said. I helped her to her feet, and she let me lead her from the room, across the landing, into her own bedroom. I laid her down, and she folded into her pillow and began to snore gently. "Good night, Momma," I said, and kissed her.

I went back to the Pumpkin Kid. I stood in *his* doorway, I stared at *him*. Let him have the nightmares about me. Because I could do anything to him that I wanted. And I went up to him, close, closer than I thought I could dare. I lifted a finger. I put it on top of his forehead. Resting it there so it was just skimming the surface—and then pressing down, pressing down hard. I took my finger away. I had left a mark. Only a little indentation, but it was there. And was there a bit of juice bleeding from it? I think there was. I said, "Good night, Pumpkin Kid," and went back downstairs to the sofa.

I felt calmer than I had in a very long time, and I slept soundly.

There are tales about the awful fates awaiting those that defy the Pumpkin Kids. We learned them at school. One of the best had been about a group of naughty little boys who had been jealous of a Pumpkin Kid and his special relationship with God and Death, and had vowed to do him harm. This would have been, I don't know, hundreds of years ago—there were lots of versions of this particular tale, and you could read about it in pop-up picture books, or see it acted out in puppet shows or pantomimes; it had given me nightmares as a little boy, but rather delicious nightmares, because you knew you would never be in danger yourself, this would never happen to you, you would never do anything so stupid as to harm a miracle child that was under the protection of Christ! And in this tale the boys lured the Pumpkin Kid into the forest, and there they killed him. They kicked him, or they stoned him, or they trapped him in a deep pit and left him to starve. But God punished them all. He destroyed the naughty boys, one by one. He wiped them off the face of the Earth—and their parents, and their brothers and their sisters, and all of their friends, every single one of them, were turned into pillars of salt.

And as those first weeks went by, it became clear—I wasn't going to be turned into a pillar of salt, and nor was Momma. And neither did the police come by (which, I thought, seemed more likely.) I couldn't work out why not. I thought at first that the disappearance of our Pumpkin Kid hadn't been reported yet—maybe the chaperones were ashamed to come forward. (Because where had the chaperones been? Why hadn't they been doing their Christ-witnessed jobs? Wasn't their carelessness enough to turn them into pillars of salt?) Our town safeguarded its store of precious Pumpkin Kids to the very best of its ability; had the theft of one become public knowledge it would have caused widespread outrage, if not actual panic. But it could only be a matter of time. Soon, surely, the disappearance would be noticed, and then an investigation would begin, and someone would point the finger at Momma. And our lives would be over, and I guess at least then so would be all the waiting.

But no one came. And as a new month began, and then another, and *still* no one came, I realized that somehow, incredibly, we must have gotten away with it. Every last Pumpkin in the town was accounted for. It was as if nothing had really happened, and there wasn't a spare one, large as life, tied up in my bedroom after all.

And some days that's precisely how Momma acted. She pretended that there was nothing untoward, that life was just the same as it had always been. She wouldn't so much as mention our special guest, let alone go to see him or ask how he was. She would go to her job at the supermarket and come back from her job at the supermarket and that was the full extent of all she was prepared to think about, thank you—her face was set as hard as stone and I knew there was no point in talking to her. But other days she was a different person. She would go to his bedside and spend all her time there, she would forget to eat or go into work. She'd stare at him in wonder, and maybe stroke his body, stroke his face. "He's beautiful," she'd say. And, "Why can't you be this beautiful?" And, "I wasn't sure I believed in God. But look at him! Now I know it's all true."

Sometimes she'd close the door on me, and I had to put my ear to the keyhole to hear her whisper to him. "Are you in there, my poor dear Da?" she'd ask. "And Momma too? I love you both. I love you, and I miss you so very much!"

But I was the one who had to look after him, who cleaned him and fed him. I would moisten a towel with water and rub it against his skin, and yet it never lost that shiny oily glow. "Where have you come from? Was it another town?" But the nearest town was a hundred miles away or more, I didn't know quite how far, but it was impossible to believe a barefooted boy could have walked that distance on his own. "Why did you come here? Tell me that at least!" He wouldn't chew his food, so I had to pour soup into his mouth, then hold my hands over his face so that it wouldn't all run out—and sometimes I made the soup piping hot and I hoped that it would burn him. "Do you think you're better than me?" And he'd never reply, he'd never so much as grunt a word, he'd stare up at me, and smirk that little smile. Of course he was better. He didn't need to answer.

The first time I cut into the Pumpkin Kid's neck I was nervous. I did it just the way I'd been shown, two nicks in the sign of the cross. But it wasn't as if I were blessed like Pastor Lewis was, I wasn't a man of God—if anything, I know, I was a sick failure who had denied His blessing. Still, the Pumpkin Kid didn't seem to mind—he actually nodded as I approached with the knife, and smiled a little wider, and stuck out his fat pulpy tongue in encouragement. I made the cuts, and I sipped at his blood. I don't know what signs I was looking for—Pastor Lewis had always been frustratingly vague about what a ripening child should taste like—but it seemed to me a little sweeter than the Christ blood I drank in church. That first time I tested him was hard, but it got easier after that—after a while I wouldn't even bother to bandage the gash, and I'd sip at the pumpkin juice until no more flowed out and I was full.

One day I stayed behind after church, just like old times. Pastor Lewis looked surprised to see me, and a little nervous too. He licked his fat lips. "It's been a while," he said. "I didn't think you liked me any more." We went back into the vestry, and it still smelled of pipe-smoke, but I also detected a heavy tang of body odor. He cut into my neck, and I refused to flinch, I had seen how bravely a real Pumpkin could take it. He guzzled at my neck for a little while, and there was the familiar not-funny tickle from his stubble, and when he pulled away his face was flushed. "Yes," he said. "Interesting. I mean, you're not ripe quite yet, but there's a little bit of pumpkin in there."

I kissed him on the lips then, and he was very surprised, and he responded, and I stuck my tongue into his mouth and felt around for a bit, but I didn't know what he was talking about, I couldn't taste any pumpkin there at all.

We had to lie down for a while after that. I spoke to him, really just to make conversation, the silence was embarrassing. I asked him how the Halloween preparations were going.

"Well, I think, yes, yes," he said. "Couple of months to go yet, but I think we're on track, some of this year's batch are ripening nicely!"

And I asked him what would happen if you had a Pumpkin Kid who was ripe and ready, and yet was somehow missed out of the ceremony. And he looked aghast, and said, "I have never missed out a child, not once." But I persisted, what would actually happen? "It's a ridiculous question," he said. "It'd be like Jesus Christ turning up late for his own crucifixion. This is what Pumpkin Children are born for. This is their purpose."

He looked quite offended, and began to get up. "I love you," I said. "I love you with all my heart, more than I have ever loved anybody." It was fun to say it, fun to see how embarrassed it made him.

"Look," Pastor Lewis said. "I'm not sure we should meet any more. Obviously, you're welcome to come to church, and take part in the Holy Sacrament. I'm not going to excommunicate you or anything, ha! But all this . . . this other stuff . . . You don't taste of pumpkin. Let me be straight with you. You don't taste of pumpkin, and you never have. I was just being kind. I didn't mind being kind to you, when you were younger. I liked it, when you were younger."

I said I quite understood. I got up, and I went home. Momma was still in her Sunday best, and she was standing at our Pumpkin Kid's bedside, and she was holding on to his hand, and her eyes were shining. She looked up as I came in to the room, and she smiled. She smiled, and she reached out to me, and I was too surprised to resist, I let her take me by the hand too. And we held that pose for a little while, as if someone was about to take a picture, but no one was going to take a picture—hand in hand in hand, like a human chain, and Momma in the middle of it all, and she looked at me, and she said, more gently than I had ever heard her, "We're a proper family at last. This is perfect. Whatever else might happen, this is perfect, right here and now."

One night the Pumpkin Kid came for me again.

I was drifting off to sleep on the sofa when I saw his outline framed in the doorway. "Come closer," I said.

His face was fatter and pulpy, and the cracks in his skin were deep, and now sheer gobbets of juice were running down his cheeks and his chin. And his face was also that of a little boy and his cheeks were smooth like a baby's and his eyes were wide with confusion and fear.

I got up. And as I approached his boy face twisted nervously, and his pumpkin face broke into an ever-wider smile. "What do you want?" I asked.

He went to the front door. He turned the handle, and the door fell open, though I was sure it had been locked. He stepped outside into the dark night. He didn't even bother to turn his head to see if I would follow. I did.

And I thought how funny he looked as he marched along—barefoot, and dressed only in that orange smock—and then I realized I was barefoot too and in silly striped pajamas, I guess I looked funny too.

I expected to feel the cold, and that the hard pavement would cut my feet, but I felt nothing.

I caught him up, and we walked side-by-side. And though we didn't talk, and he never turned to look at me, I was proud that we were together, that I'd found a friend. That I *belonged*—and the town was deserted, and the lights in every house were dark, and it wasn't just that everyone was asleep, it was as if they were all missing, or vanished, or dead. Gone for good, leaving everything for us to play with, just for us and no one else.

We turned up a side street, and then another. And soon I was in uncharted territory, I had never been to this part of the town before. The houses looked colder and more forbidding, and that was silly, because they all looked just the same as my own house, the one I had just abandoned for no good reason in the middle of the night—the one I knew I would never be able to find again unless the Pumpkin Kid helped me back, I was lost, I was lost forever. All alone, and the houses getting more densely packed and crushing in on us. And then I realized with a sudden chill that we were *not* alone—that in the distance were more children in their orange smocks—and coming at us from the left—and now from the right, from all directions—and the orange looked brown and filthy in the moonlight. Dozens of them now, and some were older teenagers like me, and some were infants. A baby was doing its best to match his pumpkin-fellows stride for stride even though its legs were embarrassingly short.

We all converged in front of one of those anonymous houses. My Pumpkin Kid gave no sign of welcome to the others, he stood still and waited until everyone was ready. And I stood with him, but now I felt out of place—and at any moment one of the children would challenge me for crashing a party to which I had clearly not been invited. I even thought then of running away, but where would I have gone? The streets would have drowned me, and I'd never be heard of again.

All together now, all the Pumpkin Kids and me. And they turned toward the house—and I turned with them. Inside the house, as if on cue, a single downstairs light switched on.

We marched up to the front door. We stepped inside.

The sitting room was much the same as at my house; the carpet was a different sort of beige.

A man sat on a hard chair, staring down at the floor. He looked up when all the children came in, maybe there was just a flicker of surprise?

"We all die alone, destined to be forgotten," he said. "Save those who choose to die, and die in good faith." I wanted to say the "Amen" afterwards, but my throat was too dry, and when I opened my mouth I couldn't speak. I thought I'd seen this man in church, but I couldn't be sure, lots of people went to church.

The man hung the rope from the ceiling. We waited. None of us tried to help. Then he climbed on to the chair, and put his head through the noose. "Well," he said to us all, "I guess this is it."

He didn't kill himself right away. I began to get bored. I think maybe some of the Pumpkin Kids did too, though their faces never changed expression; one of the Pumpkin Infants sat down on the floor, it was way past her bedtime. "I've changed my mind!" he said suddenly. "I can do that, can't I? I don't have enough faith!" Still, he kicked away the chair in the end, and he just hung there for a while, and he writhed, and his feet spun around like he thought he was riding a bicycle, and his eyes were wide and wild.

He couldn't speak, but he reached out towards us, it looked like he wanted some help. And so two of the Pumpkin Kids came forward, each took a leg, and gave one single yank downwards with all their might. There was a snap, and the man was still. It was beautiful, really.

Some of the older Pumpkin Kids extricated the man from the noose, and gently lowered him to the floor.

Then, one by one, the Kids came forward, and bent down in front of him. They touched his face. I thought at first they were paying their respects, but it was too meticulous for that. They prodded at his lips, his nose; they squeezed his jowls so that all the fat got bunched up; they traced the contours of his chin, his cheekbones, eye sockets.

And when my own Pumpkin Kid had taken his turn, he looked at me, and nodded his head.

"Oh," I said. "No, I'm good, thanks." But all the Pumpkin Kids were watching, and they were patient, and it soon became clear that until I took my part in their ritual no one was going anywhere. So I stooped down beside the corpse, and rather gingerly I wiped my hand over his face.

And at once I knew the dimensions of his skull, how to measure the gap between his eyes, the particular curvature of his jaw. I understood the span of his face fully and practically, I learned it all—and I didn't know why.

We had all now examined the man's head, and committed its exact size and shape to memory. I thought we would leave him there upon the floor, or put a sheet over his head or something. Instead we hoisted him back into the noose, and set him swinging, all ready to be found by his family the next morning.

It was over. I wanted to thank the Pumpkin Kids, for letting me share their evening with them. But I wasn't sure that was appropriate. So I nodded at them, and gave them big smiles, and they gave me big smiles in return. But to be fair, the smiles were already etched upon their faces and I couldn't be sure they were for me.

We all went our separate ways then, the children in their orange smocks fanning out across the streets as they headed home. And I went back to my own home with my own Pumpkin Kid, and as we reached the house the sun was starting to rise and the world to wake. "We don't have to go to bed just yet," I told him. "Stay with me. I'm not tired." But perhaps he *was* tired, or perhaps he just didn't fancy it—he gave me a farewell nod, then went upstairs.

In the morning I went to see him, and fed him his soup, and as usual most of it dribbled out of his mouth and on to the bed. And he was lying on his back as always, and his eyes stared at me without recognition. But I knew we had had an adventure together, and I gave his hand a friendly squeeze.

In the local newspaper the suicide was reported, and the article gave thanks that his Christ-witnessed death had passed cleanly and without complication.

III

October 1st. And out comes the bunting. I watch as the banners are hung across the streets. HAPPY HALLOWEEN, say some, and HOLY HALLOWEEN, say others, and there are streamers everywhere, and there's tinsel and colored lights, and in the shop windows there are pictures of jack-o'-lanterns and quotations from the Bible, all the best bits where Jesus mentions pumpkins.

October 6th, and 'tis the season, so I go out to buy a Halloween tree. I set it up in the sitting room, and it's a tall one this year, it nearly reaches the ceiling! Momma usually helps me with the decorations, but she's too busy upstairs, and so I do it all myself: and when I'm finished there are bright orange bulbs hanging from every branch, and on top an angel stares down in solemn judgment.

October 10th, and Momma calls out to me, she sounds so excited. "Look at him!" she cries. "I think he's ripening! I think he's nearly done!" The Kid won't tell; he grins at us, and the heavy slat of ribbed flesh growing over his eye makes it seem like he's winking. He opens his mouth and another ball of vegetable pulp plops out.

The 11th, and the papers report there's been another suicide. I feed the Pumpkin Kid his morning soup. "I guess you were busy out with your friends last night!" I say. "But next time, if you like, I'd be happy to come along too. If I wouldn't get in the way!"

The 15th. We get visited by the trick-or-treaters and the carol singers on the same night. The first take all our sweets, the second our spare change.

The 16th, and Momma says, "I'm not going to let him go. He's my miracle, and he'll stay with me forever." And then she bursts into tears, because we both know that can't be true.

The 18th. There have been three more suicides; there's always a rush on them as people get ready to celebrate Halloween. I feed the Pumpkin Kid. "Was it some sort of test?" I ask. "Didn't I do it right? I'm sorry. Let me try again. I know I didn't do it right, I'll do better next time."

The 24th, and with one week to go, Pastor Lewis tells us all in church that he has completed his inspections, and that this year there are no fewer than seven—seven!—Pumpkin Children ripe and ready. That's a bumper crop, it's going to be the best Halloween ever. And then he tells us of Mrs. Prentiss who lives on the high street, and Mrs. Watkins who lives by the common, and a couple more mothers aside, and how their pregnancies are all set for completion on October 31st, and we all pray for the health of their babies and say "Amen." Because this is the cycle of life, and God always provides new pumpkins to replenish the bounty.

The 29th. The pumpkin we have been allocated this year is waiting on our doorstep. I think it is a little knobblier than usual, it's hard to make it mimic a human head. But I do my best—I cut out a lid from the top, and pull out all the flesh within. I make sure it's good and hollow. I make the face, two triangular holes for eyes, another for the nose, and a mouth of jagged teeth opened wide in a smile. And as always, I try to think of Da. I dredge up every happy memory I have of Da, and put them into my handiwork, and though it looks nothing like him, I pretend that this head might be his. When I have finished I kiss it on the forehead, and bless it with the proper words. And I give thanks to God that He has shown us how to triumph over death, so long as we have enough faith, and are brave enough to be cruel.

I go upstairs to the Pumpkin Kid. There have been eight more suicides, one of them was our next-door neighbor. "Fuck you," I tell him.

The 30th, and it is a day of curfew and of fasting. I remember how as a child I would gobble as much as I could the evening before in preparation, but I'm not hungry this year, and nor is Momma. I guess I'm as grown-up as she is now. And at the end of the day, as we slide into another Halloween, she calls out for me, and she's lying on her bed in the dark, and when I make to turn the lights on she asks me not to.

I sit by her bed, and I listen to her breathing, and she doesn't say anything for a long while.

"Give me your hand," she says, at last. And so I do.

"I've said goodbye to our Pumpkin Child," she tells me. "We really ought to have given him a name, don't you think? That would have been nice." I agree, so right there and then we kick around a few possibilities and at last we come up with a really good one.

"I was so angry," she says, "when your father died."

"I know."

"Because we were supposed to die together."

"Yes."

"That was the dream. Matching nooses, hand-in-hand. Nice."

I think she's forgotten I'm still holding her hand, and I don't know what to do, I don't think I should squeeze it because that might get mistaken for sympathy. So I let it rest in mine like a dead weight.

"He couldn't wait. He had such faith. Oh, I used to envy him that faith. But I think he also felt. I don't know. That if he left us, didn't get in our way, that we'd be better together. Love each other even, I don't know. I don't know. I'm not," she says, "I'm not going to the Halloween ceremony tomorrow."

"No."

"I've had quite enough of magic. Come closer." Her voice has dropped to a whisper.

"Yes, Momma."

"Are you closer?"

"Yes, Momma."

She says, ever so gently, "I hate you." And she sounds so sad about it, so I can't even blame her.

I wait until she's asleep, and I say goodbye, and kiss her on the forehead just as I had my pumpkin-headed Da.

I go next door to see the Pumpkin Kid. He is shining. He is beautiful. "We've given you a name," I say, but I don't tell him what it is.

I undo his bonds at last, and only now do I see how tight they've been. They've cut into his skin, and the grooves they've left are wet with pus. "Go on," I say. "Go away. You're free. Get out of here while you can."

And his head twitches, and I don't know whether that's a shake or a nod, and his mouth creaks open wider. And I expect that from the mouth will slither another turd of vegetable pulp—but then there's a hiss, and I think it's a whisper, and I think I hear words.

I put my head close to the pumpkin mouth, and he tells me what I have to do.

Jesus always makes it rain at Halloween, it's part of the celebration. And this year it's particularly celebratory—it pisses down, and batters hard against the windows. I put on my best Halloween clothes, and a pair of galoshes. I go to see Momma, it's the respectful thing to do. "I hope to see you later, Momma," I say, and who knows? Maybe this year I even might.

I pick up the pumpkin I've carved. I light its candle, and leave for church, cupping the pumpkin under my coat to protect it from the rain.

The church is full. Usually everyone sits away from me, but there's no choice in the matter, and the family that I squeeze next to on the pew grit their teeth and grip their pumpkins and stare ahead refusing to look at me.

For my part, I grip on to a pumpkin of my own. It seems to me a sorry thing compared to the others in the church—some people have carved into theirs expressions of real personality. They've been made with great love and craft, and I can see that the eyes I've gouged aren't straight and the mouth doesn't have enough teeth. It looks nothing like my Da. It looks nothing like Momma either, come to that.

And we fall quiet as Pastor Lewis emerges from the vestry, and takes his place before us all. He opens his arms wide, as if embracing us. "Welcome," he says, "on this most hallowed of days, a time of transformation and resurrection, a time when we can all truly be one." His surplice is gleaming white; I see he's shaved off all of his stubble.

"Before we start, some good news. All the pregnancies are going well, and there's no reason not to believe that by the end of the day there'll be four more little miracles in our town. There *can* be errors, of course, but. . . ." And at that I am certain he looks at me, and the family next to me clearly think so, they glare and bristle with contempt. "But for now," says the pastor, "let's focus upon *this* year and the harvest it provides."

He pauses, licks his lips, enjoying the moment. Then, "Bring forth your offerings."

We file up the aisle then, one by one, and we place our pumpkins at the front of the church. By the time it's my turn there's a wall six pumpkins high, and it rings around the altar like a fortress, and all the candles inside the pumpkin heads shine bright and pure. I kneel, and Pastor Lewis gives me a sip of wine and places a wafer upon my tongue. "Only the best quality on this holiest of days," he tells us, and the blood is thick and its copper taste so rich, the body of Christ is fleshy and packed with flavor.

When all the pumpkins have been offered, and Christ has been completely devoured, and we are sitting back on our pews, Pastor Lewis begins the litany. We all know the words and mutter "Amens" in the right places. But somehow this year the words sound more magical, and I listen to them as though they're brand new.

"For we who are still living are of the dead. And we will soon be dead, and this gasp of life will seem as a fleeting dream. And Jesus said, 'Yea, I say unto you, you that eat of the pumpkin fruit shall this very evening dine at my father's table.' Amen. Blessed are the children of the pumpkins, for they will be both the quick and the dead, and we see death through a glass darkly and yea they are that glass. Jesus wept, amen. And God said unto Abraham, 'Take your child to the top of a mountain and slay him, for I am thy Lord and he is thy pumpkin.' Jesus wept. For the children must suffer so we elders can be free. And we sacrifice but a scrap of our future so we can hold on to our past. Amen. Abraham wept, and slew his son, and the Lord said, 'Yea, that's the idea.' For Moses said, 'Die, but be not forgotten!' Amen. 'Die, but return by grace of God, and grace of the Pumpkin Children.' Moses wept. I show you life eternal in a handful of pumpkin seeds, and those that take their lives in true faith never die alone. Amen, they wept, they all wept, we all weep forever."

"Amen," we say again.

Pastor Lewis grins then, his eyes twinkle. "Bring forth the children," he says. "Oh, I think you'll like this, they're an especially nice batch this year."

And in come the Pumpkin Kids, walking up the aisle.

There are seven of them. Do I recognize any from that night at the hanging? I cannot say for sure. When they reach the front and look out at us, I wonder whether they might recognize *me*, I feel the absurd urge to wave and get their attention. Barefoot of course, and in orange smocks that look grubby beside the pastor's surplice—and I think that's maybe the point, we are supposed to honor them but we don't want to *admire* them, they're not heroes, they're lambs to the slaughter. Pastor Lewis inspects them with the pride of a doting father, and that's perhaps just how he sees himself—and there's a little girl that can be no older than twelve, and she's standing a bit lopsided, and the pastor gets her to straighten up, and then gives us all a wink, and there's a ripple of laughter from the congregation—yes, how we love the cute little girls, the ones who *never* stand up straight!

The kids look pasty, their heads seem swollen. Are they ripe? I guess so, it's hard to tell. And the pastor says:

"The children are the future. And we disdain the future. It is a world we yet know not of."

The children file behind the pumpkin wall, and take hands, and face us. They close their eyes.

For a while, nothing. It doesn't look as if the Pumpkin Kids are even trying. There's no effort at all. We have to be patient. And then, you can see it—some of the children are clenching their teeth. The little girl begins to shake, just a bit—then the others start to shake too.

But we shouldn't be watching the children. We should be watching the pumpkins. And then someone cries out, "Look!" One of the pumpkins is beginning to change; the carved face is blurring and taking on real features—real skin, real eyes and teeth, hair. And there in the wall of the pumpkin fort there's now a fully formed human head, blinking, looking around the church for its family.

I don't know the woman who's been resurrected, but there's no need to waste time on her. Because other pumpkins are starting to follow suit. Another shimmers and resolves itself into the form of Mr. Bailey, who taught me math in school; and now there's one of my neighbors; there's Mrs. Thornhill from the drugstore; there's that man I helped to hang.

My pumpkin at last begins to shimmer, and I hope it will be Da, or maybe even Momma, but it turns into someone I've never seen before, and that can happen sometimes. The congregation are crying out now to all those they had lost, who have made it back from the dead for this special occasion—"I love you!" "I miss you!" "Darling, I think of you every day!" They jump up upon the pews, waving to get the attention of the pumpkins they know; they aren't allowed to embrace the heads, this is a Christ-witnessed festival of deep solemnity; and the heads can't reply, they have big burning candles wedged tight inside their skulls.

And the Pumpkin Kids have done it again, and we all praise the Lord, because death *isn't* the end, because the Pumpkin Kids prove it—that we get to see the dead, or at least some of them, those with faith, those brave enough to take the noose—and death looks like such a jolly thing, just see how merry the heads are, twitching and blinking and winking, just imagine what stories they might tell if only they could speak!

You might expect that the little girl would be the one to falter first. She looks so very fragile. In fact it's one of the boys, and his head suddenly cracks open. He rains juice down upon the church floor, and his body slumps forward—and the Pumpkin Kids holding his hands either side grasp tight so they won't break the chain. But we know it's the beginning of the end, the time of resurrection will soon be over—as one we call our goodbyes, each desperate for our message of love to be heard over the others. "Take care!" "Remember me!" "See you next year!" "Remember me, please remember!" The little girl breaks next, her head dissolves in a plume of orange pulp, and seconds later another boy comes apart. "Goodbye! Goodbye! Goodbye!" And we wave at the heads like cretins, and it's not as if they can wave back, and I'm waving too and I don't have anyone to wave to.

It's done. It's done. The heads freeze, they flicker. They're pumpkins once more. And the children? Pumpkins too—but their faces haven't been carved into the side, and there's no candle within. They're just pumpkins, the innards spilling out and rotting.

Pastor Lewis was right; it *was* a good Halloween, and those seven children gave us nearly two whole minutes with the dead. And for the moment there's still that buzz of celebration in the air. "Did you see Gramma?" "Did you see Poppa?" And then the disappointment; Halloween really is, finally, over. The miracle is spent. And right now we're as far from the next Halloween as it's possible to be, it'll be another long year before we get to glimpse our families again. Yet we all still sit in our pews. No one quite wants to admit there's nothing more to look forward to, that it's time to go home and get on with our lives.

Then I stand up. And even as I do so, I'm not yet sure I won't do the simple thing and leave the church and go home. I think I decide I will. But still, in spite of all, I walk up the aisle to the altar.

For a moment Pastor Lewis doesn't even register me. And then he looks baffled, he can't work this out. "What are you doing?" he hisses, as I walk through the fort of pumpkins, as I take my rightful place. As I make my announcement.

"I am a Pumpkin Kid."

The congregation doesn't know how to react. Maybe not all of them even recognize me? Then some laugh, catcall. "I am a Pumpkin Kid," I say again, "and I am ripe to bursting," and I stand my ground.

I close my eyes, and wait for something to happen. I concentrate with all my might. And I don't know how to do this, I can't just make myself special at a moment's notice. Not just because I decide I am, not just because I've had enough. And there's more laughter, and I can feel someone grab at my arm, and from the smell I guess it's Pastor Lewis.

I have no other children to hold hands with, but at the touch of the pastor my hands ball into fists, and then with all my strength I *push.* Down, deep into the rotten pumpkins, the ones that were kids just like me.

I can feel them, and I'm not alone, and I never was alone.

I realize I'm shaking quite a lot, but it doesn't hurt. I can feel the sweat running down my face, and it's sweet, and it's sticky.

I dare to open my eyes. To find out why the people are screaming.

And every pumpkin is my Da. Here he is, and it's good to see him, and I've missed him. But now he's here, he's just a dead man, isn't he? What use is his stupid dead face to me now? And every pumpkin is my Momma, and now I think every person I have ever known, and now every person I have *never* known. All the dead stare at me and howl out their pain and their fear, and for all their cries their breath is weak and won't blow their candles out. And then they're me, all the pumpkins are me, everyone is me.

And I look at Pastor Lewis, still grabbing my arm, it's like he's paralyzed, he can't let go—he's got my face, he's me. And those in the front row, and everyone at the back, yes, they're all screaming out of my mouth.

Pastor Lewis's head pops like a balloon, he was alive one moment and not the next. And doesn't it seem funny that life can become death so suddenly, all that fuss and fear and it's easy-peasy, here's death in an instant! Balloons are popping all over the church, it sounds like fireworks, it sounds like a proper celebration. And yes, I guess I shall pop as well sooner or later. I wonder what it will feel like. I wonder how long it will take. And then there's silence. There are no more balloons to burst, and I'm still here, and a part of me is disappointed.

After it's all over I'm too tired to move for quite a while, and I sit right down on the cold church floor. And I am so hungry, and there's pumpkin pulp everywhere, and so I eat some. I'm not proud of it.

The town is empty, it's so quiet.

When I get home, Momma has vanished from her noose, and I guess that's a good thing. I go upstairs to see the Pumpkin Kid and wonder whether he's popped too. He isn't there, but I find no trace of him, so maybe he got away. And he's left his orange smock on the bed, all folded up neatly and ready for use.

I sleep that night in my own bed, for the first time in ages, and for the last time in my life. The next morning I put on the orange smock, and go downstairs, and out of the front door, and out of the house. I've been told all the things I have to do, and there are lots of them, and some of them are Questionable, but what of that? I get started. It's a long walk to the next town, especially barefoot. But I'm happy. The rain has gone, and the sun is shining, and it's my birthday.

LANTERN JACK

Christopher Fowler

Christopher Fowler is the award-winning author of a number of story collections and more than thirty novels, including the popular Bryant & May series of mysteries.

He has fulfilled several schoolboy fantasies—releasing a terrible Christmas pop single, becoming a male model, posing as the villain in a Batman graphic novel, running a night club, appearing in *The Pan Books of Horror Stories*, and standing in for James Bond.

His work divides into black comedy, horror, mystery, and tales unclassifiable enough to have publishers tearing their hair out.

His often hilarious and moving autobiography, *Paperboy*, was about growing up in London in the 1950s and '60s, while *The Book of Forgotten Authors*, featuring insightful mini-essays on ninety-nine forgotten authors and their forgotten books, was based on a series of columns he wrote for the *Independent on Sunday* newspaper.

"This story came about because I needed something for Halloween," explains Fowler. "I was doing a gig at the London Metropolitan Archive, and figured I'd be on stage for fifteen minutes, tops.

"When I arrived, I found a wing-backed armchair on the stage and the organizer told me I had an hour to fill. I had no other stories on me.

"Desperate, I looked into the audience and found one of my fans there, who had another of my tales on him. I had written 'Lantern Jack' to be read aloud, and it saved the day, partly because I thesped it to the max and discovered my inner Laurence Olivier that night."

NO, PLEASE, YOU were before me. Age before beauty, ha ha. I'm in no rush to be served. The barmaid knows me, she'll get around to looking after me soon enough. This is my local. I'm always in here on special evenings. Well, there's never anything on the telly and at least you meet interesting people here. There's always someone new passing through.

I don't come in on a Saturday night because they have a DJ now and the music's too loud for me. You'd probably enjoy it, being young. I haven't seen you in here before. This place? Yes, it's unusual to find a traditional pub like this. The Jack O'Lantern has an interesting history. Well, if you're sure I'm not boring you. I like your Halloween outfit; sexy witch, very original. This place is a bit of a pet subject of mine.

We're on the site of an ancient peat bog. The strange phenomenon of gas flickering over it was called *ignis fatuus*, from which we get the flickering of the jack-o'-lantern. They built a coaching inn on the marsh in 1720. Not a good idea. Even now, there's still water seeping through the basement walls. Later it became a gin palace. That burned down, and it was rebuilt as a pub called The Duke of Wellington. Being on the corner of Southwark Street and Leather Lane, the pub was caught between two districts, one of elegant town houses and the other of terrible, reeking slums.

See this counter? It's part of the original bar. Solid teak, brass fittings. It was curved in a great horseshoe that took in all three rooms, the public, the snug, and the saloon. But the Jack was caught between two worlds. The drunken poor came in on that side in order to drown their miseries in cheap ale, and the fine gentlemen ventured in to swig down their port while visiting the brothels nearby. Oh yes, there were dozens in the backstreets. The area was notorious back then. It's all gentrified now. Urban professionals. They don't drink in here. Not posh enough for them. They'll be the first to scream when it's gone. Not that the area will ever really change. You don't change London, London changes you.

Of course, there was always trouble in here on All Hallows' Eve, right from when it first opened. One time, close to midnight, two of the king's horsemen came in and proceeded to get drunk. They mocked one of the poor ostlers who stood at the other side of the bar, and brought him over for their amusement. They challenged him to prove that he had not been born a bastard. When he couldn't do so, they told him that if he could win a game of wits, they would give him five gold sovereigns.

They placed a white swan feather on the one of the tables and seated themselves on either side of it. Then they produced a meat cleaver that belonged to the cook, sharpened it and challenged him to drop the feather into his lap before they could bring down the cleaver on his hand.

The ostler knew that the king's horsemen were employed for their strength and speed, and feared that they would cut off his fingers even though they were drunk, but once the bet had been made he couldn't refuse to go through with it. You never went back on a bet in those days.

They splayed his fingers on the table, six inches from the feather. As one of the men raised the cleaver high above his head, the other counted down from five on his pocket watch. The ostler held his hand flat and lowered his head to the level of the table, studying the feather. Then, as the countdown ended and the cleaver swooped, the ostler sucked the feather into his mouth and spat it into his lap. He won the bet. Unfortunately, the king's men were so angered that they took him outside and cut off his nose with their swords. The nose remained on the wall here for, oh, decades.

During World War II no one was much in the mood to celebrate Halloween. No female could come in alone, because it was considered immoral in those days. Well, so many men were off fighting, and most of the women around here were left behind. If they entered the pub by themselves it meant they were available, see. But there was one attractive married lady, a redhead, Marjorie somebody, who came in regularly and drank alone. None of the accompanied women would talk to her—they cut her dead. This Marjorie took no notice, just sat at the bar enjoying her drink.

But the whispering campaign took its toll. The other women said she was a tart, sitting there drinking gin and French while her husband was flying on dangerous missions over Germany. The pointed remarks grew louder, until they were directly addressed to her. Finally, Marjorie couldn't sit there any longer without answering back. She told the others that her husband had been shot down during the first weeks of the war, and that was why she came in alone, because it was his favorite place and she missed him so much.

The other women were chastened by this and felt sorry for her, but in time they became disapproving again, saying that a young widow should show remorse and respect for the dead. People were very judgmental in those days.

Then on October 31st, 1944, when she'd been at the bar longer than usual, a handsome young airman came into the pub toward the end of the evening and kissed her passionately without even introducing himself. Everyone professed to be shocked. The women said it was disgusting for her to make such a spectacle, but their disapproval turned to outrage because she slid from her stool, put her arm around his waist and went off into the foggy night with him.

It wasn't until the barman was cleaning up that night that he found the photograph of Marjorie's husband lying on the counter. And of course, it was the young airman. He'd come back to find her on All Hallows' Eve. Had he survived being shot down after all, or had the power of her love called him back from the other side, to be with her again? They never returned to the pub, so I don't suppose we'll ever know.

In the 1960s they changed the name of the pub again. It became The Groove. Psychedelic, it was, very druggy. All crimson-painted walls and rotating oil lights. Let's see, then it was Swingers, a purple plastic 1970s pick-up joint, then in the 1980s it was a gay leather bar called The Anvil, then it became The Frog 'n' Firkin, then it was a black-light techno club called ZeeQ, then it was a French-themed gastropub, La Petite Maison, and now it's back to being the Jack O'Lantern again. Always on the same site, always changing identities. But the nature of the place never changed, always the rich rubbing against the poor, the dead disturbing the living, the marsh rising up toward midnight.

See the pumpkin flickering above the bar? It's lit all year round, not just tonight. If you look carefully, it looks like you can see a skull behind the smile. It was put there one All Hallows' Eve in the 1960s. For months a sad-looking young man and his sick father would come and sit in that corner over there. The young man wanted to move in with his girlfriend, but her life was in Sheffield, and being with her meant moving away from his father. I would sit here and listen to the old man complaining about his illnesses, watching as his son got torn up inside about the decision he knew would soon have to make.

His father would sit there and cough and complain, and would catalogue the debilitating diseases from which he was suffering, but the funny thing was that he looked better with each passing week, while his son looked sicker and sicker.

I could see what was going to happen. The young man had to make a choice, and his decision coincided with his father's worst attack, although nobody knew what was wrong with him. The old man still managed to make it to the pub every night. The son made up his mind to leave, but he couldn't desert his father, even though Papa was slowly draining his life away. Finally he broke off with his girlfriend to look after his father, who looked so well in his hour of triumph that even the son became suspicious.

I heard the girl quickly married someone else. We didn't see the boy for a while, but when he finally came back in, he sat on that stool alone. It seemed the old man had fallen down the coal cellar steps at midnight on Halloween, and had twisted his head right around. The son put the jack-o'-lantern up there that very night. It even looks like the old man. . . .

The barstool didn't stay empty for long. It was taken by a vivacious young woman who turned the head of every man as she pushed open the crimson curtains into the pub. Everyone loved her, the way she laughed and enjoyed the company of men so openly, without a care in the world. She came in every evening at eight o'clock. She drank a little too much and never had any money, but being in her presence made you feel like you'd won a prize.

She wanted to fall in love with a man who would bring some order to her chaotic life, and then one day she met such a man at a party. He held a senior post in American Embassy, and gave her everything she ever wanted, a beautiful house, nice clothes, money, stability. She stopped her drinking, bore him a son, and became a model wife. His only stipulation was she should never again come into the pub. One evening he came home and found her hanging from a beam in their farmhouse. I think you can guess what night that was.

Of course, everyone in here has a story. There was a woman who used to come in once a month and get completely legless, but the landlord never banned her. I asked him why, and he told me that she was an actress hired to play drunk in bars for the Alcohol Licensing Board. They used to collect data on how often drunks were served liquor, and she came here to practice her act. The stress of her job got to her, though. One evening, she decided to have a real drink and got genuinely plastered, but the landlord thought she was just acting again. On the way home, she drove her car into a lamppost and was beheaded. Halloween again.

Look, it's like the lantern's laughing now, isn't it?

You think this pub has endured more than its fair share of tragedy? I knew them all, and I'm still here. I sit here drinking while the tragedies of others unfold around me, and I can do nothing for them, any more than they can change me. And which of us is the main character in the story? Perhaps we only ever belong at the edges of someone else's tale. We suffer, we cry, we die unnoticed, and the people we consider unimportant fail to sense our suffering because to them we are merely background colors, minor characters in their story.

Of course, I could add my own story to the list of peripheral tales. I could tell you about the bizarre death of my wife, and what happened when the newspapers discovered where I had buried—oh, but that was so long ago.

Who am I? They call me Lantern Jack. I suppose I'm the pub mascot. Only here one night a year. And only ever seen by special people.

What's that? You can see me?

Yes dear, and I'll tell you why.

Come closer.

Closer.

Let me whisper in your ear.

It means you join me tonight.

Well, I should let you get on. I shouldn't have taken up so much of your time. I'm sure you must have many important things to do . . . before midnight.

Cheers!

HALLOWEEN TREATS

Jane Yolen

Jane Yolen has been called the Hans Christian Andersen of America and the Aesop of the twentieth century. She is the author of more than 370 books, including children's fiction, poetry, short stories, graphic novels, nonfiction, fantasy, and science fiction. Her publications include *Owl Moon*, *The Devil's Arithmetic*, and *How Do Dinosaurs Say Good Night?*, while among her many honors are the Caldecott and Christopher Medals; multiple Nebula, World Fantasy, Mythopoeic, Golden Kite, and Jewish Book awards; the World Fantasy Convention's Lifetime Achievement Award, and the Science Fiction Poetry Grand Master Award.

She is also a teacher of writing and a book reviewer.

"I live in a small town in Western Massachusetts," reveals the author, "and give out writing awards to both the elementary school children and to a graduating senior at the high school. Every year about 140 kids come by my house trick-or-treating with their parents, and I hand out candy and a newly written Halloween poem. This poem was one of them.

"Last year, two girls clearly about to graduate high school knocked on the door and refused the candy. 'We've just come for the poem,' they said. *Score!!!*"

Ghouls eat their ghoulash
on Halloween night.
Ghosties eat toasties, it's true.
Gremlins eat grem-crackers,
holiday snick-snackers.
My treat will always be you.

Goblins all gobble down
gobs of gray candy,
and they like their finger-snacks, too.
Witches snatch gumdrops
plus toe jam and thumb pops,
But kiddo, my treat's always you!

Werewolves devour
each Halloween hour
their weight in boo-burgers, it's true.
And vampires veinly
drink berry-juice mainly,
but sweetie, my treat's really you.

There are dragons all dragging
snack wagons and bagging
up knight-nibbles, by ones and two.
And zombies on trains
are devouring brains.
Yet . . .
I'd rather be eating,
through wind, rain, or sleeting,
our bags of trick-treating
with you, my dear kiddo.
With you.

ACKNOWLEDGMENTS

Special thanks to Herman Graf, Kim Lim, Cat Mihos, Rebecca Eskildsen (Writers House Literary Agency), and Sarah Gerton (Curtis Brown, Ltd.) for their help with compiling this volume.

ABOUT THE EDITOR

Stephen Jones lives in London, England. A Hugo Award nominee, he is the winner of four World Fantasy Awards, three International Horror Guild Awards, five Bram Stoker Awards, twenty-one British Fantasy Awards, and a Lifetime Achievement Award from the Horror Writers Association. One of Britain's most acclaimed horror and dark fantasy writers and editors, he has more than 145 books to his credit, including *The Art of Horror Movies: An Illustrated History*, the film books of Neil Gaiman's *Coraline* and *Stardust*, *The Essential Monster Movie Guide* and *The Hellraiser Chronicles*; the nonfiction studies *Horror: 100 Best Books* and *Horror: Another 100 Best Books* (both with Kim Newman); the single-author collections *Necronomicon* and *Eldritch Tales* by H. P. Lovecraft, *The Complete Chronicles of Conan* and *Conan's Brethren* by Robert E. Howard, and *Curious Warnings: The Great Ghost Stories of M. R. James*; plus such anthologies as *Horrorology: The Lexicon of Fear*, *Fearie Tales: Stories of the Grimm and Gruesome*, *A Book of Horrors*, *The Mammoth Book of Vampire Stories by Women*, *The Lovecraft Squad* and *Zombie Apocalypse!* series, and twenty-nine volumes of *Best New Horror*. You can visit his web site at www.stephenjoneseditor.com or follow him on Facebook at "Stephen Jones-Editor."